THE GREAT
WRITERS
L I B R A R Y

Barchester Towers

"In the latter days of July in the year 185—, a most important question was for ten days hourly asked in the cathedral city of Barchester, and answered every hour in various ways – Who was to be the new Bishop?"

Barchester Towers

Anthony Trollope

Front cover: Preparing the Lesson by Thomas Graham, Bridgeman Art Library

This edition is the copyright © 1987 of Marshall Cavendish Ltd.

Published in 1987 for The Great Writers library by
Marshall Cavendish Partworks Ltd, 119 Wardour Street, London W1V 3TD.
Reprinted in 1992.
Printed and bound in Spain by Printer Industria Gráfica, Barcelona. D.L.B. 24874-1987

ISBN 0-86307-680-7

This is a facsimile reproduction of the 1891 edition published by
Longmans, Green, and Co, London and New York.

BARCHESTER TOWERS.

CHAPTER I.

WHO WILL BE THE NEW BISHOP?

IN the latter days of July in the year 185—, a most important question was for ten days hourly asked in the cathedral city of Barchester, and answered every hour in various ways — Who was to be the new Bishop?

The death of old Dr. Grantly, who had for many years filled that chair with meek authority, took place exactly as the ministry of Lord —— was going to give place to that of Lord ——. The illness of the good old man was long and lingering, and it became at last a matter of intense interest to those concerned whether the new appointment should be made by a conservative cr liberal government.

It was pretty well understood that the out-going premier had made his selection, and that if the question rested with him, the mitre would descend on the head of Archdeacon Grantly, the old bishop's son. The archdeacon had long managed the affairs of the diocese; and for some months previous to the demise of his father, rumour had confidently assigned to him the reversion of his father's honours.

Bishop Grantly died as he had lived, peaceably, slowly, without pain and without excitement. The breath ebbed from him almost imperceptibly, and for a month before his death, it was a question whether he were alive or dead.

A trying time was this for the archdeacon, for whom was designed the reversion of his father's see by those who then had the giving away of episcopal thrones. I would not be understood to say that the prime minister had in so many words promised the bishopric to Dr. Grantly. He was too discreet a man for that. There is a proverb with reference to the killing of cats, and those who know anything either of high or low government places, will be well aware that a promise may be made without positive words, and that an expectant may be put into the highest state of encouragement though the great man on whose breath he hangs may have done no more than whisper that "Mr. So-and-so is certainly a rising man."

Such a whisper had been made, and was known by those who heard it to signify that the cures of the diocese of Barchester should not be taken out of the hands of the archdeacon. The then prime minister was all in all at Oxford, and had lately passed a night at the house of the master of Lazarus. Now the master of Lazarus—which is, by the bye, in many respects the most comfortable, as well as the richest college at Oxford,—was the archdeacon's most intimate friend and most trusted counsellor. On the occasion of the prime minister's visit, Dr. Grantly was of course present, and the meeting was very gracious. On the following morning Dr. Gwynne, the master, told the archdeacon that in his opinion the thing was settled.

At this time the bishop was quite on his last legs; but the ministry also were tottering. Dr. Grantly returned from Oxford happy and elated, to resume his place in the palace, and to continue to perform for the father the last duties of a son; which, to give him his due, he performed with more tender care than was to be expected from his usual somewhat worldly manners.

A month since the physicians had named four weeks as the outside period during which breath could be supported within the body of the dying man. At the end of the month the physicians wondered, and named another fortnight. The old man lived on wine alone, but at the end of the fortnight he still lived; and the tidings of the fall of the ministry became more frequent. Sir Lamda Mewnew and Sir Omicron Pie, the two great London doctors, now came down for the fifth time, and declared, shaking their learned heads, that another week of life was impossible; and as they sat down to lunch in the episcopal dining-room, whispered to the archdeacon their own private knowledge that the ministry must fall within five days. The son returned to his father's room, and after administering with his own hands the sustaining modicum of madeira, sat down by the bedside to calculate his chances.

The ministry were to be out within five days: his father was to be dead within—No, he rejected that view of the subject. The ministry were to be out, and the diocese might probably be vacant at the same period. There was much doubt as to the names of the men who were to succeed to power, and a week must elapse before a Cabinet was formed. Would not vacancies be filled by the outgoing men during this week? Dr. Grantly had a kind of idea that such would be the case, but did not know; and then he wondered at his own ignorance on such a question.

He tried to keep his mind away from the subject, but he could not. The race was so very close, and the stakes were so very high. He then looked at the dying man's impassive, placid face. There was no sign there of death or disease; it was something thinner than of yore, somewhat grayer, and the deep lines of age more marked; but, as far as he could judge, life might yet hang there for weeks to come. Sir Lamda Mewnew and Sir Omicron Pie had thrice been wrong, and might yet be wrong thrice again. The old bishop slept during twenty of the twenty-four hours, but during the short periods of his waking moments, he knew both his son and his dear old friend, Mr. Harding, the archdeacon's father-in-law, and would thank them tenderly for their care and love. Now he lay sleeping like a baby, resting easily on his back, his mouth just open, and his few gray hairs straggling from beneath his cap; his breath was perfectly noiseless, and his thin, wan hand, which lay above the coverlid, never moved. Nothing could be easier than the old man's passage from this world to the next.

But by no means easy were the emotions of him who sat there watching. He knew it must be now or never. He was already over fifty, and there was little chance that his friends who were now leaving office would soon return to it. No probable British prime minister but he who was now in, he who was so soon to be out, would think of making a bishop of Dr. Grantly. Thus he thought long and sadly, in deep silence, and then gazed at that still living face, and then at last dared to ask himself whether he really longed for his father's death.

The effort was a salutary one, and the question was answered in a moment. The proud, wishful, worldly man, sank on his knees by the bedside, and taking the bishop's hand within his own, prayed eagerly that his sins might be forgiven him.

His face was still buried in the clothes when the door of the bed-room opened noiselessly, and Mr. Harding entered with a velvet step. Mr. Harding's attendance at that bedside had been nearly as constant as that of the archdeacon, and his ingress and egress was as much a matter of course as that of his son-in-law. He was standing close beside the archdeacon before he was perceived, and would also have knelt in prayer had he not feared that his doing so might have caused some sudden start, and have disturbed the dying man.   Dr. Grantly, however, instantly perceived him, and rose from his knees.   As he did so Mr. Harding took both his hands, and pressed them warmly.   There was more fellowship between them at that moment than there had ever been before, and it so happened that after circumstances greatly preserved the feeling. As they stood there pressing each other's hands, the tears rolled freely down their cheeks.

"God bless you, my dears,"—said the bishop with feeble voice as he woke—"God bless you—may God bless you both, my dear children:" and so he died.

There was no loud rattle in the throat, no dreadful struggle, no palpable sign of death; but the lower jaw fell a little from its place, and the eyes, which had been so constantly closed in sleep, now remained fixed and open.   Neither Mr. Harding nor Dr. Grantly knew that life was gone, though both suspected it.

"I believe it's all over," said Mr. Harding, still pressing the other's hands.   "I think—nay, I hope it is."

"I will ring the bell," said the other, speaking all but in a whisper.   "Mrs. Phillips should be here."

Mrs. Phillips, the nurse, was soon in the room, and immediately, with practised hand, closed those staring eyes.

"It's all over, Mrs. Phillips?" asked Mr. Harding.

"My lord's no more," said Mrs. Phillips, turning round and curtseying low with solemn face; "his lordship's gone more like a sleeping babby than any that I ever saw."

"It's a great relief, archdeacon," said Mr. Harding, "a great relief—dear, good, excellent old man.   Oh that our last moments may be as innocent and as peaceful as his!"

"Surely," said Mrs. Phillips.   "The Lord be praised for all his mercies; but, for a meek, mild, gentle-spoken Christian, his lordship was——" and Mrs. Phillips, with unaffected but easy grief, put up her white apron to her flowing eyes.

"You cannot but rejoice that it is over," said Mr. Harding, still consoling his friend.   The archdeacon's mind, however, had already travelled from the death chamber to the closet of the prime minister.   He had brought himself to pray for his father's life, but now that that life was done, minutes were too precious to be lost.   It was now useless to dally with the fact of the bishop's death—useless to lose perhaps everything for the pretence of a foolish sentiment.

But how was he to act while his father-in-law stood there holding his hand? how, without appearing unfeeling, was he to forget his father in the bishop—to overlook what he had lost, and think only of what he might possibly gain?

"No; I suppose not," said he, at last, in answer to Mr. Harding. "We have all expected it so long."

Mr. Harding took him by the arm and led him from the room. "We will see him again to-morrow morning," said he; "we had better leave the room now to the women." And so they went down stairs.

It was already evening and nearly dark. It was most important that the prime minister should know that night that the diocese was vacant. Everything might depend on it; and so, in answer to Mr. Harding's further consolation, the archdeacon suggested that a telegraph message should be immediately sent off to London. Mr. Harding who had really been somewhat surprised to find Dr. Grantly, as he thought, so much affected, was rather taken aback; but he made no objection. He knew that the arch-deacon had some hope of succeeding to his father's place, though he by no means knew how highly raised that hope had been.

"Yes," said Dr. Grantly, collecting himself and shaking off his weakness, "we must send a message at once; we don't know what might be the consequence of delay. Will you do it?"

"I! oh yes; certainly: I'll do anything, only I don't know exactly what it is you want."

Dr. Grantly sat down before a writing table, and taking pen and ink, wrote on a slip of paper as follows:—

"By Electric Telegraph.
"For the Earl of ——, Downing Street, or elsewhere.
"'The Bishop of Barchester is dead.'
"Message sent by the Rev. Septimus Harding."

"There," said he, "just take that to the telegraph office at the railway station, and give it in as it is; they'll probably make you copy it on to one of their own slips; that's all you'll have to do: then you'll have to pay them half-a-crown;" and the archdeacon put his hand in his pocket and pulled out the necessary sum.

Mr. Harding felt very much like an errand-boy, and also felt that he was called on to perform his duties as such at rather an unseemly time; but he said nothing, and took the slip of paper and the proffered coin.

"But you've put my name into it, archdeacon."

"Yes," said the other, "there should be the name of some clergyman you know, and what name so proper as that of so old a friend as yourself? The Earl won't look at the name, you may be sure of that; but my dear Mr. Harding, pray don't lose any time."

Mr. Harding got as far as the library door on his way to the station, when he suddenly remembered the news with which he was fraught. when he entered the poor bishop's bed-room. He had found the moment so inopportune for any mundane tidings, that he had repressed the words which were on his tongue, and immediately afterwards all recollection of the circumstance was for the time banished by the scene which had occurred.

"But, archdeacon," said he, turning back, "I forgot to tell you —The ministry are out."

"Out!" ejaculated the archdeacon, in a tone which too plainly showed his anxiety and dismay, although under the circumstances of the moment he endeavoured to control himself: "Out! who told you so?"

Mr. Harding explained that news to this effect had come down by electric telegraph, and that the tidings had been left at the palace door by Mr. Chadwick.

The archdeacon sat silent for awhile meditating, and Mr. Harding stood looking at him. "Never mind," said the archdeacon at last; "send the message all the same. The news must be sent to some one, and there is at present no one else in a position to receive it. Do it at once, my dear friend; you know I would not trouble you, were I in a state to do it myself. A few minutes' time is of the greatest importance."

Mr. Harding went out and sent the message, and it may be as well that we should follow it to its destination. Within thirty minutes of its leaving Barchester it reached the Earl of —— in his inner library. What elaborate letters, what eloquent appeals, what indignant remonstrances, he might there have to frame, at such a moment, may be conceived, but not described! How he was preparing his thunder for successful rivals, standing like a British peer with his back to the sea-coal fire, and his hands in his breeches pockets,—how his fine eye was lit up with anger, and his forehead gleamed with patriotism,—how he stamped his foot as he thought of his heavy associates,—how he all but swore as he remembered how much too clever one of them had been,—my creative readers may imagine. But was he so engaged? No: history and truth compel me to deny it. He was sitting easily in a lounging chair, conning over a Newmarket list, and by his elbow on the table was lying open an uncut French novel on which he was engaged.

He opened the cover in which the message was enclosed, and having read it, he took his pen and wrote on the back of it —

"For the Earl of ——,
"With the Earl of ——'s compliments,"

and sent it off again on its journey.

Thus terminated our unfortunate friend's chance of possessing the glories of a bishopric.

The names of many divines were given in the papers as that of the bishop elect. "The British Grandmother" declared that Dr. Gwynne was to be the man, in compliment to the late ministry. This was a heavy blow to Dr. Grantly, but he was not doomed to see himself superseded by his friend. "The Anglican Devotee" put forward confidently the claims of a great London preacher of austere doctrines ; and "The Eastern Hemisphere," an evening paper supposed to possess much official knowledge, declared in favour of an eminent naturalist, a gentleman most completely versed in the knowledge of rocks and minerals, but supposed by many to hold on religious subjects no special doctrines whatever. "The Jupiter," that daily paper, which, as we all know, is the only true source of infallibly correct information on all subjects, for a while was silent, but at last spoke out. The merits of all these candidates were discussed and somewhat irreverently disposed of, and then "The Jupiter" declared that Dr. Proudie was to be the man.

Dr. Proudie was the man. Just a month after the demise of the late bishop, Dr. Proudie kissed the Queen's hand as his successor elect.

We must beg to be allowed to draw a curtain over the sorrows of the archdeacon as he sat, sombre and sad at heart, in the study of his parsonage at Plumstead Episcopi. On the day subsequent to the despatch of the message he heard that the Earl of —— had consented to undertake the formation of a ministry, and from that moment he knew that his chance was over. Many will think that he was wicked to grieve for the loss of episcopal power, wicked to have coveted it, nay, wicked even to have thought about it, in the way and at the moments he had done so.

With such censures I cannot profess that I completely agree. The *nolo episcopari*, though still in use, is so directly at variance with the tendency of all human wishes, that it cannot be thought to express the true aspirations of rising priests in the Church of England. A lawyer does not sin in seeking to be a judge, or in compassing his wishes by all honest means. A young diplomate entertains a fair ambition when he looks forward to be the lord of a first-rate embassy ; and a poor novelist when he attempts to rival Dickens or rise above Fitzjeames, commits no fault, though he may be foolish. Sydney Smith truly said that in these recreant days we cannot expect to find the majesty of St. Paul beneath the cassock of a curate. If we look to our clergymen to be more than men, we shall probably teach ourselves to think that they are less, and can hardly hope to raise the character of the pastor by denying to him the right to entertain the aspirations of a man.

Our archdeacon was worldly — who among us is not so? He was ambitious — who among us is ashamed to own that " last infirmity of noble minds!" He was avaricious, my readers will say. No — it was for no love of lucre that he wished to be bishop of Barchester. He was his father's only child, and his father had left him great wealth. His preferment brought him in nearly three thousand a year. The bishopric, as cut down by the Ecclesiastical Commission was only five. He would be a richer man as archdeacon than he could be as bishop. But he certainly did desire to play first fiddle; he did desire to sit in full lawn sleeves among the peers of the realm; and he did desire, if the truth must out, to be called " My Lord " by his reverend brethren.

His hopes, however, were they innocent or sinful, were not fated to be realised; and Dr. Proudie was consecrated Bishop of Barchester.

CHAP. II.

HIRAM'S HOSPITAL ACCORDING TO ACT OF PARLIAMENT.

It is hardly necessary that I should here give to the public any lengthened biography of Mr. Harding, up to the period of the commencement of this tale. The public cannot have forgotten how ill that sensitive gentleman bore the attack that was made on him in the columns of the Jupiter, with reference to the income which he received as warden of Hiram's Hospital, in the city of Barchester. Nor can it yet be forgotten that a law-suit was instituted against him on the matter of that charity by Mr. John Bold, who afterwards married his, Mr. Harding's, younger and then only unmarried daughter. Under pressure of these attacks, Mr. Harding had resigned his wardenship, though strongly recommended to abstain from doing so, both by his friends and by his lawyers. He did, however, resign it, and betook himself manfully to the duties of the small parish of St. Cuthbert's, in the city, of which he was vicar, continuing also to perform those of precentor of the cathedral, a situation of small emolument which had hitherto been supposed to be joined, as a matter of course, to the wardenship of the Hospital above spoken of.

When he left the hospital from which he had been so ruthlessly driven, and settled himself down in his own modest manner in the High Street of Barchester, he had not expected that others would make more fuss about it than he was inclined to do himself; and the extent of his hope was, that the movement might have been made in time to prevent any further paragraphs in the Jupiter. His affairs, however, were not allowed to subside thus quietly, and people were quite as much inclined to talk about the disinterested sacrifice he had made, as they had before been to upbraid him for his cupidity.

The most remarkable thing that occurred, was the receipt of an autograph letter from the Archbishop of Canterbury, in which the primate very warmly praised his conduct, and begged to know what his intentions were for the future. Mr. Harding replied that he intended to be rector of St. Cuthbert's, in Barchester: and so that matter dropped. Then the newspapers took up his case, the Jupiter among the rest, and wafted his name in eulogistic strains through every reading-room in the nation. It was discovered also, that he was the author of that great musical work, Harding's Church Music,—and a new edition was spoken of, though, I believe, never printed. It is, however, certain that the work was introduced into the Royal Chapel at St. James's, and that a long criticism appeared in the Musical Scrutator, declaring that in no previous work of the kind had so much research been joined with such exalted musical ability, and asserting that the name of Harding would henceforward be known wherever the Arts were cultivated, or Religion valued.

This was high praise, and I will not deny that Mr. Harding was gratified by such flattery; for if Mr. Harding was vain on any subject, it was on that of music. But here the matter rested. The second edition, if printed, was never purchased; the copies which had been introduced into the Royal Chapel disappeared again, and were laid by in peace, with a load of similar literature. Mr. Towers, of the Jupiter, and his brethren, occupied themselves with other names, and the undying fame promised to our friend was clearly intended to be posthumous.

Mr. Harding had spent much of his time with his friend the bishop, much with his daughter Mrs. Bold, now, alas, a widow; and had almost daily visited the wretched remnant of his former subjects, the few surviving bedesmen now left at Hiram's Hospital. Six of them were still living. The number, according to old Hiram's will, should always have been twelve. But after the abdication of their warden, the bishop had appointed no successor to him, no new occupants of the charity had been nominated, and it appeared as though the hospital at Barchester would fall into abeyance, unless the powers that be should take some steps towards putting it once more into working order.

During the past five years, the powers that be had not overlooked Barchester Hospital, and sundry political doctors had taken the matter in hand. Shortly after Mr. Harding's resignation, the Jupiter had very clearly shown what ought to be done. In about half a column it had distributed the income, rebuilt the building, put an end to all bickerings, regenerated kindly feeling, provided for Mr. Harding, and placed the whole thing on a footing which could not but be satisfactory to the city and Bishop of Barchester, and to the nation at large. The wisdom of this scheme was testified by the number of letters which " Common Sense," " Veritas," and " One that loves fair play " sent to the Jupiter, all expressing admiration, and amplifying on the details given. It is singular enough that no adverse letter appeared at all, and, therefore, none of course was written.

But Cassandra was not believed, and even the wisdom of the Jupiter sometimes falls on deaf ears. Though other plans did not put themselves forward in the columns of the Jupiter, reformers of church charities were not slack to make known in various places their different nostrums for setting Hiram's Hospital on its feet again. A learned bishop took occasion, in the Upper House, to allude to the matter, intimating that he had communicated on the subject with his right reverend brother of Barchester. The radical member for Staleybridge had suggested that the funds should be alienated for the education of the agricultural poor of the country, and he amused the house by some anecdotes touching the superstition and habits of the agriculturists in question. A political pamphleteer had produced a few dozen pages, which he called "Who are John Hiram's heirs?" intending to give an infallible rule for the governance of all such establishments ; and, at last, a member of the government promised that in the next session a short bill should be introduced for regulating the affairs of Barchester, and other kindred concerns.

The next session came, and, contrary to custom, the bill came also. Men's minds were then intent on other things. The first threatenings of a huge war hung heavily over the nation, and the question as to Hiram's heirs did not appear to interest very many people either in or out of the house. The bill, however, was read and re-read, and in some undistinguished manner passed through its eleven stages without appeal or dissent. What would John Hiram have said in the matter, could he have predicted that some

forty-five gentlemen would take on themselves to make a law alter-
ing the whole purport of his will, without in the least knowing at
the moment of their making it, what it was that they were doing?
It is however to be hoped that the under-secretary for the Home
Office knew, for to him had the matter been confided.

The bill, however, did pass, and at the time at which this history
is supposed to commence, it had been ordained that there should
be, as heretofore, twelve old men in Barchester Hospital, each with
1s. 4d. a day; that there should also be twelve old women to be
located in a house to be built, each with 1s. 2d. a day; that there
should be a matron, with a house and 70l. a year; a steward with
150l. a year; and latterly, a warden with 450l. a year, who should
have the spiritual guidance of both establishments, and the
temporal guidance of that appertaining to the male sex. The
bishop, dean, and warden were, as formerly, to appoint in turn
the recipients of the charity, and the bishop was to appoint the
officers. There was nothing said as to the wardenship being held
by the precentor of the cathedral, nor a word as to Mr. Harding's
right to the situation.

It was not, however, till some months after the death of the
old bishop, and almost immediately consequent on the installation
of his successor, that notice was given that the reform was about
to be carried out. The new law and the new bishop were among
the earliest works of a new ministry, or rather of a ministry who,
having for a while given place to their opponents, had then returned to power; and the death of Dr. Grantly occurred, as we
have seen, exactly at the period of the change.

Poor Eleanor Bold! How well does that widow's cap become
her, and the solemn gravity with which she devotes herself to her
new duties. Poor Eleanor!

Poor Eleanor! I cannot say that with me John Bold was ever
a favourite. I never thought him worthy of the wife he had won.
But in her estimation he was most worthy. Hers was one of
those feminine hearts which cling to a husband, not with idolatry,
for worship can admit of no defect in its idol, but with the perfect
tenacity of ivy. As the parasite plant will follow even the defects
of the trunk which it embraces, so did Eleanor cling to and love
the very faults of her husband. She had once declared that
whatever her father did should in her eyes be right. She then
transferred her allegiance, and became ever ready to defend the
worst failings of her lord and master.

And John Bold was a man to be loved by a woman; he was
himself affectionate, he was confiding and manly; and that arro-

gance of thought, unsustained by first-rate abilities, that attempt at being better than his neighbours which jarred so painfully on the feelings of his acquaintance, did not injure him in the estimation of his wife.

Could she even have admitted that he had a fault, his early death would have blotted out the memory of it. She wept as for the loss of the most perfect treasure with which mortal woman had ever been endowed ; for weeks after he was gone the idea of future happiness in this world was hateful to her ; consolation, as it is called, was insupportable, and tears and sleep were her only relief.

But God tempers the wind to the shorn lamb. She knew that she had within her the living source of other cares. She knew that there was to be created for her another subject of weal or woe, of unutterable joy or despairing sorrow, as God in his mercy might vouchsafe to her. At first this did but augment her grief ! To be the mother of a poor infant, orphaned before it was born, brought forth to the sorrows of an ever desolate hearth, nurtured amidst tears and wailing, and then turned adrift into the world without the aid of a father's care ! There was at first no joy in this.

By degrees, however, her heart became anxious for another object, and, before its birth, the stranger was expected with all the eagerness of a longing mother. Just eight months after the father's death a second John Bold was born, and if the worship of one creature can be innocent in another, let us hope that the adoration offered over the cradle of the fatherless infant may not be imputed as a sin.

It will not be worth our while to define the character of the child, or to point out in how far the faults of the father were redeemed within that little breast by the virtues of the mother. The baby, as a baby, was all that was delightful, and I cannot foresee that it will be necessary for us to inquire into the facts of his after life. Our present business at Barchester will not occupy us above a year or two at the furthest, and I will leave it to some other pen to produce, if necessary, the biography of John Bold the Younger.

But, as a baby, this baby was all that could be desired. This fact no one attempted to deny. " Is he not delightful ? " she would say to her father, looking up into his face from her knees, her lustrous eyes overflowing with soft tears, her young face encircled by her close widow's cap and her hands on each side of the cradle in which her treasure was sleeping. The grandfather would gladly admit that the treasure was delightful, and the uncle archdeacon himself would agree, and Mrs. Grantly, Eleanor's sister, would re-echo the word with true sisterly energy; and Mary Bold —— but Mary Bold was a second worshipper at the same shrine.

The baby was really delightful; he took his food with a will, struck out his toes merrily whenever his legs were uncovered, and did not have fits. These are supposed to be the strongest points of baby perfection, and in all these our baby excelled.

And thus the widow's deep grief was softened, and a sweet balm was poured into the wound which she had thought nothing but death could heal. How much kinder is God to us than we are willing to be to ourselves! At the loss of every dear face, at the last going of every well beloved one, we all doom ourselves to an eternity of sorrow, and look to waste ourselves away in an ever-running fountain of tears. How seldom does such grief endure! how blessed is the goodness which forbids it to do so! "Let me ever remember my living friends, but forget them as soon as dead," was the prayer of a wise man who understood the mercy of God. Few perhaps would have the courage to express such a wish, and yet to do so would only be to ask for that release from sorrow, which a kind Creator almost always extends to us.

I would not, however, have it imagined that Mrs. Bold forgot her husband. She daily thought of him with all conjugal love, and enshrined his memory in the innermost centre of her heart. But yet she was happy in her baby. It was so sweet to press the living toy to her breast, and feel that a human being existed who did owe, and was to owe everything to her; whose daily food was drawn from herself; whose little wants could all be satisfied by her; whose little heart would first love her and her only; whose infant tongue would make its first effort in calling her by the sweetest name a woman can hear. And so Eleanor's bosom became tranquil, and she set about her new duties eagerly and gratefully.

As regards the concerns of the world, John Bold had left his widow in prosperous circumstances. He had bequeathed to her all that he possessed, and that comprised an income much exceeding what she or her friends thought necessary for her. It amounted to nearly a thousand a year; and when she reflected on its extent, her dearest hope was to hand it over, not only unimpaired but increased, to her husband's son, to her own darling, to the little man who now lay sleeping on her knee, happily ignorant of the cares which were to be accumulated in his behalf.

When John Bold died she earnestly implored her father to come and live with her, but this Mr. Harding declined, though for some weeks he remained with her as a visitor. He could not be prevailed upon to forego the possession of some small home of his own, and so remained in the lodgings he had first selected over a chemist's shop in the High Street of Barchester.

CHAP. III.

DR. AND MRS. PROUDIE.

THIS narrative is supposed to commence immediately after the installation of Dr. Proudie. I will not describe the ceremony, as I do not precisely understand its nature. I am ignorant whether a bishop be chaired like a member of parliament, or carried in a gilt coach like a lord mayor, or sworn in like a justice of peace, or introduced like a peer to the upper house, or led between two brethren like a knight of the garter; but I do know that every thing was properly done, and that nothing fit or becoming to a young bishop was omitted on the occasion.

Dr. Proudie was not the man to allow anything to be omitted that might be becoming to his new dignity. He understood well the value of forms, and knew that the due observance of rank could not be maintained unless the exterior trappings belonging to it were held in proper esteem. He was a man born to move in high circles; at least so he thought himself, and circumstances had certainly sustained him in this view. He was the nephew of an Irish baron by his mother's side, and his wife was the niece of a Scotch earl. He had for years held some clerical office appertaining to courtly matters, which had enabled him to live in London, and to entrust his parish to his curate. He had been preacher to the royal beefeaters, curator of theological manuscripts in the Ecclesiastical Courts, chaplain to the Queen's yeomanry guard, and almoner to his Royal Highness the Prince of Rappe-Blankenberg.

His residence in the metropolis, rendered necessary by the duties thus entrusted to him, his high connections, and the peculiar talents and nature of the man, recommended him to persons in power; and Dr. Proudie became known as a useful and rising clergyman.

Some few years since, even within the memory of many who are not yet willing to call themselves old, a liberal clergyman was a person not frequently to be met. Sydney Smith was such, and was looked on as little better than an infidel; a few others also might be named, but they were "raræ aves," and were regarded with doubt and distrust by their brethren. No man was so surely a tory as a country rector—nowhere were the powers that be so cherished as at Oxford.

When, however, Dr. Whately was made an archbishop, and Dr. Hampden some years afterwards regius professor, many wise divines saw that a change was taking place in men's minds, and that more liberal ideas would henceforward be suitable to the priests as well as to the laity. Clergymen began to be heard of who had ceased to anathematise papists on the one hand, or vilify dissenters on the other. It appeared clear that high church principles, as they are called, were no longer to be surest claims to promotion with at any rate one section of statesmen, and Dr. Proudie was one among those who early in life adapted himself to the views held by the whigs on most theological and religious subjects. He bore with the idolatry of Rome, tolerated even the infidelity of Socinianism, and was hand and glove with the Presbyterian Synods of Scotland and Ulster.

Such a man at such a time was found to be useful, and Dr. Proudie's name began to appear in the newspapers. He was made one of a commission who went over to Ireland to arrange matters preparative to the working of the national board; he became honorary secretary to another commission nominated to inquire into the revenues of cathedral chapters; and had had something to do with both the regium donum and the Maynooth grant.

It must not on this account be taken as proved that Dr. Proudie was a man of great mental powers, or even of much capacity for business, for such qualities had not been required in him. In the arrangement of those church reforms with which he was connected, the ideas and original conception of the work to be done were generally furnished by the liberal statesmen of the day, and the labour of the details was borne by officials of a lower rank. It was, however, thought expedient that the name of some clergyman should appear in such matters, and as Dr. Proudie had become known as a tolerating divine, great use of this sort was made of his name. If he did not do much active good, he never did any harm; he was amenable to those who were really in authority, and at the sittings of the various boards to which he belonged maintained a kind of dignity which had its value.

He was certainly possessed of sufficient tact to answer the purpose for which he was required without making himself troublesome; but it must not therefore be surmised that he doubted his own power, or failed to believe that he could himself take a high part in high affairs when his own turn came. He was biding his time, and patiently looking forward to the days when he himself would sit authoritative at some board, and talk and direct, and rule the roast, while lesser stars sat round and obeyed, as he had so well accustomed himself to do.

His reward and his time had now come. He was selected for the vacant bishopric, and on the next vacancy which might occur in any diocese would take his place in the House of Lords, prepared to give not a silent vote in all matters concerning the weal of the church establishment. Toleration was to be the basis on which he was to fight his battles, and in the honest courage of his heart he thought no evil would come to him in encountering even such foes as his brethren of Exeter and Oxford.

Dr. Proudie was an ambitious man, and before he was well consecrated Bishop of Barchester, he had begun to look up to archiepiscopal splendour, and the glories of Lambeth, or at any rate of Bishopsthorpe. He was comparatively young, and had, as he fondly flattered himself, been selected as possessing such gifts, natural and acquired, as must be sure to recommend him to a yet higher notice, now that a higher sphere was opened to him. Dr. Proudie was, therefore, quite prepared to take a conspicuous part in all theological affairs appertaining to these realms; and having such views, by no means intended to bury himself at Barchester as his predecessor had done. No: London should still be his ground: a comfortable mansion in a provincial city might be well enough for the dead months of the year. Indeed Dr. Proudie had always felt it necessary to his position to retire from London when other great and fashionable people did so ; but London should still be his fixed residence, and it was in London that he resolved to exercise that hospitality so peculiarly recommended to all bishops by St. Paul. How otherwise could he keep himself before the world ? how else give to the government, in matters theological, the full benefit of his weight and talents ?

This resolution was no doubt a salutary one as regarded the world at large, but was not likely to make him popular either with the clergy or people of Barchester. Dr. Grantly had always lived there ; and in truth it was hard for a bishop to be popular after Dr. Grantly. His income had averaged 9000l. a year; his successor was to be rigidly limited to 5000l. He had but one child on whom to spend his money ; Dr. Proudie had seven or eight. He had been a man of few personal expenses, and they had been confined to the tastes of a moderate gentleman; but Dr. Proudie had to maintain a position in fashionable society, and had that to do with comparatively small means. Dr. Grantly had certainly kept his carriage, as became a bishop; but his carriage, horses, and coachman, though they did very well for Barchester, would have been almost ridiculous at Westminster. Mrs. Proudie determined that her husband's equipage should not shame her, and things on which Mrs. Proudie resolved, were generally accomplished.

From all this it was likely to result that Dr. Proudie would not spend much money at Barchester; whereas his predecessor had dealt with the tradesmen of the city in a manner very much to their satisfaction. The Grantlys, father and son, had spent their money like gentlemen; but it soon became whispered in Barchester that Dr. Proudie was not unacquainted with those prudent devices by which the utmost show of wealth is produced from limited means.

In person Dr. Proudie is a good looking man; spruce and dapper, and very tidy. He is somewhat below middle height being about five feet four; but he makes up for the inches which he wants by the dignity with which he carries those which he has. It is no fault of his own if he has not a commanding eye, for he studies hard to assume it. His features are well formed, though perhaps the sharpness of his nose may give to his face in the eyes of some people an air of insignificance. If so, it is greatly redeemed by his mouth and chin, of which he is justly proud.

Dr. Proudie may well be said to have been a fortunate man, for he was not born to wealth, and he is now bishop of Barchester; but nevertheless he has his cares. He has a large family, of whom the three eldest are daughters, now all grown up and fit for fashionable life; and he has a wife. It is not my intention to breathe a word against the character of Mrs. Proudie, but still I cannot think that with all her virtues she adds much to her husband's happiness. The truth is that in matters domestic she rules supreme over her titular lord, and rules with a rod of iron. Nor is this all. Things domestic Dr. Proudie might have abandoned to her, if not voluntarily, yet willingly. But Mrs. Proudie is not satisfied with such home dominion, and stretches her power over all his movements, and will not even abstain from things spiritual. In fact, the bishop is henpecked.

The archdeacon's wife, in her happy home at Plumstead, knows how to assume the full privileges of her rank, and express her own mind in becoming tone and place. But Mrs. Grantly's sway, if sway she has, is easy and beneficent. She never shames her husband; before the world she is a pattern of obedience; her voice is never loud, nor her looks sharp: doubtless she values power, and has not unsuccessfully striven to acquire it; but she knows what should be the limits of a woman's rule.

Not so Mrs. Proudie. This lady is habitually authoritative to all, but to her poor husband she is despotic. Successful as has been his career in the eyes of the world, it would seem that in the eyes of his wife he is never right. All hope of defending himself has long passed from him; indeed he rarely even attempts self-justification; and is aware that submission produces the nearest approach to peace which his own house can ever attain.

Mrs. Proudie has not been able to sit at the boards and committees to which her husband has been called by the state; nor, as he often reflects, can she make her voice heard in the House of Lords. It may be that she will refuse to him permission to attend to this branch of a bishop's duties; it may be that she will insist on his close attendance to his own closet. He has never whispered a word on the subject to living ears, but he has already made his fixed resolve. Should such an attempt be made he will rebel. Dogs have turned against their masters, and even Neapolitans against their rulers, when oppression has been too severe. And Dr. Proudie feels within himself that if the cord be drawn too tight, he also can muster courage and resist.

The state of vassalage in which our bishop has been kept by his wife has not tended to exalt his character in the eyes of his daughters, who assume in addressing their father too much of that authority which is not properly belonging, at any rate, to them. They are, on the whole, fine engaging young ladies. They are tall and robust like their mother, whose high cheek bones, and ——, we may say auburn hair, they all inherit. They think somewhat too much of their grand uncles, who have not hitherto returned the compliment by thinking much of them. But now that their father is a bishop, it is probable that family ties will be drawn closer. Considering their connection with the church, they entertain but few prejudices against the pleasures of the world; and have certainly not distressed their parents, as too many English girls have lately done, by any enthusiastic wish to devote themselves to the seclusion of a protestant nunnery. Dr. Proudie's sons are still at school.

One other marked peculiarity in the character of the bishop's wife must be mentioned. Though not averse to the society and manners of the world, she is in her own way a religious woman; and the form in which this tendency shows itself in her is by a strict observance of Sabbatarian rule. Dissipation and low dresses during the week are, under her control, atoned for by three services, an evening sermon read by herself, and a perfect abstinence from any cheering employment on the Sunday. Unfortunately for those under her roof to whom the dissipation and low dresses are not extended, her servants namely and her husband, the compensating strictness of the Sabbath includes all. Woe betide the recreant housemaid who is found to have been listening to the honey of a sweetheart in the Regent's park, instead of the soul-stirring evening discourse of Mr. Slope. Not only is she sent adrift, but she is so sent with a character which leaves her little hope of a decent place. Woe betide the six-foot hero who escorts Mrs. Proudie to her pew in red plush breeches, if he slips away to the neighbouring beer-shop, instead of falling into the back seat appropriated to his use. Mrs. Proudie has the eyes of Argus for such offenders. Occasional drunkenness in the week may be overlooked, for six feet on low wages are hardly to be procured if the morals are always kept at a high pitch; but not even for grandeur or economy will Mrs. Proudie forgive a desecration of the Sabbath.

In such matters Mrs. Proudie allows herself to be often guided by that eloquent preacher, the Rev. Mr. Slope, and as Dr. Proudie is guided by his wife, it necessarily follows that the eminent man we have named has obtained a good deal of control over Dr. Proudie in matters concerning religion. Mr. Slope's only preferment has hitherto been that of reader and preacher in a London district church : and on the consecration of his friend the new bishop, he readily gave this up to undertake the onerous but congenial duties of domestic chaplain to his lordship.

Mr. Slope, however, on his first introduction, must not be brought before the public at the tail of a chapter.

CHAP. IV.

THE BISHOP'S CHAPLAIN.

OF the Rev. Mr. Slope's parentage I am not able to say much. I have heard it asserted that he is lineally descended from that eminent physician who assisted at the birth of Mr. T. Shandy, and that in early years he added an " e " to his name, for the sake of euphony, as other great men have done before him. If this be so, I presume he was christened Obadiah, for that is his name, in commemoration of the conflict in which his ancestor so distinguished himself. All my researches on the subject have, however, failed in enabling me to fix the date on which the family changed its religion.

He had been a sizar at Cambridge, and had there conducted himself at any rate successfully, for in due process of time he was an M.A., having university pupils under his care. From thence he was transferred to London, and became preacher at a new district church built on the confines of Baker Street. He was in this position when congenial ideas on religious subjects recommended him to Mrs. Proudie, and the intercourse had become close and confidential.

Having been thus familiarly thrown among the Misses Proudie, it was no more than natural that some softer feeling than friendship should be engendered. There have been some passages of love between him and the eldest hope, Olivia; but they have hitherto resulted in no favourable arrangement. In truth, Mr. Slope having made a declaration of affection, afterwards withdrew it on finding that the doctor had no immediate worldly funds with which to endow his child; and it may easily be conceived that Miss Proudie, after such an announcement on his part, was not readily disposed to receive any further show of affection. On the appointment of Dr. Proudie to the bishopric of Barchester, Mr. Slope's views were in truth somewhat altered. Bishops, even though they be poor, can provide for clerical children, and Mr. Slope began to regret that he had not been more disinterested. He no sooner heard the tidings of the doctor's elevation, than he recommenced his siege, not violently, indeed, but respectfully, and at a distance. Olivia Proudie, however, was a girl of spirit: she had the blood of two peers in her veins, and, better still, she had another lover on her books; so Mr. Slope sighed in vain; and the pair soon found it convenient to establish a mutual bond of inveterate hatred.

It may be thought singular that Mrs. Proudie's friendship for the young clergyman should remain firm after such an affair; but, to tell the truth, she had known nothing of it. Though very fond of Mr. Slope herself, she had never conceived the idea that either of her daughters would become so, and remembering their high birth and social advantages, expected for them matches of a different sort. Neither the gentleman nor the lady found it necessary to enlighten her. Olivia's two sisters had each known of the affair, so had all the servants, so had all the people living in the adjoining houses on either side; but Mrs. Proudie had been kept in the dark.

Mr. Slope soon comforted himself with the reflection, that as he had been selected as chaplain to the bishop, it would probably be in his power to get the good things in the bishop's gift, without troubling himself with the bishop's daughter; and he found himself able to endure the pangs of rejected love. As he sat himself down in the railway carriage, confronting the bishop and Mrs. Proudie, as they started on their first journey to Barchester, he began to form in his own mind a plan of his future life. He knew well his patron's strong points, but he knew the weak ones as well. He understood correctly enough to what attempts the new bishop's high spirit would soar, and he rightly guessed that public life would better suit the great man's taste, than the small details of diocesan duty.

He, therefore, he, Mr. Slope, would in effect be bishop of Barchester. Such was his resolve; and to give Mr. Slope his due, he had both courage and spirit to bear him out in his resolution. He knew that he should have a hard battle to fight, for the power and patronage of the see would be equally coveted by another great mind—Mrs. Proudie would also choose to be bishop of Barchester. Mr. Slope, however, flattered himself that he could out-manœuvre the lady. She must live much in London, while he would always be on the spot. She would necessarily remain ignorant of much, while he would know everything belonging to the diocese. At first, doubtless, he must flatter and cajole, perhaps yield, in some things; but he did not doubt of ultimate triumph. If all other means failed, he could join the bishop against his wife, inspire courage into the unhappy man, lay an axe to the root of the woman's power, and emancipate the husband.

Such were his thoughts as he sat looking at the sleeping pair in the railway carriage, and Mr. Slope is not the man to trouble himself with such thoughts for nothing. He is possessed of more than average abilities, and is of good courage. Though he can stoop to fawn, and stoop low indeed, if need be, he has still within him the power to assume the tyrant; and with the power he has certainly the wish. His acquirements are not of the highest order, but such as they are they are completely under control, and he knows the use of them. He is gifted with a certain kind of pulpit eloquence, not likely indeed to be persuasive with men, but powerful with the softer sex. In his sermons he deals greatly in denunciations, excites the minds of his weaker hearers with a not unpleasant terror, and leaves an impression on their minds that all mankind are in a perilous state, and all womankind too, except those who attend regularly to the evening lectures in Baker Street. His looks and tones are extremely severe, so much so that one cannot but fancy that he regards the greater part of the world as being infinitely too bad for his care. As he walks through the streets, his very face denotes his horror of the world's wickedness; and there is always an anathema lurking in the corner of his eye.

In doctrine, he, like his patron, is tolerant of dissent, if so strict a mind can be called tolerant of anything. With Wesleyan-Methodists he has something in common, but his soul trembles in agony at the iniquities of the Puseyites. His aversion is carried to things outward as well as inward. His gall rises at a new church with a high pitched roof; a full-breasted black silk waistcoat is with him a symbol of Satan; and a profane jest-book would not, in his view, more foully desecrate the church seat of a Christian, than a book of prayer printed with red letters, and ornamented with a cross on the back. Most active clergymen have their hobby, and Sunday observances are his. Sunday, however, is a word which never pollutes his mouth—it is always " the Sabbath." The " desecration of the Sabbath," as he delights to call it, is to him meat and drink :—he thrives upon that as policemen do on the general evil habits of the community. It is the loved subject of all his evening discourses, the source of all his eloquence, the secret of all his power over the female heart. To him the revelation of God appears only in that one law given for Jewish observance. To him the mercies of our Saviour speak in vain, to him in vain has been preached that sermon which fell from divine lips on the mountain— " Blessed are the meek, for they shall inherit the earth "—" Blessed are the merciful, for they shall obtain mercy." To him the New Testament is comparatively of little moment, for from it can he draw no fresh authority for that dominion which he loves to exercise over at least a seventh part of man's allotted time here below.

Mr. Slope is tall, and not ill made. His feet and hands are large, as has ever been the case with all his family, but he has a broad chest and wide shoulders to carry off these excrescences, and on the whole his figure is good. His countenance, however, is not specially prepossessing. His hair is lank, and of a dull pale reddish hue. It is always formed into three straight lumpy masses, each brushed with admirable precision, and cemented with much grease; two of them adhere closely to the sides of his face, and the other lies at right angles above them. He wears no whiskers, and is always punctiliously shaven. His face is nearly of the same colour as his hair, though perhaps a little redder : it is not unlike beef,—beef, however, one would say, of a bad quality. His forehead is capacious and high, but square and heavy, and unpleasantly shining. His mouth is large, though his lips are thin and bloodless ; and his big, prominent, pale brown eyes inspire anything but confidence. His nose, however, is his redeeming feature: it is pronounced straight and well-formed ; though I myself should have liked it better did it not possess a somewhat spongy, porous appearance, as though it had been cleverly formed out of a red coloured cork.

I never could endure to shake hands with Mr. Slope. A cold, clammy perspiration always exudes from him, the small drops are ever to be seen standing on his brow, and his friendly grasp is unpleasant.

Such is Mr. Slope — such is the man who has suddenly fallen into the midst of Barchester Close, and is destined there to assume the station which has heretofore been filled by the son of the late bishop. Think, oh, my meditative reader, what an associate we have here for those comfortable prebendaries, those gentlemanlike clerical doctors, those happy well-used well-fed minor canons, who have grown into existence at Barchester under the kindly wings of Bishop Grantly!

But not as a mere associate for these does Mr. Slope travel down to Barchester with the bishop and his wife. He intends to be, if not their master, at least the chief among them. He intends to lead, and to have followers ; he intends to hold the purse strings of the diocese, and draw round him an obedient herd of his poor and hungry brethren.

And here we can hardly fail to draw a comparison between the archdeacon and our new private chaplain ; and despite the manifold faults of the former, one can hardly fail to make it much to his advantage.

Both men are eager, much too eager, to support and increase the power of their order. Both are anxious that the world should be priest-governed, though they have probably never confessed so much, even to themselves. Both begrudge any other kind of dominion held by man over man. Dr. Grantly, if he admits the Queen's supremacy in things spiritual, only admits it as being due to the *quasi* priesthood conveyed in the consecrating qualities of her coronation ; and he regards things temporal as being by their nature subject to those which are spiritual. Mr. Slope's ideas of sacerdotal rule are of quite a different class. He cares nothing, one way or the other, for the Queen's supremacy ; these to his ears are empty words, meaning nothing. Forms he regards but little, and such titular expressions as supremacy, consecration, ordination, and the like, convey of themselves no significance to him. Let him be supreme who can. The temporal king, judge, or gaoler, can work but on the body. The spiritual master, if he have the necessary gifts, and can duly use them, has a wider field of empire. He works upon the soul. If he can make himself be believed, he can be all powerful over those who listen. If he be careful to meddle with none who are too strong in intellect, or too weak in flesh, he may indeed be supreme. And such was the ambition of Mr. Slope.

Dr. Grantly interfered very little with the worldly doings of those who were in any way subject to him. I do not mean to say that he omitted to notice misconduct among his clergy, immorality in his parish, or omissions in his family; but he was not anxious to do so where the necessity could be avoided. He was not troubled with a propensity to be curious, and as long as those around him were tainted with no heretical leaning towards dissent, as long as they fully and freely admitted the efficacy of Mother Church, he was willing that that mother should be merciful and affectionate, prone to indulgence, and unwilling to chastise. He himself enjoyed the good things of this world, and liked to let it be known that he did so. He cordially despised any brother rector who thought harm of dinner-parties, or dreaded the dangers of a moderate claret-jug; consequently dinner-parties and claret-jugs were common in the diocese. He liked to give laws and to be obeyed in them implicitly, but he endeavoured that his ordinances should be within the compass of the man, and not unpalatable to the gentleman. He had ruled among his clerical neighbours now for sundry years, and as he had maintained his power without becoming unpopular, it may be presumed that he had exercised some wisdom.

Of Mr. Slope's conduct much cannot be said, as his grand career is yet to commence; but it may be premised that his tastes will be very different from those of the archdeacon. He conceives it to be his duty to know all the private doings and desires of the flock entrusted to his care. From the poorer classes he exacts an unconditional obedience to set rules of conduct, and if disobeyed he has recourse, like his great ancestor, to the fulminations of an Ernulfus: "Thou shalt be damned in thy going in and in thy coming out — in thy eating and thy drinking," &c. &c. &c. With the rich, experience has already taught him that a different line of action is necessary. Men in the upper walks of life do not mind being cursed, and the women, presuming that it be done in delicate phrase, rather like it. But he has not, therefore, given up so important a portion of believing Christians. With the men, indeed, he is generally at variance; they are hardened sinners, on whom the voice of the priestly charmer too often falls in vain; but with the ladies, old and young, firm and frail, devout and dissipated, he is, as he conceives, all powerful. He can reprove faults with so much flattery, and utter censure in so caressing a manner, that the female heart, if it glow with a spark of low church susceptibility, cannot withstand him. In many houses he is thus an admired guest: the husbands, for their wives' sake, are fain to admit him; and when once admitted it is not easy to shake him off. He has, however, a pawing, greasy way with him, which does not endear him to those who do not value him for their souls' sake, and he is not a man to make himself at once popular in a large circle such as is now likely to surround him at Barchester.

CHAP. V.

A MORNING VISIT.

It was known that Dr. Proudie would immediately have to reappoint to the wardenship of the hospital under the act of Parliament to which allusion has been made; but no one imagined that any choice was left to him—no one for a moment thought that he could appoint any other than Mr. Harding. Mr. Harding himself, when he heard how the matter had been settled, without troubling himself much on the subject, considered it as certain that he would go back to his pleasant house and garden. And though there would be much that was melancholy, nay, almost heartrending, in such a return, he still was glad that it was to be so. His daughter might probably be persuaded to return there with him. She had, indeed, all but promised to do so, though she still entertained an idea that that greatest of mortals, that important atom of humanity, that little god upon earth, Johnny Bold her baby, ought to have a house of his own over his head.

Such being the state of Mr. Harding's mind in the matter, he did not feel any peculiar personal interest in the appointment of Dr. Proudie to the bishopric. He, as well as others at Barchester, regretted that a man should be sent among them who, they were aware, was not of their way of thinking; but Mr. Harding himself was not a bigoted man on points of church doctrine, and he was quite prepared to welcome Dr. Proudie to Barchester in a graceful and becoming manner. He had nothing to seek and nothing to fear ; he felt that it behoved him to be on good terms with his bishop, and he did not anticipate any obstacle that would prevent it.

In such a frame of mind he proceeded to pay his respects at the palace the second day after the arrival of the bishop and his chaplain. But he did not go alone. Dr. Grantly proposed to accompany him, and Mr. Harding was not sorry to have a companion, who would remove from his shoulders the burden of the conversation in such an interview. In the affair of the consecration Dr. Grantly had been introduced to the bishop, and Mr. Harding had also been there. He had, however, kept himself in the background, and he was now to be presented to the great man for the first time.

The archdeacon's feelings were of a much stronger nature. He was not exactly the man to overlook his own slighted claims, or to forgive the preference shown to another. Dr. Proudie was playing Venus to his Juno, and he was prepared to wage an internecine war against the owner of the wished-for apple, and all his satellites, private chaplains, and others.

Nevertheless, it behoved him also to conduct himself towards the intruder as an old archdeacon should conduct himself to an incoming bishop ; and though he was well aware of all Dr. Proudie's abominable opinions as regarded dissenters, church reform, the hebdomadal council, and such like ; though he disliked the man, and hated the doctrines, still he was prepared to show respect to the station of the bishop. So he and Mr. Harding called together at the palace.

His lordship was at home, and the two visitors were shown through the accustomed hall into the well-known room, where the good old bishop used to sit. The furniture had been bought at a valuation, and every chair and table, every bookshelf against the wall, and every square in the carpet, was as well known to each of them as their own bedrooms. Nevertheless they at once felt that they were strangers there. The furniture was for the most part the same, yet the place had been metamorphosed. A new sofa had been introduced, a horrid chintz affair, most unprelatical and almost irreligious : such a sofa as never yet stood in the study of any decent high church clergyman of the Church of England. The old curtains had also given way. They had, to be sure, become dingy, and that which had been originally a rich and goodly ruby had degenerated into a reddish brown. Mr. Harding, however, thought the old reddish brown much preferable to the gaudy buff-coloured trumpery moreen which Mrs. Proudie had deemed good enough for her husband's own room in the provincial city of Barchester.

Our friends found Dr. Proudie sitting on the old bishop's chair, looking very nice in his new apron; they found, too, Mr. Slope standing on the hearthrug, persuasive and eager, just as the archdeacon used to stand; but on the sofa they also found Mrs. Proudie, an innovation for which a precedent might in vain be sought in all the annals of the Barchester bishopric!

There she was, however, and they could only make the best of her. The introductions were gone through in much form. The archdeacon shook hands with the bishop, and named Mr. Harding, who received such an amount of greeting as was due from a bishop to a precentor. His lordship then presented them to his lady wife; the archdeacon first, with archidiaconal honours, and then the precentor with diminished parade. After this Mr. Slope presented himself. The bishop, it is true, did mention his name, and so did Mrs. Proudie too, in a louder tone; but Mr. Slope took upon himself the chief burden of his own introduction. He had great pleasure in making himself acquainted with Dr. Grantly; he had heard much of the archdeacon's good works in that part of the diocese in which his duties as archdeacon had been exercised (thus purposely ignoring the archdeacon's hitherto unlimited dominion over the diocese at large). He was aware that his lordship depended greatly on the assistance which Dr. Grantly would be able to give him in that portion of his diocese. He then thrust out his hand, and grasping that of his new foe, bedewed it unmercifully. Dr. Grantly in return bowed, looked stiff, contracted his eyebrows, and wiped his hand with his pocket-handkerchief. Nothing abashed, Mr. Slope then noticed the precentor, and descended to the grade of the lower clergy. He gave him a squeeze of the hand, damp indeed, but affectionate, and was very glad to make the acquaintance of Mr. ——; oh yes, Mr. Harding; he had not exactly caught the name — "Precentor in the cathedral," surmised Mr. Slope. Mr. Harding confessed that such was the humble sphere of his work. "Some parish duty as well," suggested Mr. Slope. Mr. Harding acknowledged the diminutive incumbency of St. Cuthbert's. Mr. Slope then left him alone, having condescended sufficiently, and joined the conversation among the higher powers.

There were four persons there, each of whom considered himself the most important personage in the diocese; himself, indeed, or herself, as Mrs. Proudie was one of them; and with such a difference of opinion it was not probable that they would get on pleasantly together. The bishop himself actually wore the visible apron, and trusted mainly to that—to that and his title, both being facts which could not be overlooked. The archdeacon knew his subject, and really understood the business of bishoping, which the others did not; and this was his strong ground. Mrs. Proudie had her sex to back her, and her habit of command, and was nothing daunted by the high tone of Dr. Grantly's face and figure. Mr. Slope had only himself and his own courage and tact to depend on, but he nevertheless was perfectly self-assured, and did not doubt but that he should soon get the better of weak men who trusted so much to externals, as both bishop and archdeacon appeared to do.

"Do you reside in Barchester, Dr. Grantly?" asked the lady with her sweetest smile.

Dr. Grantly explained that he lived in his own parish of Plumstead Episcopi, a few miles out of the city. Whereupon the lady hoped that the distance was not too great for country visiting, as she would be so glad to make the acquaintance of Mrs. Grantly. She would take the earliest opportunity, after the arrival of her horses at Barchester; their horses were at present in London; their horses were not immediately coming down, as the bishop would be obliged, in a few days, to return to town. Dr. Grantly was no doubt aware that the bishop was at present much called upon by the " University Improvement Committee : " indeed, the Committee could not well proceed without him, as their final report had now to be drawn up. The bishop had also to prepare a scheme for the " Manufacturing Towns Morning and Evening Sunday School Society," of which he was a patron, or president, or director, and therefore the horses would not come down to Barchester at present ; but whenever the horses did come down, she would take the earliest opportunity of calling at Plumstead Episcopi, providing the distance was not too great for country visiting.

The archdeacon made his fifth bow : he had made one at each mention of the horses; and promised that Mrs. Grantly would do herself the honour of calling at the palace on an early day. Mrs. Proudie declared that she would be delighted : she had'nt liked to ask, not being quite sure whether Mrs. Grantly had horses; besides, the distance might have been, &c. &c.

Dr. Grantly again bowed, but said nothing. He could have bought every individual possession of the whole family of the

Proudies, and have restored them as a gift, without much feeling the loss; and had kept a separate pair of horses for the exclusive use of his wife since the day of his marriage; whereas Mrs. Proudie had been hitherto jobbed about the streets of London at so much a month during the season; and at other times had managed to walk, or hire a smart fly from the livery stables.

"Are the arrangements with reference to the Sabbath-day schools generally pretty good in your archdeaconry?" asked Mr. Slope.

"Sabbath-day schools!" repeated the archdeacon with an affectation of surprise. "Upon my word, I can't tell; it depends mainly on the parson's wife and daughters. There is none at Plumstead."

This was almost a fib on the part of the archdeacon, for Mrs. Grantly has a very nice school. To be sure it is not a Sunday school exclusively, and is not so designated; but that exemplary lady always attends there an hour before church, and hears the children say their catechism, and sees that they are clean and tidy for church, with their hands washed, and their shoes tied; and Grisel and Florinda, her daughters, carry thither a basket of large buns, baked on the Saturday afternoon, and distribute them to all the children not especially under disgrace, which buns are carried home after church with considerable content, and eaten hot at tea, being then split and toasted. The children of Plumstead would indeed open their eyes if they heard their venerated pastor declare that there was no Sunday school in his parish.

Mr. Slope merely opened his eyes wider, and slightly shrugged his shoulders. He was not, however, prepared to give up his darling project.

"I fear there is a great deal of Sabbath travelling here," said he. "On looking at the 'Bradshaw,' I see that there are three trains in and three out every Sabbath. Could nothing be done to induce the company to withdraw them? Don't you think, Dr. Grantly, that a little energy might diminish the evil?"

"Not being a director, I really can't say. But if you can withdraw the passengers, the company I dare say, will withdraw the trains," said the doctor. "It's merely a question of dividends."

"But surely, Dr. Grantly," said the lady, "surely we should look at it differently. You and I, for instance, in our position: surely we should do all that we can to control so grievous a sin. Don't you think so, Mr. Harding?" and she turned to the precentor, who was sitting mute and unhappy.

Mr. Harding thought that all porters and stokers, guards,

breaksmen, and pointsmen ought to have an opportunity of going to church, and he hoped that they all had.

"But surely, surely," continued Mrs. Proudie, "surely that is not enough. Surely that will not secure such an observance of the Sabbath as we are taught to conceive is not only expedient but indispensable; surely——"

Come what come might, Dr. Grantly was not to be forced into a dissertation on a point of doctrine with Mrs. Proudie, nor yet with Mr. Slope; so without much ceremony he turned his back upon the sofa, and began to hope that Dr. Proudie had found that the palace repairs had been such as to meet his wishes.

"Yes, yes," said his lordship; upon the whole he thought so —upon the whole, he didn't know that there was much ground for complaint; the architect, perhaps, might have——but his double, Mr. Slope, who had sidled over to the bishop's chair, would not allow his lordship to finish his ambiguous speech.

"There is one point I would like to mention, Mr. Archdeacon. His lordship asked me to step through the premises, and I see that the stalls in the second stable are not perfect."

"Why—there's standing there for a dozen horses," said the archdeacon.

"Perhaps so," said the other; "indeed, I've no doubt of it; but visitors, you know, often require so much accommodation. There are so many of the bishop's relatives who always bring their own horses."

Dr. Grantly promised that due provision for the relatives' horses should be made, as far at least as the extent of the original stable building would allow. He would himself communicate with the architect.

"And the coach-house, Dr. Grantly," continued Mr. Slope; "there is really hardly room for a second carriage in the large coach-house, and the smaller one, of course, holds only one."

"And the gas," chimed in the lady; "there is no gas through the house, none whatever, but in the kitchen and passages. Surely the palace should have been fitted through with pipes for gas, and hot water too. There is no hot water laid on anywhere above the ground-floor; surely there should be the means of getting hot water in the bed-rooms without having it brought in jugs from the kitchen."

The bishop had a decided opinion that there should be pipes for hot water. Hot water was very essential for the comfort of the palace. It was, indeed, a requisite in any decent gentleman's house.

Mr. Slope had remarked that the coping on the garden wall was in many places imperfect.

Mrs. Proudie had discovered a large hole, evidently the work of rats, in the servants' hall.

The bishop expressed an utter detestation of rats. There was nothing, he believed, in this world, that he so much hated as a rat.

Mr. Slope had, moreover, observed that the locks of the out-houses were very imperfect : he might specify the coal-cellar, and the wood-house.

Mrs. Proudie had also seen that those on the doors of the servants' bedrooms were in an equally bad condition; indeed the locks all through the house were old-fashioned and unserviceable.

The bishop thought that a great deal depended on a good lock, and quite as much on the key. He had observed that the fault very often lay with the key, especially if the wards were in any way twisted.

Mr. Slope was going on with his catalogue of grievances, when he was somewhat loudly interrupted by the archdeacon, who succeeded in explaining that the diocesan architect, or rather his foreman, was the person to be addressed on such subjects ; and that he, Dr. Grantly, had inquired as to the comfort of the palace, merely as a point of compliment. He was sorry, however, that so many things had been found amiss : and then he rose from his chair to escape.

Mrs. Proudie, though she had contrived to lend her assistance in recapitulating the palatial dilapidations, had not on that account given up her hold of Mr. Harding, nor ceased from her cross-examinations as to the iniquity of Sabbatical amusements. Over and over again had she thrown out her "Surely, surely," at Mr. Harding's devoted head, and ill had that gentleman been able to parry the attack.

He had never before found himself subjected to such a nuisance. Ladies hitherto, when they had consulted him on religious subjects, had listened to what he might choose to say with some deference, and had differed, if they differed, in silence. But Mrs. Proudie interrogated him, and then lectured. "Neither thou, nor thy son, nor thy daughter, nor thy man servant, nor thy maid servant," said she, impressively, and more than once, as though Mr. Harding had forgotten the words. She shook her finger at him as she quoted the favourite law, as though menacing him with punishment; and then called upon him categorically to state whether he did not think that travelling on the Sabbath was an abomination and a desecration.

Mr. Harding had never been so hard pressed in his life. He felt that he ought to rebuke the lady for presuming so to talk to a gentleman and a clergyman many years her senior ; but he recoiled from the idea of scolding the bishop's wife, in the bishop's presence, on his first visit to the palace; moreover, to tell the truth, he was somewhat afraid of her. She, seeing him sit silent and absorbed, by no means refrained from the attack.

"I hope, Mr. Harding," said she, shaking her head slowly and solemnly, "I hope you will not leave me to think that you approve of Sabbath travelling," and she looked a look of unutterable meaning into his eyes.

There was no standing this, for Mr. Slope was now looking at him, and so was the bishop, and so was the archdeacon, who had completed his adieux on that side of the room. Mr. Harding therefore got up also, and putting out his hand to Mrs. Proudie said: "If you will come to St. Cuthbert's some Sunday, I will preach you a sermon on that subject."

And so the archdeacon and the precentor took their departure, bowing low to the lady, shaking hands with the lord, and escaping from Mr. Slope in the best manner each could. Mr. Harding was again maltreated; but Dr. Grantly swore deeply in the bottom of his heart, that no earthly consideration should ever again induce him to touch the paw of that impure and filthy animal.

And now had I the pen of a mighty poet, would I sing in epic verse the noble wrath of the archdeacon. The palace steps descend to a broad gravel sweep, from whence a small gate opens out into the street, very near the covered gateway leading into the close. The road from the palace door turns to the left, through the spacious gardens, and terminates on the London-road, half a mile from the cathedral.

Till they had both passed this small gate and entered the close, neither of them spoke a word; but the precentor clearly saw from his companion's face that a tornado was to be expected, nor was he himself inclined to stop it. Though by nature far less irritable than the archdeacon, even he was angry: he even—that mild and courteous man—was inclined to express himself in anything but courteous terms.

CHAP. VI.

WAR.

"GOOD heavens!" exclaimed the archdeacon, as he placed his foot on the gravel walk of the close, and raising his hat with one hand, passed the other somewhat violently over his now grizzled locks; smoke issued forth from the uplifted beaver as it were a cloud of wrath, and the safety-valve of his anger opened, and emitted a visible steam, preventing positive explosion and probable apoplexy. "Good heavens!"—and the archdeacon looked up to the gray pinnacles of the cathedral tower, making a mute appeal to that still living witness which had looked down on the doings of so many bishops of Barchester.

"I don't think I shall ever like that Mr. Slope," said Mr Harding.

"Like him!" roared the archdeacon, standing still for a moment to give more force to his voice; "like him!" All the ravens of the close cawed their assent. The old bells of the tower, in chiming the hour, echoed the words; and the swallows flying out from their nests mutely expressed a similar opinion. Like Mr. Slope! Why no, it was not very probable that any Barchester-bred living thing should like Mr. Slope!

"Nor Mrs. Proudie either," said Mr. Harding.

The archdeacon hereupon forgot himself. I will not follow his example, nor shock my readers by transcribing the term in which he expressed his feeling as to the lady who had been named. The ravens and the last lingering notes of the clock bells were less scrupulous, and repeated in corresponding echoes the very improper exclamation. The archdeacon again raised his hat, and another salutary escape of steam was effected.

There was a pause, during which the precentor tried to realise the fact that the wife of a bishop of Barchester had been thus designated, in the close of the cathedral, by the lips of its own archdeacon: but he could not do it.

"The bishop seems to be a quiet man enough," suggested Mr. Harding, having acknowledged to himself his own failure.

"Idiot!" exclaimed the doctor, who for the nonce was not capable of more than such spasmodic attempts at utterance.

"Well he did not seem very bright," said Mr. Harding, "and yet he has always had the reputation of a clever man. I suppose he's cautious and not inclined to express himself very freely."

The new bishop of Barchester was already so contemptible a creature in Dr. Grantly's eyes, that he could not condescend to discuss his character. He was a puppet to be played by others; a mere wax doll, done up in an apron and a shovel hat, to be stuck on a throne or elsewhere, and pulled about by wires as others chose. Dr. Grantly did not choose to let himself down low enough to talk about Dr. Proudie; but he saw that he would have to talk about the other members of his household, the coadjutor bishops, who had brought his lordship down, as it were, in a box, and were about to handle the wires as they willed. This in itself was a terrible vexation to the archdeacon. Could he have ignored the chaplain, and have fought the bishop, there would have been, at any rate, nothing degrading in such a contest. Let the Queen make whom she would bishop of Barchester; a man, or even an ape, when once a bishop, would be a respectable adversary, if he would but fight, himself. But what was such a person as Dr. Grantly to do, when such another person as Mr. Slope was put forward as his antagonist?

If he, our archdeacon, refused the combat, Mr. Slope would walk triumphant over the field, and have the diocese of Barchester under his heel.

If, on the other hand, the archdeacon accepted as his enemy the man whom the new puppet bishop put before him as such, he would have to talk about Mr. Slope, and write about Mr. Slope, and in all matters treat with Mr. Slope, as a being standing, in some degree, on ground similar to his own. He would have to meet Mr. Slope; to —— Bah! the idea was sickening. He could not bring himself to have to do with Mr. Slope.

"He is the most thoroughly bestial creature that ever I set my eyes upon," said the archdeacon.

"Who — the bishop?" asked the other, innocently.

"Bishop! no—I'm not talking about the bishop. How on earth such a creature got ordained! — they'll ordain anybody now, I know; but he's been in the church these ten years; and they used to be a little careful ten years ago."

"Oh! you mean Mr. Slope."

"Did you ever see any animal less like a gentleman?" asked Dr. Grantly.

"I can't say I felt myself much disposed to like him."

"Like him!" again shouted the doctor, and the assenting ravens again cawed an echo; "of course, you don't like him: it's not a question of liking. But what are we to do with him?"

"Do with him?" asked Mr. Harding.

"Yes — what are we to do with him? How are we to treat him? There he is, and there he'll stay. He has put his foot in that palace, and he will never take it out again till he's driven. How are we to get rid of him?"

"I don't suppose he can do us much harm."

"Not do harm!—Well, I think you'll find yourself of a different opinion before a month is gone. What would you say now, if he got himself put into the hospital? Would that be harm?"

Mr. Harding mused awhile, and then said he didn't think the new bishop would put Mr. Slope into the hospital.

"If he doesn't put him there, he'll put him somewhere else where he'll be as bad. I tell you that that man, to all intents and purposes, will be Bishop of Barchester;" and again Dr. Grantly raised his hat, and rubbed his hand thoughtfully and sadly over his head.

"Impudent scoundrel!" he continued after a while. "To dare to cross-examine me about the Sunday schools in the diocese, and Sunday travelling too : I never in my life met his equal for sheer impudence. Why, he must have thought we were two candidates for ordination !"

"I declare I thought Mrs. Proudie was the worst of the two," said Mr. Harding.

"When a woman is impertinent, one must only put up with it, and keep out of her way in future ; but I am not inclined to put up with Mr. Slope. 'Sabbath travelling!'" and the doctor attempted to imitate the peculiar drawl of the man he so much disliked : "'Sabbath travelling!' Those are the sort of men who will ruin the Church of England, and make the profession of a clergyman disreputable. It is not the dissenters or the papists that we should fear, but the set of canting, low-bred hypocrites who are wriggling their way in among us ; men who have no fixed principle, no standard ideas of religion or doctrine, but who take up some popular cry, as this fellow has done about 'Sabbath travelling.'"

Dr. Grantly did not again repeat the question aloud, but he did so constantly to himself, "What were they to do with Mr. Slope ?" How was he openly, before the world, to show that he utterly disapproved of and abhorred such a man ?

Hitherto Barchester had escaped the taint of any extreme rigour of church doctrine. The clergymen of the city and neighbourhood, though very well inclined to promote high-church principles, privileges, and prerogatives, had never committed themselves to tendencies, which are somewhat too loosely called Puseyite practices. They all preached in their black gowns, as their fathers had done before them ; they wore ordinary black cloth waistcoats ; they had no candles on their altars, either lighted or unlighted ; they made no private genuflexions, and were contented to confine themselves to such ceremonial observances as had been in vogue for the last hundred years. The services were decently and demurely read in their parish churches, chanting was confined to the cathedral, and the science of intoning was unknown. One young man who had come direct from Oxford as a curate to Plumstead had, after the lapse of two or three Sundays, made a faint attempt, much to the bewilderment of the poorer part of the congregation. Dr Grantly had not been present on the occasion ; but Mrs. Grantly who had her own opinion on the subject, immediately after the service expressed a hope that the young gentleman had not been taken ill, and offered to send him all kinds of condiments supposed to be good for a sore throat. After that there had been no more intoning at Plumstead Episcopi.

But now the archdeacon began to meditate on some strong measures of absolute opposition. Dr. Proudie and his crew were of the lowest possible order of Church of England clergymen, and therefore it behoved him, Dr. Grantly, to be of the very highest. Dr. Proudie would abolish all forms and ceremonies, and therefore Dr. Grantly felt the sudden necessity of multiplying them. Dr. Proudie would consent to deprive the church of all collective authority and rule, and therefore Dr. Grantly would stand up for the full power of convocation, and the renewal of all its ancient privileges.

It was true that he could not himself intone the service, but he could procure the co-operation of any number of gentleman-like curates well trained in the mystery of doing so.   He would not willingly alter his own fashion of dress, but he could people Bar- chester with young clergymen dressed in the longest frocks, and in the highest-breasted silk waistcoats. He certainly was not prepared to cross himself, or to advocate the real presence ; but, without going this length, there were various observances, by adopting which he could plainly show his antipathy to such men as Dr. Proudie and Mr. Slope.

All these things passed through his mind as he paced up and down the close with Mr. Harding. War, war, internecine war was in his heart. He felt that, as regarded himself and Mr. Slope, one of the two must be annihilated as far as the city of Barchester was concerned ; and he did not intend to give way until there was not left to him an inch of ground on which he could stand. He still flattered himself that he could make Barchester too hot to hold Mr. Slope, and he had no weakness of spirit to prevent his bringing about such a consummation if it were in his power.

"I suppose Susan must call at the palace," said Mr. Harding.

"Yes, she shall call there ; but it shall be once and once only. I dare say 'the horses' won't find it convenient to come out to Plumstead very soon, and when that once is done the matter may drop."

"I don't suppose Eleanor need call. I don't think Eleanor would get on at all well with Mrs. Proudie."

"Not the least necessity in life," replied the archdeacon, not without the reflection that a ceremony which was necessary for his wife, might not be at all binding on the widow of John Bold. "Not the slightest reason on earth why she should do so, if she doesn't like it. For myself, I don't think that any decent young woman should be subjected to the nuisance of being in the same room with that man."

And so the two clergymen parted, Mr. Harding going to his daughter's house, and the archdeacon seeking the seclusion of his brougham.

The new inhabitants of the palace did not express any higher opinion of their visitors than their visitors had expressed of them. Though they did not use quite such strong language as Dr. Grantly had done, they felt as much personal aversion, and were quite as well aware as he was that there would be a battle to be fought, and that there was hardly room for Proudieism in Barchester as long as Grantlyism was predominant.

Indeed, it may be doubted whether Mr. Slope had not already within his breast a better prepared system of strategy, a more accurately-defined line of hostile conduct than the archdeacon. Dr. Grantly was going to fight because he found that he hated the man. Mr. Slope had predetermined to hate the man, because he foresaw the necessity of fighting him. When he had first reviewed the *carte du pays*, previous to his entry into Barchester, the idea had occurred to him of conciliating the archdeacon, of cajoling and flattering him into submission, and of obtaining the upper hand by cunning instead of courage. A little inquiry, however, sufficed to convince him that all his cunning would fail to win over such a man as Dr. Grantly to such a mode of action as that to be adopted by Mr. Slope; and then he determined to fall back upon his courage. He at once saw that open battle against Dr. Grantly and all Dr. Grantly's adherents was a necessity of his position, and he deliberately planned the most expedient methods of giving offence.

Soon after his arrival the bishop had intimated to the dean, that with the permission of the canon then in residence, his chaplain would preach in the cathedral on the next Sunday. The canon in residence happened to be the Hon. and Rev. Dr. Vesey Stanhope, who at this time was very busy on the shores of the Lake of Como, adding to that unique collection of butterflies for which he is so famous. Or, rather, he would have been in residence but for the butterflies and other such summer-day considerations; and the vicar-choral, who was to take his place in the pulpit, by no means objected to having his work done for him by Mr. Slope.

Mr. Slope accordingly preached, and if a preacher can have satisfaction in being listened to, Mr. Slope ought to have been gratified. I have reason to think that he was gratified, and that he left the pulpit with the conviction that he had done what he intended to do when he entered it.

On this occasion the new bishop took his seat for the first time in the throne allotted to him. New scarlet cushions and drapery had been prepared, with new gilt binding and new fringe. The old carved oak-wood of the throne, ascending with its numerous grotesque pinnacles half-way up to the roof of the choir, had been washed, and dusted, and rubbed, and it all looked very smart. Ah! how often sitting there, in happy early days, on those lowly benches in front of the altar, have I whiled away the tedium of a sermon in considering how best I might thread my way up amidst those wooden towers, and climb safely to the topmost pinnacle!

All Barchester went to hear Mr. Slope; either for that or to gaze at the new bishop. All the best bonnets of the city were there, and moreover all the best glossy clerical hats. Not a stall but had its fitting occupant; for though some of the prebendaries might be away in Italy or elsewhere, their places were filled by brethren, who flocked into Barchester on the occasion. The dean was there, a heavy old man, now too old, indeed, to attend frequently in his place; and so was the archdeacon. So also were the chancellor, the treasurer, the precentor, sundry canons and minor canons, and every lay member of the choir, prepared to sing the new bishop in with due melody and harmonious expression of sacred welcome.

The service was certainly very well performed. Such was always the case at Barchester, as the musical education of the choir had been good, and the voices had been carefully selected. The psalms were beautifully chanted; the Te Deum was magnificently sung; and the litany was given in a manner, which is still to be found at Barchester, but, if my taste be correct, is to be found nowhere else. The litany in Barchester cathedral has long been the special task to which Mr. Harding's skill and voice have been devoted. Crowded audiences generally make good performers, and though Mr. Harding was not aware of any extraordinary exertion on his part, yet probably he rather exceeded his usual mark. Others were doing their best, and it was natural that he should emulate his brethren. So the service went on, and at last Mr. Slope got into the pulpit.

He chose for his text a verse from the precepts addressed by St. Paul to Timothy, as to the conduct necessary in a spiritual pastor and guide, and it was immediately evident that the good clergy of Barchester were to have a lesson.

"Study to show thyself approved unto God, a workman that needeth not to be ashamed, rightly dividing the word of truth." These were the words of his text, and with such a subject in such a place, it may be supposed that such a preacher would be listened to by such an audience. He was listened to with breathless attention, and not without considerable surprise. Whatever opinion of Mr. Slope might have been held in Barchester before he commenced his discourse, none of his hearers, when it was over, could mistake him either for a fool or a coward.

It would not be becoming were I to travestie a sermon, or even to repeat the language of it in the pages of a novel. In endeavouring to depict the characters of the persons of whom I write, I am to a certain extent forced to speak of sacred things. I trust, however, that I shall not be thought to scoff at the pulpit, though some may imagine that I do not feel all the reverence that is due to the cloth. I may question the infallibility of the teachers, but I hope that I shall not therefore be accused of doubt as to the thing to be taught.

Mr. Slope, in commencing his sermon, showed no slight tact in his ambiguous manner of hinting that, humble as he was himself, he stood there as the mouthpiece of the illustrious divine who sat opposite to him; and having premised so much, he gave forth a very accurate definition of the conduct which that prelate would rejoice to see in the clergymen now brought under his jurisdiction, It is only necessary to say, that the peculiar points insisted upon were exactly those which were most distasteful to the clergy of the diocese, and most averse to their practice and opinions; and that all those peculiar habits and privileges which have always been dear to high-church priests, to that party which is now scandalously called the high-and-dry church, were ridiculed, abused, and anathematised. Now, the clergymen of the diocese of Barchester are all of the high-and-dry church.

Having thus, according to his own opinion, explained how a clergyman should show himself approved unto God, as a workman that needeth not to be ashamed, he went on to explain how the word of truth should be divided; and here he took a rather narrow view of the question, and fetched his arguments from afar. His object was to express his abomination of all ceremonious modes of utterance, to cry down any religious feeling which might be excited, not by the sense, but by the sound of words, and in fact to insult cathedral practices. Had St. Paul spoken of rightly pronouncing instead of rightly dividing the word of truth, this part of his sermon would have been more to the purpose; but the preacher's immediate object was to preach Mr. Slope's doctrine, and not St. Paul's, and he contrived to give the necessary twist to the text with some skill.

He could not exactly say, preaching from a cathedral pulpit, that chanting should be abandoned in cathedral services. By such an assertion, he would have overshot his mark and rendered himself absurd, to the delight of his hearers. He could, however, and did, allude with heavy denunciations to the practice of intoning in parish churches, although the practice was all but unknown in the diocese; and from thence he came round to the undue preponderance, which he asserted, music had over meaning in the beautiful service which they had just heard. He was aware, he said, that the practices of our ancestors could not be abandoned at a moment's notice; the feelings of the aged would be outraged, and the minds of respectable men would be shocked. There were many, he was aware, of not sufficient calibre of thought to perceive, of not sufficient education to know, that a mode of service, which was effective when outward ceremonies were of more moment than inward feelings, had become all but barbarous at a time when inward conviction was everything, when each word of the minister's lips should fall intelligibly into the listener's heart. Formerly the religion of the multitude had been an affair of the imagination: now, in these latter days, it had become necessary that a Christian should have a reason for his faith—should not only believe, but digest — not only hear, but understand. The words of our morning service, how beautiful, how apposite, how intelligible they were, when read with simple and distinct decorum! but how much of the meaning of the words was lost when they were produced with all the meretricious charms of melody! &c. &c.

Here was a sermon to be preached before Mr. Archdeacon Grantly, Mr. Precentor Harding, and the rest of them! before a whole dean and chapter assembled in their own cathedral! before men who had grown old in the exercise of their peculiar services, with a full conviction of their excellence for all intended purposes! This too from such a man, a clerical *parvenu*, a man without a cure, a mere chaplain, an intruder among them; a fellow raked up, so said Dr. Grantly, from the gutters of Marylebone! They had to sit through it! None of them, not even Dr. Grantly, could close his ears, nor leave the house of God during the hours of service. They were under an obligation of listening, and that too, without any immediate power of reply.

There is, perhaps, no greater hardship at present inflicted on mankind in civilised and free countries, than the necessity of listening to sermons. No one but a preaching clergyman has, in these realms, the power of compelling an audience to sit silent, and be tormented. No one but a preaching clergyman can revel in platitudes, truisms, and untruisms, and yet receive, as his undisputed privilege, the same respectful demeanour as though words of impassioned eloquence, or persuasive logic, fell from his lips. Let a professor of law or physic find his place in a lecture-room, and there pour forth jejune words and useless empty phrases, and he will pour them forth to empty benches. Let a barrister attempt to talk without talking well, and he will talk but seldom. A judge's charge need be listened to per force by none but the jury, prisoner, and gaoler. A member of Parliament can be coughed down or counted out. Town-councillors can be tabooed. But no one can rid himself of the preaching clergyman. He is the bore of the age, the old man whom we Sindbads cannot shake off, the nightmare that disturbs our Sunday's rest, the incubus that overloads our religion and makes God's service distasteful. We are not forced into church! No: but we desire more than that. We desire not to be forced to stay away. We desire, nay, we are resolute, to enjoy the comfort of public worship; but we desire also that we may do so without an amount of tedium which ordinary human nature cannot endure with patience; that we may be able to leave the house of God, without that anxious longing for escape, which is the common consequence of common sermons.

With what complacency will a young parson deduce false conclusions from misunderstood texts, and then threaten us with all the penalties of Hades if we neglect to comply with the injunctions he has given us! Yes, my too self-confident juvenile friend, I do believe in those mysteries, which are so common in your mouth; I do believe in the unadulterated word which you hold there in your hand; but you must pardon me if, in some things, I doubt your interpretation. The bible is good, the prayer-book is good, nay, you yourself would be acceptable, if you would read to me some portion of those time-honoured discourses which our great divines have elaborated in the full maturity of their powers. But you must excuse me, my insufficient young lecturer, if I yawn over your imperfect sentences, your repeated phrases, your false pathos, your drawlings and denouncings, your humming and hawing, your oh-ing and ah-ing, your black gloves and your white handkerchief. To me, it all means nothing; and hours are too precious to be so wasted —— if one could only avoid it.

And here I must make a protest against the pretence, so often put forward by the working clergy, that they are overburdened by the multitude of sermons to be preached. We are all too fond of our own voices, and a preacher is encouraged in the vanity of making his heard by the privilege of a compelled audience. His sermon is the pleasant morsel of his life, his delicious moment of self-exaltation. "I have preached nine sermons this week," said a young friend to me the other day, with hand languidly raised to his brow, the picture of an overburdened martyr. "Nine this week, seven last week, four the week before. I have preached twenty-three sermons this month. It is really too much." "Too much, indeed," said I, shuddering; "too much for the strength of any one." "Yes," he answered meekly, "indeed it is; I am beginning to feel it painfully." "Would," said I, "you could feel it—would that you could be made to feel it." But he never guessed that my heart was wrung for the poor listeners.

There was, at any rate, no tedium felt in listening to Mr. Slope on the occasion in question. His subject came too home to his audience to be dull; and, to tell the truth, Mr. Slope had the gift of using words forcibly. He was heard through his thirty minutes of eloquence with mute attention and open ears; but with angry eyes, which glared round from one enraged parson to another, with wide-spread nostrils from which already burst forth fumes of indignation, and with many shufflings of the feet and uneasy motions of the body, which betokened minds disturbed, and hearts not at peace with all the world.

At last the bishop, who, of all the congregation, had been most surprised, and whose hair almost stood on end with terror, gave the blessing in a manner not at all equal to that in which he had long been practising it in his own study, and the congregation was free to go their way.

CHAP. VII.

THE DEAN AND CHAPTER TAKE COUNSEL.

ALL Barchester was in a tumult. Dr. Grantly could hardly get himself out of the cathedral porch before he exploded in his wrath. The old dean betook himself silently to his deanery, afraid to speak; and there sat, half stupefied, pondering many things in vain. Mr. Harding crept forth solitary and unhappy; and, slowly passing beneath the elms of the close, could scarcely bring himself to believe that the words which he had heard had proceeded from the pulpit of Barchester cathedral. Was he again to be disturbed? was his whole life to be shown up as a useless sham a second time? would he have to abdicate his precentorship, as he had his warden-ship, and to give up chanting, as he had given up his twelve old bedesmen? And what if he did! Some other Jupiter, some other Mr. Slope, would come and turn him out of St. Cuthbert's. Surely he could not have been wrong all his life in chanting the litany as he had done! He began, however, to have his doubts. Doubting himself was Mr. Harding's weakness. It is not, however, the usual fault of his order.

Yes! all Barchester was in a tumult. It was not only the clergy who were affected. The laity also had listened to Mr. Slope's new doctrine, all with surprise, some with indignation, and some with a mixed feeling, in which dislike of the preacher was not so strongly blended. The old bishop and his chaplains, the dean and his canons and minor canons, the old choir, and especially Mr. Harding who was at the head of it, had all been popular in Barchester. They had spent their money and done good; the poor had not been ground down; the clergy in society had neither been overbearing nor austere; and the whole repute of the city was due to its ecclesiastical importance. Yet there were those who had heard Mr. Slope with satisfaction.

It is so pleasant to receive a fillip of excitement when suffering from the dull routine of every-day life! The anthems and Te Deums were in themselves delightful, but they had been heard so often! Mr. Slope was certainly not delightful, but he was new, and, moreover, clever. They had long thought it slow, so said now many of the Barchesterians, to go on as they had done in their old humdrum way, giving ear to none of the religious changes which were moving the world without. People in advance of the age now had new ideas, and it was quite time that Barchester should go in advance. Mr. Slope might be right. Sunday certainly had not been strictly kept in Barchester, except as regarded the ca-thedral services. Indeed the two hours between services had long been appropriated to morning calls and hot luncheons. Then Sunday schools! really more ought to have been done as to Sunday schools; Sabbath-day schools Mr. Slope had called them. The late bishop had really not thought of Sunday schools as he should have done. (These people probably did not reflect that catechisms and collects are quite as hard work to the young mind as book-keeping is to the elderly; and that quite as little feeling of worship enters into the one task as the other.) And then, as regarded that great question of musical services, there might be much to be said on Mr. Slope's side of the question. It certainly was the fact, that people went to the cathedral to hear the music, &c. &c.

And so a party absolutely formed itself in Barchester on Mr. Slope's side of the question! This consisted, among the upper classes, chiefly of ladies. No man — that is, no gentleman — could possibly be attracted by Mr. Slope, or consent to sit at the feet of so abhorrent a Gamaliel. Ladies are sometimes less nice in their appreciation of physical disqualification; and, provided that a man speak to them well, they will listen, though he speak from a mouth never so deformed and hideous. Wilkes was most fortunate as a lover; and the damp, sandy-haired, saucer-eyed, red-fisted, Mr. Slope was powerful only over the female breast.

There were, however, one or two of the neighbouring clergy who thought it not quite safe to neglect the baskets in which for the nonce were stored the loaves and fishes of the diocese of Barchester. They, and they only, came to call on Mr. Slope after his performance in the cathedral pulpit. Among these Mr. Quiverful, the rector of Puddingdale, whose wife still continued to present him from year to year with fresh pledges of her love, and so to increase his cares and, it is to be hoped, his happiness equally. Who can wonder that a gentleman, with fourteen living children and a bare income of 400*l.* a year, should look after the loaves and fishes, even when they are under the thumb of a Mr. Slope?

Very soon after the Sunday on which the sermon was preached, the leading clergy of the neighbourhood held high debate together as to how Mr. Slope should be put down. In the first place he should never again preach from the pulpit of Barchester cathedral. This was Dr. Grantly's earliest dictum; and they all agreed, providing only that they had the power to exclude him. Dr. Grantly declared that the power rested with the dean and chapter, observing that no clergyman out of the chapter had a claim to preach there, saving only the bishop himself. To this the dean assented, but alleged that contests on such a subject would be unseemly; to which rejoined a meagre little doctor, one of the cathedral prebendaries, that the contest must be all on the side of Mr. Slope if every prebendary were always there ready to take his own place in the pulpit. Cunning little meagre doctor, whom it suits well to live in his own cosy house within Barchester close, and who is well content to have his little fling at Dr. Vesey Stanhope and other absentees, whose Italian villas, or enticing London homes, are more tempting than cathedral stalls and residences!

To this answered the burly chancellor, a man rather silent in deed, but very sensible, that absent prebendaries had their vicars, and that in such case the vicar's right to the pulpit was the same as that of the higher order.   To which the dean assented, groaning deeply at these truths.   Thereupon, however, the meagre doctor remarked that they would be in the hands of their minor canons, one of whom might at any hour betray his trust.   Whereon was heard from the burly chancellor an ejaculation sounding somewhat like "Pooh, pooh, pooh!" but it might be that the worthy man was but blowing out the heavy breath from his windpipe.   Why silence him at all? suggested Mr. Harding.   Let them not be ashamed to hear what any man might have to preach to them, unless he preached false doctrine; in which case, let the bishop silence him.   So spoke our friend; vainly; for human ends must be attained by human means.   But the dean saw a ray of hope out of those purblind old eyes of his.   Yes, let them tell the bishop how distasteful to them was this Mr. Slope: a new bishop just come to his seat could not wish to insult his clergy while the gloss was yet fresh on his first apron.

Then up rose Dr. Grantly; and, having thus collected the scattered wisdom of his associates, spoke forth with words of deep authority.   When I say up rose the archdeacon, I speak of the inner man, which then sprang up to more immediate action, for the doctor had, bodily, been standing all along with his back to the dean's empty ·fire-grate, and the tails of his frock coat supported over his two arms.   His hands were in his breeches pockets.

"It is quite clear that this man must not be allowed to preach again in this cathedral.   We all see that, except our dear friend here, the milk of whose nature runs so softly, that he would not have the heart to refuse the Pope the loan of his pulpit, if the Pope would come and ask it.   We must not, however, allow the man to preach again here.   It is not because his opinion on church matters may be different from ours—with that one would not quarrel.   It is because he has purposely insulted us.   When he went up into the pulpit last Sunday, his studied object was to give offence to men who had grown old in reverence of those things of which he dared to speak so slightingly.   What! to come here a stranger, a young, unknown, and unfriended stranger, and tell us, in the name of the bishop his master, that we are ignorant of our duties, old-fashioned, and useless!   I don't know whether most to admire his courage or his impudence!   And one thing I will tell you : that sermon originated solely with the man himself.   The bishop was no more a party to it than was the dean here.   You all know how grieved I am to see a bishop in this diocese holding the latitudinarian ideas by which Dr. Proudie has made himself conspicuous. You all know how greatly I should distrust the opinion of such a man. But in this matter I hold him to be blameless. I believe Dr. Proudie has lived too long among gentlemen to be guilty, or to instigate another to be guilty, of so gross an outrage. No! that man uttered what was untrue when he hinted that he was speaking as the mouthpiece of the bishop. It suited his ambitious views at once to throw down the gauntlet to us—at once to defy us here in the quiet of our own religious duties—here within the walls of our own loved cathedral—here where we have for so many years exercised our ministry without schism and with good repute. Such an attack upon us, coming from such a quarter, is abominable."

"Abominable," groaned the dean. "Abominable," muttered the meagre doctor. "Abominable," re-echoed the chancellor, uttering the sound from the bottom of his deep chest. "I really think it was," said Mr. Harding.

"Most abominable and most unjustifiable," continued the archdeacon. "But, Mr. Dean, thank God, that pulpit is still our own: your own, I should say. That pulpit belongs solely to the dean and chapter of Barchester Cathedral, and, as yet, Mr. Slope is no part of that chapter. You, Mr. Dean, have suggested that we should appeal to the bishop to abstain from forcing this man on us; but what if the bishop allow himself to be ruled by his chaplain? In my opinion, the matter is in our own hands. Mr Slope cannot preach there without permission asked and obtained, and let that permission be invariably refused. Let all participation in the ministry of the cathedral service be refused to him. Then, if the bishop choose to interfere, we shall know what answer to make to the bishop. My friend here has suggested that this man may again find his way into the pulpit by undertaking the duty of some of your minor canons; but I am sure that we may fully trust to these gentlemen to support us, when it is known that the dean objects to any such transfer."

"Of course you may," said the chancellor.

There was much more discussion among the learned conclave, all of which, of course, ended in obedience to the archdeacon's commands. They had too long been accustomed to his rule to shake it off so soon; and in this particular case they had none of them a wish to abet the man whom he was so anxious to put down.

Such a meeting as that we have just recorded is not held in such a city as Barchester unknown and untold of. Not only was the fact of the meeting talked of in every respectable house, including the palace, but the very speeches of the dean, the archdeacon, and chancellor were repeated; not without many additions and imaginary circumstances, according to the tastes and opinions of the relaters.

All, however, agreed in saying that Mr. Slope was to be debarred from opening his mouth in the cathedral of Barchester; many believed that the vergers were to be ordered to refuse him even the accommodation of a seat; and some of the most far-going advocates for strong measures, declared that his sermon was looked upon as an indictable offence, and that proceedings were to be taken against him for brawling.

The party who were inclined to defend him — the enthusiastically religious young ladies, and the middle-aged spinsters desirous of a move — of course took up his defence the more warmly on account of this attack. If they could not hear Mr. Slope in the cathedral, they would hear him elsewhere; they would leave the dull dean, the dull old prebendaries, and the scarcely less dull young minor canons, to preach to each other; they would work slippers and cushions, and hem bands for Mr. Slope, make him a happy martyr, and stick him up in some new Sion or Bethesda, and put the cathedral quite out of fashion.

Dr. and Mrs. Proudie at once returned to London. They thought it expedient not to have to encounter any personal application from the dean and chapter respecting the sermon, till the violence of the storm had expended itself; but they left Mr. Slope behind them nothing daunted, and he went about his work zealously, flattering such as would listen to his flattery, whispering religious twaddle into the ears of foolish women, ingratiating himself with the few clergy who would receive him, visiting the houses of the poor, inquiring into all people, prying into everything, and searching with his minutest eye into all palatial dilapidations. He did not, however, make any immediate attempt to preach again in the cathedral.

And so all Barchester was by the ears.

CHAP. VIII.

THE EX-WARDEN REJOICES IN HIS PROBABLE RETURN TO THE HOSPITAL.

Among the ladies in Barchester who have hitherto acknowledged Mr. Slope as their spiritual director, must not be reckoned either

the widow Bold, or her sister-in-law. On the first outbreak of
the wrath of the denizens of the close, none had been more animated against the intruder than these two ladies. And this was
natural. Who could be so proud of the musical distinction of their
own cathedral as the favourite daughter of the precentor? Who
would be so likely to resent an insult offered to the old choir?
And in such matters Miss Bold and her sister-in-law had but one
opinion.

This wrath, however, has in some degree been mitigated, and I
regret to say that these ladies allowed Mr. Slope to be his own
apologist. About a fortnight after the sermon had been preached,
they were both of them not a little surprised by hearing Mr. Slope
announced, as the page in buttons opened Mrs. Bold's drawing-
room door. Indeed, what living man could, by a mere morning
visit, have surprised them more? Here was the great enemy of
all that was good in Barchester coming into their own drawing-
room, and they had no strong arm, no ready tongue, near at hand
for their protection. The widow snatched her baby out of its
cradle into her lap, and Mary Bold stood up ready to die manfully
in that baby's behalf, should, under any circumstances, such a
sacrifice become necessary.

In this manner was Mr. Slope received. But when he left, he
was allowed by each lady to take her hand, and to make his adieux
as gentlemen do who have been graciously entertained! Yes; he
shook hands with them, and was curtseyed out courteously, the
buttoned page opening the door, as he would have done for the
best canon of them all. He had touched the baby's little hand
and blessed him with a fervid blessing; he had spoken to the
widow of her early sorrows, and Eleanor's silent tears had not
rebuked him; he had told Mary Bold that her devotion would be
rewarded, and Mary Bold had heard the praise without disgust.
And how had he done all this? how had he so quickly turned
aversion into, at any rate, acquaintance? how had he overcome
the enmity with which these ladies had been ready to receive him,
and made his peace with them so easily?

My readers will guess from what I have written that I myself
do not like Mr. Slope; but I am constrained to admit that he is a
man of parts. He knows how to say a soft word in the proper
place; he knows how to adapt his flattery to the ears of his
hearers; he knows the wiles of the serpent, and he uses them.
Could Mr. Slope have adapted his manners to men as well as to
women, could he ever have learnt the ways of a gentleman, he might
have risen to great things.

He commenced his acquaintance with Eleanor by praising her father. He had, he said, become aware that he had unfortunately offended the feelings of a man of whom he could not speak too highly ; he would not now allude to a subject which was probably too serious for drawing-room conversation, but he would say, that it had been very far from him to utter a word in disparagement of a man, of whom all the world, at least the clerical world, spoke so highly as it did of Mr. Harding. And so he went on, unsaying a great deal of his sermon, expressing his highest admiration for the precentor's musical talents, eulogising the father and the daughter and the sister-in-law, speaking in that low silky whisper which he always had specially prepared for feminine ears, and, ultimately, gaining his object. When he left, he expressed a hope that he might again be allowed to call ; and though Eleanor gave no verbal assent to this, she did not express dissent : and so Mr. Slope's right to visit at the widow's house was established.

The day after this visit Eleanor told her father of it, and expressed an opinion that Mr. Slope was not quite so black as he had been painted. Mr. Harding opened his eyes rather wider than usual when he heard what had occurred, but he said little ; he could not agree in any praise of Mr. Slope, and it was not his practice to say much evil of any one. He did not, however, like the visit, and simple-minded as he was, he felt sure that Mr. Slope had some deeper motive than the mere pleasure of making soft speeches to two ladies.

Mr. Harding, however, had come to see his daughter with other purpose than that of speaking either good or evil of Mr. Slope. He had come to tell her that the place of warden in Hiram's hospital was again to be filled up, and that in all probability he would once more return to his old home and his twelve bedesmen

"But," said, he, laughing, "I shall be greatly shorn of my ancient glory."

"Why so, papa?"

"This new act of parliament, that is to put us all on our feet again," continued he, " settles my income at four hundred and fifty pounds per annum."

"Four hundred and fifty," said she, "instead of eight hundred Well ; that is rather shabby. But still, papa, you'll have the dear old house and the garden ? "

"My dear," said he, " it's worth twice the money ; " and as he spoke he showed a jaunty kind of satisfaction in his tone and manner, and in the quick, pleasant way in which he paced Eleanor's drawing-room. "It's worth twice the money. I shall have the house and the garden, and a larger income than I can possibly want."

"At any rate, you'll have no extravagant daughter to provide for;" and as she spoke, the young widow put her arm within his, and made him sit on the sofa beside her; "at any rate you'll not have that expense."

"No, my dear; and I shall be rather lonely without her; but we won't think of that now. As regards income I shall have plenty for all I want. I shall have my old house; and I don't mind owning now that I have felt sometimes the inconvenience of living in a lodging. Lodgings are very nice for young men, but at my time of life there is a want of —— I hardly know what to call it, perhaps not respectability ——"

"Oh, papa! I'm sure there's been nothing like that. Nobody has thought it; nobody in all Barchester has been more respected than you have been since you took those rooms in High Street. Nobody! Not the dean in his deanery, or the archdeacon out at Plumstead."

"The archdeacon would not be much obliged to you if he heard you," said he, smiling somewhat at the exclusive manner in which his daughter confined her illustration to the church dignitaries of the chapter of Barchester; "but at any rate I shall be glad to get back to the old house. Since I heard that it was all settled, I have begun to fancy that I can't be comfortable without my two sitting-rooms."

"Come and stay with me, papa, till it is settled—there's a dear papa."

"Thank ye, Nelly. But no; I won't do that. It would make two movings. I shall be very glad to get back to my old men again. Alas! alas! There have six of them gone in these few last years. Six out of twelve! And the others I fear have had but a sorry life of it there. Poor Bunce, poor old Bunce!"

Bunce was one of the surviving recipients of Hiram's charity; an old man, now over ninety, who had long been a favourite of Mr. Harding's.

"How happy old Bunce will be," said Mrs. Bold, clapping her soft hands softly. "How happy they all will be to have you back again. You may be sure there will soon be friendship among them again when you are there."

"But," said he, half laughing, "I am to have new troubles, which will be terrible to me. There are to be twelve old women, and a matron. How shall I manage twelve women and a matron!"

"The matron will manage the women of course."

"And who'll manage the matron?" said he.

"She won't want to be managed. She'll be a great lady herself I suppose. But, papa, where will the matron live? She is not to live in the warden's house with you, is she?"

"Well, I hope not, my dear."

"Oh, papa, I tell you fairly, I won't have a matron for a new step-mother."

"You shan't, my dear; that is, if I can help it. But they are going to build another house for the matron and the women; and I believe they haven't even fixed yet on the site of the building."

"And have they appointed the matron?" said Eleanor.

"They haven't appointed the warden yet," replied he.

"But there's no doubt about that, I suppose," said his daughter.

Mr. Harding explained that he thought there was no doubt; that the archdeacon had declared as much, saying that the bishop and his chaplain between them had not the power to appoint any one else, even if they had the will to do so, and sufficient impudence to carry out such a will. The archdeacon was of opinion, that though Mr. Harding had resigned his wardenship, and had done so unconditionally, he had done so under circumstances which left the bishop no choice as to his re-appointment, now that the affair of the hospital had been settled on a new basis by act of parliament. Such was the archdeacon's opinion, and his father-in-law received it without a shadow of doubt.

Dr. Grantly had always been strongly opposed to Mr. Harding's resignation of the place. He had done all in his power to dissuade him from it. He had considered that Mr. Harding was bound to withstand the popular clamour with which he was attacked for receiving so large an income as eight hundred a year from such a charity, and was not even yet satisfied that his father-in-law's conduct had not been pusillanimous and undignified. He looked also on this reduction of the warden's income as a shabby, paltry scheme on the part of government for escaping from a difficulty into which it had been brought by the public press. Dr. Grantly observed that the government had no more right to dispose of a sum of four hundred and fifty pounds a year out of the income of Hiram's legacy, than of nine hundred; whereas, as he said, the bishop, dean, and chapter clearly had a right to settle what sum should be paid. He also declared that the government had no more right to saddle the charity with twelve old women than with twelve hundred; and he was, therefore, very indignant on the matter. He probably forgot when so talking that government had done nothing of the kind, and had never assumed any such might or any such right. He made the common mistake of attributing to the government, which in such matters is powerless, the doings of parliament, which in such matters is omnipotent.

But though he felt that the glory and honour of the situation of warden of Barchester hospital were indeed curtailed by the new arrangement; that the whole establishment had to a certain degree been made vile by the touch of Whig commissioners; that the place with its lessened income, its old women, and other innovations, was very different from the hospital of former days; still the archdeacon was too practical a man of the world to wish that his father-in-law, who had at present little more than 200*l*. per annum for all his wants, should refuse the situation, defiled, undignified, and commission-ridden as it was.

Mr. Harding had, accordingly, made up his mind that he would return to his old home at the hospital, and to tell the truth, had experienced almost a childish pleasure in the idea of doing so. The diminished income was to him not even the source of momentary regret. The matron and the old women did rather go against the grain; but he was able to console himself with the reflection, that, after all, such an arrangement might be of real service to the poor of the city. The thought that he must receive his re-appointment as the gift of the new bishop, and probably through the hands of Mr. Slope, annoyed him a little; but his mind was set at rest by the assurance of the archdeacon that there would be no favour in such a presentation. The re-appointment of the old warden would be regarded by all the world as a matter of course. Mr. Harding, therefore, felt no hesitation in telling his daughter that they might look upon his return to his old quarters as a settled matter.

"And you won't have to ask for it, papa."

"Certainly not, my dear. There is no ground on which I could ask for any favour from the bishop, whom, indeed, I hardly know. Nor would I ask a favour, the granting of which might possibly be made a question to be settled by Mr. Slope. No," said he, moved for a moment by a spirit very unlike his own, "I certainly shall be very glad to go back to the hospital; but I should never go there, if it were necessary that my doing so should be the subject of a request to Mr. Slope."

This little outbreak of her father's anger jarred on the present tone of Eleanor's mind. She had not learnt to like Mr. Slope, but she had learnt to think that he had much respect for her father; and she would, therefore, willingly use her efforts to induce something like good feeling between them.

"Papa," said she, "I think you somewhat mistake Mr. Slope's character."

"Do I?" said he, placidly.

"I think you do, papa. I think he intended no personal disrespect to you when he preached the sermon which made the archdeacon and the dean so angry!"

"I never supposed he did, my dear. I hope I never inquired within myself whether he did or no. Such a matter would be unworthy of any inquiry, and very unworthy of the consideration of the chapter. But I fear he intended disrespect to the ministration of God's services, as conducted in conformity with the rules of the Church of England."

"But might it not be that he thought it his duty to express his dissent from that which you, and the dean, and all of us here so much approve?"

"It can hardly be the duty of a young man rudely to assail the religious convictions of his elders in the church. Courtesy should have kept him silent, even if neither charity nor modesty could do so."

"But Mr. Slope would say that on such a subject the commands of his heavenly Master do not admit of his being silent."

"Nor of his being courteous, Eleanor?"

"He did not say that, papa."

"Believe me, my child, that Christian ministers are never called on by God's word to insult the convictions, or even the prejudices of their brethren; and that religion is at any rate not less susceptible of urbane and courteous conduct among men, than any other study which men may take up. I am sorry to say that I cannot defend Mr. Slope's sermon in the cathedral. But come, my dear, put on your bonnet, and let us walk round the dear old gardens at the hospital. I have never yet had the heart to go beyond the court-yard since we left the place. Now I think I can venture to enter."

Eleanor rang the bell, and gave a variety of imperative charges as to the welfare of the precious baby, whom, all but unwillingly, she was about to leave for an hour or so, and then sauntered forth with her father to revisit the old hospital. It had been forbidden ground to her as well as to him since the day on which they had walked forth together from its walls.

CHAP. IX.

THE STANHOPE FAMILY.

It is now three months since Dr. Proudie began his reign, and changes have already been effected in the diocese which show at least the energy of an active mind. Among other things absentee clergymen have been favoured with hints much too strong to be overlooked. Poor dear old Bishop Grantly had on this matter been too lenient, and the archdeacon had never been inclined to be severe with those who were absent on reputable pretences, and who provided for their duties in a liberal way.

Among the greatest of the diocesan sinners in this respect was Dr. Vesey Stanhope. Years had now passed since he had done a day's duty; and yet there was no reason against his doing duty except a want of inclination on his own part. He held a prebendal stall in the diocese; one of the best residences in the close; and the two large rectories of Crabtree Canonicorum, and Stogpingum. Indeed, he had the cure of three parishes, for that of Eiderdown was joined to Stogpingum. He had resided in Italy for twelve years. His first going there had been attributed to a sore throat; and that sore throat, though never repeated in any violent manner, had stood him in such stead, that it had enabled him to live in easy idleness ever since.

He had now been summoned home — not, indeed, with rough violence, or by any peremptory command, but by a mandate which he found himself unable to disregard. Mr. Slope had written to him by the bishop's desire. In the first place, the bishop much wanted the valuable co-operation of Dr. Vesey Stanhope in the diocese; in the next, the bishop thought it his imperative duty to become personally acquainted with the most conspicuous of his diocesan clergy; then the bishop thought it essentially necessary for Dr. Stanhope's own interests, that Dr. Stanhope should, at any rate for a time, return to Barchester; and lastly, it was said that so strong a feeling was at the present moment evinced by the hierarchs of the church with reference to the absence of its clerical members, that it behoved Dr. Vesey Stanhope not to allow his name to stand among those which would probably in a few months be submitted to the councils of the nation.

There was something so ambiguously frightful in this last threat that Dr. Stanhope determined to spend two or three summer months at his residence in Barchester. His rectories were inhabited by his curates, and he felt himself from disuse to be unfit for parochial duty ; but his prebendal home was kept empty for him, and he thought it probable that he might be able now and again to preach a prebendal sermon. He arrived, therefore, with all his family at Barchester, and he and they must be introduced to my readers.

The great family characteristic of the Stanhopes might probably be said to be heartlessness ; but this want of feeling was, in most of them, accompanied by so great an amount of good nature as to make itself but little noticeable to the world. They were so prone to oblige their neighbours that their neighbours failed to perceive how indifferent to them was the happiness and well-being of those around them. The Stanhopes would visit you in your sickness (provided it were not contagious), would bring you oranges, French novels, and the last new bit of scandal, and then hear of your death or your recovery with an equally indifferent composure. Their conduct to each other was the same as to the world ; they bore and forbore : and there was sometimes, as will be seen, much necessity for forbearing : but their love among themselves rarely reached above this. It is astonishing how much each of the family was able to do, and how much each did, to prevent the well-being of the other four.

For there were five in all ; the doctor, namely, and Mrs. Stanhope, two daughters, and one son. The doctor, perhaps, was the least singular and most estimable of them all, and yet such good qualities as he possessed were all negative. He was a good looking rather plethoric gentleman of about sixty years of age. His hair was snow white, very plentiful, and somewhat like wool of the finest description. His whiskers were very large and very white, and gave to his face the appearance of a benevolent sleepy old lion. His dress was always unexceptionable. Although he had lived so many years in Italy it was invariably of a decent clerical hue, but it never was hyperclerical. He was a man not given to much talking, but what little he did say was generally well said. His reading seldom went beyond romances and poetry of the lightest and not always most moral description. He was thoroughly a *bon vivant;* an accomplished judge of wine, though he never drank to excess ; and a most inexorable critic in all affairs touching the kitchen. He had had much to forgive in his own family, since a family had grown up around him, and had forgiven everything —except inattention to his dinner. His weakness in that respect was now fully understood, and his temper but seldom tried. As Dr. Stanhope was a clergyman, it may be supposed that his religious convictions made up a considerable part of his character; but this was not so. That he had religious convictions must be believed; but he rarely obtruded them, even on his children. This abstinence on his part was not systematic, but very characteristic of the man. It was not that he had predetermined never to influence their thoughts; but he was so habitually idle that his time for doing so had never come till the opportunity for doing so was gone for ever. Whatever conviction the father may have had, the children were at any rate but indifferent members of the church from which he drew his income.

Such was Dr. Stanhope. The features of Mrs. Stanhope's character were even less plainly marked than those of her lord. The *far niente* of her Italian life had entered into her very soul, and brought her to regard a state of inactivity as the only earthly good. In manner and appearance she was exceedingly prepossessing. She had been a beauty, and even now, at fifty-five, she was a handsome woman. Her dress was always perfect: she never dressed but once in the day, and never appeared till between three and four; but when she did appear, she appeared at her best. Whether the toil rested partly with her, or wholly with her hand-maid, it is not for such a one as the author even to imagine. The structure of her attire was always elaborate, and yet never over laboured. She was rich in apparel, but not bedizened with finery; her ornaments were costly, rare, and such as could not fail to attract notice, but they did not look as though worn with that purpose. She well knew the great architectural secret of decorating her constructions, and never descended to construct a decoration. But when we have said that Mrs. Stanhope knew how to dress, and used her knowledge daily, we have said all. Other purpose in life she had none. It was something, indeed, that she did not interfere with the purposes of others. In early life she had under-gone great trials with reference to the doctor's dinners; but for the last ten or twelve years her eldest daughter Charlotte had taken that labour off her hands, and she had had little to trouble her;—little, that is, till the edict for this terrible English journey had gone forth: since, then, indeed, her life had been laborious enough. For such a one, the toil of being carried from the shores of Como to the city of Barchester is more than labour enough, let the care of the carriers be ever so vigilant. Mrs. Stanhope had been obliged to have every one of her dresses taken in from the effects of the journey.

Charlotte Stanhope was at this time about thirty-five years old; and, whatever may have been her faults, she had none of those which belong particularly to old young ladies. She neither dressed young, nor talked young, nor indeed looked young. She appeared to be perfectly content with her time of life, and in no way affected the graces of youth. She was a fine young woman; and had she been a man, would have been a very fine young man. All that was done in the house, and that was not done by servants, was done by her. She gave the orders, paid the bills, hired and dismissed the domestics, made the tea, carved the meat, and managed everything in the Stanhope household. She, and she alone, could ever induce her father to look into the state of his worldly concerns. She, and she alone, could in any degree control the absurdities of her sister. She, and she alone, prevented the whole family from falling into utter disrepute and beggary. It was by her advice that they now found themselves very unpleasantly situated in Barchester.

So far, the character of Charlotte Stanhope is not unprepossessing. But it remains to be said, that the influence which she had in her family, though it had been used to a certain extent for their worldly well-being, had not been used to their real benefit, as it might have been. She had aided her father in his indifference to his professional duties, counselling him that his livings were as much his individual property as the estates of his elder brother were the property of that worthy peer. She had for years past stifled every little rising wish for a return to England which the doctor had from time to time expressed. She had encouraged her mother in her idleness in order that she herself might be mistress and manager of the Stanhope household. She had encouraged and fostered the follies of her sister, though she was always willing, and often able, to protect her from their probable result. She had done her best, and had thoroughly succeeded in spoiling her brother, and turning him loose upon the world an idle man without a profession, and without a shilling that he could call his own.

Miss Stanhope was a clever woman, able to talk on most subjects, and quite indifferent as to what the subject was. She prided herself on her freedom from English prejudice, and she might have added, from feminine delicacy. On religion she was a pure free-thinker, and with much want of true affection, delighted to throw out her own views before the troubled mind of her father. To have shaken what remained of his Church of England faith would have gratified her much; but the idea of his abandoning his preferment in the church had never once presented itself to her mind. How could he indeed, when he had no income from any other source?

But the two most prominent members of the family still remain to be described. The second child had been christened Madeline, and had been a great beauty. We need not say had been, for she was never more beautiful than at the time of which we write, though her person for many years had been disfigured by an accident. It is unnecessary that we should give in detail the early history of Madeline Stanhope. She had gone to Italy when about seventeen years of age, and had been allowed to make the most of her surpassing beauty in the saloons of Milan, and among the crowded villas along the shores of the Lake of Como. She had become famous for adventures in which her character was just not lost, and had destroyed the hearts of a dozen cavaliers without once being touched in her own. Blood had flowed in quarrels about her charms, and she heard of these encounters with pleasurable excitement. It had been told of her that on one occasion she had stood by in the disguise of a page, and had seen her lover fall.

As is so often the case, she had married the very worst of those who sought her hand. Why she had chosen Paulo Neroni, a man of no birth and no property, a mere captain in the pope's guard, one who had come up to Milan either simply as an adventurer or else as a spy, a man of harsh temper and oily manners, mean in figure, swarthy in face, and so false in words as to be hourly detected, need not now be told. When the moment for doing so came, she had probably no alternative. He, at any rate, had become her husband; and after a prolonged honeymoon among the lakes, they had gone together to Rome, the papal captain having vainly endeavoured to induce his wife to remain behind him.

Six months afterwards she arrived at her father's house a cripple, and a mother. She had arrived without even notice, with hardly clothes to cover her, and without one of those many ornaments which had graced her bridal *trousseau*. Her baby was in the arms of a poor girl from Milan, whom she had taken in exchange for the Roman maid who had accompanied her thus far, and who had then, as her mistress said, become homesick and had returned. It was clear that the lady had determined that there should be no witness to tell stories of her life in Rome.

She had fallen, she said, in ascending a ruin, and had fatally injured the sinews of her knee; so fatally, that when she stood she lost eight inches of her accustomed height; so fatally, that when she essayed to move, she could only drag herself painfully along, with protruded hip and extended foot in a manner less graceful than that of a hunchback. She had consequently made up her mind, once and for ever, that she would never stand, and never attempt to move herself.

Stories were not slow to follow her, averring that she had been cruelly ill used by Neroni, and that to his violence had she owed her accident. Be that as it may, little had been said about her husband, but that little had made it clearly intelligible to the family that Signor Neroni was to be seen and heard of no more. There was no question as to re-admitting the poor ill used beauty to her old family rights, no question as to adopting her infant daughter beneath the Stanhope roof tree. Though heartless, the Stanhopes were not selfish. The two were taken in, petted, made much of, for a time all but adored, and then felt by the two parents to be great nuisances in the house. But in the house the lady was, and there she remained, having her own way, though that way was not very conformable with the customary usages of an English clergyman.

Madame Neroni, though forced to give up all motion in the world, had no intention whatever of giving up the world itself. The beauty of her face was uninjured, and that beauty was of a peculiar kind. Her copious rich brown hair was worn in Grecian *bandeaux* round her head, displaying as much as possible of her forehead and cheeks. Her forehead, though rather low, was very beautiful from its perfect contour and pearly whiteness. Her eyes were long and large, and marvellously bright; might I venture to say, bright as Lucifer's, I should perhaps best express the depth of their brilliancy. They were dreadful eyes to look at, such as would absolutely deter any man of quiet mind and easy spirit from attempting a passage of arms with such foes. There was talent in them, and the fire of passion and the play of wit, but there was no love. Cruelty was there instead, and courage, a desire of master-hood, cunning, and a wish for mischief. And yet, as eyes, they were very beautiful. The eyelashes were long and perfect, and the long steady unabashed gaze, with which she would look into the face of her admirer, fascinated while it frightened him. She was a basilisk from whom an ardent lover of beauty could make no escape. Her nose and mouth and teeth and chin and neck and bust were perfect, much more so at twenty-eight than they had been at eighteen. What wonder that with such charms still glowing in her face, and with such deformity destroying her figure, she should resolve to be seen, but only to be seen reclining on a sofa.

Her resolve had not been carried out without difficulty. She had still frequented the opera at Milan; she had still been seen occasionally in the saloons of the *noblesse*; she had caused herself to be carried in and out from her carriage, and that in such a manner as in no wise to disturb her charms, disarrange her dress, or expose her deformities. Her sister always accompanied her and a maid, a man-servant also, and on state occasions, two. It was impossible that her purpose could have been achieved with less: and yet, poor as she was, she had achieved her purpose. And then again the more dissolute Italian youths of Milan frequented the Stanhope villa and surrounded her couch, not greatly to her father's satisfaction. Sometimes his spirit would rise, a dark spot would show itself on his cheek, and he would rebel; but Charlotte would assuage him with some peculiar triumph of her culinary art, and all again would be smooth for a while.

Madeline affected all manner of rich and quaint devices in the garniture of her room, her person, and her feminine belongings. In nothing was this more apparent than in the visiting card which she had prepared for her use. For such an article one would say that she, in her present state, could have but small need, seeing how improbable it was that she should make a morning call: but not such was her own opinion. Her card was surrounded by a deep border of gilding; on this she had imprinted, in three lines,—

> " La Signora Madeline
> " Vesey Neroni.
> — Nata Stanhope."

And over the name she had a bright gilt coronet, which certainly looked very magnificent. How she had come to concoct such a name for herself it would be difficult to explain. Her father had been christened Vesey, as another man is christened Thomas; and she had no more right to assume it than would have the daughter of a Mr. Josiah Jones to call herself Mrs. Josiah Smith, on marrying a man of the latter name. The gold coronet was equally out of place, and perhaps inserted with even less excuse. Paulo Neroni had had not the faintest title to call himself a scion of even Italian nobility. Had the pair met in England Neroni would probably have been a count; but they had met in Italy, and any such pretence on his part would have been simply ridiculous. A coronet, however, was a pretty ornament, and if it could solace a poor cripple to have such on her card, who would begrudge it to her?

Of her husband, or of his individual family, she never spoke: but with her admirers she would often allude in a mysterious way to her married life and isolated state, and, pointing to her daughter would call her the last of the blood of the emperors, thus referring Neroni's extraction to the old Roman family from which the worst of the Cæsars sprang.

The "Signora" was not without talent, and not without a certain sort of industry; she was an indomitable letter writer, and her letters were worth the postage: they were full of wit, mischief, satire, love, latitudinarian philosophy, free religion, and, sometimes, alas! loose ribaldry. The subject, however, depended entirely on the recipient, and she was prepared to correspond with any one but moral young ladies or stiff old women. She wrote also a kind of poetry, generally in Italian, and short romances, generally in French. She read much of a desultory sort of literature, and as a modern linguist had really made great proficiency. Such was the lady who had now come to wound the hearts of the men of Barchester.

Ethelbert Stanhope was in some respects like his younger sister, but he was less inestimable as a man than she as a woman. His great fault was an entire absence of that principle which should have induced him, as the son of a man without fortune, to earn his own bread. Many attempts had been made to get him to do so, but these had all been frustrated, not so much by idleness on his part, as by a disinclination to exert himself in any way not to his taste. He had been educated at Eton, and had been intended for the Church, but had left Cambridge in disgust after a single term, and notified to his father his intention to study for the bar. Preparatory to that, he thought it well that he should attend a German university, and consequently went to Leipsic. There he remained two years, and brought away a knowledge of German and a taste for the fine arts. He still, however, intended himself for the bar, took chambers, engaged himself to sit at the feet of a learned pundit, and spent a season in London. He there found that all his aptitudes inclined him to the life of an artist, and he determined to live by painting. With this object he returned to Milan, and had himself rigged out for Rome. As a painter he might have earned his bread, for he wanted only diligence to excel; but when at Rome his mind was carried away by other things: he soon wrote home for money, saying that he had been converted to the Mother Church, that he was already an acolyte of the Jesuits, and that he was about to start with others to Palestine on a mission for converting Jews. He did go to Judea, but being unable to convert the Jews, was converted by them. He again wrote home, to say that Moses was the only giver of perfect laws to the world, that the coming of the true Messiah was at hand, that great things were doing in Palestine, and that he had met one of the family of Sidonia, a most remarkable man, who was now on his way to Western Europe, and whom he had induced to deviate from his route with the object of calling at the Stanhope villa.   Ethelbert then expressed his hope that his mother and sisters would listen to this wonderful prophet.   His father he knew could not do so from pecuniary considerations.   This Sidonia, however, did not take so strong a fancy to him as another of that family once did to a young English nobleman.   At least he provided him with no heaps of gold as large as lions; so that the Judaised Ethelbert was again obliged to draw on the revenues of the Christian Church.

It is needless to tell how the father swore that he would send no more money and receive no Jew; nor how Charlotte declared that Ethelbert could not be left penniless in Jerusalem, and how "La Signora Neroni" resolved to have Sidonia at her feet. The money was sent, and the Jew did come.   The Jew did come, but he was not at all to the taste of "La Signora."   He was a dirty little old man, and though he had provided no golden lions, he had, it seems, relieved young Stanhope's necessities.   He positively refused to leave the villa till he had got a bill from the doctor on his London bankers.

Ethelbert did not long remain a Jew.   He soon re-appeared at the villa without prejudices on the subject of his religion, and with a firm resolve to achieve fame and fortune as a sculptor.   He brought with him some models which he had originated at Rome, and which really gave such fair promise that his father was induced to go to further expense in furthering these views.   Ethelbert opened an establishment, or rather took lodgings and a workshop, at Carrara, and there spoilt much marble, and made some few pretty images.   Since that period, now four years ago, he had alternated between Carrara and the villa, but his sojourns at the workshop became shorter and shorter, and those at the villa longer and longer.   'Twas no wonder; for Carrara is not a spot in which an Englishman would like to dwell.

When the family started for England he had resolved not to be left behind, and with the assistance of his elder sister had carried his point against his father's wishes.   It was necessary, he said, that he should come to England for orders.   How otherwise was he to bring his profession to account?

In personal appearance Ethelbert Stanhope was the most singular of beings.   He was certainly very handsome.   He had his sister Madeline's eyes without their stare, and without their hard cunning cruel firmness.   They were also very much lighter, and of so light and clear a blue as to make his face remarkable, if nothing else did so. On entering a room with him, Ethelbert's blue eyes would be the first thing you would see, and on leaving it almost the last you would forget. His light hair was very long and silky, coming down over his coat. His beard had been prepared in holy land, and was patriarchal. He never shaved, and rarely trimmed it. It was glossy, soft, clean, and altogether not unprepossessing. It was such, that ladies might desire to reel it off and work it into their patterns in lieu of floss silk. His complexion was fair and almost pink, he was small in height, and slender in limb, but well-made, and his voice was of peculiar sweetness.

In manner and dress he was equally remarkable. He had none of the *mauvaise honte* of an Englishman. He required no introduction to make himself agreeable to any person. He habitually addressed strangers, ladies as well as men, without any such formality, and in doing so never seemed to meet with rebuke. His costume cannot be described, because it was so various; but it was always totally opposed in every principle of colour and construction to the dress of those with whom he for the time consorted.

He was habitually addicted to making love to ladies, and did so without any scruple of conscience, or any idea that such a practice was amiss. He had no heart to touch himself, and was literally unaware that humanity was subject to such an infliction. He had not thought much about it; but, had he been asked, would have said, that ill-treating a lady's heart meant injuring her promotion in the world. His principles therefore forbade him to pay attention to a girl, if he thought any man was present whom it might suit her to marry. In this manner, his good nature frequently interfered with his amusement; but he had no other motive in abstaining from the fullest declarations of love to every girl that pleased his eye.

Bertie Stanhope, as he was generally called, was, however, popular with both sexes; and with Italians as well as English. His circle of acquaintance was very large, and embraced people of all sorts. He had no respect for rank, and no aversion to those below him. He had lived on familiar terms with English peers, German shopkeepers, and Roman priests. All people were nearly alike to him. He was above, or rather below, all prejudices. No virtue could charm him, no vice shock him. He had about him a natural good manner, which seemed to qualify him for the highest circles, and yet he was never out of place in the lowest. He had no principle, no regard for others, no self-respect, no desire to be other than a drone in the hive, if only he could, as a drone, get what honey was sufficient for him. Of honey, in his latter days, it may probably be presaged, that he will have but short allowance.

Such was the family of the Stanhopes, who, at this period, suddenly joined themselves to the ecclesiastical circle of Barchester close. Any stranger union, it would be impossible perhaps to conceive. And it was not as though they all fell down into the cathedral precincts hitherto unknown and untalked of. In such case no amalgamation would have been at all probable between the new-comers and either the Proudie set or the Grantly set. But such was far from being the case. The Stanhopes were all known by name in Barchester, and Barchester was prepared to receive them with open arms. The doctor was one of her prebendaries, one of her rectors, one of her pillars of strength; and was, moreover, counted on, as a sure ally, both by Proudies and Grantlys.

He himself was the brother of one peer, and his wife was the sister of another—and both these peers were lords of whiggish tendency, with whom the new bishop had some sort of alliance This was sufficient to give to Mr. Slope high hope that he might enlist Dr. Stanhope on his side, before his enemies could out-manœuvre him. On the other hand, the old dean had many many years ago, in the days of the doctor's clerical energies, been instrumental in assisting him in his views as to preferment; and many many years ago also, the two doctors, Stanhope and Grantly, had, as young parsons been joyous together in the common rooms of Oxford. Dr. Grantly, consequently, did not doubt but that the new comer would range himself under his banners.

Little did any of them dream of what ingredients the Stanhope family was now composed.

CHAP. X.

MRS. PROUDIE'S RECEPTION—COMMENCED.

THE bishop and his wife had only spent three or four days in Barchester on the occasion of their first visit. His lordship had, as we have seen, taken his seat on his throne; but his demeanour there, into which it had been his intention to infuse much hierarchal dignity, had been a good deal disarranged by the audacity of his chaplain's sermon. He had hardly dared to look his clergy in the face, and to declare by the severity of his countenance that in truth he meant all that his factotum was saying on his behalf ; nor yet did he dare to throw Mr. Slope over, and show to those around him that he was no party to the sermon, and would resent it.

He had accordingly blessed his people in a shambling manner, not at all to his own satisfaction, and had walked back to his palace with his mind very doubtful as to what he would say to his chaplain on the subject. He did not remain long in doubt. He had hardly doffed his lawn when the partner of all his toils entered his study, and exclaimed even before she had seated herself —

" Bishop, did you ever hear a more sublime, more spirit-moving, more appropriate discourse than that ? "

" Well, my love ; ha—hum—he! " The bishop did not know what to say.

" I hope, my lord, you don't mean to say you disapprove ? "

There was a look about the lady's eye which did not admit of my lord's disapproving at that moment. He felt that if he intended to disapprove, it must be now or never; but he also felt that it could not be now. It was not in him to say to the wife of his bosom that Mr. Slope's sermon was ill-timed, impertinent and vexatious.

" No, no," replied the bishop. " No, I can't say I disapprove — a very clever sermon and very well intended, and I dare say will do a great deal of good." This last praise was added, seeing that what he had already said by no means satisfied Mrs. Proudie.

" I hope it will," said she. " I am sure it was well deserved. Did you ever in your life, bishop, hear anything so like play-acting as the way in which Mr. Harding sings the litany? I shall beg Mr. Slope to continue a course of sermons on the subject till all that is altered. We will have at any rate, in our cathedral, a decent, godly, modest morning service. There must be no more play-acting here now ; " and so the lady rang for lunch.

The bishop knew more about cathedrals and deans, and precentors and church services than his wife did, and also more of a bishop's powers. But he thought it better at present to let the subject drop.

" My dear," said he, " I think we must go back to London on Tuesday. I find my staying here will be very inconvenient to the Government."

The bishop knew that to this proposal his wife would not object ; and he also felt that by thus retreating from the ground of battle, the heat of the fight might be got over in his absence.

" Mr. Slope will remain here, of course ? " said the lady.

" Oh, of course," said the bishop.

Thus, after less than a week's sojourn in his palace, did the bishop fly from Barchester; nor did he return to it for two months, the London season being then over. During that time Mr. Slope was not idle, but he did not again essay to preach in the cathedral. In answer to Mrs. Proudie's letters, advising a course of sermons, he had pleaded that he would at any rate wish to put off such an undertaking till she was there to hear them.

He had employed his time in consolidating a Proudie and Slope party — or rather a Slope and Proudie party, and he had not employed his time in vain. He did not meddle with the dean and chapter, except by giving them little teasing intimations of the bishop's wishes about this and the bishop's feelings about that, in a manner which was to them sufficiently annoying, but which they could not resent. He preached once or twice in a distant church in the suburbs of the city, but made no allusion to the cathedral service. He commenced the establishment of two "Bishop's Barchester Sabbath-day Schools," gave notice of a proposed "Bishop's Barchester Young Men's Sabbath Evening Lecture Room," — and wrote three or four letters to the manager of the Barchester branch railway, informing him how anxious the bishop was that the Sunday trains should be discontinued.

At the end of two months, however, the bishop and the lady reappeared; and as a happy harbinger of their return, heralded their advent by the promise of an evening party on the largest scale. The tickets of invitation were sent out from London — they were dated from Bruton Street, and were despatched by the odious Sabbath breaking railway, in a huge brown paper parcel to Mr. Slope. Everybody calling himself a gentleman, or herself a lady, within the city of Barchester, and a circle of two miles round it, was included. Tickets were sent to all the diocesan clergy, and also to many other persons of priestly note, of whose absence the bishop, or at least the bishop's wife, felt tolerably confident. It was intended, however, to be a thronged and noticeable affair, and preparations were made for receiving some hundreds.

And now there arose considerable agitation among the Grantlyites whether or no they would attend the episcopal bidding. The first feeling with them all was to send the briefest excuses both for themselves and their wives and daughters. But by degrees policy prevailed over passion. The archdeacon perceived that he would be making a false step if he allowed the cathedral clergy to give the bishop just ground of umbrage. They all met in conclave and agreed to go. They would show that they were willing to respect the office, much as they might dislike the man. They agreed to go. The old dean would crawl in, if it were but for half an hour. The chancellor, treasurer, archdeacon, prebendaries, and minor canons would all go, and would all take their wives. Mr. Harding was especially bidden to do so, resolving in his heart to keep himself far removed from Mrs. Proudie. And Mrs. Bold was determined to go, though assured by her father that there was no necessity for such a sacrifice on her part. When all Barchester was to be there, neither Eleanor nor Mary Bold understood why they should stay away. Had they not been invited separately? and had not a separate little note from the chaplain, couched in the most respectful language, been enclosed with the huge episcopal card?

And the Stanhopes would be there, one and all. Even the lethargic mother would so far bestir herself on such an occasion. They had only just arrived. The card was at the residence waiting for them. No one in Barchester had seen them; and what better opportunity could they have of showing themselves to the Barchester world? Some few old friends, such as the archdeacon and his wife, had called, and had found the doctor and his eldest daughter; but the *élite* of the family were not yet known.

The doctor indeed wished in his heart to prevent the signora from accepting the bishop's invitation; but she herself had fully determined that she would accept it. If her father was ashamed of having his daughter carried into a bishop's palace, she had no such feeling.

"Indeed, I shall," she had said to her sister who had gently endeavoured to dissuade her, by saying that the company would consist wholly of parsons and parsons' wives. "Parsons, I suppose, are much the same as other men, if you strip them of their black coats; and as to their wives, I dare say they won't trouble me. You may tell papa I don't at all mean to be left at home."

Papa was told, and felt that he could do nothing but yield. He also felt that it was useless for him now to be ashamed of his children. Such as they were, they had become such under his auspices; as he had made his bed, so he must lie upon it; as he had sown his seed, so must he reap his corn. He did not indeed utter such reflections in such language, but such was the gist of his thoughts. It was not because Madeline was a cripple that he shrank from seeing her make one of the bishop's guests; but because he knew that she would practise her accustomed lures, and behave herself in a way that could not fail of being distasteful to the propriety of Englishwomen. These things had annoyed but not shocked him in Italy. There they had shocked no one; but here in Barchester, here among his fellow parsons, he was ashamed that they should be seen. Such had been his feelings, but he repressed them. What if his brother clergymen were shocked! They could not take from him his preferment because the manners of his married daughter were too free.

La Signora Neroni had, at any rate, no fear that she would shock anybody. Her ambition was to create a sensation, to have parsons at her feet, seeing that the manhood of Barchester consisted mainly of parsons, and to send, if possible, every parson's wife home with a green fit of jealousy. None could be too old for her, and hardly any too young. None too sanctified, and none too worldly. She was quite prepared to entrap the bishop himself, and then to turn up her nose at the bishop's wife. She did not doubt of success, for she had always succeeded; but one thing was absolutely necessary, she must secure the entire use of a sofa.

The card sent to Dr. and Mrs. Stanhope and family, had been so sent in an envelope, having on the cover Mr. Slope's name. The signora soon learnt that Mrs. Proudie was not yet at the palace, and that the chaplain was managing everything. It was much more in her line to apply to him than to the lady, and she accordingly wrote him the prettiest little billet in the world. In five lines she explained everything, declared how impossible it was for her not to be desirous to make the acquaintance of such persons as the Bishop of Barchester and his wife, and she might add also of Mr. Slope, depicted her own grievous state, and concluded by being assured that Mrs. Proudie would forgive her extreme hardihood in petitioning to be allowed to be carried to a sofa. She then enclosed one of her beautiful cards. In return she received as polite an answer from Mr. Slope—a sofa should be kept in the large drawing-room, immediately at the top of the grand stairs, especially for her use.

And now the day of the party had arrived. The bishop and his wife came down from town, only on the morning of the eventful day, as behoved such great people to do; but Mr. Slope had toiled day and night to see that everything should be in right order. There had been much to do. No company had been seen in the palace since heaven knows when. New furniture had been required, new pots and pans, new cups and saucers, new dishes and plates. Mrs. Proudie had at first declared that she would condescend to nothing so vulgar as eating and drinking; but Mr. Slope had talked, or rather written her out of economy! Bishops should be given to hospitality, and hospitality meant eating and drinking. So the supper was conceded; the guests, however, were to stand as they consumed it.

There were four rooms opening into each other on the first floor of the house, which were denominated the drawing-rooms, the reception room, and Mrs. Proudie's boudoir. In olden days one of these had been Bishop Grantly's bed-room, and another his common sitting room and study. The present bishop, however, had been moved down into a back parlour, and had been given to understand, that he could very well receive his clergy in the dining-room, should they arrive in too large a flock to be admitted into his small sanctum. He had been unwilling to yield, but after a short debate had yielded.

Mrs. Proudie's heart beat high as she inspected her suite of rooms. They were really very magnificent, or at least would be so by candlelight; and they had nevertheless been got up with commendable economy. Large rooms when full of people and full of light look well, because they are large, and are full, and are light. Small rooms are those which require costly fittings and rich furniture. Mrs. Proudie knew this, and made the most of it; she had therefore a huge gas lamp with a dozen burners hanging from each of the ceilings.

People were to arrive at ten, supper was to last from twelve till one, and at half-past one every body was to be gone. Carriages were to come in at the gate in the town and depart at the gate outside. They were desired to take up at a quarter before one. It was managed excellently, and Mr. Slope was invaluable.

At half-past nine the bishop and his wife and their three daughters entered the great reception room, and very grand and very solemn they were. Mr. Slope was down stairs giving the last orders about the wine. He well understood that curates and country vicars with their belongings did not require so generous an article as the dignitaries of the close. There is a useful gradation in such things, and Marsala at 20s. a dozen did very well for the exterior supplementary tables in the corner.

"Bishop," said the lady, as his lordship sat himself down, "don't sit on that sofa, if you please; it is to be kept separate for a lady."

The bishop jumped up and seated himself on a cane-bottomed chair. "A lady?" he inquired meekly; "do you mean one particular lady, my dear?"

"Yes, Bishop, one particular lady," said his wife, disdaining to explain.

"She has got no legs, papa," said the youngest daughter, tittering.

"No legs!" said the bishop, opening his eyes.

"Nonsense, Netta, what stuff you talk," said Olivia. " She has got legs, but she can't use them. She has always to be kept lying down, and three or four men carry her about everywhere."

"Laws, how odd!" said Augusta. "Always carried about by four men! I'm sure I shouldn't like it. Am I right behind, mamma? I feel as if I was open ; " and she turned her back to her anxious parent.

"Open ! to be sure you are," said she, "and a yard of petticoat strings hanging out. I don't know why I pay such high wages to Mrs. Richards, if she can't take the trouble to see whether or no you are fit to be looked at," and Mrs. Proudie poked the strings here, and twitched the dress there, and gave her daughter a shove and a shake, and then pronounced it all right.

"But," rejoined the bishop, who was dying with curiosity about the mysterious lady and her legs, "who is it that is to have the sofa? What's her name, Netta ? "

A thundering rap at the front door interrupted the conversation. Mrs. Proudie stood up and shook herself gently, and touched her cap on each side as she looked in the mirror. Each of the girls stood on tiptoe, and re-arranged the bows on their bosoms ; and Mr. Slope rushed up stairs three steps at a time.

"But who is it, Netta ? " whispered the bishop to his youngest daughter.

"La Signora Madeline Vesey Neroni," whispered back the daughter; " and mind you don't let any one sit upon the sofa."

"La Signora Madeline Vicinironi ! " muttered, to himself, the bewildered prelate. Had he been told that the Begum of Oude was to be there, or Queen Pomara of the Western Isles, he could not have been more astonished. La Signora Madeline Vicinironi, who, having no legs to stand on, had bespoken a sofa in his drawing-room ! — who could she be ? He however could now make no further inquiry, as Dr. and Mrs. Stanhope were announced. They had been sent on out of the way a little before the time, in order that the signora might have plenty of time to get herself conveniently packed into the carriage.

The bishop was all smiles for the prebendary's wife, and the bishop's wife was all smiles for the prebendary. Mr. Slope was presented, and was delighted to make the acquaintance of one of whom he had heard so much. The doctor bowed very low, and then looked as though he could not return the compliment as regarded Mr. Slope, of whom, indeed, he had heard nothing. The doctor, in spite of his long absence, knew an English gentleman when he saw him.

And then the guests came in shoals: Mr. and Mrs. Qufverful and their three grown daughters. Mr. and Mrs. Chadwick and their three daughters. The burly chancellor and his wife and clerical son from Oxford. The meagre little doctor without incumbrance. Mr. Harding with Eleanor and Miss Bold. The dean leaning on a gaunt spinster, his only child now living with him, a lady very learned in stones, ferns, plants, and vermin, and who had written a book about petals. A wonderful woman in her way was Miss Trefoil. Mr. Finnie, the attorney, with his wife, was to be seen, much to the dismay of many who had never met him in a drawing-room before. The five Barchester doctors were all there, and old Scalpen, the retired apothecary and tooth-drawer, who was first taught to consider himself as belonging to the higher orders by the receipt of the bishop's card. Then came the archdeacon and his wife, with their elder daughter Griselda, a slim pale retiring girl of seventeen, who kept close to her mother, and looked out on the world with quiet watchful eyes, one who gave promise of much beauty when time should have ripened it.

And so the rooms became full, and knots were formed, and every new comer paid his respects to my lord and passed on, not presuming to occupy too much of the great man's attention. The archdeacon shook hands very heartily with Doctor Stanhope, and Mrs. Grantly seated herself by the doctor's wife. And Mrs. Proudie moved about with well regulated grace, measuring out the quantity of her favours to the quality of her guests, just as Mr. Slope had been doing with the wine. But the sofa was still empty, and five-and-twenty ladies and five gentlemen had been courteously warned off it by the mindful chaplain.

"Why doesn't she come?" said the bishop to himself. His mind was so preoccupied with the signora, that he hardly remembered how to behave himself *en bishop*.

At last a carriage dashed up to the hall steps with a very different manner of approach from that of any other vehicle that had been there that evening. A perfect commotion took place. The doctor, who heard it as he was standing in the drawing-room, knew that his daughter was coming, and retired into the furthest corner, where he might not see her entrance. Mrs. Proudie perked herself up, feeling that some important piece of business was in hand. The bishop was instinctively aware that La Signora Vicinironi was come at last, and Mr. Slope hurried into the hall to give his assistance.

He was, however, nearly knocked down and trampled on by the

cortège that he encountered on the hall steps. He got himself
picked up as well as he could, and followed the cortège up stairs.
The signora was carried head foremost, her head being the care of
her brother and an Italian man-servant who was accustomed to the
work; her feet were in the care of the lady's maid and the lady's
Italian page; and Charlotte Stanhope followed to see that all was
done with due grace and decorum. In this manner they climbed
easily into the drawing-room, and a broad way through the crowd
having been opened, the signora rested safely on her couch. She
had sent a servant beforehand to learn whether it was a right or a
left hand sofa, for it required that she should dress accordingly,
particularly as regarded her bracelets.

And very becoming her dress was. It was white velvet, without any other garniture than rich white lace worked with pearls
across her bosom, and the same round the armlets of her dress.
Across her brow she wore a band of red velvet, on the centre of
which shone a magnificent Cupid in mosaic, the tints of whose
wings were of the most lovely azure, and the colour of his chubby
cheeks the clearest pink. On the one arm which her position required her to expose she wore three magnificent bracelets, each of
different stones. Beneath her on the sofa, and over the cushion
and head of it, was spread a crimson silk mantle or shawl, which
went under her whole body and concealed her feet. Dressed as
she was and looking as she did, so beautiful and yet so motionless,
with the pure brilliancy of her white dress brought out and
strengthened by the colour beneath it, with that lovely head, and
those large bold bright staring eyes, it was impossible that either
man or woman should do other than look at her.

Neither man nor woman for some minutes did do other.

Her bearers too were worthy of note. The three servants were
Italian, and though perhaps not peculiar in their own country,
were very much so in the palace at Barchester. The man especially attracted notice, and created a doubt in the mind of some
whether he were a friend or a domestic. The same doubt was felt
as to Ethelbert. The man was attired in a loose fitting common
black cloth morning coat. He had a jaunty fat well-pleased clean
face, on which no atom of beard appeared, and he wore round his
neck a loose black silk neckhandkerchief. The bishop essayed to
make him a bow, but the man, who was well-trained, took no notice
of him, and walked out of the room quite at his ease, followed by
the woman and the boy.

Ethelbert Stanhope was dressed in light blue from head to foot.
He had on the loosest possible blue coat, cut square like a shooting

coat, and very short. It was lined with silk of azure blue. He had on a blue satin waistcoat, a blue neckhandkerchief which was fastened beneath his throat with a coral ring, and very loose blue trowsers which almost concealed his feet. His soft glossy beard was softer and more glossy than ever.

The bishop who had made one mistake, thought that he also was a servant, and therefore tried to make way for him to pass. But Ethelbert soon corrected the error.

CHAP. XI.

MRS. PROUDIE'S RECEPTION — CONCLUDED.

"BISHOP OF BARCHESTER, I presume?" said Bertie Stanhope, putting out his hand, frankly; "I am delighted to make your acquaintance. We are in rather close quarters here, a'nt we?"

In truth they were. They had been crowded up behind the head of the sofa : the bishop in waiting to receive his guest, and the other in carrying her; and they now had hardly room to move themselves.

The bishop gave his hand quickly, and made his little studied bow, and was delighted to make——. He could'nt go on, for he did not know whether his friend was a signor, or a count, or a prince.

"My sister really puts you all to great trouble," said Bertie.

"Not at all!" The bishop was delighted to have the opportunity of welcoming the Signora Viçinironi — so at least he said — and attempted to force his way round to the front of the sofa. He had, at any rate, learnt that his strange guests were brother and sister. The man, he presumed, must be Signor Vicinironi, — or count, or prince, as it might be. It was wonderful what good English he spoke. There was just a twang of foreign accent, and no more.

"Do you like Barchester on the whole?" asked Bertie.

The bishop, looking dignified, said that he did like Barchester.

"You've not been here very long, I believe," said Bertie.

"No — not long," said the bishop, and tried again to make his way between the back of the sofa and a heavy rector, who was staring over it at the grimaces of the signora.

"You weren't a bishop before, were you?"

Dr. Proudie explained that this was the first diocese he had held,

" Ah — I thought so," said Bertie ; " but you are changed about sometimes, a'nt you ?"

" Translations are occasionally made," said Dr. Proudie ; " but not so frequently as in former days."

" They've cut them all down to pretty nearly the same figure, haven't they?" said Bertie.

To this the bishop could not bring himself to make any answer, but again attempted to move the rector.

" But the work, I suppose, is different?" continued Bertie. " Is there much to do here, at Barchester?" This was said exactly in the tone that a young Admiralty clerk might use in asking the same question of a brother acolyte at the Treasury.

" The work of a bishop of the Church of England," said Dr. Proudie, with considerable dignity, "is not easy. The responsibility which he has to bear is very great indeed."

" Is it?" said Bertie, opening wide his wonderful blue eyes. " Well; I never was afraid of responsibility. I once had thoughts of being a bishop, myself."

" Had thoughts of being a bishop!" said Dr. Proudie, much amazed.

" That is, a parson — a parson first, you know, and a bishop afterwards. If I had once begun, I'd have stuck to it. But, on the whole, I like the Church of Rome the best."

The bishop could not discuss the point, so he remained silent.

" Now, there's my father," continued Bertie ; "he hasn't stuck to it. I fancy he didn't like saying the same thing over so often. By the bye, Bishop, have you seen my father?"

The bishop was more amazed than ever. Had he seen his father? " No," he replied ; " he had not yet had the pleasure : he hoped he might;" and, as he said so, he resolved to bear heavy on that fat, immovable rector, if ever he had the power of doing so.

" He's in the room somewhere," said Bertie, " and he'll turn up soon. By the bye, do you know much about the Jews?"

At last the bishop saw a way out. " I beg your pardon," said he ; "but I'm forced to go round the room."

" Well — I believe I'll follow in your wake," said Bertie. " Terribly hot — isn't it?" This he addressed to the fat rector with whom he had brought himself into the closest contact. " They've got this sofa into the worst possible part of the room; suppose we move it. Take care, Madeline."

The sofa had certainly been so placed that those who were behind it found great difficulty in getting out ;— there was but a narrow gangway, which one person could stop. This was a bad arrangement, and one which Bertie thought it might be well to improve.

"Take care, Madeline," said he; and turning to the fat rector added, "Just help me with a slight push."

The rector's weight was resting on the sofa, and unwittingly lent all its impetus to accelerate and increase the motion which Bertie intentionally originated. The sofa rushed from its moorings, and ran half way into the middle of the room. Mrs. Proudie was standing with Mr. Slope in front of the signora, and had been trying to be condescending and sociable; but she was not in the very best of tempers; for she found that, whenever she spoke to the lady, the lady replied by speaking to Mr. Slope. Mr. Slope was a favourite, no doubt; but Mrs. Proudie had no idea of being less thought of than the chaplain. She was beginning to be stately, stiff, and offended when unfortunately the castor of the sofa, caught itself in her lace train, and carried away there is no saying how much of her garniture. Gathers were heard to go, stitches to crack, plaits to fly open, flounces were seen to fall, and breadths to expose themselves; — a long ruin of rent lace disfigured the carpet, and still clung to the vile wheel on which the sofa moved.

So, when a granite battery is raised, excellent to the eyes of warfaring men, is its strength and symmetry admired. It is the work of years. Its neat embrasures, its finished parapets, its casemated stories, show all the skill of modern science. But, anon, a small spark is applied to the treacherous fusee — a cloud of dust arises to the heavens — and then nothing is to be seen but dirt and dust and ugly fragments.

We know what was the wrath of Juno when her beauty was despised. We know too what storms of passion even celestial minds can yield. As Juno may have looked at Paris on Mount Ida, so did Mrs. Proudie look on Ethelbert Stanhope when he pushed the leg of the sofa into her lace train.

"Oh, you idiot, Bertie!" said the signora, seeing what had been done, and what were to be the consequences.

"Idiot!" re-echoed Mrs. Proudie, as though the word were not half strong enough to express the required meaning; "I'll let him know——;" and then looking round to learn, at a glance, the worst, she saw that at present it behoved her to collect the scattered *débris* of her dress.

Bertie, when he saw what he had done, rushed over the sofa, and threw himself on one knee before the offended lady. His object, doubtless, was to liberate the torn lace from the castor; but he looked as though he were imploring pardon from a goddess.

"Unhand it, sir!" said Mrs. Proudie. From what scrap of dramatic poetry she had extracted the word cannot be said; but it must have rested on her memory, and now seemed opportunely dignified for the occasion.

"I'll fly to the looms of the fairies to repair the damage, if you'll only forgive me," said Ethelbert, still on his knees.

"Unhand it, sir!" said Mrs. Proudie, with redoubled emphasis, and all but furious wrath. This allusion to the fairies was a direct mockery, and intended to turn her into ridicule. So at least it seemed to her. "Unhand it, sir!" she almost screamed.

"It's not me; it's the cursed sofa," said Bertie, looking imploringly in her face, and holding up both his hands to show that he was not touching her belongings, but still remaining on his knees.

Hereupon the signora laughed; not loud, indeed, but yet audibly And as the tigress bereft of her young will turn with equal anger on any within reach, so did Mrs. Proudie turn upon her female guest.

"Madam!" she said — and it is beyond the power of prose to tell of the fire which flashed from her eyes.

The signora stared her full in the face for a moment, and then turning to her brother said, playfully, "Bertie, you idiot, get up."

By this time the bishop, and Mr. Slope, and her three daughters were around her, and had collected together the wide ruins of her magnificence. The girls fell into circular rank behind their mother, and thus following her and carrying out the fragments, they left the reception-rooms in a manner not altogether devoid of dignity. Mrs. Proudie had to retire and re-array herself.

As soon as the constellation had swept by, Ethelbert rose from his knees, and turning with mock anger to the fat rector, said: "After all it was your doing, sir — not mine. But perhaps you are waiting for preferment, and so I bore it."

Whereupon there was a laugh against the fat rector, in which both the bishop and the chaplain joined; and thus things got themselves again into order.

"Oh! my lord, I am so sorry for this accident," said the signora, putting out her hand so as to force the bishop to take it. "My brother is so thoughtless. Pray sit down, and let me have the pleasure of making your acquaintance. Though I am so poor a creature as to want a sofa, I am not so selfish as to require it all." Madeline could always dispose herself so as to make room for a gentleman, though, as she declared, the crinoline of her lady friends was much too bulky to be so accommodated.

"It was solely for the pleasure of meeting you that I have had myself dragged here," she continued. "Of course, with your occupation, one cannot even hope that you should have time to come to us, that is, in the way of calling. And at your English dinner-parties all is so dull and so stately. Do you know, my lord, that in coming to England my only consolation has been the thought that I should know you;" and she looked at him with the look of a she-devil.

The bishop, however, thought that she looked very like an angel and accepting the proffered seat, sat down beside her. He uttered some platitude as to his deep obligation for the trouble she had taken, and wondered more and more who she was.

"Of course you know my sad story?" she continued.

The bishop didn't know a word of it. He knew, however, or thought he knew, that she couldn't walk into a room like other people, and so made the most of that. He put on a look of ineffable distress, and said that he was aware how God had afflicted her.

The signora just touched the corner of her eyes with the most lovely of pocket-handkerchiefs. Yes, she said — she had been sorely tried—tried, she thought, beyond the common endurance of humanity; but while her child was left to her, everything was left. "Oh! my lord," she exclaimed, "you must see that infant—the last bud of a wondrous tree: you must let a mother hope that you will lay your holy hands on her innocent head, and consecrate her for female virtues. May I hope it?" said she, looking into the bishop's eye, and touching the bishop's arm with her hand.

The bishop was but a man, and said she might. After all, what was it but a request that he would confirm her daughter?—a request, indeed, very unnecessary to make, as he should do so as a matter of course, if the young lady came forward in the usual way.

"The blood of Tiberius," said the signora, in all but a whisper: "the blood of Tiberius flows in her veins. She is the last of the Neros!"

The bishop had heard of the last of the Visigoths, and had floating in his brain some indistinct idea of the last of the Mohicans, but to have the last of the Neros thus brought before him for a blessing was very staggering. Still he liked the lady: she had a proper way of thinking, and talked with more propriety than her brother. But who were they? It was now quite clear that that blue madman with the silky beard was not a Prince Vicinironi. The lady was married, and was of course one of the Vicinironi's by right of the husband. So the bishop went on learning.

"When will you see her ? " said the signora with a start.

"See whom ? " said the bishop.

"My child," said the mother.

"What is the young lady's age?" asked the bishop.

"She is just seven," said the signora.

"Oh," said the bishop, shaking his head ; "she is much too young — very much too young."

"But in sunny Italy you know, we do not count by years," and the signora gave the bishop one of her very sweetest smiles.

"But indeed, she is a great deal too young," persisted the bishop ; "we never confirm before——"

"But you might speak to her ; you might let her hear from your consecrated lips, that she is not a castaway because she is a Roman ; that she may be a Nero and yet a Christian ; that she may owe her black locks and dark cheeks to the blood of the pagan Cæsars, and yet herself be a child of grace ; you will tell her this, won't you, my friend ? "

The friend said he would, and asked if the child could say her catechism.

"No," said the signora, "I would not allow her to learn lessons such as those in a land ridden over by priests, and polluted by the idolatry of Rome. It is here, here in Barchester, that she must first be taught to lisp those holy words. Oh, that you could be her instructor ! "

Now, Dr. Proudie certainly liked the lady, but, seeing that he was a bishop, it was not probable that he was going to instruct a little girl in the first rudiments of her catechism ; so he said he'd send a teacher.

"But you'll see her, yourself, my lord ? "

The bishop said he would, but where should he call.

"At papa's house," said the signora, with an air of some little surprise at the question.

The bishop actually wanted the courage to ask her who was her papa ; so he was forced at last to leave her without fathoming the mystery. Mrs. Proudie, in her second best, had now returned to the rooms, and her husband thought it as well that he should not remain in too close conversation with the lady whom his wife appeared to hold in such slight esteem. Presently he came across his youngest daughter.

"Netta," said he, "do you know who is the father of that Signora Vicinironi ? "

"It isn't Vicinironi, papa," said Netta ; "but Vesey Neroni, and she's Doctor Stanhope's daughter But I must go and do the civil to Griselda Grantly ; I declare nobody has spoken a word to the poor girl this evening."

Dr. Stanhope ! Dr. Vesey Stanhope ! Dr. Vesey Stanhope's daughter, of whose marriage with a dissolute Italian scamp he now remembered to have heard something ! And that impertinent blue cub who had examined him as to his episcopal bearings was old Stanhope's son, and the lady who had entreated him to come and teach her child the catechism was old Stanhope's daughter ! the daughter of one of his own prebendaries ! As these things flashed across his mind, he was nearly as angry as his wife had been. Nevertheless, he could not but own that the mother of the last of the Neros was an agreeable woman.

Dr. Proudie tripped out into the adjoining room, in which were congregated a crowd of Grantlyite clergymen, among whom the archdeacon was standing pre-eminent, while the old dean was sitting nearly buried in a huge arm-chair by the fire-place. The bishop was very anxious to be gracious, and, if possible, to diminish the bitterness which his chaplain had occasioned. Let Mr. Slope do the *fortiter in re*, he himself would pour in the *suaviter in modo*.

"Pray don't stir, Mr. Dean, pray don't stir," he said, as the old man essayed to get up ; "I take it as a great kindness, your coming to such an *omnium gatherum* as this. But we have hardly got settled yet, and Mrs. Proudie has not been able to see her friends as she would wish to do. Well, Mr. Archdeacon, after all, we have not been so hard upon you at Oxford."

"No," said the archdeacon ; "you've only drawn our teeth and cut out our tongues ; you've allowed us still to breathe and swallow."

"Ha, ha, ha !" laughed the bishop ; "it's not quite so easy to cut out the tongue of an Oxford magnate, — and as for teeth, — ha, ha, ha ! Why, in the way we've left the matter, it's very odd if the heads of colleges don't have their own way quite as fully as when the hebdomadal board was in all its glory ; what do you say, Mr. Dean ?"

"An old man, my lord, never likes changes," said the dean.

"You must have been sad bunglers if it is so," said the archdeacon ; "and indeed, to tell the truth, I think you have bungled it. At any rate, you must own this ; you have not done the half what you boasted you would do."

"Now, as regards your system of professors——" began the chancellor slowly. He was never destined to get beyond such beginning.

"Talking of professors," said a soft clear voice, close behind the chancellor's elbow; "how much you Englishmen might learn from Germany; only you are all too proud."

The bishop looking round, perceived that that abominable young Stanhope had pursued him. The dean stared at him, as though he were some unearthly apparition; so also did two or three prebendaries and minor canons. The archdeacon laughed.

"The German professors are men of learning," said Mr. Harding, "but——"

"German professors!" groaned out the chancellor, as though his nervous system had received a shock which nothing but a week of Oxford air could cure.

"Yes," continued Ethelbert; not at all understanding why a German professor should be contemptible in the eyes of an Oxford don. "Not but what the name is best earned at Oxford. In Germany the professors do teach; at Oxford, I believe they only profess to do so, and sometimes not even that. You'll have those universities of yours about your ears soon, if you don't consent to take a lesson from Germany."

There was no answering this. Dignified clergymen of sixty years of age could not condescend to discuss such a matter with a young man with such clothes and such a beard.

"Have you got good water out at Plumstead, Mr. Archdeacon?" said the bishop by way of changing the conversation.

"Pretty good," said Dr. Grantly.

"But by no means so good as his wine, my lord," said a witty minor canon.

"Nor so generally used," said another; "that is for inward application."

"Ha, ha, ha!" laughed the bishop, "a good cellar of wine is a very comfortable thing in a house."

"Your German professors, sir, prefer beer, I believe," said the sarcastic little meagre prebendary.

"They don't think much of either," said Ethelbert; "and that perhaps accounts for their superiority. Now the Jewish professor——"

The insult was becoming too deep for the spirit of Oxford to endure, so the archdeacon walked off one way and the chancellor another, followed by their disciples, and the bishop and the young reformer were left together on the hearth-rug.

"I was a Jew once myself," began Bertie.

The bishop was determined not to stand another examination, or be led on any terms into Palestine; so he again remembered that he had to do something very particular, and left young

Stanhope with the dean. The dean did not get the worst of it, for Ethelbert gave him a true account of his remarkable doings in the Holy Land.

"Oh, Mr. Harding," said the bishop, overtaking the *ci-devant* warden; "I wanted to say one word about the hospital. You know, of course, that it is to be filled up."

Mr. Harding's heart beat a little, and he said that he had heard so.

"Of course," continued the bishop; "there can be only one man whom I could wish to see in that situation. I don't know what your own views may be, Mr. Harding——"

"They are very simply told, my lord," said the other; "to take the place if it be offered me, and to put up with the want of it should another man get it."

The bishop professed himself delighted to hear it; Mr. Harding might be quite sure that no other man would get it. There were some few circumstances which would in a slight degree change the nature of the duties. Mr. Harding was probably aware of this, and would, perhaps, not object to discuss the matter with Mr. Slope. It was a subject to which Mr. Slope had given a good deal of attention.

Mr. Harding felt, he knew not why, oppressed and annoyed. What could Mr. Slope do to him? He knew that there were to be changes. The nature of them must be communicated to the warden through somebody, and through whom so naturally as the bishop's chaplain? 'Twas thus he tried to argue himself back to an easy mind, but in vain.

Mr. Slope in the mean time had taken the seat which the bishop had vacated on the signora's sofa, and remained with that lady till it was time to marshal the folk to supper. Not with contented eyes had Mrs. Proudie seen this. Had not this woman laughed at her distress, and had not Mr. Slope heard it? Was she not an intriguing Italian woman, half wife and half not, full of affectation, airs, and impudence? Was she not horribly bedizened with velvet and pearls, with velvet and pearls, too, which had not been torn off her back? Above all, did she not pretend to be more beautiful than her neighbours? To say that Mrs. Proudie was jealous would give a wrong idea of her feelings. She had not the slightest desire that Mr. Slope should be in love with herself. But she desired the incense of Mr. Slope's spiritual and temporal services, and did not choose that they should be turned out of their course to such an object as Signora Neroni. She considered also that Mr. Slope ought in duty to hate the signora; and it appeared from his manner that he was very far from hating her.

"Come, Mr. Slope," she said, sweeping by, and looking all that she felt; "can't you make yourself useful? Do pray take Mrs. Grantly down to supper."

Mrs. Grantly heard and escaped. The words were hardly out of Mrs. Proudie's mouth, before the intended victim had stuck her hand through the arm of one of her husband's curates, and saved herself. What would the archdeacon have said had he seen her walking down stairs with Mr. Slope?

Mr. Slope heard also, but was by no means so obedient as was expected. Indeed, the period of Mr. Slope's obedience to Mrs. Proudie was drawing to a close. He did not wish yet to break with her, nor to break with her at all, if it could be avoided. But he intended to be master in that palace, and as she had made the same resolution it was not improbable that they might come to blows.

Before leaving the signora he arranged a little table before her, and begged to know what he should bring her. She was quite indifferent, she said—nothing—anything. It was now she felt the misery of her position, now that she must be left alone. Well, a little chicken, some ham, and a glass of champagne.

Mr. Slope had to explain, not without blushing for his patron, that there was no champagne.

Sherry would do just as well. And then Mr. Slope descended with the learned Miss Trefoil on his arm. Could she tell him, he asked, whether the ferns of Barsetshire were equal to those of Cumberland? His strongest worldly passion was for ferns — and before she could answer him he left her wedged between the door and the sideboard. It was fifty minutes before she escaped, and even then unfed.

"You are not leaving us, Mr. Slope," said the watchful lady of the house, seeing her slave escaping towards the door, with stores of provisions held high above the heads of the guests.

Mr. Slope explained that the Signora Neroni was in want of her supper.

"Pray, Mr. Slope, let her brother take it to her," said Mrs. Proudie, quite out loud. "It is out of the question that you should be so employed. Pray, Mr. Slope, oblige me; I am sure Mr Stanhope will wait upon his sister."

Ethelbert was most agreeably occupied in the furthest corner of of the room, making himself both useful and agreeable to Mrs. Proudie's youngest daughter.

"I couldn't get out, madam, if Madeline were starving for her supper," said he; "I'm physically fixed, unless I could fly."

The lady's anger was increased by seeing that her daughter also had gone over to the enemy ; and when she saw, that in spite of her remonstrances, in the teeth of her positive orders, Mr. Slope went off to the drawing-room, the cup of her indignation ran over, and she could not restrain herself. " Such manners I never saw," she said, muttering. " I cannot, and will not permit it ; " and then, after fussing and fuming for a few minutes, she pushed her way through the crowd, and followed Mr. Slope.

When she reached the room above, she found it absolutely deserted, except by the guilty pair. The signora was sitting very comfortably up to her supper, and Mr. Slope was leaning over her and administering to her wants. They had been discussing the merits of Sabbath-day schools, and the lady had suggested that as she could not possibly go to the children, she might be indulged in the wish of her heart by having the children brought to her.

"And when shall it be, Mr. Slope ? " said she.

Mr. Slope was saved the necessity of committing himself to a promise by the entry of Mrs. Proudie. She swept close up to the sofa so as to confront the guilty pair, stared full at them for a moment, and then said as she passed on to the next room, " Mr. Slope, his lordship is especially desirous of your attendance below ; you will greatly oblige me if you will join him." And so she stalked on.

Mr. Slope muttered something in reply, and prepared to go down stairs. As for the bishop's wanting him, he knew his lady patroness well enough to take that assertion at what it was worth ; but he did not wish to make himself the hero of a scene, or to become conspicuous for more gallantry than the occasion required.

" Is she always like this ? " said the signora.

" Yes—always—madam," said Mrs. Proudie, returning ; "always the same—always equally adverse to impropriety of conduct of every description ; " and she stalked back through the room again, following Mr. Slope out of the door.

The signora couldn't follow her, or she certainly would have done so. But she laughed loud, and sent the sound of it ringing through the lobby and down the stairs after Mrs. Proudie's feet. Had she been as active as Grimaldi, she could probably have taken no better revenge.

" Mr. Slope," said Mrs. Proudie, catching the delinquent at the door, " I am surprised that you should leave my company to attend on such a painted Jezebel as that."

"But she's lame, Mrs. Proudie, and cannot move. Somebody must have waited upon her."

" Lame," said Mrs. Proudie ; " I'd lame her if she belonged to

me. What business had she here at all ?—such impertinence—
such affectation."

In the hall and adjacent rooms all manner of cloaking and
shawling was going on, and the Barchester folk were getting themselves gone. Mrs. Proudie did her best to smirk at each and every
one, as they made their adieux, but she was hardly successful.
Her temper had been tried fearfully. By slow degrees, the guests
went.

"Send back the carriage quick," said Ethelbert, as Dr. and Mrs.
Stanhope took their departure.

The younger Stanhopes were left to the very last, and an uncomfortable party they made with the bishop's family. They all
went into the dining-room, and then the bishop, observing that
"the lady" was alone in the drawing-room, they followed him up.
Mrs. Proudie kept Mr. Slope and her daughters in close conversation, resolving that he should not be indulged, nor they polluted.
The bishop, in mortal dread of Bertie and the Jews, tried to
converse with Charlotte Stanhope about the climate of Italy.
Bertie and the signora had no resource but in each other.

"Did you get your supper, at last, Madeline?" said the impudent
or else mischievous young man.

"Oh, yes," said Madeline; "Mr. Slope was so very kind as to
bring it me. I fear, however, he put himself to more inconvenience
than I wished."

Mrs. Proudie looked at her, but said nothing. The meaning of
her look might have been thus translated: "If ever you find
yourself within these walls again, I'll give you leave to be as
impudent, and affected, and as mischievous as you please."

At last the carriage returned with the three Italian servants,
and La Signora Madeline Vesey Neroni was carried out, as she
had been carried in.

The lady of the palace retired to her chamber by no means
contented with the result of her first grand party at Barchester.

CHAP. XII.

SLOPE VERSUS HARDING.

Two or three days after the party, Mr. Harding received a note,
begging him to call on Mr. Slope, at the palace, at an early hour
the following morning. There was nothing uncivil in the com-

munication, and yet the tone of it was thoroughly displeasing. It was as follows :

"My dear Mr. Harding, — Will you favour me by calling on me at the palace to-morrow morning at 9.30 A.M. The bishop wishes me to speak to you touching the hospital. I hope you will excuse my naming so early an hour. I do so as my time is greatly occupied. If, however, it is positively inconvenient to you, I will change it to 10. You will, perhaps, be kind enough to let me have a note in reply.

"Believe me to be,
"My dear Mr. Harding,
"Your assured friend,
"OBH. SLOPE.

"The Palace, Monday morning,
"20th August, 185—."

Mr. Harding neither could nor would believe anything of the sort; and he thought, moreover, that Mr. Slope was rather impertinent to call himself by such a name. His assured friend, indeed ! How many assured friends generally fall to the lot of a man in this world ? And by what process are they made ? and how much of such process had taken place as yet between Mr. Harding and Mr. Slope ? Mr. Harding could not help asking himself these questions as he read and re-read the note before him. He answered it, however, as follows :

"Dear Sir, — I will call at the palace to-morrow at 9.30 A.M. as you desire.

"Truly yours,
"S. HARDING.

"High Street, Barchester, Monday."

And on the following morning, punctually at half-past nine, he knocked at the palace door, and asked for Mr. Slope.

The bishop had one small room allotted to him on the ground-floor, and Mr. Slope had another. Into this latter Mr. Harding was shown, and asked to sit down. Mr. Slope was not yet there. The ex-warden stood up at the window looking into the garden, and could not help thinking how very short a time had passed since the whole of that house had been open to him, as though he had been a child of the family, born and bred in it. He remembered how the old servants used to smile as they opened the door to him ; how the familiar butler would say, when he had been absent a few hours longer than usual, "A sight of you, Mr. Harding, is good for sore eyes ;" how the fussy housekeeper would swear that he couldn't have dined, or couldn't have breakfasted, or couldn't have lunched. And then, above all, he remembered the pleasant gleam of inward satisfaction which always spread itself over the old bishop's face, whenever his friend entered his room.

A tear came into each eye as he reflected that all this was gone. What use would the hospital be to him now? He was alone in the world, and getting old ; he would soon, very soon have to go, and leave it all, as his dear old friend had gone ;—go, and leave the hospital, and his accustomed place in the cathedral, and his haunts and pleasures, to younger and perhaps wiser men. That chanting of his ! — perhaps, in truth, the time for it had gone by. He felt as though the world were sinking from his feet ; as though this, this was the time for him to turn with confidence to those hopes which he had preached with confidence to others. "What," said he to himself, "can a man's religion be worth, if it does not support him against the natural melancholy of declining years ?" And, as he looked out through his dimmed eyes into the bright parterres of the bishop's garden, he felt that he had the support which he wanted.

Nevertheless, he did not like to be thus kept waiting. If Mr. Slope did not really wish to see him at half-past nine o'clock, why force him to come away from his lodgings with his breakfast in his throat? To tell the truth, it was policy on the part of Mr Slope. Mr. Slope had made up his mind that Mr. Harding should either accept the hospital with abject submission, or else refuse it altogether ; and had calculated that he would probably be more quick to do the latter, if he could be got to enter upon the subject in an ill-humour. Perhaps Mr. Slope was not altogether wrong in his calculation.

It was nearly ten when Mr. Slope hurried into the room, and, muttering something about the bishop and diocesan duties, shook Mr. Harding's hand ruthlessly, and begged him to be seated.

Now the air of superiority which this man assumed, did go against the grain of Mr. Harding ; and yet he did not know how to resent it. The whole tendency of his mind and disposition was opposed to any contra-assumption of grandeur on his own part, and he hadn't the worldly spirit or quickness necessary to put down insolent pretensions by downright and open rebuke, as the archdeacon would have done. There was nothing for Mr. Harding but to submit, and he accordingly did so.

"About the hospital, Mr. Harding ?" began Mr. Slope, speaking of it as the head of a college at Cambridge might speak of some sizarship which had to be disposed of.

Mr. Harding crossed one leg over another, and then one hand over the other on the top of them, and looked Mr. Slope in the face ; but he said nothing.

"It's to be filled up again," said Mr. Slope. Mr. Harding said that he had understood so.

"Of course, you know, the income will be very much reduced," continued Mr. Slope. "The bishop wished to be liberal, and he therefore told the government that he thought it ought to be put at not less than 450*l*. I think on the whole the bishop was right; for though the services required will not be of a very onerous nature, they will be more so than they were before. And it is, perhaps, well that the clergy immediately attached to the cathedral town should be made as comfortable as the extent of the ecclesiastical means at our disposal will allow. Those are the bishop's ideas, and I must say mine also."

Mr. Harding sat rubbing one hand on the other, but said not a word.

"So much for the income, Mr. Harding. The house will, of course, remain to the warden, as before. It should, however, I think, be stipulated that he should paint inside every seven years, and outside every three years, and be subject to dilapidations, in the event of vacating, either by death or otherwise. But this is a matter on which the bishop must yet be consulted."

Mr. Harding still rubbed his hands, and still sat silent, gazing up into Mr. Slope's unprepossessing face.

"Then, as to the duties," continued he, "I believe, if I am rightly informed, there can hardly be said to have been any duties hitherto," and he gave a sort of half laugh, as though to pass off the accusation in the guise of a pleasantry.

Mr. Harding thought of the happy, easy years he had passed in his old home; of the worn-out, aged men whom he had succoured; of his good intentions; and of his work, which had certainly been of the lightest. He thought of these things, doubting for a moment whether he did or did not deserve the sarcasm. He gave his enemy the benefit of the doubt, and did not rebuke him. He merely observed, very tranquilly, and perhaps with too much humility, that the duties of the situation, such as they were, had, he believed, been done to the satisfaction of the late bishop.

Mr. Slope again smiled, and this time the smile was intended to operate against the memory of the late bishop, rather than against the energy of the ex-warden ; and so it was understood by Mr. Harding. The colour rose to his cheeks, and he began to feel very angry.

"You must be aware, Mr. Harding, that things are a good deal changed in Barchester," said Mr. Slope.

Mr. Harding said that he was aware of it. "And not only in Barchester, Mr. Harding, but in the world at large. It is not only in Barchester that a new man is carrying out new measures and casting away the useless rubbish of past centuries. The same thing is going on throughout the country. Work is now required from every man who receives wages; and they who have to superintend the doing of work, and the paying of wages, are bound to see that this rule is carried out. New men, Mr. Harding, are now needed, and are now forthcoming in the church, as well as in other professions."

All this was wormwood to our old friend. He had never rated very high his own abilities or activity; but all the feelings of his heart were with the old clergy, and any antipathies of which his heart was susceptible, were directed against those new, busy, uncharitable, self-lauding men, of whom Mr. Slope was so good an example.

"Perhaps," said he, "the bishop will prefer a new man at the hospital?"

"By no means," said Mr Slope. "The bishop is very anxious that you should accept the appointment; but he wishes you should understand beforehand what will be the required duties. In the first place, a Sabbath-day school will be attached to the hospital."

"What! for the old men?" asked Mr. Harding.

"No, Mr. Harding, not for the old men, but for the benefit of the children of such of the poor of Barchester as it may suit. The bishop will expect that you shall attend this school, and the teachers shall be under your inspection and care."

Mr. Harding slipped his topmost hand off the other, and began to rub the calf of the leg which was supported.

"As to the old men," continued Mr. Slope, "and the old women who are to form a part of the hospital, the bishop is desirous that you shall have morning and evening service on the premises every Sabbath, and one week-day service; that you shall preach to them once at least on Sundays; and that the whole hospital be always collected for morning and evening prayer. The bishop thinks that this will render it unnecessary that any separate seats in the cathedral should be reserved for the hospital inmates."

Mr. Slope paused, but Mr. Harding still said nothing.

"Indeed, it would be difficult to find seats for the women; and, on the whole, Mr. Harding, I may as well say at once, that for people of that class the cathedral service does not appear to me the most useful, — even if it be so for any class of people."

"We will not discuss that, if you please," said Mr. Harding.

"I am not desirous of doing so; at least, not at the present moment. I hope, however, you fully understand the bishop's wishes about the new establishment of the hospital; and if, as I do not doubt, I shall receive from you an assurance that you accord with his lordship's views, it will give me very great pleasure to be the bearer from his lordship to you of the presentation to the appointment."

"But if I disagree with his lordship's views?" asked Mr Harding.

"But I hope you do not," said Mr. Slope.

"But if I do?" again asked the other.

"If such unfortunately should be the case, which I can hardly conceive, I presume your own feelings will dictate to you the propriety of declining the appointment."

"But if I accept the appointment, and yet disagree with the bishop, what then?"

This question rather bothered Mr. Slope. It was true that he had talked the matter over with the bishop, and had received a sort of authority for suggesting to Mr. Harding the propriety of a Sunday school, and certain hospital services; but he had no authority for saying that these propositions were to be made peremptory conditions attached to the appointment. The bishop's idea had been that Mr. Harding would of course consent, and that the school would become, like the rest of those new establishments in the city, under the control of his wife and his chaplain. Mr. Slope's idea had been more correct. He intended that Mr. Harding should refuse the situation, and that an ally of his own should get it; but he had not conceived the possibility of Mr. Harding openly accepting the appointment, and as openly rejecting the conditions.

"It is not, I presume, probable," said he, "that you will accept from the hands of the bishop a piece of preferment, with a fixed predetermination to disacknowledge the duties attached to it."

"If I become warden," said Mr. Harding, "and neglect my duty, the bishop has means by which he can remedy the grievance."

"I hardly expected such an argument from you, or I may say the suggestion of such a line of conduct," said Mr. Slope, with a great look of injured virtue.

"Nor did I expect such a proposition."

"I shall be glad at any rate to know what answer I am to make to his lordship," said Mr. Slope

"I will take an early opportunity of seeing his lordship myself," said Mr. Harding.

"Such an arrangement," said Mr. Slope, "will hardly give his lordship satisfaction. Indeed, it is impossible that the bishop should himself see every clergyman in the diocese on every subject of patronage that may arise. The bishop, I believe, did see you on the matter, and I really cannot see why he should be troubled to do so again."

"Do you know, Mr. Slope, how long I have been officiating as a clergyman in this city?" Mr. Slope's wish was now nearly fulfilled. Mr. Harding had become angry, and it was probable that he might commit himself.

"I really do not see what that has to do with the question. You cannot think the bishop would be justified in allowing you to regard as a sinecure a situation that requires an active man, merely because you have been employed for many years in the cathedral."

"But it might induce the bishop to see me, if I asked him to do so. I shall consult my friends in this matter, Mr. Slope; but I mean to be guilty of no subterfuge,—you may tell the bishop that as I altogether disagree with his views about the hospital, I shall decline the situation if I find that any such conditions are attached to it as those you have suggested;" and so saying, Mr. Harding took his hat and went his way.

Mr. Slope was contented. He considered himself at liberty to accept Mr. Harding's last speech as an absolute refusal of the appointment. At least, he so represented it to the bishop and to Mrs. Proudie.

"That is very surprising," said the bishop.

"Not at all," said Mrs. Proudie; "you little know how determined the whole set of them are to withstand your authority."

"But Mr. Harding was so anxious for it," said the bishop.

"Yes," said Mr. Slope, "if he can hold it without the slightest acknowledgment of your lordship's jurisdiction."

"That is out of the question," said the bishop.

"I should imagine it to be quite so," said the chaplain.

"Indeed, I should think so," said the lady.

"I really am sorry for it," said the bishop.

"I don't know that there is much cause for sorrow," said the lady. "Mr. Quiverful is a much more deserving man, more in need of it, and one who will make himself much more useful in the close neighbourhood of the palace."

"I suppose I had better see Quiverful?" said the chaplain.

"I suppose you had," said the bishop.

CHAP. XIII.

THE RUBBISH CART.

MR. HARDING was not a happy man as he walked down the palace pathway, and stepped out into the close. His preferment and pleasant house were a second time gone from him; but that he could endure. He had been schooled and insulted by a man young enough to be his son; but that he could put up with. He could even draw from the very injuries, which had been inflicted on him, some of that consolation which we may believe martyrs always receive from the injustice of their own sufferings, and which is generally proportioned in its strength to the extent of cruelty with which martyrs are treated. He had admitted to his daughter that he wanted the comfort of his old home, and yet he could have returned to his lodgings in the High Street, if not with exultation, at least with satisfaction, had that been all. But the venom of the chaplain's harangue had worked into his blood, and sapped the life of his sweet contentment.

"New men are carrying out new measures, and are carting away the useless rubbish of past centuries!" What cruel words these had been; and how often are they now used with all the heartless cruelty of a Slope! A man is sufficiently condemned if it can only be shown that either in politics or religion he does not belong to some new school established within the last score of years. He may then regard himself as rubbish and expect to be carted away. A man is nothing now unless he has within him a full appreciation of the new era; an era in which it would seem that neither honesty nor truth is very desirable, but in which success is the only touchstone of merit. We must laugh at every thing that is established. Let the joke be ever so bad, ever so untrue to the real principles of joking; nevertheless we must laugh — or else beware the cart. We must talk, think, and live up to the spirit of the times, and write up to it too, if that cacoethes be upon us, or else we are nought. New men and new measures, long credit and few scruples, great success or wonderful ruin, such are now the tastes of Englishmen who know how to live. Alas, alas! under such circumstances Mr. Harding could not but feel that he was an Englishman who did not know how to live. This new doctrine of Mr. Slope and the rubbish cart, new at least at Barchester, sadly disturbed his equanimity.

"The same thing is going on throughout the whole country!"
"Work is now required from every man who receives wages!"
And had he been living all his life receiving wages, and doing no
work? Had he in truth so lived as to be now in his old age
justly reckoned as rubbish fit only to be hidden away in some huge
dust hole? The school of men to whom he professes to belong,
the Grantlys, the Gwynnes, and the old high set of Oxford divines,
are afflicted with no such self-accusations as these which troubled
Mr. Harding. They, as a rule, are as satisfied with the wisdom
and propriety of their own conduct as can be any Mr. Slope, or
any Dr. Proudie, with his own. But unfortunately for himself
Mr. Harding had little of this self-reliance. When he heard himself designated as rubbish by the Slopes of the world, he had no
other resource than to make inquiry within his own bosom as to
the truth of the designation. Alas, alas! the evidence seemed
generally to go against him.

He had professed to himself in the bishop's parlour that in these
coming sources of the sorrow of age, in these fits of sad regret
from which the latter years of few reflecting men can be free,
religion would suffice to comfort him. Yes, religion could console
him for the loss of any worldly good; but was his religion of that
active sort which would enable him so to repent of misspent years
as to pass those that were left to him in a spirit of hope for the
future? And such repentance itself, is it not a work of agony
and of tears? It is very easy to talk of repentance; but a man
has to walk over hot ploughshares before he can complete it;
to be skinned alive as was St. Bartholomew; to be stuck full of
arrows as was St. Sebastian; to lie broiling on a gridiron like St.
Lorenzo! How if his past life required such repentance as this?
had he the energy to go through with it?

Mr. Harding, after leaving the palace, walked slowly for an hour
or so beneath the shady elms of the close, and then betook himself
to his daughter's house. He had at any rate made up his mind
that he would go out to Plumstead to consult Dr. Grantly, and
that he would in the first instance tell Eleanor what had occurred.

And now he was doomed to undergo another misery. Mr.
Slope had forestalled him at the widow's house. He had called
there on the preceding afternoon. He could not, he had said, deny
himself the pleasure of telling Mrs. Bold that her father was about
to return to the pretty house at Hiram's hospital. He had been
instructed by the bishop to inform Mr. Harding that the appointment would now be made at once. The bishop was of course only
too happy to be able to be the means of restoring to Mr. Harding

the preferment which he had so long adorned. And then by degrees Mr. Slope had introduced the subject of the pretty school which he hoped before long to see attached to the hospital. He had quite fascinated Mrs. Bold by his description of this picturesque, useful, and charitable appendage, and she had gone so far as to say that she had no doubt her father would approve, and that she herself would gladly undertake a class.

Any one who had heard the entirely different tone, and seen the entirely different manner in which Mr. Slope had spoken of this projected institution to the daughter and to the father, could not have failed to own that Mr. Slope was a man of genius. He said nothing to Mrs. Bold about the hospital sermons and services, nothing about the exclusion of the old men from the cathedral, nothing about dilapidation and painting, nothing about carting away the rubbish. Eleanor had said to herself that certainly she did not like Mr. Slope personally, but that he was a very active, zealous clergyman, and would no doubt be useful in Barchester. All this paved the way for much additional misery to Mr. Harding.

Eleanor put on her happiest face as she heard her father on the stairs, for she thought she had only to congratulate him; but directly she saw his face, she knew that there was but little matter for congratulation. She had seen him with the same weary look of sorrow on one or two occasions before, and remembered it well. She had seen him when he first read that attack upon himself in the Jupiter which had ultimately caused him to resign the hospital; and she had seen him also when the archdeacon had persuaded him to remain there against his own sense of propriety and honour. She knew at a glance that his spirit was in deep trouble.

"Oh, papa, what is it?" said she, putting down her boy to crawl upon the floor.

"I came to tell you, my dear," said he, "that I am going out to Plumstead: you won't come with me, I suppose?"

"To Plumstead, papa? Shall you stay there?"

"I suppose I shall, to night: I must consult the archdeacon about this weary hospital. Ah me! I wish I had never thought of it again."

"Why, papa, what is the matter?"

"I've been with Mr. Slope, my dear, and he isn't the pleasantest companion in the world, at least not to me." Eleanor gave a sort of half blush; but she was wrong if she imagined that her father in any way alluded to her acquaintance with Mr. Slope.

"Well, papa."

"He wants to turn the hospital into a Sunday school and a preaching house; and I suppose he will have his way. I do not feel myself adapted for such an establishment, and therefore, I suppose, I must refuse the appointment."

"What would be the harm of the school, papa?"

"The want of a proper schoolmaster, my dear."

"But that would of course be supplied."

"Mr. Slope wishes to supply it by making me his schoolmaster. But as I am hardly fit for such work, I intend to decline."

"Oh, papa! Mr. Slope doesn't intend that. He was here yesterday, and what he intends——"

"He was here yesterday, was he?" asked Mr. Harding.

"Yes, papa."

"And talking about the hospital?"

"He was saying how glad he would be, and the bishop too, to see you back there again. And then he spoke about the Sunday school; and to tell the truth I agreed with him; and I thought you would have done so too. Mr. Slope spoke of a school, not inside the hospital, but just connected with it, of which you would be the patron and visitor; and I thought you would have liked such a school as that; and I promised to look after it and to take a class—and it all seemed so very——. But, oh, papa! I shall be so miserable if I find I have done wrong."

"Nothing wrong at all, my dear," said he, gently, very gently rejecting his daughter's caress. "There can be nothing wrong in your wishing to make yourself useful; indeed, you ought to do so by all means. Every one must now exert himself who would not choose to go to the wall." Poor Mr. Harding thus attempted in his misery to preach the new doctrine to his child. "Himself or herself, it's all the same," he continued; "you will be quite right, my dear, to do something of this sort, but——"

"Well, papa?"

"I am not quite sure that if I were you I would select Mr. Slope for my guide."

"But I have never done so, and never shall."

"It would be very wicked of me to speak evil of him, for to tell the truth I know no evil of him; but I am not quite sure that he is honest. That he is not gentleman-like in his manners, of that I am quite sure."

"I never thought of taking him for my guide, papa."

"As for myself, my dear," continued he, "we know the old proverb—'It's bad teaching an old dog tricks.' I must decline the Sunday school, and shall therefore probably decline the hospital also. But I will first see your brother-in-law." So he took up his hat, kissed the baby, and withdrew, leaving Eleanor in as low spirits as himself.

All this was a great aggravation to his misery. He had so few with whom to sympathise, that he could not afford to be cut off from the one whose sympathy was of the most value to him. And yet it seemed probable that this would be the case. He did not own to himself that he wished his daughter to hate Mr. Slope; yet had she expressed such a feeling there would have been very little bitterness in the rebuke he would have given her for so un-charitable a state of mind. The fact, however, was that she was on friendly terms with Mr. Slope, that she coincided with his views, adhered at once to his plans, and listened with delight to his teaching. Mr. Harding hardly wished his daughter to hate the man, but he would have preferred that to her loving him.

He walked away to the inn to order a fly, went home to put up his carpet bag, and then started for Plumstead. There was, at any rate, no danger that the archdeacon would fraternise with Mr. Slope; but then he would recommend internecine war, public appeals, loud reproaches, and all the paraphernalia of open battle. Now that alternative was hardly more to Mr. Harding's taste than the other.

When Mr. Harding reached the parsonage he found that the archdeacon was out, and would not be home till dinner-time, so he began his complaint to his elder daughter. Mrs. Grantly enter-tained quite as strong an antagonism to Mr. Slope as did her husband; she was also quite as alive to the necessity of combating the Proudie faction, of supporting the old church interest of the close, of keeping in 'her own set such of the loaves and fishes as duly belonged to it; and was quite as well prepared as her lord to carry on the battle without giving or taking quarter. Not that she was a woman prone to quarrelling, or ill inclined to live at peace with her clerical neighbours; but she felt, as did the arch-deacon, that the presence of Mr. Slope in Barchester was an insult to every one connected with the late bishop, and that his assumed dominion in the diocese was a spiritual injury to her husband. Hitherto people had little guessed how bitter Mrs. Grantly could be. She lived on the best of terms with all the rectors' wives around her. She had been popular with all the ladies connected with the close. Though much the wealthiest of the ecclesiastical matrons of the county, she had so managed her affairs that her carriage and horses had given umbrage to none. She had never thrown herself among the county grandees so as to excite the envy of other clergymen's wives. She had never talked too loudly of earls and countesses, or boasted that she gave her governess sixty pounds a year, or her cook seventy. Mrs. Grantly had lived the life of a wise, discreet, peace-making woman; and the people of Barchester were surprised at the amount of military vigour she displayed as general of the feminine Grantlyite forces.

Mrs. Grantly soon learnt that her sister Eleanor had promised to assist Mr. Slope in the affairs of the hospital; and it was on this point that her attention soon fixed itself.

"How can Eleanor endure him?" said she.

"He is a very crafty man," said her father, "and his craft has been successful in making Eleanor think that he is a meek, charitable, good clergyman. God forgive me, if I wrong him, but such is not his true character in my opinion."

"His true character, indeed!" said she, with something approaching to scorn for her father's moderation. "I only hope he won't have craft enough to make Eleanor forget herself and her position."

"Do you mean marry him?" said he, startled out of his usual demeanour by the abruptness and horror of so dreadful a proposition.

"What is there so improbable in it? Of course that would be his own object if he thought he had any chance of success. Eleanor has a thousand a year entirely at her own disposal, and what better fortune could fall to Mr. Slope's lot than the transferring of the disposal of such a fortune to himself?"

"But you can't think she likes him, Susan?"

"Why not?" said Susan. "Why shouldn't she like him? He's just the sort of man to get on with a woman left as she is, with no one to look after her."

"Look after her!" said the unhappy father; "don't we look after her?"

"Ah, papa, how innocent you are! Of course it was to be expected that Eleanor should marry again. I should be the last to advise her against it, if she would only wait the proper time, and then marry at least a gentleman."

"But you don't really mean to say that you suppose Eleanor has ever thought of marrying Mr. Slope? Why, Mr. Bold has only been dead a year."

"Eighteen months," said his daughter. "But I don't suppose Eleanor has ever thought about it. It is very probable, though, that he has, and that he will try and make her do so; and that he will succeed too, if we don't take care what we are about."

This was quite a new phase of the affair to poor Mr. Harding.

To have thrust upon him as his son-in-law, as the husband of his favourite child, the only man in the world whom he really positively disliked, would be a misfortune which he felt he would not know how to endure patiently. But then, could there be any ground for so dreadful a surmise? In all worldly matters he was apt to look upon the opinion of his eldest daughter as one generally sound and trustworthy. In her appreciation of character, of motives, and the probable conduct both of men and women, she was usually not far wrong. She had early foreseen the marriage of Eleanor and John Bold; she had at a glance deciphered the character of the new bishop and his chaplain; could it possibly be that her present surmise should ever come forth as true?

"But you don't think that she likes him?" said Mr. Harding again.

"Well, papa, I can't say that I think she dislikes him as she ought to do. Why is he visiting there as a confidential friend, when he never ought to have been admitted inside the house? Why is it that she speaks to him about your welfare and your position, as she clearly has done? At the bishop's party the other night, I saw her talking to him for half an hour at the stretch."

"I thought Mr. Slope seemed to talk to nobody there but that daughter of Stanhope's," said Mr. Harding, wishing to defend his child.

"Oh, Mr. Slope is a cleverer man than you think of, papa, and keeps more than one iron in the fire."

To give Eleanor her due, any suspicion as to the slightest inclination on her part towards Mr. Slope was a wrong to her. She had no more idea of marrying Mr. Slope than she had of marrying the bishop; and the idea that Mr. Slope would present himself as a suitor had never occurred to her. Indeed, to give her her due again, she had never thought about suitors since her husband's death. But nevertheless it was true that she had overcome all that repugnance to the man which was so strongly felt for him by the rest of the Grantly faction. She had forgiven him his sermon. She had forgiven him his low church tendencies, his Sabbath schools, and puritanical observances. She had forgiven his pharisaical arrogance, and even his greasy face and oily vulgar manners. Having agreed to overlook such offences as these, why should she not in time be taught to regard Mr. Slope as a suitor?

And as to him, it must also be affirmed that he was hitherto equally innocent of the crime imputed to him. How it had come to pass that a man whose eyes were generally so widely open to everything around him had not perceived that this young widow was rich as well as beautiful, cannot probably now be explained. But such was the fact. Mr. Slope had ingratiated himself with Mrs. Bold, merely as he had done with other ladies, in order to strengthen his party in the city. He subsequently amended his error ; but it was not till after the interview between him and Mr. Harding.

CHAP. XIV.

THE NEW CHAMPION.

THE archdeacon did not return to the parsonage till close upon the hour of dinner, and there was therefore no time to discuss matters before that important ceremony. He seemed to be in an especial good humour, and welcomed his father-in-law with a sort of jovial earnestness that was usual with him when things on which he was intent were going on as he would have them.

" It's all settled, my dear," said he to his wife as he washed his hands in his dressing-room, while she, according to her wont, sat listening in the bedroom ; " Arabin has agreed to accept the living. " He'll be here next week." And the archdeacon scrubbed his hands and rubbed his face with a violent alacrity, which showed that Arabin's coming was a great point gained.

" Will he come here to Plumstead ? " said the wife.

" He has promised to stay a month with us," said the arch-deacon, " so that he may see what his parish is like. You'll like Arabin very much. He's a gentleman in every respect, and full of humour."

" He's very queer, isn't he ? " asked the lady.

" Well—he is a little odd in some of his fancies ; but there's nothing about him you won't like. He is as staunch a churchman as there is at Oxford. I really don't know what we should do without Arabin. It's a great thing for me to have him so near me ; and if anything can put Slope down, Arabin will do it."

The Reverend Francis Arabin was a fellow of Lazarus, the favoured disciple of the great Dr. Gwynne, a high churchman at all points ; so high, indeed, that at one period of his career he had all but toppled over into the cesspool of Rome ; a poet and also a polemical writer, a great pet in the common rooms at Oxford, an eloquent clergyman, a droll, odd, humorous, energetic, conscientious man, and as the archdeacon had boasted of him, a thorough gentleman. As he will hereafter be brought more closely to our notice, it is now only necessary to add, that he had just been presented to the vicarage of St. Ewold by Dr. Grantly, in whose gift as archdeacon the living lay. St. Ewold is a parish lying just without the city of Barchester. The suburbs of the new town, indeed, are partly within its precincts, and the pretty church and parsonage are not much above a mile distant from the city gate.

St. Ewold is not a rich piece of preferment—it is worth some three or four hundred a year at most, and has generally been held by a clergyman attached to the cathedral choir. The archdeacon, however, felt, when the living on this occasion became vacant, that it imperatively behoved him to aid the force of his party with some tower of strength, if any such tower could be got to occupy St. Ewold's. He had discussed the matter with his brethren in Barchester; not in any weak spirit as the holder of patronage to be used for his own or his family's benefit, but as one to whom was committed a trust, on the due administration of which much of the church's welfare might depend. He had submitted to them the name of Mr. Arabin, as though the choice had rested with them all in conclave, and they had unanimously admitted that, if Mr. Arabin would accept St. Ewold's no better choice could possibly be made.

If Mr. Arabin would accept St. Ewold's! There lay the difficulty. Mr. Arabin was a man standing somewhat prominently before the world, that is, before the Church of England world. He was not a rich man, it is true, for he held no preferment but his fellowship ; but he was a man not over anxious for riches, not married of course, and one whose time was greatly taken up in discussing, both in print and on platforms, the privileges and practices of the church to which he belonged. As the archdeacon had done battle for its temporalities, so did Mr. Arabin do battle for its spiritualities; and both had done so conscientiously; that is, not so much each for his own benefit as for that of others.

Holding such a position as Mr. Arabin did, there was much reason to doubt whether he would consent to become the parson of St. Ewold's, and Dr. Grantly had taken the trouble to go himself to Oxford on the matter. Dr. Gwynne and Dr. Grantly together had succeeded in persuading this eminent divine that duty required him to go to Barchester. There were wheels within wheels in this affair. For some time past Mr. Arabin had been engaged in a tremendous controversy with no less a person than Mr. Slope, respecting the apostolic succession. These two gentlemen had never seen each other, but they had been extremely bitter in print. Mr. Slope had endeavoured to strengthen his cause by calling Mr. Arabin an owl, and Mr. Arabin had retaliated by hinting that Mr. Slope was an infidel. This battle had been commenced in the columns of the daily Jupiter, a powerful newspaper, the manager of which was very friendly to Mr. Slope's view of the case. The matter, however, had become too tedious for the readers of the Jupiter, and a little note had therefore been appended to one of Mr. Slope's most telling rejoinders, in which it had been stated that no further letters from the reverend gentleman could be inserted except as advertisements.

Other methods of publication were, however, found less expensive than advertisements in the Jupiter ; and the war went on merrily. Mr. Slope declared that the main part of the consecration of a clergyman was the self-devotion of the inner man to the duties of the ministry. Mr. Arabin contended that a man was not consecrated at all, had, indeed, no single attribute of a clergyman, unless he became so through the imposition of some bishop's hands, who had become a bishop through the imposition of other hands, and so on in a direct line to one of the apostles. Each had repeatedly hung the other on the horns of a dilemma ; but neither seemed to be a whit the worse for the hanging ; and so the war went on merrily.

Whether or no the near neighbourhood of the foe may have acted in any way as an inducement to Mr. Arabin to accept the living of St. Ewold, we will not pretend to say ; but it had at any rate been settled in Dr. Gwynne's library, at Lazarus, that he would accept it, and that he would lend his assistance towards driving the enemy out of Barchester, or, at any rate, silencing him while he remained there. Mr. Arabin intended to keep his rooms at Oxford, and to have the assistance of a curate at St. Ewold ; but he promised to give as much time as possible to the neighbourhood of Barchester, and from so great a man Dr. Grantly was quite satisfied with such a promise. It was no small part of the satisfaction derivable from such an arrangement that Bishop Proudie would be forced to institute into a living, immediately under his own nose, the enemy of his favourite chaplain.

All through dinner the archdeacon's good humour shone brightly in his face. He ate of the good things heartily, he drank wine with his wife and daughter, he talked pleasantly of his doings at Oxford, told his father-in-law that he ought to visit Dr. Gwynne at Lazarus, and launched out again in praise of Mr. Arabin.

' Is Mr. Arabin married, papa ? " asked Griselda.

" No, my dear ; the fellow of a college-is never married."

"Is he a young man, papa ?"

"About forty, I believe," said the archdeacon.

"Oh !" said Griselda. Had her father said eighty, Mr. Arabin would not have appeared to her to be very much older.

When the two gentlemen were left alone over their wine, Mr. Harding told his tale of woe. But even this, sad as it was, did not much diminish the archdeacon's good humour, though it greatly added to his pugnacity.

"He can't do it," said Dr. Grantly over and over again, as his father-in-law explained to him the terms on which the new warden of the hospital was to be appointed ; "he can't do it. What he says is not worth the trouble of listening to. He can't alter the duties of the place."

"Who can't ?" asked the ex-warden.

"Neither the bishop nor the chaplain, nor yet the bishop's wife, who, I take it, has really more to say to such matters than either of the other two. The whole body corporate of the palace together have no power to turn the warden of the hospital into a Sunday schoolmaster."

"But the bishop has the power to appoint whom he pleases, and——"

"I don't know that ; I rather think he'll find he has no such power. Let him try it, and see what the press will say. For once we shall have the popular cry on our side. But Proudie, ass as he is, knows the world too well to get such a hornet's nest about his ears."

Mr. Harding winced at the idea of the press. He had had enough of that sort of publicity, and was unwilling to be shown up a second time either as a monster or as a martyr. He gently remarked that he hoped the newspapers would not get hold of his name again, and then suggested that perhaps it would be better that he should abandon his object. "I am getting old," said he ; "and after all I doubt whether I am fit to undertake new duties."

"New duties !" said the archdeacon : "don't I tell you there shall be no new duties ?"

"Or, perhaps, old duties either," said Mr. Harding ; "I think I will remain content as I am." The picture of Mr. Slope carting away the rubbish was still present to his mind.

The archdeacon drank off his glass of claret, and prepared himself to be energetic. " I do hope," said he, "that you are not going to be so weak as to allow such a man as Mr. Slope to deter you from doing what you know it is your duty to do. You know it is your duty to resume your place at the hospital now that parliament has so settled the stipend as to remove those difficulties which induced you to resign it. You cannot deny this; and should your timidity now prevent you from doing so, your conscience will hereafter never forgive you;" and as he finished this clause of his speech, he pushed over the bottle to his companion.

"Your conscience will never forgive you," he continued. "You resigned the place from conscientious scruples, scruples which I greatly respected, though I did not share them. All your friends respected them, and you left your old house as rich in reputation as you were ruined in fortune. It is now expected that you will return. Dr. Gwynne was saying only the other day ——"

"Dr. Gwynne does not reflect how much older a man I am now than when he last saw me."

"Old—nonsense!" said the archdeacon; "you never thought yourself old till you listened to the impudent trash of that coxcomb at the palace."

"I shall be sixty-five if I live till November," said Mr. Harding.

"And seventy-five, if you live till November ten years," said the archdeacon. "And you bid fair to be as efficient then as you were ten years ago. But for heaven's sake let us have no pretence in this matter. Your plea of old age is only a pretence. But you're not drinking your wine. It is only a pretence. The fact is, you are half afraid of this Slope, and would rather subject yourself to comparative poverty and discomfort, than come to blows with a man who will trample on you, if you let him."

"I certainly don't like coming to blows, if I can help it."

"Nor I neither—but sometimes we can't help it. This man's object is to induce you to refuse the hospital, that he may put some creature of his own into it; that he may show his power, and insult us all by insulting you, whose cause and character are so intimately bound up with that of the chapter. You owe it to us all to resist him in this, even if you have no solicitude for yourself. But surely, for your own sake, you will not be so lily-livered as to fall into this trap which he has baited for you, and let him take the very bread out of your mouth without a struggle."

Mr. Harding did not like being called lily-livered, and was rather inclined to resent it. "I doubt there is any true courage," said he, "in squabbling for money."

"If honest men did not squabble for money, in this wicked world of ours, the dishonest men would get it all; and I do not see that the cause of virtue would be much improved. No,—we must use the means which we have. If we were to carry your argument home, we might give away every shilling of revenue which the church has; and I presume you are not prepared to say that the church would be strengthened by such a sacrifice." The archdeacon filled his glass and then emptied it, drinking with much reverence a silent toast to the well-being and permanent security of those temporalities which were so dear to his soul.

"I think all quarrels between a clergyman and his bishop should be avoided," said Mr. Harding.

"I think so too; but it is quite as much the duty of the bishop to look to that as of his inferior. I tell you what, my friend; I'll see the bishop in this matter, that is, if you will allow me; and you may be sure I will not compromise you. My opinion is, that all this trash about the Sunday-schools and the sermons has originated wholly with Slope and Mrs. Proudie, and that the bishop knows nothing about it. The bishop can't very well refuse to see me, and I'll come upon him when he has neither his wife nor his chaplain by him. I think you'll find that it will end in his sending you the appointment without any condition whatever. And as to the seats in the cathedral, we may safely leave that to Mr. Dean. I believe the fool positively thinks that the bishop could walk away with the cathedral if he pleased."

And so the matter was arranged between them. Mr. Harding had come expressly for advice, and therefore felt himself bound to take the advice given him. He had known, moreover, beforehand, that the archdeacon would not hear of his giving the matter up, and accordingly though he had in perfect good faith put forward his own views, he was prepared to yield.

They therefore went into the drawing-room in good humour with each other, and the evening passed pleasantly in prophetic discussions on the future wars of Arabin and Slope. The frogs and the mice would be nothing to them, nor the angers of Agamemnon and Achilles. How the archdeacon rubbed his hands, and plumed himself on the success of his last move! He could not himself descend into the arena with Slope, but Arabin would have no such scruples. Arabin was exactly the man for such work, and the only man whom he knew that was fit for it.

The archdeacon's good humour and high buoyancy continued till, when reclining on his pillow, Mrs. Grantly commenced to give him her view of the state of affairs at Barchester. And then certainly he was startled. The last words he said that night were as follows:—

"If she does, by heaven I'll never speak to her again. She dragged me into the mire once, but I'll not pollute myself with such filth as that——" And the archdeacon gave a shudder

which shook the whole room, so violently was he convulsed with
the thought which then agitated his mind.

Now in this matter the widow Bold was scandalously ill-treated
by her relatives. She had spoken to the man three or four times,
and had expressed her willingness to teach in a Sunday-school.
Such was the full extent of her sins in the matter of Mr. Slope.
Poor Eleanor! But time will show.

The next morning Mr. Harding returned to Barchester, no
further word having been spoken in his hearing respecting Mr.
Slope's acquaintance with his younger daughter. But he observed
that the archdeacon at breakfast was less cordial than he had been
on the preceding evening.

CHAP. XV.

THE WIDOW'S SUITORS.

MR. SLOPE lost no time in availing himself of the bishop's permission to see Mr. Quiverful, and it was in his interview with this
worthy pastor that he first learned that Mrs. Bold was worth the
wooing. He rode out to Puddingdale to communicate to the
embryo warden the good will of the bishop in his favour, and
during the discussion on the matter it was not unnatural that the
pecuniary resources of Mr. Harding and his family should become
the subject of remark.

Mr. Quiverful, with his fourteen children and his four hundred
a year, was a very poor man, and the prospect of this new preferment, which was to be held together with his living, was very
grateful to him. To what clergyman so circumstanced would not
such a prospect be very grateful? But Mr. Quiverful had long
been acquainted with Mr. Harding, and had received kindness at
his hands, so that his heart misgave him as he thought of supplanting a friend at the hospital. Nevertheless, he was extremely
civil, cringingly civil, to Mr. Slope; treated him quite as the
great man; entreated this great man to do him the honour to drink
a glass of sherry, at which, as it was very poor Marsala, the now
pampered Slope turned up his nose; and ended by declaring his
extreme obligation to the bishop and Mr. Slope, and his great
desire to accept the hospital, if—if it were certainly the case that
Mr. Harding had refused it.

What man, as needy as Mr. Quiverful, would have been more disinterested?

"Mr. Harding did positively refuse it," said Mr. Slope, with a certain air of offended dignity, "when he heard of the conditions to which the appointment is now subjected. Of course, you understand, Mr. Quiverful, that the same conditions will be imposed on yourself."

Mr. Quiverful cared nothing for the conditions. He would have undertaken to preach any number of sermons Mr. Slope might have chosen to dictate, and to pass every remaining hour of his Sundays within the walls of a Sunday-school. What sacrifices, or, at any rate, what promises, would have been too much to make for such an addition to his income, and for such a house! But his mind still recurred to Mr. Harding.

"To be sure," said he; "Mr. Harding's daughter is very rich, and why should he trouble himself with the hospital?"

"You mean Mrs. Grantly," said Slope.

"I meant his widowed daughter," said the other. "Mrs. Bold has twelve hundred a year of her own, and I suppose Mr. Harding means to live with her."

"Twelve hundred a year of her own!" said Slope, and very shortly afterwards took his leave, avoiding, as far as it was possible for him to do, any further allusion to the hospital. Twelve hundred a year, said he to himself, as he rode slowly home. If it were the fact that Mrs. Bold had twelve hundred a year of her own, what a fool would he be to oppose her father's return to his old place. The train of Mr. Slope's ideas will probably be plain to all my readers. Why should he not make the twelve hundred a year his own? and if he did so, would it not be well for him to have a father-in-law comfortably provided with the good things of this world? would it not, moreover, be much more easy for him to gain the daughter, if he did all in his power to forward the father's views?

These questions presented themselves to him in a very forcible way, and yet there were many points of doubt. If he resolved to restore to Mr. Harding his former place, he must take the necessary steps for doing so at once; he must immediately talk over the bishop, quarrel on the matter with Mrs. Proudie whom he knew he could not talk over, and let Mr. Quiverful know that he had been a little too precipitate as to Mr. Harding's positive refusal. That he could effect all this, he did not doubt; but he did not wish to effect it for nothing. He did not wish to give way to Mr.

Harding, and then be rejected by the daughter. He did not wish to lose one influential friend before he had gained another.

And thus he rode home, meditating many things in his mind. It occurred to him that Mrs. Bold was sister-in-law to the arch-deacon; and that not even for twelve hundred a year would he submit to that imperious man. A rich wife was a great desideratum to him, but success in his profession was still greater; there were, moreover, other rich women who might be willing to become wives; and after all, this twelve hundred a year might, when inquired into, melt away into some small sum utterly beneath his notice. Then also he remembered that Mrs. Bold had a son.

Another circumstance also much influenced him, though it was one which may almost be said to have influenced him against his will. The vision of the Signora Neroni was perpetually before his eyes. It would be too much to say that Mr. Slope was lost in love, but yet he thought, and kept continually thinking, that he had never seen so beautiful a woman. He was a man whose nature was open to such impulses, and the wiles of the Italianised charmer had been thoroughly successful in imposing upon his thoughts. We will not talk about his heart: not that he had no heart, but because his heart had little to do with his present feelings. His taste had been pleased, his eyes charmed, and his vanity gratified. He had been dazzled by a sort of loveliness which he had never before seen, and had been caught by an easy, free, voluptuous manner which was perfectly new to him. He had never been so tempted before, and the temptation was now irresistible. He had not owned to himself that he cared for this woman more than for others around him; but yet he thought often of the time when he might see her next, and made, almost unconsciously, little cunning plans for seeing her frequently.

He had called at Dr. Stanhope's house the day after the bishop's party, and then the warmth of his admiration had been fed with fresh fuel. If the signora had been kind in her manner and flattering in her speech when lying upon the bishop's sofa, with the eyes of so many on her, she had been much more so in her mother's drawing-room, with no one present but her sister to repress either her nature or her art. Mr. Slope had thus left her quite bewildered, and could not willingly admit into his brain any scheme, a part of which would be the necessity of his abandoning all further special friendship with this lady.

And so he slowly rode along very meditative.

And here the author must beg it to be remembered that Mr. Slope was not in all things a bad man. His motives, like those of most men, were mixed; and though his conduct was generally very different from that which we would wish to praise, it was actuated perhaps as often as that of the majority of the world by a desire to do his duty. He believed in the religion which he taught, harsh, unpalatable, uncharitable as that religion was. He believed those whom he wished to get under his hoof, the Grantlys and Gwynnes of the church, to be the enemies of that religion. He believed himself to be a pillar of strength, destined to do great things; and with that subtle, selfish, ambiguous sophistry to which the minds of all men are so subject, he had taught himself to think that in doing much for the promotion of his own interests he was doing much also for the promotion of religion. But Mr. Slope had never been an immoral man. Indeed, he had resisted temptations to immorality with a strength of purpose that was creditable to him. He had early in life devoted himself to works which were not compatible with the ordinary pleasures of youth, and he had abandoned such pleasures not without a struggle. It must therefore be conceived that he did not admit to himself that he warmly admired the beauty of a married woman without heartfelt stings of conscience; and to pacify that conscience, he had to teach himself that the nature of his admiration was innocent.

And thus he rode along meditative and ill at ease. His conscience had not a word to say against his choosing the widow and her fortune. That he looked upon as a godly work rather than otherwise; as a deed which, if carried through, would redound to his credit as a Christian. On that side lay no future remorse, no conduct which he might probably have to forget, no inward stings. If it should turn out to be really the fact that Mrs. Bold had twelve hundred a year at her own disposal, Mr. Slope would rather look upon it as a duty which he owed his religion to make himself the master of the wife and the money; as a duty, too, in which some amount of self-sacrifice would be necessary. He would have to give up his friendship with the signora, his resistance to Mr. Harding, his antipathy—no, he found on mature self-examination, that he could not bring himself to give up his antipathy to Dr. Grantly. He would marry the lady as the enemy of her brother-in-law if such an arrangement suited her; if not, she must look elsewhere for a husband.

It was with such resolve as this that he reached Barchester. He would at once ascertain what the truth might be as to the lady's wealth, and having done this, he would be ruled by circumstances in his conduct respecting the hospital. If he found that he could turn round and secure the place for Mr. Harding without much self-sacrifice, he would do so; but if not, he would woo the daughter in opposition to the father. But in no case would he succumb to the archdeacon.

He saw his horse taken round to the stable, and immediately went forth to commence his inquiries. To give Mr. Slope his due, he was not a man who ever let much grass grow under his feet.

Poor Eleanor! She was doomed to be the intended victim of more schemes than one.

About the time that Mr. Slope was visiting the vicar of Puddingdale, a discussion took place respecting her charms and wealth at Dr. Stanhope's house in the close. There had been morning callers there, and people had told some truth and also some falsehood respecting the property which John Bold had left behind him. By degrees the visitors went, and as the doctor went with them, and as the doctor's wife had not made her appearance, Charlotte Stanhope and her brother were left together. He was sitting idly at the table, scrawling caricatures of Barchester notables, then yawning, then turning over a book or two, and evidently at a loss how to kill his time without much labour.

"You haven't done much, Bertie, about getting any orders," said his sister.

"Orders!" said he; "who on earth is there at Barchester to give one orders? Who among the people here could possibly think it worth his while to have his head done into marble?"

"Then you mean to give up your profession," said she.

"No, I don't," said he, going on with some absurd portrait of the bishop. "Look at that, Lotte; isn't it the little man all over, apron and all? I'd go on with my profession at once, as you call it, if the governor would set me up with a studio in London; but as to sculpture at Barchester—I suppose half the people here don't know what a torso means."

"The governor will not give you a shilling to start you in London," said Lotte. "Indeed, he can't give you what would be sufficient, for he has not got it. But you might start yourself very well, if you pleased."

"How the deuce am I to do it?" said he.

"To tell you the truth, Bertie, you'll never make a penny by any profession."

"That's what I often think myself," said he, not in the least offended. "Some men have a great gift of making money, but they can't spend it. Others can't put two shillings together, but they have a great talent for all sorts of outlay. I begin to think that my genius is wholly in the latter line."

"How do you mean to live then?" asked the sister.

"I suppose I must regard myself as a young raven, and look for heavenly manna; besides, we have all got something when the governor goes."

"Yes—you'll have enough to supply yourself with gloves and boots; that is, if the Jews have not got the possession of it all. I believe they have the most of it already. I wonder, Bertie, at your indifference; that you, with your talents and personal advantages, should never try to settle yourself in life. I look forward with dread to the time when the governor must go. Mother, and Madeline, and I,—we shall be poor enough, but you will have absolutely nothing."

"Sufficient for the day is the evil thereof," said Bertie.

"Will you take my advice?" said his sister.

"*Cela dépend*," said the brother.

"Will you marry a wife with money?"

"At any rate," said he, "I won't marry one without: wives with money a'nt so easy to get now-a-days; the parsons pick them all up."

"And a parson will pick up the wife I mean for you, if you do not look quickly about it; the wife I mean is Mrs. Bold."

"Whew-w-w-w!" whistled Bertie, "a widow!"

"She is very beautiful," said Charlotte.

"With a son and heir all ready to my hand," said Bertie.

"A baby that will very likely die," said Charlotte.

"I don't see that," said Bertie. "But however, he may live for me—I don't wish to kill him; only, it must be owned that a ready-made family is a drawback."

"There is only one after all," pleaded Charlotte.

"And that a very little one, as the maid-servant said," rejoined Bertie.

"Beggars mustn't be choosers, Bertie; you can't have everything."

"God knows I am not unreasonable," said he, "nor yet opinionated; and if you'll arrange it all for me, Lotte, I'll marry the lady. Only mark this; the money must be sure, and the income at my own disposal, at any rate for the lady's life."

Charlotte was explaining to her brother that he must make love for himself if he meant to carry on the matter, and was encouraging him to do so, by warm eulogiums on Eleanor's beauty, when the signora was brought into the drawing-room. When at home, and subject to the gaze of none but her own family, she allowed herself to be dragged about by two persons, and her two bearers now deposited her on her sofa. She was not quite so grand in her apparel as she had been at the bishop's party, but yet she was dressed with much care, and though there was a look of care and pain about her eyes, she was, even by daylight, extremely beautiful.

"Well, Madeline; so I'm going to be married," Bertie began, as soon as the servants had withdrawn.

"There's no other foolish thing left, that you haven't done," said Madeline, "and therefore you are quite right to try that."

"Oh, you think it's a foolish thing, do you?" said he. "There's Lotte advising me to marry by all means. But on such a subject your opinion ought to be the best; you have experience to guide you."

"Yes, I have," said Madeline, with a sort of harsh sadness in her tone, which seemed to say — What is it to you if I am sad? I have never asked your sympathy.

Bertie was sorry when he saw that she was hurt by what he said, and he came and squatted on the floor close before her face to make his peace with her.

"Come, Mad, I was only joking ; you know that   But in sober earnest, Lotte is advising me to marry. She wants me to marry this Mrs. Bold. She's a widow with lots of tin, a fine baby, a beautiful complexion, and the *George and Dragon* hotel up in the High Street. By Jove, Lotte, if I marry her, I'll keep the public house myself—it's just the life to suit me."

"What?" said Madeline, "that vapid swarthy creature in the widow's cap, who looked as though her clothes had been stuck on her back with a pitchfork!" The signora never allowed any woman to be beautiful.

"Instead of being vapid," said Lotte, "I call her a very lovely woman. She was by far the loveliest woman in the rooms the other night; that is, excepting you, Madeline."

Even the compliment did not soften the asperity of the maimed beauty. "Every woman is charming according to Lotte," she said; "I never knew an eye with so little true appreciation. In the first place, what woman on earth could look well in such a thing as that she had on her head?"

"Of course she wears a widow's cap; but she'll put that off when Bertie marries her."

"I don't see any of course in it," said Madeline. "The death of twenty husbands should not make me undergo such a penance. It is as much a relic of paganism as the sacrifice of a Hindoo woman at the burning of her husband's body. If not so bloody, it is quite as barbarous, and quite as useless."

"But you don't blame her for that," said Bertie. "She does it because it's the custom of the country. People would think ill of her if she didn't do it."

"Exactly," said Madeline. "She is just one of those English nonentities who would tie her head up in a bag for three months every summer, if her mother and her grandmother had tied up their heads before her. It would never occur to her, to think whether there was any use in submitting to such a nuisance."

"It's very hard, in a country like England, for a young woman to set herself in opposition to prejudices of that sort," said the prudent Charlotte.

"What you mean is, that it's very hard for a fool not to be a fool,' said Madeline.

Bertie Stanhope had been so much knocked about the world from his earliest years, that he had not retained much respect for the gravity of English customs ; but even to his mind an idea presented itself, that, perhaps in a wife, true British prejudice would not in the long run be less agreeable than Anglo-Italian freedom from restraint. He did not exactly say so, but he expressed the idea in another way.

"I fancy," said he, "that if I were to die, and then walk, I should think that my widow looked better in one of those caps than any other kind of head-dress."

"Yes—and you'd fancy also that she could do nothing better than shut herself up and cry for you, or else burn herself. But she would think differently. She'd probably wear one of those horrid she-helmets, because she'd want the courage not to do so ; but she'd wear it with a heart longing for the time when she might be allowed to throw it off. I hate such shallow false pretences. For my part, I would let the world say what it pleased, and show no grief if I felt none ;—and perhaps not, if I did."

"But wearing a widow's cap won't lessen her fortune," said Charlotte.

"Or increase it," said Madeline. "Then why on earth does she do it ? "

"But Lotte's object is to make her put it off," said Bertie.

"If it be true that she has got twelve hundred a year quite at her own disposal, and she be not utterly vulgar in her manners, I would advise you to marry her. I dare say she is to be had for the asking : and as you are not going to marry her for love, it doesn't much matter whether she is good-looking or not. As to your really marrying a woman for love, I don't believe *you* are fool enough for that."

" Oh, Madeline ! " exclaimed her sister.

" And oh, Charlotte ! " said the other.

" You don't mean to say that no man can love a woman unless he be a fool ? "

"I mean very much the same thing, — that any man who is willing to sacrifice his interest to get possession of a pretty face is a fool. Pretty faces are to be had cheaper than that. I hate your mawkish sentimentality, Lotte. You know as well as I do in what way husbands and wives generally live together; you know how far the warmth of conjugal affection can withstand the trial of a bad dinner, of a rainy day, or of the least privation which poverty brings with it; you know what freedom a man claims for himself, what slavery he would exact from his wife if he could ! And you know also how wives generally obey. Marriage means tyranny on one side and deceit on the other. I say that a man is a fool to sacrifice his interests for such a bargain. A woman, too generally, has no other way of living."

" But Bertie has no other way of living," said Charlotte.

" Then, in God's name, let him marry Mrs. Bold," said Madeline. And so it was settled between them.

But let the gentle-hearted reader be under no apprehension whatsoever. It is not destined that Eleanor shall marry Mr. Slope or Bertie Stanhope. And here, perhaps, it may be allowed to the novelist to explain his views on a very important point in the art of telling tales. He ventures to reprobate that system which goes so far to violate all proper confidence between the author and his readers, by maintaining nearly to the end of the third volume a mystery as to the fate of their favourite personage. Nay, more, and worse than this, is too frequently done. Have not often the profoundest efforts of genius been used to baffle the aspirations of the reader, to raise false hopes and false fears, and to give rise to expectations which are never to be realised ? Are not promises all but made of delightful horrors, in lieu of which the writer produces nothing but most commonplace realities in his final chapter? And is there not a species of deceit in this to which the honesty of the present age should lend no countenance ?

And what can be the worth of that solicitude which a peep into the third volume can utterly dissipate ? What the value of those literary charms which are absolutely destroyed by their enjoyment? When we have once learnt what was that picture before which was hung Mrs. Ratcliffe's solemn curtain, we feel no further interest

about either the frame or the veil. They are to us, merely a
receptacle for old bones, an inappropriate coffin, which we would
wish to have decently buried out of our sight.

And then, how grievous a thing it is to have the pleasure of
your novel destroyed by the ill-considered triumph of a previous
reader. "Oh, you needn't be alarmed for Augusta, of course she
accepts Gustavus in the end." "How very ill-natured you are,
Susan," says Kitty, with tears in her eyes; "I don't care a bit
about it now." Dear Kitty, if you will read my book, you may
defy the ill-nature of of your sister. There shall be no secret that
she can tell you. Nay, take the last chapter if you please — learn
from its pages all the results of our troubled story, and the story
shall have lost none of its interest, if indeed there be any in-
interest in it to lose.

Our doctrine is, that the author and the reader should move along
together in full confidence with each other. Let the personages
of the drama undergo ever so complete a comedy of errors among
themselves, but let the spectator never mistake the Syracusan for
the Ephesian; otherwise he is one of the dupes, and the part of a
dupe is never dignified.

I would not for the value of this chapter have it believed by a
single reader that my Eleanor could bring herself to marry Mr.
Slope, or that she should be sacrificed to a Bertie Stanhope. But
among the good folk of Barchester many believed both the one
and the other.

CHAP. XVI.

BABY WORSHIP.

"DIDDLE, diddle, diddle, diddle, dum, dum, dum," said or sung
Eleanor Bold.

"Diddle, diddle, diddle, diddle, dum, dum, dum, " continued
Mary Bold, taking up the second part in this concerted piece.

The only audience at the concert was the baby, who however
gave such vociferous applause, that the performers, presuming it to
amount to an encore, commenced again.

"Diddle, diddle, diddle, diddle, dum, dum, dum : hasn't he got
lovely legs?" said the rapturous mother.

"H'm m 'm 'm 'm," simmered Mary, burying her lips in the
little fellow's fat neck, by way of kissing him.

"H'm 'm 'm 'm 'm," simmered the mamma, burying her lips also in his fat round short legs. "He's a dawty little bold darling, so he is; and he has the nicest little pink legs in all the world, so he has;" and the simmering and the kissing went on over again, and as though the ladies were very hungry, and determined to eat him.

"Well, then, he's his own mother's own darling: well, he shall —oh, oh — Mary, Mary — did you ever see? What am I to do? My naughty, naughty, naughty, naughty little Johnny." All these energetic exclamations were elicited by the delight of the mother in finding that her son was strong enough, and mischievous enough, to pull all her hair out from under her cap. "He's been and pulled down all mamma's hair, and he's the naughtiest, naughtiest, naughtiest little man that ever, ever, ever, ever, ever——"

A regular service of baby worship was going on. Mary Bold was sitting on a low easy chair, with the boy in her lap, and Eleanor was kneeling before the object of her idolatry. As she tried to cover up the little fellow's face with her long, glossy, dark brown locks, and permitted him to pull them hither and thither, as he would, she looked very beautiful in spite of the widow's cap which she still wore. There was a quiet, enduring, grateful sweetness about her face, which grew so strongly upon those who knew her, as to make the great praise of her beauty which came from her old friends, appear marvellously exaggerated to those who were only slightly acquainted with her. Her loveliness was like that of many landscapes, which require to be often seen to be fully enjoyed. There was a depth of dark clear brightness in her eyes which was lost upon a quick observer, a character about her mouth which only showed itself to those with whom she familiarly conversed, a glorious form of head the perfect symmetry of which required the eye of an artist for its appreciation. She had none of that dazzling brilliancy, of that voluptuous Rubens beauty, of that pearly whiteness, and those vermilion tints, which immediately entranced with the power of a basilisk men who came within reach of Madeline Neroni. It was all but impossible to resist the signora, but no one was called upon for any resistance towards Eleanor. You might begin to talk to her as though she were your sister, and it would not be till your head was on your pillow, that the truth and intensity of her beauty would flash upon you; that the sweetness of her voice would come upon your ear. A sudden half-hour with the Neroni, was like falling into a pit; an evening spent with Eleanor like an unexpected ramble in some quiet fields of asphodel.

"We'll cover him up till there sha'n't be a morsel of his little 'ittle 'ittle 'ittle nose to be seen," said the mother, stretching her streaming locks over the infant's face. The child screamed with delight, and kicked till Mary Bold was hardly able to hold him.

At this moment the door opened, and Mr. Slope was announced. Up jumped Eleanor, and with a sudden quick motion of her hands pushed back her hair over her shoulders. It would have been perhaps better for her that she had not, for she thus showed more of her confusion than she would have done had she remained as she was. Mr. Slope, however, immediately recognised her loveliness, and thought to himself, that irrespective of her fortune, she would be an inmate that a man might well desire for his house, a partner for his bosom's care very well qualified to make care lie easy. Eleanor hurried out of the room to re-adjust her cap, muttering some unnecessary apology about her baby. And while she is gone, we will briefly go back and state what had been hitherto the results of Mr. Slope's meditations on his scheme of matrimony.

His inquiries as to the widow's income had at any rate been so far successful as to induce him to determine to go on with the speculation. As regarded Mr. Harding, he had also resolved to do what he could without injury to himself. To Mrs. Proudie he determined not to speak on the matter, at least not at present. His object was to instigate a little rebellion on the part of the bishop. He thought that such a state of things would be advisable not only in respect to Messrs. Harding and Quiverful, but also in the affairs of the diocese generally. Mr. Slope was by no means of opinion that Dr. Proudie was fit to rule, but he conscientiously thought it wrong that his brother clergy should be subjected to petticoat government. He therefore made up his mind to infuse a little of his spirit into the bishop, sufficient to induce him to oppose his wife, though not enough to make him altogether insubordinate.

He had therefore taken an opportunity of again speaking to his lordship about the hospital, and had endeavoured to make it appear that after all it would be unwise to exclude Mr. Harding from the appointment. Mr. Slope, however, had a harder task than he had imagined. Mrs. Proudie, anxious to assume to herself as much as possible of the merit of patronage, had written to Mrs. Quiverful, requesting her to call at the palace; and had then explained to that matron, with much mystery, condescension, and dignity, the good that was in store for her and her progeny. Indeed Mrs Proudie had been so engaged at the very time that Mr. Slope had been doing the same with the husband at Puddingdale Vicarage, and had thus in a measure committed herself. The thanks, the

humility, the gratitude, the surprise of Mrs. Quiverful had been
very overpowering; she had all but embraced the knees of her
patroness, and had promised that the prayers of fourteen unprovided babes (so Mrs. Quiverful had described her own family, the
eldest of which was a stout young woman of three-and-twenty)
should be put up to heaven morning and evening for the munificent
friend whom God had sent to them. Such incense as this was not
unpleasing to Mrs. Proudie, and she made the most of it. She
offered her general assistance to the fourteen unprovided babes, if,
as she had no doubt, she should find them worthy; expressed a
hope that the eldest of them would be fit to undertake tuition in
her Sabbath schools, and altogether made herself a very great lady
in the estimation of Mrs. Quiverful.

Having done this, she thought it prudent to drop a few words
before the bishop, letting him know that she had acquainted the
Puddingdale family with their good fortune; so that he might
perceive that he stood committed to the appointment. The husband
well understood the *ruse* of his wife, but he did not resent it. He
knew that she was taking the patronage out of his hands; he was
resolved to put an end to her interference, and re-assume his
powers. But then he thought this was not the best time to do it.
He put off the evil hour, as many a man in similar circumstances
has done before him.

Such having been the case, Mr. Slope naturally encountered a
difficulty in talking over the bishop, a difficulty indeed which he
found could not be overcome except at the cost of a general outbreak
at the palace. A general outbreak at the present moment might
be good policy, but it also might not. It was at any rate not a step
to be lightly taken. He began by whispering to the bishop that
he feared that public opinion would be against him if Mr. Harding
did not reappear at the hospital. The bishop answered with some
warmth that Mr. Quiverful had been promised the appointment on
Mr. Slope's advice. "Not promised!" said Mr. Slope. "Yes,
promised," replied the bishop, "and Mrs. Proudie has seen Mrs.
Quiverful on the subject." This was quite unexpected on the part
of Mr. Slope, but his presence of mind did not fail him, and he
turned the statement to his own account.

"Ah, my lord," said he, "we shall all be in scrapes if the ladies
interfere."

This was too much in unison with my lord's feelings to be altogether unpalatable, and yet such an allusion to interference
demanded a rebuke. My lord was somewhat astounded also,
though not altogether made miserable, by finding that there was a
point of difference between his wife and his chaplain.

I don't know what you mean by interference," said the bishop mildly. "When Mrs. Proudie heard that Mr. Quiverful was to be appointed, it was not unnatural that she should wish to see Mrs. Quiverful about the schools. I really cannot say that I see any interference."

"I only speak, my lord, for your own comfort," said Slope; "for your own comfort and dignity in the diocese. I can have no other motive. As far as personal feelings go, Mrs. Proudie is the best friend I have. I must always remember that. But still, in my present position, my first duty is to your lordship."

"I'm sure of that, Mr. Slope, I am quite sure of that;" said the bishop mollified : "and you really think that Mr. Harding should have the hospital?"

"Upon my word, I'm inclined to think so. I am quite prepared to take upon myself the blame of first suggesting Mr. Quiverful's name. But since doing so, I have found that there is so strong a feeling in the diocese in favour of Mr. Harding, that I think your lordship should give way. I hear also that Mr. Harding has modified the objections he first felt to your lordship's propositions. And as to what has passed between Mrs. Proudie and Mrs. Quiverful, the circumstance may be a little inconvenient, but I really do not think that that should weigh in a matter of so much moment."

And thus the poor bishop was left in a dreadfully undecided state as to what he should do. His mind, however, slightly inclined itself to the appointment of Mr. Harding, seeing that by such a step he should have the assistance of Mr. Slope in opposing Mrs. Proudie.

Such was the state of affairs at the palace, when Mr. Slope called at Mrs. Bold's house, and found her playing with her baby. When she ran out of the room, Mr. Slope began praising the weather to Mary Bold, then he praised the baby and kissed him, and then he praised the mother, and then he praised Miss Bold herself. Mrs. Bold, however, was not long before she came back.

"I have to apologise for calling at so very early an hour," began Mr. Slope, "but I was really so anxious to speak to you that I hope you and Miss Bold will excuse me."

Eleanor muttered something in which the words "certainly," and "of course," and "not early at all," were just audible, and then apologised for her own appearance, declaring with a smile, that her baby was becoming such a big boy that he was quite unmanageable.

"He's a great big naughty boy," said she to the child; "and

we must send him away to a great big rough romping school, where they have great big rods, and do terrible things to naughty boys who don't do what their own mammas tell them;" and she then commenced another course of kissing, being actuated thereto by the terrible idea of sending her child away which her own imagination had depicted.

"And where the masters don't have such beautiful long hair to be dishevelled," said Mr. Slope, taking up the joke and paying a compliment at the same time.

Eleanor thought he might as well have left the compliment alone; but she said nothing and looked nothing, being occupied as she was with the baby.

"Let me take him," said Mary. "His clothes are nearly off his back with his romping," and so saying she left the room with the child. Miss Bold had heard Mr. Slope say he had something pressing to say to Eleanor, and thinking that she might be *de trop*, took this opportunity of getting herself out of the room.

"Don't be long, Mary," said Eleanor, as Miss Bold shut the door.

"I am glad, Mrs. Bold, to have the opportunity of having ten minutes' conversation with you alone," began Mr. Slope. "Will you let me openly ask you a plain question?"

"Certainly," said she.

"And I am sure you will give me a plain and open answer."

"Either that or none at all," said she, laughing.

"My question is this, Mrs. Bold; is your father really anxious to go back to the hospital?"

"Why do you ask me?" said she. "Why don't you ask himself?"

"My dear Mrs. Bold, I'll tell you why. There are wheels within wheels, all of which I would explain to you, only I fear that there is not time. It is essentially necessary that I should have an answer to this question, otherwise I cannot know how to advance your father's wishes; and it is quite impossible that I should ask himself. No one can esteem your father more than I do, but I doubt if this feeling is reciprocal." It certainly was not. "I must be candid with you as the only means of avoiding ultimate consequences, which may be most injurious to Mr. Harding. I fear there is a feeling, I will not even call it a prejudice, with regard to myself in Barchester, which is not in my favour. You remember that sermon——"

"Oh! Mr. Slope, we need not go back to that," said Eleanor.

"For one moment, Mrs. Bold. It is not that I may talk of myself, but because it is so essential that you should understand how matters stand. That sermon may have been ill-judged,—it was certainly misunderstood; but I will say nothing about that now; only this, that it did give rise to a feeling against myself which your father shares with others. It may be that he has proper cause, but the result is that he is not inclined to meet me on friendly terms. I put it to yourself whether you do not know this to be the case."

Eleanor made no answer, and Mr. Slope, in the eagerness of his address, edged his chair a little nearer to the widow's seat, unperceived by her.

"Such being so," continued Mr. Slope, "I cannot ask him this question as I can ask it of you. In spite of my delinquencies since I came to Barchester you have allowed me to regard you as a friend." Eleanor made a little motion with her head which was hardly confirmatory; but Mr. Slope, if he noticed it, did not appear to do so. "To you I can speak openly, and explain the feelings of my heart. This your father would not allow. Unfortunately the bishop has thought it right that this matter of the hospital should pass through my hands. There have been some details to get up with which he would not trouble himself, and thus it has come to pass that I was forced to have an interview with your father on the matter."

"I am aware of that," said Eleanor.

"Of course," said he. "In that interview Mr. Harding left the impression on my mind that he did not wish to return to the hospital."

"How could that be?" said Eleanor, at last stirred up to forget the cold propriety of demeanour which she had determined to maintain.

"My dear Mrs. Bold, I give you my word that such was the case," said he, again getting a little nearer to her. "And what is more than that, before my interview with Mr. Harding, certain persons at the palace, I do not mean the bishop, had told me that such was the fact. I own, I hardly believed it; I own, I thought that your father would wish on every account, for conscience' sake, for the sake of those old men, for old association, and the memory of dear days long gone by, on every account I thought that he would wish to resume his duties. But I was told that such was not his wish; and he certainly left me with the impression that I had been told the truth."

"Well!" said Eleanor, now sufficiently roused on the matter.

"I hear Miss Bold's step," said Mr. Slope; "would it be asking too great a favour to beg you to——I know you can manage anything with Miss Bold."

Eleanor did not like the word manage, but still she went out, and asked Mary to leave them alone for another quarter of an hour.

"Thank you, Mrs. Bold, — I am so very grateful for this confidence. Well, I left your father with this impression. Indeed, I may say that he made me understand that he declined the appointment."

"Not the appointment," said Eleanor. "I am sure he did not decline the appointment. But he said that he would not agree, — that is, that he did not like the scheme about the schools and the services, and all that. I am quite sure he never said that he wished to refuse the place."

"Oh, Mrs. Bold!" said Mr. Slope, in a manner almost impassioned. "I would not, for the world, say to so good a daughter a word against so good a father. But you must, for his sake, let me show you exactly how the matter stands at present. Mr. Harding was a little flurried when I told him of the bishop's wishes about the school. I did so, perhaps, with the less caution because you yourself had so perfectly agreed with me on the same subject. He was a little put out and spoke warmly. 'Tell the bishop,' said he, 'that I quite disagree with him, — and shall not return to the hospital, as such conditions are attached to it.' What he said was to that effect; indeed, his words were, if anything, stronger than those. I had no alternative but to repeat them to his lordship, who said that he could look on them in no other light than a refusal. He also had heard the report that your father did not wish for the appointment, and putting all these things together, he thought he had no choice but to look for some one else. He has consequently offered the place to Mr. Quiverful."

"Offered the place to Mr. Quiverful!" repeated Eleanor, her eyes suffused with tears. "Then, Mr. Slope, there is an end of it."

"No, my friend — not so," said he. "It is to prevent such being the end of it that I am now here. I may at any rate presume that I have got an answer to my question, and that Mr. Harding is desirous of returning."

"Desirous of returning — of course he is," said Eleanor; "of course he wishes to have back his house and his income, and his place in the world; to have back what he gave up with such self-denying honesty, if he can have them without restraints on his conduct to which at his age it would be impossible that he should submit. How can the bishop ask a man of his age to turn schoolmaster to a pack of children?"

"Out of the question," said Mr. Slope, laughing slightly; "of course no such demand shall be made on your father. I can at any rate promise you that I will not be the medium of any so absurd a requisition. We wished your father to preach in the hospital, as the inmates may naturally be too old to leave it; but even that shall not be insisted on. We wished also to attach a Sabbath-day school to the hospital, thinking that such an establishment could not but be useful under the surveillance of so good a clergyman as Mr. Harding, and also under your own. But, dear Mrs. Bold; we won't talk of these things now. One thing is clear; we must do what we can to annul this rash offer the bishop has made to Mr. Quiverful. Your father wouldn't see Quiverful, would he? Quiverful is an honourable man, and would not, for a moment, stand in your father's way."

"What?" said Eleanor; "ask a man with fourteen children to give up his preferment! I am quite sure he will do no such thing."

"I suppose not," said Slope; and he again drew near to Mrs. Bold, so that now they were very close to each other. Eleanor did not think much about it, but instinctively moved away a little. How greatly would she have increased the distance could she have guessed what had been said about her at Plumstead! "I suppose not. But it is out of the question that Quiverful should supersede your father, —quite out of the question. The bishop has been too rash. An idea occurs to me, which may, perhaps, with God's blessing, put us right. My dear Mrs. Bold, would you object to seeing the bishop yourself?"

"Why should not my father see him?" said Eleanor. She had once before in her life interfered in her father's affairs, and then not to much advantage. She was older now, and felt that she should take no step in a matter so vital to him without his consent.

"Why, to tell the truth," said Mr. Slope, with a look of sorrow, as though he greatly bewailed the want of charity in his patron, "the bishop fancies that he has cause of anger against your father. I fear an interview would lead to further ill will."

"Why," said Eleanor, "my father is the mildest, the gentlest man living."

"I only know," said Slope, "that he has the best of daughters. So you would not see the bishop? As to getting an interview, I could manage that for you without the slightest annoyance to yourself."

"I could do nothing, Mr. Slope, without consulting my father."

"Ah!" said he, "that would be useless; you would then only be your father's messenger. Does anything occur to yourself? Something must be done. Your father shall not be ruined by so ridiculous a misunderstanding."

Eleanor said that nothing occurred to her, but that it was very hard; and the tears came to her eyes and rolled down her cheeks. Mr. Slope would have given much to have had the privilege of drying them; but he had tact enough to know that he had still a great deal to do before he could even hope for any privilege with Mrs. Bold.

"It cuts me to the heart to see you so grieved," said he. "But pray let me assure you that your father's interests shall not be sacrificed if it be possible for me to protect them. I will tell the bishop openly what are the facts. I will explain to him that he has hardly the right to appoint any other than your father, and will show him that if he does so he will be guilty of great injustice,— and you, Mrs. Bold, you will have the charity at any rate to believe this of me, that I am truly anxious for your father's welfare, — for his and for your own."

The widow hardly knew what answer to make. She was quite aware that her father would not be at all thankful to Mr. Slope; she had a strong wish to share her father's feelings; and yet she could not but acknowledge that Mr. Slope was very kind. Her father, who was generally so charitable to all men, who seldom spoke ill of any one, had warned her against Mr. Slope, and yet she did not know how to abstain from thanking him. What interest could he have in the matter but that which he professed? Nevertheless there was that in his manner which even she distrusted. She felt, she did not know why, that there was something about him which ought to put her on her guard.

Mr. Slope read all this in her hesitating manner just as plainly as though she had opened her heart to him. It was the talent of the man that he could so read the inward feelings of women with whom he conversed. He knew that Eleanor was doubting him, and that if she thanked him she would only do so because she could not help it; but yet this did not make him angry or even annoy him. Rome was not built in a day.

"I did not come for thanks," continued he, seeing her hesitation; "and do not want them — at any rate before they are merited. But this I do want, Mrs. Bold, that I may make to myself friends in this fold to which it has pleased God to call me as one of the humblest of his shepherds. If I cannot do so, my task here must indeed be a sad one. I will at any rate endeavour to deserve them."

"I'm sure," said she, "you will soon make plenty of friends." She felt herself obliged to say something.

"That will be nothing unless they are such as will sympathise with my feelings; unless they are such as I can reverence and admire—and love. If the best and purest turn away from me, I cannot bring myself to be satisfied with the friendship of the less estimable. In such case I must live alone."

"Oh! I'm sure you will not do that, Mr. Slope." Eleanor meant nothing, but it suited him to appear to think some special allusion had been intended.

"Indeed, Mrs. Bold, I shall live alone, quite alone as far as the heart is concerned, if those with whom I yearn to ally myself turn away from me. But enough of this; I have called you my friend, and I hope you will not contradict me. I trust the time may come when I may also call your father so. May God bless you, Mrs. Bold, you and your darling boy. And tell your father from me that what can be done for his interest shall be done."

And so he took his leave, pressing the widow's hand rather more closely than usual. Circumstances, however, seemed just then to make this intelligible, and the lady did not feel called on to resent it.

"I cannot understand him," said Eleanor to Mary Bold, a few minutes afterwards. "I do not know whether he is a good man or a bad man—whether he is true or false."

"Then give him the benefit of the doubt," said Mary, "and believe the best."

"On the whole, I think I do," said Eleanor. "I think I do believe that he means well—and if so, it is a shame that we should revile him, and make him miserable while he is among us. But, oh, Mary, I fear papa will be disappointed in the hospital."

CHAP. XVII.

WHO SHALL BE COCK OF THE WALK?

ALL this time things were going on somewhat uneasily at the palace. The hint or two which Mr. Slope had given was by no means thrown away upon the bishop. He had a feeling that if he ever meant to oppose the now almost unendurable despotism of his wife, he must lose no further time in doing so; that if he ever meant to be himself master in his own diocese, let alone his own house, he should begin at once. It would have been easier to have done so from the day of his consecration than now, but easier now than when Mrs. Proudie should have succeeded in thoroughly mastering the diocesan details. Then the proffered assistance of Mr. Slope was a great thing for him, a most unexpected and invaluable

aid. Hitherto he had looked on the two as allied forces ; and had
considered that as allies they were impregnable. He had begun to
believe that his only chance of escape would be by the advancement
of Mr. Slope to some distant and rich preferment. But now it
seemed that one of his enemies, certainly the least potent of them,
but nevertheless one very important, was willing to desert his own
camp. Assisted by Mr. Slope what might he not do? He walked
up and down his little study, almost thinking that the time might
come when he would be able to appropriate to his own use the big
room up stairs, in which his predecessor had always sat.

As he revolved these things in his mind a note was brought to
him from Archdeacon Grantly, in which that divine begged his
lordship to do him the honour of seeing him on the morrow —
would his lordship have the kindness to name an hour? Dr.
Grantly's proposed visit would have reference to the reappointment
of Mr. Harding to the wardenship of Barchester hospital. The
bishop having read his note was informed that the archdeacon's
servant was waiting for an answer.

Here at once a great opportunity offered itself to the bishop
of acting on his own responsibility. He bethought himself however of his new ally, and rang the bell for Mr. Slope. It turned
out that Mr. Slope was not in the house ; and then, greatly daring,
the bishop with his own unassisted spirit wrote a note to the archdeacon saying that he would see him, and naming an hour for
doing so. Having watched from his study-window that the
messenger got safely off from the premises with this despatch, he
began to turn over in his mind what step he should next take.

To-morrow he would have to declare to the archdeacon either
that Mr. Harding should have the appointment, or that he should
not have it. The bishop felt that he could not honestly throw
over the Quiverfuls without informing Mrs. Proudie, and he
resolved at last to brave the lioness in her den and tell her that
circumstances were such that it behoved him to reappoint Mr.
Harding. He did not feel that he should at all derogate from his
new courage by promising Mrs. Proudie that the very first piece
of available preferment at his disposal should be given to Quiverful
to atone for the injury done to him. If he could mollify the
lioness with such a sop, how happy would he think his first efforts
to have been !

Not without many misgivings did he find himself in Mrs.
Proudie's boudoir. He had at first thought of sending for her.
But it was not at all impossible that she might chose to take such
a message amiss, and then also it might be some protection to him

to have his daughters present at the interview. He found her sitting with her account books before her nibbling the end of her pencil, evidently mersed in pecuniary difficulties, and harassed in mind by the multiplicity of palatial expenses, and the heavy cost of episcopal grandeur. Her daughters were around her. Olivia was reading a novel, Augusta was crossing a note to her bosom friend in Baker Street, and Netta was working diminutive coach wheels for the bottom of a petticoat. If the bishop could get the better of his wife in her present mood, he would be a man indeed. He might then consider the victory his own for ever. After all, in such cases the matter between husband and wife stands much the same as it does between two boys at the same school, two cocks in the same yard, or two armies on the same continent. The conqueror once is generally the conqueror for ever after. The prestige of victory is every thing.

"Ahem—my dear," began the bishop, "if you are disengaged, I wished to speak to you." Mrs. Proudie put her pencil down carefully at the point to which she had dotted her figures, marked down in her memory the sum she had arrived at, and then looked up, sourly enough, into her helpmate's face. "If you are busy, another time will do as well," continued the bishop, whose courage like Bob Acres' had oozed out, now that he found himself on the ground of battle.

"What is it about, Bishop?" asked the lady.

"Well—it was about those Quiverfuls—but I see you are engaged. · Another time will do just as well for me."

"What about the Quiverfuls? It is quite understood, I believe, that they are to come to the hospital. There is to be no doubt about that, is there?" and as she spoke she kept her pencil sternly and vigorously fixed on the column of figures before her.

"Why, my dear, there is a difficulty," said the bishop.

"A difficulty!" said Mrs. Proudie, "what difficulty? The place has been promised to Mr. Quiverful, and of course he must have it. He has made all his arrangements. He has written for a curate for Puddingdale, he has spoken to the auctioneer about selling his farm, horses, and cows, and in all respects considers the place as his own. Of course he must have it."

Now, bishop, look well to thyself, and call up all the manhood that is in thee. Think how much is at stake. If now thou art not true to thy guns, no Slope can hereafter aid thee. How can he who deserts his own colours at the first smell of gunpowder expect faith in any ally. Thou thyself hast sought the battle-field; fight out the battle manfully now thou art there. Courage, bishop, courage!

Frowns cannot kill, nor can sharp words break any bones. After all the apron is thine own. She can appoint no wardens, give away no benefices, nominate no chaplains, an' thou art but true to thyself. Up, man, and at her with a constant heart.

Some little monitor within the bishop's breast so addressed him. But then there was another monitor there which advised him differently, and as follows. Remember, bishop, she is a woman, and such a woman too as thou well knowest: a battle of words with such a woman is the very mischief. Were it not better for thee to carry on this war, if it must be waged, from behind thine own table in thine own study? Does not every cock fight best on his own dunghill? Thy daughters also are here, the pledges of thy love, the fruits of thy loins; is it well that they should see thee in the hour of thy victory over their mother? nay, is it well that they should see thee in the possible hour of thy defeat? Besides, hast thou not chosen thy opportunity with wonderful little skill, indeed with no touch of that sagacity for which thou art famous? Will it not turn out that thou art wrong in this matter, and thine enemy right; that thou hast actually pledged thyself in this matter of the hospital, and that now thou wouldest turn upon thy wife because she requires from thee but the fulfilment of thy promise? Art thou not a Christian bishop, and is not thy word to be held sacred whatever be the result? Return, bishop, to thy sanctum on the lower floor, and postpone thy combative propensities for some occasion in which at least thou mayest fight the battle against odds less tremendously against thee.

All this passed within the bishop's bosom while Mrs. Proudie still sat with her fixed pencil, and the figures of her sum still enduring on the tablets of her memory. "£4 17s. 7d." she said to herself. "Of course Mr. Quiverful must have the hospital," she said out loud to her lord.

"Well, my dear, I merely wanted to suggest to you that Mr. Slope seems to think that if Mr. Harding be not appointed, public feeling in the matter would be against us, and that the press might perhaps take it up."

"Mr. Slope seems to think!" said Mrs. Proudie, in a tone of voice which plainly showed the bishop that he was right in looking for a breach in that quarter. "And what has Mr. Slope to do with it? I hope, my lord, you are not going to allow yourself to be governed by a chaplain." And now in her eagerness the lady lost her place in her account.

"Certainly not, my dear. Nothing I can assure you is less probable. But still Mr. Slope may be useful in finding how the wind blows, and I really thought that if we could give something else as good to the Quiverfuls——"

"Nonsense," said Mrs. Proudie; "it would be years before you could give them anything else that could suit them half as well, and as for the press and the public, and all that, remember there are two ways of telling a story. If Mr. Harding is fool enough to tell his tale, we can also tell ours. The place was offered to him, and he refused it. It has now been given to some one else, and there's an end of it. At least, I should think so."

"Well, my dear, I rather believe you are right;" said the bishop, and sneaking out of the room, he went down stairs, troubled in his mind as to how he should receive the archdeacon on the morrow. He felt himself not very well just at present; and began to consider that he might, not improbably, be detained in his room the next morning by an attack of bile. He was, unfortunately, very subject to bilious annoyances.

"Mr. Slope, indeed! I'll Slope him," said the indignant matron to her listening progeny. "I don't know what has come to Mr. Slope. I believe he thinks he is to be Bishop of Barchester himself, because I've taken him by the hand, and got your father to make him his domestic chaplain."

"He was always full of impudence," said Olivia; "I told you so once before, mamma." Olivia, however, had not thought him too impudent when once before he had proposed to make her Mrs. Slope.

"Well, Olivia, I always thought you liked him," said Augusta, who at that moment had some grudge against her sister. "I always disliked the man, because I think him thoroughly vulgar."

"There you're wrong," said Mrs. Proudie; "he's not vulgar at all; and what is more, he is a soul-stirring, eloquent preacher; but he must be taught to know his place if he is to remain in this house."

"He has the horridest eyes I ever saw in a man's head," said Netta; "and I tell you what, he's terribly greedy; did you see all the currant pie he ate yesterday?"

When Mr. Slope got home he soon learnt from the bishop, as much from his manner as his words, that Mrs. Proudie's behests in the matter of the hospital were to be obeyed. Dr. Proudie let fall something as to "this occasion only," and "keeping all affairs about patronage exclusively in his own hands." But he was quite decided about Mr. Harding; and as Mr. Slope did not wish to have both the prelate and the prelatess against him, he did not at present see that he could do anything but yield.

He merely remarked that he would of course carry out the bishop's views, and that he was quite sure that if the bishop trusted to his own judgment things in the diocese would certainly be well ordered. Mr. Slope knew that if you hit a nail on the head often enough, it will penetrate at last.

He was sitting alone in his room on the same evening when a light knock was made on his door, and before he could answer it the door was opened, and his patroness appeared. He was all smiles in a moment, but so was not she also. She took, however, the chair that was offered to her, and thus began her expostulation: —

"Mr. Slope, I did not at all approve your conduct the other night with that Italian woman. Any one would have thought that you were her lover."

"Good gracious, my dear madam," said Mr. Slope, with a look of horror. "Why, she is a married woman."

"That's more than I know," said Mrs. Proudie; "however she chooses to pass for such. But married or not married, such attention as you paid to her was improper. I cannot believe that you would wish to give offence in my drawing-room, Mr. Slope; but I owe it to myself and my daughters to tell you that I disapprove your conduct."

Mr. Slope opened wide his huge protruding eyes, and stared out of them with a look of well-feigned surprise. "Why, Mrs. Proudie," said he, "I did but fetch her something to eat when she said she was hungry."

"And you have called on her since," continued she, looking at the culprit with the stern look of a detective policeman in the act of declaring himself.

Mr. Slope turned over in his mind whether it would be well for him to tell this termagant at once that he should call on whom he liked, and do what he liked; but he remembered that his footing in Barchester was not yet sufficiently firm, and that it would be better for him to pacify her.

"I certainly called since at Dr. Stanhope's house, and certainly saw Madame Neroni."

"Yes, and you saw her alone," said the episcopal Argus.

"Undoubtedly, I did," said Mr. Slope, "but that was because nobody else happened to be in the room. Surely it was no fault of mine if the rest of the family were out."

"Perhaps not; but I assure you, Mr. Slope, you will fall greatly in my estimation if I find that you allow yourself to be caught by the lures of that woman. I know women better than you do, Mr

Slope, and you may believe me that that signora, as she calls herself, is not a fitting companion for a strict evangelical, unmarried
young clergyman."

· How Mr. Slope would have liked to laugh at her, had he dared!
But he did not dare. So he merely said, " I can assure you, Mrs.
Proudie, the lady in question is nothing to me."

" Well, 1 hope not, Mr. Slope. But I have considered it my
duty to give you this caution ; and now there is another thing I
feel myself called on to speak about; it is your conduct to the
bishop, Mr. Slope."

" My conduct to the bishop," said he, now truly surprised and
ignorant what the lady alluded to.

" Yes, Mr. Slope; your conduct to the bishop. It is by no
means what I would wish to see it."

" Has the bishop said anything, Mrs. Proudie ? "

" No, the bishop has said nothing. He probably thinks that
any remarks on the matter will come better from me, who first introduced you to his lordship's notice. The fact is, Mr. Slope, you
are a little inclined to take too much upon yourself."

An angry spot showed itself on Mr. Slope's cheeks, and it was
with difficulty that he controlled himself. But he did do so, and
sat quite silent while the lady went on.

" It is the fault of many young men in your position, and therefore the bishop is not inclined at present to resent it. You will,
no doubt, soon learn what is required from you, and what is not.
If you will take my advice, however, you will be careful not to
obtrude advice upon the bishop in any matter touching patronage.
If his lordship wants advice, he knows where to look for it." And
then having added to her counsel a string of platitudes as to what
was desirable and what not desirable in the conduct of a strictly
evangelical, unmarried young clergyman, Mrs. Proudie retreated,
leaving the chaplain to his thoughts.

The upshot of his thoughts was this, that there certainly was
not room in the diocese for the energies of both himself and Mrs.
Proudie, and that it behoved him quickly to ascertain whether his
energies or hers were to prevail.

CHAP. XVIII.

THE WIDOW'S PERSECUTION.

EARLY on the following morning Mr. Slope was summoned to the bishop's dressing-room, and went there fully expecting that he should find his lordship very indignant, and spirited up by his wife to repeat the rebuke which she had administered on the previous day. Mr. Slope had resolved that at any rate from him he would not stand it, and entered the dressing-room in rather a combative disposition; but he found the bishop in the most placid and gentlest of humours. His lordship complained of being rather unwell, had a slight headache, and was not quite the thing in his stomach; but there was nothing the matter with his temper.

"Oh, Slope," said he, taking the chaplain's proffered hand, "Archdeacon Grantly is to call on me this morning, and I really am not fit to see him. I fear I must trouble you to see him for me;" and then Dr. Proudie proceeded to explain what it was that must be said to Dr. Grantly. He was to be told in fact in the civilest words in which the tidings could be conveyed, that Mr. Harding having refused the wardenship, the appointment had been offered to Mr. Quiverful and accepted by him.

Mr. Slope again pointed out to his patron that he thought he was perhaps not quite wise in his decision, and this he did *sotto voce*. But even with this precaution it was not safe to say much, and during the little that he did say, the bishop made a very slight, but still a very ominous gesture with his thumb towards the door which opened from his dressing-room to some inner sanctuary. Mr. Slope at once took the hint, and said no more; but he perceived that there was to be confidence between him and his patron, that the league desired by him was to be made, and that this appointment of Mr. Quiverful was to be the last sacrifice offered on the altar of conjugal obedience. All this Mr. Slope read in the slight motion of the bishop's thumb, and he read it correctly. There was no need of parchments and seals, of attestations, explanations, and professions. The bargain was understood between them, and Mr. Slope gave the bishop his hand upon it. The bishop understood the little extra squeeze, and an intelligible gleam of assent twinkled in his eye.

"Pray be civil to the archdeacon, Mr. Slope," said he out loud; "but make him quite understand that in this matter Mr. Harding has put it out of my power to oblige him."

It would be a calumny on Mrs. Proudie to suggest that she was sitting in her bed-room with her ear at the keyhole during this interview. She had within her a spirit of decorum which prevented her from descending to such baseness. To put her ear to a key-hole or to listen at a chink, was a trick for a housemaid.

Mrs. Proudie knew this, and therefore she did not do it; but she stationed herself as near to the door as she well could, that she might, if possible, get the advantage which the housemaid would have had, without descending to the housemaid's artifice.

It was little, however, that she heard, and that little was only sufficient to deceive her. She saw nothing of that friendly pressure, perceived nothing of that concluded bargain; she did not even dream of the treacherous resolves which those two false men had made together to upset her in the pride of her station, to dash the cup from her lip before she had drank of it, to sweep away all her power before she had tasted its sweets! Traitors that they were; the husband of her bosom, and the outcast whom she had fostered and brought to the warmth of the world's brightest fireside! But neither of them had the magnanimity of this woman. Though two men have thus leagued themselves together against her, even yet the battle is not lost.

Mr. Slope felt pretty sure that Dr. Grantly would decline the honour of seeing him, and such turned out to be the case. The archdeacon, when the palace door was opened to him, was greeted by a note. Mr. Slope presented his compliments, &c. &c. The bishop was ill in his room, and very greatly regretted, &c. &c. Mr. Slope had been charged with the bishop's views, and if agreeable to the archdeacon, would do himself the honour, &c. &c. The archdeacon, however, was not agreeable, and having read his note in the hall, crumpled it up in his hand, and muttering something about sorrow for his lordship's illness, took his leave, without sending as much as a verbal message in answer to Mr. Slope's note.

"Ill!" said the archdeacon to himself as he flung himself into his brougham. "The man is absolutely a coward. He is afraid to see me. Ill, indeed!" The archdeacon was never ill himself, and did not therefore understand that any one else could in truth be prevented by illness from keeping an appointment. He regarded all such excuses as subterfuges, and in the present instance he was not far wrong.

Dr. Grantly desired to be driven to his father-in-law's lodgings in the High Street, and hearing from the servant that Mr. Harding was at his daughter's followed him to Mrs. Bold's house, and there found him. The archdeacon was fuming with rage when he got into the drawing-room, and had by this time nearly forgotten the pusillanimity of the bishop in the villany of the chaplain.

"Look at that," said he, throwing Mr. Slope's crumpled note to Mr. Harding. "I am to be told that if I choose I may have the honour of seeing Mr. Slope, and that, too, after a positive engagement with the bishop."

"But he says the bishop is ill," said Mr. Harding.

"Pshaw! You don't mean to say that you are deceived by such an excuse as that. He was well enough yesterday. Now I tell you what, I will see the bishop; and I will tell him also very plainly what I think of his conduct. I will see him, or else Barchester will soon be too hot to hold him."

Eleanor was sitting in the room, but Dr. Grantly had hardly noticed her in his anger. Eleanor now said to him, with the greatest innocence, "I wish you had seen Mr. Slope, Dr. Grantly, because I think perhaps it might have done good."

The archdeacon turned on her with almost brutal wrath. Had she at once owned that she had accepted Mr. Slope for her second husband, he could hardly have felt more convinced of her belonging body and soul to the Slope and Proudie party than he now did on hearing her express such a wish as this. Poor Eleanor!

"See him!" said the archdeacon glaring at her; "and why am I to be called on to lower myself in the world's esteem and my own by coming in contact with such a man as that? I have hitherto lived among gentlemen, and do not mean to be dragged into other company by anybody."

Poor Mr. Harding well knew what the archdeacon meant, but Eleanor was as innocent as her own baby. She could not understand how the archdeacon could consider himself to be dragged into bad company by condescending to speak to Mr. Slope for a few minutes when the interests of her father might be served by his doing so.

"I was talking for a full hour yesterday to Mr. Slope," said she, with some little assumption of dignity, "and I did not find myself lowered by it."

"Perhaps not," said he. "But if you'll be good enough to allow me, I shall judge for myself in such matters. And I tell you what, Eleanor; it will be much better for you if you will allow yourself to be guided also by the advice of those who are your friends. If you do not you will be apt to find that you have no friends left who can advise you."

Eleanor blushed up to the roots of her hair. But even now she had not the slightest idea of what was passing in the archdeacon's mind. No thought of love-making or love-receiving had yet found its way to her heart since the death of poor John Bold; and if it were possible that such a thought should spring there, the man must be far different from Mr. Slope that could give it birth.

Nevertheless Eleanor blushed deeply, for she felt she was charged with improper conduct, and she did so with the more inward pain because her father did not instantly rally to her side; that father for whose sake and love she had submitted to be the receptacle of Mr. Slope's confidence. She had given a detailed account of all that had passed to her father; and though he had not absolutely agreed with her about Mr. Slope's views touching the hospital, yet he had said nothing to make her think that she had been wrong in talking to him.

She was far too angry to humble herself before her brother-in-law. Indeed, she had never accustomed herself to be very abject before him, and they had never been confidential allies. " I do not the least understand what you mean, Dr. Grantly," said she. " I do not know that I can accuse myself of doing anything that my friends should disapprove. Mr. Slope called here expressly to ask what papa's wishes were about the hospital; and as I believe he called with friendly intentions I told him."

"Friendly intentions!" sneered the archdeacon.

"I believe you greatly wrong Mr. Slope," continued Eleanor, "but I have explained this to papa already; and as you do not seem to approve of what I say, Dr. Grantly, I will with your permission leave you and papa together," and so saying she walked slowly out of the room.

All this made Mr. Harding very unhappy. It was quite clear that the archdeacon and his wife had made up their minds that Eleanor was going to marry Mr. Slope. Mr. Harding could not really bring himself to think that she would do so, but yet he could not deny that circumstances made it appear that the man's company was not disagreeable to her. She was now constantly seeing him, and yet she received visits from no other unmarried gentleman. She always took his part when his conduct was canvassed, although she was aware how personally objectionable he was to her friends. Then, again, Mr. Harding felt that if she should choose to become Mrs. Slope, he had nothing that he could justly urge against her doing so. She had full right to please herself, and he, as a father, could not say that she would disgrace herself by marrying a clergyman who stood so well before the world as Mr. Slope did. As for quarrelling with his daughter on account of such a marriage, and separating himself from her as the archdeacon had threatened to do, that, with Mr. Harding, would be out of the question. If she should determine to marry this man, he must get over his aversion as best he could. His Eleanor, his own old companion in their old happy home, must still be the friend of his bosom, the child of his heart. Let who would cast her off, he would not. If it were fated that he should have to sit in his old age at the same table with that man whom of all men he disliked the most, he would meet his fate as best he might. Anything to him would be preferable to the loss of his daughter.

Such being his feelings, he hardly knew how to take part with Eleanor against the archdeacon, or with the archdeacon against Eleanor. It will be said that he should never have suspected her.—Alas! he never should have done so. But Mr. Harding was by no means a perfect character. In his indecision, his weakness, his proneness to be led by others, his want of self-confidence, he was very far from being perfect. And then it must be remembered that such a marriage as that which the archdeacon contemplated with disgust, which we who know Mr. Slope so well would regard with equal disgust, did not appear so monstrous to Mr. Harding, because in his charity he did not hate the chaplain as the archdeacon did, and as we do.

He was, however, very unhappy when his daughter left the room, and he had recourse to an old trick of his that was customary to him in his times of sadness. He began playing some slow tune upon an imaginary violoncello, drawing one hand slowly backwards and forwards as though he held a bow in it, and modulating the unreal cords with the other.

"She'll marry that man as sure as two and two make four," said the practical archdeacon.

"I hope not, I hope not," said the father. "But if she does, what can I say to her? I have no right to object to him."

"No right!" exclaimed Dr. Grantly.

"No right as her father. He is in my own profession, and for aught we know a good man."

To this the archdeacon would by no means assent. It was not well, however, to argue the case against Eleanor in her own drawing-room, and so they both walked forth and discussed the matter in all its bearings under the elm trees of the close. Mr. Harding also explained to his son-in-law what had been the purport, at any rate the alleged purport, of Mr. Slope's last visit to the widow. He, however, stated that he could not bring himself to believe that Mr. Slope had any real anxiety such as that he had pretended.

" I cannot forget his demeanour to myself," said Mr. Harding.
" and it is not possible that his ideas should have changed so soon."

"I see it all," said the archdeacon. "The sly *tartufe!* He
thinks to buy the daughter by providing for the father. He means
to show how powerful he is, how good he is, and how much he is
willing to do for her *beaux yeux;* yes, I see it all now. But we'll
be too many for him yet, Mr. Harding," he said, turning to his
companion with some gravity, and pressing his hand upon the
other's arm. "It would, perhaps, be better for you to lose the
hospital than get it on such terms."

"Lose it!" said Mr. Harding; "why I've lost it already. I
don't want it. I've made up my mind to do without it. I'll
withdraw altogether. I'll just go and write a line to the bishop
and tell him that I withdraw my claim altogether."

Nothing would have pleased him better than to be allowed to
escape from the trouble and difficulty in such a manner. But he
was now going too fast for the archdeacon.

"No—no—no! we'll do no such thing," said Dr. Grantly;
"we'll still have the hospital. I hardly doubt but that we'll have
it. But not by Mr. Slope's assistance. If that be necessary we'll
lose it; but we'll have it, spite of his teeth, if we can. Arabin
will be at Plumstead to-morrow ; you must come over and talk
to him."

The two now turned into the cathedral library, which was used
by the clergymen of the close as a sort of ecclesiastical club-room,
for writing sermons and sometimes letters ; also for reading theological works, and sometimes magazines and newspapers. The
theological works were not disturbed, perhaps, quite as often as
from the appearance of the building the outside public might have
been led to expect. Here the two allies settled on their course of
action. The archdeacon wrote a letter to the bishop, strongly
worded, but still respectful, in which he put forward his father-in-
law's claim to the appointment, and expressed his own regret that
he had not been able to see his lordship when he called. Of Mr.
Slope he made no mention whatsoever. It was then settled that
Mr. Harding should go out to Plumstead on the following day ;
and after considerable discussion on the matter, the archdeacon
proposed to ask Eleanor there also, so as to withdraw her, if
possible, from Mr. Slope's attentions. "A week or two," said he,
"may teach her what he is, and while she is there she will be out
of harm's way. Mr. Slope won't come there after her."

Eleanor was not a little surprised when her brother-in-law came
back and very civilly pressed her to go out to Plumstead with her

father. She instantly perceived that her father had been fighting
her battles for her behind her back. She felt thankful to him, and
for his sake she would not show her resentment to the archdeacon
by refusing his invitation. But she could not, she said, go on the
morrow; she had an invitation to drink tea at the Stanhopes
which she had promised to accept. She would, she added, go
with her father on the next day, if he would wait; or she would
follow him.

"The Stanhopes!" said Dr. Grantly; "I did not know you
were so intimate with them."

"I did not know it myself," said she, "till Miss Stanhope called
yesterday. However, I like her very much, and I have promised
to go and play chess with some of them."

"Have they a party there?" said the archdeacon, still fearful of
Mr. Slope.

"Oh, no," said Eleanor; "Miss Stanhope said there was to be
nobody at all. But she had heard that Mary had left me for a
few weeks, and she had learnt from some one that I play chess,
and so she came over on purpose to ask me to go in."

"Well, that's very friendly," said the ex-warden. "They
certainly do look more like foreigners than English people, but I
dare say they are none the worse for that."

The archdeacon was inclined to look upon the Stanhopes with
favourable eyes, and had nothing to object on the matter. It was
therefore arranged that Mr. Harding should postpone his visit to
Plumstead for one day, and then take with him Eleanor, the baby,
and the nurse.

Mr. Slope is certainly becoming of some importance in Barchester.

CHAP. XIX.

BARCHESTER BY MOONLIGHT.

THERE was much cause for grief and occasional perturbation of
spirits in the Stanhope family, but yet they rarely seemed to be
grieved or to be disturbed. It was the peculiar gift of each of
them that each was able to bear his or her own burden without
complaint, and perhaps without sympathy. They habitually looked
on the sunny side of the wall, if there was a gleam on either side
for them to look at; and, if there was none, they endured the
shade with an indifference which, if not stoical, answered the end

at which the Stoics aimed. Old Stanhope could not but feel that he had ill-performed his duties as a father and a clergyman ; and could hardly look forward to his own death without grief at the position in which he would leave his family. His income for many years had been as high as 3000*l.* a year, and yet they had among them no other provision than their mother's fortune of 10,000*l.* He had not only spent his income, but was in debt. Yet with all this, he seldom showed much outward sign of trouble.

It was the same with the mother. If she added little to the pleasures of her children she detracted still less : she neither grumbled at her lot, nor spoke much of her past or future sufferings ; as long as she had a maid to adjust her dress, and had those dresses well made, nature with her was satisfied. It was the same with the children. Charlotte never rebuked her father with the prospect of their future poverty, nor did it seem to grieve her that she was becoming an old maid so quickly ; her temper was rarely ruffled, and, if we might judge by her appearance, she was always happy. The signora was not so sweet-tempered, but she possessed much enduring courage ; she seldom complained — never, indeed, to her family. Though she had a cause for affliction which would have utterly broken down the heart of most women as beautiful as she and as devoid of all religious support, yet, she bore her suffering in silence, or alluded to it only to elicit the sympathy and stimulate the admiration of the men with whom she flirted. As to Bertie, one would have imagined from the sound of his voice and the gleam of his eye that he had not a sorrow nor a care in the world. Nor had he. He was incapable of anticipating to-morrow's griefs. The prospect of future want no more disturbed his appetite than does that of the butcher's knife disturb the appetite of the sheep.

Such was the usual tenour of their way ; but there were rare exceptions. Occasionally the father would allow an angry glance to fall from his eye, and the lion would send forth a low dangerous roar as though he meditated some deed of blood. Occasionally also Madame Neroni would become bitter against mankind, more than usually antagonistic to the world's decencies, and would seem as though she was about to break from her moorings and allow herself to be carried forth by the tide of her feelings to utter ruin and shipwreck. She, however, like the rest of them, had no real feelings, could feel no true passion. In that was her security. Before she resolved on any contemplated escapade she would make a small calculation, and generally summed up that the Stanhope villa or even Barchester close was better than the world at large.

They were most irregular in their hours. The father was

generally the earliest in the breakfast-parlour, and Charlotte would soon follow and give him his coffee; but the others breakfasted anywhere, anyhow, and at any time. On the morning after the archdeacon's futile visit to the palace, Dr. Stanhope came down stairs with an ominously dark look about his eyebrows; his white locks were rougher than usual, and he breathed thickly and loudly as he took his seat in his arm-chair. He had open letters in his hand, and when Charlotte came into the room he was still reading them. She went up and kissed him as was her wont, but he hardly noticed her as she did so, and she knew at once that something was the matter.

"What's the meaning of that?" said he, throwing over the table a letter with a Milan post-mark. Charlotte was a little frightened as she took it up, but her mind was relieved when she saw that it was merely the bill of their Italian milliner. The sum total was certainly large, but not so large as to create an important row.

"It's for our clothes, papa, for six months before we came here. The three of us can't dress for nothing, you know."

"Nothing, indeed!" said he, looking at the figures, which in Milanese denominations were certainly monstrous.

"The man should have sent it to me," said Charlotte.

"I wish he had with all my heart—if you would have paid it. I see enough in it, to know that three quarters of it are for Madeline."

"She has little else to amuse her, sir," said Charlotte with true good nature.

"And I suppose he has nothing else to amuse him," said the doctor, throwing over another letter to his daughter. It was from some member of the family of Sidonia, and politely requested the father to pay a small trifle of 700*l*., being the amount of a bill discounted in favour of Mr. Ethelbert Stanhope, and now overdue for a period of nine months.

Charlotte read the letter, slowly folded it up, and put it under the edge of the tea-tray.

"I suppose he has nothing to amuse him but discounting bills with Jews. Does he think I'll pay that?"

"I am sure he thinks no such thing," said she.

"And who does he think will pay it?"

"As far as honesty goes I suppose it won't much matter if it is never paid," said she. "I dare say he got very little of it."

"I suppose it won't much matter either," said the father, "if he goes to prison and rots there. It seems to me that that's the other alternative."

Dr. Stanhope spoke of the custom of his youth. But his daughter, though she had lived so long abroad, was much more completely versed in the ways of the English world. "If the man arrests him," said she, "he must go through the court."

It is thus, thou great family of Sidonia — it is thus that we Gentiles treat thee, when, in our extremest need, thou and thine have aided us with mountains of gold as big as lions, — and occasionally with wine-warrants and orders for dozens of dressing-cases.

"What, and become an insolvent?" said the doctor.

"He's that already," said Charlotte, wishing always to get over a difficulty.

"What a condition," said the doctor, "for the son of a clergyman of the Church of England!"

"I don't see why clergymen's sons should pay their debts more than other young men," said Charlotte.

"He's had as much from me since he left school as is held sufficient for the eldest son of many a nobleman," said the angry father.

"Well, sir," said Charlotte, "give him another chance."

"What!" said the doctor, "do you mean that I am to pay that Jew?"

"Oh no! I wouldn't pay him, he must take his chance; and if the worst comes to the worst, Bertie must go abroad. But I want you to be civil to Bertie, and let him remain here as long as we stop. He has a plan in his head, that may put him on his feet after all."

"Has he any plan for following up his profession?"

"Oh, he'll do that too; but that must follow. He's thinking of getting married."

Just at that moment the door opened, and Bertie came in whistling. The doctor immediately devoted himself to his egg, and allowed Bertie to whistle himself round to his sister's side without noticing him.

Charlotte gave a sign to him with her eye, first glancing at her father, and then at the letter, the corner of which peeped out from under the tea-tray. Bertie saw and understood, and with the quiet motion of a cat abstracted the letter, and made himself acquainted with its contents. The doctor, however, had seen him, deep as he appeared to be mersed in his egg-shell, and said in his harshest voice, "Well, sir, do you know that gentleman?"

"Yes, sir," said Bertie. "I have a sort of acquaintance with him, but none that can justify him in troubling you. If you will allow me, sir, I will answer this."

"At any rate I sha'n't," said the father, and then he added, after a pause, "Is it true, sir, that you owe the man 700*l.*?"

"Well," said Bertie, "I think I should be inclined to dispute the amount, if I were in a condition to pay him such of it as I really do owe him."

"Has he your bill for 700*l.*?" said the father, speaking very loudly and very angrily.

"Well, I believe he has," said Bertie; "but all the money I ever got from him was 150*l.*"

"And what became of the 550*l.*?"

"Why, sir, the commission was 100*l.* or so, and I took the remainder in paving-stones and rocking-horses."

"Paving stones and rocking-horses!" said the doctor, "where are they?"

"Oh, sir, I suppose they are in London somewhere—but I'll inquire if you wish for them."

"He's an idiot," said the doctor, "and it's sheer folly to waste more money on him. Nothing can save him from ruin;" and so saying, the unhappy father walked out of the room.

"Would the governor like to have the paving-stones?" said Bertie to his sister.

"I'll tell you what," said she, "if you don't take care, you will find yourself loose upon the world without even a house over your head: you don't know him as well as I do. He's very angry."

Bertie stroked his big beard, sipped his tea, chatted over his misfortunes in a half comic, half serious tone, and ended by promising his sister that he would do his very best to make himself agreeable to the widow Bold. Then Charlotte followed her father to his own room and softened down his wrath, and persuaded him to say nothing more about the Jew bill discounter, at any rate for a few weeks. He even went so far as to say he would pay the 700*l.*, or at any rate settle the bill, if he saw a certainty of his son's securing for himself anything like a decent provision in life Nothing was said openly between them about poor Eleanor : but the father and the daughter understood each other.

They all met together in the drawing-room at nine o'clock, in perfect good humour with each other ; and about that hour Mrs. Bold was announced. She had never been in the house before, though she had of course called; and now she felt it strange to find herself there in her usual evening dress, entering the drawing-room of these strangers in this friendly unceremonious way, as though she had known them all her life. But in three minutes they made her at home. Charlotte tripped down stairs and took her bonnet from her, and Bertie came to relieve her from her shawl, and the signora smiled on her as she could smile when she chose to be gracious, and the old doctor shook hands with her in a kind benedictory manner that went to her heart at once, and made her feel that he must be a good man.

She had not been seated for above five minutes when the door again opened, and Mr. Slope was announced. She felt rather surprised, because she was told that nobody was to be there, and it was very evident from the manner of some of them, that Mr. Slope was unexpected. But still there was not much in it. In such invitations a bachelor or two more or less are always spoken of as nobodies, and there was no reason why Mr. Slope should not drink tea at Dr. Stanhope's as well as Eleanor herself. He, however, was very much surprised and not very much gratified at finding that his own embryo spouse made one of the party. He had come there to gratify himself by gazing on Madame Neroni's beauty, and listening to and returning her flattery: and though he had not owned as much to himself, he still felt that if he spent the evening as he had intended to do, he might probably not thereby advance his suit with Mrs. Bold.

The signora, who had no idea of a rival, received Mr. Slope with her usual marks of distinction. As he took her hand, she made some confidential communication to him in a low voice, declaring that she had a plan to communicate to him after tea, and was evidently prepared to go on with her work of reducing the chaplain to a state of captivity. Poor Mr. Slope was rather beside himself. He thought that Eleanor could not but have learnt from his demeanour that he was an admirer of her own, and he had also flattered himself that the idea was not unacceptable to her. What would she think of him if he now devoted himself to a married woman!

But Eleanor was not inclined to be severe in her criticisms on him in this respect, and felt no annoyance of any kind, when she found herself seated between Bertie and Charlotte Stanhope. She had no suspicion of Mr. Slope's intentions; she had no suspicion even of the suspicion of other people; but still she felt well pleased not to have Mr. Slope too near to her.

And she was not ill-pleased to have Bertie Stanhope near her. It was rarely indeed that he failed to make an agreeable impression on strangers. With a bishop indeed who thought much of his own dignity it was possible that he might fail, but hardly with a young and pretty woman. He possessed the tact of becoming instantly intimate with women without giving rise to any fear of impertinence. He had about him somewhat of the propensities of a tame cat. It seemed quite natural that he should be petted, caressed, and treated with familiar good nature, and that in return he should purr, and be sleek and graceful, and above all never show his claws. Like other tame cats, however, he had his claws, and sometimes made them dangerous.

When tea was over Charlotte went to the open window and declared loudly that the full harvest moon was much too beautiful to be disregarded, and called them all to look at it. To tell the truth, there was but one there who cared much about the moon's beauty, and that one was not Charlotte; but she knew how valuable an aid to her purpose the chaste goddess might become, and could easily create a little enthusiasm for the purpose of the moment. Eleanor and Bertie were soon with her. The doctor was now quiet in his arm-chair, and Mrs. Stanhope in hers, both prepared for slumber.

"Are you a Whewellite or a Brewsterite, or a t'othermanite, Mrs. Bold?" said Charlotte, who knew a little about everything, and had read about a third of each of the books to which she alluded.

"Oh!" said Eleanor; "I have not read any of the books, but I feel sure that there is one man in the moon at least, if not more."

"You don't believe in the pulpy gelatinous matter?" said Bertie.

"I heard about that," said Eleanor; "and I really think it's almost wicked to talk in such a manner. How can we argue about God's power in the other stars from the laws which he has given for our rule in this one?"

"How indeed!" said Bertie. "Why shouldn't there be a race of salamanders in Venus? and even if there be nothing but fish in Jupiter, why shouldn't the fish there be as wide awake as the men and women here?"

"That would be saying very little for them," said Charlotte. "I am for Dr. Whewell myself; for I do not think that men and women are worth being repeated in such countless worlds. There may be souls in other stars, but I doubt their having any bodies attached to them. But come, Mrs. Bold, let us put our bonnets on and walk round the close. If we are to discuss sidereal questions, we shall do so much better under the towers of the cathedral, than stuck in this narrow window."

Mrs. Bold made no objection, and a party was made to walk out. Charlotte Stanhope well knew the rule as to three being no company, and she had therefore to induce her sister to allow Mr. Slope to accompany them.

"Come, Mr. Slope," she said; "I'm sure you'll join us. We shall be in again in a quarter of an hour, Madeline."

Madeline read in her eye all that she had to say, knew her object, and as she had to depend on her sister for so many of her amusements, she felt that she must yield. It was hard to be left alone while others of her own age walked out to feel the soft influence of the bright night, but it would be harder still to be without the sort of sanction which Charlotte gave to all her flirtations and intrigues. Charlotte's eye told her that she must give up just at present for the good of the family, and so Madeline obeyed.

But Charlotte's eyes said nothing of the sort to Mr. Slope. He had no objection at all to the *tête-à-tête* with the signora, which the departure of the other three would allow him, and gently whispered to her, "I shall not leave you alone."

"Oh, yes," said she; "go — pray go, pray go, for my sake. Do not think that I am so selfish. It is understood that nobody is kept within for me. You will understand this too when you know me better. Pray join them, Mr. Slope, but when you come in speak to me for five minutes before you leave us."

Mr. Slope understood that he was to go, and he therefore joined the party in the hall. He would have had no objection at all to this arrangement, if he could have secured Mrs. Bold's arm; but this of course was out of the question. Indeed, his fate was very soon settled, for no sooner had he reached the hall-door than Miss Stanhope put her hand within his arm, and Bertie walked off with Eleanor just as naturally as though she were already his own property.

And so they sauntered forth: first they walked round the close, according to their avowed intent; then they went under the old arched gateway below St. Cuthbert's little church, and then they turned behind the grounds of the bishop's palace, and so on till they came to the bridge just at the edge of the town, from which passers-by can look down into the gardens of Hiram's Hospital; and here Charlotte and Mr. Slope, who were in advance, stopped till the other two came up to them. Mr. Slope knew that the gable-ends and old brick chimneys which stood up so prettily in the moonlight, were those of Mr. Harding's late abode, and would not have stopped on such a spot, in such company, if he could have avoided it; but Miss Stanhope would not take the hint which he tried to give.

"This is a very pretty place, Mrs. Bold," said Charlotte; "by far the prettiest place near Barchester. I wonder your father gave it up."

It was a very pretty place, and now by the deceitful light of the moon looked twice larger, twice prettier, twice more antiquely picturesque than it would have done in truth-telling daylight. Who does not know the air of complex multiplicity and the mysterious interesting grace which the moon always lends to old gabled buildings half surrounded, as was the hospital, by fine trees! As seen from the bridge on the night of which we are speaking, Mr. Harding's late abode did look very lovely; and though Eleanor did not grieve at her father's having left it, she felt at the moment an intense wish that he might be allowed to return.

"He is going to return to it almost immediately, is he not?" asked Bertie.

Eleanor made no immediate reply. Many such a question passes unanswered, without the notice of the questioner; but such was not now the case. They all remained silent as though expecting her to reply, and after a moment or two, Charlotte said, "I believe it is settled that Mr. Harding returns to the hospital, is it not?"

"I don't think anything about it is settled yet," said Eleanor.

"But it must be a matter of course," said Bertie; "that is, if your father wishes it; who else on earth could hold it after what has occurred?"

Eleanor quietly made her companion understand that the matter was one which she could not discuss in the present company; and then they passed on; Charlotte said she would go a short way up the hill out of the town so as to look back upon the towers of the cathedral, and as Eleanor lent upon Bertie's arm for assistance in the walk, she told him how the matter stood between her father and the bishop.

"And, he," said Bertie, pointing on to Mr. Slope, "what part does he take in it?"

Eleanor explained how Mr. Slope had at first endeavoured to tyrannise over her father, but how he had latterly come round, and done all he could to talk the bishop over in Mr. Harding's favour. "But my father," said she, "is hardly inclined to trust him; they all say he is so arrogant to the old clergymen of the city."

"Take my word for it," said Bertie, "your father is right. If I am not very much mistaken, that man is both arrogant and false."

They strolled up to the top of the hill, and then returned through the fields by a footpath which leads by a small wooden bridge, or rather a plank with a rustic rail to it, over the river to the other side of the cathedral from that at which they had started. They had thus walked round the bishop's grounds, through which the river runs, and round the cathedral and adjacent fields, and it was past eleven before they reached the doctor's door.

"It is very late," said Eleanor, "it will be a shame to disturb your mother again at such an hour."

"Oh," said Charlotte, laughing, "you won't disturb mamma; I dare say she is in bed by this time, and Madeline would be furious if you did not come in and see her. Come, Bertie, take Mrs. Bold's bonnet from her."

They went up stairs, and found the signora alone, reading She looked somewhat sad and melancholy, but not more so perhaps than was sufficient to excite additional interest in the bosom of Mr. Slope; and she was soon deep in whispered intercourse with that happy gentleman, who was allowed to find a resting-place on her sofa. The signora had a way of whispering that was peculiarly her own, and was exactly the reverse of that which prevails among great tragedians. The great tragedian hisses out a positive whisper, made with bated breath, and produced by inarticulated tongue-formed sounds, but yet he is audible through the whole house. The signora however used no hisses, and produced all her words in a clear silver tone, but they could only be heard by the ear into which they were poured.

Charlotte hurried and skurried about the room hither and thither, doing, or pretending to do many things; and then saying something about seeing her mother, ran up stairs. Eleanor was thus left alone with Bertie, and she hardly felt an hour fly by her. To give Bertie his due credit, he could not have played his cards better. He did not make love to her, nor sigh, nor look languishing; but he was amusing and familiar, yet respectful; and when he left Eleanor at her own door at one o'clock, which he did by the bye with the assistance of the now jealous Slope, she thought that he was one of the most agreeable men, and the Stanhopes decidedly the most agreeable family, that she had ever met.

CHAP. XX.

MR. ARABIN.

THE Rev. Francis Arabin, fellow of Lazarus, late professor of poetry at Oxford, and present vicar of St. Ewold, in the diocese of Barchester, must now be introduced personally to the reader.

And as he will fill a conspicuous place in the volume, it is desirable
that he should be made to stand before the reader's eye by the aid
of such portraiture as the author is able to produce.

It is to be regretted that no mental method of daguerreotype or
photography has yet been discovered, by which the characters of
men can be reduced to writing and put into grammatical language
with an unerring precision of truthful description. How often
does the novelist feel, ay, and the historian also and the biographer,
that he has conceived within his mind and accurately depicted on
the tablet of his brain the full character and personage of a man,
and that nevertheless, when he flies to pen and ink to perpetuate
the portrait, his words forsake, elude, disappoint, and play the
deuce with him, till at the end of a dozen pages the man described
has no more resemblance to the man conceived than the sign-board
at the corner of the street has to the Duke of Cambridge?

And yet such mechanical descriptive skill would hardly give
more satisfaction to the reader than the skill of the photographer
does to the anxious mother desirous to possess an absolute duplicate
of her beloved child. The likeness is indeed true; but it is a dull,
dead, unfeeling, inauspicious likeness. The face is indeed there,
and those looking at it will know at once whose image it is; but
the owner of the face will not be proud of the resemblance.

There is no royal road to learning; no short cut to the acquire-
ment of any valuable art. Let photographers and daguerreotypers
do what they will, and improve as they may with further skill on
that which skill has already done, they will never achieve a
portrait of the human face divine. Let biographers, novelists, and
the rest of us groan as we may under the burdens which we so
often feel too heavy for our shoulders, we must either bear them
up like men, or own ourselves too weak for the work we have
undertaken. There is no way of writing well and also of writing
easily.

Labor omnia vincit improbus. Such should be the chosen
motto of every labourer, and it may be that labour, if adequately
enduring, may suffice at last to produce even some not untrue
resemblance of the Rev. Francis Arabin.

Of his doings in the world, and of the sort of fame which he has
achieved, enough has been already said. It has also been said
that he is forty years of age, and still unmarried. He was the
younger son of a country gentleman of small fortune in the north
of England. At an early age he went to Winchester, and was
intended by his father for New College; but though studious as
a boy, he was not studious within the prescribed limits; and at

the age of eighteen he left school with a character for talent, but without a scholarship. All that he had obtained, over and above the advantage of his character, was a gold medal for English verse, and hence was derived a strong presumption on the part of his friends that he was destined to add another name to the imperishable list of English poets.

From Winchester he went to Oxford, and was entered as a commoner at Balliol. Here his special career very soon commenced. He utterly eschewed the society of fast men, gave no wine parties, kept no horses, rowed no boats, joined no rows, and was the pride of his college tutor. Such at least was his career till he had taken his little go ; and then he commenced a course of action which, though not less creditable to himself as a man, was hardly so much to the taste of the tutor. He became a member of a vigorous debating society, and rendered himself remarkable there for humorous energy. Though always in earnest, yet his earnestness was always droll. To be true in his ideas, unanswerable in his syllogisms, and just in his aspirations was not enough for him. He had failed, failed in his own opinion as well as that of others when others came to know him, if he could not reduce the arguments of his opponents to an absurdity, and conquer both by wit and reason. To say that his object was ever to raise a laugh, would be most untrue. He hated such common and unnecessary evidence of satisfaction on the part of his hearers. A joke that required to be laughed at was, with him, not worth uttering. He could appreciate by a keener sense than that of his ears the success of his wit, and would see in the eyes of his auditory whether or no he was understood and appreciated.

He had been a religious lad before he left school. That is, he had addicted himself to a party in religion, and having done so had received that benefit which most men do who become partisans in such a cause. We are much too apt to look at schism in our church as an unmitigated evil. Moderate schism, if there may be such a thing, at any rate calls attention to the subject, draws in supporters who would otherwise have been inattentive to the matter, and teaches men to think upon religion. How great an amount of good of this description has followed that movement in the Church of England which commenced with the publication of Froude's Remains !

As a boy young Arabin took up the cudgels on the side of the Tractarians, and at Oxford he sat for a while at the feet of the great Newman. To this cause he lent all his faculties. For it he concocted verses, for it he made speeches, for it he scintillated the brightest sparks of his quiet wit. For it he ate and drank and dressed, and had his being. In due process of time he took his degree, and wrote himself B.A., but he did not do so with any remarkable amount of academical éclat. He had occupied himself too much with high church matters, and the polemics, politics, and outward demonstrations usually concurrent with high churchmanship, to devote himself with sufficient vigour to the acquisition of a double first. He was not a double first, nor even a first class man ; but he revenged himself on the university by putting firsts and double firsts out of fashion for the year, and laughing down a species of pedantry which at the age of twenty-three leaves no room in a man's mind for graver subjects than conic sections or Greek accents.

Greek accents, however, and conic sections were esteemed necessaries at Balliol, and there was no admittance there for Mr. Arabin within the list of its fellows. Lazarus, however, the richest and most comfortable abode of Oxford dons, opened its bosom to the young champion of a church militant. Mr. Arabin was ordained, and became a fellow soon after taking his degree, and shortly after that was chosen professor of poetry.

And now came the moment of his great danger. After many mental struggles, and an agony of doubt which may be well surmised, the great prophet of the Tractarians confessed himself a Roman Catholic. Mr. Newman left the Church of England, and with him carried many a waverer. He did not carry off Mr. Arabin, but the escape which that gentleman had was a very narrow one. He left Oxford for a while that he might meditate in complete peace on the step which appeared to him to be all but unavoidable, and shut himself up in a little village on the sea-shore of one of our remotest counties, that he might learn by communing with his own soul whether or no he could with a safe conscience remain within the pale of his mother church.

Things would have gone badly with him there had he been left entirely to himself. Every thing was against him: all his worldly interests required him to remain a Protestant ; and he looked on his worldly interests as a legion of foes, to get the better of whom was a point of extremest honour. In his then state of ecstatic agony such a conquest would have cost him little; he could easily have thrown away all his livelihood ; but it cost him much to get over the idea that by choosing the Church of England he should be open in his own mind to the charge that he had been led to such a choice by unworthy motives. Then his heart was against him : he loved with a strong and eager love the man who had hitherto been his guide, and yearned to follow his footsteps. His tastes were against him: the ceremonies and pomps of the Church of Rome, their august feasts and solemn fasts, invited his imagination and pleased his eye. His flesh was against him: how great an aid would it be to a poor, weak, wavering man to be constrained to high moral duties, self-denial, obedience, and chastity by laws which were certain in their enactments, and not to be broken without loud, palpable, unmistakable sin! Then his faith was against him: he required to believe so much; panted so eagerly to give signs of his belief; deemed it so insufficient to wash himself simply in the waters of Jordan; that some great deed, such as that of forsaking everything for a true church, had for him allurements almost past withstanding.

Mr. Arabin was at this time a very young man, and when he left Oxford for his far retreat was much too confident in his powers of fence, and too apt to look down on the ordinary sense of ordinary people, to expect aid in the battle that he had to fight from any chance inhabitants of the spot which he had selected. But Providence was good to him; and there, in that all but desolate place, on the storm-beat shore of that distant sea, he met one who gradually calmed his mind, quieted his imagination, and taught him something of a Christian's duty. When Mr. Arabin left Oxford, he was inclined to look upon the rural clergymen of most English parishes almost with contempt. It was his ambition, should he remain within the fold of their church, to do somewhat towards redeeming and rectifying their inferiority, and to assist in infusing energy and faith into the hearts of Christian ministers, who were, as he thought, too often satisfied to go through life without much show of either.

And yet it was from such a one that Mr. Arabin in his extremest need received that aid which he so much required. It was from the poor curate of a small Cornish parish that he first learnt to know that the highest laws for the governance of a Christian's duty must act from within and not from without; that no man can become a serviceable servant solely by obedience to written edicts; and that the safety which he was about to seek within the gates of Rome was no other than the selfish freedom from personal danger which the bad soldier attempts to gain who counterfeits illness on the eve of battle.

Mr. Arabin returned to Oxford a humbler but a better and a happier man; and from that time forth he put his shoulder to the wheel as a clergyman of the Church for which he had been educated. The intercourse of those among whom he familiarly lived kept him staunch to the principles of that system of the Church to which he had always belonged. Since his severance from Mr. Newman, no one had had so strong an influence over him as the head of his college. During the time of his expected apostacy, Dr. Gwynne had not felt much predisposition in favour of the young fellow. Though a High Churchman himself within moderate limits, Dr. Gwynne felt no sympathy with men who could not satisfy their faiths with the Thirty-nine Articles. He regarded the enthusiasm of such as Newman as a state of mind more nearly allied to madness than to religion; and when he saw it evinced by very young men, was inclined to attribute a good deal of it to vanity. Dr. Gwynne himself, though a religious man, was also a thoroughly practical man of the world, and he regarded with no favourable eye the tenets of any one who looked on the two things as incompatible. When he found that Mr. Arabin was a half Roman, he began to regret all he had done towards bestowing a fellowship on so unworthy a recipient; and when again he learnt that Mr. Arabin would probably complete his journey to Rome, he regarded with some satisfaction the fact that in such case the fellowship would be again vacant.

When, however, Mr. Arabin returned and professed himself a confirmed Protestant, the master of Lazarus again opened his arms to him, and gradually he became the pet of the college. For some little time he was saturnine, silent, and unwilling to take any prominent part in university broils; but gradually his mind recovered, or rather made, its tone, and he became known as a man always ready at a moment's notice to take up the cudgels in opposition to anything that savoured of an evangelical bearing. He was great in sermons, great on platforms, great at after dinner conversations, and always pleasant as well as great. He took delight in elections, served on committees, opposed tooth and nail all projects of university reform, and talked jovially over his glass of port of the ruin to be anticipated by the Church, and of the sacrilege daily committed by the Whigs. The ordeal through which he had gone, in resisting the blandishments of the lady of Rome, had certainly done much towards the strengthening of his character. Although in small and outward matters he was self-confident enough, nevertheless in things affecting the inner man he aimed at a humility of spirit which would never have been attractive to him but for that visit to the coast of Cornwall. This visit he now repeated every year.

Such is an interior view of Mr. Arabin at the time when he accepted the living of St. Ewold. Exteriorly, he was not a remarkable person. He was above the middle height, well made, and very active. His hair, which had been jet black, was now tinged with gray, but his face bore no sign of years. It would perhaps be wrong to say that he was handsome, but his face was, nevertheless, pleasant to look upon. The cheek bones were rather too high for beauty, and the formation of the forehead too massive and heavy: but the eyes, nose, and mouth were perfect. There was a continual play of lambent fire about his eyes, which gave promise of either pathos or humour whenever he essayed to speak, and that promise was rarely broken. There was a gentle play about his mouth which declared that his wit never descended to sarcasm, and that there was no ill-nature in his repartee.

Mr. Arabin was a popular man among women, but more so as a general than a special favourite. Living as a fellow at Oxford, marriage with him had been out of the question, and it may be doubted whether he had ever allowed his heart to be touched. Though belonging to a church in which celibacy is not the required lot of its ministers, he had come to regard himself as one of those clergymen to whom to be a bachelor is almost a necessity. He had never looked for parochial duty, and his career at Oxford was utterly incompatible with such domestic joys as a wife and nursery. He looked on women, therefore, in the same light that one sees them regarded by many Romish priests. He liked to have near him that which was pretty and amusing, but women generally were little more to him than children. He talked to them without putting out all his powers, and listened to them without any idea that what he should hear from them could either actuate his conduct or influence his opinion.

Such was Mr. Arabin, the new vicar of St. Ewold, who is going to stay with the Grantlys, at Plumstead Episcopi.

Mr. Arabin reached Plumstead the day before Mr. Harding and Eleanor, and the Grantly family were thus enabled to make his acquaintance and discuss his qualifications before the arrival of the other guests. Griselda was surprised to find that he looked so young; but she told Florinda her younger sister, when they had retired for the night, that he did not talk at all like a young man: and she decided, with the authority that seventeen has over sixteen, that he was not at all nice, although his eyes were lovely. As usual, sixteen implicitly acceded to the dictum of seventeen in such a matter, and said that he certainly was not nice. They then branched off on the relative merits of other clerical bachelors in the vicinity, and both determined without any feeling of jealousy between them that a certain Rev. Augustus

Green was by many degrees the most estimable of the lot. The gentleman in question had certainly much in his favour, as, having a comfortable allowance from his father, he could devote the whole proceeds of his curacy to violet gloves and unexceptionable neck ties. Having thus fixedly resolved that the new comer had nothing about him to shake the pre-eminence of the exalted Green, the two girls went to sleep in each other's arms, contented with themselves and the world.

Mrs. Grantly at first sight came to much the same conclusion about her husband's favourite as her daughters had done, though, in seeking to measure his relative value, she did not compare him to Mr. Green ; indeed, she made no comparison by name between him and any one else ; but she remarked to her husband that one person's swans were very often another person's geese, thereby clearly showing that Mr. Arabin had not yet proved his qualifications in swanhood to her satisfaction.

" Well, Susan," said he, rather offended at hearing his friend spoken of so disrespectfully, " if you take Mr. Arabin for a goose, I cannot say that I think very highly of your discrimination."

" A goose! No, of course, he's not a goose. I've no doubt he's a very clever man. But you're so matter-of-fact, archdeacon, when it suits your purpose, that one can't trust oneself to any *façon de parler.* I've no doubt Mr. Arabin is a very valuable man—at Oxford, and that he'll be a good vicar at St. Ewold. All I mean is, that having passed one evening with him, I don't find him to be absolutely a paragon. In the first place, if I am not mistaken, he is a little inclined to be conceited."

" Of all the men that I know intimately," said the archdeacon, " Arabin is, in my opinion, the most free from any taint of self-conceit. His fault is that he's too diffident."

" Perhaps so," said the lady ; " only I must own I did not find it out this evening."

Nothing further was said about him. Dr. Grantly thought that his wife was abusing Mr. Arabin merely because he had praised him ; and Mrs. Grantly knew that it was useless arguing for or against any person in favour of or in opposition to whom the archdeacon had already pronounced a strong opinion.

In truth they were both right. Mr. Arabin was a diffident man in social intercourse with those whom he did not intimately know ; when placed in situations which it was his business to fill, and discussing matters with which it was his duty to be conversant, Mr. Arabin was from habit brazen-faced enough. When standing on a platform in Exeter Hall, no man would be less mazed than he by the eyes of the crowd before him; for such was the work which his profession had called on him to perform ; but he shrank from a strong expression of opinion in general society, and his doing so not uncommonly made it appear that he considered the company not worth the trouble of his energy. He was averse to dictate when the place did not seem to him to justify dictation ; and as those subjects on which people wished to hear him speak were such as he was accustomed to treat with decision, he generally shunned the traps there were laid to allure him into discussion, and, by doing so, not unfrequently subjected himself to such charges as those brought against him by Mrs. Grantly.

Mr. Arabin, as he sat at his open window, enjoying the delicious moonlight and gazing at the gray towers of the church, which stood almost within the rectory grounds, little dreamed that he was the subject of so many friendly or unfriendly criticisms. Considering how much we are all given to discuss the characters of others, and discuss them often not in the strictest spirit of charity, it is singular how little we are inclined to think that others can speak ill-naturedly of us, and how angry and hurt we are when proof reaches us that they have done so. It is hardly too much to say that we all of us occasionally speak of our dearest friends in a manner in which those dearest friends would very little like to hear themselves mentioned; and that we nevertheless expect that our dearest friends shall invariably speak of us as though they were blind to all our faults, but keenly alive to every shade of our virtues.

It did not occur to Mr. Arabin that he was spoken of at all. It seemed to him, when he compared himself with his host, that he was a person of so little consequence to any, that he was worth no one's words or thoughts. He was utterly alone in the world as regarded domestic ties and those inner familiar relations which are hardly possible between others than husbands and wives, parents and children, or brothers and sisters. He had often discussed with himself the necessity of such bonds for a man's happiness in this world, and had generally satisfied himself with the answer that happiness in this world is not a necessity. Herein he deceived himself, or rather tried to do so. He, like others, yearned for the enjoyment of whatever he saw enjoyable ; and though he attempted, with the modern stoicism of so many Christians, to make himself believe that joy and sorrow were matters which here should be held as perfectly indifferent, these things were not indifferent to him. He was tired of his Oxford rooms and his college life. He regarded the wife and children of his friend with something like envy; he all but coveted the pleasant drawing-room, with its pretty windows opening on to lawns and flower-beds, the apparel of the comfortable house, and — above all — the air of home which encompassed it all.

It will be said that no time can have been so fitted for such desires on his part as this, when he had just possessed himself of a country parish, of a living among fields and gardens, of a house which a wife would grace. It is true there was a difference between the opulence of Plumstead and the modest economy of St. Ewold; but surely Mr. Arabin was not a man to sigh after wealth! Of all men, his friends would have unanimously declared he was the last to do so. But how little our friends know us! In his period of stoical rejection of this world's happiness, he had cast from him as utter dross all anxiety as to fortune. He had, as it were, proclaimed himself to be indifferent to promotion, and those who chiefly admired his talents, and would mainly have exerted themselves to secure to them their deserved reward, had taken him at his word. And now, if the truth must out, he felt himself disappointed — disappointed not by them but by himself. The day-dream of his youth was over, and at the age of forty he felt that he was not fit to work in the spirit of an apostle. He had mistaken himself, and learned his mistake when it was past remedy. He had professed himself indifferent to mitres and diaconal residences, to rich livings and pleasant glebes, and now he had to own to himself that he was sighing for the good things of other men, on whom in his pride he had ventured to look down.

Not for wealth, in its vulgar sense, had he ever sighed; not for the enjoyment of rich things had he ever longed; but for the allotted share of worldly bliss, which a wife, and children, and happy home could give him, for that usual amount of comfort which he had ventured to reject as unnecessary for him, he did now feel that he would have been wiser to have searched.

He knew that his talents, his position, and his friends would have won for him promotion, had he put himself in the way of winning it. Instead of doing so, he had allowed himself to be persuaded to accept a living which would give him an income of some 300l. a year, should he, by marrying, throw up his fellowship. Such, at the age of forty, was the worldly result of labour, which the world had chosen to regard as successful. The world also thought that Mr. Arabin was, in his own estimation, sufficiently paid. Alas! alas! the world was mistaken; and Mr. Arabin was beginning to ascertain that such was the case.

And here, may I beg the reader not to be hard in his judgment upon this man. Is not the state at which he has arrived, the natural result of efforts to reach that which is not the condition of humanity? Is not modern stoicism, built though it be on Christianity, as great an outrage on human nature as was the stoicism of the ancients? The philosophy of Zeno was built on true laws, but on true laws misunderstood, and therefore misapplied. It is the same with our Stoics here, who would teach us that wealth and worldly comfort and happiness on earth are not worth the search. Alas, for a doctrine which can find no believing pupils and no true teachers!

The case of Mr. Arabin was the more singular, as he belonged to a branch of the Church of England well inclined to regard its temporalities with avowed favour, and had habitually lived with men who were accustomed to much worldly comfort. But such was his idiosyncrasy, that these very facts had produced within him, in early life, a state of mind that was not natural to him. He was content to be a High Churchman, if he could be so on principles of his own, and could strike out a course showing a marked difference from those with whom he consorted. He was ready to be a partisan as long as he was allowed to have a course of action and of thought unlike that of his party. His party had indulged him, and he began to feel that his party was right and himself wrong, just when such a conviction was too late to be of service to him. He discovered, when such discovery was no longer serviceable, that it *would* have been worth his while to have worked for the usual pay assigned to work in this world, and have earned a wife and children, with a carriage for them to sit in; to have earned a pleasant dining-room, in which his friends could drink his wine, and the power of walking up the high street of his country town, with the knowledge that all its tradesmen would have gladly welcomed him within their doors. Other men arrived at those convictions in their start in life, and so worked up to them. To him they had come when they were too late to be of use.

It has been said that Mr. Arabin was a man of pleasantry; and it may be thought that such a state of mind as that described, would be antagonistic to humour. But surely such is not the case. Wit is the outward mental casing of the man, and has no more to do with the inner mind of thoughts and feelings than have the rich brocaded garments of the priest at the altar with the asceticism of the anchorite below them, whose skin is tormented with sackcloth, and whose body is half flayed with rods. Nay, will not such a one often rejoice more than any other in the rich show of his outer apparel? Will it not be food for his pride to feel that he groans inwardly, while he shines outwardly? So it is with the mental efforts which men make. Those which they show forth daily to the world are often the opposites of the inner workings of the spirit.

In the archdeacon's drawing-room, Mr. Arabin had sparkled with his usual unaffected brilliancy, but when he retired to his bed-room, he sat there sad, at his open window, repining within himself that he also had no wife, no bairns, no soft sward of lawn duly mown for him to lie on, no herd of attendant curates, no bowings from the banker's clerks, no rich rectory. That apostleship that he had thought of had evaded his grasp, and he was now only vicar of St. Ewold's, with a taste for a mitre. Truly he had fallen between two stools.

CHAP. XXI.

ST. EWOLD'S PARSONAGE.

WHEN Mr. Harding and Mrs. Bold reached the rectory on the following morning, the archdeacon and his friend were at St. Ewold's. They had gone over that the new vicar might inspect his church, and be introduced to the squire, and were not expected back before dinner. Mr. Harding rambled out by himself, and strolled, as was his wont at Plumstead, about the lawn and round the church; and as he did so, the two sisters naturally fell into conversation about Barchester.

There was not much sisterly confidence between them. Mrs. Grantly was ten years older than Eleanor, and had been married while Eleanor was yet a child. They had never, therefore, poured into each other's ears their hopes and loves; and now that one was a wife and the other a widow, it was not probable that they would begin to do so. They lived too much asunder to be able to fall into that kind of intercourse which makes confidence between sisters almost a necessity; and, moreover, that which is so easy at eighteen is often very difficult at twenty-eight. Mrs. Grantly knew this, and did not, therefore, expect confidence from her sister; and yet she longed to ask her whether in real truth Mr. Slope was agreeable to her.

It was by no means difficult to turn the conversation to Mr. Slope. That gentleman had become so famous at Barchester, had so much to do with all clergymen connected with the city, and was so specially concerned in the affairs of Mr. Harding, that it would have been odd if Mr. Harding's daughters had not talked about him. Mrs. Grantly was soon abusing him, which she did with her whole heart; and Mrs. Bold was nearly as eager to defend him. She positively disliked the man, would have been delighted to learn that he had taken himself off so that she should never see him again, had indeed almost a fear of him, and yet she constantly found herself taking his part. The abuse of other people, and abuse of a nature that she felt to be unjust, imposed this necessity on her, and at last made Mr. Slope's defence an habitual course of argument with her.

From Mr. Slope the conversation turned to the Stanhopes, and Mrs. Grantly was listening with some interest to Eleanor's account of the family, when it dropped out that Mr. Slope made one of the party.

"What!" said the lady of the rectory, "was Mr. Slope there too?"

Eleanor merely replied that such had been the case.

"Why, Eleanor, he must be very fond of you, I think; he seems to follow you everywhere."

Even this did not open Eleanor's eyes. She merely laughed, and said that she imagined Mr. Slope found other attraction at Dr. Stanhope's. And so they parted. Mrs. Grantly felt quite convinced that the odious match would take place; and Mrs. Bold as convinced that that unfortunate chaplain, disagreeable as he must be allowed to be, was more sinned against than sinning.

The archdeacon of course heard before dinner that Eleanor had remained the day before in Barchester with the view of meeting Mr. Slope, and that she had so met him. He remembered how she had positively stated that there were to be no guests at the Stanhopes, and he did not hesitate to accuse her of deceit. Moreover, the fact, or rather presumed fact, of her being deceitful on such a matter, spoke but too plainly in evidence against her as to her imputed crime of receiving Mr. Slope as a lover.

"I am afraid that anything we can do will be too late," said the archdeacon. "I own I am fairly surprised. I never liked your sister's taste with regard to men; but still I did not give her credit for —— ugh!"

"And so soon, too," said Mrs. Grantly, who thought more, perhaps, of her sister's indecorum in having a lover before she had put off her weeds, than her bad taste in having such a lover as Mr. Slope.

"Well, my dear, I shall be sorry to be harsh, or to do anything that can hurt your father; but, positively, neither that man nor his wife shall come within my doors."

Mrs. Grantly sighed, and then attempted to console herself and her lord by remarking that, after all, the thing was not accomplished yet. Now that Eleanor was at Plumstead, much might be done to wean her from her fatal passion. Poor Eleanor!

The evening passed off without anything to make it remarkable. Mr. Arabin discussed the parish of St. Ewold with the archdeacon, and Mrs. Grantly and Mr. Harding, who knew the personages of the parish, joined in. Eleanor also knew them, but she said little. Mr. Arabin did not apparently take much notice of her, and she was not in a humour to receive at that time with any special grace any special favourite of her brother-in-law. Her first idea on reaching her bed-room was that a much pleasanter family party might be met at Dr. Stanhope's than at the rectory. She began to think that she was getting tired of clergymen and their respectable humdrum wearisome mode of living, and that, after all, people in the outer world, who had lived in Italy, London, or elsewhere, need not necessarily be regarded as atrocious and abominable. The Stanhopes, she had thought, were a giddy, thoughtless, extravagant set of people; but she had seen nothing wrong about them, and had, on the other hand, found that they thoroughly knew how to make their house agreeable. It was a thousand pities, she thought, that the archdeacon should not have a little of the same *savoir vivre*. Mr. Arabin, as we have said, did not apparently take much notice of her; but yet he did not go to bed without feeling that he had been in company with a very pretty woman; and as is the case with most bachelors, and some married men, regarded the prospect of his month's visit at Plumstead in a pleasanter light, when he learnt that a very pretty woman was to share it with him.

Before they all retired it was settled that the whole party should drive over on the following day to inspect the parsonage at St. Ewold. The three clergymen were to discuss dilapidations, and the two ladies were to lend their assistance in suggesting such changes as might be necessary for a bachelor's abode. Accordingly, soon after breakfast, the carriage was at the door. There was only room for four inside, and the archdeacon got upon the box. Eleanor found herself opposite to Mr. Arabin, and was, therefore, in a manner forced into conversation with him. They were soon on comfortable terms together; and had she thought about it, she would have thought that, in spite of his black cloth, Mr. Arabin would not have been a bad addition to the Stanhope family party.

Now that the archdeacon was away, they could all trifle. Mr. Harding began by telling them in the most innocent manner imaginable an old legend about Mr. Arabin's new parish. There was, he said, in days of yore, an illustrious priestess of St. Ewold, famed through the whole country for curing all manner of diseases. She had a well, as all priestesses have ever had, which well was extant to this day, and shared in the minds of many of the people the sanctity which belonged to the consecrated ground of the parish church. Mr. Arabin declared that he should look on such tenets on the part of his parishioners as anything but orthodox. And Mrs. Grantly replied that she so entirely disagreed with him as to think that no parish was in a proper state that had not its priestess as well as its priest. "The duties are never well done," said she, "unless they are so divided."

"I suppose, papa," said Eleanor, "that in the olden times the priestess bore all the sway herself. Mr. Arabin, perhaps, thinks that such might be too much the case now if a sacred lady were admitted within the parish."

"I think, at any rate," said he, "that it is safer to run no such risk. No priestly pride has ever exceeded that of sacerdotal females. A very lowly curate I might, perhaps, essay to rule; but a curatess would be sure to get the better of me."

"There are certainly examples of such accidents happening, said Mrs. Grantly. "They do say that there is a priestess at Barchester who is very imperious in all things touching the altar. Perhaps the fear of such a fate as that is before your eyes."

When they were joined by the archdeacon on the gravel before the vicarage, they descended again to grave dulness. Not that Archdeacon Grantly was a dull man; but his frolic humours were of a cumbrous kind; and his wit, when he was witty, did not generally extend itself to his auditory. On the present occasion he was soon making speeches about wounded roofs and walls, which he declared to be in want of some surgeon's art. There was not a partition that he did not tap, nor a block of chimneys that he did not narrowly examine; all water-pipes, flues, cisterns, and sewers underwent an investigation; and he even descended, in the care of his friend, so far as to bore sundry boards in the floors with a bradawl.

Mr. Arabin accompanied him through the rooms, trying to look wise in such domestic matters, and the other three also followed. Mrs. Grantly showed that she had not herself been priestess of a parish twenty years for nothing, and examined the bells and window panes in a very knowing way.

" You will, at any rate, have a beautiful prospect out of your own window, if this is to be your private sanctum," said Eleanor. She was standing at the lattice of a little room up stairs, from which the view certainly was very lovely. It was from the back of the vicarage, and there was nothing to interrupt the eye between the house and the glorious gray pile of the cathedral. The intermediate ground, however, was beautifully studded with timber. In the immediate foreground ran the little river which afterwards skirted the city ; and, just to the right of the cathedral, the pointed gables and chimneys of Hiram's Hospital peeped out of the elms which encompass it.

" Yes," said he, joining her. " I shall have a beautifully complete view of my adversaries. I shall sit down before the hostile town, and fire away at them at a very pleasant distance. I shall just be able to lodge a shot in the hospital, should the enemy ever get possession of it ; and as for the palace, I have it within full range."

" I never saw anything like you clergymen," said Eleanor ; " you are always thinking of fighting each other."

" Either that," said he, " or else supporting each other. The pity is that we cannot do the one without the other. But are we not here to fight? Is not ours a church militant? What is all our work but fighting, and hard fighting, if it be well done ? "

" But not with each other."

" That's as it may be. The same complaint which you make of me for battling with another clergyman of our own church, the Mohammedan would make against me for battling with the error of a priest of Rome. Yet, surely, you would not be inclined to say that I should be wrong to do battle with such as him. A pagan, too, with his multiplicity of gods, would think it equally odd that the Christian and the Mohammedan should disagree."

" Ah! but you wage your wars about trifles so bitterly."

" Wars about trifles," said he, " are always bitter, especially among neighbours. When the differences are great, and the parties comparative strangers, men quarrel with courtesy. What combatants are ever so eager as two brothers ? "

" But do not such contentions bring scandal on the church ? "

" More scandal would fall on the church if there were no such contentions. We have but one way to avoid them — that of acknowledging a common head of our church, whose word on all points of doctrine shall be authoritative. Such a termination of our difficulties is alluring enough. It has charms which are irresistible to many, and all but irresistible, I own, to me."

"You speak now of the Church of Rome?" said Eleanor.

"No," said he, "not necessarily of the Church of Rome; but of *a* church with *a* head. Had it pleased God to vouchsafe to us such a church our path would have been easy. But easy paths have not been thought good for us." He paused and stood silent for a while, thinking of the time when he had so nearly sacrificed all he had, his powers of mind, his free agency, the fresh running waters of his mind's fountain, his very inner self, for an easy path in which no fighting would be needed; and then he continued: — "What you say is partly true; our contentions do bring on us some scandal. The outer world, though it constantly reviles us for our human infirmities, and throws in our teeth the fact that being clergymen we are still no more than men, demands of us that we should do our work with godlike perfection. There is nothing godlike about us: we differ from each other with the acerbity common to man — we triumph over each other with human frailty — we allow differences on subjects of divine origin to produce among us antipathies and enmities which are anything but divine. This is all true. But what would you have in place of it? There is no infallible head for a church on earth. This dream of believing man has been tried, and we see in Italy and in Spain what has come of it. Grant that there are and have been no bickerings within the pale of the Pope's Church. Such an assumption would be utterly untrue; but let us grant it, and then let us say which church has incurred the heavier scandals."

There was a quiet earnestness about Mr. Arabin, as he half acknowledged and half defended himself from the charge brought against him, which surprised Eleanor. She had been used all her life to listen to clerical discussion; but the points at issue between the disputants had so seldom been of more than temporal significance as to have left on her mind no feeling of reverence for such subjects. There had always been a hard worldly leaven of the love either of income or of power in the strains she had heard; there had been no panting for the truth; no aspirations after religious purity. It had always been taken for granted by those around her that they were indubitably right, that there was no ground for doubt, that the hard uphill work of ascertaining what the duty of a clergyman should be had been already accomplished in full; and that what remained for an active militant parson to do, was to hold his own against all comers. Her father, it is true, was an exception to this; but then he was so essentially antimilitant in all things, that she classed him in her own mind apart from all others. She had never argued the matter within herself, or considered whether this common tone was or was not faulty; but she was sick of it without knowing that she was so. And now she found to her surprise and not without a certain pleasurable excitement, that this new comer among them spoke in a manner very different from that to which she was accustomed.

"It is so easy to condemn," said he, continuing the thread of his thoughts "I know no life that must be so delicious as that of a writer for newspapers, or a leading member of the opposition — to thunder forth accusations against men in power; show up the worst side of everything that is produced; to pick holes in every coat; to be indignant, sarcastic, jocose, moral, or supercilious; to damn with faint praise, or crush with open calumny! What can be so easy as this when the critic has to be responsible for nothing? You condemn what I do; but put yourself in my position and do the reverse, and then see if I cannot condemn you."

"Oh! Mr. Arabin, I do not condemn you."

"Pardon me, you do, Mrs. Bold—you as one of the world; you are now the opposition member; you are now composing your leading article, and well and bitterly you do it. 'Let dogs delight to bark and bite;' you fitly begin with an elegant quotation; 'but if we are to have a church at all, in heaven's name let the pastors who preside over it keep their hands from each other's throats. Lawyers can live without befouling each other's names; doctors do not fight duels. Why is it that clergymen alone should indulge themselves in such unrestrained liberty of abuse against each other?' and so you go on reviling us for our ungodly quarrels, our sectarian propensities, and scandalous differences. It will, however, give you no trouble to write another article next week in which we, or some of us, shall be twitted with an unseemly apathy in matters of our vocation. It will not fall on you to reconcile the discrepancy; your readers will never ask you how the poor parson is to be urgent in season and out of season, and yet never come in contact with men who think widely differently from him. You, when you condemn this foreign treaty, or that official arrangement, will have to incur no blame for the graver faults of any different measure. It is so easy to condemn; and so pleasant too; for eulogy charms no listeners as detraction does."

Eleanor only half followed him in his raillery, but she caught his meaning. "I know I ought to apologise for presuming to criticise you," she said; "but I was thinking with sorrow of the ill-will that has lately come among us at Barchester, and I spoke more freely than I should have done."

"Peace on earth and good-will among men, are, like heaven.

promises for the future;" said he, following rather his own thoughts than hers. "When that prophecy is accomplished, there will no longer be any need for clergymen."

Here they were interrupted by the archdeacon, whose voice was heard from the cellar shouting to the vicar.

"Arabin, Arabin,"—and then turning to his wife, who was apparently at his elbow—"where has he gone to? This cellar is perfectly abominable. It would be murder to put a bottle of wine into it till it has been roofed, walled, and floored. How on earth old Goodenough ever got on with it, I cannot guess. But then Goodenough never had a glass of wine that any man could drink."

"What is it, archdeacon?" said the vicar, running down stairs, and leaving Eleanor above to her meditations.

"This cellar must be roofed, walled, and floored," repeated the archdeacon. "Now mind what I say, and don't let the architect persuade you that it will do; half of these fellows know nothing about wine. This place as it is now would be damp and cold in winter, and hot and muggy in summer. I wouldn't give a straw for the best wine that ever was vinted, after it had lain here a couple of years."

Mr. Arabin assented, and promised that the cellar should be reconstructed according to the archdeacon's receipt.

"And, Arabin, look here; was such an attempt at a kitchen grate ever seen?"

"The grate is really very bad," said Mrs. Grantly; "I am sure the priestess won't approve of it, when she is brought home to the scene of her future duties. Really, Mr. Arabin, no priestess accustomed to such an excellent well as that above could put up with such a grate as this."

"If there must be a priestess at St. Ewold's at all, Mrs. Grantly, I think we will leave her to her well, and not call down her divine wrath on any of the imperfections rising from our human poverty. However, I own I am amenable to the attractions of a well-cooked dinner, and the grate shall certainly be changed."

By this time the archdeacon had again ascended, and was now in the dining-room. "Arabin," said he, speaking in his usual loud clear voice, and with that tone of dictation which was so common to him; "you must positively alter this dining-room, that is, remodel it altogether; look here, it is just sixteen feet by fifteen; did anybody ever hear of a dining-room of such proportions!" and the archdeacon stepped the room long-ways and cross-ways with ponderous steps, as though a certain amount of ecclesiastical dignity could be imparted even to such an occupation as that by the manner of doing it. "Barely sixteen; you may call it a square."

"It would do very well for a round table," suggested the ex-warden.

Now there was something peculiarly unorthodox in the arch-deacon's estimation in the idea of a round table. He had always been accustomed to a goodly board of decent length, comfortably elongating itself according to the number of the guests, nearly black with perpetual rubbing, and as bright as a mirror. Now round dinner tables are generally of oak, or else of such new construction as not to have acquired the peculiar hue which was so pleasing to him. He connected them with what he called the nasty new fangled method of leaving a cloth on the table, as though to warn people that they were not to sit long. In his eyes there was something democratic and parvenue in a round table. He imagined that dissenters and calico-printers chiefly used them, and perhaps a few literary lions more conspicuous for their wit than their gentility. He was a little flurried at the idea of such an article being introduced into the diocese by a protégé of his own, and at the instigation of his father-in-law.

"A round dinner-table," said he, with some heat, "is the most abominable article of furniture that ever was invented. I hope that Arabin has more taste than to allow such a thing in his house."

Poor Mr. Harding felt himself completely snubbed, and of course said nothing further; but Mr. Arabin who had yielded submissively in the small matters of the cellar and kitchen grate, found himself obliged to oppose reforms which might be of a nature too expensive for his pocket.

"But it seems to me, archdeacon, that I can't very well lengthen the room without pulling down the wall, and if I pull down the wall, I must build it up again; then if I throw out a bow on this side, I must do the same on the other, then if I do it for the ground floor, I must carry it up to the floor above. That will be putting a new front to the house, and will cost, I suppose, a couple of hundred pounds. The ecclesiastical commissioners will hardly assist me when they hear that my grievance consists in having a dining room only sixteen feet long."

The archdeacon proceeded to explain that nothing would be easier than adding six feet to the front of the dining-room, without touching any other room in the house. Such irregularities of construction in small country houses were, he said, rather graceful than otherwise, and he offered to pay for the whole thing out of his own pocket if it cost more than forty pounds. Mr. Arabin, however, was firm, and, although the archdeacon fussed and fumed about it, would not give way.

Forty pounds, he said, was a matter of serious moment to him, and his friends, if under such circumstances they would be good-natured enough to come to him at all, must put up with the misery of a square room. He was willing to compromise matters by disclaiming any intention of having a round table.

"But," said Mrs. Grantly, "what if the priestess insists on having both the rooms enlarged?"

"The priestess in that case must do it for herself, Mrs. Grantly."

"I have no doubt she will be well able to do so," replied the lady; "to do that and many more wonderful things. I am quite sure that the priestess of St. Ewold, when she does come, won't come empty-handed."

Mr. Arabin, however, did not appear well inclined to enter into speculative expenses on such a chance as this, and therefore, any material alterations in the house, the cost of which could not fairly be made to lie at the door either of the ecclesiastical commissioners or of the estate of the late incumbent, were tabooed. With this essential exception, the archdeacon ordered, suggested, and carried all points before him in a manner very much to his own satisfaction. A close observer, had there been one there, might have seen that his wife had been quite as useful in the matter as himself. No one knew better than Mrs. Grantly the appurtenances necessary to a comfortable house. She did not, however, think it necessary to lay claim to any of the glory which her lord and master was so ready to appropriate as his own.

Having gone through their work effectually and systematically, the party returned to Plumstead well satisfied with their expedition.

CHAP. XXII.

THE THORNES OF ULLATHORNE.

On the following Sunday Mr. Arabin was to read himself in at his new church. It was agreed at the rectory that the archdeacon should go over with him and assist at the reading-desk, and that Mr. Harding should take the archdeacon's duty at Plumstead Church. Mrs. Grantly had her school and her buns to attend to, and professed that she could not be spared; but Mrs. Bold was to accompany them. It was further agreed also, that they would lunch at the squire's house, and return home after the afternoon service.

Wilfred Thorne, Esq., of Ullathorne, was the squire of St. Ewold's; or rather the squire of Ullathorne; for the domain of the modern landlord was of wider notoriety than the fame of the ancient saint. He was a fair specimen of what that race has come to in our days, which a century ago was, as we are told, fairly represented by Squire Western. If that representation be a true one, few classes of men can have made faster strides in improvement. Mr. Thorne, however, was a man possessed of quite a sufficient number of foibles to lay him open to much ridicule. He was still a bachelor, being about fifty, and was not a little proud of his person. When living at home at Ullathorne there was not much room for such pride, and there therefore he always looked like a gentleman, and like that which he certainly was, the first man in his parish. But during the month or six weeks which he annually spent in London, he tried so hard to look like a great man there also, which he certainly was not, that he was put down as a fool by many at his club. He was a man of considerable literary attainment in a certain way and on certain subjects. His favourite authors were Montaigne and Burton, and he knew more perhaps than any other man in his own county, and the next to it, of the English essayists of the two last centuries. He possessed complete sets of the "Idler," the "Spectator," the "Tatler," the "Guardian," and the "Rambler;" and would discourse by hours together on the superiority of such publications to anything which has since been produced in our Edinburghs and Quarterlies. He was a great proficient in all questions of genealogy, and knew enough of almost every gentleman's family in England to say of what blood and lineage were descended all those who had any claim to be considered as possessors of any such luxuries. For blood and lineage he himself had a most profound respect. He counted back his own ancestors to some period long antecedent to the Conquest; and could tell you, if you would listen to him, how it had come to pass that they, like Cedric the Saxon, had been permitted to hold their own among the Norman barons. It was not, according to his showing, on account of any weak complaisance on the part of his family towards their Norman neighbours. Some Ealfried of Ullathorne once fortified his own castle, and held out, not only that, but the then existing cathedral of Barchester also, against one Geoffrey De Burgh, in the time of King John; and Mr. Thorne possessed the whole history of the siege written on vellum, and illuminated in a most costly manner. It little signified that no one could read the writing, as, had that been possible, no one could have understood the language. Mr. Thorne could, however, give you all the particulars in good English, and had no objection to do so.

It would be unjust to say that he looked down on men whose families were of recent date. He did not do so. He frequently consorted with such, and had chosen many of his friends from among them. But he looked on them as great millionaires are apt to look on those who have small incomes; as men who have Sophocles at their fingers' ends regard those who know nothing of Greek. They might doubtless be good sort of people, entitled to much praise for virtue, very admirable for talent, highly respectable in every way; but they were without the one great good gift. Such was Mr. Thorne's way of thinking on this matter; nothing could atone for the loss of good blood; nothing could neutralise its good effects. Few indeed were now possessed of it, but the possession was on that account the more precious. It was very pleasant to hear Mr. Thorne descant on this matter. Were you in your ignorance to surmise that such a one was of a good family because the head of his family was a baronet of an old date, he would open his eyes with a delightful look of affected surprise, and modestly remind you that baronetcies only dated from James I. He would gently sigh if you spoke of the blood of the Fitzgeralds and De Burghs; would hardly allow the claims of the Howards and Lowthers; and has before now alluded to the Talbots as a family who had hardly yet achieved the full honours of a pedigree.

In speaking once of a wide spread race whose name had received the honours of three coronets, scions from which sat for various constituencies, some one of whose members had been in almost every cabinet formed during the present century, a brilliant race such as there are few in England, Mr. Thorne had called them all " dirt." He had not intended any disrespect to these men. He admired them in many senses, and allowed them their privileges without envy. He had merely meant to express his feeling that the streams which ran through their veins were not yet purified by time to that perfection, had not become so genuine an ichor, as to be worthy of being called blood in the genealogical sense.

When Mr. Arabin was first introduced to him, Mr. Thorne had immediately suggested that he was one of the Arabins of Uphill Stanton. Mr. Arabin replied that he was a very distant relative of the family alluded to. To this Mr. Thorne surmised that the relationship could not be very distant. Mr. Arabin assured him that it was so distant that the families knew nothing of each other. Mr. Thorne laughed his gentle laugh at this, and told Mr. Arabin that there was now existing no branch of his family separated from the parent stock at an earlier date than the reign of Elizabeth; and that therefore Mr. Arabin could not call himself distant. Mr. Arabin himself was quite clearly an Arabin of Uphill Stanton.

"But," said the vicar, "Uphill Stanton has been sold to the De Greys, and has been in their hands for the last fifty years."

"And when it has been there one hundred and fifty, if it unluckily remain there so long," said Mr. Thorne, "your descendants will not be a whit the less entitled to describe themselves as being of the family of Uphill Stanton. Thank God, no De Grey can buy that — and, thank God — no Arabin. and no Thorne, can sell it."

In politics, Mr. Thorne was an unflinching conservative. He looked on those fifty-three Trojans, who, as Mr. Dod tells us, censured free trade in November, 1852, as the only patriots left among the public men of England. When that terrible crisis of free trade had arrived, when the repeal of the corn laws was carried by those very men whom Mr. Thorne had hitherto regarded as the only possible saviours of his country, he was for a time paralysed. His country was lost; but that was comparatively a small thing. Other countries had flourished and fallen, and the human race still went on improving under God's providence. But now all trust in human faith must for ever be at an end. Not only must ruin come, but it must come through the apostasy of those who had been regarded as the truest of true believers. Politics in England, as a pursuit for gentlemen, must be at an end. Had Mr. Thorne been trodden under foot by a Whig, he could have borne it as a Tory and a martyr; but to be so utterly thrown over and deceived by those he had so earnestly supported, so thoroughly trusted, was more than he could endure and live. He therefore ceased to live as a politician, and refused to hold any converse with the world at large on the state of the country.

Such were Mr. Thorne's impressions for the first two or three years after Sir Robert Peel's apostasy; but by degrees his temper, as did that of others, cooled down. He began once more to move about, to frequent the bench and the market, and to be seen at dinners, shoulder to shoulder with some of those who had so cruelly betrayed him. It was a necessity for him to live, and that plan of his for avoiding the world did not answer. He, however, and others around him who still maintained the same staunch principles of protection — men like himself, who were too true to flinch at the cry of a mob — had their own way of consoling themselves. They were, and felt themselves to be, the only true depositaries left of certain Eleusinian mysteries, of certain deep and wondrous services of worship by which alone the gods could be rightly approached. To them and them only was it now given to know these things, and to perpetuate them, if that might still be done, by the careful and secret education of their children.

We have read how private and peculiar forms of worship have been carried on from age to age in families, which to the outer world have apparently adhered to the services of some ordinary church. And so by degrees it was with Mr. Thorne. He learnt at length to listen calmly while protection was talked of as a thing dead, although he knew within himself that it was still quick with a mystic life. Nor was he without a certain pleasure that such knowledge though given to him should be debarred from the multitude. He became accustomed to hear, even among country gentlemen, that free trade was after all not so bad, and to hear this without dispute, although conscious within himself that everything good in England had gone with his old palladium. He had within him something of the feeling of Cato, who gloried that he could kill himself because Romans were no longer worthy of their name. Mr. Thorne had no thought of killing himself, being a Christian, and still possessing his 4000*l.* a year ; but the feeling was not on that account the less comfortable.

Mr. Thorne was a sportsman, and had been active though not outrageous in his sports. Previous to the great downfall of politics in his county, he had supported the hunt by every means in his power. He had preserved game till no goose or turkey could show a tail in the parish of St. Ewold's. He had planted gorse covers with more care than oaks and larches. He had been more anxious for the comfort of his foxes than of his ewes and lambs. No meet had been more popular than Ullathorne ; no man's stables had been more liberally open to the horses of distant men than Mr. Thorne's; no man had said more, written more, or done more to keep the club up. The theory of protection could expand itself so thoroughly in the practices of a county hunt ! But when the great ruin came ; when the noble master of the Barsetshire hounds supported the recreant minister in the House of Lords, and basely surrendered his truth, his manhood, his friends, and his honour for the hope of a garter, then Mr. Thorne gave up the hunt. He did not cut his covers, for that would not have been the act of a gen·

tleman. He did not kill his foxes, for that according to his light would have been murder. He did not say that his covers should not be drawn, or his earths stopped, for that would have been illegal according to the by-laws prevailing among country gentlemen. But he absented himself from home on the occasion of every meet at Ullathorne, left the covers to their fate, and could not be persuaded to take his pink coat out of the press, or his hunters out of his stable. This lasted for two years, and then by degrees he came round. He first appeared at a neighbouring meet on a pony, dressed in his shooting coat, as though he had trotted in by accident; then he walked up one morning on foot to see his favourite gorse drawn, and when his groom brought his mare out by chance, he did not refuse to mount her. He was next persuaded, by one of the immortal fifty-three, to bring his hunting materials over to the other side of the county, and take a fortnight with the hounds there; and so gradually he returned to his old life. But in hunting as in other things he was only supported by an inward feeling of mystic superiority to those with whom he shared the common breath of outer life.

Mr. Thorne did not live in solitude at Ullathorne. He had a sister, who was ten years older than himself, and who participated in his prejudices and feelings so strongly, that she was a living caricature of all his foibles. She would not open a modern quarterly, did not choose to see a magazine in her drawing-room, and would not have polluted her fingers with a shred of the "Times" for any consideration. She spoke of Addison, Swift, and Steele, as though they were still living, regarded De Foe as the best known novelist of his country, and thought of Fielding as a young but meritorious novice in the fields of romance. In poetry, she was familiar with names as late as Dryden, and had once been seduced into reading the "Rape of the Lock;" but she regarded Spenser as the purest type of her country's literature in this line. Genealogy was her favourite insanity. Those things which are the pride of most genealogists were to her contemptible. Arms and mottoes set her beside herself. Ealfried of Ullathorne had wanted no motto to assist him in cleaving to the brisket Geoffrey De Burgh; and Ealfried's great grandfather, the gigantic Ullafrid, had required no other arms than those which nature gave him to hurl from the top of his own castle a cousin of the base invading Norman. To her all modern English names were equally insignificant: Hengist, Horsa, and such like, had for her ears the only true savour of nobility. She was not contented unless she could go beyond the Saxons; and would certainly have christened her children, had she had children, by the names of the ancient Britons. In some respects she was not unlike Scott's Ulrica, and had she been given to cursing, she would certainly have done so in the names of Mista, Skogula, and Zernebock. Not having submitted to the embraces of any polluting Norman, as poor Ulrica had done, and having assisted no parricide, the milk of human kindness was not curdled in her bosom. She never cursed, therefore, but blessed rather. This, however, she did in a strange uncouth Saxon manner that would have been unintelligible to any peasants but her own.

As a politician, Miss Thorne had been so thoroughly disgusted with public life by base deeds long antecedent to the Corn Law question, that that had but little moved her. In her estimation her brother had been a fast young man, hurried away by a too ardent temperament into democratic tendencies. Now happily he was brought to sounder views by seeing the iniquity of the world. She had not yet reconciled herself to the Reform Bill, and still groaned in spirit over the defalcations of the Duke as touching the Catholic Emancipation. If asked whom she thought the Queen should take as her counsellor, she would probably have named Lord Eldon ; and when reminded that that venerable man was no longer present in the flesh to assist us, she would probably have answered with a sigh that none now could help us but the dead.

In religion, Miss Thorne was a pure Druidess. We would not have it understood by that, that she did actually in these latter days assist at any human sacrifices, or that she was in fact hostile to the Church of Christ. She had adopted the Christian religion as a milder form of the worship of her ancestors, and always appealed to her doing so as evidence that she had no prejudices against reform, when it could be shown that reform was salutary. This reform was the most modern of any to which she had as yet acceded, it being presumed that British ladies had given up their paint and taken to some sort of petticoats before the days of St. Augustine. That further feminine step in advance which combines paint and petticoats together, had not found a votary in Miss Thorne.

But she was a Druidess in this, that she regretted she knew not what in the usages and practices of her Church. She sometimes talked and constantly thought of good things gone by, though she had but the faintest idea of what those good things had been. She imagined that a purity had existed which was now gone ; that a piety had adorned our pastors and a simple docility our people, for which it may be feared history gave her but little true warrant. She was accustomed to speak of Cranmer as though he had been the firmest and most simple-minded of martyrs, and of Elizabeth as though the pure Protestant faith of her people had been the one anxiety of her life. It would have been cruel to undeceive her, had it been possible; but it would have been impossible to make her believe that the one was a time-serving priest, willing to go any length to keep his place, and that the other was in heart a papist, with this sole proviso, that she should be her own pope.

And so Miss Thorne went on sighing and regretting, looking back to the divine right of kings as the ruling axiom of a golden age, and cherishing, low down in the bottom of her heart of hearts, a dear unmentioned wish for the restoration of some exiled Stuart. Who would deny her the luxury of her sighs, or the sweetness of her soft regrets!

In her person and her dress she was perfect, and well she knew her own perfection. She was a small elegantly made old woman, with a face from which the glow of her youth had not departed without leaving some streaks of a roseate hue. She was proud of her colour, proud of her grey hair which she wore in short crisp curls peering out all around her face from the dainty white lace cap. To think of all the money that she spent in lace used to break the heart of poor Mrs. Quiverful with her seven daughters. She was proud of her teeth, which were still white and numerous, proud of her bright cheery eye, proud of her short jaunty step, and very proud of the neat, precise, small feet with which those steps were taken. She was proud also, ay, very proud, of the rich brocaded silk in which it was her custom to ruffle through her drawing-room.

We know what was the custom of the lady of Branksome—

> "Nine-and-twenty knights of fame
> Hung their shields in Branksome Hall."

The lady of Ullathorne was not so martial in her habits, but hardly less costly. She might have boasted that nine-and-twenty silken skirts might have been produced in her chamber, each fit to stand alone. The nine-and-twenty shields of the Scottish heroes were less independent, and hardly more potent to withstand any attack that might be made on them. Miss Thorne when fully dressed might be said to have been armed cap-a-pie, and she was always fully dressed, as far as was ever known to mortal man.

For all this rich attire Miss Thorne was not indebted to the generosity of her brother. She had a very comfortable independence of her own, which she divided among juvenile relatives, the milliners, and the poor, giving much the largest share to the latter. It may be imagined, therefore, that with all her little follies she was not unpopular. All her follies have, we believe, been told. Her virtues were too numerous to describe, and not sufficiently interesting to deserve description.

While we are on the subject of the Thornes, one word must be said of the house they lived in. It was not a large house, nor a fine house, nor perhaps to modern ideas a very commodious house ; but by those who love the peculiar colour and peculiar ornaments of genuine Tudor architecture it was considered a perfect gem. We beg to own ourselves among the number, and therefore take this opportunity to express our surprise that so little is known by English men and women of the beauties of English architecture. The ruins of the Colosseum, the Campanile at Florence, St. Mark's, Cologne, the Bourse and Notre Dame, are with our tourists as familiar as household words ; but they know nothing of the glories of Wiltshire, Dorsetshire, and Somersetshire. Nay, we much question whether many noted travellers, men who have pitched their tents perhaps under Mount Sinai, are not still ignorant that there are glories in Wiltshire, Dorsetshire, and Somersetshire. We beg that they will go and see.

Mr. Thorne's house was called Ullathorne Court, and was properly so called ; for the house itself formed two sides of a quadrangle, which was completed on the other two sides by a wall about twenty feet high. This wall was built of cut stone, rudely cut indeed, and now much worn, but of a beautiful rich tawny yellow colour, the effect of that stonecrop of minute growth, which it had taken three centuries to produce. The top of this wall was ornamented by huge round stone balls of the same colour as the wall itself. Entrance into the court was had through a pair of iron gates, so massive that no one could comfortably open or close them, consequently they were rarely disturbed. From the gateway two paths led obliquely across the court ; that to the left reaching the hall-door, which was in the corner made by the angle of the house, and that to the right leading to the back entrance, which was at the further end of the longer portion of the building.

With those who are now adepts in contriving house accommodation, it will militate much against Ullathorne Court, that no carriage could be brought to the hall-door. If you enter Ullathorne at all, you must do so, fair reader, on foot, or at least in a bath-chair. No vehicle drawn by horses ever comes within that iron gate. But this is nothing to the next horror that will encounter you. On entering the front door, which you do by no very grand portal, you find yourself immediately in the dining-room. What,—no hall? exclaims my luxurious friend, accustomed to all the comfortable appurtenances of modern life. Yes, kind sir ; a noble hall, if you will but observe it; a true old English hall of excellent dimensions for a country gentleman's family ; but, if you please, no dining-parlour.

Both Mr. and Miss Thorne were proud of this peculiarity of their dwelling, though the brother was once all but tempted by his friends to alter it. They delighted in the knowledge that they, like Cedric, positively dined in their true hall, even though they so dined tête-à-tête. But though they had never owned, they had felt and endeavoured to remedy the discomfort of such an arrangement. A huge screen partitioned off the front door and a portion of the hall, and from the angle so screened off a second door led into a passage, which ran along the larger side of the house next to the courtyard. Either my reader or I must be a bad hand at topography, if it be not clear that the great hall forms the ground-floor of the smaller portion of the mansion, that which was to your left as you entered the iron gate, and that it occupies the whole of this wing of the building. It must be equally clear that it looks out on a trim mown lawn, through three quadrangular windows with stone mullions, each window divided into a larger portion at the bottom, and a smaller portion at the top, and each portion again divided into five by perpendicular stone supporters. There may be windows which give a better light than such as these, and it may be, as my utilitarian friend observes, that the giving of light is the desired object of a window. I will not argue the point with him. Indeed I cannot. But I shall not the less die in the assured conviction that no sort or description of window is capable of imparting half so much happiness to mankind as that which had been adopted at Ullathorne Court. What—not an oriel? says Miss Diana de Midellage. No, Miss Diana ; not even an oriel, beautiful as is an oriel window. It has not about it so perfect a feeling of quiet English homely comfort. Let oriel windows grace a college, or the half public mansion of a potent peer ; but for the sitting room of quiet country ladies, of ordinary homely folk, nothing can equal the square mullioned windows of the Tudor architects.

The hall was hung round with family female insipidities by Lely, and unprepossessing male Thornes in red coats by Kneller ; each Thorne having been let into a panel in the wainscoting, in the proper manner. At the further end of the room was a huge fire-place, which afforded much ground of difference between the brother and sister. An antiquated grate that would hold about a hundred weight of coal, had been stuck on to the hearth, by Mr. Thorne's father. This hearth had of course been intended for the consumption of wood fagots, and the iron dogs for the purpose were still standing, though half buried in the masonry of the grate. Miss Thorne was very anxious to revert to the dogs. The dear good old creature was always glad to revert to anything, and had she been systematically indulged, would doubtless in time have reflected that fingers were made before forks, and have reverted accordingly. But in the affairs of the fire-place, Mr. Thorne would not revert. Country gentlemen around him, all had comfortable grates in their dining-rooms. He was not exactly the man to have suggested a modern usage; but he was not so far prejudiced as to banish those which his father had prepared for his use. Mr. Thorne had, indeed, once suggested that with very little contrivance the front door might have been so altered, as to open at least into the passage; but on hearing this, his sister Monica, such was Miss Thorne's name, had been taken ill, and had remained so for a week. Before she came down stairs she received a pledge from her brother that the entrance should never be changed in her lifetime.

At the end of the hall opposite to the fire-place a door led into the drawing-room, which was of equal size, and lighted with precisely similar windows. But yet the aspect of the room was very different. It was papered, and the ceiling, which in the hall showed the old rafters, was whitened and finished with a modern cornice. Miss Thorne's drawing-room, or, as she always called it, withdrawing-room, was a beautiful apartment. The windows opened on to the full extent of the lovely trim garden; immediately before the windows were plots of flowers in stiff, stately, stubborn little beds, each bed surrounded by a stone coping of its own; beyond, there was a low parapet wall, on which stood urns and images, fawns, nymphs, satyrs, and a whole tribe of Pan's followers; and then again, beyond that, a beautiful lawn sloped away to a sunk fence which divided the garden from the park. Mr. Thorne's study was at the end of the drawing-room, and beyond that were the kitchen and the offices. Doors opened into both Miss Thorne's withdrawing-room and Mr. Thorne's sanctum from the passage above alluded to; which, as it came to the latter room, widened itself so as to make space for the huge black oak stairs, which led to the upper regions.

Such was the interior of Ullathorne Court. But having thus described it, perhaps somewhat too tediously, we beg to say that it is not the interior to which we wish to call the English tourist's attention, though we advise him to lose no legitimate opportunity of becoming acquainted with it in a friendly manner. It is the outside of Ullathorne that is so lovely. Let the tourist get admission at least into the garden, and fling himself on that soft sward just opposite to the exterior angle of the house. He will there get the double frontage, and enjoy that which is so lovely — the expanse of architectural beauty without the formal dulness of one long line.

It is the colour of Ullathorne that is so remarkable. It is all of that delicious tawny hue which no stone can give, unless it has on it the vegetable richness of centuries. Strike the wall with your hand, and you will think that the stone has on it no covering, but rub it carefully, and you will find that the colour comes off upon your finger. No colourist that ever yet worked from a palette has been able to come up to this rich colouring of years crowding themselves on years.

Ullathorne is a high building for a country house, for it possesses three stories; and in each story, the windows are of the same sort as that described, though varying in size, and varying also in their lines athwart the house. Those of the ground floor are all uniform in size and position. But those above are irregular both in size and place, and this irregularity gives a bizarre and not unpicturesque appearance to the building. Along the top, on every side, runs a low parapet, which nearly hides the roof, and at the corners are more figures of fawns and satyrs.

Such is Ullathorne House. But we must say one word of the approach to it, which shall include all the description which we mean to give of the church also. The picturesque old church of St. Ewold's stands immediately opposite to the iron gates which open into the court, and is all but surrounded by the branches of the lime trees, which form the avenue leading up to the house from both sides. This avenue is magnificent, but it would lose much of its value in the eyes of many proprietors, by the fact that the road through it is not private property. It is a public lane between hedge rows, with a broad grass margin on each side of the road, from which the lime trees spring. Ullathorne Court, therefore, does not stand absolutely surrounded by its own grounds, though Mr. Thorne is owner of all the adjacent land. This, however, is the source of very little annoyance to him. Men, when they are acquiring property, think much of such things, but they who live where their ancestors have lived for years, do not feel the misfortune. It never occurred either to Mr. or Miss Thorne that they were not sufficiently private, because the world at large might, if it so wished, walk or drive by their iron gates. That part of the world which availed itself of the privilege was however very small.

Such a year or two since were the Thornes of Ullathorne. Such, we believe, are the inhabitants of many an English country home. May it be long before their number diminishes.

CHAP. XXIII.

MR. ARABIN READS HIMSELF IN AT ST. EWOLD'S.

ON the Sunday morning the archdeacon with his sister-in-law and Mr Arabin drove over to Ullathorne, as had been arranged. On their way thither the new vicar declared himself to be considerably disturbed in his mind at the idea of thus facing his parishioners for the first time. He had, he said, been always subject to *mauvaise honte* and an annoying degree of bashfulness, which often unfitted him for any work of a novel description; and now he felt this so strongly that he feared he should acquit himself badly in St. Ewold's reading-desk. He knew, he said, that those sharp little eyes of Miss Thorne would be on him, and that they would not approve. All this the archdeacon greatly ridiculed. He himself knew not, and had never known, what it was to be shy. He could not conceive that Miss Thorne, surrounded as she would be by the peasants of Ullathorne and a few of the poorer inhabitants of the suburbs of Barchester, could in any way affect the composure of a man well accustomed to address the learned congregation of St. Mary's at Oxford, and he laughed accordingly at the idea of Mr. Arabin's modesty.

Thereupon Mr. Arabin commenced to subtilise. The change, he said, from St. Mary's to St. Ewold's was quite as powerful on the spirits as would be that from St. Ewold's to St. Mary's. Would not a peer who, by chance of fortune, might suddenly be driven to herd among navvies be as afraid of the jeers of his companions, as would any navvy suddenly exalted to a seat among the peers? Whereupon the archdeacon declared with a loud laugh that he would tell Miss Thorne that her new minister had likened her to a navvy. Eleanor, however, pronounced such a conclusion to be unfair; a comparison might be very just in its proportions which did not at all assimilate the things compared. But Mr. Arabin went on subtilising, regarding neither the archdeacon's raillery nor Eleanor's defence. A young lady, he said, would execute with most perfect self-possession a difficult piece of music in a room crowded with strangers, who would not be able to express herself in intelligible language, even on any ordinary subject and among her most intimate friends, if she were required to do so standing on a box somewhat elevated among them. It was all an affair of education, and he at forty found it difficult to educate himself anew.

Eleanor dissented on the matter of the box; and averred she could speak very well about dresses, or babies, or legs of mutton from any box, provided it were big enough for her to stand upon without fear, even though all her friends were listening to her The archdeacon was sure she would not be able to say a word, but this proved nothing in favour of Mr. Arabin. Mr. Arabin said that he would try the question out with Mrs. Bold, and get her on a box some day when the rectory might be full of visitors. To this Eleanor assented, making condition that the visitors should be of their own set, and the archdeacon cogitated in his mind, whether by such a condition it was intended that Mr. Slope should be included, resolving also that, if so, the trial would certainly never take place in the rectory drawing-room at Plumstead.

And so arguing, they drove up to the iron gates of Ullathorne Court.

Mr. and Miss Thorne were standing ready dressed for church in the hall, and greeted their clerical visitors with cordiality. The archdeacon was an old favourite. He was a clergyman of the old school, and this recommended him to the lady. He had always been an opponent of free trade as long as free trade was an open question; and now that it was no longer so, he, being a clergyman, had not been obliged, like most of his lay Tory companions, to read his recantation. He could therefore be regarded as a supporter of the immaculate fifty-three, and was on this account a favourite with Mr. Thorne. The little bell was tinkling, and the rural population of the parish were standing about the lane, leaning on the church stile, and against the walls of the old court, anxious to get a look at their new minister as he passed from the house to the rectory. The archdeacon's servant had already preceded them thither with the vestments.

They all went forth together; and when the ladies passed into the church the three gentlemen tarried a moment in the lane, that Mr. Thorne might name to the vicar with some kind of one-sided introduction, the most leading among his parishioners.

"Here are our churchwardens, Mr. Arabin; Farmer Greenacre and Mr. Stiles. Mr. Stiles has the mill as you go into Barchester; and very good churchwardens they are."

"Not very severe, I hope," said Mr. Arabin: the two ecclesiastical officers touched their hats, and each made a leg in the approved rural fashion, assuring the vicar that they were very glad to have the honour of seeing him, and adding that the weather was very good for the harvest. Mr. Stiles being a man somewhat versed in town life, had an impression of his own dignity, and did not quite like leaving his pastor under the erroneous idea that he being a churchwarden kept the children in order during church time. 'Twas thus he understood Mr. Arabin's allusion to his severity, and hastened to put matters right by observing that "Sexton Clodheve looked to the younguns, and perhaps sometimes there may be a thought too much stick going on during sermon." Mr. Arabin's bright eye twinkled as he caught that of the archdeacon's; and he smiled to himself as he observed how ignorant his officers were of the nature of their authority, and of the surveillance which it was their duty to keep even over himself.

Mr. Arabin read the lessons and preached. It was enough to put a man a little out, let him have been ever so used to pulpit reading, to see the knowing way in which the farmers cocked their ears, and set about a mental criticism as to whether their new minister did or did not fall short of the excellence of him who had lately departed from them. A mental and silent criticism it was for the existing moment, but soon to be made public among the elders of St. Ewold's over the green graves of their children and forefathers. The excellence, however, of poor old Mr. Goodenough had not been wonderful, and there were few there who did not deem that Mr. Arabin did his work sufficiently well, in spite of the slightly nervous affection which at first impeded him, and which nearly drove the archdeacon beside himself.

But the sermon was the thing to try the man. It often surprises us that very young men can muster courage to preach for the first time to a strange congregation. Men who are as yet but little more than boys, who have but just left, what indeed we may not call a school, but a seminary intended for their tuition as scholars, whose thoughts have been mostly of boating, cricketing, and wine parties, ascend a rostrum high above the heads of the submissive crowd, not that they may read God's word to those below, but that they may preach their own word for the edification of their hearers. It seems strange to us that they are not stricken dumb by the new and awful solemnity of their position. How am I, just turned twenty-three, who have never yet passed ten thoughtful days since the power of thought first came to me, how am I to instruct these greybeards, who with the weary thinking of so many years have approached so near the grave ? Can I teach them their duty ? Can I explain to them that which I so imperfectly understand, that which years of study may have made so plain to them ? Has my newly acquired privilege, as one of God's ministers, imparted to me as yet any fitness for the wonderful work of a preacher ?

It must be supposed that such ideas do occur to young clergymen, and yet they overcome, apparently with ease, this difficulty which to us appears to be all but insurmountable. We have never been subjected in the way of ordination to the power of a bishop's hands. It may be that there is in them something that sustains the spirit and banishes the natural modesty of youth. But for ourselves we must own that the deep affection which Dominie Sampson felt for his young pupils has not more endeared him to us than the bashful spirit which sent him mute and inglorious from the pulpit when he rose there with the futile attempt to preach God's gospel.

There is a rule in our church which forbids the younger order of our clergymen to perform a certain portion of the service. The absolution must be read by a minister in priest's orders. If there be no such minister present, the congregation can have the benefit of no absolution but that which each may succeed in administering to himself. The rule may be a good one, though the necessity for it hardly comes home to the general understanding. But this forbearance on the part of youth would be much more appreciated if it were extended likewise to sermons. The only danger would be that congregations would be too anxious to prevent their young clergymen from advancing themselves in the ranks of the ministry. Clergymen who could not preach would be such blessings that they would be bribed to adhere to their incompetence.

Mr. Arabin, however, had not the modesty of youth to impede him, and he succeeded with his sermon even better than with the lessons. He took for his text two verses out of the second epistle of St. John, "Whosoever transgresseth, and abideth not in the doctrine of Christ, hath not God. He that abideth in the doctrine of Christ he hath both the Father and Son. If there come any unto you and bring not this doctrine, receive him not into your house, neither bid him God speed." He told them that the house of theirs to which he alluded was this their church in which he now addressed them for the first time; that their most welcome and proper manner of bidding him God speed would be their patient obedience to his teaching of the gospel; but that he could put forward no claim to such conduct on their part unless he taught them the great Christian doctrine of works and faith combined. On this he enlarged, but not very amply, and after twenty minutes succeeded in sending his new friends home to their baked mutton and pudding well pleased with their new minister.

Then came the lunch at Ullathorne. As soon as they were in the hall Miss Thorne took Mr. Arabin's hand, and assured him that she received him into her house, into the temple, she said, in which she worshipped, and bade him God speed with all her heart. Mr. Arabin was touched, and squeezed the spinster's hand without uttering a word in reply. Then Mr. Thorne expressed a hope that Mr. Arabin found the church easy to fill, and Mr. Arabin having replied that he had no doubt he should do so as soon as he had learnt to pitch his voice to the building, they all sat down to the good things before them.

Miss Thorne took special care of Mrs. Bold. Eleanor still wore her widow's weeds, and therefore had about her that air of grave and sad maternity which is the lot of recent widows. This opened the soft heart of Miss Thorne, and made her look on her young guest as though too much could not be done for her. She heaped chicken and ham upon her plate, and poured out for her a full bumper of port wine. When Eleanor, who was not sorry to get it, had drunk a little of it, Miss Thorne at once essayed to fill it again. To this Eleanor objected, but in vain. Miss Thorne winked and nodded and whispered, saying that it was the proper thing and must be done, and that she knew all about it; and so she desired Mrs. Bold to drink it up, and not mind any body.

"It is your duty, you know, to support yourself," she said into the ear of the young mother; "there's more than yourself depending on it;" and thus she coshered up Eleanor with cold fowl and port wine. How it is that poor men's wives, who have no cold fowl and port wine on which to be coshered up, nurse their children without difficulty, whereas the wives of rich men, who eat and drink everything that is good, cannot do so, we will for the present leave to the doctors and the mothers to settle between them.

And then Miss Thorne was great about teeth. Little Johnny Bold had been troubled for the last few days with his first incipient masticator, and, with that freemasonry which exists among ladies, Miss Thorne became aware of the fact before Eleanor had half finished her wing.   The old lady prescribed at once a receipt which had been much in vogue in the young days of her grandmother, and warned Eleanor with solemn voice against the fallacies of modern medicine.

"Take his coral, my dear," said she, "and rub it well with carrot-juice; rub it till the juice dries on it, and then give it him to play with ——"

"But he hasn't got a coral," said Eleanor.

"Not got a coral!" said Miss Thorne, with almost angry vehemence.   "Not got a coral — how can you expect that he should cut his teeth ?   Have you got Daffy's Elixir ? "

Eleanor explained that she had not.   It had not been ordered by Mr. Rerechild, the Barchester doctor whom she employed ; and then the young mother mentioned some shockingly modern succedaneum, which Mr. Rerechild's new lights had taught him to recommend.

Miss Thorne looked awfully severe.   "Take care, my dear," said she, "that the man knows what he's about; take care he doesn't destroy your little boy.   But " — and she softened into sorrow as she said it, and spoke more in pity than in anger — "but I don't know who there is in Barchester now that you can trust.   Poor dear old Doctor Bumpwell, indeed ——"

"Why, Miss Thorne, he died when I was a little girl."

"Yes, my dear, he did, and an unfortunate day it was for Barchester.   As to those young men that have come up since" (Mr. Rerechild, by the bye, was quite as old as Miss Thorne herself), "one doesn't know where they came from or who they are, or whether they know anything about their business or not."

"I think there are very clever men in Barchester," said Eleanor.

"Perhaps there may be ; only I don't know them; and it's admitted on all sides that medical men arn't now what they used to be. They used to be talented, observing, educated men.   But now any whipper-snapper out of an apothecary's shop can call himself a doctor.   I believe no kind of education is now thought necessary."

Eleanor was herself the widow of a medical man, and felt a little inclined to resent all these hard sayings.   But Miss Thorne was so essentially good-natured that it was impossible to resent anything she said.   She therefore sipped her wine and finished her chicken.

"At any rate, my dear, don't forget the carrot-juice, and by all means get him a coral at once.   My grandmother Thorne had the best teeth in the county, and carried them to the grave with her at eighty. I have heard her say it was all the carrot-juice. She couldn't bear the Barchester doctors. Even poor old Dr. Bumpwell didn't please her." It clearly never occurred to Miss Thorne that some fifty years ago Dr. Bumpwell was only a rising man, and therefore as much in need of character in the eyes of the then ladies of Ullathorne, as the present doctors were in her own.

The archdeacon made a very good lunch, and talked to his host about turnip-drillers and new machines for reaping; while the host, thinking it only polite to attend to a stranger, and fearing that perhaps he might not care about turnip crops on a Sunday, mooted all manner of ecclesiastical subjects.

"I never saw a heavier lot of wheat, Thorne, than you've got there in that field beyond the copse. I suppose that's guano," said the archdeacon.

"Yes, guano. I get it from Bristol myself. You'll find you often have a tolerable congregation of Barchester people out here, Mr. Arabin. They are very fond of St. Ewold's, particularly of an afternoon, when the weather is not too hot for the walk."

"I am under an obligation to them for staying away to-day, at any rate," said the vicar. "The congregation can never be too small for a maiden sermon."

"I got a ton and a half at Bradley's in High Street," said the archdeacon, "and it was a complete take in. I don't believe there was five hundred-weight of guano in it."

"That Bradley never has anything good," said Miss Thorne, who had just caught the name during her whisperings with Eleanor. "And such a nice shop as there used to be in that very house before he came. Wilfred, don't you remember what good things old Ambleoff used to have?"

"There have been three men since Ambleoff's time," said the archdeacon, "and each as bad as the other. But who gets it for you at Bristol, Thorne?"

"I ran up myself this year and bought it out of the ship. I am afraid as the evenings get shorter, Mr. Arabin, you'll find the reading desk too dark. I must send a fellow with an axe and make him lop off some of those branches."

Mr. Arabin declared that the morning light at any rate was perfect, and deprecated any interference with the lime trees. And then they took a stroll out among the trim parterres, and Mr. Arabin explained to Mrs. Bold the difference between a naiad and a dryad, and dilated on vases and the shapes of urns. Miss Thorne busied herself among her pansies; and her brother, finding it quite impracticable to give anything of a peculiarly Sunday tone to the conversation, abandoned the attempt, and had it out with the archdeacon about the Bristol guano.

At three o'clock they again went into church; and now Mr. Arabin read the service and the archdeacon preached. Nearly the same congregation was present, with some adventurous pedestrians from the city, who had not thought the heat of the mid-day August sun too great to deter them. The archdeacon took his text from the Epistle to Philemon. " I beseech thee for my son Onesimus, whom I have begotten in my bonds." From such a text it may be imagined the kind of sermon which Dr. Grantly preached, and on the whole it was neither dull, nor bad, nor out of place.

He told them that it had become his duty to look about for a pastor for them, to supply the place of one who had been long among them; and that in this manner he regarded as a son him whom he had selected, as St. Paul had regarded the young disciple whom he sent forth. Then he took a little merit to himself for having studiously provided the best man he could without reference to patronage or favour; but he did not say that the best man according to his views was he who was best able to subdue Mr. Slope, and make that gentleman's situation in Barchester too hot to be comfortable. As to the bonds, they had consisted in the exceeding struggle which he had made to get a good clergyman for them. He deprecated any comparison between himself and St. Paul, but said that he was entitled to beseech them for their good will towards Mr. Arabin, in the same manner that the apostle had besought Philemon and his household with regard to Onesimus.

The archdeacon's sermon, text, blessing and all, was concluded within the half hour. Then they shook hands with their Ulla-thorne friends, and returned to Plumstead. 'Twas thus that Mr. Arabin read himself in at St. Ewold's.

CHAP. XXIV.

MR. SLOPE MANAGES MATTERS VERY CLEVERLY AT PUDDINGDALE.

THE next two weeks passed pleasantly enough at Plumstead. The whole party there assembled seemed to get on well together. Eleanor made the house agreeable, and the archdeacon and Mrs. Grantly seemed to have forgotten her iniquity as regarded

Mr. Slope. **Mr.** Harding had his violoncello, and played to them while his daughters accompanied him. Johnny Bold, by the help either of Mr. Rerechild or else by that of his coral and carrot-juice, got through his teething troubles. There had been gaieties too of all sorts. They had dined at Ullathorne, and the Thornes had dined at the Rectory. Eleanor had been duly put to stand on her box, and in that position had found herself quite unable to express her opinion on the merits of flounces, such having been the subject given to try her elocution. Mr. Arabin had of course been much in his own parish, looking to the doings at his vicarage, calling on his parishioners, and taking on himself the duties of his new calling. But still he had been every evening at Plumstead, and Mrs. Grantly was partly willing to agree with her husband that he was a pleasant inmate in a house.

They had also been at a dinner party at Dr. Stanhope's, of which Mr. Arabin had made one. He also, moth-like, burnt his wings in the flames of the signora's candle. Mrs. Bold, too, had been there, and had felt somewhat displeased with the taste, want of taste she called it, shown by Mr. Arabin in paying so much attention to Madame Neroni. It was as infallible that Madeline should displease and irritate the women, as that she should charm and captivate the men. The one result followed naturally on the other. It was quite true that Mr. Arabin had been charmed. He thought her a very clever and a very handsome woman; he thought also that her peculiar affliction entitled her to the sympathy of all. He had never, he said, met so much suffering joined to such perfect beauty and so clear a mind. 'Twas thus he spoke of the signora coming home in the archdeacon's carriage; and Eleanor by no means liked to hear the praise. It was, however, exceedingly unjust of her to be angry with Mr. Arabin, as she had herself spent a very pleasant evening with Bertie Stanhope, who had taken her down to dinner, and had not left her side for one moment after the gentlemen came out of the dining room. It was unfair that she should amuse herself with Bertie and yet begrudge her new friend his license of amusing himself with Bertie's sister. And yet she did so. She was half angry with him in the carriage, and said something about meretricious manners. Mr. Arabin did not understand the ways of women very well, or else he might have flattered himself that Eleanor was in love with him.

But Eleanor was not in love with him. How many shades there are between love and indifference, and how little the graduated scale is understood! She had now been nearly three weeks in the same house with Mr. Arabin, and had received much of his attention, and listened daily to his conversation. He had usually devoted at least some portion of his evening to her exclusively. At Dr. Stanhope's he had devoted himself exclusively to another. It does not require that a woman should be in love to be irritated at this ; it does not require that she should even acknowledge to herself that it is unpleasant to her. Eleanor had no such self-knowledge. She thought in her own heart that it was only on Mr. Arabin's account that she regretted that he could condescend to be amused by the signora. " I thought he had more mind," she said to herself, as she sat watching her baby's cradle on her return from the party. " After all, I believe Mr. Stanhope is the pleasanter man of the two." Alas for the memory of poor John Bold ! Eleanor was not in love with Bertie Stanhope, nor was she in love with Mr. Arabin. But her devotion to her late husband was fast fading, when she could revolve in her mind, over the cradle of his infant, the faults and failings of other aspirants to her favour.

Will any one blame my heroine for this ? Let him or her rather thank God for all His goodness,—for His mercy endureth for ever.

Eleanor, in truth, was not in love ; neither was Mr. Arabin. Neither indeed was Bertie Stanhope, though he had already found occasion to say nearly as much as that he was. The widow's cap had prevented him from making a positive declaration, when otherwise he would have considered himself entitled to do so on a third or fourth interview. It was, after all but a small cap now, and had but little of the weeping-willow left in its construction. It is singular how these emblems of grief fade away by unseen gradations. Each pretends to be the counterpart of the forerunner, and yet the last little bit of crimped white crape that sits so jauntily on the back of the head, is as dissimilar to the first huge mountain of woe which disfigured the face of the weeper, as the state of the Hindoo is to the jointure of the English dowager.

But let it be clearly understood that Eleanor was in love with no one, and that no one was in love with Eleanor. Under these circumstances her anger against Mr. Arabin did not last long, and before two days were over they were both as good friends as ever. She could not but like him, for every hour spent in his company was spent pleasantly. And yet she could not quite like him, for there was always apparent in his conversation a certain feeling on his part that he hardly thought it worth his while to be in earnest. It was almost as though he were playing with a child. She knew well enough that he was in truth a sober thoughtful man, who in some matters and on some occasions could endure an agony of earnestness. And yet to her he was always gently playful. Could she have seen his brow once clouded she might have learnt to love him.

So things went on at Plumstead, and on the whole not unpleasantly, till a huge storm darkened the horizon, and came down upon the inhabitants of the rectory with all the fury of a waterspout. It was astonishing how in a few minutes the whole face of the heavens was changed. The party broke up from breakfast in perfect harmony; but fierce passions had arisen before the evening, which did not admit of their sitting at the same board for dinner. To explain this, it will be necessary to go back a little.

It will be remembered that the bishop expressed to Mr. Slope in his dressing-room, his determination that Mr. Quiverful should be confirmed in his appointment to the hospital, and that his lordship requested Mr. Slope to communicate this decision to the archdeacon. It will also be remembered that the archdeacon had indignantly declined seeing Mr. Slope, and had instead, written a strong letter to the bishop, in which he all but demanded the situation of warden for Mr. Harding. To this letter the archdeacon received an immediate formal reply from Mr. Slope, in which it was stated, that the bishop had received and would give his best consideration to the archdeacon's letter.

The archdeacon felt himself somewhat checkmated by this reply. What could he do with a man who would neither see him, nor argue with him by letter, and who had undoubtedly the power of appointing any clergyman he pleased? He had consulted with Mr. Arabin, who had suggested the propriety of calling in the aid of the master of Lazarus. "If," said he, "you and Dr. Gwynne formally declare your intention of waiting upon the bishop, the bishop will not dare to refuse to see you; and if two such men as you are see him together, you will probably not leave him without carrying your point."

The archdeacon did not quite like admitting the necessity of his being backed by the master of Lazarus before he could obtain admission into the episcopal palace of Barchester; but still he felt that the advice was good, and he resolved to take it. He wrote again to the bishop, expressing a hope that nothing further would be done in the matter of the hospital, till the consideration promised by his lordship had been given, and then sent off a warm appeal to his friend the master, imploring him to come to Plumstead and assist in driving the bishop into compliance. The master had rejoined, raising some difficulty, but not declining; and the archdeacon had again pressed his point, insisting on the necessity for immediate action. Dr. Gwynne unfortunately had the gout, and could therefore name no immediate day, but still agreed to come, if it should be finally found necessary. So the matter stood, as regarded the party at Plumstead.

But Mr. Harding had another friend fighting his battle for him, quite as powerful as the master of Lazarus, and this was Mr. Slope. Though the bishop had so pertinaciously insisted on giving way to his wife in the matter of the hospital, Mr. Slope did not think it necessary to abandon his object. He had, he thought, daily more and more reason to imagine that the widow would receive his overtures favourably, and he could not but feel that Mr. Harding at the hospital, and placed there by his means, would be more likely to receive him as a son-in-law, than Mr. Harding growling in opposition and disappointment under the archdeacon's wing at Plumstead. Moreover, to give Mr. Slope due credit, he was actuated by greater motives even than these. He wanted a wife, and he wanted money, but he wanted power more than either. He had fully realised the fact that he must come to blows with Mrs. Proudie. He had no desire to remain in Barchester as her chaplain. Sooner than do so, he would risk the loss of his whole connection with the diocese. What! was he to feel within him the possession of no ordinary talents; was he to know himself to be courageous, firm, and, in matters where his conscience did not interfere, unscrupulous; and yet be contented to be the working factotum of a woman-prelate? Mr. Slope had higher ideas of his own destiny. Either he or Mrs. Proudie must go to the wall; and now had come the time when he would try which it should be.

The bishop had declared that Mr. Quiverful should be the new warden. As Mr. Slope went down stairs prepared to see the archdeacon if necessary, but fully satisfied that no such necessity would arise, he declared to himself that Mr. Harding should be warden. With the object of carrying this point, he rode over to Puddingdale, and had a further interview with the worthy expectant of clerical good things. Mr. Quiverful was on the whole a worthy man. The impossible task of bringing up as ladies and gentlemen fourteen children on an income which was insufficient to give them with decency the common necessaries of life, had had an effect upon him not beneficial either to his spirit, or his keen sense of honour. Who can boast that he would have supported such a burden with a different result? Mr. Quiverful was an honest, pains-taking, drudging man; anxious, indeed, for bread and meat, anxious for means to quiet his butcher and cover with returning smiles the now sour countenance of the baker's wife, but anxious also to be right with his own conscience. He was not careful, as another might be who sat on an easier worldly seat, to stand well with those around him, to shun a breath which might sully his name, or a rumour which might affect his honour. He could not afford such niceties of conduct, such moral luxuries. It must suffice for him to be ordinarily honest according to the ordinary honesty of the world's ways, and to let men's tongues wag as they would.

He had felt that his brother clergymen, men whom he had known for the last twenty years, looked coldly on him from the first moment that he had shown himself willing to sit at the feet of Mr. Slope; he had seen that their looks grew colder still, when it became bruited about that he was to be the bishop's new warden at Hiram's hospital. This was painful enough; but it was the cross which he was doomed to bear. He thought of his wife, whose last new silk dress was six years in wear. He thought of all his young flock, whom he could hardly take to church with him on Sundays, for there were not decent shoes and stockings for them all to wear. He thought of the well-worn sleeves of his own black coat, and of the stern face of the draper from whom he would fain ask for cloth to make another, did he not know that the credit would be refused him. Then he thought of the comfortable house in Barchester, of the comfortable income, of his boys sent to school, of his girls with books in their hands instead of darning needles, of his wife's face again covered with smiles, and of his daily board again covered with plenty. He thought of these things; and do thou also, reader, think of them, and then wonder, if thou canst, that Mr. Slope had appeared to him to possess all those good gifts which could grace a bishop's chaplain. "How beautiful upon the mountains are the feet of him that bringeth good tidings."

Why, moreover, should the Barchester clergy have looked coldly on Mr. Quiverful? Had they not all shown that they regarded with complacency the loaves and fishes of their mother church? Had they not all, by some hook or crook, done better for themselves than he had done? They were not burdened as he was burdened. Dr. Grantly had five children, and nearly as many thousands a year on which to feed them. It was very well for him to turn up his nose at a new bishop who could do nothing for him, and a chaplain who was beneath his notice; but it was cruel in a man so circumstanced to set the world against the father of fourteen children because he was anxious to obtain for them an honourable support! He, Mr. Quiverful, had not asked for the wardenship; he had not even accepted it till he had been assured that Mr. Harding had refused it. How hard then that he should be blamed for doing that which not to have done would have argued a most insane imprudence?

Thus in this matter of the hospital poor Mr. Quiverful had his trials; and he had also his consolations. On the whole the consolations were the more vivid of the two. The stern draper heard of the coming promotion, and the wealth of his warehouse was at Mr. Quiverful's disposal. Coming events cast their shadows before, and the coming event of Mr. Quiverful's transference to Barchester produced a delicious shadow in the shape of a new outfit for Mrs. Quiverful and her three elder daughters. Such consolations come home to the heart of a man, and quite home to the heart of a woman. Whatever the husband might feel, the wife cared nothing for frowns of dean, archdeacon, or prebendary. To her the outsides and insides of her husband and fourteen children were everything. In her bosom every other ambition had been swallowed up in that maternal ambition of seeing them and him and herself duly clad and properly fed. It had come to that with her that life had now no other purpose. She recked nothing of the imaginary rights of others. She had no patience with her husband when he declared to her that he could not accept the hospital unless he knew that Mr. Harding had refused it. Her husband had no right to be Quixotic at the expense of fourteen children. The narrow escape of throwing away his good fortune which her lord had had, almost paralysed her. Now, indeed, they had received the full promise not only from Mr. Slope, but also from Mrs. Proudie. Now, indeed, they might reckon with safety on their good fortune. But what if all had been lost? · What if her fourteen bairns had been resteeped to the hips in poverty by the morbid sentimentality of their father? Mrs. Quiverful was just at present a happy woman, but yet it nearly took her breath away when she thought of the risk they had run.

"I don't know what your father means when he talks so much of what is due to Mr. Harding," she said to her eldest daughter. "Does he think that Mr. Harding would give him 450l. a year out of fine feeling? And what signifies it whom he offends, as long as he gets the place? He does not expect anything better. It passes me to think how your father can be so soft, while everybody around him is so griping."

Thus, while the outer world was accusing Mr. Quiverful of rapacity for promotion and of disregard to his honour, the inner world of his own household was falling foul of him, with equal vehemence, for his willingness to sacrifice their interest to a false feeling of sentimental pride. It is astonishing how much difference the point of view makes in the aspect of all that we look at!

Such were the feelings of the different members of the family at Puddingdale on the occasion of Mr. Slope's second visit. Mrs. Quiverful, as soon as she saw his horse coming up the avenue from the vicarage gate, hastily packed up her huge basket of needlework, and hurried herself and her daughter out of the room in which she was sitting with her husband. "It's Mr. Slope," she said. "He's come to settle with you about the hospital. I do hope we shall now be able to move at once." And she hastened to bid the maid of all work go to the door, so that the welcome great man might not be kept waiting.

Mr. Slope thus found Mr. Quiverful alone. Mrs. Quiverful went off to her kitchen and back settlements with anxious beating heart, almost dreading that there might be some slip between the cup of her happiness and the lip of her fruition, but yet comforting herself with the reflection that after what had taken place, any such slip could hardly be possible.

Mr. Slope was all smiles as he shook his brother clergyman's hand, and said that he had ridden over because he thought it right at once to put Mr. Quiverful in possession of the facts of the matter regarding the wardenship of the hospital. As he spoke, the poor expectant husband and father saw at a glance that his brilliant hopes were to be dashed to the ground, and that his visitor was now there for the purpose of unsaying what on his former visit he had said. There was something in the tone of the voice, something in the glance of the eye, which told the tale. Mr. Quiverful knew it all at once. He maintained his self-possession, however, smiled with a slight unmeaning smile, and merely said that he was obliged to Mr. Slope for the trouble he was taking.

"It has been a troublesome matter from first to last," said Mr. Slope; "and the bishop has hardly known how to act. Between ourselves — but mind this of course must go no further, Mr. Quiverful."

Mr. Quiverful said that of course it should not. "The truth is, that poor Mr. Harding has hardly known his own mind. You remember our last conversation, no doubt."

Mr. Quiverful assured him that he remembered it very well indeed.

"You will remember that I told you that Mr. Harding had refused to return to the hospital."

Mr. Quiverful declared that nothing could be more distinct on his memory.

"And acting on this refusal, I suggested that you should take the hospital," continued Mr. Slope.

"I understood you to say that the bishop had authorised you to offer it to me."

"Did I? did I go so far as that? Well, perhaps it may be, that in my anxiety in your behalf I did commit myself further than I should have done. So far as my own memory serves me, I don't think I did go quite so far as that. But I own I was very anxious that you should get it; and I may have said more than was quite prudent."

"But," said Mr. Quiverful, in his deep anxiety to prove his case, "my wife received as distinct a promise from Mrs. Proudie as one human being could give to another."

Mr. Slope smiled, and gently shook his head. He meant that smile for a pleasant smile, but it was diabolical in the eyes of the man he was speaking to. "Mrs. Proudie!" he said. "If we are to go to what passes between the ladies in these matters, we shall really be in a nest of troubles from which we shall never extricate ourselves. Mrs. Proudie is a most excellent lady, kind-hearted, charitable, pious, and in every way estimable. But, my dear Mr. Quiverful, the patronage of the diocese is not in her hands."

Mr. Quiverful for a moment sat panic-stricken and silent. "Am I to understand, then, that I have received no promise?" he said, as soon as he had sufficiently collected his thoughts.

"If you will allow me, I will tell you exactly how the matter rests. You certainly did receive a promise conditional on Mr. Harding's refusal. I am sure you will do me the justice to remember that you yourself declared that you could accept the appointment on no other condition than the knowledge that Mr. Harding had declined it."

"Yes," said Mr. Quiverful; "I did say that, certainly."

"Well; it now appears that he did not refuse it."

"But surely you told me, and repeated it more than once, that he had done so in your own hearing."

"So I understood him. But it seems I was in error. But don't for a moment, Mr. Quiverful, suppose that I mean to throw you over. No. Having held out my hand to a man in your position, with your large family and pressing claims, I am not now going to draw it back again. I only want you to act with me fairly and honestly."

"Whatever I do, I shall endeavour at any rate to act fairly," said the poor man, feeling that he had to fall back for support on the spirit of martyrdom within him.

"I am sure you will," said the other. "I am sure you have no wish to obtain possession of an income which belongs by all right to another. No man knows better than you do Mr. Harding's history, or can better appreciate his character. Mr. Harding is very desirous of returning to his old position, and the bishop feels that he is at the present moment somewhat hampered, though of course he is not bound, by the conversation which took place on the matter between you and me."

"Well," said Mr. Quiverful, dreadfully doubtful as to what his conduct under such circumstances should be, and fruitlessly striving to harden his nerves with some of that instinct of self-preservation which made his wife so bold.

"The wardenship of this little hospital is not the only thing in the bishop's gift, Mr. Quiverful, nor is it by many degrees the best. And his lordship is not the man to forget any one whom he has once marked with approval. If you would allow me to advise you as a friend ——"

"Indeed I shall be most grateful to you," said the poor vicar of Puddingdale ——

"I should advise you to withdraw from any opposition to Mr. Harding's claims. If you persist in your demand, I do not think you will ultimately succeed. Mr. Harding has all but a positive right to the place. But if you will allow me to inform the bishop that you decline to stand in Mr. Harding's way, I think I may promise you — though, by the bye, it must not be taken as a formal promise — that the bishop will not allow you to be a poorer man than you would have been had you become warden."

Mr. Quiverful sat in his arm chair silent, gazing at vacancy. What was he to say? All this that came from Mr. Slope was so true. Mr. Harding had a right to the hospital. The bishop had a great many good things to give away. Both the bishop and Mr. Slope would be excellent friends and terrible enemies to a man in his position. And then he had no proof of any promise; he could not force the bishop to appoint him.

"Well, Mr. Quiverful, what do you say about it?"

"Oh, of course, whatever you think fit, Mr. Slope. It's a great disappointment, a very great disappointment. I won't deny that I am a very poor man, Mr. Slope."

"In the end, Mr. Quiverful, you will find that it will have been better for you."

The interview ended in Mr. Slope receiving a full renunciation from Mr. Quiverful of any claim he might have to the appointment in question. It was only given verbally and without witnesses; but then the original promise was made in the same way.

Mr. Slope again assured him that he should not be forgotten, and then rode back to Barchester, satisfied that he would now be able to mould the bishop to his wishes.

CHAP. XXV.

FOURTEEN ARGUMENTS IN FAVOUR OF MR. QUIVERFUL'S CLAIMS.

WE have most of us heard of the terrible anger of a lioness when, surrounded by her cubs, she guards her prey. Few of us wish to disturb the mother of a litter of puppies when mouthing a bone in the midst of her young family. Medea and her children are familiar to us, and so is the grief of Constance. Mrs. Quiverful, when she first heard from her husband the news which he had to impart, felt within her bosom all the rage of a lioness, the rapacity of the hound, the fury of the tragic queen, and the deep despair of the bereaved mother.

Doubting, but yet hardly fearing, what might have been the tenor of Mr. Slope's discourse, she rushed back to her husband as soon as the front door was closed behind the visitor. It was well for Mr. Slope that he so escaped, — the anger of such a woman, at such a moment, would have cowed even him. As a general rule, it is highly desirable that ladies should keep their temper; a woman when she storms always makes herself ugly, and usually ridiculous also. There is nothing so odious to man as a virago. Though Theseus loved an Amazon, he showed his love but roughly; and from the time of Theseus downward, no man ever wished to have his wife remarkable rather for forward prowess than retiring gentleness. A low voice "is an excellent thing in woman."

Such may be laid down as a very general rule; and few women should allow themselves to deviate from it, and then only on rare occasions. But if there be a time when a woman may let her hair to the winds, when she may loose her arms, and scream out trumpet-tongued to the ears of men, it is when nature calls out within her not for her own wants, but for the wants of those whom her womb has borne, whom her breasts have suckled, for those who look to her for their daily bread as naturally as man looks to his Creator.

There was nothing poetic in the nature of Mrs. Quiverful. She was neither a Medea nor a Constance. When angry, she spoke out her anger in plain words, and in a tone which might have been modulated with advantage ; but she did so, at any rate, without affectation. Now, without knowing it, she rose to a tragic vein.

"Well, my dear; we are not to have it." Such were the words with which her ears were greeted when she entered the parlour, still hot from the kitchen fire. And the face of her husband spoke even more plainly than his words :—

> " E'en such a man, so faint, so spiritless,
> So dull, so dead in look, so woe-begone,
> Drew Priam's curtain in the dead of night."

"What !" said she, — and Mrs. Siddons could not have put more passion into a single syllable, — "What ! not have it ? who says so ?" And she sat opposite to her husband, with her elbows on the table, her hands clasped together, and her coarse, solid, but once handsome face stretched over it towards him.

She sat as silent as death while he told his story, and very dreadful to him her silence was. He told it very lamely and badly, but still in such a manner that she soon understood the whole of it.

"And so you have resigned it ?" said she.

"I have had no opportunity of accepting it," he replied. "I had no witnesses to Mr. Slope's offer, even if that offer would bind the bishop. It was better for me, on the whole, to keep on good terms with such men than to fight for what I should never get !"

"Witnesses !" she screamed, rising quickly to her feet, and walking up and down the room. "Do clergymen require witnesses to their words ? He made the promise in the bishop's name, and if it is to be broken, I'll know the reason why. Did he not positively say that the bishop had sent him to offer you the place ? "

"He did, my dear. But that is now nothing to the purpose."

"It is everything to the purpose, Mr. Quiverful. Witnesses indeed ! and then to talk of *your* honour being questioned, because you wish to provide for fourteen children. It is everything to the purpose ; and so they shall know, if I scream it into their ears from the town cross of Barchester."

"You forget, Letitia, that the bishop has so many things in his gift. We must wait a little longer. That is all."

"Wait ! Shall we feed the children by waiting. Will waiting put George, and Tom, and Sam, out into the world? Will it enable my poor girls to give up some of their drudgery ? Will waiting make Bessy and Jane fit even to be governesses ? Will waiting pay for the things we got in Barchester last week ?"

"It is all we can do, my dear. The disappointment is as much

to me as to you ; and yet, God knows, I feel it more for your sake
than my own."

Mrs. Quiverful was looking full into her husband's face, and
saw a small hot tear appear on each of those furrowed cheeks.
This was too much for her woman's heart. He also had risen
and was standing with his back to the empty grate. She rushed
towards him, and, seizing him in her arms, sobbed aloud upon his
bosom.

"You are too good, too soft, too yielding," she said at last.
"These men, when they want you, they use you like a cat's-paw ;
and when they want you no longer, they throw you aside like an
old shoe. This is twice they have treated you so."

"In one way this will be all for the better," argued he. "It
will make the bishop feel that he is bound to do something for me."

"At any rate, he shall hear of it," said the lady, again revert-
ing to her more angry mood. "At any rate he shall hear of it,
and that loudly ; and so shall she. She little knows Letitia
Quiverful, if she thinks I will sit down quietly with the loss after
all that passed between us at the palace. If there's any feeling
within her, I'll make her ashamed of herself,"—and she paced the
room again, stamping the floor as she went with her fat heavy foot.
"Good heavens ! what a heart she must have within her to treat
in such a way as this the father of fourteen unprovided children !"

Mr. Quiverful proceeded to explain that he didn't think that
Mrs. Proudie had had anything to do with it.

"Don't tell me," said Mrs. Quiverful; "I know more about it
than that. Doesn't all the world know that Mrs. Proudie is bishop
of Barchester, and that Mr. Slope is merely her creature? Wasn't
it she that made me the promise, just as though the thing was in
her own particular gift? I tell you, it was that woman who sent
him over here to-day, because, for some reason of her own, she
wants to go back from her word."

"My dear, you're wrong—"

"Now, Q., don't be so soft," she continued. "Take my word for
it, the bishop knows no more about it than Jemima does." Jemima
was the two-year-old. "And if you'll take my advice, you'll lose
no time in going over and seeing him yourself."

Soft, however, as Mr. Quiverful might be, he would not allow
himself to be talked out of his opinion on this occasion ; and proceeded with much minuteness to explain to his wife the tone in
which Mr. Slope had spoken of Mrs. Proudie's interference in
diocesan matters. As he did so, a new idea gradually instilled
itself into the matron's head, and a new course of conduct pre-

sented itself to her judgment. What if, after all, Mrs. Proudie knew nothing of this visit of Mr. Slope's? In that case, might it not be possible that that lady would still be staunch to her in this matter, still stand her friend, and, perhaps, possibly carry her through in opposition to Mr. Slope? Mrs. Quiverful said nothing as this vague hope occurred to her, but listened with more than ordinary patience to what her husband had to say. While he was still explaining that in all probability the world was wrong in its estimation of Mrs. Proudie's power and authority, she had fully made up her mind as to her course of action. She did not, however, proclaim her intention. She shook her head ominously as he continued his narration ; and when he had completed she rose to go, merely observing that it was cruel, cruel treatment. She then asked him if he would mind waiting for a late dinner instead of dining at their usual hour of three, and, having received from him a concession on this point, she proceeded to carry her purpose into execution.

She determined that she would at once go to the palace; that she would do so, if possible, before Mrs. Proudie could have had an interview with Mr. Slope ; and that she would be either submissive, piteous and pathetic, or else indignant, violent and exacting, according to the manner in which she was received.

She was quite confident in her own power. Strengthened as she was by the pressing wants of fourteen children, she felt that she could make her way through legions of episcopal servants, and force herself, if need be, into the presence of the lady who had so wronged her. She had no shame about it, no *mauvaise honte,* no dread of archdeacons. She would, as she declared to her husband, make her wail heard in the market-place if she did not get redress and justice. It might be very well for an unmarried young curate to be shamefaced in such matters ; it might be all right that a snug rector, really in want of nothing, but still looking for better preferment, should carry on his affairs decently under the rose. But Mrs. Quiverful, with fourteen children, had given over being shamefaced, and, in some things, had given over being decent. If it were intended that she should be ill used in the manner proposed by Mr. Slope, it should not be done under the rose. All the world should know of it.

In her present mood, Mrs. Quiverful was not over careful about her attire. She tied her bonnet under her chin, threw her shawl over her shoulders, armed herself with the old family cotton umbrella, and started for Barchester. A journey to the palace was not quite so easy a thing for Mrs. Quiverful as for our friend at

Plumstead. Plumstead is nine miles from Barchester, and Puddingdale is but four. But the archdeacon could order round his brougham, and his high-trotting fast bay gelding would take him into the city within the hour. There was no brougham in the coach-house of Puddingdale Vicarage, no bay horse in the stables. There was no method of locomotion for its inhabitants but that which nature has assigned to man.

Mrs. Quiverful was a broad heavy woman, not young, nor given to walking. In her kitchen, and in the family dormitories, she was active enough; but her pace and gait were not adapted for the road. A walk into Barchester and back in the middle of an August day would be to her a terrible task, if not altogether impracticable. There was living in the parish, about half a mile from the vicarage on the road to the city, a decent, kindly farmer, well to do as regards this world, and so far mindful of the next that he attended his parish church with decent regularity. To him Mrs. Quiverful had before now appealed in some of her more pressing family troubles, and had not appealed in vain. At his door she now presented herself, and, having explained to his wife that most urgent business required her to go at once to Barchester, begged that Farmer Subsoil would take her thither in his tax-cart. The farmer did not reject her plan; and, as soon as Prince could be got into his collar, they started on their journey.

Mrs. Quiverful did not mention the purpose of her business, nor did the farmer alloy his kindness by any unseemly questions. She merely begged to be put down at the bridge going into the city, and to be taken up again at the same place in the course of two hours. The farmer promised to be punctual to his appointment, and the lady, supported by her umbrella, took the short cut to the close, and in a few minutes was at the bishop's door.

Hitherto she had felt no dread with regard to the coming interview. She had felt nothing but an indignant longing to pour forth her claims, and declare her wrongs, if those claims were not fully admitted. But now the difficulty of her situation touched her a little. She had been at the palace once before, but then she went to give grateful thanks. Those who have thanks to return for favours received find easy admittance to the halls of the great. Such is not always the case with men, or even with women, who have favours to beg. Still less easy is access for those who demand the fulfilment of promises already made.

Mrs. Quiverful had not been slow to learn the ways of the world. She knew all this, and she knew also that her cotton umbrella and all but ragged shawl would not command respect in the eyes of the palatial servants. If she were too humble, she knew well that she would never succeed. To overcome by imperious overbearing with such a shawl as hers upon her shoulders, and such a bonnet on her head, would have required a personal bearing very superior to that with which nature had endowed her. Of this also Mrs. Quiverful was aware. She must make it known that she was the wife of a gentleman and a clergyman, and must yet condescend to conciliate.

The poor lady knew but one way to overcome these difficulties at the very threshold of her enterprise, and to this she resorted. Low as were the domestic funds at Puddingdale, she still retained possession of half-a-crown, and this she sacrificed to the avarice of Mrs. Proudie's metropolitan sesquipedalian serving-man. She was, she said, Mrs. Quiverful of Puddingdale, the wife of the Rev. Mr. Quiverful. She wished to see Mrs. Proudie. It was indeed quite indispensable that she should see Mrs. Proudie. James Fitzplush looked worse than dubious, did not know whether his lady were out, or engaged, or in her bed-room; thought it most probable she was subject to one of these or to some other cause that would make her invisible; but Mrs. Quiverful could sit down in the waiting-room while inquiry was being made of Mrs. Proudie's maid.

"Look here, my man," said Mrs. Quiverful; "I must see her;" and she put her card and half-a-crown — think of it, my reader, think of it; her last half-crown — into the man's hand, and sat herself down on a chair in the waiting-room.

Whether the bribe carried the day, or whether the bishop's wife really chose to see the vicar's wife, it boots not now to inquire The man returned, and begging Mrs. Quiverful to follow him, ushered her into the presence of the mistress of the diocese.

Mrs. Quiverful at once saw that her patroness was in a smiling humour. Triumph sat throned upon her brow, and all the joys of dominion hovered about her curls. Her lord had that morning contested with her a great point. He had received an invitation to spend a couple of days with the archbishop. His soul longed for the gratification. Not a word, however, in his grace's note alluded to the fact of his being a married man; and, if he went at all, he must go alone. This necessity would have presented no insurmountable bar to the visit, or have militated much against the pleasure, had he been able to go without any reference to Mrs. Proudie. But this he could not do. He could not order his portmanteau to be packed, and start with his own man, merely telling the lady of his heart that he would probably be back on Saturday. There are men — may we not rather say monsters?

— who do such things; and there are wives — may we not rather say slaves? — who put up with such usage. But Doctor and Mrs. Proudie were not among the number.

The bishop, with some beating about the bush, made the lady understand that he very much wished to go. The lady, without any beating about the bush, made the bishop understand that she wouldn't hear of it. It would be useless here to repeat the arguments that were used on each side, and needless to record the result. Those who are married will understand very well how the battle was lost and won; and those who are single will never understand it till they learn the lesson which experience alone can give. When Mrs. Quiverful was shown into Mrs. Proudie's room, that lady had only returned a few minutes from her lord. But before she left him she had seen the answer to the archbishop's note written and sealed. No wonder that her face was wreathed with smiles as she received Mrs. Quiverful.

She instantly spoke of the subject which was so near the heart of her visitor. "Well, Mrs. Quiverful," said she, "is it decided yet when you are to move into Barchester?"

"That woman," as she had an hour or two since been called, became instantly re-endowed with all the graces that can adorn a bishop's wife. Mrs. Quiverful immediately saw that her business was to be piteous, and that nothing was to be gained by indignation; nothing, indeed, unless she could be indignant in company with her patroness.

"Oh, Mrs. Proudie," she began, "I fear we are not to move to Barchester at all."

"Why not?" said that lady sharply, dropping at a moment's notice her smiles and condescension, and turning with her sharp quick way to business which she saw at a glance was important.

And then Mrs. Quiverful told her tale. As she progressed in the history of her wrongs she perceived that the heavier she leant upon Mr. Slope the blacker became Mrs. Proudie's brow, but that such blackness was not injurious to her own cause. When Mr. Slope was at Puddingdale vicarage that morning she had regarded him as the creature of the lady-bishop; now she perceived that they were enemies. She admitted her mistake to herself without any pain or humiliation. She had but one feeling, and that was confined to her family. She cared little how she twisted and turned among these new comers at the bishop's palace so long as she could twist her husband into the warden's house. She cared not which was her friend or which was her enemy, if only she could get this preferment which she so sorely wanted.

She told her tale, and Mrs. Proudie listened to it almost in silence. She told how Mr. Slope had cozened her husband into resigning his claim, and had declared that it was the bishop's will that none but Mr. Harding should be warden. Mrs. Proudie's brow became blacker and blacker. At last she started from her chair, and begging Mrs. Quiverful to sit and wait for her return, marched out of the room.

"Oh, Mrs. Proudie, it's for fourteen children—for fourteen children." Such was the burden that fell on her ear as she closed the door behind her.

CHAP. XXVI.

MRS. PROUDIE WRESTLES AND GETS A FALL.

It was hardly an hour since Mrs. Proudie had left her husband's apartment victorious, and yet so indomitable was her courage that she now returned thither panting for another combat. She was greatly angry with what she thought was his duplicity. He had so clearly given her a promise on this matter of the hospital. He had been already so absolutely vanquished on that point. Mrs. Proudie began to feel that if every affair was to be thus discussed and battled about twice and even thrice, the work of the diocese would be too much even for her.

Without knocking at the door she walked quickly into her husband's room, and found him seated at his office table, with Mr. Slope opposite to him. Between his fingers was the very note which he had written to the archbishop in her presence——and it was open! Yes, he had absolutely violated the seal which had been made sacred by her approval. They were sitting in deep conclave, and it was too clear that the purport of the archbishop's invitation had been absolutely canvassed again, after it had been already debated and decided on in obedience to her behests! Mr. Slope rose from his chair, and bowed slightly. The two opposing spirits looked each other fully in the face, and they knew that they were looking each at an enemy.

"What is this, bishop, about Mr. Quiverful?" said she, coming to the end of the table and standing there.

Mr. Slope did not allow the bishop to answer, but replied himself. "I have been out to Puddingdale this morning, ma'am, and have seen Mr. Quiverful. Mr. Quiverful has abandoned his claim to the hospital, because he is now aware that Mr. Harding is desirous to fill his old place.   Under these circumstances I have strongly advised his lordship to nominate Mr. Harding."

"Mr. Quiverful has not abandoned anything," said the lady, with a very imperious voice.   "His lordship's word has been pledged to him, and it must be respected."

The bishop still remained silent.   He was anxiously desirous of making his old enemy bite the dust beneath his feet.   His new ally had told him that nothing was more easy for him than to do so.   The ally was there now at his elbow to help him, and yet his courage failed him.   It is so hard to conquer when the prestige of former victories is all against one.   It is so hard for the cock who has once been beaten out of his yard to resume his courage and again take a proud place upon a dunghill.

"Perhaps I ought not to interfere," said Mr. Slope, "but yet ——"

"Certainly you ought not," said the infuriated dame.

"But yet," continued Mr. Slope, not regarding the interruption, "I have thought it my imperative duty to recommend the bishop not to slight Mr. Harding's claims."

"Mr. Harding should have known his own mind," said the lady.

"If Mr. Harding be not replaced at the hospital, his lordship will have to encounter much ill will, not only in the diocese, but in the world at large.   Besides, taking a higher ground, his lordship, as I understand, feels it to be his duty to gratify, in this matter, so very worthy a man and so good a clergyman as Mr. Harding."

"And what is to become of the Sabbath-day school, and of the Sunday services in the hospital?" said Mrs. Proudie, with something very nearly approaching to a sneer on her face.

"I understand that Mr. Harding makes no objection to the Sabbath-day school," said Mr. Slope.   "And as to the hospital services, that matter will be best discussed after his appointment. If he has any permanent objection, then, I fear, the matter must rest."

"You have a very easy conscience in such matters, Mr. Slope," said she.

"I should not have an easy conscience," he rejoined, "but a conscience very far from being easy, if anything said or done by me should lead the bishop to act unadvisedly in this matter.   It is clear that in the interview I had with Mr. Harding, I misunderstood him ——"

"And it is equally clear that you have misunderstood Mr.

Quiverful," said she, now at the top of her wrath. " What business have you at all with these interviews ? Who desired you to go to Mr. Quiverful this morning ? Who commissioned you to manage this affair ? Will you answer me, sir ? — who sent you to Mr. Quiverful this morning ? "

There was a dead pause in the room. Mr. Slope had risen from his chair, and was standing with his hand on the back of it, looking at first very solemn and now very black. Mrs. Proudie was standing as she had at first placed herself, at the end of the table, and as she interrogated her foe she struck her hand upon it with almost more than feminine vigour. The bishop was sitting in his easy chair twiddling his thumbs, turning his eyes now to his wife, and now to his chaplain, as each took up the cudgels. How comfortable it would be if they could fight it out between them without the necessity of any interference on his part ; fight it out so that one should kill the other utterly, as far as diocesan life was concerned, so that he, the bishop, might know clearly by whom it behoved him to be led. There would be the comfort of quiet in either case ; but if the bishop had a wish as to which might prove the victor, that wish was certainly not antagonistic to Mr. Slope.

" Better the d —— you know than the d —— you don't know," is an old saying, and perhaps a true one ; but the bishop had not yet realised the truth of it.

" Will you answer me, sir ? " she repeated. " Who instructed you to call on Mr. Quiverful this morning ? " There was another pause. " Do you intend to answer me, sir ? "

" I think, Mrs. Proudie, that under all the circumstances it will be better for me not to answer such a question," said Mr. Slope. Mr. Slope had many tones in his voice, all duly under his command ; among them was a sanctified low tone, and a sanctified loud tone ; and he now used the former.

" Did any one send you, sir ? "

" Mrs. Proudie," said Mr. Slope, " I am quite aware how much I owe to your kindness. I am aware also what is due by courtesy from a gentleman to a lady. But there are higher considerations than either of those, and I hope I shall be forgiven if I now allow myself to be actuated solely by them. My duty in this matter is to his lordship, and I can admit of no questioning but from him. He has approved of what I have done, and you must excuse me if I say, that having that approval and my own, I want none other."

What horrid words were these which greeted the ear of Mrs. Proudie ? The matter was indeed too clear. There was premeditated mutiny in the camp. Not only had ill-conditioned minds become insubordinate by the fruition of a little power, but sedition had been overtly taught and preached. The bishop had not yet been twelve months in his chair, and rebellion had already reared her hideous head within the palace. Anarchy and misrule would quickly follow, unless she took immediate and strong measures to put down the conspiracy which she had detected.

"Mr. Slope," she said, with slow and dignified voice, differing much from that which she had hitherto used, "Mr. Slope, I will trouble you, if you please, to leave the apartment. I wish to speak to my lord alone."

Mr. Slope also felt that everything depended on the present interview. Should the bishop now be repetticoated, his thraldom would be complete and for ever. The present moment was peculiarly propitious for rebellion. The bishop had clearly committed himself by breaking the seal of the answer to the archbishop; he had therefore fear to influence him. Mr. Slope had told him that no consideration ought to induce him to refuse the archbishop's invitation; he had therefore hope to influence him. He had accepted Mr. Quiverful's resignation, and therefore dreaded having to renew that matter with his wife. He had been screwed up to the pitch of asserting a will of his own, and might possibly be carried on till by an absolute success he should have been taught how possible it was to succeed. Now was the moment for victory or rout. It was now that Mr. Slope must make himself master of the diocese, or else resign his place and begin his search for fortune again. He saw all this plainly. After what had taken place any compromise between him and the lady was impossible. Let him once leave the room at her bidding, and leave the bishop in her hands, and he might at once pack up his portmanteau and bid adieu to episcopal honours, Mrs. Bold, and the Signora Neroni.

And yet it was not so easy to keep his ground when he was bidden by a lady to go.; or to continue to make a third in a party between a husband and wife when the wife expressed a wish for a *tête-à-tête* with her husband.

"Mr. Slope," she repeated, "I wish to be alone with my lord."

"His lordship has summoned me on most important diocesan business," said Mr. Slope, glancing with uneasy eye at Dr. Proudie. He felt that he must trust something to the bishop, and yet that trust was so woefully ill-placed. "My leaving him at the present moment is, I fear, impossible."

"Do you bandy words with me, you ungrateful man?" said she. "My lord, will you do me the favour to beg Mr. Slope to leave the room?"

My lord scratched his head, but for the moment said nothing. This was as much as Mr. Slope expected from him, and was on the whole, for him, an active exercise of marital rights.

"My lord," said the lady, "is Mr. Slope to leave this room, or am I?"

Here Mrs. Proudie made a false step. She should not have alluded to the possibility of retreat on her part. She should not have expressed the idea that her order for Mr. Slope's expulsion could be treated otherwise than by immediate obedience. In answer to such a question the bishop naturally said in his own mind, that as it was necessary that one should leave the room, per- haps it might be as well that Mrs. Proudie did so. He did say so in his own mind, but externally he again scratched his head and again twiddled his thumbs.

Mrs. Proudie was boiling over with wrath. Alas, alas! could she but have kept her temper as her enemy did, she would have conquered as she had ever conquered. But divine anger got the better of her, as it has done of other heroines, and she fell.

"My lord," said she, "am I to be vouchsafed an answer or am I not?"

At last he broke his deep silence and proclaimed himself a Slopeite. "Why, my dear," said he, "Mr. Slope and I are very busy."

That was all. There was nothing more necessary. He had gone to the battle-field, stood the dust and heat of the day, en- countered the fury of the foe, and won the victory. How easy is success to those who will only be true to themselves!

Mr. Slope saw at once the full amount of his gain, and turned on the vanquished lady a look of triumph which she never forgot and never forgave. Here he was wrong. He should have looked humbly at her, and with meek entreating eye have deprecated her anger. He should have said by his glance that he asked pardon for his success, and that he hoped forgiveness for the stand which he had been forced to make in the cause of duty. So might he perchance have somewhat mollified that imperious bosom, and pre- pared the way for future terms. But Mr. Slope meant to rule without terms. Ah, forgetful, inexperienced man! Can you cause that little trembling victim to be divorced from the woman that possesses him? Can you provide that they shall be separated at bed and board? Is he not flesh of her flesh and bone of her bone, and must he not so continue? It is very well now for you to stand your ground, and triumph as she is driven ignominiously from the room; but can you be present when those curtains are drawn, when that awful helmet of proof has been tied beneath the chin, when the small remnants of the bishop's prowess shall be cowed by the tassel above his head? Can you then intrude yourself when the wife wishes "to speak to my lord alone?"

But for the moment Mr. Slope's triumph was complete; for Mrs. Proudie without further parley left the room, and did not forget to shut the door after her. Then followed a close conference between the new allies, in which was said much which it astonished Mr. Slope to say and the bishop to hear. And yet the one said it and the other heard it without ill will. There was no mincing of matters now. The chaplain plainly told the bishop that the world gave him credit for being under the governance of his wife; that his credit and character in the diocese were suffering; that he would surely get himself into hot water if he allowed Mrs. Proudie to interfere in matters which were not suitable for a woman's powers; and in fact that he would become contemptible if he did not throw off the yoke under which he groaned. The bishop at first hummed and hawed, and affected to deny the truth of what was said. But his denial was not stout and quickly broke down. He soon admitted by silence his state of vassalage, and pledged himself, with Mr. Slope's assistance, to change his courses. Mr. Slope also did not make out a bad case for himself. He explained how it grieved him to run counter to a lady who had always been his patroness, who had befriended him in so many ways, who had, in fact, recommended him to the bishop's notice; but, as he stated, his duty was now imperative; he held a situation of peculiar confidence, and was immediately and especially attached to the bishop's person. In such a situation his conscience required that he should regard solely the bishop's interests, and therefore he had ventured to speak out.

The bishop took this for what it was worth, and Mr. Slope only intended that he should do so. It gilded the pill which Mr. Slope had to administer, and which the bishop thought would be less bitter than that other pill which he had so long been taking.

"My lord," had his immediate reward, like a good child. He was instructed to write and at once did write another note to the archbishop accepting his grace's invitation. This note Mr. Slope, more prudent than the lady, himself took away and posted with his own hands. Thus he made sure that this act of self-jurisdiction should be as nearly as possible a *fait accompli*. He begged, and coaxed, and threatened the bishop with a view of making him also write at once to Mr. Harding; but the bishop, though temporarily emancipated from his wife, was not yet enthralled to Mr. Slope.

He said, and probably said truly, that such an offer must be made in some official form; that he was not yet prepared to sign the form; and that he should prefer seeing Mr. Harding before he did so. Mr. Slope might, however, beg Mr. Harding to call upon him. Not disappointed with his achievement Mr. Slope went his way. He first posted the precious note which he had in his pocket, and then pursued other enterprises in which we must follow him in other chapters.

Mrs. Proudie, having received such satisfaction as was to be derived from slamming her husband's door, did not at once betake herself to Mrs. Quiverful. Indeed for the first few moments after her repulse she felt that she could not again see that lady. She would have to own that she had been beaten, to confess that the diadem had passed from her brow, and the sceptre from her hand! No, she would send a message to her with the promise of a letter on the next day or the day after. Thus resolving, she betook herself to her bed-room; but here she again changed her mind. The air of that sacred enclosure somewhat restored her courage, and gave her more heart. As Achilles warmed at the sight of his armour, as Don Quixote's heart grew strong when he grasped his lance, so did Mrs. Proudie look forward to fresh laurels, as her eye fell on her husband's pillow. She would not despair. Having so resolved, she descended with dignified mien and refreshed countenance to Mrs. Quiverful.

This scene in the bishop's study took longer in the acting than in the telling. We have not, perhaps, had the whole of the conversation. At any rate Mrs. Quiverful was beginning to be very impatient, and was thinking that farmer Subsoil would be tired of waiting for her, when Mrs. Proudie returned. Oh! who can tell the palpitations of that maternal heart, as the suppliant looked into the face of the great lady to see written there either a promise of house, income, comfort and future competence, or else the doom of continued and ever increasing poverty. Poor mother! poor wife! there was little there to comfort you!

"Mrs. Quiverful," thus spoke the lady with considerable austerity, and without sitting down herself, "I find that your husband has behaved in this matter in a very weak and foolish manner."

Mrs. Quiverful immediately rose upon her feet, thinking it disrespectful to remain sitting while the wife of the bishop stood. But she was desired to sit down again, and made to do so, so that Mrs. Proudie might stand and preach over her. It is generally considered an offensive thing for a gentleman to keep his seat while another is kept standing before him, and we presume the same law holds with regard to ladies. It often is so felt; but we are inclined to say that it never produces half the discomfort cr half the feeling of implied inferiority that is shown by a great man who desires his visitor to be seated while he himself speaks from his legs. Such a solecism in good breeding, when construed into English, means this: "The accepted rules of courtesy in the world require that I should offer you a seat; if I did not do so, you would bring a charge against me in the world of being arrogant and ill-mannered; I will obey the world; but, nevertheless, I will not put myself on an equality with you. You may sit down, but I won't sit with you. Sit, therefore, at my bidding, and I'll stand and talk at you!"

This was just what Mrs. Proudie meant to say; and Mrs. Quiverful, though she was too anxious and too flurried thus to translate the full meaning of the manœuvre, did not fail to feel its effect. She was cowed and uncomfortable, and a second time essayed to rise from her chair.

"Pray be seated, Mrs. Quiverful, pray keep your seat. Your husband, I say, has been most weak and most foolish. It is impossible, Mrs. Quiverful, to help people who will not help themselves. I much fear that I can now do nothing for you in this matter."

"Oh! Mrs. Proudie,—don't say so," said the poor woman again jumping up.

"*Pray* be seated Mrs. Quiverful. I much fear that I can do nothing further for you in this matter. Your husband has, in a most unaccountable manner, taken upon himself to resign that which I was empowered to offer him. As a matter of course, the bishop expects that his clergy shall know their own minds. What he may ultimately do—what we may finally decide on doing—I cannot now say. Knowing the extent of your family—"

"Fourteen children, Mrs. Proudie, fourteen of them! and barely bread,—barely bread! It's hard for the children of a clergyman, it's hard for one who has always done his duty respectably!" Not a word fell from her about herself; but the tears came streaming down her big coarse cheeks, on which the dust of the August road had left its traces.

Mrs. Proudie has not been portrayed in these pages as an agreeable or an amiable lady. There has been no intention to impress the reader much in her favour. It is ordained that all novels should have a male and a female angel, and a male and a female devil. If it be considered that this rule is obeyed in these pages, the latter character must be supposed to have fallen to the lot of Mrs.

Proudie. But she was not all devil. There was a heart inside
that stiff-ribbed bodice, though not, perhaps, of large dimensions,
and certainly not easily accessible. Mrs. Quiverful, however, did
gain access, and Mrs. Proudie proved herself a woman. Whether
it was the fourteen children with their probable bare bread and
their possible bare backs, or the respectability of the father's work,
or the mingled dust and tears on the mother's face, we will not
pretend to say. But Mrs. Proudie was touched.

She did not show it as other women might have done. She did
not give Mrs. Quiverful eau-de-Cologne, or order her a glass of
wine. She did not take her to her toilet table, and offer her the
use of brushes and combs, towels and water. She did not say soft
little speeches and coax her kindly back to equanimity. Mrs.
Quiverful, despite her rough appearance, would have been as
amenable to such little tender cares as any lady in the land. But
none such were forthcoming. Instead of this, Mrs. Proudie
slapped one hand upon the other, and declared, — not with an oath ;
for as a lady and a Sabbatarian and a she-bishop, she could not
swear, — but with an adjuration, that "she wouldn't have it done."

The meaning of this was that she wouldn't have Mr. Quiverful's
promised appointment cozened away by the treachery of Mr. Slope
and the weakness of her husband. This meaning she very soon
explained to Mrs. Quiverful.

"Why was your husband such a fool," said she, now dismounted
from her high horse and sitting confidentially down close to her
visitor, "as to take the bait which that man threw to him? If
he had not been so utterly foolish, nothing could have prevented
your going to the hospital."

Poor Mrs. Quiverful was ready enough with her own tongue in
accusing her husband to his face of being soft, and perhaps did
not always speak of him to her children quite so respectfully as
she might have done. But she did not at all like to hear him
abused by others, and began to vindicate him, and to explain that
of course he had taken Mr. Slope to be an emissary from Mrs.
Proudie herself ; that Mr. Slope was thought to be peculiarly her
friend ; and that, therefore, Mr. Quiverful would have been failing
in respect to her had he assumed to doubt what Mr. Slope had said.

Thus mollified Mrs. Proudie again declared that "she would not
have it done," and at last sent Mrs. Quiverful home with an
assurance that, to the furthest stretch of her power and influence
in the palace, the appointment of Mr. Quiverful should be insisted
on. As she repeated the word "insisted," she thought of the
bishop in his night-cap, and with compressed lips slightly shook

her head. Oh! my aspiring pastors, divines to whose ears *nolo episcopari* are the sweetest of words, which of you would be a bishop on such terms as these ?

Mrs. Quiverful got home in the farmer's cart, not indeed with a light heart, but satisfied that she had done right in making her visit.

CHAP. XXVII.

A LOVE SCENE.

MR. SLOPE, as we have said, left the palace with a feeling of considerable triumph. Not that he thought that his difficulties were all over ; he did not so deceive himself ; but he felt that he had played his first move well, as well as the pieces on the board would allow ; and that he had nothing with which to reproach himself. He first of all posted the letter to the archbishop, and having made that sure he proceeded to push the advantage which he had gained. Had Mrs. Bold been at home, he would have called on her ; but he knew that she was at Plumstead, so he wrote the following note. It was the beginning of what, he trusted, might be a long and tender series of epistles.

"My dear Mrs. Bold, — You will understand perfectly that I cannot at present correspond with your father. I heartily wish that I could, and hope the day may be not long distant when mists shall have cleared away, and we may know each other. But I cannot preclude myself from the pleasure of sending you these few lines to say that Mr. Q. has to-day, in my presence, resigned any title that he ever had to the wardenship of the hospital, and that the bishop has assured me that it is his intention to offer it to your esteemed father.

"Will you, with my respectful compliments, ask him, who I believe is now a fellow-visitor with you, to call on the bishop either on Wednesday or Thursday, between ten and one. *This is by the bishop's desire.* If you will so far oblige me as to let me have a line naming either day, and the hour which will suit Mr. Harding, I will take care that the servants shall have orders to show him in without delay. Perhaps I should say no more, — but still I wish you could make your father understand that no subject will be mooted between his lordship and him, which will refer at all to the method in which he may choose to perform his duty. I, for one, am persuaded that no clergyman could perform it more satisfactorily than he did, or than he will do again.

"On a former occasion I was indiscreet and much too impatient, considering your father's age and my own. I hope he will not now refuse my apology. I still hope also that, with your aid and sweet pious labours, we may live to attach such a Sabbath school to the old endowment, as may, by God's grace and furtherance, be a blessing to the poor of this city.

"You will see at once that this letter is confidential. The subject, of course, makes it so. But, equally of course, it is for your parent's eye as well as for your own, should you think proper to show it to him.

"I hope my darling little friend Johnny is as strong as ever, — dear little fellow. Does he still continue his rude assaults on those beautiful long silken tresses?

"I can assure you your friends miss you from Barchester sorely; but it would be cruel to begrudge you your sojourn among flowers and fields during this truly sultry weather.

"Pray believe me, my dear Mrs. Bold,
"Yours most sincerely,
"OBADIAH SLOPE.

"Barchester, Friday."

Now this letter, taken as a whole, and with the consideration that Mr. Slope wished to assume a great degree of intimacy with Eleanor, would not have been bad, but for the allusion to the tresses. Gentlemen do not write to ladies about their tresses, unless they are on very intimate terms indeed. But Mr. Slope could not be expected to be aware of this. He longed to put a little affection into his epistle, and yet he thought it injudicious, as the letter would, he knew, be shown to Mr. Harding. He would have insisted that the letter should be strictly private and seen by no eyes but Eleanor's own, had he not felt that such an injunction would have been disobeyed. He therefore restrained his passion, did not sign himself "yours affectionately," and contented himself instead with the compliment to the tresses.

Having finished his letter, he took it to Mrs. Bold's house, and learning there, from the servant, that things were to be sent out to Plumstead that afternoon, left it, with many injunctions, in her hands.

We will now follow Mr. Slope so as to complete the day with him, and then return to his letter and its momentous fate in the next chapter.

There is an old song which gives us some very good advice about courting : —

> "It's gude to be off with the auld luve
> Before ye be on wi' the new."

Of the wisdom of this maxim Mr. Slope was ignorant, and accordingly, having written his letter to Mrs. Bold, he proceeded to call upon the Signora Neroni. Indeed it was hard to say which was the old love and which the new, Mr. Slope having been smitten with both so nearly at the same time. Perhaps he thought it not amiss to have two strings to his bow. But two strings to Cupid's bow are always dangerous to him on whose behalf they are to be used. A man should remember that between two stools he may fall to the ground.

But in sooth Mr. Slope was pursuing Mrs. Bold in obedience to his better instincts, and the signora in obedience to his worser. Had he won the widow and worn her, no one could have blamed him. You, O reader, and I, and Eleanor's other friends would have received the story of such a winning with much disgust and disappointment; but we should have been angry with Eleanor, not with Mr. Slope. Bishop, male and female, dean and chapter and diocesan clergy in full congress, could have found nothing to disapprove of in such an alliance. Convocation itself, that mysterious and mighty synod, could in no wise have fallen foul of it. The possession of 1000*l.* a year and a beautiful wife would not at all have hurt the voice of the pulpit charmer, or lessened the grace and piety of the exemplary clergyman.

But not of such a nature were likely to be his dealings with the Signora Neroni. In the first place he knew that her husband was living, and therefore he could not woo her honestly. Then again she had nothing to recommend her to his honest wooing had such been possible. She was not only portionless, but also from misfortune unfitted to be chosen as the wife of any man who wanted a useful mate. Mr. Slope was aware that she was a helpless, hopeless cripple.

But Mr. Slope could not help himself. He knew that he was wrong in devoting his time to the back drawing-room in Dr. Stanhope's house. He knew that what took place there would if divulged utterly ruin him with Mrs. Bold. He knew that scandal would soon come upon his heels and spread abroad among the black coats of Barchester some tidings, exaggerated tidings, of the sighs which he poured into the lady's ears. He knew that he was acting against the recognised principles of his life, against those laws of conduct by which he hoped to achieve much higher success. But as we have said, he could not help himself. Passion, for the first time in his life, passion was too strong for him.

As for the signora, no such plea can be put forward for her, for in truth she cared no more for Mr. Slope than she did for twenty others who had been at her feet before him. She willingly, nay greedily, accepted his homage. He was the finest fly that Barchester had hitherto afforded to her web ; and the signora was a powerful spider that made wondrous webs, and could in no way live without catching flies. Her taste in this respect was abominable, for she had no use for the victims when caught. She could not eat them matrimonially, as young lady-flies do whose webs are most frequently of their mothers' weaving. Nor could she devour them by any escapade of a less legitimate description. Her unfortunate affliction precluded her from all hope of levanting with a lover. It would be impossible to run away with a lady who required three servants to move her from a sofa.

The signora was subdued by no passion. Her time for love was gone. She had lived out her heart, such heart as she had ever had, in her early years, at an age when Mr. Slope was thinking of the second book of Euclid and his unpaid bill at the buttery hatch. In age the lady was younger than the gentleman; but in feelings, in knowledge of the affairs of love, in intrigue, he was immeasurably her junior. It was necessary to her to have some man at her feet. It was the one customary excitement of her life. She delighted in the exercise of power which this gave her ; it was now nearly the only food for her ambition ; she would boast to her sister that she could make a fool of any man, and the sister, as little imbued with feminine delicacy as herself, good naturedly thought it but fair that such amusement should be afforded to a poor invalid who was debarred from the ordinary pleasures of life.

Mr. Slope was madly in love, but hardly knew it. The signora spitted him, as a boy does a cockchafer on a cork, that she might enjoy the energetic agony of his gyrations. And she knew very well what she was doing.

Mr. Slope having added to his person all such adornments as are possible to a clergyman making a morning visit, such as a clean neck tie, clean handkerchief, new gloves, and a *soupçon* of not unnecessary scent, called about three o'clock at the doctor's door. At about this hour the signora was almost always alone in the back-drawing room. The mother had not come down. The doctor was out or in his own room. Bertie was out, and Charlotte at any rate left the room if any one called whose object was specially with her sister. Such was her idea of being charitable and sisterly.

Mr. Slope, as was his custom, asked for Mr. Stanhope, and was told, as was the servant's custom, that the signora was in the drawing-room. Upstairs he accordingly went. He found her, as he always did, lying on her sofa with a French volume before her, and a beautiful little inlaid writing case open on her table. At the moment of his entrance she was in the act of writing.

"Ah my friend," said she, putting out her left hand to him across her desk, "I did not expect you to-day and was this very instant writing to you——"

Mr. Slope, taking the soft fair delicate hand in his, and very soft and fair and delicate it was, bowed over it his huge red head and kissed it. It was a sight to see, a deed to record if the author could fitly do it, a picture to put on canvass. Mr. Slope was big, awkward, cumbrous, and having his heart in his pursuit was ill at ease. The lady was fair, as we have said, and delicate ; every thing about her was fine and refined ; her hand in his looked like a rose lying among carrots, and when he kissed it he looked as a cow might do on finding such a flower among her food. She was graceful as a couchant goddess, and, moreover, as self-possessed as Venus must have been when courting Adonis.

Oh, that such grace and such beauty should have condescended to waste itself on such a pursuit!

"I was in the act of writing to you," said she, "but now my scrawl may go into the basket ;" and she raised the sheet of gilded note paper from off her desk as though to tear it.

"Indeed it shall not," said he, laying the embargo of half a stone weight of human flesh and blood upon the devoted paper. "Nothing that you write for my eyes, signora, shall be so desecrated," and he took up the letter, put that also among the carrots and fed on it, and then proceeded to read it.

"Gracious me ! Mr. Slope," said she, " I hope you don't mean to say that you keep all the trash I write to you. Half my time I don't know what I write, and when I do, I know it is only fit for the back of the fire. I hope you have not that ugly trick of keeping letters."

"At any rate, I don't throw them into a waste-paper basket. If destruction is their doomed lot, they perish worthily, and are burnt on a pyre, as Dido was of old."

"With a steel pen stuck through them, of course," said she, "to make the simile more complete. Of all the ladies of my acquaintance I think Lady Dido was the most absurd. Why did she not do as Cleopatra did ? Why did she not take out her ships and insist on going with him? She could not bear to lose the land she had got by a swindle; and then she could not bear the loss of her lover. So she fell between two stools. Mr. Slope, whatever you do, never mingle love and business."

Mr. Slope blushed up to his eyes, and over his mottled forehead to the very roots of his hair. He felt sure that the signora knew all about his intentions with reference to Mrs. Bold. His conscience told him that he was detected. His doom was to be spoken; he was to be punished for his duplicity, and rejected by the beautiful creature before him. Poor man. He little dreamt that had all his intentions with reference to Mrs. Bold been known to the signora, it would only have added zest to that lady's amusement. It was all very well to have Mr. Slope at her feet, to show her power by making an utter fool of a clergyman, to gratify her own infidelity by thus proving the little strength which religion had in controlling the passions even of a religious man; but it would be an increased gratification if she could be made to understand that she was at the same time alluring her victim away from another, whose love if secured would be in every way beneficent and salutary.

The signora had indeed discovered with the keen instinct of such a woman, that Mr. Slope was bent on matrimony with Mrs. Bold, but in alluding to Dido she had not thought of it. She instantly perceived, however, from her lover's blushes, what was on his mind, and was not slow in taking advantage of it.

She looked him full in the face, not angrily, nor yet with a smile, but with an intense and overpowering gaze; and then holding up her forefinger, and slightly shaking her head she said:—

" Whatever you do, my friend, do not mingle love and business. Either stick to your treasure and your city of wealth, or else follow your love like a true man. But never attempt both. If you do, you'll have to die with a broken heart as did poor Dido. Which is it to be with you, Mr. Slope, love or money?"

Mr. Slope was not so ready with a pathetic answer as he usually was with touching episodes in his extempore sermons. He felt that he ought to say something pretty, something also that should remove the impression on the mind of his lady love. But he was rather put about how to do it.

" Love," said he, " true overpowering love, must be the strongest passion a man can feel; it must control every other wish, and put aside every other pursuit. But with me love will never act in that way unless it be returned;" and he threw upon the signora a look of tenderness which was intended to make up for all the deficiencies of his speech.

"Take my advice," said she. "Never mind love. After all, what is it? The dream of a few weeks. That is all its joy. The disappointment of a life is its Nemesis. Who was ever successful in true love? Success in love argues that the love is false. True love is always despondent or tragical. Juliet loved, Haidee loved, Dido loved, and what came of it? Troilus loved and ceased to be a man."

"Troilus loved and was fooled," said the more manly chaplain. "A man may love and yet not be a Troilus. All women are not Cressids."

"No; all women are not Cressids. The falsehood is not always on the woman's side. Imogen was true, but how was she rewarded? Her lord believed her to be the paramour of the first he who came near her in his absence. Desdemona was true and was smothered. Ophelia was true and went mad. There is no happiness in love, except at the end of an English novel. But in wealth, money, houses, lands, goods and chattels, in the good things of this world, yes, in them there is something tangible, something that can be retained and enjoyed."

"Oh, no," said Mr. Slope, feeling himself bound to enter some protest against so very unorthodox a doctrine, "this world's wealth will make no one happy."

"And what will make you happy — you — you?" said she, raising herself up, and speaking to him with energy across the table. "From what source do you look for happiness? Do not say that you look for none? I shall not believe you. It is a search in which every human being spends an existence."

"And the search is always in vain," said Mr. Slope. "We look for happiness on earth, while we ought to be content to hope for it in heaven."

"Pshaw! you preach a doctrine which you know you don't believe. It is the way with you all. If you know that there is no earthly happiness, why do you long to be a bishop or a dean? Why do you want lands and income?"

"I have the natural ambition of a man," said he.

"Of course you have, and the natural passions; and therefore I say that you don't believe the doctrine you preach. St. Paul was an enthusiast. He believed so that his ambition and passions did not war against his creed. So does the Eastern fanatic who passes half his life erect upon a pillar. As for me, I will believe in no belief that does not make itself manifest by outward signs. I will think no preaching sincere that is not recommended by the practice of the preacher."

Mr. Slope was startled and horrified, but he felt that he could not answer. How could he stand up and preach the lessons of his

Master, being there as he was, on the devil's business? He was a true believer, otherwise this would have been nothing to him. He had audacity for most things, but he had not audacity to make a plaything of the Lord's word. All this the signora understood, and felt much interest as she saw her cockchafer whirl round upon her pin.

"Your wit delights in such arguments," said he, "but your heart and your reason do not go along with them."

"My heart!" said she; "you quite mistake the principles of my composition if you imagine that there is such a thing about me." After all, there was very little that was false in anything that the signora said. If Mr. Slope allowed himself to be deceived it was his own fault. Nothing could have been more open than her declarations about herself.

The little writing table with her desk was still standing before her, a barrier, as it were, against the enemy. She was sitting as nearly upright as she ever did, and he had brought a chair close to the sofa, so that there was only the corner of the table between him and her. It so happened that as she spoke her hand lay upon the table, and as Mr. Slope answered her he put his hand upon hers.

"No heart!" said he. "That is a heavy charge which you bring against yourself, and one of which I cannot find you guilty——"

She withdrew her hand, not quickly and angrily, as though insulted by his touch, but gently and slowly.

"You are in no condition to give a verdict on the matter," said she, "as you have not tried me. No; don't say that you intend doing so, for you know you have no intention of the kind; nor indeed have I either. As for you, you will take your vows where they will result in something more substantial than the pursuit of such a ghostlike, ghastly love as mine——"

"Your love should be sufficient to satisfy the dream of a monarch," said Mr. Slope, not quite clear as to the meaning of his words.

"Say an archbishop, Mr. Slope," said she. Poor fellow! she was very cruel to him. He went round again upon his cork on this allusion to his profession. He tried, however to smile, and gently accused her of joking on a matter, which was, he said, to him of such vital moment.

"Why—what gulls do you men make of us," she replied. "How you fool us to the top of our bent; and of all men you clergymen are the most fluent of your honeyed caressing words. Now look me in the face, Mr. Slope, boldly and openly."

Mr. Slope did look at her with a languishing loving eye, and as he did so, he again put forth his hand to get hold of hers.

"I told you to look at me boldly, Mr. Slope; but confine your boldness to your eyes."

"Oh, Madeline!" he sighed.

"Well, my name is Madeline," said she; "but none except my own family usually call me so. Now look me in the face, Mr. Slope. Am I to understand that you say you love me?"

Mr. Slope never had said so. If he had come there with any formed plan at all, his intention was to make love to the lady without uttering any such declaration. It was, however, quite impossible that he should now deny his love. He had, therefore, nothing for it, but to go down on his knees distractedly against the sofa, and swear that he did love her with a love passing the love of man.

The signora received the assurance with very little palpitation or appearance of surprise. "And now answer me another question," said she; "when are you to be married to my dear friend Eleanor Bold?"

Poor Mr. Slope went round and round in mortal agony. In such a condition as his it was really very hard for him to know what answer to give. And yet no answer would be his surest condemnation. He might as well at once plead guilty to the charge brought against him.

"And why do you accuse me of such dissimulation?" said he.

"Dissimulation! I said nothing of dissimulation. I made no charge against you, and make none. Pray don't defend yourself to me. You swear that you are devoted to my beauty, and yet you are on the eve of matrimony with another. I feel this to be rather a compliment. It is to Mrs. Bold that you must defend yourself. That you may find difficult; unless, indeed, you can keep her in the dark. You clergymen are cleverer than other men."

"Signora, I have told you that I loved you, and now you rail at me?"

"Rail at you. God bless the man; what would he have? Come, answer me this at your leisure,—not without thinking now, but leisurely and with consideration,—Are you not going to be married to Mrs. Bold?"

"I am not," said he. And as he said it, he almost hated, with an exquisite hatred, the woman whom he could not help loving with an exquisite love.

"But surely you are a worshipper of hers?"

"I am not," said Mr. Slope, to whom the word worshipper was peculiarly distasteful. The signora had conceived that it would be so.

"I wonder at that," said she. "Do you not admire her? To my eye she is the perfection of English beauty. And then she is rich too. I should have thought she was just the person to attract you. Come, Mr. Slope, let me give you advice on this matter. Marry the charming widow; she will be a good mother to your children, and an excellent mistress of a clergyman's household."

"Oh, signora, how can you be so cruel?"

"Cruel," said she, changing the voice of banter which she had been using for one which was expressively earnest in its tone; "is that cruelty?"

"How can I love another, while my heart is entirely your own?"

"If that were cruelty, Mr. Slope, what might you say of me if I were to declare that I returned your passion? What would you think if I bound you even by a lover's oath to do daily penance at this couch of mine? What can I give in return for a man's love? Ah, dear friend, you have not realised the conditions of my fate."

Mr. Slope was not on his knees all this time. After his declaration of love he had risen from them as quickly as he thought consistent with the new position which he now filled, and as he stood was leaning on the back of his chair. This outburst of tenderness on the signora's part quite overcame him, and made him feel for the moment that he could sacrifice everything to be assured of the love of the beautiful creature before him, maimed, lame, and already married as she was.

"And can I not sympathise with your lot?" said he, now seating himself on her sofa, and pushing away the table with his foot.

"Sympathy is so near to pity!" said she. "If you pity me, cripple as I am, I shall spurn you from me."

"Oh, Madeline, I will only love you," and again he caught her hand and devoured it with kisses. Now she did not draw it from him, but sat there as he kissed it, looking at him with her great eyes, just as a great spider would look at a great fly that was quite securely caught.

"Suppose Signor Neroni were to come to Barchester," said she, "would you make his acquaintance?"

"Signor Neroni!" said he.

"Would you introduce him to the bishop, and Mrs. Proudie, and the young ladies?" said she, again having recourse to that horrid quizzing voice which Mr. Slope so particularly hated.

"Why do you ask such a question?" said he.

"Because it is necessary that you should know that there is a Signor Neroni. I think you had forgotten it."

"If I thought that you retained for that wretch one particle of the love of which he was never worthy, I would die before I would distract you by telling you what I feel. No! were your husband the master of your heart, I might perhaps love you; but you should never know it."

"My heart again! how you talk. And you consider then, that if a husband be not master of his wife's heart, he has no right to her fealty; if a wife ceases to love, she may cease to be true. Is that your doctrine on this matter, as a minister of the Church of England?"

Mr. Slope tried hard within himself to cast off the pollution with which he felt that he was defiling his soul. He strove to tear himself away from the noxious siren that had bewitched him. But he could not do it. He could not be again heart free. He had looked for rapturous joy in loving this lovely creature, and he already found that he met with little but disappointment and self-rebuke. He had come across the fruit of the Dead Sea, so sweet and delicious to the eye, so bitter and nauseous to the taste. He had put the apple to his mouth, and it had turned to ashes between his teeth. Yet he could not tear himself away. He knew, he could not but know, that she jeered at him, ridiculed his love, and insulted the weakness of his religion. But she half permitted his adoration, and that half permission added such fuel to his fire that all the fountain of his piety could not quench it. He began to feel savage, irritated, and revengeful. He meditated some severity of speech, some taunt that should cut her, as her taunts cut him. He reflected as he stood there for a moment, silent before her, that if he desired to quell her proud spirit, he should do so by being prouder even than herself; that if he wished to have her at his feet suppliant for his love it behoved him to conquer her by indifference. All this passed through his mind. As far as dead knowledge went, he knew, or thought he knew, how a woman should be tamed. But when he essayed to bring his tactics to bear, he failed like a child. What chance has dead knowledge with experience in any of the transactions between man and man? What possible chance between man and woman? Mr. Slope loved furiously, insanely, and truly ; but he had never played the game of love. The signora did not love at all, but she was up to every move of the board. It was Philidor pitted against a school-boy.

And so she continued to insult him, and he continued to bear it.

"Sacrifice the world for love!" said she, in answer to some renewed vapid declaration of his passion ; "how often has the same thing been said, and how invariably with the same falsehood!"

"Falsehood," said he. "Do you say that I am false to you? do you say that my love is not real?"

"False? of course it is false, false as the father of falsehood—if indeed falsehoods need a sire and are not self-begotten since the world began. You are ready to sacrifice the world for love? Come, let us see what you will sacrifice. I care nothing for nuptial vows. The wretch, I think you were kind enough to call him so, whom I swore to love and obey, is so base that he can only be thought of with repulsive disgust. In the council chamber of my heart I have divorced him. To me that is as good as though aged lords had gloated for months over the details of his licentious life. I care nothing for what the world can say. Will you be as frank? Will you take me to your home as your wife? Will you call me Mrs. Slope before bishop, dean, and prebendaries?" The poor tortured wretch stood silent, not knowing what to say. "What! you won't do that. Tell me, then, what part of the world is it that you will sacrifice for my charms?"

"Were you free to marry, I would take you to my house to-morrow and wish no higher privilege."

"I am free," said she, almost starting up in her energy. For though there was no truth in her pretended regard for her clerical admirer, there was a mixture of real feeling in the scorn and satire with which she spoke of love and marriage generally. "I am free; free as the winds. Come; will you take me as I am? Have your wish; sacrifice the world, and prove yourself a true man."

Mr. Slope should have taken her at her word. She would have drawn back, and he would have had the full advantage of the offer. But he did not. Instead of doing so, he stood wrapt in astonishment, passing his fingers through his lank red hair, and thinking as he stared upon her animated countenance that her wondrous beauty grew more and more wonderful as he gazed on it. "Ha! ha! ha!" she laughed out loud. "Come, Mr. Slope; don't talk of sacrificing the world again. People beyond one-and-twenty should never dream of such a thing. You and I, if we have the dregs of any love left in us, if we have the remnants of a passion remaining in our hearts, should husband our re-sources better. We are not in our *première jeunesse*. The world is a very nice place. Your world, at any rate, is so. You have all manner of fat rectories to get, and possible bishoprics to enjoy. Come, confess; on second thoughts you would not sacrifice such things for the smiles of a lame lady?"

It was impossible for him to answer this. In order to be in any way dignified, he felt that he must be silent.

"Come," said she — "don't boody with me: don't be angry because I speak out some home truths. Alas, the world, as I have found it, has taught me bitter truths. Come, tell me that I am forgiven. Are we not to be friends?" and she again put out her hand to him.

He sat himself down in the chair beside her, and took her proffered hand and leant over her.

"There," said she, with her sweetest softest smile — a smile to withstand which a man should be cased in triple steel, "there; seal your forgiveness on it," and she raised it towards his face. He kissed it again and again, and stretched over her as though desirous of extending the charity of his pardon beyond the hand that was offered to him. She managed, however, to check his ardour. For one so easily allured as this poor chaplain, her hand was surely enough.

"Oh, Madeline!" said he, "tell me that you love me — do you — do you love me?"

"Hush," said she. "There is my mother's step. Our *tête-à-tête* has been of monstrous length. Now you had better go. But we shall see you soon again, shall we not?"

Mr. Slope promised that he would call again on the following day.

"And, Mr. Slope," she continued, "pray answer my note. You have it in your hand, though I declare during these two hours you have not been gracious enough to read it. It is about the Sabbath school and the children. You know how anxious I am to have them here. I have been learning the catechism myself, on purpose. You must manage it for me next week. I will teach them, at any rate, to submit themselves to their spiritual pastors and masters."

Mr. Slope said but little on the subject of Sabbath schools, but he made his adieu, and betook himself home with a sad heart, troubled mind, and uneasy conscience.

CHAP. XXVIII.

MRS. BOLD IS ENTERTAINED BY DR. AND MRS. GRANTLY AT PLUMSTEAD.

IT will be remembered that Mr. Slope, when leaving his *billet doux* at the house of Mrs. Bold, had been informed that it would be sent out to her at Plumstead that afternoon. The archdeacon and Mr. Harding had in fact come into town together in the brougham, and it had been arranged that they should call for Eleanor's parcels as they left on their way home. Accordingly they did so call, and the maid, as she handed to the coachman a small basket and large bundle carefully and neatly packed, gave in at the carriage window Mr. Slope's epistle. The archdeacon, who was sitting next to the window, took it, and immediately recognised the hand-writing of his enemy.

"Who left this?" said he.

"Mr. Slope called with it himself, your reverence," said the girl; "and was very anxious that missus should have it to-day."

So the brougham drove off, and the letter was left in the archdeacon's hand. He looked at it as though he held a basket of adders. He could not have thought worse of the document had he read it and discovered it to be licentious and atheistical. He did, moreover, what so many wise people are accustomed to do in similar circumstances; he immediately condemned the person to whom the letter was written, as though she were necessarily a *particeps criminis*.

Poor Mr. Harding, though by no means inclined to forward Mr. Slope's intimacy with his daughter, would have given anything to have kept the letter from his son-in-law. But that was now impossible. There it was in his hand; and he looked as thoroughly disgusted as though he were quite sure that it contained all the rhapsodies of a favoured lover.

"It's very hard on me," said he, after awhile, "that this should go on under my roof."

Now here the archdeacon was certainly most unreasonable. Having invited his sister-in-law to his house, it was a natural consequence that she should receive her letters there. And if Mr. Slope chose to write to her, his letter would, as a matter of course, be sent after her. Moreover, the very fact of an invitation to one's, house implies confidence on the part of the inviter. He had shown that he thought Mrs. Bold to be a fit person to stay with him by his asking her to do so, and it was most cruel to her that he should complain of her violating the sanctity of his roof-tree, when the laches committed were none of her committing.

Mr. Harding felt this; and felt also that when the archdeacon talked thus about his roof, what he said was most offensive to himself as Eleanor's father. If Eleanor did receive a letter from Mr. Slope what was there in that to pollute the purity of Dr. Grantly's household? He was indignant that his daughter should be so judged and so spoken of; and he made up his mind that even as Mrs. Slope she must be dearer to him than any other creature on God's earth. He almost broke out, and said as much ; but for the moment he restrained himself.

"Here," said the archdeacon, handing the offensive missile to his father-in-law ; "I am not going to be the bearer of his love letters. You are her father, and may do as you think fit with it."

By doing as he thought fit with it, the archdeacon certainly meant that Mr. Harding would be justified in opening and reading the letter, and taking any steps which might in consequence be necessary. To tell the truth, Dr. Grantly did feel rather a stronger curiosity than was justified by his outraged virtue, to see the contents of the letter. Of course he could not open it himself, but he wished to make Mr. Harding understand that he, as Eleanor's father, would be fully justified in doing so. The idea of such a proceeding never occurred to Mr. Harding. His authority over Eleanor ceased when she became the wife of John Bold. He had not the slightest wish to pry into her correspondence. He consequently put the letter into his pocket, and only wished that he had been able to do so without the archdeacon's knowledge. They both sat silent during half the journey home, and then Dr. Grantly said, "Perhaps Susan had better give it to her. She can explain to her sister, better than either you or I can do, how deep is the disgrace of such an acquaintance."

"I think you are very hard upon Eleanor," replied Mr. Harding "I will not allow that she has disgraced herself, nor do I think it likely that she will do so. She has a right to correspond with whom she pleases, and I shall not take upon myself to blame her because she gets a letter from Slope."

"I suppose," said Dr. Grantly, "you don't wish her to marry the man. I suppose you'll admit that she would disgrace herself if she did do so."

"I do not wish her to marry him," said the perplexed father ; "I do not like him, and do not think he would make a good husband. But if Eleanor chooses to do so, I shall certainly not think that she disgraces herself."

"Good heavens!" exclaimed Dr. Grantly, and threw himself back into the corner of his brougham. Mr. Harding said nothing more, but commenced playing a dirge, with an imaginary fiddle bow upon an imaginary violoncello, for which there did not appear to be quite room enough in the carriage ; and he continued the tune, with sundry variations, till he arrived at the rectory door.

The archdeacon had been meditating sad things in his mind. Hitherto he had always looked on his father-in-law as a true partisan, though he knew him to be a man devoid of all the combative qualifications for that character. He had felt no fear that Mr. Harding would go over to the enemy, though he had never counted much on the ex-warden's prowess in breaking the hostile ranks. Now, however, it seemed that Eleanor, with her wiles, had completely trepanned and bewildered her father, cheated him out of his judgment, robbed him of the predilections and tastes of his life, and caused him to be tolerant of a man whose arrogance and vulgarity would, a few years since, have been unendurable to him. That the whole thing was as good as arranged between Eleanor and Mr. Slope there was no longer any room to doubt. That Mr. Harding knew that such was the case, even this could hardly be doubted. It was too manifest that he at any rate suspected it, and was prepared to sanction it.

And to tell the truth, such was the case. Mr. Harding disliked Mr. Slope as much as it was in his nature to dislike any man. Had his daughter wished to do her worst to displease him by a second marriage, she could hardly have succeeded better than by marrying Mr. Slope. But, as he said to himself now very often, what right had he to condemn her if she did nothing that was really wrong? If she liked Mr. Slope it was her affair. It was indeed miraculous to him that a woman with such a mind, so educated, so refined, so nice in her tastes, should like such a man. Then he asked himself whether it was possible that she did so?

Ah, thou weak man; most charitable, most Christian, but weakest of men! Why couldst thou not have asked herself? Was she not the daughter of thy loins, the child of thy heart, the best beloved to thee of all humanity? Had she not proved to thee, by years of closest affection, her truth and goodness and filial obedience? And yet, knowing and feeling all this, thou couldst endure to go groping in darkness, hearing her named in strains which wounded thy loving heart, and being unable to defend her as thou shouldst have done!

Mr. Harding had not believed, did not believe, that his daughter meant to marry this man; but he feared to commit himself to such an opinion. If she did do it there would be then no means of retreat. The wishes of his heart were—First, that there should be no truth in the archdeacon's surmises; and in this wish he would have fain trusted entirely, had he dared so to do; Secondly, that the match might be prevented, if unfortunately, it had been contemplated by Eleanor; Thirdly, that should she be so infatuated as to marry this man, he might justify his conduct, and declare that no cause existed for his separating himself from her.

He wanted to believe her incapable of such a marriage; he wanted to show that he so believed of her; but he wanted also to be able to say hereafter, that she had done nothing amiss, if she should unfortunately prove herself to be different from what he thought her to be.

Nothing but affection could justify such fickleness; but affection did justify it. There was but little of the Roman about Mr. Harding. He could not sacrifice his Lucretia even though she should be polluted by the accepted addresses of the clerical Tarquin at the palace. If Tarquin could be prevented, well and good; but if not, the father would still open his heart to his daughter, and accept her as she presented herself, Tarquin and all.

Dr. Grantly's mind was of a stronger calibre, and he was by no means deficient in heart. He loved with an honest genuine love his wife and children and friends. He loved his father-in-law; and was quite prepared to love Eleanor too, if she would be one of his party, if she would be on his side, if she would regard the Slopes and the Proudies as the enemies of mankind, and acknowledge and feel the comfortable merits of the Gwynnes and Arabins. He wished to be what he called "safe" with all those whom he had admitted to the penetralia of his house and heart. He could luxuriate in no society that was deficient in a certain feeling of faithful staunch high-churchism, which to him was tantamount to freemasonry. He was not strict in his lines of definition. He endured without impatience many different shades of Anglo-church conservatism; but with the Slopes and Proudies he could not go on all fours.

He was wanting in, moreover, or perhaps it would be more correct to say, he was not troubled by that womanly tenderness which was so peculiar to Mr. Harding. His feelings towards his friends were, that while they stuck to him he would stick to them; that he would work with them shoulder and shoulder; that he would be faithful to the faithful. He knew nothing of that beautiful love which can be true to a false friend.

And thus these two men, each miserable enough in his own way, returned to Plumstead.

It was getting late when they arrived there, and the ladies had already gone up to dress. Nothing more was said as the two parted in the hall. As Mr. Harding passed to his own room he knocked at Eleanor's door and handed in the letter. The archdeacon hurried to his own territory, there to unburden his heart to his faithful partner.

What colloquy took place between the marital chamber and the adjoining dressing-room shall not be detailed. The reader, now intimate with the persons concerned, can well imagine it. The whole tenor of it also might be read in Mrs. Grantly's brow as she came down to dinner.

Eleanor, when she received the letter from her father's hand, had no idea from whom it came. She had never seen Mr. Slope's hand-writing, or if so had forgotten it; and did not think of him as she twisted the letter as people do twist letters when they do not immediately recognise their correspondents either by the writing or the seal. She was sitting at her glass brushing her hair, and rising every other minute to play with her boy who was sprawling on the bed, and who engaged pretty nearly the whole attention of the maid as well as of his mother.

At last, sitting before her toilet table, she broke the seal, and turning over the leaf saw Mr. Slope's name. She first felt surprised, and then annoyed, and then anxious. As she read it she became interested. She was so delighted to find that all obstacles to her father's return to the hospital were apparently removed that she did not observe the fulsome language in which the tidings were conveyed. She merely perceived that she was commissioned to tell her father that such was the case, and she did not realise the fact that such a communication should not have been made, in the first instance, to her by an unmarried young clergyman. She felt, on the whole, grateful to Mr. Slope, and anxious to get on her dress that she might run with the news to her father. Then she came to the allusion to her own pious labours, and she said in her heart that Mr. Slope was an affected ass. Then she went on again and was offended by her boy being called Mr. Slope's darling — he was nobody's darling but her own; or at any rate not the darling of a disagreeable stranger like Mr. Slope. Lastly she arrived at the tresses and felt a qualm of disgust. She looked up in the glass, and there they were before her, long and silken, certainly, and very beautiful. I will not say but that she knew them to be so, but she felt angry with them and brushed them roughly and carelessly. She crumpled the letter up with angry violence, and resolved, almost without thinking of it, that she would not show it to her father. She would merely tell him the contents of it. She then comforted herself again with her boy, had her dress fastened, and went down to dinner.

As she tripped down the stairs she began to ascertain that there was some difficulty in her situation. She could not keep from her father the news about the hospital, nor could she comfortably confess the letter from Mr. Slope before the Grantlys. Her father

had already gone down. She had heard his step upon the lobby.
She resolved therefore to take him aside, and tell him her little bit
of news. Poor girl ! she had no idea how severely the unfortunate letter had already been discussed.

When she entered the drawing room the whole party were there,
including Mr. Arabin, and the whole party looked glum and sour.
The two girls sat silent and apart as though they were aware that
something was wrong. Even Mr. Arabin was solemn and silent.
Eleanor had not seen him since breakfast. He had been the whole
day at St. Ewold's, and such having been the case it was natural
that he should tell how matters were going on there. He did
nothing of the kind, however, but remained solemn and silent.
They were all solemn and silent. Eleanor knew in her heart that
they had been talking about her, and her heart misgave her as she
thought of Mr. Slope and his letter. At any rate she felt it to be
quite impossible to speak to her father alone while matters were
in this state.

Dinner was soon announced and Dr. Grantly, as was his wont,
gave Eleanor his arm. But he did so as though the doing it were
an outrage on his feelings rendered necessary by sternest necessity. With quick sympathy Eleanor felt this, and hardly put her
fingers on his coat sleeve. It may be guessed in what way the
dinner-hour was passed. Dr. Grantly said a few words to Mr.
Arabin, Mr. Arabin said a few words to Mrs. Grantly, she said a
few words to her father, and he tried to say a few words to
Eleanor. She felt that she had been tried and found guilty of
something, though she knew not what. She longed to say out to
them all, " Well, what is it that I have done ; out with it, and let
me know my crime ; for heaven's sake let me hear the worst of
it ;" but she could not. She could say nothing, but sat there
silent, half feeling that she was guilty, and trying in vain to pretend even to eat her dinner.

At last the cloth was drawn, and the ladies were not long following it. When they were gone the gentlemen were somewhat more
sociable but not much so. They could not of course talk over
Eleanor's sins. The archdeacon had indeed so far betrayed his
sister-in-law as to whisper into Mr. Arabin's ear in the study, as
they met there before dinner, a hint of what he feared. He did so
with the gravest and saddest of fears, and Mr. Arabin became
grave and apparently sad enough as he heard it. He opened his
eyes and his mouth and said in a sort of whisper "Mr. Slope !" in
the same way as he might have said "The Cholera !" had his
friend told him that that horrid disease was in his nursery. "I

fear so, I fear so," said the archdeacon, and then together they left the room.

We will not accurately analyse Mr. Arabin's feelings on receipt of such astounding tidings. It will suffice to say that he was surprised, vexed. sorrowful, and ill at ease. He had not perhaps thought very much about Eleanor, but he had appreciated her influence, and had felt that close intimacy with her in a country house was pleasant to him, and also beneficial. He had spoken highly of her intelligence to the archdeacon, and had walked about the shrubberies with her, carrying her boy on his back. When Mr. Arabin had called Johnny his darling, Eleanor was not angry.

Thus the three men sat over their wine, all thinking of the same subject, but unable to speak of it to each other. So we will leave them, and follow the ladies into the drawing-room.

Mrs. Grantly had received a commission from her husband, and had undertaken it with some unwillingness. He had desired her to speak gravely to Eleanor, and to tell her that, if she persisted in her adherence to Mr. Slope, she could no longer look for the countenance of her present friends. Mrs. Grantly probably knew her sister better than the doctor did, and assured him that it would be in vain to talk to her. The only course likely to be of any service in her opinion was to keep Eleanor away from Barchester. Perhaps she might have added, for she had a very keen eye in such things, that there might also be ground for hope in keeping Eleanor near Mr. Arabin. Of this, however, she said nothing. But the archdeacon would not be talked over; he spoke much of his conscience, and declared that if Mrs. Grantly would not do it he would. So instigated, the lady undertook the task, stating, however, her full conviction that her interference would be worse than useless. And so it proved.

As soon as they were in the drawing-room Mrs. Grantly found some excuse for sending her girls away, and then began her task. She knew well that she could exercise but very slight authority over her sister. Their various modes of life, and the distance between their residences, had prevented any very close confidence. They had hardly lived together since Eleanor was a child. Eleanor had moreover, especially in latter years, resented in a quiet sort of way the dictatorial authority which the archdeacon seemed to exercise over her father, and on this account had been unwilling to allow the archdeacon's wife to exercise authority over herself.

"You got a note just before dinner, I believe," began the eldest sister.

Eleanor acknowledged that she had done so, and felt that she turned red as she acknowledged it. She would have given any-thing to have kept her colour, but the more she tried to do so the more signally she failed.

"Was it not from Mr. Slope?"

Eleanor said that the letter was from Mr. Slope.

"Is he a regular correspondent of yours, Eleanor?"

"Not exactly," said she, already beginning to feel angry at the cross-examination. She determined, and why it would be difficult to say, that nothing should induce her to tell her sister Susan what was the subject of the letter. Mrs. Grantly, she knew, was instigated by the archdeacon, and she would not plead to any arraignment made against her by him.

'But, Eleanor dear, why do you get letters from Mr. Slope at all, knowing, as you do, he is a person so distasteful to papa, and to the archdeacon, and indeed to all your friends?"

"In the first place, Susan, I don't get letters from him; and in the next place, as Mr. Slope wrote the one letter which I have got, and as I only received it, which I could not very well help doing, as papa handed it to me, I think you had better ask Mr. Slope instead of me."

"What was his letter about, Eleanor?"

"I cannot tell you," said she, "because it was confidential. It was on business respecting a third person."

"It was in no way personal to yourself, then?"

"I won't exactly say that, Susan," said she, getting more and more angry at her sister's questions.

"Well, I must say it's rather singular," said Mrs. Grantly, affecting to laugh, "that a young lady in your position should receive a letter from an unmarried gentleman of which she will not tell the contents, and which she is ashamed to show to her sister."

"I am not ashamed," said Eleanor blazing up; "I am not ashamed of anything in the matter; only I do not choose to be cross-examined as to my letters by any one."

"Well, dear," said the other, " I cannot but tell you that I do not think Mr. Slope a proper correspondent for you."

"If he be ever so improper, how can I help his having written to me? But you are all prejudiced against him to such an extent, that that which would be kind and generous in another man is odious and impudent in him. I hate a religion that teaches one to be so onesided in one's charity."

"I am sorry, Eleanor, that you hate the religion you find here; but surely you should remember that in such matters the archdeacon must know more of the world than you do. I don't ask you to respect or comply with me, although I am, unfortunately, so many years your senior ; but surely, in such a matter as this, you might consent to be guided by the archdeacon. He is most anxious to be your friend if you will let him."

" In such a matter as what ? " said Eleanor very testily. "Upon my word I don't know what this is all about."

" We all want you to drop Mr. Slope."

" You all want me to be as illiberal as yourselves. That I shall never be. I see no harm in Mr. Slope's acquaintance, and I shall not insult the man by telling him that I do. He has thought it necessary to write to me, and I do not want the archdeacon's advice about the letter. If I did I would ask it."

" Then, Eleanor, it is my duty to tell you," and now she spoke with a tremendous gravity, " that the archdeacon thinks that such a correspondence is disgraceful, and that he cannot allow it to go on in his house."

Eleanor's eyes flashed fire as she answered her sister, jumping up from her seat as she did so. " You may tell the archdeacon that wherever I am I shall receive what letters I please and from whom I please. And as for the word disgraceful, if Dr. Grantly has used it of me he has been unmanly and inhospitable," and she walked off to the door. "When papa comes from the dining-room I will thank you to ask him to step up to my bed-room. I will show him Mr. Slope's letter, but I will show it to no one else." And so saying she retreated to her baby.

She had no conception of the crime with which she was charged. The idea that she could be thought by her friends to regard Mr. Slope as a lover, had never flashed upon her. She conceived that they were all prejudiced and illiberal in their persecution of him, and therefore she would not join in the persecution, even though she greatly disliked the man.

Eleanor was very angry as she seated herself in a low chair by her open window at the foot of her child's bed. " To dare to say I have disgraced myself," she repeated to herself more than once. " How papa can put up with that man's arrogance ! I will certainly not sit down to dinner in his house again unless he begs my pardon for that word." And then a thought struck her that Mr. Arabin might perchance hear of her " disgraceful " correspondence with Mr. Slope, and she turned crimson with pure vexation. Oh, if she had known the truth ? If she could have conceived that Mr. Arabin had been informed as a fact that she was going to marry Mr. Slope !

She had not been long in her room before her father joined her. As he left the drawing-room Mrs. Grantly took her husband into the recess of the window, and told him how signally she had failed.

"I will speak to her myself before I go to bed," said the archdeacon.

"Pray do no such thing," said she; "you can do no good and will only make an unseemly quarrel in the house. You have no idea how headstrong she can be."

The archdeacon declared that as to that he was quite indifferent. He knew his duty and would do it. Mr. Harding was weak in the extreme in such matters. He would not have it hereafter on his conscience that he had not done all that in him lay to prevent so disgraceful an alliance. It was in vain that Mrs. Grantly assured him that speaking to Eleanor angrily would only hasten such a crisis, and render it certain if at present there were any doubt. He was angry, self-willed, and sore. The fact that a lady of his household had received a letter from Mr. Slope had wounded his pride in the sorest place, and nothing could control him.

Mr. Harding looked worn and woebegone as he entered his daughter's room. These sorrows worried him sadly. He felt that if they were continued he must go to the wall in the manner so kindly prophesied to him by the chaplain. He knocked gently at his daughter's door, waited till he was distinctly bade to enter, and then appeared as though he and not she were the suspected criminal.

Eleanor's arm was soon within his, and she had soon kissed his forehead and caressed him, not with joyous but with eager love. "Oh, papa," she said, "I do so want to speak to you. They have been talking about me down stairs to-night; don't you know they have, papa?"

Mr. Harding confessed with a sort of murmur that the archdeacon had been speaking of her.

"I shall hate Dr. Grantly soon —"

"Oh my dear!"

"Well; I shall. I cannot help it. He is so uncharitable, so unkind, so suspicious of every one that does not worship himself: and then he is so monstrously arrogant to other people who have a right to their opinions as well as he has to his own."

"He is an earnest eager man, my dear: but he never means to be unkind."

"He is unkind, papa, most unkind. There, I got that letter from Mr. Slope before dinner. It was you yourself who gave it to me. There; pray read it. It is all for you. It should have been addressed to you. You know how they have been talking about it down stairs. You know how they behaved to me at dinner. And since dinner Susan has been preaching to me, till I could not remain in the room with her. Read it, papa ; and then say whether that is a letter that need make Dr. Grantly so outrageous."

Mr. Harding took his arm from his daughter's waist, and slowly read the letter. She expected to see his countenance lit with joy as he learnt that his path back to the hospital was made so smooth ; but she was doomed to disappointment, as had once been the case before on a somewhat similar occasion. His first feeling was one of unmitigated disgust that Mr. Slope should have chosen to interfere in his behalf. He had been anxious to get back to the hospital, but he would have infinitely sooner resigned all pretensions to the place, than have owed it in any manner to Mr. Slope's influence in his favour. Then he thoroughly disliked the tone of Mr. Slope's letter; it was unctuous, false, and unwholesome, like the man. He saw, which Eleanor had failed to see, that much more had been intended than was expressed. The appeal to Eleanor's pious labours as separate from his own grated sadly against his feelings as a father. And then when he came to the "darling boy" and the "silken tresses," he slowly closed and folded the letter in despair. It was impossible that Mr. Slope should so write unless he had been encouraged. It was impossible Eleanor should have received such a letter, and have received it without annoyance, unless she were willing to encourage him. So at least Mr. Harding argued to himself.

How hard it is to judge accurately of the feelings of others. Mr. Harding, as he came to the close of the letter, in his heart condemned his daughter for indelicacy, and it made him miserable to do so. She was not responsible for what Mr. Slope might write. True. But then she expressed no disgust at it. She had rather expressed approval of the letter as a whole. She had given it to him to read, as a vindication for herself and also for him. The father's spirits sank within him as he felt that he could not acquit her.

And yet it was the true feminine delicacy of Eleanor's mind which brought her on this condemnation. Listen to me, ladies, and I beseech *you* to acquit her. She thought of this man, this lover of whom she was so unconscious, exactly as her father did, exactly as the Grantlys did. At least she esteemed him personally as they did. But she believed him to be in the main an honest man, and one truly inclined to assist her father. She felt herself bound, after what had passed, to show this letter

to Mr. Harding. She thought it necessary that he should know
what Mr. Slope had to say. But she did not think it necessary
to apologise for, or condemn, or even allude to the vulgarity, of
the man's tone, which arose, as does all vulgarity, from ignorance. It was nauseous to her to have a man like Mr. Slope
commenting on her personal attractions; and she did not think it
necessary to dilate with her father upon what was nauseous.
She never supposed they could disagree on such a subject. It would
have been painful for her to point it out, painful for her to speak
strongly against a man of whom, on the whole, she was anxious
to think and speak well. In encountering such a man she had
encountered what was disagreeable, as she might do in walking
the streets. But in such encounters she never thought it necessary to dwell on what disgusted her.

And he, foolish weak loving man, would not say one word,
though one word would have cleared up everything. There
would have been a deluge of tears, and in ten minutes every one
in the house would have understood how matters really were.
The father would have been delighted. The sister would have
kissed her sister and begged a thousand pardons. The archdeacon
would have apologised and wondered, and raised his eyebrows,
and gone to bed a happy man. And Mr. Arabin — Mr. Arabin
would have dreamt of Eleanor, have awoke in the morning with
ideas of love, and retired to rest the next evening with schemes of
marriage. But, alas! all this was not to be.

Mr. Harding slowly folded the letter, handed it back to her,
kissed her forehead and bade God bless her. He then crept
slowly away to his own room.

As soon as he had left the passage another knock was given at
Eleanor's door, and Mrs. Grantly's very demure own maid,
entering on tiptoe, wanted to know would Mrs. Bold be so kind as
to speak to the archdeacon for two minutes, in the archdeacon's
study, if not disagreeable. The archdeacon's compliments, and he
wouldn't detain her two minutes.

Eleanor thought it was very disagreeable; she was tired and
fagged and sick at heart; her present feelings towards Dr. Grantly
were anything but those of affection. She was, however, no
coward, and therefore promised to be in the study in five minutes.
So she arranged her hair, tied on her cap, and went down with a
palpitating heart.

CHAP. XXIX.

A SERIOUS INTERVIEW.

THERE are people who delight in serious interviews, especially when to them appertains the part of offering advice or administering rebuke, and perhaps the archdeacon was one of these. Yet on this occasion he did not prepare himself for the coming conversation with much anticipation of pleasure. Whatever might be his faults he was not an inhospitable man, and he almost felt that he was sinning against hospitality in upbraiding Eleanor in his own house. Then, also he was not quite sure that he would get the best of it. His wife had told him that he decidedly would not, and he usually gave credit to what his wife said. He was, however, so convinced of what he considered to be the impropriety of Eleanor's conduct, and so assured also of his own duty in trying to check it, that his conscience would not allow him to take his wife's advice and go to bed quietly.

Eleanor's face as she entered the room was not such as to reassure him. As a rule she was always mild in manner and gentle in conduct; but there was that in her eye which made it not an easy task to scold her. In truth she had been little used to scolding. No one since her childhood had tried it but the archdeacon, and he had generally failed when he did try it. He had never done so since her marriage; and now, when he saw her quiet easy step, as she entered his room, he almost wished that he had taken his wife's advice.

He began by apológising for the trouble he was giving her. She begged him not to mention it, assured him that walking down stairs was no trouble to her at all, and then took a seat and waited patiently for him to begin his attack.

"My dear Eleanor," he said, "I hope you believe me when I assure you that you have no sincerer friend than I am." To this Eleanor answered nothing, and therefore he proceeded. "If you had a brother of your own I should not probably trouble you with what I am going to say. . But as it is I cannot but think that it must be a comfort to you to know that you have near you one who is as anxious for your welfare as any brother of your own could be."

"I never had a brother," said she.

"I know you never had, and it is therefore that I speak to you."

"I never had a brother," she repeated; "but I have hardly felt the want. Papa has been to me both father and brother."

"Your father is the fondest and most affectionate of men. But—"

"He is—the fondest and most affectionate of men, and the best of counsellors. While he lives I can never want advice."

This rather put the archdeacon out. He could not exactly contradict what his sister-in-law said about her father; and yet he did not at all agree with her. He wanted her to understand that he tendered his assistance because her father was a soft good-natured gentleman, not sufficiently knowing in the ways of the world; but he could not say this to her. So he had to rush into the subject matter of his proffered counsel without any acknowledgment on her part that she could need it, or would be grateful for it.

"Susan tells me that you received a letter this evening from Mr. Slope."

"Yes; papa brought it in the brougham. Did he not tell you?"

"And Susan says that you objected to let her know what it was about."

"I don't think she asked me. But had she done so I should not have told her. I don't think it nice to be asked about one's letters. If one wishes to show them one does so without being asked."

"True. Quite so. What you say is quite true. But is not the fact of your receiving letters from Mr. Slope, which you do not wish to show to your friends, a circumstance which must excite some—some surprise—some suspicion—"

"Suspicion!" said she, not speaking above her usual voice, speaking still in a soft womanly tone, but yet with indignation; "suspicion! and who suspects me, and of what?" And then there was a pause, for the archdeacon was not quite ready to explain the ground of his suspicion. "No, Dr. Grantly, I did not choose to show Mr. Slope's letter to Susan. I could not show it to any one till papa had seen it. If you have any wish to read it now, you can do so," and she handed the letter to him over the table.

This was an amount of compliance which he had not at all expected, and which rather upset him in his tactics. However, he took the letter, perused it carefully, and then refolding it, kept it on the table under his hand. To him it appeared to be in almost every respect the letter of a declared lover; it seemed to corroborate his worst suspicions; and the fact of Eleanor's showing it to him was all but tantamount to a declaration on her part, that it was her pleasure to receive love-letters from Mr. Slope. He almost entirely overlooked the real subject-matter of the epistle; so intent was he on the forthcoming courtship and marriage.

"I'll thank you to give it me back, if you please, Dr. Grantly."

He took it in his hand and held it up, but made no immediate overture to return it. "And Mr. Harding has seen this?" said he.

"Of course he has," said she; "it was written that he might see it. It refers solely to his business — of course I showed it to him."

"And, Eleanor, do you think that that is a proper letter for you — for a person in your condition — to receive from Mr. Slope?"

"Quite a proper letter," said she, speaking, perhaps, a little out of obstinacy; probably forgetting at the moment the objectionable mention of her silken curls.

"Then, Eleanor, it is my duty to tell you that I wholly differ from you."

"So I suppose," said she, instigated now by sheer opposition and determination not to succumb. "You think Mr. Slope is a messenger direct from Satan. I think he is an industrious, well meaning clergyman. It's a pity that we differ as we do. But, as we do differ, we had probably better not talk about it."

Here Eleanor undoubtedly put herself in the wrong. She might probably have refused to talk to Dr. Grantly on the matter in dispute without any impropriety; but having consented to listen to him, she had no business to tell him that he regarded Mr. Slope as an emissary from the evil one; nor was she justified in praising Mr. Slope, seeing that in her heart of hearts she did not think well of him. She was, however, wounded in spirit, and angry and bitter. She had been subjected to contumely and cross-questioning and ill-usage through the whole evening. No one, not even Mr. Arabin, not even her father, had been kind to her. All this she attributed to the prejudice and conceit of the archdeacon, and therefore she resolved to set no bounds to her antagonism to him. She would neither give nor take quarter. He had greatly presumed in daring to question her about her correspondence, and she was determined to show that she thought so.

"Eleanor, you are forgetting yourself," said he, looking very sternly at her. "Otherwise you would never tell me that I conceive any man to be a messenger from Satan."

"But you do," said she. "Nothing is too bad for him. Give me that letter, if you please;" and she stretched out her hand and

took it from him. "He has been doing his best to serve papa
doing more than any of papa's friends could do; and yet, because
he is the chaplain of a bishop whom you don't like, you speak of
him as though he had no right to the usage of a gentleman."

"He has done nothing for your father."

"I believe that he has done a great deal; and, as far as I am
concerned, I am grateful to him. Nothing that you can say can
prevent my being so. I judge people by their acts, and his, as far
as I can see them, are good." She then paused for a moment.
"If you have nothing further to say, I shall be obliged by being
permitted to say good night—I am very tired."

Dr. Grantly had, as he thought, done his best to be gracious to
his sister-in-law. He had endeavoured not to be harsh to her,
and had striven to pluck the sting from his rebuke. But he did
not intend that she should leave him without hearing him.

"I have something to say, Eleanor; and I fear I must trouble
you to hear it. You profess that it is quite proper that you should
receive from Mr. Slope such letters as that you have in your hand.
Susan and I think very differently. You are, of course, your own
mistress, and much as we both must grieve should anything
separate you from us, we have no power to prevent you from taking
steps which may lead to such a separation. If you are so wilful
as to reject the counsel of your friends, you must be allowed to
cater for yourself. But Eleanor, I may at any rate ask you this.
Is it worth your while to break away from all those you have
loved—from all who love you—for the sake of Mr. Slope?"

"I don't know what you mean, Dr. Grantly; I don't know what
you're talking about. I don't want to break away from anybody."

"But you will do so if you connect yourself with Mr. Slope.
Eleanor, I must speak out to you. You must choose between your
sister and myself and our friends, and Mr. Slope and his friends.
I say nothing of your father, as you may probably understand his
feelings better than I do."

"What do you mean, Dr. Grantly? What am I to understand?
I never heard such wicked prejudice in my life."

"It is no prejudice, Eleanor. I have known the world longer
than you have done. Mr. Slope is altogether beneath you. You
ought to know and feel that he is so. Pray—pray think of this
before it is too late."

"Too late!"

"Or if you will not believe me, ask Susan; you cannot think
she is prejudiced against you. Or even consult your father, he is
not prejudiced against you. Ask Mr. Arabin ———"

"You haven't spoken to Mr. Arabin about this!" said she, jumping up and standing before him.

"Eleanor, all the world in and about Barchester will be speaking of it soon."

"But have you spoken to Mr. Arabin about me and Mr. Slope?"

"Certainly I have, and he quite agrees with me."

"Agrees with what?" said she. "I think you are trying to drive me mad."

"He agrees with me and Susan that it is quite impossible you should be received at Plumstead as Mrs. Slope."

Not being favourites with the tragic muse we do not dare to attempt any description of Eleanor's face when she first heard the name of Mrs. Slope pronounced as that which would or should or might at some time appertain to herself. The look, such as it was, Dr. Grantly did not soon forget. For a moment or two she could find no words to express her deep anger and deep disgust; and, indeed, at this conjuncture, words did not come to her very freely.

"How dare you be so impertinent?" at last she said; and then hurried out of the room, without giving the archdeacon the opportunity of uttering another word. It was with difficulty she contained herself till she reached her own room; and then locking the door, she threw herself on her bed and sobbed as though her heart would break.

But even yet she had no conception of the truth. She had no idea that her father and her sister had for days past conceived in sober earnest the idea that she was going to marry this man. She did not even then believe that the archdeacon thought that she would do so. By some manœuvre of her brain, she attributed the origin of the accusation to Mr. Arabin, and as she did so her anger against him was excessive, and the vexation of her spirit almost unendurable. She could not bring herself to think that the charge was made seriously. It appeared to her most probable that the archdeacon and Mr. Arabin had talked over her objectionable acquaintance with Mr. Slope; that Mr. Arabin, in his jeering, sarcastic way, had suggested the odious match as being the severest way of treating with contumely her acquaintance with his enemy; and that the archdeacon, taking the idea from him, thought proper to punish her by the allusion. The whole night she lay awake thinking of what had been said, and this appeared to be the most probable solution.

But the reflection that Mr. Arabin should have in any way mentioned her name in connection with that of Mr. Slope was overpowering; and the spiteful ill-nature of the archdeacon, in repeating the charge to her, made her wish to leave his house almost before the day had broken. One thing was certain : nothing should make her stay there beyond the following morning, and nothing should make her sit down to breakfast in company with Dr. Grantly. When she thought of the man whose name had been linked with her own, she cried from sheer disgust. It was only because she would be thus disgusted, thus pained and shocked and cut to the quick, that the archdeacon had spoken the horrid word. He wanted to make her quarrel with Mr. Slope, and therefore he had outraged her by his abominable vulgarity. She determined that at any rate he should know that she appreciated it.

Nor was the archdeacon a bit better satisfied with the result of his serious interview than was Eleanor. He gathered from it, as indeed he could hardly fail to do, that she was very angry with him ; but he thought that she was thus angry, not because she was suspected of an intention to marry Mr. Slope, but because such an intention was imputed to her as a crime. Dr. Grantly regarded this supposed union with disgust; but it never occurred to him that Eleanor was outraged, because she looked at it exactly in the same light.

He returned to his wife vexed and somewhat disconsolate, but, nevertheless, confirmed in his wrath against his sister-in-law. "Her whole behaviour," said he, "has been most objectionable. She handed me his love letter to read as though she were proud of it. And she is proud of it. She is proud of having this slavering, greedy man at her feet. She will throw herself and John Bold's money into his lap; she will ruin her boy, disgrace her father and you, and be a wretched miserable woman."

His spouse who was sitting at her toilet table, continued her avocations, making no answer to all this. She had known that the archdeacon would gain nothing by interfering; but she was too charitable to provoke him by saying so while he was in such deep sorrow.

"This comes of a man making such a will as that of Bold's," he continued. "Eleanor is no more fitted to be trusted with such an amount of money in her own hands than is a charity-school girl." Still Mrs. Grantly made no reply. "But I have done my duty; I can do nothing further. I have told her plainly that she cannot be allowed to form a link of connection between me and that man. From henceforward it will not be in my power to make her welcome at Plumstead. I cannot have Mr. Slope's love letters coming here. Susan, I think you had better let her understand that as her mind on this subject seems to be irrevocably fixed, it will be better for all parties that she should return to Barchester."

Now Mrs. Grantly was angry with Eleanor, nearly as angry as her husband; but she had no idea of turning her sister out of the house. She, therefore, at length spoke out, and explained to the archdeacon, in her own mild seducing way, that he was fuming and fussing and fretting himself very unnecessarily. She declared that things, if left alone, would arrange themselves much better than he could arrange them ; and at last succeeded in inducing him to go to bed in a somewhat less inhospitable state of mind.

On the following morning Eleanor's maid was commissioned to send word into the dining-room that her mistress was not well enough to attend prayers, and that she would breakfast in her own room. Here she was visited by her father and declared to him her intention of returning immediately to Barchester. He was hardly surprised by the announcement. All the household seemed to be aware that something had gone wrong. Every one walked about with subdued feet, and people's shoes seemed to creak more than usual. There was a look of conscious intelligence on the faces of the women: and the men attempted, but in vain, to converse as though nothing were the matter. All this had weighed heavily on the heart of Mr. Harding ; and when Eleanor told him that her immediate return to Barchester was a necessity, he merely sighed piteously, and said that he would be ready to accompany her.

But here she objected strenuously. She had a great wish, she said, to go alone; a great desire that it might be seen that her father was not implicated in her quarrel with Dr. Grantly. To this at last he gave way; but not a word passed between them about Mr. Slope—not a word was said, not a question asked as to the serious interview on the preceding evening. There was, indeed, very little confidence between them, though neither of them knew why it should be so. Eleanor once asked him whether he would not call upon the bishop; but he answered rather tartly that he did not know—he did not think he should, but he could not say just at present. And so they parted. Each was miserably anxious for some show of affection, for some return of confidence, for some sign of the feeling that usually bound them together. But none was given. The father could not bring himself to question his daughter about her supposed lover ; and the daughter would not sully her mouth by repeating the odious word with which Dr. Grantly had roused her wrath. And so they parted.

There was some trouble in arranging the method of Eleanor's

return. She begged her father to send for a postchaise; but when Mrs. Grantly heard of this, she objected strongly. If Eleanor would go away in dudgeon with the archdeacon, why should she let all the servants and all the neighbourhood know that she had done so? So at last Eleanor consented to make use of the Plumstead carriage; and as the archdeacon had gone out immediately after breakfast and was not to return till dinner-time, she also consented to postpone her journey till after lunch, and to join the family at that time. As to the subject of the quarrel not a word was said by any one. The affair of the carriage was arranged by Mr. Harding, who acted as Mercury between the two ladies; they, when they met, kissed each other very lovingly, and then sat down each to her crochet work as though nothing was amiss in all the world.

CHAP. XXX.

ANOTHER LOVE SCENE.

BUT there was another visitor at the rectory whose feelings in this unfortunate matter must be somewhat strictly analysed. Mr. Arabin had heard from his friend of the probability of Eleanor's marriage with Mr. Slope with amazement, but not with incredulity. It has been said that he was not in love with Eleanor, and up to this period this certainly had been true. But as soon as he heard that she loved some one else, he began to be very fond of her himself. He did not make up his mind that he wished to have her for his wife; he had never thought of her, and did not now think of her, in connection with himself; but he experienced an inward indefinable feeling of deep regret, a gnawing sorrow, an unconquerable depression of spirits, and also a species of self-abasement that he—he, Mr. Arabin—had not done something to prevent that other he, that vile he, whom he so thoroughly despised, from carrying off this sweet prize.

Whatever man may have reached the age of forty unmarried without knowing something of such feelings must have been very successful or else very cold-hearted.

Mr. Arabin had never thought of trimming the sails of his bark so that he might sail as convoy to this rich argosy. He had seen that Mrs. Bold was beautiful, but he had not dreamt of making her beauty his own. He knew that Mrs. Bold was rich, but he had had no more idea of appropriating her wealth than that of

Dr. Grantly. He had discovered that Mrs. Bold was intelligent, warm-hearted, agreeable, sensible, all, in fact, that a man could wish his wife to be ; but the higher were her attractions, the greater her claims to consideration, the less had he imagined that he might possibly become the possessor of them. Such had been his instinct rather than his thoughts, so humble and so diffident. Now his diffidence was to be rewarded by his seeing this woman, whose beauty was to his eyes perfect, whose wealth was such as to have deterred him from thinking of her, whose widowhood would have silenced him had he not been so deterred, by his seeing her become the prey of —— Obadiah Slope !

On the morning of Mrs. Bold's departure he got on his horse to ride over to St. Ewold's. As he rode he kept muttering to himself a line from Van Artevelde,

> "How little flattering is woman's love."

And then he strove to recall his mind and to think of other affairs, his parish, his college, his creed — but his thoughts would rever; to Mr. Slope and the Flemish chieftain. —

> "When we think upon it,
> How little flattering is woman's love,
> Given commonly to whosoe'er is nearest
> And propped with most advantage."

It was not that Mrs. Bold should marry any one but him ; he had not put himself forward as a suitor ; but that she should marry Mr. Slope — and so he repeated over again—

> "Outward grace
> Nor inward light is needful — day by day
> Men wanting both are mated with the best
> And loftiest of God's feminine creation,
> Whose love takes no distinction but of gender,
> And ridicules the very name of choice."

And so he went on, troubled much in his mind.

He had but an uneasy ride of it that morning, and little good did he do at St. Ewold's.

The necessary alterations in his house were being fast completed, and he walked through the rooms, and went up and down the stairs, and rambled through the garden ; but he could not wake himself to much interest about them. He stood still at every window to look out and think upon Mr. Slope. At almost every window he had before stood and chatted with Eleanor. She and Mrs. Grantly had been there continually, and while Mrs. Grantly had been giving orders, and seeing that orders had been complied with, he and Eleanor had conversed on all things appertaining to a clergyman's profession. He thought how often he had laid down the law to her, and how sweetly she had borne with his somewhat dictatorial decrees. He remembered her listening intelligence, her gentle but quick replies, her interest in all that concerned the church, in all that concerned him ; and then he struck his riding whip against the window sill, and declared to himself that it was impossible that Eleanor Bold should marry Mr. Slope.

And yet he did not really believe, as he should have done, that it was impossible. He should have known her well enough to feel that it was truly impossible. He should have been aware that Eleanor had that within her which would surely protect her from such degradation. But he, like so many others, was deficient in confidence in woman. He said to himself over and over again that it was impossible that Eleanor Bold should become Mrs. Slope, and yet he believed that she would do so. And so he rambled about, and could do and think of nothing. He was thoroughly uncomfortable, thoroughly ill at ease, cross with himself, and every body else, and feeding in his heart on animosity towards Mr. Slope. This was not as it should be, as he knew and felt; but he could not help himself. In truth Mr. Arabin was now in love with Mrs. Bold, though ignorant of the fact himself. He was in love, and, though forty years old, was in love without being aware of it. He fumed and fretted, and did not know what was the matter, as a youth might do at one-and-twenty. And so having done no good at St. Ewold's, he rode back much earlier than was usual with him, instigated by some inward unacknowledged hope that he might see Mrs. Bold before she left.

Eleanor had not passed a pleasant morning. She was irritated with every one, and not least with herself. She felt that she had been hardly used, but she felt also that she had not played her own cards well. She should have held herself so far above suspicion as to have received her sister's innuendoes and the archdeacon's lecture with indifference. She had not done this, but had shown herself angry and sore, and was now ashamed of her own petulance, and yet unable to discontinue it.

The greater part of the morning she had spent alone ; but after a while her father joined her. He had fully made up his mind that, come what come might, nothing should separate him from his younger daughter. It was a hard task for him to reconcile himself to the idea of seeing her at the head of Mr. Slope's table ; but he got through it. Mr. Slope, as he argued to himself, was a respectable man and a clergyman; and he, as Eleanor's father, had no right even to endeavour to prevent her from marrying such a one. He longed to tell her how he had determined to prefer her to all the world, how he was prepared to admit that she was not wrong, how thoroughly he differed from Dr. Grantly; but he could not bring himself to mention Mr. Slope's name. There was yet a chance that they were all wrong in their surmise! and, being thus in doubt, he could not bring himself to speak openly to her on the subject.

He was sitting with her in the drawing-room, with his arm round her waist, saying every now and then some little soft words of affection, and working hard with his imaginary fiddle-bow, when Mr. Arabin entered the room. He immediately got up, and the two made some trite remarks to each other, neither thinking of what he was saying, while Eleanor kept her seat on the sofa mute and moody. Mr. Arabin was included in the list of those against whom her anger was excited. He, too, had dared to talk about her acquaintance with Mr. Slope; he, too, had dared to blame her for not making an enemy of his enemy. She had not intended to see him before her departure, and was now but little inclined to be gracious.

There was a feeling through the whole house that something was wrong. Mr. Arabin, when he saw Eleanor, could not succeed in looking or in speaking as though he knew nothing of all this. He could not be cheerful and positive and contradictory with her, as was his wont. He had not been two minutes in the room before he felt that he had done wrong to return; and the moment he heard her voice, he thoroughly wished himself back at St. Ewold's. Why, indeed, should he have wished to have aught further to say to the future wife of Mr. Slope?

"I am sorry to hear that you are to leave us so soon," said he, striving in vain to use his ordinary voice. In answer to this she muttered something about the necessity of her being in Barchester, and betook herself most industriously to her crochet work.

Then there was a little more trite conversation between Mr. Arabin and Mr. Harding; trite, and hard, and vapid, and senseless. Neither of them had anything to say to the other, and yet neither at such a moment liked to remain silent. At last Mr. Harding, taking advantage of a pause, escaped out of the room, and Eleanor and Mr. Arabin were left together.

"Your going will be a great break-up to our party," said he.

She again muttered something which was all but inaudible; but kept her eyes fixed upon her work.

"We have had a very pleasant month here," said he; "at least I have; and I am sorry it should be so soon over."

"I have already been from home longer than I intended," said she; "and it is time that I should return."

"Well, pleasant hours and pleasant days must come to an end. It is a pity that so few of them are pleasant; or perhaps, rather "——

"It is a pity, certainly, that men and women do so much to destroy the pleasantness of their days," said she, interrupting him. "It is a pity that there should be so little charity abroad."

"Charity should begin at home," said he; and he was proceeding to explain that he as a clergyman could not be what she would call charitable at the expense of those principles which he considered it his duty to teach, when he remembered that it would be worse than vain to argue on such a matter with the future wife of Mr. Slope. "But you are just leaving us," he continued, "and I will not weary your last hour with another lecture. As it is, I fear I have given you too many."

"You should practise as well as preach, Mr. Arabin?"

"Undoubtedly I should. So should we all. All of us who presume to teach are bound to do our utmost towards fulfilling our own lessons. I thoroughly allow my deficiency in doing so: but I do not quite know now to what you allude. Have you any special reason for telling me now that I should practise as well as preach?"

Eleanor made no answer. She longed to let him know the cause of her anger, to upbraid him for speaking of her disrespectfully, and then at last to forgive him, and so part friends. She felt that she would be unhappy to leave him in her present frame of mind; but yet she could hardly bring herself to speak to him of Mr. Slope. And how could she allude to the innuendo thrown out by the archdeacon, and thrown out, as she believed, at the instigation of Mr. Arabin? She wanted to make him know that he was wrong, to make him aware that he had ill-treated her, in order that the sweetness of her forgiveness might be enhanced. She felt that she liked him too well to be contented to part with him in displeasure; and yet she could not get over her deep displeasure without some explanation, some acknowledgment on his part, some assurance that he would never again so sin against her.

"Why do you tell me that I should practise what I preach?" continued he.

"All men should do so."

"Certainly. That is as it were understood and acknowledged.

But you do not say so to all men, or to all clergymen. The advice, good as it is, is not given except in allusion to some special deficiency. If you will tell me my special deficiency, I will endeavour to profit by the advice."

She paused for a while, and then, looking full in his face, she said, "You are not bold enough, Mr. Arabin, to speak out to me openly and plainly, and yet you expect me, a woman, to speak openly to you. Why did you speak calumny of me to Dr. Grantly behind my back?"

"Calumny!" said he, and his whole face became suffused with blood; "what calumny? If I have spoken calumny of you, I will beg your pardon, and his to whom I spoke it, and God's pardon also. But what calumny have I spoken of you to Dr. Grantly?"

She also blushed deeply. She could not bring herself to ask him whether he had not spoken of her as another man's wife. "You know that best yourself," said she; "but I ask you as a man of honour, if you have not spoken of me as you would not have spoken of your own sister; or rather I will not ask you," she continued, finding that he did not immediately answer her. "I will not put you to the necessity of answering such a question. Dr. Grantly has told me what you said."

"Dr. Grantly certainly asked me for my advice, and I gave it. He asked me "——

"I know he did, Mr. Arabin. He asked you whether he would be doing right to receive me at Plumstead, if I continued my acquaintance with a gentleman who happens to be personally disagreeable to yourself and to him?"

"You are mistaken, Mrs. Bold. I have no personal knowledge of Mr. Slope; I never met him in my life."

"You are not the less individually hostile to him. It is not for me to question the propriety of your enmity; but I had a right to expect that my name should not have been mixed up in your hostilities. This has been done, and been done by you in a manner the most injurious and the most distressing to me as a woman. I must confess, Mr. Arabin, that from you I expected a different sort of usage."

As she spoke she with difficulty restrained her tears; but she did restrain them. Had she given way and sobbed aloud, as in such cases a woman should do, he would have melted at once, implored her pardon, perhaps knelt at her feet and declared his love. Everything would have been explained, and Eleanor would have gone back to Barchester with a contented mind. How easily would she have forgiven and forgotten the archdeacon's suspicions had she but heard the whole truth from Mr. Arabin. But then where would have been my novel? She did not cry, and Mr. Arabin did not melt.

"You do me an injustice," said he. "My advice was asked by Dr. Grantly, and I was obliged to give it."

"Dr. Grantly has been most officious, most impertinent. I have as complete a right to form my acquaintance as he has to form his. What would you have said, had I consulted you as to the propriety of my banishing Dr. Grantly from my house because he knows Lord Tattenham Corner? I am sure Lord Tattenham is quite as objectionable an acquaintance for a clergyman as Mr. Slope is for a clergyman's daughter."

"I do not know Lord Tattenham Corner."

"No; but Dr. Grantly does. It is nothing to me if he knows all the young lords on every racecourse in England. I shall not interfere with him; nor shall he with me."

"I am sorry to differ with you, Mrs. Bold; but as you have spoken to me on this matter, and especially as you blame me for what little I said on the subject, I must tell you that I do differ from you. Dr. Grantly's position as a man in the world gives him a right to choose his own acquaintances, subject to certain influences. If he chooses them badly, those influences will be used. If he consorts with persons unsuitable to him, his bishop will interfere. What the bishop is to Dr. Grantly, Dr. Grantly is to you."

"I deny it. I utterly deny it," said Eleanor, jumping from her seat, and literally flashing before Mr. Arabin, as she stood on the drawing-room floor. He had never seen her so excited, he had never seen her look half so beautiful.

"I utterly deny it," said she. "Dr. Grantly has no sort of jurisdiction over me whatsoever. Do you and he forget that I am not altogether alone in the world? Do you forget that I have a father? Dr. Grantly, I believe, always has forgotten it."

"From you, Mr. Arabin," she continued, "I would have listened to advice, because I should have expected it to have been given as one friend may advise another; not as a schoolmaster gives an order to a pupil. I might have differed from you; on this matter I should have done so; but had you spoken to me in your usual manner and with your usual freedom I should not have been angry. But now —— was it manly of you, Mr. Arabin, to speak of me in this way ——, so disrespectful — so ——? I cannot bring myself to repeat what you said. You must understand what I feel. Was it just of you to speak of me in such a way, and to advise my sister's husband to turn me out of my sister's house, because I chose to know a man of whose doctrine you disapprove?"

"I have no alternative left to me, Mrs. Bold," said he, standing with his back to the fire-place, looking down intently at the carpet pattern, and speaking with a slow measured voice, "but to tell you plainly what did take place between me and Dr. Grantly."

"Well," said she, finding that he paused for a moment.

"I am afraid that what I may say may pain you."

"It cannot well do so more than what you have already done," said she.

"Dr. Grantly asked me whether I thought it would be prudent for him to receive you in his house as the wife of Mr. Slope, and I told him that I thought it would be imprudent. Believing it to be utterly impossible that Mr. Slope and ——"

"Thank you, Mr. Arabin, that is sufficient. I do not want to know your reasons," said she, speaking with a terribly calm voice. "I have shown to this gentleman the common-place civility of a neighbour; and because I have done so, because I have not indulged against him in all the rancour and hatred which you and Dr. Grantly consider due to all clergymen who do not agree with yourselves, you conclude that I am to marry him; — or rather you do not conclude so—no rational man could really come to such an outrageous conclusion without better ground; — you have not thought so—but, as I am in a position in which such an accusation must be peculiarly painful, it is made in order that I may be terrified into hostility against this enemy of yours."

As she finished speaking, she walked to the drawing-room window and stepped out into the garden. Mr. Arabin was left in the room, still occupied in counting the pattern on the carpet. He had, however, distinctly heard and accurately marked every word that she had spoken. Was it not clear from what she had said, that the archdeacon had been wrong in imputing to her any attachment to Mr. Slope ? Was it not clear that Eleanor was still free to make another choice ? It may seem strange that he should for a moment have had a doubt; and yet he did doubt. She had not absolutely denied the charge ; she had not expressly said that it was untrue. Mr. Arabin understood little of the nature of a woman's feelings, or he would have known how improbable it was that she should make any clearer declaration than she had done. Few men do understand the nature of a woman's heart, till years have robbed such understanding of its value. And it is well that it should be so, or men would triumph too easily.

Mr. Arabin stood counting the carpet, unhappy, wretchedly unhappy, at the hard words that had been spoken to him; and yet happy, exquisitely happy, as he thought that after all the woman whom **he** so regarded was not to become the wife of the man whom he so much disliked. As he stood there he began to be aware that he was himself in love. Forty years had passed over his head, and as yet woman's beauty had never given him an uneasy hour. His present hour was very uneasy.

Not that he remained there for half or a quarter of that time. In spite of what Eleanor had said, Mr. Arabin was, in truth, a manly man. Having ascertained that he loved this woman, and having now reason to believe that she was free to receive his love, at least if she pleased to do so, he followed her into the garden to make such wooing as he could.

He was not long in finding her. She was walking to and fro beneath the avenue of elms that stood in the archdeacon's grounds, skirting the churchyard. What had passed between her and Mr. Arabin, had not, alas, tended to lessen the acerbity of her spirit. She was very angry; more angry with him than with any one. How could he have so misunderstood her? She had been so intimate with him, had allowed him such latitude in what he had chosen to say to her, had complied with his ideas, cherished his views, fostered his precepts, cared for his comforts, made much of him in every way in which a pretty woman can make much of an unmarried man without committing herself or her feelings! She had been doing this, and while she had been doing it he had regarded her as the affianced wife of another man.

As she passed along the avenue, every now and then an unbidden tear would force itself on her cheek, and as she raised her hand to brush it away she stamped with her little foot upon the sward with very spite to think that she had been so treated.

Mr. Arabin was very near to her when she first saw him, and she turned short round and retraced her steps down the avenue, trying to rid her cheeks of all trace of the tell-tale tears. It was a needless endeavour, for Mr. Arabin was in a state of mind that hardly allowed him to observe such trifles. He followed her down the walk, and overtook her just as she reached the end of it.

He had not considered how he would address her; he had not thought what he would say. He had only felt that it was wretchedness to him to quarrel with her, and that it would be happiness to be allowed to love her. And yet he could not lower himself by asking her pardon. He had done her no wrong. He had not calumniated her, not injured her, as she had accused him of doing. He could not confess sins of which he had not been guilty. He could only let the past be past, and ask her as to her and his hopes for the future.

"I hope we are not to part as enemies?" said he.

"There shall be no enmity on my part," said Eleanor; "I endeavour to avoid all enmities. It would be a hollow pretence were I to say that there can be true friendship between us after what has just passed. People cannot make their friends of those whom they despise."

"And am I despised?"

"*I* must have been so before you could have spoken of me as you did. And I was deceived, cruelly deceived. I believed that you thought well of me ; I believed that you esteemed me."

"Thought well of you and esteemed you!" said he. "In justifying myself before you, I must use stronger words than those." He paused for a moment, and Eleanor's heart beat with painful violence within her bosom as she waited for him to go on. "I have esteemed, do esteem you, as I never yet esteemed any woman. Think well of you! I never thought to think so well, so much of any human creature. Speak calumny of you! Insult you! Wilfully injure you! I wish it were my privilege to shield you from calumny, insult, and injury. Calumny! ah, me. 'Twere almost better that it were so. Better than to worship with a sinful worship; sinful and vain also." And then he walked along beside her, with his hands clasped behind his back, looking down on the grass beneath his feet, and utterly at a loss how to express his meaning. And Eleanor walked beside him determined at least to give him no assistance.

"Ah me!" he uttered at last, speaking rather to himself than to her. "Ah me! these Plumstead walks were pleasant enough, if one could have but heart's ease ; but without that the dull dead stones of Oxford were far preferable; and St. Ewold's too; Mrs. Bold, I am beginning to think that I mistook myself when I came hither. A Romish priest now would have escaped all this. Oh, Father of heaven! how good for us would it be, if thou couldest vouchsafe to us a certain rule."

"And have we not a certain rule, Mr. Arabin?"

"Yes—yes, surely; 'Lead us not into temptation but deliver us from evil.' But what is temptation? what is evil? Is this evil,—is this temptation?"

Poor Mr. Arabin! It would not come out of him, that deep true love of his. He could not bring himself to utter it in plain language that would require and demand an answer. He knew not how to say to the woman by his side, "Since the fact is that you do not love that other man, that you are not to be his wife, can you love me, will you be my wife?" These were the words which were in his heart, but with all his sighs he could not draw them to his lips. He would have given anything, everything for power to ask this simple question; but glib as was his tongue in pulpits and on platforms, now he could not find a word wherewith to express the plain wish of his heart.

And yet Eleanor understood him as thoroughly as though he had declared his passion with all the elegant fluency of a practised Lothario. With a woman's instinct she followed every bend of his mind, as he spoke of the pleasantness of Plumstead and the stones of Oxford, as he alluded to the safety of the Romish priest and the hidden perils of temptation. She knew that it all meant love. She knew that this man at her side, this accomplished scholar, this practised orator, this great polemical combatant, was striving and striving in vain to tell her that his heart was no longer his own.

She knew this, and felt a sort of joy in knowing it; and yet she would not come to his aid. He had offended her deeply, had treated her unworthily, the more unworthily seeing that he had learnt to love her, and Eleanor could not bring herself to abandon her revenge. She did not ask herself whether or no she would ultimately accept his love. She did not even acknowledge to herself that she now perceived it with pleasure. At the present moment it did not touch her heart; it merely appeased her pride and flattered her vanity. Mr. Arabin had dared to associate her name with that of Mr. Slope, and now her spirit was soothed by finding that he would fain associate it with his own. And so she walked on beside him inhaling incense, but giving out no sweetness in return.

"Answer me this," said Mr. Arabin, stopping suddenly in his walk, and stepping forward so that he faced his companion. "Answer me this one question. You do not love Mr. Slope? you do not intend to be his wife?"

Mr. Arabin certainly did not go the right way to win such a woman as Eleanor Bold. Just as her wrath was evaporating, as it was disappearing before the true warmth of his untold love, he re-kindled it by a most useless repetition of his original sin. Had he known what he was about he should never have mentioned Mr. Slope's name before Eleanor Bold, till he had made her all his own. Then, and not till then, he might have talked of Mr. Slope with as much triumph as he chose.

"I shall answer no such question," said she; "and what is more, I must tell you that nothing can justify your asking it. Good morning!"

And so saying she stepped proudly across the lawn, and passing through the drawing-room window joined her father and sister at lunch in the dining-room. Half an hour afterwards she was in the carriage, and so she left Plumstead without again seeing Mr. Arabin.

His walk was long and sad among the sombre trees that over-shadowed the churchyard. He left the archdeacon's grounds that he might escape attention, and sauntered among the green hillocks under which lay at rest so many of the once loving swains and forgotten beauties of Plumstead. To his ears Eleanor's last words sounded like a knell never to be reversed. He could not compre-hend that she might be angry with him, indignant with him, re-morseless with him, and yet love him. He could not make up his mind whether or no Mr. Slope was in truth a favoured rival. If not, why should she not have answered his question?

Poor Mr. Arabin — untaught, illiterate, boorish, ignorant man! That at forty years of age you should know so little of the work-ings of a woman's heart!

CHAP. XXXI.

THE BISHOP'S LIBRARY.

AND thus the pleasant party at Plumstead was broken up. It had been a very pleasant party as long as they had all remained in good humour with one another. Mrs. Grantly had felt her house to be gayer and brighter than it had been for many a long day, and the archdeacon had been aware that the month had passed pleasantly without attributing the pleasure to any other special merits than those of his own hospitality. Within three or four days of Eleanor's departure Mr. Harding had also returned, and Mr. Arabin had gone to Oxford to spend one week there previous to his settling at the vicarage of St. Ewold's. He had gone laden with many messages to Dr. Gwynne touching the iniquity of the doings in Barchester palace, and the peril in which it was believed the hospital still stood in spite of the assurances contained in Mr. Slope's inauspicious letter.

During Eleanor's drive into Barchester she had not much op-portunity of reflecting on Mr. Arabin. She had been constrained to divert her mind both from his sins and his love by the necessity of conversing with her sister and maintaining the appearance of parting with her on good terms. When the carriage reached her own door, and while she was in the act of giving her last kiss to her sister and nieces, Mary Bold ran out and exclaimed,

"Oh! Eleanor,—have you heard?—oh! Mrs. Grantly, have you heard what has happened? The poor dean!"

'Good heavens!" said Mrs. Grantly; "what—what has happened?"

"This morning at nine he had a fit of apoplexy, and he has not spoken since. I very much fear that by this time he is no more."

Mrs. Grantly had been very intimate with the dean, and was therefore much shocked. Eleanor had not known him so well; nevertheless she was sufficiently acquainted with his person and manners to feel startled and grieved also at the tidings she now received. "I will go at once to the deanery," said Mrs. Grantly; "the archdeacon, I am sure, will be there. If there is any news to send you I will let Thomas call before he leaves town." And so the carriage drove off, leaving Eleanor and her baby with Mary Bold.

Mrs. Grantly had been quite right. The archdeacon was at the deanery. He had come into Barchester that morning by himself, not caring to intrude himself upon Eleanor, and he also immediately on his arrival had heard of the dean's fit. There was, as we have before said, a library or reading room connecting the cathedral with the dean's house. This was generally called the bishop's library, because a certain bishop of Barchester was supposed to have added it to the cathedral. It was built immediately over a portion of the cloisters, and a flight of stairs descended from it into the room in which the cathedral clergymen put their surplices on and off. As it also opened directly into the dean's house, it was the passage through which that dignitary usually went to his public devotions. Who had or had not the right of entry into it, it might be difficult to say; but the people of Barchester believed that it belonged to the dean, and the clergymen of Barchester believed that it belonged to the chapter.

On the morning in question most of the resident clergymen who constituted the chapter, and some few others, were here assembled, and among them as usual the archdeacon towered with high authority. He had heard of the dean's fit before he was over the bridge which led into the town, and had at once come to the well known clerical trysting place. He had been there by eleven o'clock, and had remained ever since. From time to time the medical men who had been called in came through from the deanery into the library, uttered little bulletins, and then returned. There was it appears very little hope of the old man's rallying, indeed no hope of any thing like a final recovery. The only question was whether he must die at once speechless, unconscious, stricken to death by his first heavy fit; or whether by due aid of medical skill he might not be so far brought back to this world as to become conscious of his state, and enabled to address one prayer to his Maker before he was called to meet Him face to face at the judgment seat.

Sir Omicron Pie had been sent for from London. That great man had shown himself a wonderful adept at keeping life still moving within an old man's heart in the case of good old Bishop Grantly, and it might be reasonably expected that he would be equally successful with a dean. In the mean time Dr. Fillgrave and Mr. Rerechild were doing their best; and poor Miss Trefoil sat at the head of her father's bed, longing, as in such cases daughters do long, to be allowed to do something to show her love; if it were only to chafe his feet with her hands, or wait in menial offices on those autocratic doctors; anything so that now in the time of need she might be of use.

The archdeacon alone of the attendant clergy had been admitted for a moment into the sick man's chamber. He had crept in with creaking shoes, had said with smothered voice a word of consolation to the sorrowing daughter, had looked on the distorted face of his old friend with solemn but yet eager scrutinising eye, as though he said in his heart "and so some day it will probably be with me;" and then having whispered an unmeaning word or two to the doctors, had creaked his way back again into the library.

"He'll never speak again, I fear," said the archdeacon as he noiselessly closed the door, as though the unconscious dying man, from whom all sense had fled, would have heard in his distant chamber the spring of the lock which was now so carefully handled.

"Indeed! indeed! is he so bad?" said the meagre little prebendary, turning over in his own mind all the probable candidates for the deanery, and wondering whether the archdeacon would think it worth his while to accept it. "The fit must have been very violent."

"When a man over seventy has a stroke of apoplexy, it seldom comes very lightly," said the burly chancellor.

"He was an excellent, sweet-tempered man," said one of the vicars choral. "Heaven knows how we shall repair his loss."

"He was indeed," said a minor canon; "and a great blessing to all those privileged to take a share of the services of our cathedral. I suppose the government will appoint, Mr. Archdeacon. I trust we may have no stranger."

"We will not talk about his successor," said the archdeacon, "while there is yet hope."

"Oh no, of course not," said the minor canon. "It would be exceedingly indecorous! but——"

"I know of no man," said the meagre little prebendary, "who has better interest with the present government than Mr. Slope."

"Mr. Slope!" said two or three at once almost sotto voce. "Mr. Slope dean of Barchester!"

"Pooh!" exclaimed the burly chancellor.

"The bishop would do anything for him," said the little prebendary.

"And so would Mrs. Proudie," said the vicar choral.

"Pooh!" said the chancellor.

The archdeacon had almost turned pale at the idea. What if Mr. Slope should become dean of Barchester? To be sure there was no adequate ground, indeed no ground at all, for presuming that such a desecration could even be contemplated. But nevertheless it was on the cards. Dr. Proudie had interest with the government, and the man carried as it were Dr. Proudie in his pocket. How should they all conduct themselves if Mr. Slope were to become dean of Barchester? The bare idea for a moment struck even Dr. Grantly dumb.

"It would certainly not be very pleasant for us to have Mr. Slope at the deanery," said the little prebendary, chuckling inwardly at the evident consternation which his surmise had created.

"About as pleasant and as probable as having you in the palace," said the chancellor.

"I should think such an appointment highly improbable," said the minor canon, "and, moreover, extremely injudicious. Should not you, Mr. Archdeacon?"

"I should presume such a thing to be quite out of the question," said the archdeacon; "but at the present moment I am thinking rather of our poor friend who is lying so near us than of Mr. Slope."

"Of course, of course," said the vicar choral with a very solemn air; "of course you are. So are we all. Poor Dr. Trefoil; the best of men, but——"

"It's the most comfortable dean's residence in England," said a second prebendary. "Fifteen acres in the grounds. It is better than many of the bishops' palaces."

"And full two thousand a year," said the meagre doctor.

"It is cut down to 1200l." said the chancellor.

"No," said the second prebendary. "It is to be fifteen. A special case was made."

"No such thing," said the chancellor.

"You'll find I'm right," said the prebendary.

"I'm sure I read it in the report," said the minor canon.

"Nonsense," said the chancellor. "They couldn't do it. There were to be no exceptions but London and Durham."

"And Canterbury and York," said the vicar choral, modestly.

"What do you say, Grantly?" said the meagre little doctor.

"Say about what?" said the archdeacon, who had been looking as though he were thinking about his friend the dean, but who had in reality been thinking about Mr. Slope.

"What is the next dean to have, twelve or fifteen?"

"Twelve," said the archdeacon authoritatively, thereby putting an end at once to all doubt and dispute among his subordinates as far as that subject was concerned.

"Well, I certainly thought it was fifteen," said the minor canon.

"Pooh!" said the burly chancellor. At this moment the door opened, and in came Dr. Fillgrave.

"How is he?" "Is he conscious?" "Can he speak?" "I hope not dead?" "No worse news, doctor, I trust?" "I hope, I trust, something better, doctor?" said half a dozen voices all at once, each in a tone of extremest anxiety. It was pleasant to see how popular the good old dean was among his clergy.

"No change, gentlemen; not the slightest change—but a telegraphic message has arrived—Sir Omicron Pie will be here by the 9.15 P.M. train. If any man can do anything Sir Omicron Pie will do it. But all that skill can do has been done."

"We are sure of that, Dr. Fillgrave," said the archdeacon; "we are quite sure of that. But yet you know ——"

"Oh! quite right," said the doctor, "quite right—I should have done just the same—I advised it at once. I said to Rerechild at once that with such a life and such a man, Sir Omicron should be summoned—of course I knew expense was nothing—so distinguished, you know, and so popular. Nevertheless, all that human skill can do has been done."

Just at this period Mrs. Grantly's carriage drove into the close, and the archdeacon went down to confirm the news which she had heard before.

"By the 9.15 P.M. train Sir Omicron Pie did arrive. And in the course of the night a sort of consciousness returned to the poor old dean. Whether this was due to Sir Omicron Pie is a question on which it may be well not to offer an opinion. Dr. Fillgrave was very clear in his own mind, but Sir Omicron himself is thought to have differed from that learned doctor. At any rate Sir Omicron expressed an opinion that the dean had yet some days to live.

For the eight or ten next days, accordingly, the poor dean remained in the same state, half conscious and half comatose, and the attendant clergy began to think that no new appointment would be necessary for some few months to come.

CHAP. XXXII.

A NEW CANDIDATE FOR ECCLESIASTICAL HONOURS.

THE dean's illness occasioned much mental turmoil in other places besides the deanery and adjoining library; and the idea which occurred to the meagre little prebendary about Mr. Slope did not occur to him alone.

The bishop was sitting listlessly in his study when the news reached him of the dean's illness. It was brought to him by Mr. Slope, who of course was not the last person in Barchester to hear it. It was also not slow in finding its way to Mrs. Proudie's ears. It may be presumed that there was not just then much friendly intercourse between these two rival claimants for his lordship's obedience. Indeed, though living in the same house, they had not met since the stormy interview between them in the bishop's study on the preceding day.

On that occasion Mrs. Proudie had been defeated. That the prestige of continual victory should have been torn from her standards was a subject of great sorrow to that militant lady; but though defeated, she was not overcome. She felt that she might yet recover her lost ground, that she might yet hurl Mr. Slope down to the dust from which she had picked him, and force her sinning lord to sue for pardon in sackcloth and ashes.

On that memorable day, memorable for his mutiny and rebellion against her high behests, he had carried his way with a high hand, and had really begun to think it possible that the days of his slavery were counted. He had begun to hope that he was now about to enter into a free land, a land delicious with milk which he himself might quaff, and honey which would not tantalise him by being only honey to the eye. When Mrs. Proudie banged the door, as she left his room, he felt himself every inch a bishop. To be sure his spirit had been a little cowed by his chaplain's subsequent lecture; but on the whole he was highly pleased with himself, and flattered himself that the worst was over. " Ce n'est que le premier pas qui coûte," he reflected ; and now that the first step had been so magnanimously taken, all the rest would follow easily.

He met his wife as a matter of course at dinner, where little or nothing was said that could ruffle the bishop's happiness. His daughters and the servants were present and protected him.

He made one or two trifling remarks on the subject of his projected visit to the archbishop, in order to show to all concerned that he intended to have his own way ; and the very servants perceiving the change transferred a little of their reverence from their mistress to their master. All which the master perceived ; and so also did the mistress. But Mrs. Proudie bided her time.

After dinner he returned to his study where Mr. Slope soon found him, and there they had tea together and planned many things. For some few minutes the bishop was really happy ; but as the clock on the chimney piece warned him that the stilly hours of night were drawing on, as he looked at his chamber candlestick and knew that he must use it, his heart sank within him again. He was as a ghost, all whose power of wandering free through these upper regions ceases at cock-crow ; or rather he was the opposite of the ghost, for till cock-crow he must again be a serf. And would that be all ? Could he trust himself to come down to breakfast a free man in the morning.

He was nearly an hour later than usual, when he betook himself to his rest. Rest ! what rest ? However, he took a couple of glasses of sherry, and mounted the stairs. Far be it from us to follow him thither. There are some things which no novelist, no historian, should attempt ; some few scenes in life's drama which even no poet should dare to paint. Let that which passed between Dr. Proudie and his wife on this night be understood to be among them.

He came down the following morning a sad and thoughtful man. He was attenuated in appearance ; one might almost say emaciated. I doubt whether his now grizzled locks had not palpably become more grey than on the preceding evening. At any rate he had aged materially. Years do not make a man old gradually and at an even pace. Look through the world and see if this is not so always, except in those rare cases in which the human being lives and dies without joys and without sorrows, like a vegetable. A man shall be possessed of florid youthful blooming health till, it matters not what age. Thirty—forty—fifty, then comes some nipping frost, some period of agony, that robs the fibres of the body of their succulence, and the hale and hearty man is counted among the old.

He came down and breakfasted alone; Mrs. Proudie being indisposed took her coffee in her bed-room, and her daughters waited upon her there. He ate his breakfast alone, and then, hardly knowing what he did, he betook himself to his usual seat in his study. He tried to solace himself with his coming visit to the archbishop. That effort of his own free will at any rate remained to him as an enduring triumph. But somehow, now that he had achieved it, he did not seem to care so much about it. It was his ambition that had prompted him to take his place at the archiepiscopal table, and his ambition was now quite dead within him.

He was thus seated when Mr. Slope made his appearance, with breathless impatience.

"My lord, the dean is dead."

"Good heavens!" exclaimed the bishop, startled out of his apathy by an announcement so sad and so sudden.

"He is either dead or now dying. He has had an apoplectic fit, and I am told that there is not the slightest hope; indeed, I do not doubt that by this time he is no more."

Bells were rung, and servants were immediately sent to inquire. In the course of the morning, the bishop, leaning on his chaplain's arm, himself called at the deanery door. Mrs. Proudie sent to Miss Trefoil all manner of offers of assistance. The Miss Proudies sent also, and there was immense sympathy between the palace and the deanery. The answer to all inquiries was unvaried. The dean was just the same; and Sir Omicron Pie was expected down by the 9.15 P. M. train.

And then Mr. Slope began to meditate, as others also had done, as to who might possibly be the new dean; and it occurred to him, as it had also occurred to others, that it might be possible that he should be the new dean himself. And then the question as to the twelve hundred, or fifteen hundred, or two thousand, ran in his mind, as it had run through those of the other clergymen in the cathedral library.

Whether it might be two thousand, or fifteen or twelve hundred, it would in any case undoubtedly be a great thing for him, if he could get it. The gratification to his ambition would be greater even than that of his covetousness. How glorious to out-top the archdeacon in his own cathedral city; to sit above prebendaries and canons, and have the cathedral pulpit and all the cathedral services altogether at his own disposal!

But it might be easier to wish for this than to obtain it. Mr.

Slope, however, was not without some means of forwarding his views, and he at any rate did not let the grass grow under his feet. In the first place he thought—and not vainly—that he could count upon what assistance the bishop could give him. He immediately changed his views with regard to his patron ; he made up his mind that if he became dean, he would hand his lordship back again to his wife's vassalage ; and he thought it possible that his lordship might not be sorry to rid himself of one of his mentors. Mr. Slope had also taken some steps towards making his name known to other men in power. There was a certain chief-commissioner of national schools who at the present moment was presumed to stand especially high in the good graces of the government big wigs, and with him Mr. Slope had contrived to establish a sort of epistolary intimacy. He thought that he might safely apply to Sir Nicholas Fitzwhiggin ; and he felt sure that if Sir Nicholas chose to exert himself, the promise of such a piece of preferment would be had for the asking for.

Then he also had the press at his bidding, or flattered himself that he had so. The daily Jupiter had taken his part in a very thorough manner in those polemical contests of his with Mr. Arabin ; he had on more than one occasion absolutely had an in-terview with a gentleman on the staff of that paper, who, if not the editor, was as good as the editor ; and had long been in the habit of writing telling letters on all manner of ecclesiastical abuses, which he signed with his initials, and sent to his editorial friend with private notes signed in his own name. Indeed, he and Mr. Towers—such was the name of the powerful gentleman of the press with whom he was connected—were generally very amiable with each other. Mr. Slope's little productions were always printed and occasionally commented upon ; and thus, in a small sort of way, he had become a literary celebrity. This public life had great charms for him, though it certainly also had its draw-backs. On one occasion, when speaking in the presence of re-porters, he had failed to uphold and praise and swear by that special line of conduct which had been upheld and praised and sworn by in the Jupiter, and then he had been much surprised and at the moment not a little irritated to find himself lacerated most unmercifully by his old ally. He was quizzed and bespattered and made a fool of, just as though, or rather worse than if, he had been a constant enemy instead of a constant friend. He had hitherto not learnt that a man who aspires to be on the staff of the Jupiter must surrender all individuality. But ultimately this little casti-gation had broken no bones between him and his friend Mr

Towers. Mr. Slope was one of those who understood the world too well to show himself angry with such a potentate as the Jupiter. He had kissed the rod that scourged him, and now thought that he might fairly look for his reward. He determined that he would at once let Mr. Towers know that he was a candidate for the place which was about to become vacant. More than one piece of preferment had lately been given away much in accordance with advice tendered to the government in the columns of the Jupiter.

But it was incumbent on Mr. Slope first to secure the bishop. He specially felt that it behoved him to do this before the visit to the archbishop was made. It was really quite providential that the dean should have fallen ill just at the very nick of time. If Dr. Proudie could be instigated to take the matter up warmly, he might manage a good deal while staying at the archbishop's palace. Feeling this very strongly Mr. Slope determined to sound the bishop that very afternoon. He was to start on the following morning to London, and therefore not a moment could be lost with safety.

He went into the bishop's study about five o'clock, and found him still sitting alone. It might have been supposed that he had hardly moved since the little excitement occasioned by his walk to the dean's door. He still wore on his face that dull dead look of half unconscious suffering. He was doing nothing, reading nothing, thinking of nothing, but simply gazing on vacancy when Mr. Slope for the second time that day entered his room.

"Well, Slope," said he, somewhat impatiently; for, to tell the truth, he was not anxious just at present to have much conversation with Mr. Slope.

"Your lordship will be sorry to hear that as yet the poor dean has shown no sign of amendment."

"Oh—ah—hasn't he? Poor man! I'm sure I'm very sorry. I suppose Sir Omicron has not arrived yet?"

"No; not till the 9.15 P.M. train."

"I wonder they didn't have a special. They say Dr. Trefoil is very rich."

"Very rich, I believe," said Mr. Slope. "But the truth is, all the doctors in London can do no good; no other good than to show that every possible care has been taken. Poor Dr. Trefoil is not long for this world, my lord."

"I suppose not—I suppose not."

"Oh no; indeed, his best friends could not wish that he should outlive such a shock, for his intellects cannot possibly survive it."

"Poor man! poor man!" said the bishop.

"It will naturally be a matter of much moment to your lordship who is to succeed him," said Mr. Slope. "It would be a great thing if you could secure the appointment for some person of your own way of thinking on important points. The party hostile to us are very strong here in Barchester — much too strong."

"Yes, yes. If poor Dr. Trefoil is to go, it will be a great thing to get a good man in his place."

"It will be everything to your lordship to get a man on whose co-operation you can reckon. Only think what trouble we might have if Dr. Grantly, or Dr. Hyandry, or any of that way of thinking, were to get it."

"It is not very probable that Lord —— will give it to any of that school; why should he?"

"No. Not probable; certainly not; but it's possible. Great interest will probably be made. If I might venture to advise your lordship, I would suggest that you should discuss the matter with his grace next week. I have no doubt that your wishes, if made known and backed by his grace, would be paramount with Lord ——."

"Well, I don't know that; Lord —— has always been very kind to me, very kind. But I am unwilling to interfere in such matters unless asked. And indeed, if asked, I don't know whom, at this moment, I should recommend."

Mr. Slope, even Mr. Slope, felt at the present rather abashed. He hardly knew how to frame his little request in language sufficiently modest. He had recognised and acknowledged to himself the necessity of shocking the bishop in the first instance by the temerity of his application, and his difficulty was how best to remedy that by his adroitness and eloquence. "I doubted myself," said he, "whether your lordship would have any one immediately in your eye, and it is on this account that I venture to submit to you an idea that I have been turning over in my own mind. If poor Dr. Trefoil must go, I really do not see why, with your lordship's assistance, I should not hold the preferment myself."

"You!" exclaimed the bishop, in a manner that Mr. Slope could hardly have considered complimentary.

The ice was now broken, and Mr. Slope became fluent enough. "I have been thinking of looking for it. If your lordship will press the matter on the archbishop, I do not doubt but I shall succeed. You see I shall be the first to move, which is a great matter. Then I can count upon assistance from the public press : my name is known, I may say, somewhat favourably known to that portion of the press which is now most influential with the government, and I have friends also in the government. But, nevertheless, it is to you, my lord, that I look for assistance. It is from your hands that I would most willingly receive the benefit. And, which should ever be the chief consideration in such matters, you must know better than any other person whatsoever what qualifications I possess."

The bishop sat for a while dumbfounded. Mr. Slope dean of Barchester ! The idea of such a transformation of character would never have occurred to his own unaided intellect. At first he went on thinking why, for what reasons, on what account, Mr. Slope should be dean of Barchester. But by degrees the direction of his thoughts changed, and he began to think why, for what reasons, on what account, Mr. Slope should not be dean of Barchester. As far as he himself, the bishop, was concerned, he could well spare the services of his chaplain. That little idea of using Mr. Slope as a counterpoise to his wife had well nigh evaporated. He had all but acknowledged the futility of the scheme. If indeed he could have slept in his chaplain's bed-room instead of his wife's, there might have been something in it. But —— ——. And thus as Mr. Slope was speaking, the bishop began to recognise the idea that that gentleman might become dean of Barchester without impropriety ; not moved, indeed, by Mr. Slope's eloquence, for he did not follow the tenor of his speech ; but led thereto by his own cogitations.

"I need not say," continued Mr. Slope, "that it would be my chief desire to act in all matters connected with the cathedral as far as possible in accordance with your views. I know your lordship so well (and I hope you know me well enough to have the same feelings), that I am satisfied that my being in that position would add materially to your own comfort, and enable you to extend the sphere of your useful influence. As I said before, it is most desirable that there should be but one opinion among the dignitaries of the same diocese. I doubt much whether I would accept such an appointment in any diocese in which I should be constrained to differ much from the bishop. In this case there would be a delightful uniformity of opinion."

Mr. Slope perfectly well perceived that the bishop did not follow a word that he said, but nevertheless he went on talking. He knew it was necessary that Dr. Proudie should recover from his surprise, and he knew also that he must give him the opportunity of appearing to have been persuaded by argument. So he went on, and produced a multitude of fitting reasons all tending to show that no one on earth could make so good a dean of Barchester as himself, that the government and the public would assuredly co-incide in desiring that he, Mr. Slope, should be dean of Barchester ; but that for high considerations of ecclesiastical polity it would be especially desirable that this piece of preferment should be so bestowed through the instrumentality of the bishop of the diocese.

"But I really don't know what I could do in the matter," said the bishop.

"If you would mention it to the archbishop; if you could tell his grace that you consider such an appointment very desirable, that you have it much at heart with a view to putting an end to schism in the diocese ; if you did this with your usual energy, you would probably find no difficulty in inducing his grace to promise that he would mention it to Lord ——. Of course you would let the archbishop know that I am not looking for the preferment solely through his intervention ; that you do not exactly require him to ask it as a favour ; that you expect that I shall get it through other sources, as is indeed the case ; but that you are very anxious that his grace should express his approval of such an ar-rangement to Lord ——."

It ended in the bishop promising to do as he was bid. Not that he so promised without a stipulation. "About that hospital," he said, in the middle of the conference. "I was never so troubled in my life;" which was about the truth. "You haven't spoken to Mr. Harding since I saw you?"

Mr. Slope assured his patron that he had not.

"Ah well, then—I think upon the whole it will be better to let Quiverful have it. It has been half promised to him, and he has a large family and is very poor. I think on the whole it will be better to make out the nomination for Mr. Quiverful."

"But, my lord," said Mr. Slope, still thinking that he was bound to make a fight for his own view on this matter and remembering that it still behoved him to maintain his lately acquired supremacy over Mrs. Proudie, lest he should fail in his views regarding the deanery,—"but, my lord, I am really much afraid ——"

"Remember, Mr. Slope," said the bishop, "I can hold out no sort of hope to you in this matter of succeeding poor Dr. Trefoil. I will certainly speak to the archbishop, as you wish it, but I cannot think ——"

"Well, my lord," said Mr. Slope, fully understanding the bishop and in his turn interrupting him, " perhaps your lordship is right about Mr. Quiverful. I have no doubt I can easily arrange matters with Mr. Harding, and I will make out the nomination for your signature as you direct."

" Yes, Slope, I think that will be best; and you may be sure that any little that I can do to forward your views shall be done."

And so they parted.

Mr. Slope had now much business on his hands. He had to make his daily visit to the signora. This common prudence should have now induced him to omit, but he was infatuated; and could not bring himself to be commonly prudent. He determined therefore that he would drink tea at the Stanhopes'; and he determined also, or thought that he determined, that having done so he would go thither no more. He had also to arrange his matters with Mrs. Bold. He was of opinion that Eleanor would grace the deanery as perfectly as she would the chaplain's cottage; and he thought, moreover, that Eleanor's fortune would excellently repair any dilapidations and curtailments in the dean's stipend. which might have been made by that ruthless ecclesiastical commission.

Touching Mrs. Bold his hopes now soared high. Mr. Slope was one of that numerous multitude of swains who think that all is fair in love, and he had accordingly not refrained from using the services of Mrs. Bold's own maid. From her he had learnt much of what had taken place at Plumstead; not exactly with truth, for " the own maid" had not been able to divine the exact truth, but with some sort of similitude to it. He had been told that the archdeacon and Mrs. Grantly and Mr. Harding and Mr. Arabin had all quarrelled with " missus" for having received a letter from Mr. Slope; that " missus" had positively refused to give the letter up; that she had received from the archdeacon the option of giving up either Mr. Slope and his letter, or else the society of Plumstead rectory; and that " missus" had declared with much indignation, that " she didn't care a straw for the society of Plumstead rectory," and that she wouldn't give up Mr. Slope for any of them.

Considering the source from whence this came, it was not quite so untrue as might have been expected. It showed pretty plainly what had been the nature of the conversation in the servants' hall; and coupled as it was with the certainty of Eleanor's sudden return, it appeared to Mr. Slope to be so far worthy of credit as to justify him in thinking that the fair widow would in all human probability accept his offer.

All this work was therefore to be done. It was desirable he thought that he should make his offer before it was known that Mr.

Quiverful was finally appointed to the hospital. In his letter to Eleanor he had plainly declared that Mr. Harding was to have the appointment. It would be very difficult to explain this away; and were he to write another letter to Eleanor, telling the truth and throwing the blame on the bishop, it would naturally injure him in her estimation. He determined therefore to let that matter disclose itself as it would, and to lose no time in throwing himself at her feet.

Then he had to solicit the assistance of Sir Nicholas Fitzwhiggin and Mr. Towers, and he went directly from the bishop's presence to compose his letters to those gentlemen. As Mr. Slope was esteemed an adept at letter writing, they shall be given in full.

"(Private.)   "Palace, Barchester, Sept. 185—.

"My dear Sir Nicholas,—I hope that the intercourse which has been between us will preclude you from regarding my present application as an intrusion. You cannot I imagine have yet heard that poor dear old Dr. Trefoil has been seized with apoplexy. It is a subject of profound grief to every one in Barchester, for he has always been an excellent man—excellent as a man and as a clergyman. He is, however, full of years, and his life could not under any circumstances have been much longer spared. You may probably have known him.

"There is, it appears, no probable chance of his recovery. Sir Omicron Pie is, I believe, at present with him. At any rate the medical men here have declared that one or two days more must limit the tether of his mortal coil. I sincerely trust that his soul may wing its flight to that haven where it may for ever be at rest and for ever be happy.

"The bishop has been speaking to me about the preferment, and he is anxious that it should be conferred on me. I confess that I can hardly venture, at my age, to look for such advancement; but I am so far encouraged by his lordship, that I believe I shall be induced to do so. His lordship goes to —— to-morrow, and is intent on mentioning the subject to the archbishop.

"I know well how deservedly great is your weight with the present government. In any matter touching church preferment you would of course be listened to. Now that the matter has been put into my head, I am of course anxious to be successful. If you can assist me by your good word, you will confer on me one additional favour.

"I had better add, that Lord —— cannot as yet know of this piece of preferment having fallen in, or rather of its certainty of falling (for poor dear Dr. Trefoil is past hope). Should Lord ——— first hear it from you, that might probably be thought to give you a fair claim to express your opinion.

"Of course our grand object is, that we should all be of one opinion in church matters. This is most desirable at Barchester; it is this that makes our good bishop so anxious about it. You may probably think it expedient to point this out to Lord ——— if it shall be in your power to oblige me by mentioning the subject to his lordship.

"Believe me, my dear Sir Nicholas,
"Your most faithful servant,
"OBADIAH SLOPE."

His letter to Mr. Towers was written in quite a different strain. Mr. Slope conceived that he completely understood the difference in character and position of the two men whom he addressed. He knew that for such a man as Sir Nicholas Fitzwhiggin a little flummery was necessary, and that it might be of the easy every-day description. Accordingly his letter to Sir Nicholas was written *currente calamo*, with very little trouble. But to such a man as Mr. Towers it was not so easy to write a letter that should be effective and yet not offensive, that should carry its point without undue interference. It was not difficult to flatter Dr. Proudie or Sir Nicholas Fitzwhiggin, but very difficult to flatter Mr. Towers without letting the flattery declare itself. This, however, had to be done. Moreover, this letter must, in appearance at least, be written without effort, and be fluent, unconstrained, and demonstrative of no doubt or fear on the part of the writer. Therefore the epistle to Mr. Towers was studied, and recopied, and elaborated at the cost of so many minutes, that Mr. Slope had hardly time to dress himself and reach Dr. Stanhope's that evening.

When despatched it ran as follows:—

"(Private.)　　　　　　　　　"Barchester. Sept. 185—."

(He purposely omitted any allusion to the "palace," thinking that Mr. Towers might not like it. A great man, he remembered, had been once much condemned for dating a letter from Windsor Castle.)

"My dear Sir,—We were all a good deal shocked here this morning by hearing that poor old Dean Trefoil had been stricken with apoplexy. The fit took him about 9 A.M. I am writing now to save the post, and he is still alive, but past all hope, or possibility I believe, of living. Sir Omicron Pie is here, or will be very shortly; but all that even Sir Omicron can do, is to ratify the sentence of his less distinguished brethren that nothing can be done. Poor Dr. Trefoil's race on this side the grave is run. I do not know whether you knew him. He was a good, quiet, charitable man, of the old school of course, as any clergyman over seventy years of age must necessarily be.

"But I do not write merely with the object of sending you such news as this: doubtless some one of your Mercuries will have seen and heard and reported so much; I write, as you usually do yourself, rather with a view to the future than to the past.

"Rumour is already rife here as to Dr. Trefoil's successor, and among those named as possible future deans your humble servant is, I believe, not the least frequently spoken of; in short I am looking for the preferment. You may probably know that since Bishop Proudie came to this diocese I have exerted myself here a good deal; and I may certainly say not without some success. He and I are nearly always of the same opinion on points of doctrine as well as church discipline, and therefore I have had, as his confidential chaplain, very much in my own hands; but I confess to you that I have a higher ambition than to remain the chaplain of any bishop.

"There are no positions in which more energy is now needed than those of our deans. The whole of our enormous cathedral establishments have been allowed to go to sleep, — nay, they are all but dead, and ready for the sepulchre! And yet of what prodigious moment they might be made, if, as was intended, they were so managed as to lead the way and show an example for all our parochial clergy!

"The bishop here is most anxious for my success; indeed, he goes to-morrow to press the matter on the archbishop. I believe also I may count on the support of at least one most effective member of the government. But I confess that the support of the Jupiter, if I be thought worthy of it, would be more gratifying to me than any other; more gratifying if by it I should be successful; and more gratifying also, if, although so supported, I should be unsuccessful.

"The time has, in fact, come in which no government can venture to fill up the high places of the Church in defiance of the public press. The age of honourable bishops and noble deans has gone by; and any clergyman, however humbly born, can now hope for success, if his industry, talent, and character be sufficient to call forth the manifest opinion of the public in his favour.

"At the present moment we all feel that any counsel given in such matters by the Jupiter has the greatest weight—is, indeed, generally followed; and we feel also—I am speaking of clergymen of my own age and standing—that it should be so. There can be no patron less interested than the Jupiter, and none that more thoroughly understands the wants of the people.

"I am sure you will not suspect me of asking from you any support which the paper with which you are connected cannot conscientiously give me. My object in writing is to let you know that I am a candidate for the appointment. It is for you to judge whether or no you can assist my views. I should not, of course, have written to you on such a matter had I not believed (and I have had good reason so to believe) that the Jupiter approves of my views on ecclesiastical polity.

"The bishop expresses a fear that I may be considered too young for such a station, my age being thirty-six. I cannot think that at the present day any hesitation need be felt on such a point. The public has lost its love for antiquated servants. If a man will ever be fit to do good work he will be fit at thirty-six years of age.

"Believe me very faithfully yours,
"OBADIAH SLOPE.

" T. TOWERS, ESQ
"——Court,
"Middle Temple."

Having thus exerted himself, Mr. Slope posted his letters, and passed the remainder of the evening at the feet of his mistress.

Mr. Slope will be accused of deceit in his mode of canvassing. It will be said that he lied in the application he made to each of his three patrons. I believe it must be owned that he did so. He could not hesitate on account of his youth, and yet be quite assured that he was not too young. He could not count chiefly on the bishop's support, and chiefly also on that of the newspaper. He did not think that the bishop was going to —— to press the matter on the archbishop. It must be owned that in his canvassing Mr. Slope was as false as he well could be.

Let it, however, be asked of those who are conversant with such matters, whether he was more false than men usually are on such occasions. We English gentlemen hate the name of a lie; but how often do we find public men who believe each other's words?

CHAP. XXXIII.

MRS. PROUDIE VICTRIX.

THE next week passed over at Barchester with much apparent tranquillity. The hearts, however, of some of the inhabitants were not so tranquil as the streets of the city. The poor old dean still continued to live, just as Sir Omicron Pie had prophesied that he would do, much to the amazement, and some thought disgust, of Dr. Fillgrave. The bishop still remained away. He had stayed a day or two in town, and had also remained longer at the arch-bishop's than he had intended. Mr. Slope had as yet received no line in answer to either of his letters; but he had learnt the cause of this. Sir Nicholas was stalking a deer, or attending the Queen, in the Highlands; and even the indefatigable Mr. Towers had stolen an autumn holiday, and had made one of the yearly tribe who now ascend Mont Blanc. Mr. Slope learnt that he was not expected back till the last day of September.

Mrs. Bold was thrown much with the Stanhopes, of whom she became fonder and fonder. If asked, she would have said that Charlotte Stanhope was her especial friend, and so she would have thought. But, to tell the truth, she liked Bertie nearly as well; she had no more idea of regarding him as a lover than she would have had of looking at a big tame dog in such a light. Bertie had become very intimate with her, and made little speeches to her, and said little things of a sort very different from the speeches and sayings of other men. But then this was almost always done before his sisters; and he, with his long silken beard, his light blue eyes and strange dress, was so unlike other men. She admitted him to a kind of familiarity which she had never known with any one else, and of which she by no means understood the danger. She blushed once at finding that she had called him Bertie, and on the same day only barely remembered her position in time to check her-self from playing upon him some personal practical joke to which she was instigated by Charlotte.

In all this Eleanor was perfectly innocent, and Bertie Stanhope could hardly be called guilty. But every familiarity into which Eleanor was entrapped was deliberately planned by his sister. She knew well how to play her game, and played it without mercy; she knew, none so well, what was her brother's character, and she would have handed over to him the young widow, and the young widow's money, and the money of the widow's child, without remorse. With her pretended friendship and warm cordiality, she strove to connect Eleanor so closely with her brother as to make it impossible that she should go back even if she wished it. But Charlotte Stanhope knew really nothing of Eleanor's character; did not even understand that there were such characters. She did not comprehend that a young and pretty woman could be playful and familiar with a man such as Bertie Stanhope, and yet have no idea in her head, no feeling in her heart, that she would have been ashamed to own to all the world. Charlotte Stanhope did not in the least conceive that her new friend was a woman whom nothing could entrap into an inconsiderate marriage, whose mind would have revolted from the slightest impropriety had she been aware that any impropriety existed.

Miss Stanhope, however, had tact enough to make herself and her father's house very agreeable to Mrs. Bold. There was with them all an absence of stiffness and formality which was peculiarly agreeable to Eleanor after the great dose of clerical arrogance which she had lately been constrained to take. She played chess with them, walked with them, and drank tea with them; studied or pretended to study astronomy; assisted them in writing stories in rhyme, in turning prose tragedy into comic verse, or comic stories into would-be tragic poetry. She had no idea before that she had any such talents. She had not conceived the possibility of her doing such things as she now did. She found with the Stanhopes new amusements and employments, new pursuits, which in themselves could not be wrong, and which were exceedingly alluring.

Is it not a pity that people who are bright and clever should so often be exceedingly improper? and that those who are never improper should so often be dull and heavy? Now Charlotte Stanhope was always bright, and never heavy: but then her propriety was doubtful.

But during all this time Eleanor by no means forgot Mr. Arabin, nor did she forget Mr. Slope. She had parted from Mr. Arabin in her anger. She was still angry at what she regarded as his impertinent interference; but nevertheless she looked forward to meeting him again, and also looked forward to forgiving him. The words that Mr. Arabin had uttered still sounded in her ears. She knew that if not intended for a declaration of love, they did signify that he loved her; and she felt also that if he ever did make such a declaration, it might be that she should not receive it unkindly. She was still angry with him, very angry with him; so angry that she would bite her lip and stamp her foot as she thought of what he had said and done. But nevertheless she yearned to let him know that he was forgiven; all that she required was that he should own that he had sinned.

She was to meet him at Ullathorne on the last day of the present month. Miss Thorne had invited all the country round to a breakfast on the lawn. There were to be tents, and archery, and dancing for the ladies on the lawn, and for the swains and girls in the paddock. There were to be fiddlers and fifers, races for the boys, poles to be climbed, ditches full of water to be jumped over, horse-collars to be grinned through (this latter amusement was an addition of the stewards, and not arranged by Miss Thorne in the original programme), and every game to be played which, in a long course of reading, Miss Thorne could ascertain to have been played in the good days of Queen Elizabeth. Everything of more modern growth was to be tabooed, if possible. On one subject Miss Thorne was very unhappy. She had been turning in her mind the matter of a bull-ring, but could not succeed in making anything of it. She would not for the world have done, or allowed to be done, anything that was cruel; as to the promoting the torture of a bull for the amusement of her young neighbours, it need hardly be said that Miss Thorne would be the last to think of it. And yet there was something so charming in the name. A bull-ring, however, without a bull would only be a memento of the decadence of the times, and she felt herself constrained to abandon the idea. Quintains, however, she was determined to have, and had poles and swivels and bags of flour prepared accordingly. She would no doubt have been anxious for something small in the way of a tournament; but, as she said to her brother, that had been tried, and the age had proved itself too decidedly inferior to its fore-runners to admit of such a pastime. Mr. Thorne did not seem to participate much in her regret, feeling perhaps that a full suit of chain-armour would have added but little to his own personal comfort.

This party at Ullathorne had been planned in the first place as a sort of welcoming to Mr. Arabin on his entrance into St. Ewold's parsonage; an intended harvest-home gala for the labourers and their wives and children had subsequently been amalgamated with it, and thus it had grown to its present dimensions. All the Plumstead party had of course been asked, and at the time of the invitation Eleanor had intended to have gone with her sister. Now her plans were altered, and she was going with the Stanhopes. The Proudies were also to be there; and as Mr. Slope had not been included in the invitation to the palace, the signora, whose impudence never deserted her, asked permission of Miss Thorne to bring him.

This permission Miss Thorne gave, having no other alternative; but she did so with a trembling heart, fearing Mr. Arabin would be offended. Immediately on his return she apologised, almost with tears, so dire an enmity was presumed to rage between the two gentlemen. But Mr. Arabin comforted her by an assurance that he should meet Mr. Slope with the greatest pleasure imaginable, and made her promise that she would introduce them to each other.

But this triumph of Mr. Slope's was not so agreeable to Eleanor, who since her return to Barchester had done her best to avoid him. She would not give way to the Plumstead folk when they so ungenerously accused her of being in love with this odious man ; but, nevertheless, knowing that she was so accused, she was fully alive to the expediency of keeping out of his way and dropping him by degrees. She had seen very little of him since her return. Her servant had been instructed to say to all visitors that she was out. She could not bring herself to specify Mr. Slope particularly, and in order to avoid him she had thus debarred herself from all her friends. She had excepted Charlotte Stanhope, and by degrees a few others also. Once she had met him at the Stanhopes'; but, as a rule, Mr. Slope's visits there were made in the morning, and hers in the evening. On that one occasion Charlotte had managed to preserve her from any annoyance. This was very good-natured on the part of Charlotte, as Eleanor thought, and also very sharp-witted, as Eleanor had told her friend nothing of her reasons for wishing to avoid that gentleman. The fact, however, was, that Charlotte had learnt from her sister that Mr. Slope would probably put himself forward as a suitor for the widow's hand, and she was consequently sufficiently alive to the expediency of guarding Bertie's future wife from any danger in that quarter.

Nevertheless the Stanhopes were pledged to take Mr. Slope with them to Ullathorne. An arrangement was therefore necessarily made, which was very disagreeable to Eleanor. Dr. Stanhope, with herself, Charlotte, and Mr. Slope, were to go together, and Bertie was to follow with his sister Madeline. It was clearly visible by Eleanor's face that this assortment was very disagreeable to her; and Charlotte, who was much encouraged thereby in her own little plan, made a thousand apologies.

"I see you don't like it, my dear," said she, " but we could not manage otherwise. Bertie would give his eyes to go with you, but Madeline cannot possibly go without him. Nor could we possibly put Mr. Slope and Madeline in the same carriage without any one else. They'd both be ruined for ever, you know, and not admitted inside Ullathorne gates, I should imagine, after such an impropriety."

"Of course that wouldn't do," said Eleanor; "but couldn't I go in the carriage with the signora and your brother?"

"Impossible!" said Charlotte. "When she is there, there is only room for two." The signora, in truth, did not care to do her travelling in the presence of strangers.

"Well, then," said Eleanor, "you are all so kind, Charlotte, and so good to me, that I am sure you won't be offended; but I think I'll not go at all."

"Not go at all!—what nonsense!—indeed you shall." It had been absolutely determined in family council that Bertie should propose on that very occasion.

"Or I can take a fly," said Eleanor. "You know I am not embarrassed by so many difficulties as you young ladies; I can go alone."

"Nonsense! my dear. Don't think of such a thing; after all it is only for an hour or so; and, to tell the truth, I don't know what it is you dislike so. I thought you and Mr. Slope were great friends. What is it you dislike?"

"Oh! nothing particular," said Eleanor; "only I thought it would be a family party."

"Of course it would be much nicer, much more snug, if Bertie could go with us. It is he that is badly treated. I can assure you he is much more afraid of Mr. Slope than you are. But you see Madeline cannot go out without him,—and she, poor creature, goes out so seldom! I am sure you don't begrudge her this, though her vagary does knock about our own party a little."

Of course Eleanor made a thousand protestations, and uttered a thousand hopes that Madeline would enjoy herself. And of course she had to give way, and undertake to go in the carriage with Mr. Slope. In fact, she was driven either to do this, or to explain why she would not do so. Now she could not bring herself to explain to Charlotte Stanhope all that had passed at Plumstead.

But it was to her a sore necessity. She thought of a thousand little schemes for avoiding it; she would plead illness, and not go at all; she would persuade Mary Bold to go although not asked, and then make a necessity of having a carriage of her own to take her sister-in-law; anything, in fact, she could do, rather than be seen by Mr. Arabin getting out of the same carriage with Mr. Slope. However, when the momentous morning came she had no scheme matured, and then Mr. Slope handed her into Dr. Stanhope's carriage, and following her steps, sat opposite to her.

The bishop returned on the eve of the Ullathorne party, and was received at home with radiant smiles by the partner of all his cares. On his arrival he crept up to his dressing-room with somewhat of a palpitating heart; he had overstayed his allotted time by three days, and was not without much fear of penalties. Nothing, however, could be more affectionately cordial than the greeting he received: the girls came out and kissed him in a manner that was quite soothing to his spirit; and Mrs. Proudie, "albeit, unused to the melting mood," squeezed him in her arms, and almost in words called him her dear, darling, good, pet, little bishop. All this was a very pleasant surprise.

Mrs. Proudie had somewhat changed her tactics; not that she had seen any cause to disapprove of her former line of conduct, but she had now brought matters to such a point that she calculated that she might safely do so. She had got the better of Mr. Slope, and she now thought well to show her husband that when allowed to get the better of everybody, when obeyed by him and permitted to rule over others, she would take care that he should have his reward. Mr. Slope had not a chance against her; not only could she stun the poor bishop by her midnight anger, but she could assuage and soothe him, if she so willed, by daily indulgences. She could furnish his room for him, turn him out as smart a bishop as any on the bench, give him good dinners, warm fires, and an easy life; all this she would do if he would but be quietly obedient. But if not,——! To speak sooth, however, his sufferings on that dreadful night had been so poignant, as to leave him little spirit for further rebellion.

As soon as he had dressed himself she returned to his room. "I hope you enjoyed yourself at——," said she, seating herself on one side of the fire while he remained in his arm-chair on the other, stroking the calves of his legs. It was the first time he had had a fire in his room since the summer, and it pleased him; for the good bishop loved to be warm and cozy. Yes, he said, he had enjoyed himself very much. Nothing could be more polite than the archbishop; and Mrs. Archbishop had been equally charming.

Mrs. Proudie was delighted to hear it; nothing, she declared, pleased her so much as to think

> "Her bairn respectit like the lave."

She did not put it precisely in these words, but what she said came to the same thing; and then, having petted and fondled her little man sufficiently, she proceeded to business.

"The poor dean is still alive," said she.

"So I hear, so I hear," said the bishop. "I'll go to the deanery directly after breakfast to-morrow."

"We are going to this party at Ullathorne to morrow morning, my dear; we must be there early, you know,—by twelve o'clock I suppose."

"Oh,—ah!" said the bishop; "then I'll certainly call the next day."

"Was much said about it at——?" asked Mrs. Proudie.

"About what?" said the bishop.

"Filling up the dean's place," said Mrs. Proudie. As she spoke a spark of the wonted fire returned to her eye, and the bishop felt himself to be a little less comfortable than before.

"Filling up the dean's place; that is, if the dean dies ?—very little, my dear. It was mentioned, just mentioned."

"And what did you say about it, bishop?"

"Why, I said that I thought that if, that is, should—should the dean die, that is, I said I thought——" As he went on stammering and floundering, he saw that his wife's eye was fixed sternly on him. Why should he encounter such evil for a man whom he loved so slightly as Mr. Slope? Why should he give up his enjoyments and his ease, and such dignity as might be allowed to him, to fight a losing battle for a chaplain? The chaplain after all, if successful, would be as great a tyrant as his wife. Why fight at all? why contend? why be uneasy? From that moment he determined to fling Mr. Slope to the winds, and take the goods the gods provided.

"I am told," said Mrs. Proudie, speaking very slowly, "that Mr. Slope is looking to be the new dean."

"Yes,—certainly, I believe he is," said the bishop.

"And what does the archbishop say about that?" asked Mrs. Proudie.

"Well, my dear, to tell the truth, I promised Mr. Slope to speak to the archbishop. Mr. Slope spoke to me about it. It is very arrogant of him, I must say,—but that is nothing to me."

"Arrogant!" said Mrs. Proudie; "it is the most impudent piece of pretension I ever heard of in my life. Mr. Slope Dean of Barchester, indeed! And what did you do in the matter, bishop?"

"Why, my dear, I did speak to the archbishop."

"You don't mean to tell me," said Mrs. Proudie, "that you are going to make yourself ridiculous by lending your name to such a preposterous attempt as this? Mr. Slope Dean of Barchester, indeed!" And she tossed her head, and put her arms a-kimbo, with an air of confident defiance that made her husband quite sure that Mr. Slope never would be Dean of Barchester. In truth, Mrs. Proudie was all but invincible; had she married Petruchio, it may be doubted whether that arch wife-tamer would have been able to keep her legs out of those garments which are presumed by men to be peculiarly unfitted for feminine use.

"It is preposterous, my dear."

"Then why have you endeavoured to assist him?"

"Why,—my dear, I haven't assisted him—much."

"But why have you done it at all? why have you mixed your name up in anything so ridiculous? What was it you did say to the archbishop?"

"Why, I just did mention it; I just did say that—that in the event of the poor dean's death, Mr. Slope would—would——"

"Would what?"

"I forget how I put it,—would take it if he could get it; something of that sort. I didn't say much more than that."

"You shouldn't have said anything at all. And what did the archbishop say?"

"He didn't say anything; he just bowed and rubbed his hands. Somebody else came up at the moment, and as we were discussing the new parochial universal school committee, the matter of the new dean dropped; after that I didn't think it wise to renew it."

"Renew it! I am very sorry you ever mentioned it. What will the archbishop think of you?"

"You may be sure, my dear, the archbishop thought very little about it."

"But why did you think about it, bishop? how could you think of making such a creature as that Dean of Barchester?—Dean of Barchester! I suppose he'll be looking for a bishopric some of these days,—a man that hardly knows who his own father was; a man that I found without bread to his mouth, or a coat to his back. Dean of Barchester, indeed! I'll dean him."

Mrs. Proudie considered herself to be in politics a pure Whig: all her family belonged to the Whig party. Now, among all ranks of Englishmen and Englishwomen (Mrs. Proudie should, I think, be ranked among the former, on the score of her great strength of mind), no one is so hostile to lowly born pretenders to high station as the pure Whig.

The bishop thought it necessary to exculpate himself. "Why, my dear," said he, "it appeared to me that you and Mr. Slope did not get on quite so well as you used to do."

"Get on!" said Mrs. Proudie, moving her foot uneasily on the hearth-rug, and compressing her lips in a manner that betokened much danger to the subject of their discourse.

"I began to find that he was objectionable to you," — Mrs. Proudie's foot worked on the hearth-rug with great rapidity, — "and that you would be more comfortable if he was out of the palace," — Mrs. Proudie smiled, as a hyena may probably smile before he begins his laugh, — "and therefore I thought that if he got this place, and so ceased to be my chaplain, you might be pleased at such an arrangement."

And then the hyena laughed out. Pleased at such an arrangement! pleased at having her enemy converted into a dean with twelve hundred a year! Medea, when she describes the customs of her native country (I am quoting from Robson's edition), assures her astonished auditor that in her land captives, when taken, are eaten. "You pardon them?" says Medea. "We do indeed," says the mild Grecian. "We eat them!" says she of Colchis, with terrific energy. Mrs. Proudie was the Medea of Barchester; she had no idea of not eating Mr. Slope. Pardon him! merely get rid of him! make a dean of him! It was not so they did with their captives in her country, among people of her sort! Mr. Slope had no such mercy to expect; she would pick him to the very last bone.

"Oh, yes, my dear, of course he'll cease to be your chaplain," said she. "After what has passed, that must be a matter of course. I couldn't for a moment think of living in the same house with such a man. Besides, he has shown himself quite unfit for such a situation; making broils and quarrels among the clergy, getting you, my dear, into scrapes, and taking upon himself as though he were as good as bishop himself. Of course he'll go. But because he leaves the palace, that is no reason why he should get into the deanery."

"Oh, of course not!" said the bishop; "but to save appearances you know, my dear ——"

"I don't want to save appearances; I want Mr. Slope to appear just what he is — a false, designing, mean, intriguing man. I have my eye on him; he little knows what I see. He is misconducting himself in the most disgraceful way with that lame Italian woman. That family is a disgrace to Barchester, and Mr. Slope is a disgrace to Barchester! If he doesn't look well to it, he'll have his gown stripped off his back instead of having a dean's hat on his head. Dean, indeed! The man has gone mad with arrogance."

The bishop said nothing further to excuse either himself or his chaplain, and having shown himself passive and docile was again taken into favour. They soon went to dinner, and he spent the pleasantest evening he had had in his own house for a long time. His daughter played and sang to him as he sipped his coffee and read his newspaper, and Mrs. Proudie asked good-natured little questions about the archbishop; and then he went happily to bed, and slept as quietly as though Mrs. Proudie had been Griselda herself. While shaving himself in the morning and preparing for the festivities of Ullathorne, he fully resolved to run no more tilts against a warrior so fully armed at all points as was Mrs. Proudie.

CHAP. XXXIV

OXFORD.—THE MASTER AND TUTOR OF LAZARUS.

Mr. ARABIN, as we have said, had but a sad walk of it under the trees of Plumstead churchyard. He did not appear to any of the family till dinner time, and then he seemed, as far as their judgment went, to be quite himself. He had, as was his wont, asked himself a great many questions, and given himself a great many answers; and the upshot of this was that he had set himself down for an ass. He had determined that he was much too old and much too rusty to commence the manœuvres of love-making; that he had let the time slip through his hands which should have been used for such purposes; and that now he must lie on his bed as he had made it. Then he asked himself whether in truth he did love this woman; and he answered himself, not without a long struggle, but at last honestly, that he certainly did love her. He then asked himself whether he did not also love her money; and he again answered himself that he did so. But here he did not answer honestly. It was and ever had been his weakness to look for impure motives for his own conduct. No doubt, circumstanced as he was, with a small living and a fellowship, accustomed as he had been to collegiate luxuries and expensive comforts, he might have hesitated to marry a penniless woman had he felt ever so strong a predilection for the woman herself; no doubt Eleanor's fortune put all such difficulties out of the question; but it was equally without doubt that his love for her had crept upon him without the slightest idea on his part that he could ever benefit his own condition by sharing her wealth.

When he had stood on the hearth-rug, counting the pattern, and counting also the future chances of his own life, the remembrances of Mrs. Bold's comfortable income had not certainly damped his first assured feeling of love for her. And why should it have done so? Need it have done so with the purest of men? Be that as it may, Mr. Arabin decided against himself; he decided that it had done so in his case, and that he was not the purest of men.

He also decided, which was more to his purpose, that Eleanor did not care a straw for him, and that very probably she did care a straw for his rival. Then he made up his mind not to think of her any more, and went on thinking of her till he was almost in a state to drown himself in the little brook which ran at the bottom of the archdeacon's grounds.

And ever and again his mind would revert to the Signora Neroni, and he would make comparisons between her and Eleanor Bold, not always in favour of the latter. The signora had listened to him, and flattered him, and believed in him; at least she had told him so. Mrs. Bold had also listened to him, but had never flattered him; had not always believed in him: and now had broken from him in violent rage. The signora, too, was the more lovely woman of the two, and had also the additional attraction of her affliction; for to him it was an attraction.

But he never could have loved the Signora Neroni as he felt that he now loved Eleanor! and so he flung stones into the brook, instead of flinging in himself, and sat down on its margin as sad a gentleman as you shall meet in a summer's day.

He heard the dinner-bell ring from the churchyard, and he knew that it was time to recover his self-possession. He felt that he was disgracing himself in his own eyes, that he had been idling his time and neglecting the high duties which he had taken upon himself to perform. He should have spent this afternoon among the poor at St Ewold's, instead of wandering about at Plumstead, an ancient love-lorn swain, dejected and sighing, full of imaginary sorrows and Wertherian grief. He was thoroughly ashamed of himself, and determined to lose no time in retrieving his character, so damaged in his own eyes. Thus when he appeared at dinner he was as animated as ever, and was the author of most of the conversation which graced the archdeacon's board on that evening. Mr. Harding was ill at ease and sick at heart, and did not care to appear more comfortable than he really was; what little he did say was said to his daughter. He thought that the archdeacon and Mr. Arabin had leagued together against Eleanor's comfort; and his wish now was to break away from the pair, and undergo in his Barchester lodgings whatever Fate had in store for him. He hated the name of the hospital; his attempt to regain his-lost inheritance there had brought upon him so much suffering. As far as he was concerned, Mr. Quiverful was now welcome to the place.

And the archdeacon was not very lively. The poor dean's illness was of course discussed in the first place. Dr. Grantly did not mention Mr. Slope's name in connexion with the expected event of Dr. Trefoil's death; he did not wish to say anything about Mr. Slope just at present, nor did he wish to make known his sad surmises; but the idea that his enemy might possibly become Dean of Barchester made him very gloomy. Should such an event take place, such a dire catastrophe come about, there would be an end to his life as far as his life was connected with the city of Barchester. He must give up all his old haunts, all his old habits, and live quietly as a retired rector at Plumstead. It had been a severe trial for him to have Dr. Proudie in the palace; but with Mr. Slope also in the deanery, he felt that he should be unable to draw his breath in Barchester close.

Thus it came to pass that in spite of the sorrow at his heart, Mr. Arabin was apparently the gayest of the party. Both Mr. Harding and Mrs. Grantly were in a slight degree angry with him on account of his want of gloom. To the one it appeared as though he were triumphing at Eleanor's banishment, and to the other that he was not affected as he should have been by all the sad circumstances of the day, Eleanor's obstinacy, Mr. Slope's success, and the poor dean's apoplexy. And so they were all at cross purposes.

Mr. Harding left the room almost together with the ladies, and then the archdeacon opened his heart to Mr. Arabin. He still harped upon the hospital. "What did that fellow mean," said he. "by saying in his letter to Mrs. Bold, that if Mr. Harding would call on the bishop it would be all right? Of course I would not be guided by anything he might say; but still it may be well that Mr. Harding should see the bishop. It would be foolish to let the thing slip through our fingers because Mrs. Bold is determined to make a fool of herself."

Mr. Arabin hinted that he was not quite so sure that Mrs. Bold would make a fool of herself. He said that he was not convinced that she did regard Mr. Slope so warmly as she was supposed to do. The archdeacon questioned and cross-questioned him about this, but elicited nothing; and at last remained firm in his own conviction that he was destined, *malgré lui*, to be the brother-in-law of Mr. Slope. Mr. Arabin strongly advised that Mr. Harding should take no step regarding the hospital in connexion with, or in consequence of, Mr. Slope's letter. " If the bishop really means to confer the appointment on Mr. Harding," argued Mr. Arabin, " he will take care to let him have some other intimation than a message conveyed through a letter to a lady.   Were Mr. Harding to present himself at the palace he might merely be playing Mr. Slope's game ; " and thus it was settled that nothing should be done till the great Dr. Gwynne's arrival, or at any rate without that potentate's sanction.

It was droll to observe how these men talked of Mr. Harding as though he were a puppet, and planned their intrigues and small ecclesiastical manœuvres in reference to Mr. Harding's future position, without dreaming of taking him into their confidence. There was a comfortable house and income in question, and it was very desirable, and certainly very just, that Mr. Harding should have them ; but that, at present, was not the main point ; it was expedient to beat the bishop, and if possible to smash Mr. Slope. Mr. Slope had set up, or was supposed to have set up, a rival candidate.   Of all things the most desirable would have been to have had Mr. Quiverful's appointment published to the public, and then annulled by the clamour of an indignant world, loud in the defence of Mr. Harding's rights.   But of such an event the chance was small ; a slight fraction only of the world would be indignant, and that fraction would be one not accustomed to loud speaking.   And then the preferment had in a sort of way been offered to Mr. Harding, and had in a sort of way been refused by him.

Mr. Slope's wicked, cunning hand had been peculiarly conspicuous in the way in which this had been brought to pass, and it was the success of Mr. Slope's cunning which was so painfully grating to the feelings of the archdeacon.   That which of all things he most dreaded was that he should be out-generalled by Mr. Slope : and just at present it appeared probable that Mr. Slope would turn his flank, steal a march on him, cut off his provisions, carry his strong town by a *coup de main,* and at last beat him thoroughly in a regular pitched battle.   The archdeacon felt that his flank had been turned when desired to wait on Mr. Slope instead of the bishop, that a march had been stolen when Mr. Harding was induced to refuse the bishop's offer, that his provisions would be cut off when Mr. Quiverful got the hospital, that Eleanor was the strong town doomed to be taken, and that Mr. Slope, as Dean of Barchester, would be regarded by all the world as the conqueror in the final conflict.

Dr. Gwynne was the *Deus ex machina* who was to come down upon the Barchester stage, and bring about deliverance from these terrible evils. But how can melodramatic *dénouements* be properly brought about, how can vice and Mr. Slope be punished, and virtue and the archdeacon be rewarded, while the avenging god is laid up with the gout? In the mean time evil may be triumphant, and poor innocence, transfixed to the earth by an arrow from Dr. Proudie's quiver, may lie dead upon the ground, not to be resuscitated even by Dr. Gwynne.

Two or three days after Eleanor's departure, Mr. Arabin went to Oxford, and soon found himself closeted with the august head of his college. It was quite clear that Dr. Gwynne was not very sanguine as to the effects of his journey to Barchester, and not over anxious to interfere with the bishop. He had had the gout, but was very nearly convalescent, and Mr. Arabin at once saw that had the mission been one of which the master thoroughly approved, he would before this have been at Plumstead.

As it was, Dr. Gwynne was resolved on visiting his friend, and willingly promised to return to Barchester with Mr. Arabin. He could not bring himself to believe that there was any probability that Mr. Slope would be made Dean of Barchester. Rumour, he said, had reached, even his ears, not at all favourable to that gentleman's character, and he expressed himself strongly of opinion that any such appointment was quite out of the question. At this stage of the proceedings, the master's right-hand man, Tom Staple, was called in to assist at the conference. Tom Staple was the Tutor of Lazarus, and moreover a great man at Oxford. Though universally known by a species of nomenclature so very undignified, Tom Staple was one who maintained a high dignity in the University. He was, as it were, the leader of the Oxford tutors, a body of men who consider themselves collectively as being by very little, if at all, second in importance to the heads themselves. It is not always the case that the master, or warden, or provost, or principal can hit it off exactly with his tutor. A tutor is by no means indisposed to have a will of his own. But at Lazarus they were great friends and firm allies at the time of which we are writing.

Tom Staple was a hale strong man of about forty-five; short in stature, swarthy in face, with strong sturdy black hair, and crisp black beard, of which very little was allowed to show itself in shape of whiskers. He always wore a white neckcloth, clean indeed, but not tied with that scrupulous care which now distinguishes some of our younger clergy. He was, of course, always clothed in a seemly suit of solemn black. Mr. Staple was a decent cleanly liver, not over addicted to any sensuality; but nevertheless a somewhat warmish hue was beginning to adorn his nose, the peculiar effect, as his friends averred, of a certain pipe of port, introduced into the cellars of Lazarus the very same year in which the tutor entered it as a freshman. There was also, perhaps, a little redolence of port wine, as it were the slightest possible twang, in Mr. Staple's voice.

In these latter days Tom Staple was not a happy man ; University reform had long been his bugbear, and now was his bane. It was not with him as with most others, an affair of politics, respecting which, when the need existed, he could, for parties' sake or on behalf of principle, maintain a certain amount of necessary zeal ; it was not with him a subject for dilettante warfare, and courteous common-place opposition. To him it was life and death. The *statu quo* of the University was his only idea of life, and any reformation was as bad to him as death. He would willingly have been a martyr in the cause, had the cause admitted of martyrdom.

At the present day, unfortunately, public affairs will allow of no martyrs, and therefore it is that there is such a deficiency of zeal. Could gentlemen of 10,000*l.* a year have died on their own doorsteps in defence of protection, no doubt some half-dozen glorious old baronets would have so fallen, and the school of protection would at this day have been crowded with scholars. Who can fight strenuously in any combat in which there is no danger ? Tom Staple would have willingly been impaled before a Committee of the House, could he by such self-sacrifice have infused his own spirit into the component members of the hebdomadal board.

Tom Staple was one of those who in his heart approved of the credit system which had of old been in vogue between the students and tradesmen of the University. He knew and acknowledged to himself that it was useless in these degenerate days publicly to contend with the Jupiter on such a subject. The Jupiter had undertaken to rule the University, and Tom Staple was well aware that the Jupiter was too powerful for him. But in secret, and among his safe companions, he would argue that the system of credit was an ordeal good for young men to undergo.

The bad men, said he, the weak and worthless, blunder into danger and burn their feet ; but the good men, they who have any character, they who have that within them which can reflect credit on their Alma Mater, they come through scatheless. What merit will there be to a young man to get through safely, if he be guarded and protected and restrained like a school-boy ? By so doing, the period of the ordeal is only postponed, and the manhood of the man will be deferred from the age of twenty to that of twenty-four. If you bind him with leading-strings at college, he will break loose while eating for the bar in London ; bind him there, and he will break loose afterwards, when he is a married man.   The wild oats must be sown somewhere.   'Twas thus that Tom Staple would argue of young men ; not, indeed, with much consistency, but still with some practical knowledge of the subject gathered from long experience.

And now Tom Staple proffered such wisdom as he had for the assistance of Dr. Gwynne and Mr. Arabin.

" Quite out of the question," said he, arguing that Mr. Slope could not possibly be made the new Dean of Barchester.

" So I think," said the master. " He has no standing, and, if all I hear be true, very little character."

" As to character," said Tom Staple, " I don't think much of that. They rather like loose parsons for deans ; a little fast living, or a dash of infidelity, is no bad recommendation to a cathedral close. But they couldn't make Mr. Slope ; the last two deans have been Cambridge men ; you'll not show me an instance of their making three men running from the same University. We don't get our share, and never shall, I suppose ; but we must at least have one out of three."

" Those sort of rules are all gone by now," said Mr. Arabin.

" Everything has gone by, I believe," said Tom Staple. " The cigar has been smoked out, and we are the ashes."

" Speak for yourself, Staple," said the master.

" I speak for all," said the tutor, stoutly. " It is coming to that, that there will be no life left anywhere in the country.   No one is any longer fit to rule himself, or those belonging to him. The Government is to find us all in everything, and the press is to find the Government.   Nevertheless, Mr. Slope won't be Dean of Barchester."

" And who will be warden of the hospital ? " said Mr. Arabin.

" I hear that Mr. Quiverful is already appointed," said Tom Staple.

" I think not," said the master. " And I think, moreover, that Dr. Proudie will not be so short-sighted as to run against such a rock : Mr. Slope should himself have sense enough to prevent it."

" But perhaps Mr. Slope may have no objection to see his patron on a rock," said the suspicious tutor.

" What could he get by that ? " asked Mr. Arabin.

" It is impossible to see the doubles of such a man," said Mr. Staple. " It seems quite clear that Bishop Proudie is altogether in his hands, and it is equally clear that he has been moving heaven and earth to get this Mr. Quiverful into the hospital, although he must know that such an appointment would be most damaging to the bishop. It is impossible to understand such a man, and dreadful to think," added Tom Staple, sighing deeply, "that the welfare and fortunes of good men may depend on his intrigues."

Dr. Gwynne or Mr. Staple were not in the least aware, nor even was Mr. Arabin, that this Mr. Slope, of whom they were talking, had been using his utmost efforts to put their own candidate into the hospital ; and that in lieu of being permanent in the palace, his own expulsion therefrom had been already decided on by the high powers of the diocese.

"I'll tell you what," said the tutor, "if this Quiverful is thrust into the hospital and Dr. Trefoil does die, I should not wonder if the Government were to make Mr. Harding Dean of Barchester. They would feel bound to do something for him after all that was said when he resigned.

Dr. Gwynne at the moment made no reply to this suggestion ; but it did not the less impress itself on his mind. If Mr. Harding could not be warden of the hospital, why should he not be Dean of Barchester ?

And so the conference ended without any very fixed resolution, and Dr. Gwynne and Mr. Arabin prepared for their journey to Plumstead on the morrow.

CHAP. XXXV.

MISS THORNE'S FÊTE CHAMPÊTRE.

THE day of the Ullathorne party arrived, and all the world were there ; or at least so much of the world as had been included in Miss Thorne's invitation. As we have said, the bishop returned home on the previous evening, and on the same evening, and by the same train, came Dr. Gwynne and Mr. Arabin from Oxford. The archdeacon with his brougham was in waiting for the Master of Lazarus, so that there was a goodly show of church dignitaries on the platform of the railway.

The Stanhope party was finally arranged in the odious manner already described, and Eleanor got into the doctor's carriage full of apprehension and presentiment of further misfortune, whereas Mr. Slope entered the vehicle elate with triumph.

He had received that morning a very civil note from Sir Nicholas

Fitzwhiggin; not promising much indeed; but then Mr. Slope knew, or fancied that he knew, that it was not etiquette for government officers to make promises. Though Sir Nicholas promised nothing he implied a good deal; declared his conviction that Mr. Slope would make an excellent dean, and wished him every kind of success. To be sure he added that, not being in the cabinet, he was never consulted on such matters, and that even if he spoke on the subject his voice would go for nothing. But all this Mr. Slope took for the prudent reserve of official life. To complete his anticipated triumphs, another letter was brought to him just as he was about to start to Ullathorne.

Mr. Slope also enjoyed the idea of handing Mrs. Bold out of Dr. Stanhope's carriage before the multitude at Ullathorne gate, as much as Eleanor dreaded the same ceremony. He had fully made up his mind to throw himself and his fortune at the widow's feet, and had almost determined to select the present propitious morning for doing so. The signora had of late been less than civil to him. She had indeed admitted his visits, and listened, at any rate without anger, to his love; but she had tortured him and reviled him, jeered at him and ridiculed him, while she allowed him to call her the most beautiful of living women, to kiss her hand, and to proclaim himself with reiterated oaths her adorer, her slave, and worshipper.

Miss Thorne was in great perturbation, yet in great glory, on the morning of the gala day. Mr. Thorne also, though the party was none of his giving, had much heavy work on his hands. But perhaps the most overtasked, the most anxious, and the most effective of all the Ullathorne household was Mr. Plomacy, the steward. This last personage had, in the time of Mr. Thorne's father, when the Directory held dominion in France, gone over to Paris with letters in his boot heel for some of the royal party; and such had been his good luck that he had returned safe. He had then been very young and was now very old, but the exploit gave him a character for political enterprise and secret discretion which still availed him as thoroughly as it had done in its freshest gloss. Mr. Plomacy had been steward of Ullathorne for more than fifty years, and a very easy life he had had of it. Who could require much absolute work from a man who had carried safely at his heel that which if discovered would have cost him his head? Consequently Mr. Plomacy had never worked hard, and of latter years had never worked at all. He had a taste for timber, and therefore he marked the trees that were to be cut down, he had a taste for gardening, and would therefore allow no shrub to be planted or bed to be made without his express sanction. In these matters he was sometimes driven to run counter to his mistress, but he rarely allowed his mistress to carry the point against him.

But on occasions such as the present Mr. Plomacy came out strong. He had the honour of the family at heart; he thoroughly appreciated the duties of hospitality; and therefore, when gala doings were going on, always took the management into his own hands and reigned supreme over master and mistress.

To give Mr. Plomacy his due, old as he was, he thoroughly understood such work as he had in hand, and did it well.

The order of the day was to be as follows. The quality, as the upper classes in rural districts are designated by the lower with so much true discrimination, were to eat a breakfast, and the non-quality were to eat a dinner. Two marquees had been erected for these two banquets, that for the quality on the esoteric or garden side of a certain deep ha-ha; and that for the non-quality on the exoteric or paddock side of the same. Both were of huge dimensions; that on the outer side was, one may say, on an egregious scale; but Mr. Plomacy declared that neither would be sufficient. To remedy this, an auxiliary banquet was prepared in the dining-room, and a subsidiary board was to be spread *sub dio* for the accommodation of the lower class of yokels on the Ullathorne property.

No one who has not had a hand in the preparation of such an affair can understand the manifold difficulties which Miss Thorne encountered in her project. Had she not been made throughout of the very finest whalebone, riveted with the best Yorkshire steel, she must have sunk under them. Had not Mr. Plomacy felt how much was justly expected from a man who at one time carried the destinies of Europe in his boot, he would have given way; and his mistress, so deserted, must have perished among her poles and canvass.

In the first place there was a dreadful line to be drawn. Who were to dispose themselves within the ha-ha, and who without? To this the unthinking will give an off-hand answer, as they will to every ponderous question. Oh, the bishop and such like within the ha-ha; and Farmer Greenacre and such like without. True, my unthinking friend; but who shall define these such-likes? It is in such definitions that the whole difficulty of society consists. To seat the bishop on an arm chair on the lawn and place Farmer Geeenacre at the end of a long table in the paddock is easy enough; but where will you put Mrs. Lookaloft, whose husband, though a tenant on the estate, hunts in a red coat, whose daughters go to a fashionable seminary in Barchester, who calls her farm house Rosebank, and who has a pianoforte in her drawing-room? The Misses Lookaloft, as they call themselves, won't sit contented among the bumpkins. Mrs. Lookaloft won't squeeze her fine clothes on a bench and talk familiarly about cream and ducklings to good Mrs. Greenacre. And yet Mrs. Lookaloft is no fit companion and never has been the associate of the Thornes and the Grantlys. And if Mrs. Lookaloft be admitted within the sanctum of fashionable life, if she be allowed with her three daughters to leap the ha-ha, why not the wives and daughters of other families also? Mrs. Greenacre is at present well contented with the paddock, but she might cease to be so if she saw Mrs. Lookaloft on the lawn. And thus poor Miss Thorne had a hard time of it.

And how was she to divide her guests between the marquee and the parlour? She had a countess coming, an Honourable John and an Honourable George, and a whole bevy of Ladies Amelia, Rosina, Margaretta, &c.; she had a leash of baronets with their baronnettes; and, as we all know, she had a bishop. If she put them on the lawn, no one would go into the parlour; if she put them into the parlour, no one would go into the tent. She thought of keeping the old people in the house, and leaving the lawn to the lovers. She might as well have seated herself at once in a hornet's nest. Mr. Plomacy knew better than this. "Bless your soul, Ma'am," said he, "there won't be no old ladies; not one, barring yourself and old Mrs. Clantantram."

Personally Miss Thorne accepted this distinction in her favour as a compliment to her good sense; but nevertheless she had no desire to be closeted on the coming occasion with Mrs. Clantantram. She gave up all idea of any arbitrary division of her guests, and determined if possible to put the bishop on the lawn and the countess in the house, to sprinkle the baronets, and thus divide the attractions. What to do with the Lookalofts even Mr. Plomacy could not decide. They must take their chance. They had been specially told in the invitation that all the tenants had been invited; and they might probably have the good sense to stay away if they objected to mix with the rest of the tenantry.

Then Mr. Plomacy declared his apprehension that the Honourable Johns and Honourable Georges would come in a sort of amphibious costume, half morning half evening, satin neckhandkerchiefs, frock coats, primrose gloves, and polished boots; and that, being so dressed, they would decline riding at the quintain, or taking part in any of the athletic games which Miss Thorne had prepared with so much fond care   If the Lord Johns and

Lord Georges didn't ride at the quintain, Miss Thorne might be sure that nobody else would.

"But," said she, in dolorous voice, all but overcome by her cares; "it was specially signified that there were to be sports."

"And so there will be, of course," said Mr. Plomacy. "They'll all be sporting with the young ladies in the laurel walks. Them's the sports they care most about now-a-days. If you gets the young men at the quintain, you'll have all the young women in the pouts."

"Can't they look on, as their great grandmothers did before them?" said Miss Thorne.

"It seems to me that the ladies ain't contented with looking now-a-days. Whatever the men do they'll do. If you'll have side saddles on the nags, and let them go at the quintain too, it'll answer capital, no doubt."

Miss Thorne made no reply. She felt that she had no good ground on which to defend her sex of the present generation from the sarcasm of Mr. Plomacy. She had once declared, in one of her warmer moments, "that now-a-days the gentlemen were all women, and the ladies all men." She could not alter the debased character of the age. But, such being the case, why should she take on herself to cater for the amusement of people of such degraded tastes? This question she asked herself more than once, and she could only answer herself with a sigh. There was her own brother Wilfred, on whose shoulders rested all the ancient honours of Ullathorne house; it was very doubtful whether even he would consent to "go at the quintain," as Mr. Plomacy not injudiciously expressed it.

And now the morning arrived. The Ullathorne household was early on the move. Cooks were cooking in the kitchen long before daylight, and men were dragging out tables and hammering red baize on to benches at the earliest dawn. With what dread eagerness did Miss Thorne look out at the weather as soon as the parting veil of night permitted her to look at all! In this respect at any rate there was nothing to grieve her. The glass had been rising for the last three days, and the morning broke with that dull chill steady grey haze which in autumn generally presages a clear and dry day. By seven she was dressed and down. Miss Thorne knew nothing of the modern luxury of *déshabilles*. She would as soon have thought of appearing before her brother without her stockings as without her stays; and Miss Thorne's stays were no trifle.

And yet there was nothing for her to do when down. She

fidgeted out to the lawn, and then back into the kitchen. She put on her high-heeled clogs, and fidgeted out into the paddock. Then she went into the small home park where the quintain was erected. The pole and cross bar and the swivel, and the target and the bag of flour were all complete. She got up on a carpenter's bench and touched the target with her hand; it went round with beautiful ease; the swivel had been oiled to perfection. She almost wished to take old Plomacy at his word, to get on a side saddle and have a tilt at it herself. What must a young man be, thought she, who could prefer maundering among laurel trees with a wishy-washy school girl to such fun as this? "Well," said she aloud to herself, "one man can take a horse to water, but a thousand can't make him drink. There it is. If they haven't the spirit to enjoy it, the fault shan't be mine;" and so she returned to the house.

At a little after eight her brother came down, and they had a sort of scrap breakfast in his study. The tea was made without the customary urn, and they dispensed with the usual rolls and toast. Eggs also were missing, for every egg in the parish had been whipped into custards, baked into pies, or boiled into lobster salad. The allowance of fresh butter was short, and Mr. Thorne was obliged to eat the leg of a fowl without having it deviled in the manner he loved.

"I have been looking at the quintain, Wilfred," said she, "and it appears to be quite right."

"Oh,— ah ; yes ;" said he, "It seemed to be so yesterday when I saw it." Mr. Thorne was beginning to be rather bored by his sister's love of sports, and had especially no affection for this quintain post.

"I wish you'd just try it after breakfast," said she. "You could have the saddle put on Mark Antony, and the pole is there all handy. You can take the flour bag off, you know, if you think Mark Antony won't be quick enough," added Miss Thorne, seeing that her brother's countenance was not indicative of complete accordance with her little proposition.

Now Mark Antony was a valuable old hunter, excellently suited to Mr. Thorne's usual requirements, steady indeed at his fences, but extremely sure, very good in deep ground, and safe on the roads. But he had never yet been ridden at a quintain, and Mr. Thorne was not inclined to put him to the trial, either with or without the bag of flour. He hummed and hawed, and finally declared that he was afraid Mark Antony would shy.

"Then try the cob," said the indefatigable Miss Thorne.

" He's in physic," said Wilfred.

" There's the Beelzebub colt," said his sister ; " I know he's in the stable, because I saw Peter exercising him just now."

" My dear Monica, he's so wild, that it's as much as I can do to manage him at all. He'd destroy himself and me too, if I attempted to ride him at such a rattletrap as that."

A rattletrap ! The quintain that she had put up with so much anxious care; the game that she had prepared for the amusement of the stalwart yeomen of the country; the sport that had been honoured by the affection of so many of their ancestors ! It cut her to the heart to hear it so denominated by her own brother. There were but the two of them left together in the world ; and it had ever been one of the rules by which Miss Thorne had regulated her conduct through life, to say nothing that could provoke her brother. She had often had to suffer from his indifference to time-honoured British customs ; but she had always suffered in silence. It was part of her creed that the head of the family should never be upbraided in his own house ; and Miss Thorne had lived up to her creed. Now, however, she was greatly tried The colour mounted to her ancient cheek, and the fire blazed in her still bright eye; but yet she said nothing. She resolved that at any rate, to him nothing more should be said about the quintain that day.

She sipped her tea in silent sorrow, and thought with painful regret of the glorious days when her great ancestor Ealfried had successfully held Ullathorne against a Norman invader. There was no such spirit now left in her family except that small useless spark which burnt in her own bosom. And she herself, was not she at this moment intent on entertaining a descendant of those very Normans, a vain proud countess with a frenchified name, who would only think that she graced Ullathorne too highly by entering its portals ? Was it likely that an honourable John, the son of an Earl De Courcy, should ride at a quintain in company with Saxon yeomen ? And why should she expect her brother to do that which her brother's guests would decline to do ? "

Some dim faint idea of the impracticability of her own views flitted across her brain. Perhaps it was necessary that races doomed to live on the same soil should give way to each other, and adopt each other's pursuits. Perhaps it was impossible that after more than five centuries of close intercourse, Normans should remain Normans, and Saxons, Saxons. Perhaps after all her neighbours were wiser than herself. Such ideas did occasionally present themselves to Miss Thorne's mind, and make her sad enough. But it never occurred to her that her favourite quintain was but a modern copy of a Norman knight's amusement, an adaptation of the noble tourney to the tastes and habits of the Saxon yeomen. Of this she was ignorant, and it would have been cruelty to instruct her.

When Mr. Thorne saw the tear in her eye, he repented himself of his contemptuous expression. By him also it was recognised as a binding law that every whim of his sister was to be respected. He was not perhaps so firm in his observances to her, as she was in hers to him. But his intentions were equally good, and whenever he found that he had forgotten them it was matter of grief to him.

" My dear Monica," said he, " I beg your pardon ; I don't in the least mean to speak ill of the game. When I called it a rattletrap, I merely meant that it was so for a man of my age. You know you always forget that I an't a young man."

" I am quite sure you are not an old man, Wilfred," said she, accepting the apology in her heart, and smiling at him with the tear still on her cheek.

" If I was five-and-twenty, or thirty," continued he, " I should like nothing better than riding at the quintain all day."

" But you are not too old to hunt or to shoot," said she. " If you can jump over a ditch and hedge I am sure you could turn the quintain round."

" But when I ride over the hedges, my dear — and it isn't very often I do that — but when I do ride over the hedges there isn't any bag of flour coming after me. Think how I'd look taking the countess out to breakfast with the back of my head all covered with meal."

Miss Thorne said nothing further. She didn't like the allusion to the countess. She couldn't be satisfied with the reflection that the sports of Ullathorne should be interfered with by the personal attentions necessary for a Lady De Courcy. But she saw that it was useless for her to push the matter further. It was conceded that Mr. Thorne was to be spared the quintain ; and Miss Thorne determined to trust wholly to a youthful knight of hers, an immense favourite, who, as she often declared, was a pattern to the young men of the age, and an excellent sample of an English yeoman.

This was Farmer Greenacre's eldest son ; who, to tell the truth, had from his earliest years taken the exact measure of Miss Thorne's foot. In his boyhood he had never failed to obtain from her, apples, pocket money, and forgiveness for his numerous trespasses; and now in his early manhood he got privileges and immunities which were equally valuable. He was allowed a day or two's shooting in September; he schooled the squire's horses; got slips of trees out of the orchard, and roots of flowers out of the garden; and had the fishing of the little river altogether in his own hands. He had undertaken to come mounted on a nag of his father's, and show the way at the quintain post. Whatever young Greenacre did the others would do after him. The juvenile Lookalofts might stand aloof, but the rest of the youth of Ullathorne would be sure to venture if Harry Greenacre showed the way. And so Miss Thorne made up her mind to dispense with the noble Johns and Georges, and trust, as her ancestors had done before her, to the thews and sinews of native Ullathorne growth.

At about nine the lower orders began to congregate in the paddock and park, under the surveillance of Mr. Plomacy and the head gardener and head groom, who were sworn in as his deputies, and were to assist him in keeping the peace and promoting the sports. Many of the younger inhabitants of the neighbourhood, thinking that they could not have too much of a good thing, had come at a very early hour, and the road between the house and the church had been thronged for some time before the gates were thrown open.

And then another difficulty of huge dimensions arose, a difficulty which Mr. Plomacy had indeed foreseen and for which he was in some sort provided. Some of those who wished to share Miss Thorne's hospitality were not so particular as they should have been as to the preliminary ceremony of an invitation. They doubtless conceived that they had been overlooked by accident; and instead of taking this in dudgeon, as their betters would have done, they good-naturedly put up with the slight, and showed that they did so by presenting themselves at the gate in their Sunday best.

Mr. Plomacy, however, well knew who were welcome and who were not. To some, even though uninvited, he allowed ingress. "Don't be too particular, Plomacy," his mistress had said; "especially with the children. If they live anywhere near, let them in."

Acting on this hint, Mr. Plomacy did let in many an eager urchin, and a few tidily dressed girls with their swains, who in no way belonged to the property. But to the denizens of the city he was inexorable. Many a Barchester apprentice made his appearance there that day, and urged with piteous supplication that he had been working all the week in making saddles and boots for the use of Ullathorne, in compounding doses for the horses, or cutting up carcases for the kitchen. No such claim was allowed. Mr. Plomacy knew nothing about the city apprentices; he was to admit the tenants and labourers on the estate; Miss Thorne wasn't going to take in the whole city of Barchester; and so on.

Nevertheless, before the day was half over, all this was found to be useless. Almost anybody who chose to come made his way into the park, and the care of the guardians was transferred to the tables on which the banquet was spread. Even here there was many an unauthorised claimant for a place, of whom it was impossible to get quit without more commotion than the place and food were worth.

CHAP. XXXVI.

ULLATHORNE SPORTS. — ACT I.

THE trouble in civilised life of entertaining company, as it is called too generally without much regard to strict veracity, is so great that it cannot but be matter of wonder that people are so fond of attempting it. It is difficult to ascertain what is the *quid pro quo*. If they who give such laborious parties, and who endure such toil and turmoil in the vain hope of giving them successfully, really enjoyed the parties given by others, the matter could be understood. A sense of justice would induce men and women to undergo, in behalf of others, those miseries which others had undergone in their behalf. But they all profess that going out is as great a bore as receiving; and to look at them when they are out, one cannot but believe them.

Entertain! Who shall have sufficient self-assurance, who shall feel sufficient confidence in his own powers to dare to boast that he can entertain his company? A clown can sometimes do so, and sometimes a dancer in short petticoats and stuffed pink legs; occasionally, perhaps, a singer. But beyond these, success in this art of entertaining is not often achieved. Young men and girls linking themselves kind with kind, pairing like birds in spring because nature wills it, they, after a simple fashion, do entertain each other. Few others even try.

Ladies, when they open their houses, modestly confessing, it may be presumed, their own incapacity, mainly trust to wax candles and upholstery. Gentlemen seem to rely on their white waistcoats. To these are added, for the delight of the more sensual, champagne and such good things of the table as fashion allows to be still considered as comestible. Even in this respect the world is deteriorating. All the good soups are now tabooed; and at the houses of one's accustomed friends, small barristers, doctors, government clerks, and such like, (for we cannot all of us always live as grandees, surrounded by an elysium of livery servants), one gets a cold potato handed to one as a sort of finale to one's slice of mutton. Alas! for those happy days when one could say to one's neighbourhood, "Jones, shall I give you some mashed turnip? — may I trouble you for a little cabbage?" And then the pleasure of drinking wine with Mrs. Jones and Miss Smith; with all the Joneses and all the Smiths! These latter-day habits are certainly more economical.

Miss Thorne, however, boldly attempted to leave the modern beaten track, and made a positive effort to entertain her guests. Alas! she did so with but moderate success. They had all their own way of going, and would not go her way. She piped to them, but they would not dance. She offered to them good honest household cake, made of currants and flour and eggs and sweetmeat; but they would feed themselves on trashy wafers from the shop of the Barchester pastry-cook, on chalk and gum and adulterated sugar. Poor Miss Thorne! yours is not the first honest soul that has vainly striven to recall the glories of happy days gone by! If fashion suggests to a Lady De Courcy that when invited to a *déjeûner* at twelve she ought to come at three, no eloquence of thine will teach her the advantage of a nearer approach to punctuality.

She had fondly thought that when she called on her friends to come at twelve, and specially begged them to believe that she meant it, she would be able to see them comfortably seated in their tents at two. Vain woman — or rather ignorant woman — ignorant of the advances of that civilisation which the world had witnessed while she was growing old. At twelve she found herself alone, dressed in all the glory of the newest of her many suits of raiment; with strong shoes however, and a serviceable bonnet on her head, and a warm rich shawl on her shoulders. Thus clad she peered out into the tent, went to the ha-ha, and satisfied herself that at any rate the youngsters were amusing themselves, spoke a word to Mrs. Greenacre over the ditch, and took one look at the quintain. Three or four young farmers were turning the machine round and round, and poking at the bag of flour in a manner not at all intended by the inventor of the game; but no mounted sportsmen were there. Miss Thorne looked at her watch. It was only fifteen minutes past twelve, and it was understood that Harry Greenacre was not to begin till the half hour.

Miss Thorne returned to her drawing-room rather quicker than was her wont, fearing that the countess might come and find none to welcome her. She need not have hurried, for no one was there. At half-past twelve she peeped into the kitchen; at a quarter to one she was joined by her brother; and just then the first fashionable arrival took place. Mrs. Clantantram was announced.

No announcement was necessary, indeed; for the good lady's voice was heard as she walked across the court-yard to the house scolding the unfortunate postilion who had driven her from Barchester. At the moment, Miss Thorne could not but be thankful that the other guests were more fashionable, and were thus spared the fury of Mrs. Clantantram's indignation.

"Oh Miss Thorne, look here!" said she, as soon as she found herself in the drawing-room; "do look at my roquelaure! It's clean spoilt, and for ever. I wouldn't but wear it because I knew you wished us all to be grand to-day; and yet I had my misgivings. Oh dear, oh dear! It was five-and-twenty shillings a yard."

The Barchester post horses had misbehaved in some unfortunate manner just as Mrs. Clantantram was getting out of the chaise, and had nearly thrown her under the wheel.

Mrs. Clantantram belonged to other days, and therefore, though she had but little else to recommend her, Miss Thorne was to a certain extent fond of her. She sent the roquelaure away to be cleaned, and lent her one of her best shawls out of her own wardrobe.

The next comer was Mr. Arabin, who was immediately informed of Mrs. Clantantram's misfortune, and of her determination to pay neither master nor post-boy; although, as she remarked, she intended to get her lift home before she made known her mind upon that matter. Then a good deal of rustling was heard in the sort of lobby that was used for the ladies' outside cloaks; and the door having been thrown wide open, the servant announced, not in the most confident of voices, Mrs. Lookaloft, and the Miss Lookalofts, and Mr. Augustus Lookaloft.

Poor man!—we mean the footman. He knew, none better, that Mrs. Lookaloft had no business there, that she was not wanted there, and would not be welcome. But he had not the courage to tell a stout lady with a low dress, short sleeves, and satin at eight shillings a yard, that she had come to the wrong tent; he had not dared to hint to young ladies with white dancing shoes and long gloves, that there was a place ready for them in the paddock. And thus Mrs. Lookaloft carried her point, broke through the guards, and made her way into the citadel. That she would have to pass an uncomfortable time there, she had surmised before. But nothing now could rob her of the power of boasting that she had consorted on the lawn with the squire and Miss Thorne, with a countess, a bishop, and the county grandees, while Mrs. Greenacre and such like were walking about with the ploughboys in the park. It was a great point gained by Mrs. Lookaloft, and it might be fairly expected that from this time forward the tradesmen of Barchester would, with undoubting pens, address her husband as T. Lookaloft, Esquire.

Mrs. Lookaloft's pluck carried her through everything, and she walked triumphant into the Ullathorne drawing-room; but her children did feel a little abashed at the sort of reception they met with. It was not in Miss Thorne's heart to insult her own guests; but neither was it in her disposition to overlook such effrontery.

"Oh, Mrs. Lookaloft, is this you," said she; "and your daughters and son? Well, we're very glad to see you; but I'm sorry you've come in such low dresses, as we are all going out of doors. Could we lend you anything?"

"Oh dear no! thank ye, Miss Thorne," said the mother; "the girls and myself are quite used to low dresses, when we're out."

"Are you, indeed?" said Miss Thorne shuddering; but the shudder was lost on Mrs. Lookaloft.

"And where's Lookaloft?" said the master of the house, coming up to welcome his tenant's wife. Let the faults of the family be what they would, he could not but remember that their rent was well paid; he was therefore not willing to give them a cold shoulder.

"Such a headache, Mr. Thorne!" said Mrs. Lookaloft. "In fact he couldn't stir, or you may be certain on such a day he would not have absented hisself."

"Dear me," said Miss Thorne. "If he is so ill, I'm sure you'd wish to be with him."

"Not at all!" said Mrs. Lookaloft. "Not at all, Miss Thorne. It is only bilious you know, and when he's that way he can bear nobody nigh him."

The fact however was that Mr. Lookaloft, having either more sense or less courage than his wife, had not chosen to intrude on Miss Thorne's drawing-room; and as he could not very well have gone among the plebeians while his wife was with the patricians, he thought it most expedient to remain at Rosebank.

Mrs. Lookaloft soon found herself on a sofa, and the Miss Lookalofts on two chairs, while Mr. Augustus stood near the door ; and here they remained till in due time they were seated all four together at the bottom of the dining-room table.

Then the Grantlys came ; the archdeacon and Mrs. Grantly and the two girls, and Dr. Gwynne and Mr. Harding ; and as ill luck would have it, they were closely followed by Dr. Stanhope's carriage. As Eleanor looked out of the carriage window, she saw her brother-in-law helping the ladies out, and threw herself back into her seat, dreading to be discovered. She had had an odious journey. Mr. Slope's civility had been more than ordinarily greasy ; and now, though he had not in fact said anything which she could notice, she had for the first time entertained a suspicion that he was intending to make love to her. Was it after all true that she had been conducting herself in a way that justified the world in thinking that she liked the man? After all, could it be possible that the archdeacon and Mr. Arabin were right, and that she was wrong? Charlotte Stanhope had also been watching Mr. Slope, and had come to the conclusion that it behoved her brother to lose no further time, if he meant to gain the widow. She almost regretted that it had not been contrived that Bertie should be at Ullathorne before them.

Dr. Grantly did not see his sister-in-law in company with Mr. Slope, but Mr. Arabin did. Mr. Arabin came out with Mr. Thorne to the front door to welcome Mrs. Grantly, and he remained in the courtyard till all their party had passed on. Eleanor hung back in the carriage as long as she well could, but she was nearest to the door, and when Mr. Slope, having alighted, offered her his hand, she had no alternative but to take it. Mr. Arabin, standing at the open door while Mrs. Grantly was shaking hands with some one within, saw a clergyman alight from the carriage whom he at once knew to be Mr. Slope, and then he saw this clergyman hand out Mrs. Bold. Having seen so much, Mr. Arabin, rather sick at heart, followed Mrs. Grantly into the house.

Eleanor was, however, spared any further immediate degradation, for Dr. Stanhope gave her his arm across the courtyard, and Mr. Slope was fain to throw away his attention upon Charlotte.

They had hardly passed into the house, and from the house to the lawn, when, with a loud rattle and such noise as great men and great women are entitled to make in their passage through the world, the Proudies drove up. It was soon apparent that no every-day comer was at the door. One servant whispered to another that it was the bishop, and the word soon ran through all the hangers-on and strange grooms and coachmen about the place.

There was quite a little cortège to see the bishop and his "lady" walk across the courtyard, and the good man was pleased to see that the church was held in such respect in the parish of St. Ewold's.

And now the guests came fast and thick, and the lawn began to be crowded, and the room to be full. Voices buzzed, silk rustled against silk, and muslin crumpled against muslin. Miss Thorne became more happy than she had been, and again bethought her of her sports. There were targets and bows and arrows prepared at the further end of the lawn. Here the gardens of the place encroached with a somewhat wide sweep upon the paddock, and gave ample room for the doings of the toxophilites. Miss Thorne got together such daughters of Diana as could bend a bow, and marshalled them to the targets. There were the Grantly girls and the Proudie girls and the Chadwick girls, and the two daughters of the burly chancellor, and Miss Knowle; and with them went Frederick and Augustus Chadwick, and young Knowle of Knowle park, and Frank Foster of the Elms, and Mr. Vellem Deeds the dashing attorney of the High Street, and the Rev. Mr. Green, and the Rev. Mr. Brown, and the Rev. Mr. White, all of whom, as in duty bound, attended the steps of the three Miss Proudies.

"Did you ever ride at the quintain, Mr. Foster?" said Miss Thorne, as she walked with her party, across the lawn.

"The quintain?" said young Foster, who considered himself a dab at horsemanship. "Is it a sort of gate, Miss Thorne?"

Miss Thorne had to explain the noble game she spoke of, and Frank Foster had to own that he never had ridden at the quintain.

"Would you like to come and see?" said Miss Thorne. "There'll be plenty here without you, if you like it."

"Well, I don't mind," said Frank; "I suppose the ladies can come too."

"Oh yes," said Miss Thorne; "those who like it; I have no doubt they'll go to see your prowess, if you'll ride, Mr. Foster."

Mr. Foster looked down at a most unexceptionable pair of pantaloons, which had arrived from London only the day before. They were the very things, at least he thought so, for a picnic or fête champêtre; but he was not prepared to ride in them. Nor was he more encouraged than had been Mr. Thorne, by the idea of being attacked from behind by the bag of flour which Miss Thorne had graphically described to him.

"Well, I don't know about riding, Miss Thorne," said he; "I fear I'm not quite prepared."

Miss Thorne sighed, but said nothing further. She left the

toxophilites to their bows and arrows, and returned towards the house.   But as she passed by the entrance to the small park, she thought that she might at any rate encourage the yeomen by her presence, as she could not induce her more fashionable guests to mix with them in their manly amusements.   Accordingly she once more betook herself to the quintain post.

Here to her great delight she found Harry Greenacre ready mounted, with his pole in his hand, and a lot of comrades standing round him, encouraging him to the assault.   She stood at a little distance and nodded to him in token of her good pleasure.

" Shall I begin, ma'am ? " said Harry, fingering his long staff in a rather awkward way, while his horse moved uneasily beneath him, not accustomed to a rider armed with such a weapon.

" Yes, yes," said Miss Thorne, standing triumphant as the queen of beauty, on an inverted tub which some chance had brought thither from the farm-yard.

" Here goes then," said Harry, as he wheeled his horse round to get the necessary momentum of a sharp gallop.   The quintain post stood right before him, and the square board at which he was to tilt was fairly in his way.   If he hit that duly in the middle, and maintained his pace as he did so, it was calculated that he would be carried out of reach of the flour bag, which, suspended at the other end of the cross-bar on the post, would swing round when the board was struck.   It was also calculated that if the rider did not maintain his pace, he would get a blow from the flour bag just at the back of his head, and bear about him the signs of his awkwardness to the great amusement of the lookers-on.

Harry Greenacre did not object to being powdered with flour in the service of his mistress, and therefore gallantly touched his steed with his spur, having laid his lance in rest to the best of his ability.   But his ability in this respect was not great, and his appurtenances probably not very good ; consequently, he struck his horse with his pole unintentionally on the side of the head as he started.   The animal swerved and shied, and galloped off wide of the quintain.   Harry, well accustomed to manage a horse, but not to do so with a twelve-foot rod on his arm, lowered his right hand to the bridle and thus the end of the lance came to the ground, and got between the legs of the steed.   Down came rider and steed and staff.   Young Greenacre was thrown some six feet over the horse's head, and poor Miss Thorne almost fell off her tub in a swoon.

" Oh gracious, he's killed," shrieked a woman who was near him when he fell.

"The Lord be good to him! his poor mother, his poor mother!" said another.

"Well, drat them dangerous plays all the world over," said an old crone.

"He has broke his neck sure enough, if ever man did," said a fourth.

Poor Miss Thorne. She heard all this and yet did not quite swoon. She made her way through the crowd as best she could, sick herself almost to death. Oh, his mother — his poor mother! how could she ever forgive herself. The agony of that moment was terrific. She could hardly get to the place where the poor lad was lying, as three or four men in front were about the horse which had risen with some difficulty; but at last she found herself close to the young farmer.

"Has he marked himself? for heaven's sake tell me that; has he marked his knees?" said Harry, slowly rising and rubbing his left shoulder with his right hand, and thinking only of his horse's legs. Miss Thorne soon found that he had not broken his neck, nor any of his bones, nor been injured in any essential way. But from that time forth she never instigated any one to ride at a quintain.

Eleanor left Dr. Stanhope as soon as she could do so civilly, and went in quest of her father whom she found on the lawn in company with Mr. Arabin. She was not sorry to find them together. She was anxious to disabuse at any rate her father's mind as to this report which had got abroad respecting her, and would have been well pleased to have been able to do the same with regard to Mr. Arabin. She put her own through her father's arm, coming up behind his back, and then tendered her hand also to the vicar of St. Ewold's.

"And how did you come?" said Mr. Harding, when the first greeting was over.

"The Stanhopes brought me," said she; "their carriage was obliged to come twice, and has now gone back for the signora." As she spoke she caught Mr. Arabin's eye, and saw that he was looking pointedly at her with a severe expression. She understood at once the accusation contained in his glance. It said as plainly as an eye could speak, "Yes, you came with the Stanhopes, but you did so in order that you might be in company with Mr. Slope."

"Our party," said she, still addressing her father, "consisted of the doctor and Charlotte Stanhope, myself, and Mr. Slope." As she mentioned the last name she felt her father's arm quiver slightly beneath her touch. At the same moment Mr. Arabin turned away from them, and joining his hands behind his back strolled slowly away by one of the paths.

"Papa," said she, "it was impossible to help coming in the same carriage with Mr. Slope ; it was quite impossible. I had promised to come with them before I dreamt of his coming, and afterwards I could not get out of it without explaining and giving rise to talk. You weren't at home, you know ; I couldn't possibly help it." She said all this so quickly that by the time her apology was spoken she was quite out of breath.

"I don't know why you should have wished to help it, my dear," said her father.

"Yes, papa, you do ; you must know, you do know all the things they said at Plumstead. I am sure you do. You know all the archdeacon said. How unjust he was ; and Mr. Arabin too. He's a horrid man, a horrid odious man, but——"

"Who is an odious man, my dear ? Mr. Arabin ?"

"No ; but Mr. Slope. You know I mean Mr. Slope. He's the most odious man I ever met in my life, and it was most unfortunate my having to come here in the same carriage with him. But how could I help it ?"

A great weight began to move itself off Mr. Harding's mind. So, after all, the archdeacon with all his wisdom, and Mrs. Grantly with all her tact, and Mr. Arabin with all his talent, were in the wrong. His own child, his Eleanor, the daughter of whom he was so proud was not to become the wife of a Mr. Slope. He had been about to give his sanction to the marriage, so certified had he been of the fact ; and now he learnt that this imputed lover of Eleanor's was at any rate as much disliked by her as by any one of the family. Mr. Harding, however, was by no means sufficiently a man of the world to conceal the blunder he had made. He could not pretend that he had entertained no suspicion ; he could not make believe that he had never joined the archdeacon in his surmises. He was greatly surprised, and gratified beyond measure, and he could not help showing that such was the case.

"My darling girl," said he, "I am so delighted, so overjoyed. My own child ; you have taken such a weight off my mind."

"But surely, papa, *you* didn't think——"

"I didn't know what to think, my dear. The archdeacon told me that——"

"The archdeacon !" said Eleanor, her face lighting up with passion. "A man like the archdeacon might, one would think, be better employed than in traducing his sister-in-law, and creating bitterness between a father and his daughter !"

"He did'nt mean to do that, Eleanor."

"What did he mean then? Why did he interfere with me, and fill your mind with such falsehood?"

"Never mind it now, my child; never mind it now. We shall all know you better now."

"Oh, papa, that you should have thought it! that you should have suspected me!"

"I don't know what you mean by suspicion, Eleanor. There would be nothing disgraceful, you know; nothing wrong in such a marriage. Nothing that could have justified my interfering as your father." And Mr. Harding would have proceeded in his own defence to make out that Mr. Slope after all was a very good sort of man, and a very fitting second husband for a young widow, had he not been interrupted by Eleanor's greater energy.

"It would be disgraceful," said she; "it would be wrong; it would be abominable. Could I do such a horrid thing, I should expect no one to speak to me. Ugh——" and she shuddered as she thought of the matrimonial torch which her friends had been so ready to light on her behalf. "I don't wonder at Dr. Grantly; I don't wonder at Susan; but, oh, papa, I do wonder at you. How could you, how could you believe it?" Poor Eleanor, as she thought of her father's defalcation, could resist her tears no longer, and was forced to cover her face with her handkerchief.

The place was not very opportune for her grief. They were walking through the shrubberies, and there were many people near them. Poor Mr. Harding stammered out his excuse as best he could, and Eleanor with an effort controlled her tears, and returned her handkerchief to her pocket. She did not find it difficult to forgive her father, nor could she altogether refuse to join him in the returning gaiety of spirit to which her present avowal gave rise. It was such a load off his heart to think that he should not be called on to welcome Mr. Slope as his son-in-law. It was such a relief to him to find that his daughter's feelings and his own were now, as they ever had been, in unison. He had been so unhappy for the last six weeks about this wretched Mr. Slope! He was so indifferent as to the loss of the hospital, so thankful for the recovery of his daughter, that, strong as was the ground for Eleanor's anger, she could not find it in her heart to be long angry with him.

"Dear papa," she said, hanging closely to his arm, "never suspect me again: promise me that you never will. Whatever I do, you may be sure I shall tell you first; you may be sure I shall consult you."

And Mr. Harding did promise, and owned his sin, and promised again. And so, while he promised amendment and she uttered forgiveness, they returned together to the drawing-room windows.

And what had Eleanor meant when she declared that *whatever she did*, she would tell her father first ? What was she thinking of doing ?

So ended the first act of the melodrama which Eleanor was called on to perform this day at Ullathorne.

CHAP. XXXVII.

THE SIGNORA NERONI, THE COUNTESS DE COURCY, AND MRS. PROUDIE MEET EACH OTHER AT ULLATHORNE.

AND now there were new arrivals. Just as Eleanor reached the drawing-room the signora was being wheeled into it. She had been brought out of the carriage into the dining-room and there placed on a sofa, and was now in the act of entering the other room, by the joint aid of her brother and sister, Mr. Arabin, and two servants in livery. She was all in her glory, and looked so pathetically happy, so full of affliction and grace, was so beautiful, so pitiable, and so charming, that it was almost impossible not to be glad she was there.

Miss Thorne was unaffectedly glad to welcome her. In fact, the signora was a sort of lion ; and though there was no drop of the Leohunter blood in Miss Thorne's veins, she nevertheless did like to see attractive people at her house. The signora was attractive, and on her first settlement in the dining-room she had whispered two or three soft feminine words into Miss Thorne's ear, which, at the moment, had quite touched that lady's heart.

" Oh, Miss Thorne ; where is Miss Thorne ? " she said, as soon as her attendants had placed her in her position just before one of the windows, from whence she could see all that was going on upon the lawn ; " How am I to thank you for permitting a creature like me to be here ? But if you knew the pleasure you give me, I am sure you would excuse the trouble I bring with me." And as she spoke she squeezed the spinster's little hand between her own.

" We are delighted to see you here," said Miss Thorne ; " you give us no trouble at all, and we think it a great favour conferred by you to come and see us ; don't we Wilfred ? "

" A very great favour indeed," said Mr. Thorne, with a gallant bow, but of a somewhat less cordial welcome than that conceded by his sister. Mr. Thorne had heard perhaps more of the antecedents of his guest than his sister had done, and had not as yet undergone the power of the signora's charms.

But while the mother of the last of the Neros was thus in her full splendour, with crowds of people gazing at her and the *élite* of the company standing round her couch, her glory was paled by the arrival of the Countess De Courcy. Miss Thorne had now been waiting three hours for the countess, and could not therefore but show very evident gratification when the arrival at last took place. She and her brother of course went off to welcome the titled grandees, and with them, alas, went many of the signora's admirers.

"Oh, Mr. Thorne," said the countess, while in the act of being disrobed of her fur cloaks, and re-robed in her gauze shawls, "what dreadful roads you have; perfectly frightful."

It happened that Mr. Thorne was way-warden for the district, and not liking the attack, began to excuse his roads.

"Oh yes, indeed they are," said the countess, not minding him in the least, "perfectly dreadful; are they not, Margaretta? Why, my dear Miss Thorne, we left Courcy Castle just at eleven; it was only just past eleven, was it not, John? and ——"

"Just past one, I think you mean," said the Honourable John, turning from the group and eyeing the signora through his glass. The signora gave him back his own, as the saying is, and more with it; so that the young nobleman was forced to avert his glance, and drop his glass.

"I say, Thorne," whispered he, "who the deuce is that on the sofa?"

Dr. Stanhope's daughter," whispered back Mr. Thorne. " Signora Neroni, she calls herself.'

"Whew-ew-ew!" whistled the Honourable John. "The devil she is! I have heard no end of stories about that filly. You must positively introduce me, Thorne; you positively must."

Mr. Thorne, who was respectability itself, did not quite like having a guest about whom the Honourable John De Courcy had heard no end of stories; but he couldn't help himself. He merely resolved that before he went to bed he would let his sister know somewhat of the history of the lady she was so willing to welcome. The innocence of Miss Thorne, at her time of life, was perfectly charming; but even innocence may be dangerous.

"John may say what he likes," continued the countess, urging her excuses to Miss Thorne; "I am sure we were past the castle gate before twelve, weren't we, Margaretta?"

"Upon my word I don't know," said the Lady Margaretta, "for I was half asleep. But I do know that I was called sometime in the middle of the night, and was dressing myself before daylight."

Wise people, when they are in the wrong, always put them-selves right by finding fault with the people against whom they have sinned. Lady De Courcy was a wise woman; and therefore, having treated Miss Thorne very badly by staying away till three o'clock, she assumed the offensive and attacked Mr. Thorne's roads. Her daughter, not less wise, attacked Miss Thorne's early hours. The art of doing this is among the most precious of those usually cultivated by persons who know how to live. There is no with-standing it. Who can go systematically to work, and having done battle with the primary accusation and settled that, then bring forward a counter-charge and support that also? Life is not long enough for such labours. A man in the right relies easily on his rectitude, and therefore goes about unarmed. His very strength is his weakness. A man in the wrong knows that he must look to his weapons; his very weakness is his strength. The one is never prepared for combat, the other is always ready. There-fore it is that in this world the man that is in the wrong almost invariably conquers the man that is in the right, and invariably despises him.

A man must be an idiot or else an angel, who after the age of forty shall attempt to be just to his neighbours. Many like the Lady Margaretta have learnt their lesson at a much earlier age. But this of course depends on the school in which they have been taught.

Poor Miss Thorne was altogether overcome. She knew very well that she had been ill treated, and yet she found herself making apologies to Lady De Courcy. To do her ladyship justice, she re-ceived them very graciously, and allowed herself with her train of daughters to be led towards the lawn.

There were two windows in the drawing-room wide open for the countess to pass through; but she saw that there was a woman on a sofa, at the third window, and that that woman had, as it were, a following attached to her. Her ladyship therefore deter-mined to investigate the woman. The De Courcys were heredi-tarily short sighted, and had been so for thirty centuries at least. So Lady De Courcy, who when she entered the family had adopted the family habits, did as her son had done before her, and taking her glass to investigate the Signora Neroni, pressed in among the gentlemen who surrounded the couch, and bowed slightly to those whom she chose to honour by her acquaintance.

In order to get to the window she had to pass close to the front of the couch, and as she did so she stared hard at the occupant. The occupant in return stared hard at the countess. The countess who since her countess-ship commenced had been accustomed to see all eyes, not royal, ducal or marquesal, fall before her own, paused as she went on, raised her eyebrows, and stared even harder than before. But she had now to do with one who cared little for countesses. It was, one may say, impossible for mortal man or woman to abash Madeline Neroni. She opened her large bright lustrous eyes wider and wider, till she seemed to be all eyes. She gazed up into the lady's face, not as though she did it with an effort, but as if she delighted in doing it. She used no glass to assist her effrontery, and needed none. The faintest possible smile of derision played round her mouth, and her nostrils were slightly dilated, as if in sure anticipation of her triumph. And it was sure. The Countess De Courcy, in spite of her thirty centuries and De Courcy castle, and the fact that Lord De Courcy was grand master of the ponies to the Prince of Wales, had not a chance with her. At first the little circlet of gold wavered in the countess's hand, then the hand shook, then the circlet fell, the countess's head tossed itself into the air, and the countess's feet shambled out to the lawn. She did not however go so fast but what she heard the signora's voice, asking —

" Who on earth is that woman, Mr. Slope ? "

" That is Lady De Courcy."

" Oh, ah. I might have supposed so. Ha, ha, ha. Well, that's as good as a play."

It was as good as a play to any there who had eyes to observe it, and wit to comment on what they observed.

But the Lady De Courcy soon found a congenial spirit on the lawn. There she encountered Mrs. Proudie, and as Mrs. Proudie was not only the wife of a bishop, but was also the cousin of an earl, Lady De Courcy considered her to be the fittest companion she was likely to meet in that assemblage. They were accordingly delighted to see each other. Mrs. Proudie by no means despised a countess, and as this countess lived in the county and within a sort of extensive visiting distance of Barchester, she was glad to have this opportunity of ingratiating herself.

" My dear Lady De Courcy, I am so delighted," said she, looking as little grim as it was in her nature to do. " I hardly expected to see you here. It is such a distance, and then you know, such a crowd."

"And such roads, Mrs. Proudie! I really wonder how the people ever get about. But I don't suppose they ever do."

"Well, I really don't know; but I suppose not. The Thornes don't, I know," said Mrs. Proudie. "Very nice person, Miss Thorne, isn't she?"

"Oh, delightful, and so queer; I've known her these twenty years. A great pet of mine is dear Miss Thorne. She is so very strange, you know. She always makes me think of the Esquimaux and the Indians. Isn't her dress quite delightful?"

"Delightful," said Mrs. Proudie; "I wonder now whether she paints. Did you ever see such colour?"

"Oh, of course," said Lady De Courcy; "that is, I have no doubt she does. But, Mrs. Proudie, who is that woman on the sofa by the window? just step this way and you'll see her, there _____" and the countess led her to a spot where she could plainly see the signora's well-remembered face and figure.

She did not however do so without being equally well seen by the signora. "Look, look," said that lady to Mr. Slope, who was still standing near to her; "see the high spiritualities and temporalities of the land in league together, and all against poor me. I'll wager my bracelet, Mr. Slope, against your next sermon, that they've taken up their position there on purpose to pull me to pieces. Well, I can't rush to the combat, but I know how to protect myself if the enemy come near me."

But the enemy knew better. They could gain nothing by contact with the Signora Neroni, and they could abuse her as they pleased at a distance from her on the lawn.

"She's that horrid Italian woman, Lady De Courcy; you must have heard of her."

"What Italian woman?" said her ladyship, quite alive to the coming story; "I don't think I've heard of any Italian woman coming into the country. She doesn't look Italian either."

"Oh, you must have heard of her," said Mrs. Proudie. "No, she's not absolutely Italian. She is Dr. Stanhope's daughter— Dr. Stanhope the prebendary; and she calls herself the Signora Neroni."

"Oh-h-h-h!" exclaimed the countess.

"I was sure you had heard of her," continued Mrs. Proudie. "I don't know anything about her husband. They do say that some man named Neroni is still alive. I believe she did marry such a man abroad, but I do not at all know who or what he was."

"Ah-h-h-h!" said the countess, shaking her head with much intelligence, as every additional "h" fell from her lips. "I know all about it now. I have heard George mention her. George knows all about her. George heard about her in Rome.

"She's an abominable woman, at any rate," said Mrs. Proudie.

"Insufferable," said the countess.

"She made her way into the palace once, before I knew anything about her; and I cannot tell you how dreadfully indecent her conduct was."

"Was it?" said the delighted countess.

"Insufferable," said the prelatess.

"But why does she lie on a sofa?" asked Lady De Courcy.

"She has only one leg," replied Mrs. Proudie.

"Only one leg!" said Lady De Courcy, who felt to a certain degree dissatisfied that the signora was thus incapacitated. "Was she born so?"

"Oh, no," said Mrs. Proudie,—and her ladyship felt somewhat recomforted by the assurance,—"she had two. But that Signor Neroni beat her, I believe, till she was obliged to have one amputated. At any rate, she entirely lost the use of it."

"Unfortunate creature!" said the countess, who herself knew something of matrimonial trials.

"Yes," said Mrs. Proudie; "one would pity her, in spite of her past bad conduct, if she now knew how to behave herself. But she does not. She is the most insolent creature I ever put my eyes on."

"Indeed she is," said Lady De Courcy.

"And her conduct with men is so abominable, that she is not fit to be admitted into any lady's drawing-room."

"Dear me!" said the countess, becoming again excited, happy, and merciless.

"You saw that man standing near her,—the clergyman with the red hair?"

"Yes, yes."

"She has absolutely ruined that man. The bishop, or I should rather take the blame on myself, for it was I,—I brought him down from London to Barchester. He is a tolerable preacher, an active young man, and I therefore introduced him to the bishop. That woman, Lady De Courcy has got hold of him, and has so disgraced him, that I am forced to require that he shall leave the palace; and I doubt very much whether he won't lose his gown!"

"Why what an idiot the man must be!" said the countess.

"You don't know the intriguing villany of that woman," said Mrs. Proudie, remembering her torn flounces.

"But you say she has only got one leg!"

"She is as full of mischief as tho' she had ten. Look at her eyes, Lady De Courcy. Did you ever see such eyes in a decent woman's head?"

"Indeed I never did, Mrs. Proudie."

"And her effrontery, and her voice; I quite pity her poor father, who is really a good sort of man."

"Dr. Stanhope, isn't he?"

"Yes, Dr. Stanhope. He is one of our prebendaries,—a good quiet sort of man himself. But I am surprised that he should let his daughter conduct herself as she does."

"I suppose he can't help it," said the countess.

"But a clergyman, you know, Lady De Courcy! He should at any rate prevent her from exhibiting in public, if he cannot induce her to behave at home. But he is to be pitied. I believe he has a desperate life of it with the lot of them. That apish-looking man there, with the long beard and the loose trousers,—he is the woman's brother. He is nearly as bad as she is. They are both of them infidels."

"Infidels!" said Lady De Courcy, "and their father a prebendary!"

"Yes, and likely to be the new dean too," said Mrs. Proudie.

"Oh, yes, poor dear Dr. Trefoil!" said the countess, who had once in her life spoken to that gentleman; "I was so distressed to hear it, Mrs. Proudie. And so Dr. Stanhope is to be the new dean! He comes of an excellent family, and I wish him success in spite of his daughter. Perhaps, Mrs. Proudie, when he is dean they'll be better able to see the error of their ways."

To this Mrs. Proudie said nothing. Her dislike of the Signora Neroni was too deep to admit of her even hoping that that lady should see the error of her ways. Mrs. Proudie looked on the signora as one of the lost,—one of those beyond the reach of Christian charity, and was therefore able to enjoy the luxury of hating her, without the drawback of wishing her eventually well out of her sins.

Any further conversation between these congenial souls was prevented by the advent of Mr. Thorne, who came to lead the countess to the tent. Indeed, he had been desired to do so some ten minutes since; but he had been delayed in the drawing-room by the signora. She had contrived to detain him, to get him near to her sofa, and at last to make him seat himself on a chair close to her beautiful arm. The fish took the bait, was hooked, and caught, and landed. Within that ten minutes he had heard the whole of the signora's history in such strains as she chose to use in telling it. He learnt from the lady's own lips the whole of that mysterious tale to which the Honourable George had merely alluded. He discovered that the beautiful creature lying before him had been more sinned against than sinning. She had owned to him that she had been weak, confiding and indifferent to the world's opinion, and that she had therefore been ill-used, deceived and evil spoken of. She had spoken to him of her mutilated limb, her youth destroyed in its fullest bloom, her beauty robbed of its every charm, her life blighted, her hopes withered ; and as she did so, a tear dropped from her eye to her cheek. She had told him of these things, and asked for his sympathy.

What could a good-natured genial Anglo-Saxon Squire Thorne do but promise to sympathise with her ? Mr. Thorne did promise to sympathise ; promised also to come and see the last of the Neros, to hear more of those fearful Roman days, of those light and innocent but dangerous hours which flitted by so fast on the shores of Como, and to make himself the confidant of the signora's sorrows.

We need hardly say that he dropped all idea of warning his sister against the dangerous lady. He had been mistaken ; never so much mistaken in his life. He had always regarded that Honourable George as a coarse brutal-minded young man ; now he was more convinced than ever that he was so. It was by such men as the Honourable George that the reputations of such women as Madeline Neroni were imperilled and damaged. He would go and see the lady in her own house ; he was fully sure in his own mind of the soundness of his own judgment ; if he found her, as he believed he should do, an injured well-disposed warm-hearted woman, he would get his sister Monica to invite her out to Ullathorne.

"No," said she, as at her instance he got up to leave her, and declared that he himself would attend upon her wants ; " no, no, my friend ; I positively put a veto upon your doing so. What, in your own house, with an assemblage round you such as there is here ! Do you wish to make every woman hate me and every man stare at me ? I lay a positive order on you not to come near me again to-day. Come and see me at home. It is only at home that I can talk ;· it is only at hcme that I really can live and enjoy myself. My days of going out, days such as these, are rare indeed. Come and see me at home, Mr. Thorne, and then I will not bid you to leave me."

It is, we believe, common with young men of five and twenty to look on their seniors—on men of, say, double their own age— as so many stocks and stones,—stocks and stones, that is, in regard to feminine beauty. There never was a greater mistake. Women, indeed, generally know better; but on this subject men of one age are thoroughly ignorant of what is the very nature of mankind of other ages. No experience of what goes on in the world, no reading of history, no observation of life, has any effect in teaching the truth. Men of fifty don't dance mazurkas, being generally too fat and wheezy; nor do they sit for the hour together on river banks at their mistresses' feet, being somewhat afraid of rheumatism. But for real true love, love at first sight, love to devotion, love that robs a man of his sleep, love that "will gaze an eagle blind," love that "will hear the lowest sound when the suspicious tread of theft is stopped," love that is "like a Hercules, still climbing trees in the Hesperides,"—we believe the best age is from forty-five to seventy; up to that, men are generally given to mere flirting.

At the present moment Mr. Thorne, *ætat.* fifty, was over head and ears in love at first sight with the Signora Madeline Vesey Neroni, *nata* Stanhope.

Nevertheless he was sufficiently master of himself to offer his arm with all propriety to Lady De Courcy, and the countess graciously permitted herself to be led to the tent. Such had been Miss Thorne's orders, as she had succeeded in inducing the bishop to lead old Lady Knowle to the top of the dining-room. One of the baronets was sent off in quest of Mrs. Proudie, and found that lady on the lawn not in the best of humours. Mr. Thorne and the countess had left her too abruptly; she had in vain looked about for an attendant chaplain, or even a stray curate; they were all drawing long bows with the young ladies at the bottom of the lawn, or finding places for their graceful co-toxophilites in some snug corner of the tent. In such position Mrs. Proudie had been wont in earlier days to fall back upon Mr. Slope; but now she could never fall back upon him again. She gave her head one shake as she thought of her lone position, and that shake was as good as a week deducted from Mr. Slope's longer sojourn in Barchester. Sir Harkaway Gorse, however, relieved her present misery, though his doing so by no means mitigated the sinning chaplain's doom.

And now the eating and drinking began in earnest. Dr. Grantly, to his great horror, found himself leagued to Mrs. Clantantram. Mrs. Clantantram had a great regard for the archdeacon, which was not cordially returned; and when she, coming up to him, whispered in his ear, "Come, archdeacon, I'm sure you won't begrudge an old friend the favour of your arm," and then proceeded to tell him the whole history of her roquelaure, he resolved that he would shake her off before he was fifteen minutes older. But latterly the archdeacon had not been successful in his resolutions; and on the present occasion Mrs. Clantantram stuck to him till the banquet was over.

Dr. Gwynne got a baronet's wife, and Mrs. Grantly fell to the lot of a baronet. Charlotte Stanhope attached herself to Mr. Harding in order to make room for Bertie, who succeeded in sitting down in the dining-room next to Mrs. Bold. To speak sooth, now that he had love in earnest to make, his heart almost failed him.

Eleanor had been right glad to avail herself of his arm, seeing that Mr. Slope was hovering nigh her. In striving to avoid that terrible Charybdis of a Slope she was in great danger of falling into an unseen Scylla on the other hand, that Scylla being Bertie Stanhope. Nothing could be more gracious than she was to Bertie. She almost jumped at his proffered arm. Charlotte perceived this from a distance, and triumphed in her heart; Bertie felt it, and was encouraged; Mr. Slope saw it, and glowered with jealousy. Eleanor and Bertie sat down to table in the dining-room; and as she took her seat at his right hand, she found that Mr. Slope was already in possession of the chair at her own.

As these things were going on in the dining-room, Mr. Arabin was hanging enraptured and alone over the signora's sofa; and Eleanor from her seat could look through the open door and see that he was doing so.

CHAP. XXXVIII.

THE BISHOP BREAKFASTS, AND THE DEAN DIES.

THE bishop of Barchester said grace over the well-spread board in the Ullathorne dining-room; and while he did so the last breath was flying from the dean of Barchester as he lay in his sick room in the deanery. When the bishop of Barchester raised his first glass of champagne to his lips, the deanship of Barchester was a good thing in the gift of the prime minister. Before the bishop of Barchester had left the table, the minister of the day was made aware of the fact at his country seat in Hampshire, and had already turned over in his mind the names of five very respectable aspirants for the preferment. It is at present only necessary to say that Mr. Slope's name was not among the five.

" 'Twas merry in the hall when the beards wagged all;" and the clerical beards wagged merrily in the hall of Ullathorne that day. It was not till after the last cork had been drawn, the last speech made, the last nut cracked, that tidings reached and were whispered about that the poor dean was no more. It was well for the happiness of the clerical beards that this little delay took place, as otherwise decency would have forbidden them to wag at all.

But there was one sad man among them that day. Mr. Arabin's beard did not wag as it should have done. He had come there hoping the best, striving to think the best, about Eleanor; turning over in his mind all the words he remembered to have fallen from her about Mr. Slope, and trying to gather from them a conviction unfavourable to his rival. He had not exactly resolved to come that day to some decisive proof as to the widow's intention; but he had meant, if possible, to re-cultivate his friendship with Eleanor; and in his present frame of mind any such re-cultivation must have ended in a declaration of love.

He had passed the previous night alone at his new parsonage, and it was the first night that he had so passed. It had been dull and sombre enough. Mrs. Grantly had been right in saying that a priestess would be wanting at St. Ewold's. He had sat there alone with his glass before him, and then with his teapot, thinking about Eleanor Bold. As is usual in such meditations, he did little but blame her; blame her for liking Mr. Slope, and blame her for not liking him; blame her for her cordiality to himself, and blame her for her want of cordiality; blame her for being stubborn, head-strong, and passionate; and yet the more he thought of her the higher she rose in his affection. If only it should turn out, if only it could be made to turn out, that she had defended Mr. Slope, not from love, but on principle, all would be right. Such principle in itself would be admirable, loveable, womanly; he felt that he could be pleased to allow Mr. Slope just so much favour as that. But if —— And then Mr. Arabin poked his fire most unnecessarily, spoke crossly to his new parlour-maid who came in for the tea-things, and threw himself back in his chair determined to go to sleep. Why had she been so stiffnecked when asked a plain question? She could not but have known in what light he regarded her. Why had she not answered a plain question, and so put an end to his misery? Then, instead of going to sleep in his arm-chair, Mr. Arabin walked about the room as though he had been possessed.

On the following morning, when he attended Miss Thorne's behests he was still in a somewhat confused state. His first duty had been to converse with Mrs. Clantantram, and that lady had found it impossible to elicit the slightest sympathy from him on the subject of her roquelaure. Miss Thorne had asked him whether Mrs. Bold was coming with the Grantlys; and the two names of Bold and Grantly together had nearly made him jump from his seat.

He was in this state of confused uncertainty, hope, and doubt, when he saw Mr. Slope, with his most polished smile, handing Eleanor out of her carriage. He thought of nothing more. He never considered whether the carriage belonged to her or to Mr. Slope, or to any one else to whom they might both be mutually obliged without any concert between themselves. This sight in his present state of mind was quite enough to upset him and his resolves. It was clear as noonday. Had he seen her handed into a carriage by Mr. Slope at a church door with a white veil over her head, the truth could not be more manifest. He went into the house, and, as we have seen, soon found himself walking with Mr. Harding. Shortly afterwards Eleanor came up; and then he had to leave his companion, and either go about alone or find another. While in this state he was encountered by the archdeacon.

"I wonder," said Dr. Grantly, "if it be true that Mr. Slope and Mrs. Bold came here together. Susan says she is almost sure she saw their faces in the same carriage as she got out of her own."

Mr. Arabin had nothing for it but to bear his testimony to the correctness of Mrs. Grantly's eyesight.

"It is perfectly shameful," said the archdeacon; "or I should rather say, shameless. She was asked here as my guest; and if she be determined to disgrace herself, she should have feeling enough not to do so before my immediate friends. I wonder how that man got himself invited. I wonder whether she had the face to bring him."

To this Mr. Arabin could answer nothing, nor did he wish to answer anything. Though he abused Eleanor to himself, he did not choose to abuse her to any one else, nor was he well pleased to hear any one else speak ill of her. Dr. Grantly, however, was very angry, and did not spare his sister-in-law. Mr. Arabin therefore left him as soon as he could, and wandered back into the house.

He had not been there long, when the signora was brought in. For some time he kept himself out of temptation, and merely hovered round her at a distance; but as soon as Mr. Thorne had left her, he yielded himself up to the basilisk, and allowed himself to be made prey of.

It is impossible to say how the knowledge had been acquired, but the signora had a sort of instinctive knowledge that Mr. Arabin was an admirer of Mrs. Bold. Men hunt foxes by the aid of dogs, and are aware that they do so by the strong organ of smell with which the dog is endowed. They do not, however, in the least comprehend how such a sense can work with such acuteness. The organ by which women instinctively, as it were, know and feel how other women are regarded by men, and how also men are regarded by other women, is equally strong, and equally incomprehensible. A glance, a word, a motion, suffices : by some such acute exercise of her feminine senses the signora was aware that Mr. Arabin loved Eleanor Bold ; and therefore, by a further exercise of her peculiar feminine propensities, it was quite natural for her to entrap Mr. Arabin into her net.

The work was half done before she came to Ullathorne, and when could she have a better opportunity of completing it ? She had had almost enough of Mr. Slope, though she could not quite resist the fun of driving a very sanctimonious clergyman to madness by a desperate and ruinous passion. Mr. Thorne had fallen too easily to give much pleasure in the chase. His position as a man of wealth might make his alliance of value, but as a lover he was very second-rate. We may say that she regarded him somewhat as a sportsman does a pheasant. The bird is so easily shot, that he would not be worth the shooting were it not for the very respectable appearance that he makes in a larder. The signora would not waste much time in shooting Mr. Thorne, but still he was worth bagging for family uses.

But Mr. Arabin was game of another sort. The signora was herself possessed of quite sufficient intelligence to know that Mr. Arabin was a man more than usually intellectual. She knew also, that as a clergyman he was of a much higher stamp than Mr. Slope, and that as a gentleman he was better educated than Mr. Thorne. She would never have attempted to drive Mr. Arabin into ridiculous misery as she did Mr. Slope, nor would she think it possible to dispose of him in ten minutes as she had done with Mr. Thorne.

Such were her reflections about Mr. Arabin. As to Mr. Arabin, it cannot be said that he reflected at all about the signora. He knew that she was beautiful, and he felt that she was able to charm him. He required charming in his present misery, and therefore he went and stood at the head of her couch. She knew all about it. Such were her peculiar gifts. It was her nature to see that he required charming, and it was her province to charm him. As the Eastern idler swallows his dose of opium, as the London reprobate swallows his dose of gin, so with similar desires and for similar reasons did Mr. Arabin prepare to swallow the charms of the Signora Neroni.

"Why an't you shooting with bows and arrows, Mr. Arabin?" said she, when they were nearly alone together in the drawing-room; "or talking with young ladies in shady bowers, or turning your talents to account in some way? What was a bachelor like you asked here for? Don't you mean to earn your cold chicken and champagne? Were I you, I should be ashamed to be so idle."

Mr. Arabin murmured some sort of answer. Though he wished to be charmed, he was hardly yet in a mood to be playful in return.

"Why, what ails you, Mr. Arabin?" said she. "Here you are in your own parish; Miss Thorne tells me that her party is given expressly in your honour; and yet you are the only dull man at it. Your friend Mr. Slope was with me a few minutes since, full of life and spirits; why don't you rival him?"

It was not difficult for so acute an observer as Madeline Neroni to see that she had hit the nail on the head and driven the bolt home. Mr. Arabin winced visibly before her attack, and she knew at once that he was jealous of Mr. Slope.

"But I look on you and Mr. Slope as the very antipodes of men," said she. "There is nothing in which you are not each the reverse of the other, except in belonging to the same profession; and even in that you are so unlike as perfectly to maintain the rule. He is gregarious, you are given to solitude. He is active, you are passive. He works, you think. He likes women, you despise them. He is fond of position and power, and so are you, but for directly different reasons. He loves to be praised, you very foolishly abhor it. He will gain his rewards, which will be an insipid useful wife, a comfortable income, and a reputation for sanctimony. You will also gain yours."

"Well, and what will they be?" said Mr. Arabin, who knew that he was being flattered, and yet suffered himself to put up with it. "What will be my rewards?"

"The heart of some woman whom you will be too austere to own that you love, and the respect of some few friends which you will be too proud to own that you value."

"Rich rewards," said he; "but of little worth if they are to be so treated."

"Oh, you are not to look for such success as awaits Mr. Slope. He is born to be a successful man. He suggests to himself an object, and then starts for it with eager intention. Nothing will deter him from his pursuit. He will have no scruples, no fears, no hesitation. His desire is to be a bishop with a rising family,

the wife will come first, and in due time the apron. You will see
all this, and then ——"

"Well, and what then?"

"Then you will begin to wish that you had done the same."

Mr. Arabin looked placidly out at the lawn, and resting his
shoulder on the head of the sofa, rubbed his chin with his hand.
It was a trick he had when he was thinking deeply ; and what the
signora said made him think. Was it not all true? Would he
not hereafter look back, if not at Mr. Slope, at some others, perhaps
not equally gifted with himself, who had risen in the world while
he had lagged behind, and then wish that he had done the same?

"Is not such the doom of all speculative men of talent?" said
she. "Do they not all sit rapt as you now are, cutting imaginary
silken cords with their fine edges, while those not so highly tem-
pered sever the every-day Gordian knots of the world's struggle,
and win wealth and renown? Steel too highly polished, edges too
sharp, do not do for this world's work, Mr. Arabin."

Who was this woman that thus read the secrets of his heart,
and re-uttered to him the unwelcome bodings of his own soul?
He looked full into her face when she had done speaking, and said,
"Am I one of those foolish blades, too sharp and too fine to do a
useful day's work?"

"Why do you let the Slopes of the world out-distance you?"
said she. "Is not the blood in your veins as warm as his? does
not your pulse beat as fast? Has not God made you a man, and
intended you to do a man's work here, ay, and to take a man's
wages also?"

Mr. Arabin sat ruminating and rubbing his face, and wondering
why these things were said to him ; but he replied nothing. The
signora went on—

"The greatest mistake any man ever made is to suppose that
the good things of the world are not worth the winning. And it
is a mistake so opposed to the religion which you preach! Why
does God permit his bishops one after another to have their five
thousands and ten thousands a year if such wealth be bad and not
worth having? Why are beautiful things given to us, and luxuries
and pleasant enjoyments, if they be not intended to be used?
They must be meant for some one, and what is good for a layman
cannot surely be bad for a clerk. You try to despise these good
things, but you only try ; you don't succeed."

"Don't I?" said Mr. Arabin, still musing, and not knowing what
he said.

"I ask you the question ; do you succeed?"

Mr. Arabin looked at her piteously. It seemed to him as though he were being interrogated by some inner spirit of his own, to whom he could not refuse an answer, and to whom he did not dare to give a false reply.

"Come, Mr. Arabin, confess; do you succeed? Is money so contemptible? Is worldly power so worthless? Is feminine beauty a trifle to be so slightly regarded by a wise man?"

"Feminine beauty!" said he, gazing into her face, as though all the feminine beauty in the world were concentrated there. "Why do you say I do not regard it?"

"If you look at me like that, Mr. Arabin, I shall alter my opinion—or should do so, were I not of course aware that I have no beauty of my own worth regarding."

The gentleman blushed crimson, but the lady did not blush at all. A slightly increased colour animated her face, just so much so as to give her an air of special interest. She expected a compliment from her admirer, but she was rather grateful than otherwise by finding that he did not pay it to her. Messrs. Slope and Thorne, Messrs. Brown, Jones and Robinson, they all paid her compliments. She was rather in hopes that she would ultimately succeed in inducing Mr. Arabin to abuse her.

"But your gaze," said she, "is one of wonder, and not of admiration. You wonder at my audacity in asking you such questions about yourself."

"Well, I do rather," said he.

"Nevertheless I expect an answer, Mr. Arabin. Why were women made beautiful if men are not to regard them?"

"But men do regard them," he replied.

"And why not you?"

"You are begging the question, Madame Neroni."

"I am sure I shall beg nothing, Mr. Arabin, which you will·not grant, and I do beg for an answer. Do you not as a rule think women below your notice as companions? Let us see. There is the widow Bold looking round at you from her chair this minute. What would you say to her as a companion for life?"

Mr. Arabin, rising from his position, leaned over the sofa and looked through the drawing-room door to the place where Eleanor was seated between Bertie Stanhope and Mr. Slope. She at once caught his glance, and averted her own. She was not pleasantly placed in her present position. Mr. Slope was doing his best to attract her attention; and she was striving to prevent his doing so by talking to Mr. Stanhope, while her mind was intently fixed on Mr. Arabin and Madame Neroni. Bertie Stanhope endeavoured to take advantage of her favours, but he was thinking more of the manner in which he would by-and-by throw himself at her feet, than of amusing her at the present moment.

"There," said the signora. "She was stretching her beautiful neck to look at you, and now you have disturbed her. Well I declare, I believe I am wrong about you; I believe that you do think Mrs. Bold a charming woman. Your looks seem to say so; and by her looks I should say that she is jealous of me. Come, Mr. Arabin, confide in me, and if it is so, I'll do all in my power to make up the match."

It is needless to say that the signora was not very sincere in her offer. She was never sincere on such subjects. She never expected others to be so, nor did she expect others to think her so. Such matters were her playthings, her billiard table, her hounds and hunters, ner waltzes and polkas, her picnics and summer-day excursions. She had little else to amuse her, and therefore played at love-making in all its forms. She was now playing at it with Mr. Arabin, and did not at all expect the earnestness and truth of his answer.

"All in your power would be nothing," said he; "for Mrs. Bold is, I imagine, already engaged to another."

'Then you own the impeachment yourself."

"You cross-question me rather unfairly," he replied, "and I do not know why I answer you at all. Mrs. Bold is a very beautiful woman, and as intelligent as beautiful. It is impossible to know her without admiring her."

"So you think the widow a very beautiful woman?"

"Indeed I do."

"And one that would grace the parsonage of St. Ewold's."

"One that would well grace any man's house."

"And you really have the effrontery to tell me this," said she; "to tell me, who, as you very well know, set up to be a beauty myself, and who am at this very moment taking such an interest in your affairs, you really have the effrontery to tell me that Mrs. Bold is the most beautiful woman you know."

"I did not say so," said Mr. Arabin; "you are more beautiful——"

"Ah, come now, that is something like. I thought you could not be so unfeeling."

"You are more beautiful, perhaps more clever."

"Thank you, thank you, Mr. Arabin. I knew that you and I should be friends."

"But——"

"Not a word further. I will not hear a word further. If you talk till midnight, you cannot improve what you have said."

"But Madame Neroni, Mrs. Bold——"

"I will not hear a word about Mrs. Bold. Dread thoughts of strychnine did pass across my brain, but she is welcome to the second place."

"Her place——"

"I won't hear anything about her or her place. I am satisfied, and that is enough. But, Mr. Arabin, I am dying with hunger; beautiful and clever as I am, you know I cannot go to my food, and yet you do not bring it to me."

This at any rate was so true as to make it necessary that Mr. Arabin should act upon it, and he accordingly went into the dining-room and supplied the signora's wants.

"And yourself?" said she.

"Oh," said he, "I am not hungry; I never eat at this hour."

"Come, come, Mr. Arabin, don't let love interfere with your appetite. It never does with mine. Give me half a glass more champagne, and then go to the table. Mrs. Bold will do me an injury if you stay talking to me any longer."

Mr. Arabin did as he was bid. He took her plate and glass from her, and going into the dining-room, helped himself to a sand-wich from the crowded table and began munching it in a corner.

As he was doing so, Miss Thorne, who had hardly sat down for a moment, came into the room, and seeing him standing, was greatly distressed.

"Oh, my dear Mr. Arabin," said she, "have you never sat down yet? I am so distressed. You of all men too."

Mr. Arabin assured her that he had only just come into the room.

"That is the very reason why you should lose no more time. Come, I'll make room for you. Thank 'ee, my dear," she said, seeing that Mrs. Bold was making an attempt to move from her chair, "but I would not for worlds see you stir, for all the ladies would think it necessary to follow. But, perhaps, if Mr. Stanhope has done—just for a minute, Mr Stanhope—till I can get another chair."

And so Bertie had to rise to make way for his rival. This he did, as he did everything, with an air of good-humoured pleasantry which made it impossible for Mr. Arabin to refuse the proffered seat.

"His bishopric let another take," said Bertie; the quotation being certainly not very appropriate, either for the occasion or the person spoken to. "I have eaten and am satisfied. Mr. Arabin, pray take my chair. I wish for your sake that it really was a bishop's seat."

Mr. Arabin did sit down, and as he did so, Mrs. Bold got up as though to follow her neighbour.

"Pray, pray don't move," said Miss Thorne, almost forcing Eleanor back into her chair. "Mr. Stanhope is not going to leave us. He will stand behind you like a true knight as he is. And now I think of it, Mr. Arabin, let me introduce you to Mr. Slope. Mr. Slope, Mr. Arabin." And the two gentlemen bowed stiffly to each other across the lady whom they both intended to marry, while the other gentleman who also intended to marry her stood behind, watching them.

The two had never met each other before, and the present was certainly not a good opportunity for much cordial conversation, even if cordial conversation between them had been possible. As it was, the whole four who formed the party seemed as though their tongues were tied. Mr. Slope, who was wide awake to what he hoped was his coming opportunity, was not much concerned in the interest of the moment. His wish was to see Eleanor move, that he might pursue her. Bertie was not exactly in the same frame of mind ; the evil day was near enough ; there was no reason why he should precipitate it. He had made up his mind to marry Eleanor Bold if he could, and was resolved to-day to take the first preliminary step towards doing so. But there was time enough before him. He was not going to make an offer of marriage over the table-cloth. Having thus good-naturedly made way for Mr. Arabin, he was willing also to let him talk to the future Mrs. Stanhope as long as they remained in their present position.

Mr. Arabin, having bowed to Mr. Slope, began eating his food without saying a word further. He was full of thought, and though he ate he did so unconsciously.

But poor Eleanor was the most to be pitied. The only friend on whom she thought she could rely, was Bertie Stanhope, and he, it seemed, was determined to desert her. Mr. Arabin did not attempt to address her. She said a few words in reply to some remarks from Mr. Slope, and then feeling the situation too much for her, started from her chair in spite of Miss Thorne, and hurried from the room. Mr. Slope followed her, and young Stanhope lost the occasion.

Madeline Neroni, when she was left alone, could not help pondering much on the singular interview she had had with this singular man. Not a word that she had spoken to him had been intended by her to be received as true, and yet he had answered her in the very spirit of truth. He had done so, and she had been aware that he had so done. She had wormed from him his secret; and he, debarred as it would seem from man's usual privilege of lying, had innocently laid bare his whole soul to her. He loved Eleanor Bold, but Eleanor was not in his eye so beautiful as herself. He would fain have Eleanor for his wife, but yet he had acknowledged that she was the less gifted of the two. The man had literally been unable to falsify his thoughts when questioned, and had been compelled to be true *malgrè lui*, even when truth must have been so disagreeable to him.

This teacher of men, this Oxford pundit, this double-distilled quintessence of university perfection, this writer of religious treatises, this speaker of ecclesiastical speeches, had been like a little child in her hands ; she had turned him inside out, and read his very heart as she might have done that of a young girl. She could not but despise him for his facile openness, and yet she liked him for it too. It was a novelty to her, a new trait in a man's character. She felt also that she could never so completely make a fool of him as she did of the Slopes and Thornes. She felt that she never could induce Mr. Arabin to make protestations to her that were not true, or to listen to nonsense that was mere nonsense.

It was quite clear that Mr. Arabin was heartily in love with Mrs. Bold, and the signora, with very unwonted good nature, began to turn it over in her mind whether she could not do him a good turn. Of course Bertie was to have the first chance. It was an understood family arrangement that her brother was, if possible, to marry the widow Bold. Madeline knew too well his necessities and what was due to her sister to interfere with so excellent a plan, as long as it might be feasible. But she had strong suspicion that it was not feasible. She did not think it likely that Mrs. Bold would accept a man in her brother's position, and she had frequently said so to Charlotte. She was inclined to believe that Mr. Slope had more chance of success; and with her it would be a labour of love to rob Mr. Slope of his wife.

And so the signora resolved, should Bertie fail, to do a good-natured act for once in her life, and give up Mr. Arabin to the woman whom he loved.

CHAP. XXXIX.

THE LOOKALOFTS AND THE GREENACRES.

On the whole, Miss Thorne's provision for the amusement and feeding of the outer classes in the exoteric paddock was not unsuccessful.

Two little drawbacks to the general happiness did take place, but they were of a temporary nature, and apparent rather than real. The first was the downfall of young Harry Greenacre, and the other the uprise of Mrs. Lookaloft and her family.

As to the quintain, it became more popular among the boys on foot, than it would ever have been among the men on horseback, even had young Greenacre been more successful. It was twirled round and round till it was nearly twirled out of the ground; and the bag of flour was used with great gusto in powdering the backs and heads of all who could be coaxed within its vicinity.

Of course it was reported all through the assemblage that Harry was dead, and there was a pathetic scene between him and his mother when it was found that he had escaped scatheless from the fall. A good deal of beer was drunk on the occasion, and the quintain was "dratted" and "bothered," and very generally anathematised by all the mothers who had young sons likely to be placed in similar jeopardy. But the affair of Mrs. Lookaloft was of a more serious nature.

"I do tell 'ee plainly,—face to face,—she be there in madam's drawing-room; herself and Gussy, and them two walloping gals, dressed up to their very eyeses." This was said by a very positive, very indignant, and very fat farmer's wife, who was sitting on the end of a bench leaning on the handle of a huge cotton umbrella.

"But you didn't zee her, Dame Guffern?" said Mrs. Greenacre, whom this information, joined to the recent peril undergone by her son, almost overpowered. Mr. Greenacre held just as much land as Mr. Lookaloft, paid his rent quite as punctually, and his opinion in the vestry-room was reckoned to be every whit as good. Mrs. Lookaloft's rise in the world had been wormwood to Mrs. Greenacre. She had no taste herself for the sort of finery which had converted Barleystubb farm into Rosebank, and which had occasionally graced Mr. Lookaloft's letters with the dignity of esquirehood. She had no wish to convert her own homestead into Violet Villa, or to see her goodman go about with a new-fangled handle to his name. But it was a mortal injury to her that Mrs. Lookaloft should be successful in her hunt after such honours. She had abused and ridiculed Mrs. Lookaloft to the extent of her little power. She had pushed against her going out of church, and had excused herself with all the easiness of equality. " Ah, dame, I axes pardon; but you be grown so mortal stout these times." She had inquired with apparent cordiality of Mr. Lookaloft, after " the woman that owned him," and had, as she thought, been on the whole able to hold her own pretty well against her aspiring neighbour. Now, however, she found herself distinctly put into a separate and inferior class. Mrs. Lookaloft was asked into the Ullathorne drawing-room merely because she called her house Rosebank, and had talked over her husband into buying pianos and silk dresses instead of putting his money by to stock farms for his sons.

Mrs. Greenacre, much as she reverenced Miss Thorne, and highly as she respected her husband's landlord, could not but look on this as an act of injustice done to her and hers. Hitherto the Lookalofts had never been recognised as being of a different class from the Greenacres. Their pretensions were all self-pretensions, their finery was all paid for by themselves and not granted to them by others. The local sovereigns of the vicinity, the district fountains of honour, had hitherto conferred on them the stamp of no rank. Hitherto their crinoline petticoats, late hours, and mincing gait had been a fair subject of Mrs. Greenacre's raillery, and this raillery had been a safety valve for her envy. Now, however, and from henceforward, the case would be very different. Now the Lookalofts would boast that their aspirations had been sanctioned by the gentry of the country; now they would declare with some show of truth that their claims to peculiar consideration had been recognised. They had sat as equal guests in the presence of bishops and baronets; they had been curtseyed to by Miss Thorne on her own drawing-room carpet; they were about to sit down to table in company with a live countess! Bab Lookaloft, as she had always been called by the young Greenacres in the days of their juvenile equality, might possibly sit next to the Honourable George, and that wretched Gussy might be permitted to hand a custard to the Lady Margaretta De Courcy.

The fruition of those honours, or such of them as fell to the lot of the envied family, was not such as should have caused much envy. The attention paid to the Lookalofts by the De Courcys was very limited, and the amount of entertainment which they received from the bishop's society was hardly in itself a recompense for the dull monotony of their day. But of what they endured Mrs. Greenacre took no account; she thought only of what she considered they must enjoy, and of the dreadfully exalted tone of living which would be manifested by the Rosebank family, as the consequence of their present distinction.

"But did 'ee zee 'em there, dame, did 'ee zee 'em there with your own eyes?" asked poor Mrs. Greenacre; still hoping that there might be some ground for doubt.

"And how could I do that, unless so be I was there myself?" asked Mrs. Guffern. "I didn't zet eyes on none of them this blessed morning, but I zee'd them as did. You know our John; well, he will be for keeping company with Betsey Rusk, madam's own maid, you know. And Betsey isn't none of your common kitchen wenches. So Betsey, she come out to our John, you know, and she's always vastly polite to me, is Betsey Rusk, I must say. So before she took so much as one turn with John, she told me every ha'porth that was going on up in the house."

"Did she now?" said Mrs. Greenacre.

"Indeed she did," said Mrs. Guffern.

"And she told you them people was up there in the drawing-room?"

"She told me she zee'd them come in,—that they was dressed finer by half nor any of the family, with all their neckses and buzoms stark naked as a born babby."

"The minxes!" exclaimed Mrs. Greenacre, who felt herself more put about by this than any other mark of aristocratic distinction which her enemies had assumed.

"Yes, indeed," continued Mrs. Guffern, "as naked as you please, while all the quality was dressed just as you and I be, Mrs. Greenacre."

"Drat their impudence," said Mrs. Greenacre, from whose well-covered bosom all milk of human kindness was receding, as far as the family of the Lookalofts were concerned.

"So says I," said Mrs. Guffern; "and so says my goodman, Thomas Guffern, when he hear'd it. 'Molly,' says he to me, 'if ever you takes to going about o' mornings with yourself all naked in them ways, I begs you won't come back no more to the old house.' So says I, 'Thomas, no more I wull.' 'But,' says he, 'drat it, how the deuce does she manage with her rheumatiz, and she not a rag on her:'" and Mrs. Guffern laughed loudly as she thought of Mrs. Lookaloft's probable sufferings from rheumatic attacks.

"But to liken herself that way to folk that ha' blood in their veins," said Mrs. Greenacre.

"Well, but that warn't all neither that Betsey told. There they all swelled into madam's drawing-room, like so many turkey cocks, as much as to say, 'and who dare say no to us?' and Gregory was thinking of telling of 'em to come down here, only his heart failed him 'cause of the grand way they was dressed. So in they went; but madam looked at them as glum as death."

"Well now," said Mrs. Greenacre, greatly relieved, "so they wasn't axed different from us at all then?"

"Betsey says that Gregory says that madam wasn't a bit too well pleased to see them where they was, and that, to his believing, they was expected to come here just like the rest of us."

There was great consolation in this. Not that Mrs. Greenacre was altogether satisfied. She felt that justice to herself demanded that Mrs. Lookaloft should not only not be encouraged, but that she should also be absolutely punished. What had been done at that scriptural banquet, of which Mrs. Greenacre so often read the account to her family? Why had not Miss Thorne boldly gone to the intruder and said, "Friend, thou hast come up hither to high places not fitted to thee. Go down lower, and thou wilt find thy mates." Let the Lookalofts be treated at the present moment with ever so cold a shoulder, they would still be enabled to boast hereafter of their position, their aspirations, and their honour.

"Well, with all her grandeur, I do wonder that she be so mean," continued Mrs. Greenacre, unable to dismiss the subject. "Did you hear, goodman?" she went on, about to repeat the whole story to her husband who then came up. "There's dame Lookaloft and Bab and Gussy and the lot of 'em all sitting as grand as fivepence in madam's drawing-room, and they not axed no more nor you nor me. Did you ever hear tell the like o' that?"

"Well, and what for shouldn't they?" said Farmer Greenacre.

"Likening theyselves to the quality, as though they was estated folk, or the like o' that!" said Mrs. Guffern.

"Well, if they likes it and madam likes it, they's welcome for me," said the farmer. "Now I likes this place better, cause I be more at home like, and don't have to pay for them fine clothes for the missus. Every one to his taste, Mrs. Guffern, and if neighbour Lookaloft thinks that he has the best of it, he's welcome."

Mrs. Greenacre sat down by her husband's side to begin the heavy work of the banquet, and she did so in some measure with restored tranquillity, but nevertheless she shook her head at her gossip to show that in this instance she did not quite approve of her husband's doctrine.

"And I'll tell 'ee what, dames," continued he; "if so be that we

cannot enjoy the dinner that madam gives us because Mother
Lookaloft is sitting up there on a grand sofa, I think we ought all
to go home. If we greet at that, what'll we do when true sorrow
comes across us? How would you be now, dame, if the boy
there had broke his neck when he got the tumble?"

Mrs. Greenacre was humbled and said nothing further on the
matter. But let prudent men, such as Mr. Greenacre, preach as
they will, the family of the Lookalofts certainly does occasion a
good deal of heart-burning in the world at large.

It was pleasant to see Mr. Plomacy, as leaning on his stout stick
he went about among the rural guests, acting as a sort of head
constable as well as master of the revels. "Now, young 'un, if
you can't manage to get along without that screeching, you'd
better go to the other side of the twelve-acre field, and take your
dinner with you. Come, girls, what do you stand there for,
twirling of your thumbs? come out, and let the lads see you ;
you've no need to be so ashamed of your faces. Hollo! there, who
are you? how did you make your way in here?"

This last disagreeable question was put to a young man of about
twenty-four, who did not, in Mr. Plomacy's eye, bear sufficient
vestiges of a rural education and residence.

"If you please, your worship, Master Barrell the coachman let
me in at the church wicket, 'cause I do be working mostly al'ays
for the family."

"Then Master Barrell the coachman may let you out again,"
said Mr. Plomacy, not even conciliated by the magisterial dignity
which had been conceded to him. "What's your name? and
what trade are you, and who do you work for?"

"I'm Stubbs, your worship, Bob Stubbs ; and—and—and——"

"And what's your trade, Stubbs?"

"Plaisterer, please your worship."

"I'll plaister you, and Barrell too ; you'll just walk out of this
'ere field as quick as you walked in. We don't want no plaisterers ;
when we do, we'll send for 'em. Come, my buck, walk."

Stubbs the plasterer was much downcast at this dreadful edict.
He was a sprightly fellow, and had contrived since his egress into
the Ullathorne elysium to attract to himself a forest nymph, to
whom he was whispering a plasterer's usual soft nothings, when he
was encountered by the great Mr. Plomacy. It was dreadful to
be thus dissevered from his dryad, and sent howling back to a
Barchester pandemonium just as the nectar and ambrosia were
about to descend on the fields of asphodel. He began to try what
prayers would do, but city prayers were vain against the great

rural potentate. Not only did Mr. Plomacy order his exit, but raising his stick to show the way which led to the gate that had been left in the custody of that false Cerberus Barrell, proceeded himself to see the edict of banishment carried out.

The goddess Mercy, however, the sweetest goddess that ever sat upon a cloud, and the dearest to poor frail erring man, appeared on the field in the person of Mr. Greenacre. Never was interceding goddess more welcome.

" Come, man," said Mr. Greenacre, " never stick at trifles such a day as this. I know the lad well. Let him bide at my axing. Madam won't miss what he can eat and drink, I know."

Now Mr. Plomacy and Mr. Greenacre were sworn friends. Mr. Plomacy had at his own disposal as comfortable a room as there was in Ullathorne House; but he was a bachelor, and alone there; and, moreover, smoking in the house was not allowed even to Mr. Plomacy. His moments of truest happiness were spent in a huge arm-chair in the warmest corner of Mrs. Greenacre's beautifully clean front kitchen. 'Twas there that the inner man dissolved itself, and poured itself out in streams of pleasant chat; 'twas there that he was respected and yet at his ease; 'twas there, and perhaps there only, that he could unburden himself from the ceremonies of life without offending the dignity of those above him, or incurring the familiarity of those below. 'Twas there that his long pipe was always to be found on the accustomed chimney board, not only permitted but encouraged.

Such being the state of the case, it was not to be supposed that Mr. Plomacy could refuse such a favour to Mr. Greenacre; but nevertheless he did not grant it without some further show of austere authority.

" Eat and drink, Mr. Greenacre! No. It's not what he eats and drinks; but the example such a chap shows, coming in where he's not invited — a chap of his age too. He too that never did a day's work about Ullathorne since he was born. Plaisterer! I'll plaister him ! "

" He worked long enough for me, then, Mr. Plomacy. And a good hand he is at setting tiles as any in Barchester," said the other, not sticking quite to veracity, as indeed mercy never should. " Come, come, let him alone to-day, and quarrel with him to-morrow. You wouldn't shame him before his lass there ? "

"It goes against the grain with me, then," said Mr. Plomacy. " And take care, you Stubbs, and behave yourself. If I hear a row I shall know where it comes from. I'm up to you Barchester journeymen ; I know what stuff you're made of.'

And so Stabbs went off happy, pulling at the forelock of his shock head of hair in honour of the steward's clemency, and giving another double pull at it in honour of the farmer's kindness. And as he went he swore within his grateful heart, that if ever Farmer Greenacre wanted a day's work done for nothing, he was the lad to do it for him. Which promise it was not probable that he would ever be called on to perform.

But Mr. Plomacy was not quite happy in his mind, for he thought of the unjust steward, and began to reflect whether he had not made for himself friends of the mammon of unrighteousness. This, however, did not interfere with the manner in which he performed his duties at the bottom of the long board; nor did Mr. Greenacre perform his the worse at the top on account of the good wishes of Stubbs the plasterer. Moreover, the guests did not think it anything amiss when Mr. Plomacy, rising to say grace, prayed that God would make them all truly thankful for the good things which Madam Thorne in her great liberality had set before them!

All this time the quality in the tent on the lawn were getting on swimmingly; that is, if champagne without restriction can enable quality folk to swim. Sir Harkaway Gorse proposed the health of Miss Thorne, and likened her to a blood race-horse, always in condition, and not to be tired down by any amount of work. Mr. Thorne returned thanks, saying he hoped his sister would always be found able to run when called upon, and then gave the health and prosperity of the De Courcy family. His sister was very much honoured by seeing so many of them at her poor board. They were all aware that important avocations made the absence of the earl necessary. As his duty to his prince had called him from his family hearth, he, Mr. Thorne, could not venture to regret that he did not see him at Ullathorne; but nevertheless he would venture to say — that was to express a wish — an opinion he meant to say —— And so Mr. Thorne became somewhat gravelled, as country gentlemen in similar circumstances usually do; but he ultimately sat down, declaring that he had much satisfaction in drinking the noble earl's health, together with that of the countess, and all the family of De Courcy castle.

And then the Honourable George returned thanks. We will not follow him through the different periods of his somewhat irregular eloquence. Those immediately in his neighbourhood found it at first rather difficult to get him on his legs, but much greater difficulty was soon experienced in inducing him to resume his seat. One of two arrangements should certainly be made in these days: either let all speech-making on festive occasions be utterly tabooed and made as it were impossible; or else let those who are to exercise the privilege be first subjected to a competing examination before the civil service examining commissioners. As it is now, the Honourable Georges do but little honour to our exertions in favour of British education.

In the dining-room the bishop went through the honours of the day with much more neatness and propriety. He also drank Miss Thorne's health, and did it in a manner becoming the bench which he adorned. The party there, was perhaps a little more dull, a shade less lively than that in the tent. But what was lost in mirth, was fully made up in decorum.

And so the banquets passed off at the various tables with great eclat and universal delight.

CHAP. XL.

ULLATHORNE SPORTS.—ACT II.

"THAT which has made them drunk, has made me bold." 'Twas thus that Mr. Slope encouraged himself, as he left the dining-room in pursuit of Eleanor. He had not indeed seen in that room any person really intoxicated; but there had been a good deal of wine drunk, and Mr. Slope had not hesitated to take his share, in order to screw himself up to the undertaking which he had in hand. He is not the first man who has thought it expedient to call in the assistance of Bacchus on such an occasion.

Eleanor was out through the window, and on the grass before she perceived that she was followed. Just at that moment the guests were nearly all occupied at the tables. Here and there were to be seen a constant couple or two, who preferred their own sweet discourse to the jingle of glasses, or the charms of rhetoric which fell from the mouths of the Honourable George and the bishop of Barchester; but the grounds were as nearly vacant as Mr. Slope could wish them to be.

Eleanor saw that she was pursued, and as a deer, when escape is no longer possible, will turn to bay and attack the hounds, so did she turn upon Mr. Slope.

"Pray don't let me take you from the room," said she, speaking with all the stiffness which she knew how to use. "I have come out to look for a friend. I must beg of you, Mr. Slope, to go back."

But Mr. Slope would not be thus entreated. He had observed all day that Mrs. Bold was not cordial to him, and this had to a certain extent oppressed him. But he did not deduce from this any assurance that his aspirations were in vain. He saw that she was angry with him. Might she not be so because he had so long tampered with her feelings,—might it not arise from his having, as he knew was the case, caused her name to be bruited about in conjunction with his own, without having given her the opportunity of confessing to the world that henceforth their names were to be one and the same? Poor lady! He had within him a certain Christian conscience-stricken feeling of remorse on this head. It might be that he had wronged her by his tardiness. He had, however, at the present moment imbibed too much of Mr. Thorne's champagne to have any inward misgivings. He was right in repeating the boast of Lady Macbeth : he was not drunk ; but he was bold enough for anything. It was a pity that in such a state he could not have encountered Mrs. Proudie.

"You must permit me to attend you," said he; "I could not think of allowing you to go alone."

"Indeed you must, Mr. Slope," said Eleanor still very stiffly; "for it is my special wish to be alone."

The time for letting the great secret escape him had already come. Mr. Slope saw that it must be now or never, and he was determined that it should be now. This was not his first attempt at winning a fair lady. He had been on his knees, looked un-utterable things with his eyes, and whispered honeyed words before this. Indeed he was somewhat an adept at these things, and had only to adapt to the perhaps different taste of Mrs. Bold the well-remembered rhapsodies which had once so much gratified Olivia Proudie.

"Do not ask me to leave you, Mrs. Bold," said he with an im-passioned look, impassioned and sanctified as well, with that sort of look which is not uncommon with gentlemen of Mr. Slope's school, and which may perhaps be called the tender-pious. "Do not ask me to leave you, till I have spoken a few words with which my heart is full ; which I have come hither purposely to say."

Eleanor saw how it was now. She knew directly what it was she was about to go through, and very miserable the knowledge made her. Of course she could refuse Mr. Slope, and there would be an end of that, one might say. But there would not be an end of it as far as Eleanor was concerned. The very fact of Mr. Slope's making an offer to her would be a triumph to the archdeacon, and in a great measure a vindication of Mr. Arabin's conduct. The widow could not bring herself to endure with patience the idea that she had been in the wrong. She had defended Mr. Slope, she had declared herself quite justified in admitting him among her acquaintance, had ridiculed the idea of his considering himself as more than an acquaintance, and had resented the archdeacon's caution in her behalf: now it was about to be proved to her in a manner sufficiently disagreeable that the archdeacon had been right, and she herself had been entirely wrong.

"I don't know what you can have to say to me, Mr. Slope, that you could not have said when we were sitting at table just now;" and she closed her lips, and steadied her eyeballs, and looked at him in a manner that ought to have frozen him.

But gentlemen are not easily frozen when they are full of champagne, and it would not at any time have been easy to freeze Mr. Slope.

"There are things, Mrs. Bold, which a man cannot well say before a crowd; which perhaps he cannot well say at any time; which indeed he may most fervently desire to get spoken, and which he may yet find it almost impossible to utter. It is such things as these, that I now wish to say to you;" and then the tender-pious look was repeated, with a little more emphasis even than before.

Eleanor had not found it practicable to stand stock still before the dining-room window, and there receive his offer in full view of Miss Thorne's guests. She had therefore in self-defence walked on, and thus Mr. Slope had gained his object of walking with her. He now offered her his arm.

"Thank you, Mr. Slope, I am much obliged to you; but for the very short time that I shall remain with you I shall prefer walking alone."

"And must it be so short?" said he; "must it be —"

"Yes," said Eleanor, interrupting him; "as short as possible, if you please, sir."

"I had hoped, Mrs. Bold — I had hoped —"

"Pray hope nothing, Mr. Slope, as far as I am concerned; pray do not; I do not know, and need not know what hope you mean. Our acquaintance is very slight, and will probably remain so. Pray, pray let that be enough; there is at any rate no necessity for us to quarrel."

Mrs. Bold was certainly treating Mr. Slope rather cavalierly, and he felt it so. She was rejecting him before he had offered himself, and informed him at the same time that he was taking a great deal too much on himself to be so familiar. She did not even make an attempt

> "From such a sharp and waspish word as 'no'
>   To pluck the sting."

He was still determined to be very tender and very pious, seeing that in spite of all Mrs. Bold had said to him, he not yet abandoned hope ; but he was inclined also to be somewhat angry. The widow was bearing herself, as he thought, with too high a hand, was speaking of herself in much too imperious a tone. She had clearly no idea that an honour was being conferred on her. Mr. Slope would be tender as long as he could, but he began to think, if that failed, it would not be amiss if he also mounted himself for a while on his high horse. Mr. Slope could undoubtedly be very tender, but he could be very savage also, and he knew his own abilities.

"That is cruel," said he, "and unchristian too. The worst of us are all still bidden to hope. What have I done that you should pass on me so severe a sentence?" and then he paused a moment, during which the widow walked steadily on with measured step, saying nothing further.

"Beautiful woman," at last he burst forth ; "beautiful woman, you cannot pretend to be ignorant that I adore you. Yes, Eleanor, yes, I love you. I love you with the truest affection which man can bear to woman. Next to my hopes of heaven are my hopes of possessing you." (Mr. Slope's memory here played him false, or he would not have omitted the deanery.) "How sweet to walk to heaven with you by my side, with you for my guide, mutual guides. Say, Eleanor, dearest Eleanor, shall we walk that sweet path together?"

Eleanor had no intention of ever walking together with Mr. Slope on any other path than that special one of Miss Thorne's which they now occupied ; but as she had been unable to prevent the expression of Mr. Slope's wishes and aspirations, she resolved to hear him out to the end, before she answered him.

"Ah! Eleanor," he continued, and it seemed to be his idea that as he had once found courage to pronounce her Christian name, he could not utter it often enough. "Ah! Eleanor, will it not be sweet, with the Lord's assistance, to travel hand in hand through this mortal valley which his mercies will make pleasant to us, till hereafter we shall dwell together at the foot of his throne?

And then a more tenderly pious glance than ever beamed from the lover's eyes.   "Ah ! Eleanor—"

" My name, Mr. Slope, is Mrs. Bold," said Eleanor, who, though determined to hear out the tale of his love, was too much disgusted by his blasphemy to be able to bear much more of it.

" Sweetest angel, be not so cold," said he, and as he said it the champagne broke forth, and he contrived to pass his arm round her waist.   He did this with considerable cleverness, for up to this point Eleanor had contrived with tolerable success to keep her distance from him.   They had got into a walk nearly enveloped by shrubs, and Mr. Slope therefore no doubt considered that as they were now alone it was fitting that he should give her some outward demonstration of that affection of which he talked so much. It may perhaps be presumed that the same stamp of measures had been found to succeed with Olivia Proudie.   Be this as it may, it was not successful with Eleanor Bold.

She sprang from him as she would have jumped from an adder, but she did not spring far ; not, indeed, beyond arm's length ; and then, quick as thought, she raised her little hand and dealt him a box on the ear with such right good will, that it sounded among the trees like a miniature thunder-clap.

And now it is to be feared that every well-bred reader of these pages will lay down the book with disgust, feeling that, after all, the heroine is unworthy of sympathy.   She is a hoyden, one will say.   At any rate she is not a lady, another will exclaim.   I have suspected her all through, a third will declare ; she has no idea of the dignity of a matron ; or of the peculiar propriety which her position demands.   At one moment she is romping with young Stanhope ; then she is making eyes at Mr. Arabin ; anon she comes to fisty-cuffs with a third lover ; and all before she is yet a widow of two years' standing.

She cannot altogether be defended ; and yet it may be averred that she is not a hoyden, not given to romping, nor prone to boxing. It were to be wished devoutly that she had not struck Mr. Slope in the face.   In doing so she derogated from her dignity and committed herself.   Had she been educated in Belgravia, had she been brought up by any sterner mentor than that fond father, had she lived longer under the rule of a husband, she might, perhaps, have saved herself from this great fault.   As it was, the provocation was too much for her, the temptation to instant resentment of the insult too strong.   She was too keen in the feeling of independence a feeling dangerous for a young woman, but one in which her position peculiarly tempted her to indulge.   And then Mr. Slope's face, tinted with a deeper dye than usual by the wine he had drunk, simpering and puckering itself with pseudo piety and tender grimaces, seemed specially to call for such punishment. She had, too, a true instinct as to the man; he was capable of rebuke in this way and in no other. To him the blow from her little hand was as much an insult as a blow from a man would have been to another. It went direct to his pride. He conceived himself lowered in his dignity, and personally outraged. He could almost have struck at her again in his rage. Even the pain was a great annoyance to him, and the feeling that his clerical character had been wholly disregarded, sorely vexed him.

There are such men; men who can endure no taint on their personal self-respect, even from a woman;—men whose bodies are to themselves such sacred temples, that a joke against them is desecration, and a rough touch downright sacrilege. Mr. Slope was such a man; and, therefore, the slap on the face that he got from Eleanor was, as far as he was concerned, the fittest rebuke which could have been administered to him.

But, nevertheless, she should not have raised her hand against the man. Ladies' hands, so soft, so sweet, so delicious to the touch, so graceful to the eye, so gracious in their gentle doings, were not made to belabour men's faces. The moment the deed was done Eleanor felt that she had sinned against all propriety, and would have given little worlds to recall the blow. In her first agony of sorrow she all but begged the man's pardon. Her next impulse, however, and the one which she obeyed, was to run away.

"I never, never will speak another word to you," she said, gasping with emotion and the loss of breath which her exertion and violent feelings occasioned her, and so saying she put foot to the ground and ran quickly back along the path to the house.

But how shall I sing the divine wrath of Mr. Slope, or how invoke the tragic muse to describe the rage which swelled the celestial bosom of the bishop's chaplain? Such an undertaking by no means befits the low-heeled buskin of modern fiction. The painter put a veil over Agamemnon's face when called on to depict the father's grief at the early doom of his devoted daughter. The god, when he resolved to punish the rebellious winds, abstained from mouthing empty threats. We will not attempt to tell with what mighty surgings of the inner heart Mr. Slope swore to revenge himself on the woman who had disgraced him, nor will we vainly strive to depict his deep agony of soul.

There he is, however, alone in the garden walk, and we must contrive to bring him out of it. He was not willing to come forth quite at once. His cheek was stinging with the weight of Eleanor's fingers, and he fancied that every one who looked at him would be able to see on his face the traces of what he had endured. He stood awhile, becoming redder and redder with rage. He stood motionless, undecided, glaring with his eyes, thinking of the pains and penalties of Hades, and meditating how he might best devote his enemy to the infernal gods with all the passion of his accustomed eloquence. He longed in his heart to be preaching at her. 'Twas thus that he was ordinarily avenged of sinning mortal men and women. Could he at once have ascended his Sunday rostrum and fulminated at her such denunciations as his spirit delighted in, his bosom would have been greatly eased.

But how preach to Mr. Thorne's laurels, or how preach indeed at all in such a vanity fair as this now going on at Ullathorne? And then he began to feel a righteous disgust at the wickedness of the doings around him. He had been justly chastised for lending, by his presence, a sanction to such worldly lures. The gaiety of society, the mirth of banquets, the laughter of the young, and the eating and drinking of the elders were, for awhile, without excuse in his sight. What had he now brought down upon himself by sojourning thus in the tents of the heathen? He had consorted with idolaters round the altars of Baal; and therefore a sore punishment had come upon him. He then thought of the Signora Neroni, and his soul within him was full of sorrow. He had an inkling — a true inkling — that he was a wicked, sinful man; but it led him in no right direction; he could admit no charity in his heart. He felt debasement coming on him, and he longed to shake it off, to rise up in his stirrup, to mount to high places and great power, that he might get up into a mighty pulpit and preach to the world a loud sermon against Mrs. Bold.

There he stood fixed to the gravel for about ten minutes. Fortune favoured him so far that no prying eyes came to look upon him in his misery. Then a shudder passed over his whole frame; he collected himself, and slowly wound his way round to the lawn, advancing along the path and not returning in the direction which Eleanor had taken. When he reached the tent he found the bishop standing there in conversation with the master of Lazarus. His lordship had come out to air himself after the exertion of his speech.

"This is very pleasant — very pleasant, my lord, is it not?" said Mr. Slope with his most gracious smile, and pointing to the tent; "very pleasant. It is delightful to see so many persons enjoying themselves so thoroughly.'

Mr. Slope thought he might force the bishop to introduce him to Dr. Gwynne. A very great example had declared and practised the wisdom of being everything to everybody, and Mr. Slope was desirous of following it. His maxim was never to lose a chance. The bishop, however, at the present moment was not very anxious to increase Mr. Slope's circle of acquaintance among his clerical brethren. He had his own reasons for dropping any marked allusion to his domestic chaplain, and he therefore made his shoulder rather cold for the occasion.

"Very, very," said he without turning round, or even deigning to look at Mr. Slope. "And therefore, Dr. Gwynne, I really think that you will find that the hebdomadal board will exercise as wide and as general an authority as at the present moment. I, for one, Dr. Gwynne ——"

"Dr. Gwynne," said Mr. Slope, raising his hat, and resolving not to be outwitted by such an insignificant little goose as the bishop of Barchester.

The master of Lazarus also raised his hat and bowed very politely to Mr. Slope. There is not a more courteous gentleman in the queen's dominions than the master of Lazarus.

"My lord," said Mr. Slope; "pray do me the honour of introducing me to Dr. Gwynne. The opportunity is too much in my favour to be lost."

The bishop had no help for it. "My chaplain, Dr. Gwynne," said he; "my present chaplain, Mr. Slope." He certainly made the introduction as unsatisfactory to the chaplain as possible, and by the use of the word present, seemed to indicate that Mr. Slope might probably not long enjoy the honour which he now held. But Mr. Slope cared nothing for this. He understood the innuendo, and disregarded it. It might probably come to pass that he would be in a situation to resign his chaplaincy before the bishop was in a situation to dismiss him from it. What need the future dean of Barchester care for the bishop, or for the bishop's wife? Had not Mr. Slope, just as he was entering Dr. Stanhope's carriage, received an all important note from Tom Towers of the Jupiter? had he not that note this moment in his pocket?

So disregarding the bishop, he began to open out a conversation with the master of Lazarus.

But suddenly an interruption came, not altogether unwelcome to Mr. Slope. One of the bishop's servants came up to his master's shoulder with a long, grave face, and whispered into the bishop's ear.

"What is it, John?" said the bishop.

"The dean, my lord; he is dead."

Mr. Slope had no further desire to converse with the master of Lazarus, and was very soon on his road back to Barchester.

Eleanor, as we have said, having declared her intention of never holding further communication with Mr. Slope, ran hurriedly back towards the house. The thought, however, of what she had done grieved her greatly, and she could not abstain from bursting into tears. 'Twas thus she played the second act in that day's melodrame.

CHAP. XLI.

MRS. BOLD CONFIDES HER SORROW TO HER FRIEND MISS STANHOPE.

WHEN Mrs. Bold came to the end of the walk and faced the lawn, she began to bethink herself what she should do. Was she to wait there till Mr. Slope caught her, or was she to go in among the crowd with tears in her eyes and passion in her face? She might in truth have stood there long enough without any reasonable fear of further immediate persecution from Mr. Slope; but we are all inclined to magnify the bugbears which frighten us. In her present state of dread she did not know of what atrocity he might venture to be guilty. Had any one told her a week ago that he would have put his arm round her waist at this party of Miss Thorne's, she would have been utterly incredulous. Had she been informed that he would be seen on the following Sunday walking down the High-street in a scarlet coat and top-boots, she would not have thought such a phenomenon more improbable.

But this improbable iniquity he had committed; and now there was nothing she could not believe of him. In the first place it was quite manifest that he was tipsy; in the next place, it was to be taken as proved that all his religion was sheer hypocrisy; and finally the man was utterly shameless. She therefore stood watching for the sound of his footfall, not without some fear that he might creep out at her suddenly from among the bushes.

As she thus stood, she saw Charlotte Stanhope at a little distance from her walking quickly across the grass. Eleanor's handkerchief was in her hand, and putting it to her face so as to conceal her tears, she ran across the lawn and joined her friend.

"Oh, Charlotte," she said, almost too much out of breath to speak very plainly; "I am so glad I have found you."

"Glad you have found me!" said Charlotte, laughing: "that's a good joke. Why Bertie and I have been looking for you everywhere. He swears that you have gone off with Mr. Slope, and is now on the point of hanging himself."

"Oh, Charlotte, don't," said Mrs. Bold.

"Why, my child, what on earth is the matter with you!" said Miss Stanhope, perceiving that Eleanor's hand trembled on her own arm, and finding also that her companion was still half choked by tears. "Goodness heaven! something has distressed you. What is it? What can I do for you?"

Eleanor answered her only by a sort of spasmodic gurgle in her throat. She was a good deal upset, as people say, and could not at the moment collect herself.

"Come here, this way, Mrs. Bold; come this way, and we shall not be seen. What has happened to vex you so? What can I do for you? Can Bertie do anything?"

"Oh, no, no, no, no," said Eleanor. "There is nothing to be done. Only that horrid man ——"

"What horrid man?" asked Charlotte.

There are some moments in life in which both men and women feel themselves imperatively called on to make a confidence; in which not to do so requires a disagreeable resolution and also a disagreeable suspicion. There are people of both sexes who never make confidences; who are never tempted by momentary circumstances to disclose their secrets; but such are generally dull, close, unimpassioned spirits, "gloomy gnomes, who live in cold dark mines." There was nothing of the gnome about Eleanor; and she therefore resolved to tell Charlotte Stanhope the whole story about Mr. Slope.

"That horrid man; that Mr. Slope," said she: "did you not see that he followed me out of the dining-room?"

"Of course I did, and was sorry enough; but I could not help it. I knew you would be annoyed. But you and Bertie managed it badly between you."

"It was not his fault nor mine either. You know how I disliked the idea of coming in the carriage with that man."

"I am sure I am very sorry if that has led to it."

"I don't know what has led to it," said Eleanor, almost crying again. "But it has not been my fault."

"But what has he done, my dear?"

"He's an abominable, horrid, hypocritical man, and it would serve him right to tell the bishop all about it."

"Believe me, if you want to do him an injury, you had far better tell Mrs. Proudie. But what did he do, Mrs. Bold?"

"Ugh!" exclaimed Eleanor.

"Well, I must confess he's not very nice," said Charlotte Stanhope.

"Nice!" said Eleanor. "He is the most fulsome, fawning, abominable man I ever saw. What business had he to come to me?—I that never gave him the slightest tittle of encouragement —I that always hated him, though I did take his part when others ran him down."

"That's just where it is, my dear. He has heard that, and therefore fancied that of course you were in love with him."

This was wormwood to Eleanor. It was in fact the very thing which all her friends had been saying for the last month past; and which experience now proved to be true. Eleanor resolved within herself that she would never again take any man's part. The world with all its villany, and all its ill-nature, might wag as it liked; she would not again attempt to set crooked things straight.

"But what did he do, my dear?" said Charlotte, who was really rather interested in the subject.

"He—he—he—"

"Well—come, it can't have been anything so very horrid, for the man was not tipsy."

"Oh, I am sure he was," said Eleanor. "I am sure he must have been tipsy."

"Well, I declare I didn't observe it. But what was it, my love?"

"Why, I believe I can hardly tell you. He talked such horrid stuff that you never heard the like; about religion, and heaven, and love.—Oh, dear,—he is such a nasty man."

"I can easily imagine the sort of stuff he would talk. Well,— and then—?"

"And then—he took hold of me."

"Took hold of you?"

"Yes,—he somehow got close to me, and took hold of me—"

"By the waist?"

"Yes," said Eleanor shuddering.

"And then—"

"Then I jumped away from him, and gave him a slap on the face; and ran away along the path, till I saw you."

"Ha, ha, ha!" Charlotte Stanhope laughed heartily at the finale to the tragedy. It was delightful to her to think that Mr. Slope had had his ears boxed. She did not quite appreciate the feeling which made her friend so unhappy at the result of the interview. To her thinking, the matter had ended happily enough as regarded the widow, who indeed was entitled to some sort of triumph among her friends. Whereas to Mr. Slope would be due all those jibes and jeers which would naturally follow such an affair. His friends would ask him whether his ears tingled whenever he saw a widow; and he would be cautioned that beautiful things were made to be looked at, and not to be touched.

Such were Charlotte Stanhope's views on such matters; but she did not at the present moment clearly explain them to Mrs. Bold. Her object was to endear herself to her friend; and therefore, having had her laugh, she was ready enough to offer sympathy. Could Bertie do anything? Should Bertie speak to the man, and warn him that in future he must behave with more decorum? Bertie, indeed, she declared, would be more angry than any one else when he heard to what insult Mrs. Bold had been subjected.

"But you won't tell him?" said Mrs. Bold with a look of horror.

"Not if you don't like it," said Charlotte; "but considering everything, I would strongly advise it. If you had a brother, you know, it would be unnecessary. But it is very right that Mr. Slope should know that you have somebody by you that will, and can protect you."

"But my father is here."

"Yes, but it is so disagreeable for clergymen to have to quarrel with each other; and circumstanced as your father is just at this moment, it would be very inexpedient that there should be anything unpleasant between him and Mr. Slope. Surely you and Bertie are intimate enough for you to permit him to take your part."

Charlotte Stanhope was very anxious that her brother should at once on that very day settle matters with his future wife. Things had now come to that point between him and his father, and between him and his creditors, that he must either do so, or leave Barchester; either do that, or go back to his unwashed associates, dirty lodgings, and poor living at Carrara. Unless he could provide himself with an income, he must go to Carrara, or to ——. His father the prebendary had not said this in so many words, but had he done so, he could not have signified it more plainly.

Such being the state of the case, it was very necessary that no more time should be lost. Charlotte had seen her brother's apathy, when he neglected to follow Mrs. Bold out of the room, with anger which she could hardly suppress. It was grievous to think that

Mr. Slope should have so distanced him. Charlotte felt that she had played her part with sufficient skill. She had brought them together and induced such a degree of intimacy, that her brother was really relieved from all trouble and labour in the matter. And moreover, it was quite plain that Mrs. Bold was very fond of Bertie. And now it was plain enough also that he had nothing to fear from his rival Mr. Slope.

There was certainly an awkwardness in subjecting Mrs. Bold to a second offer on the same day. It would have been well perhaps to have put the matter off for a week, could a week have been spared. But circumstances are frequently too peremptory to be arranged as we would wish to arrange them; and such was the case now. This being so, could not this affair of Mr. Slope's be turned to advantage? Could it not be made the excuse for bringing Bertie and Mrs. Bold into still closer connection; into such close connection that they could not fail to throw themselves into each other's arms? Such was the game which Miss Stanhope now at a moment's notice resolved to play.

And very well she played it. In the first place, it was arranged that Mr. Slope should not return in the Stanhopes' carriage to Barchester. It so happened that Mr. Slope was already gone, but of that of course they knew nothing. The signora should be induced to go first, with only the servants and her sister, and Bertie should take Mr. Slope's place in the second journey. Bertie was to be told in confidence of the whole affair, and when the carriage was gone off with its first load, Eleanor was to be left under Bertie's special protection, so as to insure her from any further aggression from Mr. Slope. While the carriage was getting ready, Bertie was to seek out that gentleman and make him understand that he must provide himself with another conveyance back to Barchester. Their immediate object should be to walk about together in search of Bertie. Bertie, in short, was to be the Pegasus on whose wings they were to ride out of their present dilemma.

There was a warmth of friendship and cordial kindliness in all this, that was very soothing to the widow; but yet, though she gave way to it, she was hardly reconciled to doing so. It never occurred to her, that now that she had killed one dragon, another was about to spring up in her path; she had no remote idea that she would have to encounter another suitor in her proposed protector, but she hardly liked the thought of putting herself so much into the hands of young Stanhope. She felt that if she wanted protection, she should go to her father. She felt that she should ask him to provide a carriage for her back to Barchester. Mrs.

Clantantram she knew would give her a seat. She knew that she should not throw herself entirely upon friends whose friendship dated as it were but from yesterday. But yet she could not say "no," to one who was so sisterly in her kindness, so eager in her good nature, so comfortably sympathetic as Charlotte Stanhope. And thus she gave way to all the propositions made to her.

They first went into the dining-room, looking for their champion, and from thence to the drawing-room. Here they found Mr. Arabin, still hanging over the signora's sofa; or, rather, they found him sitting near her head, as a physician might have sat, had the lady been his patient. There was no other person in the room. The guests were some in the tent, some few still in the dining-room, some at the bows and arrows, but most of them walking with Miss Thorne through the park, and looking at the games that were going on.

All that had passed, and was passing between Mr. Arabin and the lady, it is unnecessary to give in detail. She was doing with him as she did with all others. It was her mission to make fools of men, and she was pursuing her mission with Mr. Arabin. She had almost got him to own his love for Mrs. Bold, and had subsequently almost induced him to acknowledge a passion for herself. He, poor man, was hardly aware what he was doing or saying, hardly conscious whether he was in heaven or in hell. So little had he known of female attractions of that peculiar class which the signora owned, that he became affected with a kind of temporary delirium, when first subjected to its power. He lost his head rather than his heart, and toppled about mentally, reeling in his ideas as a drunken man does on his legs. She had whispered to him words that really meant nothing, but which coming from such beautiful lips, and accompanied by such lustrous glances, seemed to have a mysterious significance, which he felt though he could not understand.

In being thus be-sirened, Mr. Arabin behaved himself very differently from Mr. Slope. The signora had said truly, that the two men were the contrasts of each other ; that the one was all for action, the other all for thought. Mr. Slope, when this lady laid upon his senses the overpowering breath of her charms, immediately attempted to obtain some fruition, to achieve some mighty triumph. He began by catching at her hand, and progressed by kissing it. He made vows of love, and asked for vows in return. He promised everlasting devotion, knelt before her, and swore that had she been on Mount Ida, Juno would have had no cause to hate the offspring of Venus. But Mr. Arabin uttered no oaths, kept his hand mostly in his trousers pocket, and had no more thought of kissing Madam Neroni, than of kissing the Countess De Courcy.

As soon as Mr. Arabin saw Mrs. Bold enter the room, he blushed and rose from his chair; then he sat down again, and then again got up. The signora saw the blush at once, and smiled at the poor victim, but Eleanor was too much confused to see anything.

"Oh, Madeline," said Charlotte, "I want to speak to you particularly; we must arrange about the carriage, you know;" and she stooped down to whisper to her sister. Mr. Arabin immediately withdrew to a little distance, and as Charlotte had in fact much to explain before she could make the new carriage arrangement intelligible, he had nothing to do but to talk to Mrs. Bold.

"We have had a very pleasant party," said he, using the tone he would have used had he declared that the sun was shining very brightly, or the rain falling very fast.

"Very," said Eleanor, who never in her life had passed a more unpleasant day.

"I hope Mr. Harding has enjoyed himself."

"Oh, yes, very much," said Eleanor, who had not seen her father since she parted from him soon after her arrival.

"He returns to Barchester to-night, I suppose."

"Yes, I believe so; that is, I think he is staying at Plumstead."

"Oh, staying at Plumstead," said Mr. Arabin.

"He came from there this morning. I believe he is going back; he didn't exactly say, however."

"I hope Mrs. Grantly is quite well."

"She seemed to be quite well. She is here; that is, unless she has gone away."

"Oh, yes, to be sure. I was talking to her. Looking very well indeed." Then there was a considerable pause; for Charlotte could not at once make Madeline understand why she was to be sent home in a hurry without her brother.

"Are you returning to Plumstead, Mrs. Bold?" Mr. Arabin merely asked this by way of making conversation, but he immediately perceived that he was approaching dangerous ground.

"No," said Mrs. Bold, very quietly; "I am going home to Barchester."

"Oh, ah, yes. I had forgotten that you had returned." And then Mr. Arabin, finding it impossible to say anything further, stood silent till Charlotte had completed her plans, and Mrs. Bold stood equally silent, intently occupied as it appeared in the arrangement of her rings.

And yet these two people were thoroughly in love with each

other; and though one was a middle-aged clergyman, and the other a lady at any rate past the wishy-washy bread-and-butter period of life, they were as unable to tell their own minds to each other as any Damon and Phillis, whose united ages would not make up that to which Mr. Arabin had already attained.

Madeline Neroni consented to her sister's proposal, and then the two ladies again went off in quest of Bertie Stanhope.

CHAP. XLII.

ULLATHORNE SPORTS.—ACT III.

AND now Miss Thorne's guests were beginning to take their departure, and the amusement of those who remained was becoming slack. It was getting dark, and ladies in morning costumes were thinking that if they were to appear by candle-light they ought to readjust themselves. Some young gentlemen had been heard to talk so loud that prudent mammas determined to retire judiciously, and the more discreet of the male sex, whose libations had been moderate, felt that there was not much more left for them to do.

Morning parties, as a rule, are failures. People never know how to get away from them gracefully. A picnic on an island or a mountain or in a wood may perhaps be permitted. There is no master of the mountain bound by courtesy to bid you stay while in his heart he is longing for your departure. But in a private house or in private grounds a morning party is a bore. One is called on to eat and drink at unnatural hours. One is obliged to give up the day which is useful, and is then left without resource for the evening which is useless. One gets home fagged and *désœuvré*, and yet at an hour too early for bed. There is no comfortable resource left. Cards in these genteel days are among the things tabooed, and a rubber of whist is impracticable.

All this began now to be felt. Some young people had come with some amount of hope that they might get up a dance in the evening, and were unwilling to leave till all such hope was at an end. Others, fearful of staying longer than was expected, had ordered their carriages early, and were doing their best to go, solicitous for their servants and horses. The countess and her noble brood were among the first to leave, and as regarded the Hon. George, it was certainly time that he did so. Her ladyship was in a great fret and fume. Those horrid roads would, she was sure, be the death of her if unhappily she were caught in them by the dark night. The lamps she was assured were good, but no lamp could withstand the jolting of the roads of East Barsetshire. The De Courcy property lay in the western division of the county.

Mrs. Proudie could not stay when the countess was gone. So the bishop was searched for by the Revs. Messrs. Grey and Green, and found in one corner of the tent enjoying himself thoroughly in a disquisition on the hebdomadal board. He obeyed, however, the behests of his lady without finishing the sentence in which he was promising to Dr. Gwynne that his authority at Oxford should remain unimpaired; and the episcopal horses turned their noses towards the palatial stables. Then the Grantlys went. Before they did so, Mr. Harding managed to whisper a word into his daughter's ear. Of course, he said he would undeceive the Grantlys as to that foolish rumour about Mr. Slope.

"No, no, no," said Eleanor; "pray do not—pray wait till I see you. You will be home in a day or two, and then I will explain to you everything."

"I shall be home to-morrow," said he.

"I am so glad," said Eleanor. "You will come and dine with me, and then we shall be so comfortable."

Mr. Harding promised. He did not exactly know what there was to be explained, or why Dr. Grantly's mind should not be disabused of the mistake into which he had fallen; but nevertheless he promised. He owed some reparation to his daughter, and he thought that he might best make it by obedience.

And thus the people were thinning off by degrees, as Charlotte and Eleanor walked about in quest of Bertie. Their search might have been long, had they not happened to hear his voice. He was comfortably ensconced in the ha-ha, with his back to the sloping side, smoking a cigar, and eagerly engaged in conversation with some youngster from the further side of the county, whom he had never met before, who was also smoking under Bertie's pupilage, and listening with open ears to an account given by his companion of some of the pastimes of Eastern clime.

"Bertie, I am seeking you everywhere," said Charlotte. "Come up here at once."

Bertie looked up out of the ha-ha, and saw the two ladies before him. As there was nothing for him but to obey, he got up and threw away his cigar. From the first moment of his acquaintance with her he had liked Eleanor Bold. Had he been left to his own devices, had she been penniless, and had it then been quite out of the question that he should marry her, he would most probably have fallen violently in love with her. But now he could not help regarding her somewhat as he did the marble workshops at Carrara, as he had done his easel and palette, as he had done the lawyer's chambers in London; in fact, as he had invariably regarded everything by which it had been proposed to him to obtain the means of living. Eleanor Bold appeared before him, no longer as a beautiful woman, but as a new profession called matrimony. It was a profession indeed requiring but little labour, and one in which an income was insured to him. But nevertheless he had been as it were goaded on to it; his sister had talked to him of Eleanor, just as she had talked of busts and portraits. Bertie did not dislike money, but he hated the very thought of earning it. He was now called away from his pleasant cigar to earn it, by offering himself as a husband to Mrs. Bold. The work indeed was made easy enough; for in lieu of his having to seek the widow, the widow had apparently come to seek him.

He made some sudden absurd excuse to his auditor, and then throwing away his cigar, climbed up the wall of the ha-ha and joined the ladies on the lawn.

"Come and give Mrs. Bold an arm," said Charlotte, "while I set you on a piece of duty which, as a preux chevalier, you must immediately perform. Your personal danger will, I fear, be insignificant, as your antagonist is a clergyman."

Bertie immediately gave his arm to Eleanor, walking between her and his sister. He had lived too long abroad to fall into the Englishman's habit of offering each an arm to two ladies at the same time; a habit, by the bye, which foreigners regard as an approach to bigamy, or a sort of incipient Mormonism.

The little history of Mr. Slope's misconduct was then told to Bertie by his sister, Eleanor's ears tingling the while. And well they might tingle. If it were necessary to speak of the outrage at all, why should it be spoken of to such a person as Mr. Stanhope, and why in her own hearing? She knew she was wrong, and was unhappy and dispirited, and yet she could think of no way to extricate herself, no way to set herself right. Charlotte spared her as much as she possibly could, spoke of the whole thing as though Mr. Slope had taken a glass of wine too much, said that of course there would be nothing more about it, but that steps must be taken to exclude Mr. Slope from the carriage.

"Mrs. Bold need be under no alarm about that," said Bertie,

"for Mr. Slope has gone this hour past. He told me that business made it necessary that he should start at once for Barchester."

"He is not so tipsy, at any rate, but what he knows his fault," said Charlotte. "Well, my dear, that is one difficulty over. Now I'll leave you with your true knight, and get Madeline off as quickly as I can. The carriage is here, I suppose, Bertie?"

"It has been here for the last hour."

"That's well. Good bye, my dear. Of course you'll come in to tea. I shall trust to you to bring her, Bertie; even by force if necessary." And so saying, Charlotte ran off across the lawn, leaving her brother alone with the widow.

As Miss Stanhope went off, Eleanor bethought herself that, as Mr. Slope had taken his departure, there no longer existed any necessity for separating Mr. Stanhope from his sister Madeline, who so much needed his aid. It had been arranged that he should remain so as to preoccupy Mr. Slope's place in the carriage, and act as a social policeman to effect the exclusion of that disagreeable gentleman. But Mr. Slope had effected his own exclusion, and there was no possible reason now why Bertie should not go with his sister. At least Eleanor saw none, and she said as much.

"Oh, let Charlotte have her own way," said he. "She has arranged it, and there will be no end of confusion, if we make another change. Charlotte always arranges everything in our house; and rules us like a despot."

"But the signora?" said Eleanor.

"Oh, the signora can do very well without me. Indeed, she will have to do without me," he added, thinking rather of his studies in Carrara, than of his Barchester hymeneals.

"Why, you are not going to leave us?" asked Eleanor.

It has been said that Bertie Stanhope was a man without principle. He certainly was so. He had no power of using active mental exertion to keep himself from doing evil. Evil had no ugliness in his eyes; virtue no beauty. He was void of any of these feelings which actuate men to do good. But he was perhaps equally void of those which actuate men to do evil. He got into debt with utter recklessness, thinking nothing as to whether the tradesmen would ever be paid or not. But he did not invent active schemes of deceit for the sake of extracting the goods of others. If a man gave him credit, that was the man's look-out; Bertie Stanhope troubled himself nothing further. In borrowing money he did the same; he gave people references to "his governor;" told them that the "old chap" had a good income;

and agreed to pay sixty per cent. for the accommodation. All
this he did without a scruple of conscience; but then he never
contrived active villany.

In this affair of his marriage, it had been represented to him as
a matter of duty that he ought to put himself in possession of Mrs.
Bold's hand and fortune; and at first he had so regarded it.
About her he had thought but little. It was the customary thing
for men situated as he was to marry for money, and there was no
reason why he should not do what others around him did. And
so he consented. But now he began to see the matter in another
light. He was setting himself down to catch this woman, as a cat
sits to catch a mouse. He was to catch her, and swallow her up,
her and her child, and her houses and land, in order that he might
live on her instead of on his father. There was a cold, calculating,
cautious cunning about this quite at variance with Bertie's
character. The prudence of the measure was quite as antagonistic
to his feelings as the iniquity.

And then, should he be successful, what would be the reward?
Having satisfied his creditors with half of the widow's fortune, he
would be allowed to sit down quietly at Barchester, keeping
economical house with the remainder. His duty would be to rock
the cradle of the late Mr. Bold's child, and his highest excitement
a demure party at Plumstead rectory, should it ultimately turn
out that the archdeacon would be sufficiently reconciled to receive
him.

There was very little in the programme to allure such a man as
Bertie Stanhope. Would not the Carrara workshop, or whatever
worldly career fortune might have in store for him, would not
almost anything be better than this? The lady herself was undoubtedly all that was desirable; but the most desirable lady
becomes nauseous when she has to be taken as a pill. He was
pledged to his sister, however, and let him quarrel with whom he
would, it behoved him not to quarrel with her. If she were lost
to him all would be lost that he could ever hope to derive henceforward from the paternal roof-tree. His mother was apparently
indifferent to his weal or woe, to his wants or his warfare. His
father's brow got blacker and blacker from day to day, as the old
man looked at his hopeless son. And as for Madeline—poor
Madeline, whom of all of them he liked the best,—she had enough
to do to shift for herself. No; come what might, he must cling to
his sister and obey her behests, let them be ever so stern; or at
the very least seem to obey them. Could not some happy deceit
bring him through in this matter so that he might save appearances

with his sister, and yet not betray the widow to her ruin? What if he made a confederate of Eleanor? 'Twas in this spirit that Bertie Stanhope set about his wooing.

"But you are not going to leave Barchester?" asked Eleanor.

"I do not know," he replied; "I hardly know yet what I am going to do. But it is at any rate certain that I must do something."

"You mean about your profession?" said she.

"Yes, about my profession, if you can call it one."

"And is it not one?" said Eleanor. "Were I a man, I know none I should prefer to it, except painting. And I believe the one is as much in your power as the other."

"Yes, just about equally so," said Bertie, with a little touch of inward satire directed at himself. He knew in his heart that he would never make a penny by either.

"I have often wondered, Mr. Stanhope, why you do not exert yourself more," said Eleanor, who felt a friendly fondness for the man with whom she was walking. "But I know it is very impertinent in me to say so."

"Impertinent!" said he. "Not so, but much too kind. It is much too kind in you to take any interest in so idle a scamp."

"But you are not a scamp, though you are perhaps idle; and I do take an interest in you; a very great interest," she added, in a voice which almost made him resolve to change his mind. "And when I call you idle, I know you are only so for the present moment. Why can't you settle steadily to work here in Barchester?"

"And make busts of the bishop, dean and chapter? or perhaps, if I achieve a great success, obtain a commission to put up an elaborate tombstone over a prebendary's widow, a dead lady with a Grecian nose, a bandeau, and an intricate lace veil; lying of course on a marble sofa, from among the legs of which Death will be creeping out and poking at his victim with a small toasting-fork."

Eleanor laughed; but yet she thought that if the surviving prebendary paid the bill, the object of the artist as a professional man would, in a great measure, be obtained.

"I don't know about the dean and chapter and the prebendary's widow," said Eleanor. "Of course you must take them as they come. But the fact of your having a great cathedral in which such ornaments are required, could not but be in your favour."

"No real artist could descend to the ornamentation of a cathedral," said Bertie, who had his ideas of the high ecstatic ambition of art, as indeed all artists have, who are not in receipt of a good income. "Buildings should be fitted to grace the sculpture, not the sculpture to grace the building."

"Yes, when the work of art is good enough to merit it. Do you, Mr. Stanhope, do something sufficiently excellent, and we ladies of Barchester will erect for it a fitting receptacle. Come, what shall the subject be?"

"I'll put you in your pony chair, Mrs. Bold, as Dannecker put Ariadne on her lion. Only you must promise to sit for me."

"My ponies are too tame, I fear, and my broad-brimmed straw hat will not look so well in marble as the lace veil of the prebendary's wife."

"If you will not consent to that, Mrs. Bold, I will consent to try no other subject in Barchester."

"You are determined, then, to push your fortune in other lands?"

"I am determined," said Bertie, slowly and significantly, as he tried to bring up his mind to a great resolve; "I am determined in this matter to be guided wholly by you."

"Wholly by me!" said Eleanor, astonished at, and not quite liking, his altered manner.

"Wholly by you," said Bertie, dropping his companion's arm, and standing before her on the path. In their walk they had come exactly to the spot in which Eleanor had been provoked into slapping Mr. Slope's face. Could it be possible that this place was peculiarly unpropitious to her comfort? could it be possible that she should here have to encounter yet another amorous swain?

"If you will be guided by me, Mr. Stanhope, you will set yourself down to steady and persevering work, and you will be ruled by your father as to the place in which it will be most advisable for you to do so."

"Nothing could be more prudent, if only it were practicable. But now, if you will let me, I will tell you how it is that I will be guided by you, and why. Will you let me tell you?"

"I really do not know what you can have to tell."

"No,—you cannot know. It is impossible that you should. But we have been very good friends, Mrs. Bold, have we not?"

"Yes, I think we have," said she, observing in his demeanour an earnestness very unusual with him.

"You were kind enough to say just now that you took an interest in me, and I was perhaps vain enough to believe you."

"There is no vanity in that; I do so as your sister's brother,— and as my own friend also."

"Well, I don't deserve that you should feel so kindly towards me," said Bertie; "but upon my word I am very grateful for it," and he paused awhile, hardly knowing how to introduce the subject that he had in hand.

And it was no wonder that he found it difficult. He had to make known to his companion the scheme that had been prepared to rob her of her wealth; he had to tell her that he had intended to marry her without loving her, or else that he loved her without intending to marry her; and he had also to bespeak from her not only his own pardon, but also that of his sister, and induce Mrs. Bold to protest in her future communion with Charlotte that an offer had been duly made to her and duly rejected.

Bertie Stanhope was not prone to be very diffident of his own conversational powers, but it did seem to him that he was about to tax them almost too far. He hardly knew where to begin, and he hardly knew where he should end.

By this time Eleanor was again walking on slowly by his side, not taking his arm as she had heretofore done, but listening very intently for whatever Bertie might have to say to her.

"I wish to be guided by you," said he; "and, indeed, in this matter, there is no one else who can set me right."

"Oh, that must be nonsense," said she.

"Well, listen to me now, Mrs. Bold; and if you can help it, pray don't be angry with me."

"Angry!" said she.

"Oh, indeed you will have cause to be so. You know how very much attached to you my sister Charlotte is."

Eleanor acknowledged that she did.

"Indeed she is; I never knew her to love any one so warmly on so short an acquaintance. You know also how well she loves me?"

Eleanor now made no answer, but she felt the blood tingle in her cheek as she gathered from what he said the probable result of this double-barrelled love on the part of Miss Stanhope.

"I am her only brother, Mrs. Bold, and it is not to be wondered at that she should love me. But you do not yet know Charlotte,— you do not know how entirely the well-being of our family hangs on her. Without her to manage for us, I do not know how we should get on from day to day. You cannot yet have observed all this."

Eleanor had indeed observed a good deal of this; she did not however now say so, but allowed him to proceed with his story.

"You cannot therefore be surprised that Charlotte should be most anxious to do the best for us all."

Eleanor said that she was not at all surprised.

"And she has had a very difficult game to play, Mrs. Bold— a very difficult game. Poor Madeline's unfortunate marriage and terrible accident, my mother's ill health, my father's absence from

England, and last, and worst perhaps, my own roving, idle spirit have almost been too much for her. You cannot wonder if among all her cares one of the foremost is to see me settled in the world."

Eleanor on this occasion expressed no acquiescence. She certainly supposed that a formal offer was to be made, and could not but think that so singular an exordium was never before made by a gentleman in a similar position. Mr. Slope had annoyed her by the excess of his ardour. It was quite clear that no such danger was to be feared from Mr. Stanhope. Prudential motives alone actuated him. Not only was he about to make love because his sister told him, but he also took the precaution of explaining all this before he began. 'Twas thus, we may presume, that the matter presented itself to Mrs. Bold.

When he had got so far, Bertie began poking the gravel with a little cane which he carried. He still kept moving on, but very slowly, and his companion moved slowly by his side, not inclined to assist him in the task the performance of which appeared to be difficult to him.

"Knowing how fond she is of yourself, Mrs. Bold, cannot you imagine what scheme should have occurred to her?"

"I can imagine no better scheme, Mr. Stanhope, than the one I proposed to you just now."

"No," said he, somewhat lack-a-daisically; "I suppose that would be the best; but Charlotte thinks another plan might be joined with it.—She wants me to marry you."

A thousand remembrances flashed across Eleanor's mind all in a moment,—how Charlotte had talked about and praised her brother, how she had continually contrived to throw the two of them together, how she had encouraged all manner of little intimacies, how she had with singular cordiality persisted in treating Eleanor as one of the family. All this had been done to secure her comfortable income for the benefit of one of the family!

Such a feeling as this is very bitter when it first impresses itself on a young mind. To the old such plots and plans, such matured schemes for obtaining the goods of this world without the trouble of earning them, such long-headed attempts to convert "tuum" into "meum," are the ways of life to which they are accustomed. 'Tis thus that many live, and it therefore behoves all those who are well to do in the world to be on their guard against those who are not. With them it is the success that disgusts, not the attempt. But Eleanor had not yet learnt to look on her money as a source of danger; she had not begun to regard herself as fair game to be hunted down by hungry gentlemen. She had enjoyed the society of the Stanhopes, she had greatly liked the cordiality of Charlotte, and had been happy in her new friends. Now she saw the cause of all this kindness, and her mind was opened to a new phase of human life.

"Miss Stanhope," said she, haughtily, "has been contriving for me a great deal of honour, but she might have saved herself the trouble. I am not sufficiently ambitious."

"Pray don't be angry with her, Mrs. Bold," said he, "or with me either."

"Certainly not with you, Mr. Stanhope," said she, with considerable sarcasm in her tone. "Certainly not with you."

"No, — nor with her," said he, imploringly.

"And why, may I ask you, Mr. Stanhope, have you told me this singular story? For I may presume I may judge by your manner of telling it, that—that—that you and your sister are not exactly of one mind on the subject."

"No, we are not."

"And if so," said Mrs. Bold, who was now really angry with the unnecessary insult which she thought had been offered to her, "and if so, why has it been worth your while to tell me all this?"

"I did once think, Mrs. Bold, — that you — that you——'

The widow now again became entirely impassive, and would not lend the slightest assistance to her companion.

"I did once think that you perhaps might, — might have been taught to regard me as more than a friend."

"Never!" said Mrs. Bold, "never. If I have ever allowed myself to do anything to encourage such an idea, I have been very much to blame, — very much to blame indeed."

"You never have," said Bertie, who really had a good-natured anxiety to make what he said as little unpleasant as possible. "You never have, and I have seen for some time that I had no chance; but my sister's hopes ran higher. I have not mistaken you, Mrs. Bold, though perhaps she has."

"Then why have you said all this to me?"

"Because I must not anger her."

"And will not this anger her? Upon my word, Mr. Stanhope, I do not understand the policy of your family. Oh, how I wish I was at home!" And as she expressed the wish, she could restrain herself no longer, but burst out into a flood of tears.

Poor Bertie was greatly moved. "You shall have the carriage to yourself going home," said he; "at least you and my father. As for me I can walk, or for the matter of that it does not much signify what I do." He perfectly understood that part of Eleanor's

grief arose from the apparent necessity of her going back to Barchester in the carriage with her second suitor.

This somewhat mollified her. "Oh, Mr. Stanhope," said she,
"why should you have made me so miserable? What will you
have gained by telling me all this?"

He had not even yet explained to her the most difficult part of his
proposition; he had not told her that she was to be a party to the
little deception which he intended to play off upon his sister. This
suggestion had still to be made, and as it was absolutely necessary,
he proceeded to make it.

We need not follow him through the whole of his statement.
At last, and not without considerable difficulty, he made Eleanor
understand why he had let her into his confidence, seeing that he
no longer intended her the honour of a formal offer. At last he
made her comprehend the part which she was destined to play in
this little family comedy.

But when she did understand it, she was only more angry with
him than ever: more angry, not only with him, but with Charlotte
also. Her fair name was to be bandied about between them in
different senses, and each sense false. She was to be played off by
the sister against the father; and then by the brother against the
sister. Her dear friend Charlotte, with all her agreeable sympathy
and affection, was striving to sacrifice her for the Stanhope family
welfare; and Bertie, who, as he now proclaimed himself, was over
head and ears in debt, completed the compliment of owning that
he did not care to have his debts paid at so great a sacrifice of
himself. Then she was asked to conspire together with this unwilling suitor, for the sake of making the family believe that he
had in obedience to their commands done his best to throw himself thus away!

She lifted up her face when he had finished, and looking at
him with much dignity, even through her tears, she said—

"I regret to say it, Mr. Stanhope; but after what has passed, I
believe that all intercourse between your family and myself had
better cease."

"Well, perhaps it had," said Bertie naïvely; "perhaps that
will be better, at any rate for a time; and then Charlotte will
think you are offended at what I have done."

"And now I will go back to the house, if you please," said
Eleanor. "I can find my way by myself, Mr. Stanhope: after
what has passed," she added, "I would rather go alone."

"But I must find the carriage for you, Mrs. Bold, and I must
tell my father that you will return with him alone, and I must

make some excuse to him for not going with you; and I must bid the servant put you down at your own house, for I suppose you will not now choose to see them again in the close."

There was a truth about this, and a perspicuity in making arrangements for lessening her immediate embarrassment, which had some effect in softening Eleanor's anger. So she suffered herself to walk by his side over the now deserted lawn, till they came to the drawing-room window. There was something about Bertie Stanhope, which gave him, in the estimation of every one, a different standing from that which any other man would occupy under similar circumstances. Angry as Eleanor was, and great as was her cause for anger, she was not half as angry with him as she would have been with any one else. He was apparently so simple, so good-natured, so unaffected and easy to talk to, that she had already half-forgiven him before he was at the drawing-room window. When they arrived there, Dr. Stanhope was sitting nearly alone with Mr. and Miss Thorne; one or two other unfortunates were there, who from one cause or another were still delayed in getting away; but they were every moment getting fewer in number.

As soon as he had handed Eleanor over to his father, Bertie started off to the front gate, in search of the carriage, and there waited leaning patiently against the front wall, and comfortably smoking a cigar, till it came up. When he returned to the room Dr. Stanhope and Eleanor were alone with their hosts.

"At last, Miss Thorne," said he cheerily, "I have come to relieve you. Mrs. Bold and my father are the last roses of the very delightful summer you have given us, and desirable as Mrs. Bold's society always is, now at least you must be glad to see the last flowers plucked from the tree."

Miss Thorne declared that she was delighted to have Mrs. Bold and Dr. Stanhope still with her; and Mr. Thorne would have said the same, had he not been checked by a yawn, which he could not suppress.

"Father, will you give your arm to Mrs. Bold?" said Bertie: and so the last adieux were made, and the prebendary led out Mrs. Bold, followed by his son.

"I shall be home soon after you," said he, as the two got into the carriage.

"Are you not coming in the carriage?" said the father.

"No, no; I have some one to see on the road, and shall walk. John, mind you drive to Mrs. Bold's house first."

Eleanor looking out of the window, saw him with his hat in his hand, bowing to her with his usual gay smile, as though nothing had happened to mar the tranquillity of the day. It was many a long year before she saw him again. Dr. Stanhope hardly spoke to her on her way home; and she was safely deposited by John at her own hall-door, before the carriage drove into the close.

And thus our heroine played the last act of that day's melodrame.

CHAP. XLIII.

MR. AND MRS. QUIVERFUL ARE MADE HAPPY. MR. SLOPE IS ENCOURAGED BY THE PRESS.

BEFORE she started for Ullathorne, Mrs. Proudie, careful soul, caused two letters to be written, one by herself and one by her lord, to the inhabitants of Puddingdale vicarage, which made happy the hearth of those within it.

As soon as the departure of the horses left the bishop's stable-groom free for other services, that humble denizen of the diocese started on the bishop's own pony with the two despatches. We have had so many letters lately that we will spare ourselves these That from the bishop was simply a request that Mr. Quiverful would wait upon his lordship the next morning at 11 A.M.; and that from the lady was as simply a request that Mrs. Quiverful would do the same by her, though it was couched in somewhat longer and more grandiloquent phraseology.

It had become a point of conscience with Mrs. Proudie to urge the settlement of this great hospital question. She was resolved that Mr. Quiverful should have it. She was resolved that there should be no more doubt or delay, no more refusals and resignations, no more secret negotiations carried on by Mr. Slope on his own account in opposition to her behests.

"Bishop," she said, immediately after breakfast, on the morning of that eventful day, "have you signed the appointment yet?"

"No, my dear, not yet; it is not exactly signed as yet."

"Then do it," said the lady.

The bishop did it; and a very pleasant day indeed he spent at Ullathorne. And when he got home he had a glass of hot negus in his wife's sitting-room, and read the last number of the "Little Dorrit" of the day with great inward satisfaction. Oh, husbands, oh, my marital friends, what great comfort is there to be derived from a wife well obeyed!

Much perturbation and flutter, high expectation and renewed hopes, were occasioned at Puddingdale, by the receipt of these episcopal despatches. Mrs. Quiverful, whose careful ear caught the sound of the pony's feet as he trotted up to the vicarage kitchen door, brought them in hurriedly to her husband. She was at the moment concocting the Irish stew destined to satisfy the noonday wants of fourteen young birds, let alone the parent couple. She had taken the letters from the man's hands between the folds of her capacious apron, so as to save them from the contamination of the stew, and in this guise she brought them to her husband's desk.

They at once divided the spoil, each taking that addressed to the other. "Quiverful," said she with impressive voice, "you are to be at the palace at eleven to-morrow."

"And so are you, my dear," said he, almost gasping with the importance of the tidings: and then they exchanged letters.

"She'd never have sent for me again," said the lady, "if it wasn't all right."

"Oh! my dear, don't be too certain," said the gentleman. "Only think if it should be wrong."

"She'd never have sent for me, Q., if it wasn't all right,' again argued the lady. "She's stiff and hard and proud as pie-crust, but I think she's right at bottom." Such was Mrs. Quiverful's verdict about Mrs. Proudie, to which in after times she always adhered. People when they get their income doubled usually think that those through whose instrumentality this little ceremony is performed are right at bottom.

"Oh Letty!" said Mr. Quiverful, rising from his well-worn seat.

"Oh Q.!" said Mrs. Quiverful: and then the two, unmindful of the kitchen apron, the greasy fingers, and the adherent Irish stew, threw themselves warmly into each other's arms.

"For heaven's sake don't let any one cajole you out of it again," said the wife.

"Let me alone for that," said the husband, with a look of almost fierce determination, pressing his fist as he spoke rigidly on his desk, as though he had Mr. Slope's head below his knuckles, and meant to keep it there.

"I wonder how soon it will be," said she.

"I wonder whether it will be at all," said he, still doubtful.

"Well, I won't say too much," said the lady. "The cup has

slipped twice before, and it may fall altogether this time; but I'll not believe it. He'll give you the appointment to-morrow. You'll find he will."

"Heaven send he may," said Mr. Quiverful, solemnly. And who that considers the weight of the burden on this man's back, will say that the prayer was an improper one? There were fourteen of them—fourteen of them living—as Mrs. Quiverful had so powerfully urged in the presence of the bishop's wife. As long as promotion cometh from any human source, whether north or south, east or west, will not such a claim as this hold good, in spite of all our examination tests, *detur digniori's* and optimist tendencies? It is fervently to be hoped that it may. Till we can become divine we must be content to be human, lest in our hurry for a change we sink to something lower.

And then the pair sitting down lovingly together, talked over all their difficulties, as they so often did, and all their hopes, as they so seldom were enabled to do.

"You had better call on that man, Q., as you come away from the palace," said Mrs. Quiverful, pointing to an angry call for money from the Barchester draper, which the postman had left at the vicarage that morning. Cormorant that he was, unjust, hungry cormorant! When rumour first got abroad that the Quiverfuls were to go to the hospital, this fellow with fawning eagerness had pressed his goods upon the wants of the poor clergyman. He had done so, feeling that he should be paid from the hospital funds, and flattering himself that a man with fourteen children, and money wherewithal to clothe them, could not but be an excellent customer. As soon as the second rumour reached him, he applied for his money angrily.

And "the fourteen"—or such of them as were old enough to hope and discuss their hopes, talked over their golden future. The tall-grown girls whispered to each other of possible Barchester parties, of possible allowances for dress, of a possible piano — the one they had in the vicarage was so weather-beaten with the storms of years and children as to be no longer worthy of the name — of the pretty garden, and the pretty house. 'Twas of such things it most behoved them to whisper.

And the younger fry, they did not content themselves with whispers, but shouted to each other of their new play-ground beneath our dear ex-warden's well-loved elms, of their future own gardens, of marbles to be procured in the wished-for city, and of the rumour which had reached them of a Barchester school.

'Twas in vain that their cautious mother tried to instil into their breasts the very feeling she had striven to banish from that of their father; 'twas in vain that she repeated to the girls that "there's many a slip 'twixt the cup and the lip;" 'twas in vain she attempted to make the children believe that they were to live at Puddingdale all their lives. Hopes mounted high and would not have themselves quelled. The neighbouring farmers heard the news, and came in to congratulate them. 'Twas Mrs. Quiverful herself who had kindled the fire, and in the first outbreak of her renewed expectations she did it so thoroughly, that it was quite past her power to put it out again.

Poor matron! good honest matron! doing thy duty in the state to which thou hast been called, heartily if not contentedly; let the fire burn on;—on this occasion the flames will not scorch; they shall warm thee and thine. 'Tis ordained that that husband of thine, that Q. of thy bosom, shall reign supreme for years to come over the bedesmen of Hiram's hospital.

And the last in all Barchester to mar their hopes, had he heard and seen all that passed at Puddingdale that day, would have been Mr. Harding. What wants had he to set in opposition to those of such a regiment of young ravens? There are fourteen of them living! with him at any rate, let us say, that that argument would have been sufficient for the appointment of Mr. Quiverful.

In the morning, Q. and his wife kept their appointments with that punctuality which bespeaks an expectant mind. The friendly farmer's gig was borrowed, and in that they went, discussing many things by the way. They had instructed the household to expect them back by one, and injunctions were given to the eldest pledge to have ready by that accustomed hour the remainder of the huge stew which the provident mother had prepared on the previous day. The hands of the kitchen clock came round to two, three, four, before the farmer's gig-wheels were again heard at the vicarage gate. With what palpitating hearts were the returning wanderers greeted!

"I suppose, children, you all thought we were never coming back any more?" said the mother, as she slowly let down her solid foot till it rested on the step of the gig. "Well, such a day as we've had!" and then leaning heavily on a big boy's shoulder, she stepped once more on terra firma.

There was no need for more than the tone of her voice to tell them that all was right. The Irish stew might burn itself to cinders now.

Then there was such kissing and hugging, such crying and laughing. Mr. Quiverful could not sit still at all, but kept walking from room to room, then out into the garden, then down the avenue into the road, and then back again to his wife. She, however, lost no time so idly.

"We must go to work at once, girls; and that in earnest. Mrs. Proudie expects us to be in the hospital house on the 15th of October."

Had Mrs. Proudie expressed a wish that they should all be there on the next morning, the girls would have had nothing to say against it.

"And when will the pay begin?" asked the eldest boy

"To-day, my dear," said the gratified mother.

"Oh,—that is jolly," said the boy.

"Mrs. Proudie insisted on our going down to the house," continued the mother; "and when there I thought I might save a journey by measuring some of the rooms and windows; so I got a knot of tape from Bobbins. Bobbins is as civil as you please, now."

"I wouldn't thank him," said Letty the younger.

"Oh, it's the way of the world, my dear. They all do just the same. You might just as well be angry with the turkey cock for gobbling at you. It's the bird's nature." And as she enunciated to her bairns the upshot of her practical experience, she pulled from her pocket the portions of tape which showed the length and breadth of the various rooms at the hospital house.

And so we will leave her happy in her toils.

The Quiverfuls had hardly left the palace, and Mrs. Proudie was still holding forth on the matter to her husband, when another visitor was announced in the person of Dr. Gwynne. The master of Lazarus had asked for the bishop, and not for Mrs. Proudie, and therefore, when he was shown into the study, he was surprised rather than rejoiced to find the lady there.

But we must go back a little, and it shall be but a little, for a difficulty begins to make itself manifest in the necessity of disposing of all our friends in the small remainder of this one volume. Oh, that Mr. Longman would allow me a fourth! It should transcend the other three as the seventh heaven transcends all the lower stages of celestial bliss.

Going home in the carriage that evening from Ullathorne, Dr. Gwynne had not without difficulty brought round his friend the archdeacon to a line of tactics much less bellicose than that which his own taste would have preferred. "It will be unseemly in us to show ourselves in a bad humour: and moreover we have no power in this matter, and it will therefore be bad policy to act as though we had." 'Twas thus the master of Lazarus argued. "If," he continued, "the bishop be determined to appoint another to the hospital, threats will not prevent him, and threats should not be lightly used by an archdeacon to his bishop. If he will place a stranger in the hospital, we can only leave him to the indignation of others. It is probable that such a step may not eventually injure your father-in-law. I will see the bishop, if you will allow me,—alone." At this the archdeacon winced visibly; "yes, alone; for so I shall be calmer: and then I shall at any rate learn what he does mean to do in the matter."

The archdeacon puffed and blew, put up the carriage window and then put it down again, argued the matter up to his own gate, and at last gave way. Everybody was against him, his own wife, Mr. Harding, and Dr. Gwynne.

"Pray keep him out of hot water, Dr. Gwynne," Mrs. Grantly had said to her guest. "My dearest madam, I'll do my best," the courteous master had replied. 'Twas thus he did it; and earned for himself the gratitude of Mrs. Grantly.

And now we may return to the bishop's study.

Dr. Gwynne had certainly not foreseen the difficulty which here presented itself. He,—together with all the clerical world of England, — had heard it rumoured about that Mrs. Proudie did not confine herself to her wardrobes, still-rooms, and laundries; but yet it had never occurred to him that if he called on a bishop at one o'clock in the day, he could by any possibility find him closeted with his wife; or that if he did so, the wife would remain longer than necessary to make her curtsey. It appeared, however, as though in the present case Mrs. Proudie had no idea of retreating.

The bishop had been very much pleased with Dr. Gwynne on the preceding day, and of course thought that Dr. Gwynne had been as much pleased with him. He attributed the visit solely to compliment, and thought it an extremely gracious and proper thing for the master of Lazarus to drive over from Plumstead specially to call at the palace so soon after his arrival in the country. The fact that they were not on the same side either in politics or doctrines made the compliment the greater. The bishop, therefore, was all smiles. And Mrs. Proudie, who liked people with good handles to their names, was also very well disposed to welcome the master of Lazarus.

"We had a charming party at Ullathorne, Master, had we not?" said she. "I hope Mrs. Grantly got home without fatigue."

Dr. Gwynne said that they had all been a little tired, but were none the worse this morning.

"An excellent person, Miss Thorne," suggested the bishop.

"And an exemplary Christian, I am told," said Mrs. Proudie.

Dr. Gwynne declared that he was very glad to hear it.

"I have not seen her Sabbath-day schools yet," continued the lady, "but I shall make a point of doing so before long."

Dr. Gwynne merely bowed at this intimation. He had heard something of Mrs. Proudie and her Sunday schools, both from Dr. Grantly and Mr. Harding.

"By the bye, Master," continued the lady, "I wonder whether Mrs. Grantly would like me to drive over and inspect her Sabbath-day school. I hear that it is most excellently kept."

Dr. Gwynne really could not say. He had no doubt Mrs. Grantly would be most happy to see Mrs. Proudie any day Mrs. Proudie would do her the honour of calling: that was, of course, if Mrs. Grantly should happen to be at home.

A slight cloud darkened the lady's brow. She saw that her offer was not taken in good part. This generation of unregenerated vipers was still perverse, stiffnecked, and hardened in their iniquity. "The archdeacon, I know," said she, "sets his face against these institutions."

At this Dr. Gwynne laughed slightly. It was but a smile. Had he given his cap for it he could not have helped it.

Mrs. Proudie frowned again. "'Suffer little children, and forbid them not,'" said she. "Are we not to remember that, Dr. Gwynne? 'Take heed that ye despise not one of these little ones.' Are we not to remember that, Dr. Gwynne?" And at each of these questions she raised at him her menacing forefinger.

"Certainly, madam, certainly," said the master, "and so does the archdeacon, I am sure, on week days as well as on Sundays."

"On week days you can't take heed not to despise them," said Mrs. Proudie, "because then they are out in the fields. On week days they belong to their parents, but on Sundays they ought to belong to the clergyman." And the finger was again raised.

The master began to understand and to share the intense disgust which the archdeacon always expressed when Mrs. Proudie's name was mentioned. What was he to do with such a woman as this? To take his hat and go would have been his natural resource; but then he did not wish to be foiled in his object.

"My lord," said he, "I wanted to ask you a question on business, if you could spare me one moment's leisure. I know I must apologise for so disturbing you; but in truth I will not detain you five minutes."

"Certainly, Master, certainly," said the bishop; "my time is quite yours,—pray make no apology, pray make no apology."

"You have a great deal to do just at the present moment, bishop. Do not forget how extremely busy you are at present," said Mrs. Proudie, whose spirit was now up ; for she was angry with her visitor.

"I will not delay his lordship much above a minute," said the master of Lazarus, rising from his chair, and expecting that Mrs. Proudie would now go, or else that the bishop would lead the way into another room.

But neither event seemed likely to occur, and Dr. Gwynne stood for a moment silent in the middle of the room.

"Perhaps it's about Hiram's hospital?" suggested Mrs. Proudie.

Dr. Gwynne, lost in astonishment, and not knowing what else on earth to do, confessed that his business with the bishop was connected with Hiram's hospital.

"His lordship has finally conferred the appointment on Mr Quiverful this morning," said the lady.

Dr. Gwynne made a simple reference to the bishop, and finding that the lady's statement was formally confirmed, he took his leave. "That comes of the reform bill," he said to himself as he walked down the bishop's avenue. "Well, at any rate the Greek play bishops were not so bad as that."

It has been said that Mr. Slope, as he started for Ullathorne, received a despatch from his friend, Mr. Towers, which had the effect of putting him in that high good-humour which subsequent events somewhat untowardly damped. It ran as follows. Its shortness will be its sufficient apology.

"My dear Sir, — I wish you every success. I don't know that I can help you, but if I can, I will.

"Yours ever,
"T. T.
"30/9/185—

There was more in this than in all Sir Nicholas Fitzwhiggin's flummery ; more than in all the bishop's promises, even had they been ever so sincere ; more than in any archbishop's good word, even had it been possible to obtain it. Tom Towers would do for him what he could.

Mr. Slope had from his youth upwards been a firm believer in the public press. He had dabbled in it himself ever since he had taken his degree, and regarded it as the great arranger and distributor of all future British terrestrial affairs whatever. He had not yet arrived at the age, an age which sooner or later comes to most of us, which dissipates the golden dreams of youth. He delighted in the idea of wresting power from the hands of his country's magnates, and placing it in a custody which was at any rate nearer to his own reach. Sixty thousand broad sheets dispersing themselves daily among his reading fellow-citizens, formed in his eyes a better depôt for supremacy than a throne at Windsor, a cabinet in Downing Street, or even an assembly at Westminster. And on this subject we must not quarrel with Mr. Slope, for the feeling is too general to be met with disrespect.

Tom Towers was as good, if not better than his promise. On the following morning the Jupiter, spouting forth public opinion with sixty thousand loud clarions, did proclaim to the world that Mr. Slope was the fitting man for the vacant post. It was pleasant for Mr. Slope to read the following lines in the Barchester news-room, which he did within thirty minutes after the morning train from London had reached the city.

"It is just now five years since we called the attention of our readers to the quiet city of Barchester. From that day to this, we have in no way meddled with the affairs of that happy ecclesiastical community. Since then, an old bishop has died there, and a young bishop has been installed; but we believe we did not do more than give some customary record of the interesting event. Nor are we now about to meddle very deeply in the affairs of the diocese. If any of the chapter feel a qualm of conscience on reading thus far, let it be quieted. Above all, let the mind of the new bishop be at rest. We are now not armed for war, but approach the reverend towers of the old cathedral with an olive-branch in our hands.

"It will be remembered that at the time alluded to, now five years past, we had occasion to remark on the state of a charity in Barchester called Hiram's hospital. We thought that it was maladministered, and that the very estimable and reverend gentleman who held the office of warden was somewhat too highly paid for duties which were somewhat too easily performed. This gentleman — and we say it in all sincerity and with no touch of sarcasm — had never looked on the matter in this light before. We do not wish to take praise to ourselves whether praise be due to us or not. But the consequence of our remark was, that the warden did look into the matter, and finding on so doing that he himself could come to no other opinion than that expressed by us, he very creditably threw up the appointment. The then bishop as creditably declined to fill the vacancy till the affair was put on a better footing. Parliament then took it up; and we have now the satisfaction of informing our readers that Hiram's hospital will be immediately re-opened under new auspices. Heretofore, provision was made for the maintenance of twelve old men. This will now be extended to the fair sex, and twelve elderly women, if any such can be found in Barchester, will be added to the establishment. There will be a matron; there will, it is hoped, be schools attached for the poorest of the children of the poor, and there will be a steward. The warden, for there will still be a warden, will receive an income more in keeping with the extent of the charity than that heretofore paid. The stipend we believe will be 450l. We may add that the excellent house which the former warden inhabited will still be attached to the situation.

"Barchester hospital cannot perhaps boast a world-wide reputation; but as we adverted to its state of decadence, we think it right also to advert to its renaissance. May it go on and prosper. Whether the salutary reform which has been introduced within its walls has been carried as far as could have been desired, may be doubtful. The important question of the school appears to be somewhat left to the discretion of the new warden. This might have been made the most important part of the establishment, and the new warden, whom we trust we shall not offend by the freedom of our remarks, might have been selected with some view to his fitness as schoolmaster. But we will not now look a gift horse in the mouth. May the hospital go on and prosper! The situation of warden has of course been offered to the gentleman who so honourably vacated it five years since; but we are given to understand that he has declined it. Whether the ladies who have been introduced, be in his estimation too much for his powers of control, whether it be that the diminished income does not offer to him sufficient temptation to resume his old place, or that he has in the meantime assumed other clerical duties, we do not know. We are, however, informed that he has refused the offer, and that the situation has been accepted by Mr. Quiverful, the vicar of Puddingdale.

"So much we think is due to Hiram redivivus. But while we are on the subject of Barchester, we will venture with all respectful humility to express our opinion on another matter, connected with the ecclesiastical polity of that ancient city. Dr. Trefoil, the dean, died yesterday. A short record of his death, giving his age, and the various pieces of preferment which he has at different times held, will be found in another column of this paper. The only fault we knew in him was his age, and as that is a crime of which we all hope to be guilty, we will not bear heavily on it. May he rest in peace! But though the great age of an expiring dean cannot be made matter of reproach, we are not inclined to look on such a fault as at all pardonable in a dean just brought to the birth. We do hope that the days of sexagenarian appointments are past. If we want deans, we must want them for some purpose. That purpose will necessarily be better fulfilled by a man of forty than by a man of sixty. If we are to pay deans at all, we are to pay them for some sort of work. That work, be it what it may, will be best performed by a workman in the prime of life. Dr. Trefoil, we see, was eighty when he died. As we have as yet completed no plan for pensioning superannuated clergymen, we do not wish to get rid of any existing deans of that age. But we prefer having as few such as possible. If a man of seventy be now appointed, we beg to point out to Lord —— that he will be past all use in a year or two, if indeed he be not so at the present moment. His lordship will allow us to remind him that all men are not evergreens like himself.

"We hear that Mr. Slope's name has been mentioned for this preferment. Mr. Slope is at present chaplain to the bishop. A better man could hardly be selected. He is a man of talent, young, active, and conversant with the affairs of the cathedral; he is moreover, we conscientiously believe, a truly pious clergyman. We know that his services in the city of Barchester have been highly appreciated. He is an eloquent preacher and a ripe scholar. Such a selection as this would go far to raise the confidence of the public in the present administration of church patronage, and would teach men to believe that from henceforth the establishment of our church will not afford easy couches to worn-out clerical voluptuaries."

Standing at a reading-desk in the Barchester news-room, Mr. Slope digested this article with considerable satisfaction. What was therein said as to the hospital was now comparatively matter of indifference to him. He was certainly glad that he had not succeeded in restoring to the place the father of that virago who had so audaciously outraged all decency in his person; and was so far satisfied. But Mrs. Proudie's nominee was appointed, and he was so far dissatisfied. His mind, however, was now soaring above Mrs. Bold or Mrs. Proudie. He was sufficiently conversant with the tactics of the Jupiter to know that the pith of the article would lie in the last paragraph. The place of honour was given to him, and it was indeed as honourable as even he could have wished. He was very grateful to his friend Mr. Towers, and with full heart looked forward to the day when he might entertain him in princely style at his own full-spread board in the deanery dining-room.

It had been well for Mr. Slope that Dr. Trefoil had died in the autumn. Those caterers for our morning repast, the staff of the Jupiter, had been sorely put to it for the last month to find a sufficiency of proper pabulum. Just then there was no talk of a new American president. No wonderful tragedies had occurred on railway trains in Georgia, or elsewhere. There was a dearth of broken banks, and a dead dean with the necessity for a live one was a godsend. Had Dr. Trefoil died in June, Mr. Towers would probably not have known so much about the piety of Mr. Slope.

And here we will leave Mr. Slope for a while in his triumph; explaining, however, that his feelings were not altogether of a triumphant nature. His rejection by the widow, or rather the method of his rejection, galled him terribly. For days to come he positively felt the sting upon his cheek, whenever he thought of what had been done to him. He could not refrain from calling her by harsh names, speaking to himself as he walked through the streets of Barchester. When he said his prayers, he could not bring himself to forgive her. When he strove to do so, his mind recoiled from the attempt, and in lieu of forgiving ran off in a double spirit of vindictiveness, dwelling on the extent of the injury he had received. And so his prayers dropped senseless from his lips.

And then the signora; what would he not have given to be able to hate her also? As it was, he worshipped the very sofa on which she was ever lying. And thus it was not all rose colour with Mr. Slope, although his hopes ran high.

CHAP. XLIV.

MRS. BOLD AT HOME.

POOR Mrs. Bold, when she got home from Ullathorne on the evening of Miss Thorne's party, was very unhappy, and moreover, very tired. Nothing fatigues the body so much as weariness of spirit, and Eleanor's spirit was indeed weary.

Dr. Stanhope had civilly but not very cordially asked her in to tea, and her manner of refusal convinced the worthy doctor that he need not repeat the invitation. He had not exactly made himself a party to the intrigue which was to convert the late Mr. Bold's patrimony into an income for his hopeful son, but he had been well aware what was going on. And he was well aware also when he perceived that Bertie declined accompanying them home in the carriage, that the affair had gone off.

Eleanor was very much afraid that Charlotte would have darted out upon her, as the prebendary got out at his own door, but Bertie had thoughtfully saved her from this, by causing the carriage to go round by her own house. This also Dr. Stanhope understood, and allowed to pass by without remark.

When she got home, she found Mary Bold in the drawing-room with the child in her lap. She rushed forward, and, throwing herself on her knees, kissed the little fellow till she almost frightened him.

"Oh, Mary, I am so glad you did not go. It was an odious party."

Now the question of Mary's going had been one greatly mooted between them. Mrs. Bold, when invited, had been the guest of the Grantlys, and Miss Thorne, who had chiefly known Eleanor at the hospital or at Plumstead rectory, had forgotten all about Mary Bold. Her sister-in-law had implored her to go under her wing, and had offered to write to Miss Thorne, or to call on her. But Miss Bold had declined. In fact, Mr. Bold had not been very popular with such people as the Thornes, and his sister would not go among them unless she were specially asked to do so.

"Well then," said Mary, cheerfully, "I have the less to regret."

"You have nothing to regret; but oh! Mary, I have—so much —so much;"—and then she began kissing her boy, whom her caresses had roused from his slumbers. When she raised her head, Mary saw that the tears were running down her cheeks.

"Good heavens, Eleanor, what is the matter? what has happened to you?— Eleanor—dearest Eleanor—what is the matter?" and Mary got up with the boy still in her arms.

"Give him to me—give him to me," said the young mother. "Give him to me, Mary," and she almost tore the child out of her sister's arms. The poor little fellow murmured somewhat at the disturbance, but nevertheless nestled himself close into his mother's bosom.

"Here, Mary, take the cloak from me. My own, own darling, darling, darling jewel. You are not false to me. Everybody else is false; everybody else is cruel. Mamma will care for nobody, nobody, nobody, but her own, own, own little man;" and she again kissed and pressed the baby, and cried till the tears ran down over the child's face.

"Who has been cruel to you, Eleanor?" said Mary. "I hope I have not."

Now, in this matter, Eleanor had great cause for mental uneasiness. She could not certainly accuse her loving sister-in-law of cruelty; but she had to do that which was more galling; she had to accuse herself of imprudence against which her sister-in-law had warned her. Miss Bold had never encouraged Eleanor's acquaintance with Mr. Slope, and she had positively discouraged the friendship of the Stanhopes as far as her usual gentle mode of speaking had permitted. Eleanor had only laughed at her, however, when she said that she disapproved of married women who lived apart from their husbands, and suggested that Charlotte Stanhope never went to church. Now, however, Eleanor must either hold her tongue, which was quite impossible, or confess herself to have been utterly wrong, which was nearly equally so. So she staved off the evil day by more tears, and consoled herself by inducing little Johnny to rouse himself sufficiently to return her caresses.

"He is a darling—as true as gold. What would mamma do without him? Mamma would lie down and die if she had not her own Johnny Bold to give her comfort." This and much more she said of the same kind, and for a time made no other answer to Mary's inquiries.

This kind of consolation from the world's deceit is very common. Mothers obtain it from their children, and men from their dogs. Some men even do so from their walking-sticks, which is just as rational. How is it that we can take joy to ourselves in that we are not deceived by those who have not attained the art to deceive us? In a true man, if such can be found, or a true woman, much consolation may indeed be taken.

In the caresses of her child, however, Eleanor did receive consolation; and may ill befall the man who would begrudge it to her. The evil day, however, was only postponed. She had to tell her disagreeable tale to Mary, and she had also to tell it to her father. Must it not, indeed, be told to the whole circle of her acquaintance before she could be made to stand all right with them? At the present moment there was no one to whom she could turn for comfort. She hated Mr. Slope; that was a matter of course, in that feeling she revelled. She hated and despised the Stanhopes; but that feeling distressed her greatly. She had, as it were, separated herself from her old friends to throw herself into the arms of this family; and then how had they intended to use her? She could hardly reconcile herself to her own father, who had believed ill of her. Mary Bold had turned Mentor. That she could have forgiven had the Mentor turned out to be in the wrong; but Mentors in the right are not to be pardoned. She could not but hate the archdeacon; and now she hated him worse than ever, for she must in some sort humble herself before him. She hated her sister, for she was part and parcel of the archdeacon. And she would have hated Mr. Arabin if she could. He had pretended to regard her, and yet before her face he had hung over that Italian woman as though there had been no beauty in the world but hers—no other woman worth a moment's attention. And Mr. Arabin would have to learn all this about Mr. Slope ! She told herself that she hated him, and she knew that she was lying to herself as she did so. She had no consolation but her baby, and of that she made the most. Mary, though she could not surmise what it was that had so violently affected her sister-in-law, saw at once that her grief was too great to be kept under control, and waited patiently till the child should be in his cradle.

"You'll have some tea, Eleanor," she said.

"Oh, I don't care," said she; though in fact she must have been very hungry, for she had eaten nothing at Ullathorne.

Mary quietly made the tea, and buttered the bread, laid aside the cloak, and made things look comfortable.

"He's fast asleep," said she, "you're very tired; let me take him up to bed."

But Eleanor would not let her sister touch him. She looked wistfully at her baby's eyes, saw that they were lost in the deepest slumber, and then made a sort of couch for him on the sofa. She was determined that nothing should prevail upon her to let him out of her sight that night.

"Come, Nelly," said Mary, "don't be cross with me. I at least have done nothing to offend you."

"I an't cross," said Eleanor.

"Are you angry then? Surely you can't be angry with me."

"No, I an't angry; at least not with you."

"If you are not, drink the tea I have made for you. I am sure you must want it."

Eleanor did drink it, and allowed herself to be persuaded. She ate and drank, and as the inner woman was recruited she felt a little more charitable towards the world at large. At last she found words to begin her story, and before she went to bed, she had made a clean breast of it and told everything—everything, that is, as to the lovers she had rejected: of Mr. Arabin she said not a word.

"I know I was wrong," said she, speaking of the blow she had given to Mr. Slope; "but I didn't know what he might do, and I had to protect myself."

"He richly deserved it," said Mary.

"Deserved it!" said Eleanor, whose mind as regarded Mr. Slope was almost bloodthirsty. "Had I stabbed him with a dagger, he would have deserved it. But what will they say about it at Plumstead?"

"I don't think I should tell them," said Mary. Eleanor began to think that she would not.

There could have been no kinder comforter than Mary Bold. There was not the slightest dash of triumph about her when she heard of the Stanhope scheme, nor did she allude to her former opinion when Eleanor called her late friend Charlotte a base, designing woman. She re-echoed all the abuse that was heaped on Mr. Slope's head, and never hinted that she had said as much before. "I told you so, I told you so!" is the croak of a true Job's comforter. But Mary, when she found her friend lying in her sorrow and scraping herself with potsherds, forbore to argue and to exult. Eleanor acknowledged the merit of the forbearance, and at length allowed herself to be tranquillised.

On the next day she did not go out of the house. Barchester she thought would be crowded with Stanhopes and Slopes; perhaps also with Arabins and Grantlys. Indeed there was hardly any one among her friends whom she could have met, without some cause of uneasiness.

In the course of the afternoon she heard that the dean was dead; and she also heard that Mr. Quiverful had been finally appointed to the hospital.

In the evening her father came to her, and then the story, or as much of it as she could bring herself to tell him, had to be repeated. He was not in truth much surprised at Mr. Slope's effrontery; but he was obliged to act as though he had been, to save his daughter's feelings. He was, however, anything but skilful in his deceit, and she saw through it.

"I see," said she, "that you think it only in the common course of things that Mr. Slope should have treated me in this way." She had said nothing to him about the embrace, nor yet of the way in which it had been met.

"I do not think it at all strange," said he, "that any one should admire my Eleanor."

"It is strange to me," said she, "that any man should have so much audacity, without ever having received the slightest encouragement."

To this Mr. Harding answered nothing. With the archdeacon

it would have been the text for a rejoinder, which would not have disgraced Bildad the Shuhite.

"But you'll tell the archdeacon?" asked Mr. Harding.

"Tell him what?" said she sharply.

"Or Susan?" continued Mr. Harding. "You'll tell Susan you'll let them know that they wronged you in supposing that this man's addresses would be agreeable to you."

"They may find that out their own way," said she; "I shall not ever willingly mention Mr. Slope's name to either of them."

"But I may."

"I have no right to hinder you from doing anything that may be necessary to your own comfort, but pray do not do it for my sake. Dr. Grantly never thought well of me, and never will. I don't know now that I am even anxious that he should do so."

And then they went to the affair of the hospital. "But is it true, papa?"

"What, my dear?" said he. "About the dean? Yes, I fear quite true. Indeed I know there is no doubt about it."

"Poor Miss Trefoil. I am so sorry for her. But I did not mean that," said Eleanor. "But about the hospital, papa?"

"Yes, my dear. I believe it is true that Mr. Quiverful is to have it."

"Oh, what a shame!"

"No, my dear, not at all, not at all a shame: I am sure I hope it will suit him."

"But, papa, you know it is a shame. After all your hopes, all your expectations to get back to your old house, to see it given away in this way to a perfect stranger!"

"My dear, the bishop had a right to give it to whom he pleased."

"I deny that, papa. He had no such right. It is not as though you were a candidate for a new piece of preferment. If the bishop has a grain of justice —"

"The bishop offered it to me on his terms, and as I did not like the terms, I refused it. After that, I cannot complain."

"Terms! he had no right to make terms."

"I don't know about that; but it seems he had the power. But to tell you the truth, Nelly, I am as well satisfied as it is. When the affair became the subject of angry discussion, I thoroughly wished to be rid of it altogether."

"But you did want to go back to the old house, papa. You told me so yourself."

"Yes, my dear, I did. For a short time I did wish it. And I was foolish in doing so. I am getting old now; and my chief worldly wish is for peace and rest. Had I gone back to the hospital, I should have had endless contentions with the bishop, contentions with his chaplain, and contentions with the arch-deacon. I am not up to this now, I am not able to meet such troubles; and therefore I am not ill-pleased to find myself left to the little church of St. Cuthbert's. I shall never starve," added he, laughing, "as long as you are here."

"But will you come and live with me, papa?" she said earnestly, taking him by both his hands. "If you will do that, if you will promise that, I will own that you are right."

"I will dine with you to-day at any rate."

"No, but live here altogether. Give up that close, odious little room in High Street."

"My dear, it's a very nice little room; and you are really quite uncivil."

"Oh, papa, don't joke. It's not a nice place for you. You say you are growing old, though I am sure you are not."

"Am not I, my dear?"

"No, papa, not old — not to say old. But you are quite old enough to feel the want of a decent room to sit in. You know how lonely Mary and I are here. You know nobody ever sleeps in the big front bed-room. It is really unkind of you to remain up there alone, when you are so much wanted here."

"Thank you, Nelly — thank you. But, my dear—"

"If you had been living here, papa, with us, as I really think you ought to have done, considering how lonely we are, there would have been none of all this dreadful affair about Mr. Slope."

Mr. Harding, however, did not allow himself to be talked over into giving up his own and only little *pied à terre* in the High Street. He promised to come and dine with his daughter, and stay with her, and visit her, and do everything but absolutely live with her. It did not suit the peculiar feelings of the man to tell his daughter that though she had rejected Mr. Slope, and been ready to reject Mr. Stanhope, some other more favoured suitor would probably soon appear; and that on the appearance of such a suitor the big front bed-room might perhaps be more frequently in re-quisition than at present. But doubtless such an idea crossed his mind, and added its weight to the other reasons which made him decide on still keeping the close, odious little room in High Street.

The evening passed over quietly and in comfort. Eleanor was always happier with her father than with any one else. He had not, perhaps, any natural taste for baby-worship, but he was always ready to sacrifice himself, and therefore made an excellent third in a trio with his daughter and Mary Bold in singing the praises of the wonderful child.

They were standing together over their music in the evening, the baby having again been put to bed upon the sofa, when the servant brought in a very small note in a beautiful pink envelope. It quite filled the room with perfume as it lay upon the small salver. Mary Bold and Mrs. Bold were both at the piano, and Mr. Harding was sitting close to them, with the violoncello between his legs ; so that the elegancy of the epistle was visible to them all.

"Please, ma'am, Dr. Stanhope's coachman says he is to wait for an answer," said the servant.

Eleanor got very red in the face as she took the note in her hand. She had never seen the writing before. Charlotte's epistles, to which she was well accustomed, were of a very different style and kind. She generally wrote on large note-paper ; she twisted up her letters into the shape and sometimes into the size of cocked hats ; she addressed them in a sprawling manly hand, and not unusually added a blot or a smudge, as though such were her own peculiar sign-manual. The address of this note was written in a beautiful female hand, and the gummed wafer bore on it an impress of a gilt coronet. Though Eleanor had never seen such a one before, she guessed that it came from the signora. Such epistles were very numerously sent out from any house in which the signora might happen to be dwelling, but they were rarely addressed to ladies. When the coachman was told by the lady's maid to take the letter to Mrs. Bold, he openly expressed his opinion that there was some mistake about it. Whereupon the lady's maid boxed the coachman's ears. Had Mr. Slope seen in how meek a spirit the coachman took the rebuke, he might have learnt a useful lesson, both in philosophy and religion.

The note was as follows. It may be taken as a faithful promise that no further letter whatever shall be transcribed at length in these pages.

"My dear Mrs. Bold,—May I ask you, as a great favour, to call on me to-morrow ? You can say what hour will best suit you ; but quite early, if you can. I need hardly say that if I could call upon you I should not take this liberty with you.

"I partly know what occurred the other day, and I promise you that you shall meet with no annoyance if you will come to me. My brother leaves us for London to-day ; from thence he goes to Italy.

"It will probably occur to you that I should not thus intrude on you, unless I had that to say to you which may be of considerable moment. Pray therefore excuse me, even if you do not grant my request, and believe me,

"Very sincerely yours,
"M. VESEY NERONI.

"Thursday Evening."

The three of them sat in consultation on this epistle for some ten or fifteen minutes, and then decided that Eleanor should write a line saying that she would see the signora the next morning, at twelve o'clock.

CHAP. XLV.

THE STANHOPES AT HOME.

WE must now return to the Stanhopes, and see how they behaved themselves on their return from Ullathorne.

Charlotte, who came back in the first homeward journey with her sister, waited in palpitating expectation till the carriage drove up to the door a second time. She did not run down or stand at the window, or show in any outward manner that she looked for anything wonderful to occur; but, when she heard the carriage-wheels, she stood up with erect ears, listening for Eleanor's footfall on the pavement or the cheery sound of Bertie's voice welcoming her in. Had she heard either, she would have felt that all was right; but neither sound was there for her to hear. She heard only her father's slow step, as he ponderously let himself down from the carriage, and slowly walked along the hall, till he got into his own private room on the ground floor. "Send Miss Stanhope to me," he said to the servant.

"There's something wrong now," said Madeline, who was lying on her sofa in the back drawing-room.

"It's all up with Bertie," replied Charlotte. "I know, I know,' she said to the servant, as he brought up the message. "Tell my father I will be with him immediately."

"Bertie's wooing has gone astray," said Madeline; "I knew it would."

"It has been his own fault then. She was ready enough, I am

quite sure," said Charlotte, with that sort of ill-nature which is
not uncommon when one woman speaks of another.

"What will you say to him now?" By "him," the signora
meant their father.

"That will be as I find him. He was ready to pay two hundred
pounds for Bertie, to stave off the worst of his creditors, if this
marriage had gone on. Bertie must now have the money instead,
and go and take his chance."

"Where is he now?"

"Heaven knows! smoking in the bottom of Mr. Thorne's ha-ha,
or philandering with some of those Miss Chadwicks. Nothing
will ever make an impression on him. But he'll be furious if I
don't go down."

"No; nothing ever will. But don't be long, Charlotte, for I
want my tea."

And so Charlotte went down to her father. There was a very
black cloud on the old man's brow; blacker than his daughter
could ever yet remember to have seen there. He was sitting in
his own arm-chair, not comfortably over the fire, but in the middle
of the room, waiting till she should come and listen to him.

"What has become of your brother?" he said, as soon as the
door was shut.

"I should rather ask you," said Charlotte. "I left you both at
Ullathorne, when I came away. What have you done with Mrs.
Bold?"

"Mrs. Bold! nonsense. The woman has gone home as she
ought to do. And heartily glad I am that she should not be
sacrificed to so heartless a reprobate."

"Oh, papa!"

"A heartless reprobate! Tell me now where he is, and what
he is going to do. I have allowed myself to be fooled between
you. Marriage, indeed! Who on earth that has money, or credit,
or respect in the world to lose, would marry him?"

"It is no use your scolding me, papa. I have done the best I
could for him and you."

"And Madeline is nearly as bad," said the prebendary, who was
in truth very, very angry

"Oh, I suppose we are all bad," replied Charlotte.

The old man emitted a huge leonine sigh. If they were all bad,
who had made them so? If they were unprincipled, selfish,
and disreputable, who was to be blamed for the education which
had had so injurious an effect?

"I know you'll ruin me among you," said he.

"Why, papa, what nonsense that is. You are living within your income this minute, and if there are any new debts, I don't know of them. I am sure there ought to be none, for we are dull enough here."

"Are those bills of Madeline's paid?"

"No, they are not. Who was to pay them?"

"Her husband may pay them."

"Her husband! would you wish me to tell her you say so? Do you wish to turn her out of your house?"

"I wish she would know how to behave herself."

"Why, what on earth has she done now? Poor Madeline! To-day is only the second time she has gone out since we came to this vile town."

He then sat silent for a time, thinking in what shape he would declare his resolve. "Well, papa," said Charlotte, "shall I stay here, or may I go up-stairs and give mamma her tea?"

"You are in your brother's confidence. Tell me what he is going to do?"

"Nothing, that I am aware of."

"Nothing—nothing! nothing but eat and drink, and spend every shilling of my money he can lay his hands upon. I have made up my mind, Charlotte. He shall eat and drink no more in this house."

"Very well. Then I suppose he must go back to Italy."

"He may go where he pleases."

"That's easily said, papa; but what does it mean? You can't let him ——"

"It means this," said the doctor, speaking more loudly than was his wont, and with wrath flashing from his eyes; "that as sure as God rules in heaven, I will not maintain him any longer in idleness."

"Oh, ruling in heaven!" said Charlotte. "It is no use talking about that. You must rule him here on earth; and the question is, how you can do it. You can't turn him out of the house penniless, to beg about the street."

"He may beg where he likes."

"He must go back to Carrara. That is the cheapest place he can live at, and nobody there will give him credit for above two or three hundred pauls. But you must let him have the means of going."

"As sure as ——"

"Oh, papa, don't swear. You know you must do it. You were ready to pay two hundred pounds for him if this marriage came off. Half that will start him to Carrara."

"What? give him a hundred pounds!"

"You know we are all in the dark, papa," said she, thinking it expedient to change the conversation. "For anything we know, he may be at this moment engaged to Mrs. Bold."

"Fiddlestick," said the father, who had seen the way in which Mrs. Bold had got into the carriage, while his son stood apart without even offering her his hand.

"Well, then, he must go to Carrara," said Charlotte.

Just at this moment the lock of the front door was heard, and Charlotte's quick ears detected her brother's cat-like step in the hall. She said nothing, feeling that for the present Bertie had better keep out of her father's way. But Dr. Stanhope also heard the sound of the lock.

"Who's that?" he demanded. Charlotte made no reply, and he asked again, "Who is that that has just come in? Open the door. Who is it?"

"I suppose it is Bertie."

"Bid him come here," said the father. But Bertie, who was close to the door and heard the call, required no further bidding, but walked in with a perfectly unconcerned and cheerful air. It was this peculiar *insouciance* which angered Dr. Stanhope, even more than his son's extravagance.

"Well, sir?" said the doctor.

"And how did you get home, sir, with your fair companion?" said Bertie. "I suppose she is not up-stairs, Charlotte?"

"Bertie," said Charlotte, "papa is in no humour for joking. He is very angry with you."

"Angry!" said Bertie, raising his eyebrows, as though he had never yet given his parent cause for a single moment's uneasiness.

"Sit down, if you please, sir," said Dr. Stanhope very sternly, but not now very loudly. "And I'll trouble you to sit down too, Charlotte. Your mother can wait for her tea a few minutes."

Charlotte sat down on the chair nearest to the door, in somewhat of a perverse sort of manner; as much as though she would say—Well, here I am; you shan't say I don't do what I am bid; but I'll be whipped if I give way to you. And she was determined not to give way. She too was angry with Bertie; but she was not the less ready on that account to defend him from his father. Bertie also sat down. He drew his chair close to the library-table, upon which he put his elbow, and then resting his face comfortably on one hand, he began drawing little pictures on a sheet of paper with the other. Before the scene was over he had completed admirable figures of Miss Thorne, Mrs. Proudie, and Lady De Courcy, and begun a family piece to comprise the whole set of the Lookalofts.

"Would it suit you, sir," said the father, "to give me some idea as to what your present intentions are? — what way of living you propose to yourself?"

"I'll do anything you can suggest, sir," replied Bertie.

"No, I shall suggest nothing further. My time for suggesting has gone by. I have only one order to give, and that is, that you leave my house."

"To-night?" said Bertie; and the simple tone of the question left the doctor without any adequately dignified method of reply.

"Papa does not quite mean to-night," said Charlotte, "at least I suppose not."

"To-morrow, perhaps," suggested Bertie.

"Yes, sir, to-morrow," said the doctor. "You shall leave this to-morrow."

"Very well, sir. Will the 4.30 P.M. train be soon enough?" and Bertie, as he asked, put the finishing touch to Miss Thorne's high-heeled boots.

"You may go how and when and where you please, so that you leave my house to-morrow. You have disgraced me, sir; you have disgraced yourself, and me, and your sisters."

"I am glad at least, sir, that I have not disgraced my mother," said Bertie.

Charlotte could hardly keep her countenance; but the doctor's brow grew still blacker than ever. Bertie was executing his *chef d'œuvre* in the delineation of Mrs. Proudie's nose and mouth.

"You are a heartless reprobate, sir; a heartless, thankless, good-for-nothing reprobate. I have done with you. You are my son — that I cannot help; but you shall have no more part or parcel in me as my child, nor I in you as your father."

"Oh, papa, papa! you must not, shall not say so," said Charlotte.

"I will say so, and do say so," said the father, rising from his chair. "And now leave the room, sir."

"Stop, stop," said Charlotte; "why don't you speak, Bertie? why don't you look up and speak? It is your manner that makes papa so angry."

"He is perfectly indifferent to all decency, to all propriety," said the doctor; and then he shouted out, "Leave the room, sir! Do you hear what I say?"

"Papa, papa, I will not let you part so. I know you will be sorry for it." And then she added, getting up and whispering into his ear, "Is he only to blame? Think of that. We have made our own bed, and, such as it is, we must lie on it. It is no use for us to quarrel among ourselves," and as she finished her whisper Bertie finished off the countess's bustle, which was so well done that it absolutely seemed to be swaying to and fro on the paper with its usual lateral motion.

"My father is angry at the present time," said Bertie, looking up for a moment from his sketches, "because I am not going to marry Mrs. Bold. What can I say on the matter? It is true that I am not going to marry her. In the first place —— "

"That is not true, sir," said Dr. Stanhope; "but I will not argue with you."

"You were angry just this moment because I would not speak," said Bertie, going on with a young Lookaloft.

"Give over drawing," said Charlotte, going up to him and taking the paper from under his hand. The caricatures, however, she preserved, and showed them afterwards to the friends of the Thornes, the Proudies, and De Courcys. Bertie, deprived of his occupation, threw himself back in his chair and waited further orders.

"I think it will certainly be for the best that Bertie should leave this at once, perhaps to-morrow," said Charlotte; "but pray, papa, let us arrange some scheme together."

"If he will leave this to-morrow, I will give him 10l., and he shall be paid 5l. a month by the banker at Carrara as long as he stays permanently in that place."

"Well, sir! it won't be long," said Bertie; "for I shall be starved to death in about three months."

"He must have marble to work with," said Charlotte.

"I have plenty there in the studio to last me three months," said Bertie. "It will be no use attempting anything large in so limited a time; unless I do my own tombstone."

Terms, however, were ultimately come to, somewhat more liberal than those proposed, and the doctor was induced to shake hands with his son, and bid him good night. Dr. Stanhope would not go up to tea, but had it brought to him in his study by his daughter.

But Bertie went up-stairs and spent a pleasant evening. He finished the Lookalofts, greatly to the delight of his sisters, though the manner of portraying their *décolleté* dresses was not the most refined. Finding how matters were going, he by degrees allowed it to escape from him that he had not pressed his suit upon the widow in a very urgent way.

"I suppose, in point of fact, you never proposed at all?" said Charlotte.

"Oh, she understood that she might have me if she wished," said he.

"And she didn't wish," said the signora.

"You have thrown me over in the most shameful manner," said Charlotte. "I suppose you told her all about my little plan?"

"Well, it came out somehow; at least the most of it."

"There's an end of that alliance," said Charlotte; "but it doesn't matter much. I suppose we shall all be back at Como soon."

"I am sure I hope so," said the signora; "I'm sick of the sight of black coats. If that Mr. Slope comes here any more, he'll be the death of me."

"You've been the ruin of him, I think," said Charlotte.

"And as for a second black-coated lover of mine, I am going to make a present of him to another lady with most singular disinterestedness."

The next day, true to his promise, Bertie packed up and went off by the 4.30 P.M. train, with 20l. in his pocket, bound for the marble quarries of Carrara. And so he disappears from our scene.

At twelve o'clock on the day following that on which Bertie went, Mrs. Bold, true also to her word, knocked at Dr. Stanhope's door with a timid hand and palpitating heart. She was at once shown up to the back drawing-room, the folding doors of which were closed, so that in visiting the signora Eleanor was not necessarily thrown into any communion with those in the front room. As she went up the stairs, she saw none of the family, and was so far saved much of the annoyance which she had dreaded.

"This is very kind of you, Mrs. Bold; very kind, after what has happened," said the lady on the sofa with her sweetest smile.

"You wrote in such a strain that I could not but come to you."

"I did, I did; I wanted to force you to see me."

"Well, signora; I am here."

"How cold you are to me. But I suppose I must put up with that. I know you think you have reason to be displeased with us all. Poor Bertie! if you knew all, you would not be angry with him."

"I am not angry with your brother—not in the least. But I hope you did not send for me here to talk about him."

"If you are angry with Charlotte, that is worse; for you have no warmer friend in all Barchester. But I did *not* send for you to talk about this,—pray bring your chair nearer, Mrs. Bold, so that I may look at you. It is so unnatural to see you keeping so far off from me."

Eleanor did as she was bid, and brought her chair close to the sofa.

"And now, Mrs. Bold, I am going to tell you something which you may perhaps think indelicate ; but yet I know that I am right in doing so."

Hereupon Mrs. Bold said nothing, but felt inclined to shake in her chair. The signora, she knew, was not very particular, and that which to her appeared to be indelicate might to Mrs. Bold appear to be extremely indecent.

"I believe you know Mr. Arabin?"

Mrs. Bold would have given the world not to blush, but her blood was not at her own command. She did blush up to her forehead, and the signora, who had made her sit in a special light in order that she might watch her, saw that she did so.

"Yes,—I am acquainted with him. That is, slightly. He is an intimate friend of Dr. Grantly, and Dr. Grantly is my brother-in-law."

"Well ; if you know Mr. Arabin, I am sure you must like him. I know and like him much. Everybody that knows him must like him."

Mrs. Bold felt it quite impossible to say anything in reply to this. Her blood was rushing about her body she knew not how or why. She felt as though she were swinging in her chair ; and she knew that she was not only red in the face, but also almost suffocated with heat. However, she sat still and said nothing.

"How stiff you are with me, Mrs. Bold," said the signora ; "and I the while am doing for you all that one woman can do to serve another."

A kind of thought came over the widow's mind that perhaps the signora's friendship was real, and that at any rate it could not hurt her ; and another kind of thought, a glimmering of a thought, came to her also,—that Mr. Arabin was too precious to be lost. She despised the signora ; but might she not stoop to conquer? It should be but the smallest fraction of a stoop!

"I don't want to be stiff ; " she said, " but your questions are so very singular."

"Well, then, I will ask you one more singular still," said Madeline Neroni, raising herself on her elbow and turning her own face full upon her companion's. "Do you love him, love him with all your heart and soul, with all the love your bosom can feel? For I can tell you that he loves you, adores you, worships you, thinks of you and nothing else, is now thinking of you as he attempts to write his sermon for next Sunday's preaching. What would I not give to be loved in such a way by such a man, that is, if I were an object fit for any man to love!"

Mrs. Bold got up from her seat and stood speechless before the woman who was now addressing her in this impassioned way. When the signora thus alluded to herself, the widow's heart was softened, and she put her own hand, as though caressingly, on that of her companion which was resting on the table. The signora grasped it and went on speaking.

"What I tell you is God's own truth; and it is for you to use it as may be best for your own happiness. But you must not betray me. He knows nothing of this. He knows nothing of my knowing his inmost heart. He is simple as a child in these matters. He told me his secret in a thousand ways because he could not dissemble; but he does not dream that he has told it. You know it now, and I advise you to use it."

Eleanor returned the pressure of the other's hand with an infinitesimal *soupçon* of a squeeze.

"And remember," continued the signora, "he is not like other men. You must not expect him to come to you with vows and oaths and pretty presents, to kneel at your feet, and kiss your shoestrings. If you want that, there are plenty to do it; but he won't be one of them." Eleanor's bosom nearly burst with a sigh; but Madeline, not heeding her, went on. "With him, yea will stand for yea, and nay for nay. Though his heart should break for it, the woman who shall reject him once, will have rejected him once and for all. Remember that. And now, Mrs. Bold, I will not keep you, for you are fluttered. I partly guess what use you will make of what I have said to you. If ever you are a happy wife in that man's house, we shall be far away; but I shall expect you to write me one line to say that you have forgiven the sins of the family."

Eleanor half whispered that she would, and then, without uttering another word, crept out of the room, and down the stairs, opened the front door for herself without hearing or seeing any one, and found herself in the close.

It would be difficult to analyse Eleanor's feelings as she walked home. She was nearly stupefied by the things that had been said to her. She felt sore that her heart should have been so searched and riddled by a comparative stranger, by a woman whom she had never liked and never could like. She was mortified that the man whom she owned to herself that she loved should have concealed his love from her and shown it to another. There was much to vex her proud spirit. But there was, nevertheless, an under-stratum of joy in all this which buoyed her up wondrously. She tried if she could disbelieve what Madame Neroni had said to her; but she found that she could not. It was true; it must be true. She could not, would not, did not doubt it.

On one point she fully resolved to follow the advice given her. If it should ever please Mr. Arabin to put such a question to her as that suggested, her "yea" should be "yea." Would not all her miseries be at an end, if she could talk of them to him openly, with her head resting on his shoulder?

CHAP. XLVI.

MR. SLOPE'S PARTING INTERVIEW WITH THE SIGNORA.

On the following day the signora was in her pride. She was dressed in her brightest of morning dresses, and had quite a *levée* round her couch. It was a beautifully bright October afternoon; all the gentlemen of the neighbourhood were in Barchester, and those who had the entry of Dr. Stanhope's house were in the signora's back drawing-room. Charlotte and Mrs. Stanhope were in the front room, and such of the lady's squires as could not for the moment get near the centre of attraction had to waste their fragrance on the mother and sister.

The first who came and the last to leave was Mr. Arabin. This was the second visit he had paid to Madame Neroni since he had met her at Ullathorne. He came he knew not why, to talk about he knew not what. But, in truth, the feelings which now troubled him were new to him, and he could not analyse them. It may seem strange that he should thus come dangling about Madame Neroni because he was in love with Mrs. Bold; but it was nevertheless the fact; and though he could not understand why he did so, Madame Neroni understood it well enough.

She had been gentle and kind to him, and had encouraged his staying. Therefore he stayed on. She pressed his hand when he first greeted her; she made him remain near her; and whispered to him little nothings. And then her eye, brilliant and bright, now mirthful, now melancholy, and invincible in either way! What man with warm feelings, blood unchilled, and a heart not guarded by a triple steel of experience could have withstood those eyes! The lady, it is true, intended to do him no mortal injury, she merely chose to inhale a slight breath of incense before she handed the casket over to another. Whether Mrs. Bold would willingly have spared even so much is another question.

And then came Mr. Slope. All the world now knew that Mr. Slope was a candidate for the deanery, and that he was generally considered to be the favourite. Mr. Slope, therefore, walked rather largely upon the earth. He gave to himself a portly air, such as might become a dean, spoke but little to other clergymen, and shunned the bishop as much as possible. How the meagre little prebendary, and the burly chancellor, and all the minor canons and vicars choral, ay, and all the choristers too, cowered and shook and walked about with long faces when they read or heard of that article in the Jupiter. Now were coming the days when nothing would avail to keep the impure spirit from the cathedral pulpit. That pulpit would indeed be his own. Precentors, vicars, and choristers might hang up their harps on the willows. Ichabod! Ichabod! the glory of their house was departing from them.

Mr. Slope, great as he was with embryo grandeur, still came to see the signora. Indeed, he could not keep himself away. He dreamed of that soft hand which he had kissed so often, and of that imperial brow which his lips had once pressed, and he then dreamed also of further favours.

And Mr. Thorne was there also. It was the first visit he had ever paid to the signora, and he made it not without due preparation. Mr. Thorne was a gentleman usually precise in his dress, and prone to make the most of himself in an unpretending way. The grey hairs in his whiskers were eliminated perhaps once a month; those on his head were softened by a mixture which we will not call a dye; it was only a wash. His tailor lived in St. James's Street, and his bootmaker at the corner of that street and Piccadilly. He was particular in the article of gloves, and the getting up of his shirts was a matter not lightly thought of in the Ullathorne laundry. On the occasion of the present visit he had rather overdone his usual efforts, and caused some little uneasiness to his sister, who had not hitherto received very cordially the proposition for a lengthened visit from the signora at Ullathorne.

There were others also there—young men about the city who had not much to do, and who were induced by the lady's charms to neglect that little; but all gave way to Mr. Thorne, who was somewhat of a grand signior, as a country gentleman always is in a provincial city.

"Oh, Mr. Thorne, this is so kind of you!" said the signora.

" You promised to come ; but I really did not expect it. I thought you country gentlemen never kept your pledges."

" Oh, yes, sometimes," said Mr. Thorne, looking rather sheepish, and making his salutations a little too much in the style of the last century.

" You deceive none but your consti—stit—stit ; what do you call the people that carry you about in chairs and pelt you with eggs and apples when they make you a member of Parliament ? "

" One another also, sometimes, signora," said Mr. Slope, with a deanish sort of smirk on his face. " Country gentlemen do deceive one another sometimes, don't they, Mr. Thorne ? "

Mr. Thorne gave him a look which undeaned him completely for the moment ; but he soon remembered his high hopes, and recovering himself quickly, sustained his probable coming dignity by a laugh at Mr. Thorne's expense.

" I never deceive a lady, at any rate," said Mr. Thorne ; "especially when the gratification of my own wishes is so strong an inducement to keep me true, as it now is."

Mr. Thorne went on thus awhile with antediluvian grimaces and compliments which he had picked up from Sir Charles Grandison, and the signora at every grimace and at every bow smiled a little smile and bowed a little bow. Mr. Thorne, however, was kept standing at the foot of the couch, for the new dean sat in the seat of honour near the table. Mr. Arabin the while was standing with his back to the fire, his coat tails under his arms, gazing at her with all his eyes—not quite in vain, for every now and again a glance came up at him, bright as a meteor out of heaven.

" Oh, Mr. Thorne, you promised to let me introduce my little girl to you. Can you spare a moment ?—will you see her now ? "

Mr. Thorne assured her that he could, and would see the young lady with the greatest pleasure in life. " Mr. Slope, might I trouble you to ring the bell ? " said she ; and when Mr. Slope got up she looked at Mr. Thorne and pointed to the chair. Mr. Thorne, however, was much too slow to understand her, and Mr. Slope would have recovered his seat had not the signora, who never chose to be unsuccessful, somewhat summarily ordered him out of it.

" Oh, Mr. Slope, I must ask you to let Mr. Thorne sit here just for a moment or two. I am sure you will pardon me. We can take a liberty with you this week. Next week, you know, when you move into the dean's house, we shall all be afraid of you."

Mr. Slope, with an air of much indifference, rose from his seat, and, walking into the next room, became greatly interested in Mrs. Stanhope's worsted work.

And then the child was brought in. She was a little girl, about eight years of age, like her mother, only that her enormous eyes were black, and her hair quite jet. Her complexion, too, was very dark, and bespoke her foreign blood. She was dressed in the most outlandish and extravagant way in which clothes could be put on a child's back. She had great bracelets on her naked little arms, a crimson fillet braided with gold round her head, and scarlet shoes with high heels. Her dress was all flounces, and stuck out from her as though the object were to make it lie off horizontally from her little hips. It did not nearly cover her knees; but this was atoned for by a loose pair of drawers, which seemed made throughout of lace; then she had on pink silk stockings. It was thus that the last of the Neros was habitually dressed at the hour when visitors were wont to call.

"Julia, my love," said the mother,—Julia was ever a favourite name with the ladies of that family. "Julia, my love, come here. I was telling you about the beautiful party poor mamma went to. This is Mr. Thorne; will you give him a kiss, dearest?"

Julia put up her face to be kissed, as she did to all her mother's visitors; and then Mr. Thorne found that he had got her, and, which was much more terrific to him, all her finery, into his arms. The lace and starch crumpled against his waistcoat and trowsers, the greasy black curls hung upon his cheek, and one of the bracelet clasps scratched his ear. He did not at all know how to hold so magnificent a lady, nor holding her what to do with her. However, he had on other occasions been compelled to fondle little nieces and nephews, and now set about the task in the mode he always had used.

"Diddle, diddle, diddle, diddle," said he, putting the child on one knee, and working away with it as though he were turning a knife-grinder's wheel with his foot.

"Mamma, mamma," said Julia, crossly, "I don't want to be diddle diddled. Let me go, you naughty old man, you."

Poor Mr. Thorne put the child down quietly on the ground, and drew back his chair; Mr. Slope, who had returned to the pole star that attracted him, laughed aloud; Mr. Arabin winced and shut his eyes; and the signora pretended not to hear her daughter.

"Go to Aunt Charlotte, lovey," said the mamma, "and ask her if it is not time for you to go out."

But little Miss Julia, though she had not exactly liked the nature of Mr. Thorne's attention, was accustomed to be played

with by gentlemen, and did not relish the idea of being sent so
soon to her aunt.

"Julia, go when I tell you, my dear." But Julia still went
pouting about the room. "Charlotte, do come and take her,"
said the signora. "She must go out; and the days get so short
now." And thus ended the much-talked-of interview between Mr.
Thorne and the last of the Neros.

Mr. Thorne recovered from the child's crossness sooner than
from Mr. Slope's laughter. He could put up with being called an
old man by an infant, but he did not like to be laughed at by the
bishop's chaplain, even though that chaplain was about to become
a dean. He said nothing, but he showed plainly enough that he
was angry.

The signora was ready enough to avenge him. "Mr. Slope,"
said she, "I hear that you are triumphing on all sides."

"How so?" said he, smiling. He did not dislike being talked
to about the deanery, though, of course, he strongly denied the
imputation.

"You carry the day both in love and war." Mr. Slope hereupon did not look quite so satisfied as he had done.

"Mr. Arabin," continued the signora, "don't you think Mr.
Slope is a very lucky man?"

"Not more so than he deserves, I am sure," said Mr. Arabin.

"Only think, Mr. Thorne, he is to be our new dean; of course
we all know that."

"Indeed, signora," said Mr. Slope, "we all know nothing about
it. I can assure you I myself——"

"He *is* to be the new dean—there is no manner of doubt of it,
Mr. Thorne."

"Hum!" said Mr. Thorne.

"Passing over the heads of old men like my father and Archdeacon Grantly——"

"Oh—oh!" said Mr. Slope.

"The archdeacon would not accept it," said Mr. Arabin;
whereupon Mr. Slope smiled abominably, and said, as plainly as a
look could speak, that the grapes were sour.

"Going over all our heads," continued the signora; "for, of
course, I consider myself one of the chapter."

"If I am ever dean," said Mr. Slope—"that is, were I ever
to become so, I should glory in such a canoness."

"Oh, Mr. Slope, stop; I haven't half done. There is another
canoness for you to glory in. Mr. Slope is not only to have the
deanery, but a wife to put in it."

Mr. Slope again looked disconcerted.

"A wife with a large fortune too. It never rains but it pours, does it, Mr. Thorne?"

"No, never," said Mr. Thorne, who did not quite relish talking about Mr. Slope and his affairs.

"When will it be, Mr. Slope?"

"When will what be?" said he.

"Oh! we know when the affair of the dean will be: a week will settle that. The new hat, I have no doubt, has been already ordered. But when will the marriage come off?"

"Do you mean mine or Mr. Arabin's?" said he, striving to be facetious.

"Well, just then I meant yours, though, perhaps, after all, Mr. Arabin's may be first. But we know nothing of him. He is too close for any of us. Now all is open and above board with you; which, by the bye, Mr. Arabin, I beg to tell you I like much the best. He who runs can read that Mr. Slope is a favoured lover. Come, Mr. Slope, when is the widow to be made Mrs. Dean?"

To Mr. Arabin this badinage was peculiarly painful; and yet he could not tear himself away and leave it. He believed, still believed with that sort of belief which the fear of a thing engenders, that Mrs. Bold would probably become the wife of Mr. Slope. Of Mr. Slope's little adventure in the garden he knew nothing. For aught he knew, Mr. Slope might have had an adventure of quite a different character. He might have thrown himself at the widow's feet, been accepted, and then returned to town a jolly, thriving wooer. The signora's jokes were bitter enough to Mr. Slope, but they were quite as bitter to Mr. Arabin. He still stood leaning against the fire-place, fumbling with his hands in his trowsers pockets.

"Come, come, Mr. Slope, don't be so bashful," continued the signora. "We all know that you proposed to the lady the other day at Ullathorne. Tell us with what words she accepted you. Was it with a simple 'yes,' or with two 'no no's,' which make an affirmative? or did silence give consent? or did she speak out with that spirit which so well becomes a widow, and say openly, 'By my troth, sir, you shall make me Mrs. Slope as soon as it is your pleasure to do so?'"

Mr. Slope had seldom in his life felt himself less at his ease. There sat Mr. Thorne, laughing silently. There stood his old antagonist, Mr. Arabin, gazing at him with all his eyes. There round the door between the two rooms were clustered a little group of people, including Miss Stanhope and the Rev. Messrs. Gray and Green, all listening to his discomfiture. He knew that it depended solely on his own wit whether or no he could throw the joke back upon the lady. He knew that it stood him to do so if he possibly could; but he had not a word. "'Tis conscience that makes cowards of us all." He felt on his cheek the sharp points of Eleanor's fingers, and did not know who might have seen the blow, who might have told the tale to this pestilent woman who took such delight in jeering him. He stood there, therefore, red as a carbuncle and mute as a fish; grinning just sufficiently to show his teeth; an object of pity.

But the signora had no pity; she knew nothing of mercy. Her present object was to put Mr. Slope down, and she was determined to do it thoroughly, now that she had him in her power.

"What, Mr. Slope, no answer? Why it can't possibly be that the woman has been fool enough to refuse you? She can't surely be looking out after a bishop. But I see how it is, Mr. Slope. Widows are proverbially cautious. You should have let her alone till the new hat was on your head; till you could show her the key of the deanery."

"Signora," said he at last, trying to speak in a tone of dignified reproach, "you really permit yourself to talk on solemn subjects in a very improper way."

"Solemn subjects—what solemn subject? Surely a dean's hat is not such a solemn subject."

"I have no aspirations such as those you impute to me. Perhaps you will drop the subject."

"Oh certainly, Mr. Slope; but one word first. Go to her again with the prime minister's letter in your pocket. I'll wager my shawl to your shovel she does not refuse you then."

"I must say, signora, that I think you are speaking of the lady in a very unjustifiable manner."

"And one other piece of advice, Mr. Slope; I'll only offer you one other;" and then she commenced singing—

> "It's gude to be merry and wise, Mr. Slope;
>   It's gude to be honest and true;
> 'It's gude to be off with the old love— Mr. Slope,
>   Before you are on with the new.—

Ha, ha, ha!"

And the signora, throwing herself back on her sofa, laughed merrily. She little recked how those who heard her would, in their own imaginations, fill up the little history of Mr. Slope's first love. She little cared that some among them might attribute to her the honour of his earlier admiration. She was tired of Mr. Slope and wanted to get rid of him; she had ground for anger with him, and she chose to be revenged.

How Mr. Slope got out of that room he never himself knew. He did succeed ultimately, and probably with some assistance, in getting his hat and escaping into the air. At last his love for the signora was cured. Whenever he again thought of her in his dreams, it was not as of an angel with azure wings. He connected her rather with fire and brimstone, and though he could still believe her to be a spirit, he banished her entirely out of heaven, and found a place for her among the infernal gods. When he weighed in the balance, as he not seldom did, the two women to whom he had attached himself in Barchester, the pre-eminent place in his soul's hatred was usually allotted to the signora.

CHAP. XLVII.

THE DEAN ELECT.

DURING the entire next week Barchester was ignorant who was to be its new dean on Sunday morning. Mr. Slope was decidedly the favourite; but he did not show himself in the cathedral, and then he sank a point or two in the betting. On Monday, he got a scolding from the bishop in the hearing of the servants, and down he went till nobody would have him at any price; but on Tuesday he received a letter, in an official cover, marked private, by which he fully recovered his place in the public favour. On Wednesday, he was said to be ill, and that did not look well; but on Thursday morning he went down to the railway station, with a very jaunty air; and when it was ascertained that he had taken a first-class ticket for London, there was no longer any room for doubt on the matter.

While matters were in this state of ferment at Barchester, there was not much mental comfort at Plumstead. Our friend the archdeacon had many grounds for inward grief. He was much displeased at the result of Dr. Gwynne's diplomatic mission to the palace, and did not even scruple to say to his wife that had he gone himself, he would have managed the affair much better. His wife did not agree with him, but that did not mend the matter.

Mr. Quiverful's appointment to the hospital was, however, a *fail accompli*, and Mr. Harding's acquiescence in that appointment was not less so. Nothing would induce Mr. Harding to make a public appeal against the bishop; and the Master of Lazarus quite approved of his not doing so.

"I don't know what has come to the Master," said the archdeacon over and over again. "He used to be ready enough to stand up for his order."

"My dear archdeacon," Mrs. Grantly would say in reply, "what is the use of always fighting? I really think the Master is right." The Master, however, had taken steps of his own, of which neither the archdeacon nor his wife knew anything.

Then Mr. Slope's successes were henbane to Dr. Grantly; and Mrs. Bold's improprieties were as bad. What would be all the world to Archdeacon Grantly if Mr. Slope should become Dean of Barchester and marry his wife's sister! He talked of it, and talked of it till he was nearly ill. Mrs. Grantly almost wished that the marriage were done and over, so that she might hear no more about it.

And there was yet another ground of misery which cut him to the quick, nearly as closely as either of the others. That paragon of a clergyman, whom he had bestowed upon St. Ewold's, that college friend of whom he had boasted so loudly, that ecclesiastical knight before whose lance Mr. Slope was to fall and bite the dust, that worthy bulwark of the church as it should be, that honoured representative of Oxford's best spirit, was — so at least his wife had told him half a dozen times — misconducting himself!

Nothing had been seen of Mr. Arabin at Plumstead for the last week, but a good deal had, unfortunately, been heard of him. As soon as Mrs. Grantly had found herself alone with the archdeacon, on the evening of the Ullathorne party, she had expressed herself very forcibly as to Mr. Arabin's conduct on that occasion. He had, she declared, looked and acted and talked very unlike a decent parish clergyman. At first the archdeacon had laughed at this, and assured her that she need not trouble herself; that Mr. Arabin would be found to be quite safe. But by degrees he began to find that his wife's eyes had been sharper than his own. Other people coupled the signora's name with that of Mr. Arabin. The meagre little prebendary who lived in the close, told him to a nicety how often Mr. Arabin had visited at Dr. Stanhope's, and how long he had remained on the occasion of each visit. He had asked after Mr. Arabin at the cathedral library, and an officious little vicar choral had offered to go and see whether he could be found at Dr. Stanhope's. Rumour, when she has contrived to sound the first note on her trumpet, soon makes a loud peal audible enough. It was too clear that Mr. Arabin had succumbed to the Italian woman, and that the archdeacon's credit would suffer fearfully if something were not done to rescue the brand from the burning. Besides, to give the archdeacon his due, he was really attached to Mr. Arabin, and grieved greatly at his back-sliding.

They were sitting, talking over their sorrows, in the drawing-room before dinner on the day after Mr. Slope's departure for London; and on this occasion Mrs. Grantly spoke out her mind freely. She had opinions of her own about parish clergymen, and now thought it right to give vent to them.

"If you would have been led by me, archdeacon, you would never have put a bachelor into St. Ewold's."

"But, my dear, you don't mean to say that all bachelor clergy-men misbehave themselves."

"I don't know that clergymen are so much better than other men," said Mrs. Grantly. "It's all very well with a curate whom you have under your own eye, and whom you can get rid of if he persists in improprieties."

"But Mr. Arabin was a fellow, and couldn't have had a wife."

"Then I would have found some one who could."

"But, my dear, are fellows never to get livings?"

"Yes, to be sure they are, when they get engaged. I never would put a young man into a living unless he were married, or engaged to be married. Now here is Mr. Arabin. The whole responsibility lies upon you."

"There is not at this moment a clergyman in all Oxford more respected for morals and conduct than Arabin."

"Oh, Oxford!" said the lady, with a sneer. "What men choose to do at Oxford, nobody ever hears of. A man may do very well at Oxford who would bring disgrace on a parish; and, to tell you the truth, it seems to me that Mr. Arabin is just such a man."

The archdeacon groaned deeply, but he had no further answer to make.

"You really must speak to him, archdeacon. Only think what the Thornes will say if they hear that their parish clergyman spends his whole time philandering with this woman."

The archdeacon groaned again. He was a courageous man, and knew well enough how to rebuke the younger clergymen of the diocese, when necessary. But there was that about Mr.

Arabin which made the doctor feel that it would be very difficult to rebuke him with good effect.

"You can advise him to find a wife for himself, and he will understand well enough what that means," said Mrs. Grantly.

The archdeacon had nothing for it but groaning. There was Mr. Slope; he was going to be made dean; he was going to take a wife; he was about to achieve respectability and wealth; an excellent family mansion, and a family carriage; he would soon be among the comfortable *élite* of the ecclesiastical world of Barchester; whereas his own *protégé*, the true scion of the true church, by whom he had sworn, would be still but a poor vicar, and that with a very indifferent character for moral conduct! It might be all very well recommending Mr. Arabin to marry, but how would Mr. Arabin when married support a wife!

Things were ordering themselves thus in Plumstead drawing-room when Dr. and Mrs. Grantly were disturbed in their sweet discourse by the quick rattle of a carriage and pair of horses on the gravel sweep. The sound was not that of visitors, whose private carriages are generally brought up to country-house doors with demure propriety, but betokened rather the advent of some person or persons who were in a hurry to reach the house, and had no intention of immediately leaving it. Guests invited to stay a week, and who were conscious of arriving after the first dinner bell, would probably approach in such a manner. So might arrive an attorney with the news of a granduncle's death, or a son from college with all the fresh honours of a double first. No one would have had himself driven up to the door of a country house in such a manner who had the slightest doubt of his own right to force an entry.

"Who is it?" said Mrs. Grantly, looking at her husband.

"Who on earth can it be?" said the archdeacon to his wife. He then quietly got up and stood with the drawing-room door open in his hand. "Why, it's your father!"

It was indeed Mr. Harding, and Mr. Harding alone. He had come by himself in a post-chaise with a couple of horses from Barchester, arriving almost after dark, and evidently full of news. His visits had usually been made in the quietest manner; he had rarely presumed to come without notice, and had always been driven up in a modest old green fly, with one horse, that hardly made itself heard as it crawled up to the hall door.

"Good gracious, Warden, is it you?" said the archdeacon, forgetting in his surprise the events of the last few years. "But come in; nothing the matter, I hope."

"We are very glad you are come, papa," said his daughter. "I'll go and get your room ready at once."

"I an't warden, archdeacon," said Mr. Harding. "Mr. Quiverful is warden."

"Oh, I know, I know," said the archdeacon, petulantly. "I forgot all about it at the moment. Is anything the matter?"

"Don't go this moment, Susan," said Mr. Harding; "I have something to tell you."

"The dinner bell will ring in five minutes," said she.

"Will it?" said Mr. Harding. "Then, perhaps, I had better wait." He was big with news which he had come to tell, but which he knew could not be told without much discussion. He had hurried away to Plumstead as fast as two horses could bring him; and now, finding himself there, he was willing to accept the reprieve which dinner would give him.

"If you have anything of moment to tell us," said the archdeacon, "pray let us hear it at once. Has Eleanor gone off?"

"No, she has not," said Mr. Harding, with a look of great displeasure.

"Has Slope been made dean?"

"No, he has not; but —"

"But what?" said the archdeacon, who was becoming very impatient.

"They have —"

"They have what?" said the archdeacon.

"They have offered it to me," said Mr. Harding, with a modesty which almost prevented his speaking.

"Good heavens!" said the archdeacon, and sank back exhausted in an easy-chair.

"My dear, dear father," said Mrs. Grantly, and threw her arms round her father's neck.

"So I thought I had better come out and consult with you at once," said Mr. Harding.

"Consult!" shouted the archdeacon. 'But, my dear Harding, I congratulate you with my whole heart — with my whole heart; I do indeed. I never heard anything in my life that gave me so much pleasure;" and he got hold of both his father-in-law's hands, and shook them as though he were going to shake them off, and walked round and round the room, twirling a copy of the Jupiter over his head, to show his extreme exultation.

"But —" began Mr. Harding.

"But me no buts," said the archdeacon. "I never was so happy in my life. It was just the proper thing to do. Upon my honour

I'll never say another word against Lord —— the longest day I have to live."

"That's Dr. Gwynne's doing, you may be sure," said Mrs. Grantly, who greatly liked the Master of Lazarus, he being an orderly married man with a large family.

"I suppose it is," said the archdeacon.

"Oh, papa, I am so truly delighted!" said Mrs. Grantly, getting up and kissing her father.

"But, my dear," said Mr. Harding.—It was all in vain that he strove to speak; nobody would listen to him.

"Well, Mr. Dean," said the archdeacon, triumphing; "the deanery gardens will be some consolation for the hospital elms. Well, poor Quiverful! I won't begrudge him his good fortune any longer."

"No, indeed," said Mrs. Grantly. "Poor woman, she has fourteen children. I am sure I am very glad they have got it."

"So am I," said Mr. Harding.

"I would give twenty pounds," said the archdeacon, "to see how Mr. Slope will look when he hears it." The idea of Mr. Slope's discomfiture formed no small part of the archdeacon's pleasure.

At last Mr. Harding was allowed to go up-stairs and wash his hands, having, in fact, said very little of all that he had come out to Plumstead on purpose to say. Nor could anything more be said till the servants were gone after dinner. The joy of Dr. Grantly was so uncontrollable that he could not refrain from calling his father-in-law Mr. Dean before the men; and therefore it was soon matter of discussion in the lower regions how Mr. Harding, instead of his daughter's future husband, was to be the new dean, and various were the opinions on the matter. The cook and butler, who were advanced in years, thought that it was just as it should be; but the footman and lady's maid, who were younger, thought it was a great shame that Mr. Slope should lose his chance.

"He's a mean chap all the same," said the footman; "and it an't along of him that I says so. But I always did admire the missus's sister; and she'd well become the situation."

While these were the ideas down-stairs, a very great difference of opinion existed above. As soon as the cloth was drawn and the wine on the table, Mr. Harding made for himself an opportunity of speaking. It was, however, with much inward troubling that he said:—

"It's very kind of Lord ——, very kind, and I feel it deeply, most deeply. I am, I must confess, gratified by the offer—"

"I should think so," said the archdeacon.

"But, all the same, I am afraid that I can't accept it."

The decanter almost fell from the archdeacon's hand upon the table ; and the start he made was so great as to make his wife jump up from her chair. Not accept the deanship! If it really ended in this, there would be no longer any doubt that his father-in-law was demented. The question now was whether a clergyman with low rank, and preferment amounting to less than 200*l.* a year, should accept high rank, 1200*l.* a year, and one of the most desirable positions which his profession had to afford!

" What !" said the archdeacon, gasping for breath, and staring at his guest as though the violence of his emotion had almost thrown him into a fit.

" What !"

" I do not find myself fit for new duties," urged Mr. Harding.

"New duties! what duties ?" said the archdeacon, with unintended sarcasm.

" Oh, papa," said Mrs. Grantly, "nothing can be easier than what a dean has to do. Surely you are more active than Dr. Trefoil."

" He won't have half as much to do as he has at present," said Dr. Grantly.

" Did you see what the Jupiter said the other day about young men ? "

" Yes ; and I saw that the Jupiter said all that it could to induce the appointment of Mr. Slope. Perhaps you would wish to see Mr. Slope made dean."

Mr. Harding made no reply to this rebuke, though he felt it strongly. He had not come over to Plumstead to have further contention with his son-in-law about Mr. Slope, so he allowed it to pass by.

" I know I cannot make you understand my feeling," he said, "for we have been cast in different moulds. I may wish that I had your spirit and energy and power of combating ; but I have not. Every day that is added to my life increases my wish for peace and rest."

" And where on earth can a man have peace and rest if not in a deanery ? " said the archdeacon.

" People will say that I am too old for it."

" Good heavens! people ! what people ? What need you care for any people ? "

" But I think myself I am too old for any new place."

" Dear papa," said Mrs. Grantly, " men ten years older than you are appointed to new situations day after day."

" My dear," said he, " it is impossible that I should make you understand my feelings, nor do I pretend to any great virtue in the matter. The truth is, I want the force of character which might enable me to stand against the spirit of the times. The call on all sides now is for young men, and I have not the nerve to put myself in opposition to the demand. Were the Jupiter, when it hears of my appointment, to write article after article, setting forth my incompetency, I am sure it would cost me my reason. I ought to be able to bear with such things, you will say. Well, my dear, I own that I ought. But I feel my weakness, and I know that I can't. And, to tell you the truth, I know no more than a child what the dean has to do."

"Pshaw!" exclaimed the archdeacon.

"Don't be angry with me, archdeacon: don't let us quarrel about it, Susan. If you knew how keenly I feel the necessity of having to disoblige you in this matter, you would not be angry with me."

This was a dreadful blow to Dr. Grantly. Nothing could possibly have suited him better than having Mr. Harding in the deanery. Though he had never looked down on Mr. Harding on account of his recent poverty, he did fully recognise the satisfaction of having those belonging to him in comfortable positions. It would be much more suitable that Mr. Harding should be dean of Barchester than vicar of St. Cuthbert's and precentor to boot. And then the great discomfiture of that arch enemy of all that was respectable in Barchester, of that new low-church clerical *parvenu* that had fallen amongst them, that alone would be worth more, almost, than the situation itself. It was frightful to think that such unhoped-for good fortune should be marred by the absurd crotchets and unwholesome hallucinations by which Mr. Harding allowed himself to be led astray. To have the cup so near his lips and then to lose the drinking of it, was more than Dr. Grantly could endure.

And yet it appeared as though he would have to endure it. In vain he threatened and in vain he coaxed. Mr. Harding did not indeed speak with perfect decision of refusing the proffered glory, but he would not speak with anything like decision of accepting it. When pressed again and again, he would again and again allege that he was wholly unfitted to new duties. It was in vain that the archdeacon tried to insinuate, though he could not plainly declare, that there were no new duties to perform. It was in vain he hinted that in all cases of difficulty he, the archdeacon, was willing and able to guide a weak-minded dean. Mr. Harding seemed to have a foolish idea, not only that there were new duties to do, but that no one should accept the place who was not himself prepared to do them.

The conference ended in an understanding that Mr. Harding should at once acknowledge the letter he had received from the minister's private secretary, and should beg that he might be allowed two days to make up his mind ; and that during those two days the matter should be considered.

On the following morning the archdeacon was to drive Mr. Harding back to Barchester.

CHAP. XLVIII.

MISS THORNE SHOWS HER TALENT AT MATCH-MAKING.

On Mr. Harding's return to Barchester from Plumstead, which was effected by him in due course in company with the archdeacon, more tidings of a surprising nature met him. He was, during the journey, subjected to such a weight of unanswerable argument, all of which went to prove that it was his bounden duty not to inter-fere with the paternal government that was so anxious to make him a dean, that when he arrived at the chemist's door in High Street, he hardly knew which way to turn himself in the matter. But, perplexed as he was, he was doomed to further perplexity. He found a note there from his daughter begging him most urgently to come to her immediately.   But we must again go back a little in our story.

Miss Thorne had not been slow to hear the rumours respecting Mr. Arabin, which had so much disturbed the happiness of Mrs. Grantly.   And she, also, was unhappy to think that her parish clergyman should be accused of worshipping a strange goddess. She, also, was of opinion, that rectors and vicars should all be married, and with that good-natured energy which was characteristic of her, she put her wits to work to find a fitting match for Mr. Arabin.   Mrs. Grantly, in this difficulty, could think of no better remedy than a lecture from the archdeacon. Miss Thorne thought that a young lady, marriageable, and with a dowry, might be of more efficacy.   In looking through the catalogue of her unmarried friends, who might possibly be in want of a husband, and might also be fit for such promotion as a country parsonage affords, she could think of no one more eligible than Mrs. Bold ; and, consequently, losing no time, she went into Barchester on the day of Mr. Slope's discomfiture, the same day that her brother had had his interesting interview with the last of the Neros, and invited Mrs. Bold to bring her nurse and baby to Ullathorne and make them a protracted visit.

Miss Thorne suggested a month or two, intending to use her influence afterwards in prolonging it so as to last out the winter, in order that Mr. Arabin might have an opportunity of becoming fairly intimate with his intended bride. " We'll have Mr. Arabin too," said Miss Thorne to herself; "and before the spring they'll know each other; and in twelve or eighteen months' time, if all goes well, Mrs. Bold will be domiciled at St. Ewold's; " and then the kind-hearted lady gave herself some not undeserved praise for her match-making genius.

Eleanor was taken a little by surprise, but the matter ended in her promising to go to Ullathorne for at any rate a week or two; and on the day previous to that on which her father drove out to Plumstead, she had had herself driven out to Ullathorne.

Miss Thorne would not perplex her with her embryo lord on that same evening, thinking that she would allow her a few hours to make herself at home; but on the following morning Mr. Arabin arrived. "And now," said Miss Thorne to herself, "I must contrive to throw them in each other's way." That same day, after dinner, Eleanor, with an assumed air of dignity which she could not maintain, with tears that she could not suppress, with a flutter which she could not conquer, and a joy which she could not hide, told Miss Thorne that she was engaged to marry Mr. Arabin, and that it behoved her to get back home to Barchester as quick as she could.

To say simply that Miss Thorne was rejoiced at the success of the scheme, would give a very faint idea of her feelings on the occasion. My readers may probably have dreamt before now that they have had before them some terribly long walk to accomplish, some journey of twenty or thirty miles, an amount of labour frightful to anticipate, and that immediately on starting they have ingeniously found some accommodating short cut which has brought them without fatigue to their work's end in five minutes. Miss Thorne's waking feelings were somewhat of the same nature. My readers may perhaps have had to do with children, and may on some occasion have promised to their young charges some great gratification intended to come off, perhaps at the end of the winter, or at the beginning of summer. The impatient juveniles, however, will not wait, and clamorously demand their treat before they go to bed. Miss Thorne had a sort of feeling that her children were equally unreasonable. She was like an inexperienced gunner, who has ill calculated the length of the train that he has laid. The gunpowder exploded much too soon, and poor Miss Thorne felt that she was blown up by the strength of her own petar.

Miss Thorne had had lovers of her own, but they had been gentlemen of old-fashioned and deliberate habits. Miss Thorne's heart also had not always been hard, though she was still a virgin spinster ; but it had never yielded in this way at the first assault. She had intended to bring together a middle-aged studious clergyman, and a discreet matron who might possibly be induced to marry again ; and in doing so she had thrown fire among tinder. Well, it was all as it should be, but she did feel perhaps a little put out by the precipitancy of her own success; and perhaps a little vexed at the readiness of Mrs. Bold to be wooed.

She said, however, nothing about it to any one, and ascribed it all to the altered manners of the new age. Their mothers and grandmothers were perhaps a little more deliberate; but it was admitted on all sides that things were conducted very differently now than in former times. For aught Miss Thorne knew of the matter, a couple of hours might be quite sufficient under the new régime to complete that for which she in her ignorance had allotted twelve months.

But we must not pass over the wooing so cavalierly. It has been told, with perhaps tedious accuracy, how Eleanor disposed of two of her lovers at Ullathorne ; and it must also be told with equal accuracy, and if possible with less tedium, how she encountered Mr. Arabin.

It cannot be denied that when Eleanor accepted Miss Thorne's invitation, she remembered that Ullathorne was in the parish of St. Ewold's. Since her interview with the signora she had done little else than think about Mr. Arabin, and the appeal that had been made to her. She could not bring herself to believe or try to bring herself to believe, that what she had been told was untrue. Think of it how she would, she could not but accept it as a fact that Mr. Arabin was fond of her ; and then when she went further, and asked herself the question, she could not but accept it as a fact also that she was fond of him. If it were destined for her to be the partner of his hopes and sorrows, to whom could she look for friendship so properly as to Miss Thorne ? This invitation was like an ordained step towards the fulfilment of her destiny, and when she also heard that Mr. Arabin was expected to be at Ullathorne on the following day, it seemed as though all the world were conspiring in her favour. Well, did she not deserve it ? In that affair of Mr. Slope, had not all the world conspired against her ?

She could not, however, make herself easy and at home. When in the evening after dinner Miss Thorne expatiated on the excellence of Mr. Arabin's qualities, and hinted that any little rumour which might be ill-naturedly spread abroad concerning him really meant nothing, Mrs. Bold found herself unable to answer. When Miss Thorne went a little further and declared that she did not know a prettier vicarage-house in the county than St. Ewold's, Mrs. Bold, remembering the projected bow-window and the projected priestess, still held her tongue ; though her ears tingled with the conviction that all the world knew that she was in love with Mr. Arabin. Well ; what would that matter if they could only meet and tell each other what each now longed to tell?

And they did meet. Mr. Arabin came early in the day, and found the two ladies together at work in the drawing-room. Miss Thorne, who had she known all the truth would have vanished into air at once, had no conception that her immediate absence would be a blessing, and remained chatting with them till luncheon-time. Mr. Arabin could talk about nothing but the Signora Neroni's beauty, would discuss no people but the Stanhopes. This was very distressing to Eleanor, and not very satisfactory to Miss Thorne. But yet there was evidence of innocence in his open avowal of admiration.

And then they had lunch, and then Mr. Arabin went out on parish duty, and Eleanor and Miss Thorne were left to take a walk together.

"Do you think the Signora Neroni is so lovely as people say ? " Eleanor asked as they were coming home.

"She is very beautiful certainly, very beautiful," Miss Thorne answered ; "but I do not know that any one considers her lovely. She is a woman all men would like to look at ; but few I imagine would be glad to take her to their hearths, even were she unmarried and not afflicted as she is."

There was some little comfort in this. Eleanor made the most of it till she got back to the house. She was then left alone in the drawing-room, and just as it was getting dark Mr. Arabin came in.

It was a beautiful afternoon in the beginning of October, and Eleanor was sitting in the window to get the advantage of the last daylight for her novel. There was a fire in the comfortable room, but the weather was not cold enough to make it attractive;

and as she could see the sun set from where she sat, she was not very attentive to her book.

Mr. Arabin when he entered stood awhile with his back to the fire in his usual way, merely uttering a few common-place remarks about the beauty of the weather, while he plucked up courage for more interesting converse. It cannot probably be said that he had resolved then and there to make an offer to Eleanor. Men we believe seldom make such resolves. Mr. Slope and Mr. Stanhope had done so, it is true; but gentlemen generally propose without any absolutely defined determination as to their doing so. Such was now the case with Mr. Arabin.

"It is a lovely sunset," said Eleanor, answering him on the dreadfully trite subject which he had chosen.

Mr. Arabin could not see the sunset from the hearth-rug, so he had to go close to her.

"Very lovely," said he, standing modestly so far away from her as to avoid touching the flounces of her dress. Then it appeared that he had nothing further to say; so after gazing for a moment in silence at the brightness of the setting sun, he returned to the fire.

Eleanor found that it was quite impossible for herself to commence a conversation. In the first place she could find nothing to say; words, which were generally plenty enough with her, would not come to her relief. And, moreover, do what she would, she could hardly prevent herself from crying.

"Do you like Ullathorne?" said Mr. Arabin, speaking from the safely distant position which he had assumed on the hearth-rug.

"Yes, indeed, very much!"

"I don't mean Mr. and Miss Thorne. I know you like them; but the style of the house. There is something about old-fashioned mansions, built as this is, and old-fashioned gardens, that to me is especially delightful."

"I like everything old-fashioned," said Eleanor; "old-fashioned things are so much the honestest."

"I don't know about that," said Mr. Arabin, gently laughing. "That is an opinion on which very much may be said on either side. It is strange how widely the world is divided on a subject which so nearly concerns us all, and which is so close beneath our eyes. Some think that we are quickly progressing towards perfection, while others imagine that virtue is disappearing from the earth."

"And you, Mr. Arabin, what do you think?" said Eleanor. She felt somewhat surprised at the tone which his conversation was taking, and yet she was relieved at his saying something which enabled herself to speak without showing her own emotion.

"What do I think, Mrs. Bold?" and then he rumbled his money with his hands in his trowsers pockets, and looked and spoke very little like a thriving lover. "It is the bane of my life that on important subjects I acquire no fixed opinion. I think, and think, and go on thinking; and yet my thoughts are running ever in different directions. I hardly know whether or no we do lean more confidently than our fathers did on those high hopes to which we profess to aspire."

"I think the world grows more worldly every day," said Eleanor.

"That is because you see more of it than when you were younger. But we should hardly judge by what we see,—we see so very very little." There was then a pause for a while, during which Mr. Arabin continued to turn over his shillings and half-crowns. "If we believe in Scripture, we can hardly think that mankind in general will now be allowed to retrograde."

Eleanor, whose mind was certainly engaged otherwise than on the general state of mankind, made no answer to this. She felt thoroughly dissatisfied with herself. She could not force her thoughts away from the topic on which the signora had spoken to her in so strange a way, and yet she knew that she could not converse with Mr. Arabin in an unrestrained natural tone till she did so. She was most anxious not to show to him any special emotion, and yet she felt that if he looked at her he would at once see that she was not at ease.

But he did not look at her. Instead of doing so, he left the fire-place and began walking up and down the room. Eleanor took up her book resolutely; but she could not read, for there was a tear in her eye, and do what she would it fell on her cheek. When Mr. Arabin's back was turned to her she wiped it away; but another was soon coursing down her face in its place. They would come; not a deluge of tears that would have betrayed her at once, but one by one, single monitors. Mr. Arabin did not observe her closely, and they passed unseen.

Mr. Arabin, thus pacing up and down the room, took four or five turns before he spoke another word, and Eleanor sat equally silent with her face bent over her book. She was afraid that her tears would get the better of her, and was preparing for an escape from the room, when Mr. Arabin in his walk stood opposite to her. He did not come close up, but stood exactly on the spot to which his course brought him, and then, with his hands under his coat tails, thus made his confession.

"Mrs. Bold," said he, "I owe you retribution for a great offence of which I have been guilty towards you." Eleanor's heart beat so that she could not trust herself to say that he had never been guilty of any offence. So Mr. Arabin thus went on.

"I have thought much of it since, and I am now aware that I was wholly unwarranted in putting to you a question which I once asked you. It was indelicate on my part, and perhaps unmanly. No intimacy which may exist between myself and your connection, Dr. Grantly, could justify it. Nor could the acquaintance which existed between ourselves." This word acquaintance struck cold on Eleanor's heart. Was this to be her doom after all? "I therefore think it right to beg your pardon in a humble spirit, and I now do so."

What was Eleanor to say to him? She could not say much, because she was crying, and yet she must say something. She was most anxious to say that something graciously, kindly, and yet not in such a manner as to betray herself. She had never felt herself so much at a loss for words.

"Indeed I took no offence, Mr. Arabin."

"Oh, but you did! And had you not done so, you would not have been yourself. You were as right to be offended, as I was wrong so to offend you. I have not forgiven myself, but I hope to hear that you forgive me."

She was now past speaking calmly, though she still continued to hide her tears, and Mr. Arabin, after pausing a moment in vain for her reply, was walking off towards the door. She felt that she could not allow him to go unanswered without grievously sinning against all charity; so, rising from her seat, she gently touched his arm and said: "Oh, Mr. Arabin, do not go till I speak to you! I do forgive you. You know that I forgive you."

He took the hand that had so gently touched his arm, and then gazed into her face as if he would peruse there, as though written in a book, the whole future destiny of his life; and as he did so, there was a sober sad seriousness in his own countenance, which Eleanor found herself unable to sustain. She could only look down upon the carpet, let her tears trickle as they would, and leave her hand within his.

It was but for a minute that they stood so, but the duration of that minute was sufficient to make it ever memorable to them both. Eleanor was sure now that she was loved. No words, be their eloquence what it might, could be more impressive than that eager, melancholy gaze.

Why did he look so into her eyes? Why did he not speak to her? Could it be that he looked for her to make the first sign?

And he, though he knew but little of women, even he knew that he was loved. He had only to ask and it would be all his own, that inexpressible loveliness, those ever speaking but yet now mute eyes, that feminine brightness and eager loving spirit which had so attracted him since first he had encountered it at St. Ewold's. It might, must all be his own now. On no other supposition was it possible that she should allow her hand to remain thus clasped within his own. He had only to ask. Ah! but that was the difficulty. Did a minute suffice for all this? Nay, perhaps it might be more than a minute.

"Mrs. Bold—" at last he said, and then stopped himself.

If he could not speak, how was she to do so? He had called her by her name, the same name that any merest stranger would have used! She withdrew her hand from his, and moved as though to return to her seat. "Eleanor!" he then said, in his softest tone, as though the courage of a lover were as yet but half assumed, as though he were still afraid of giving offence by the freedom which he took. She looked slowly, gently, almost piteously up into his face. There was at any rate no anger there to deter him.

"Eleanor!" he again exclaimed; and in a moment he had her clasped to his bosom. How this was done, whether the doing was with him or her, whether she had flown thither conquered by the tenderness of his voice, or he with a violence not likely to give offence had drawn her to his breast, neither of them knew; nor can I declare. There was now that sympathy between them which hardly admitted of individual motion. They were one and the same,—one flesh,—one spirit,—one life.

"Eleanor, my own Eleanor, my own, my wife!" She ventured to look up at him through her tears, and he, bowing his face down over hers, pressed his lips upon her brow; his virgin lips, which, since a beard first grew upon his chin, had never yet tasted the luxury of a woman's cheek.

She had been told that her yea must be yea, or her nay, nay; but she was called on for neither the one nor the other. She told Miss Thorne that she was engaged to Mr. Arabin, but no such words had passed between them, no promises had been asked or given.

"Oh, let me go," said she; "let me go now. I am too happy to remain,—let me go, that I may be alone." He did not try to hinder her, he did not repeat the kiss; he did not press another on her lips. He might have done so had he been so minded. She was now all his own. He took his arm from round her waist, his arm that was trembling with a new delight, and let her go. She fled like a roe to her own chamber, and then, having turned the bolt, she enjoyed the full luxury of her love. She idolised, almost worshipped this man who had so meekly begged her pardon. And he was now her own. Oh, how she wept and cried and laughed, as the hopes and fears and miseries of the last few weeks passed in remembrance through her mind.

Mr. Slope! That any one should have dared to think that she who had been chosen by him could possibly have mated herself with Mr. Slope! That they should have dared to tell him, also, and subject her bright happiness to such needless risk! And then she smiled with joy as she thought of all the comforts that she could give him; not that he cared for comforts, but that it would be so delicious for her to give.

She got up and rang for her maid that she might tell her little boy of his new father; and in her own way she did tell him. She desired her maid to leave her, in order that she might be alone with her child; and then, while he lay sprawling on the bed, she poured forth the praises, all unmeaning to him, of the man she had selected to guard his infancy.

She could not be happy, however, till she had made Mr. Arabin take the child to himself, and thus, as it were, adopt him as his own. The moment the idea struck her she took the baby up in her arms, and, opening her door, ran quickly down to the drawing-room. She at once found, by his step still pacing on the floor, that he was there; and a glance within the room told her that he was alone. She hesitated a moment, and then hurried in with her precious charge.

Mr. Arabin met her in the middle of the room. "There," said she, breathless with her haste; "there, take him — take him and love him."

Mr. Arabin took the little fellow from her, and kissing him again and again, prayed God to bless him. "He shall be all as my own — all as my own," said he. Eleanor, as she stooped to take back her child, kissed the hand that held him, and then rushed back with her treasure to her chamber.

It was thus that Mr. Harding's younger daughter was won for the second time. At dinner neither she nor Mr. Arabin were very bright, but their silence occasioned no remark. In the drawing-room, as we have before said, she told Miss Thorne what had occurred. The next morning she returned to Barchester, and Mr. Arabin went over with his budget of news to the archdeacon. As Doctor Grantly was not there, he could only satisfy himself by telling Mrs. Grantly how that he intended himself the honour of becoming her brother-in-law. In the ecstasy of her joy at hearing such tidings, Mrs. Grantly vouchsafed him a warmer welcome than any he had yet received from Eleanor.

"Good heavens!" she exclaimed—it was the general exclamation of the rectory. "Poor Eleanor! Dear Eleanor! What a monstrous injustice has been done her!—Well, it shall all be made up now." And then she thought of the signora. "What lies people tell," she said to herself.

But people in this matter had told no lies at all.

CHAP. XLIX.

THE BELZEBUB COLT.

WHEN Miss Thorne left the dining-room, Eleanor had formed no intention of revealing to her what had occurred; but when she was seated beside her hostess on the sofa the secret dropped from her almost unawares. Eleanor was but a bad hypocrite, and she found herself quite unable to continue talking about Mr. Arabin as though he were a stranger, while her heart was full of him. When Miss Thorne, pursuing her own scheme with discreet zeal, asked the young widow whether, in her opinion, it would not be a good thing for Mr. Arabin to get married, she had nothing for it but to confess the truth. "I suppose it would," said Eleanor, rather sheepishly. Whereupon Miss Thorne amplified on the idea. "Oh, Miss Thorne," said Eleanor, "he is going to be married: I am engaged to him."

Now Miss Thorne knew very well that there had been no such engagement when she had been walking with Mrs. Bold in the morning. She had also heard enough to be tolerably sure that there had been no preliminaries to such an engagement. She was, therefore, as we have before described, taken a little by surprise. But, nevertheless, she embraced her guest, and cordially congratulated her.

Eleanor had no opportunity of speaking another word to Mr. Arabin that evening, except such words as all the world might hear; and these, as may be supposed, were few enough. Miss Thorne did her best to leave them in privacy; but Mr. Thorne, who knew nothing of what had occurred, and another guest, a friend of his, entirely interfered with her good intentions. So poor Eleanor had to go to bed without one sign of affection. Her state, nevertheless, was not to be pitied.

The next morning she was up early. It was probable, she thought, that by going down a little before the usual hour of breakfast, she might find Mr. Arabin alone in the dining-room. Might it not be that he also would calculate that an interview would thus be possible? Thus thinking, Eleanor was dressed a full hour before the time fixed in the Ullathorne household for morning prayers. She did not at once go down. She was afraid to seem to be too anxious to meet her lover; though, heaven knows, her anxiety was intense enough. She therefore sat herself down at her window, and repeatedly looking at her watch, nursed her child till she thought she might venture forth.

When she found herself at the dining-room door, she stood a moment, hesitating to turn the handle; but when she heard Mr. Thorne's voice inside she hesitated no longer. Her object was defeated, and she might now go in as soon as she liked without the slightest imputation on her delicacy. Mr. Thorne and Mr. Arabin were standing on the hearth-rug, discussing the merits of the Belzebub colt; or rather, Mr. Thorne was discussing, and Mr. Arabin was listening. That interesting animal had rubbed the stump of his tail against the wall of his stable, and occasioned much uneasiness to the Ullathorne master of the horse. Had Eleanor but waited another minute, Mr. Thorne would have been in the stables.

Mr. Thorne, when he saw his lady guest, repressed his anxiety. The Belzebub colt must do without him. And so the three stood, saying little or nothing to each other, till at last the master of the house, finding that he could no longer bear his present state of suspense respecting his favourite young steed, made an elaborate apology to Mrs. Bold, and escaped. As he shut the door behind him, Eleanor almost wished that he had remained. It was not that she was afraid of Mr. Arabin, but she hardly yet knew how to address him.

He, however, soon relieved her from her embarrassment. He came up to her, and taking both her hands in his, he said: " So, Eleanor, you and I are to be man and wife. Is it so?"

She looked up into his face, and her lips formed themselves into a single syllable. She uttered no sound, but he could read the affirmative plainly in her face.

" It is a great trust," said he; "a very great trust."

"It is—it is," said Eleanor, not exactly taking what he had said in the sense that he had meant. "It is a very, very great trust, and I will do my utmost to deserve it."

"And I also will do my utmost to deserve it," said Mr. Arabin, very solemnly. And then, winding his arm round her waist, he stood there gazing at the fire, and she with her head leaning on his shoulder, stood by him, well satisfied with her position. They neither of them spoke, or found any want of speaking. All that was needful for them to say had been said. The yea, yea, had been spoken by Eleanor in her own way—and that way had been perfectly satisfactory to Mr. Arabin.

And now it remained to them each to enjoy the assurance of the other's love. And how great that luxury is! How far it surpasses any other pleasure which God has allowed to his creatures! And to a woman's heart how doubly delightful!

When the ivy has found its tower, when the delicate creeper has found its strong wall, we know how the parasite plants grow and prosper. They were not created to stretch forth their branches alone, and endure without protection the summer's sun and the winter's storm. Alone they but spread themselves on the ground, and cower unseen in the dingy shade. But when they have found their firm supporters, how wonderful is their beauty; how all pervading and victorious! What is the turret without its ivy, or the high garden-wall without the jasmine which gives it its beauty and fragrance? The hedge without the honeysuckle is but a hedge.

There is a feeling still half existing, but now half conquered by the force of human nature, that a woman should be ashamed of her love till the husband's right to her compels her to acknowledge it. We would fain preach a different doctrine. A woman should glory in her love; but on that account let her take the more care that it be such as to justify her glory.

Eleanor did glory in hers, and she felt, and had cause to feel, that it deserved to be held as glorious. She could have stood there for hours with his arm round her, had fate and Mr. Thorne permitted it. Each moment she crept nearer to his bosom, and felt more and more certain that there was her home. What now to her was the archdeacon's arrogance, her sister's coldness, or her dear father's weakness? What need she care for the duplicity of such friends as Charlotte Stanhope? She had found the strong shield that should guard her from all wrongs, the trusty pilot that should henceforward guide her through the shoals and rocks. She would give up the heavy burden of her independence, and once more assume the position of a woman, and the duties of a trusting and loving wife.

And he, too, stood there fully satisfied with his place. They were both looking intently on the fire, as though they could read there their future fate, till at last Eleanor turned her face towards his. "How sad you are," she said, smiling; and indeed his face was, if not sad, at least serious. "How sad you are, love!"

"Sad," said he, looking down at her; "no, certainly not sad." Her sweet loving eyes were turned towards him, and she smiled softly as he answered her. The temptation was too strong even for the demure propriety of Mr. Arabin, and, bending over her, he pressed his lips to hers.

Immediately after this, Mr. Thorne appeared, and they were both delighted to hear that the tail of the Belzebub colt was not materially injured.

It had been Mr. Harding's intention to hurry over to Ullathorne as soon as possible after his return to Barchester, in order to secure the support of his daughter in his meditated revolt against the arch-deacon as touching the deanery; but he was spared the additional journey by hearing that Mrs. Bold had returned unexpectedly home. As soon as he had read her note he started off, and found her waiting for him in her own house.

How much each of them had to tell the other, and how certain each was that the story which he or she had to tell would astonish the other!

"My dear, I am so anxious to see you," said Mr. Harding, kissing his daughter.

"Oh, papa, I have so much to tell you!" said the daughter, returning the embrace.

"My dear, they have offered me the deanery!" said Mr. Harding, anticipating by the suddenness of the revelation the tidings which Eleanor had to give him.

"Oh, papa," said she, forgetting her own love and happiness in her joy at the surprising news; "oh, papa, can it be possible? Dear papa, how thoroughly, thoroughly happy that makes me!"

"But, my dear, I think it best to refuse it."

"Oh, papa!"

"I am sure you will agree with me, Eleanor, when I explain it to you. You know, my dear, how old I am. If I live, I——"

"But, papa, I must tell you about myself."

"Well, my dear."

"I do so wonder how you'll take it."

"Take what?"

"If you don't rejoice at it, if it doesn't make you happy, if you don't encourage me, I shall break my heart."

"If that be the case, Nelly, I certainly will encourage you."

"But I fear you won't. I do so fear you won't. And yet you can't but think I am the most fortunate woman living on God's earth."

"Are you, dearest? Then I certainly will rejoice with you. Come, Nelly, come to me, and tell me what it is."

"I am going ——"

He led her to the sofa, and seating himself beside her, took both her hands in his. "You are going to be married, Nelly. Is not that it?"

"Yes," she said, faintly. "That is if you will approve;" and then she blushed as she remembered the promise which she had so lately volunteered to him, and which she had so utterly forgotten in making her engagement with Mr. Arabin.

Mr. Harding thought for a moment who the man could be whom he was to be called upon to welcome as his son-in-law. A week since he would have had no doubt whom to name. In that case he would have been prepared to give his sanction, although he would have done so with a heavy heart. Now he knew that at any rate it would not be Mr. Slope, though he was perfectly at a loss to guess who could possibly have filled the place. For a moment he thought that the man might be Bertie Stanhope, and his very soul sank within him.

"Well, Nelly?"

"Oh, papa, promise to me that, for my sake, you will love him."

"Come, Nelly, come; tell me who it is."

"But will you love him, papa?"

"Dearest, I must love any one that you love." Then she turned her face to his, and whispered into his ear the name of Mr. Arabin.

No man that she could have named could have more surprised or more delighted him. Had he looked round the world for a son-in-law to his taste, he could have selected no one whom he would have preferred to Mr. Arabin. He was a clergyman; he held a living in the neighbourhood; he was of a set to which all Mr. Harding's own partialities most closely adhered; he was the great friend of Dr. Grantly; and he was, moreover, a man of whom Mr. Harding knew nothing but what he approved. Nevertheless, his surprise was so great as to prevent the immediate expression of his joy. He had never thought of Mr. Arabin in connection with his daughter; he had never imagined that they had any feeling in common. He had feared that his daughter had been made hostile to clergymen of Mr. Arabin's stamp by her intolerance of the archdeacon's pretensions. Had he been put to wish, he might have wished for Mr. Arabin for a son-in-law; but had he been put to guess, the name would never have occurred to him.

"Mr. Arabin!" he exclaimed; "impossible!"

"Oh, papa, for heaven's sake don't say anything against him! If you love me, don't say anything against him. Oh, papa, it's done, and mustn't be undone—oh, papa!"

Fickle Eleanor! where was the promise that she would make no choice for herself without her father's approval? She had chosen, and now demanded his acquiescence. "Oh, papa, isn't he good? isn't he noble? isn't he religious, highminded, everything that a good man possibly can be?" and she clung to her father, beseeching him for his consent.

"My Nelly, my child, my own daughter! He is; he is noble and good and highminded; he is all that a woman can love and a man admire. He shall be my son, my own son. He shall be as close to my heart as you are. My Nelly, my child, my happy, happy child!"

We need not pursue the interview any further. By degrees they returned to the subject of the new promotion. Eleanor tried to prove to him, as the Grantlys had done, that his age could be no bar to his being a very excellent dean; but those arguments had now even less weight on him than before. He said little or nothing, but sat meditative. Every now and then he would kiss his daughter, and say "yes," or "no," or "very true," or "well, my dear, I can't quite agree with you there," but he could not be got to enter sharply into the question of "to be, or not to be" dean of Barchester. Of her and her happiness of Mr. Arabin and his virtues, he would talk as much as Eleanor desired; and, to tell the truth, that was not a little; but about the deanery he would now say nothing further. He had got a new idea into his head— Why should not Mr. Arabin be the new dean?

CHAP. L.

THE ARCHDEACON IS SATISFIED WITH THE STATE OF AFFAIRS.

THE archdeacon, in his journey into Barchester, had been assured by Mr. Harding that all their prognostications about Mr. Slope and Eleanor were groundless. Mr. Harding, however, had found it very difficult to shake his son-in-law's faith in his own acuteness. The matter had, to Dr. Grantly, been so plainly corroborated by such patent evidence, borne out by such endless circumstances, that he at first refused to take as true the positive statement which Mr. Harding made to him of Eleanor's own disavowal of the impeachment. But at last he yielded in a qualified way. He brought himself to admit that he would at the present regard his past convictions as a mistake; but in doing this he so guarded himself, that if, at any future time, Eleanor should come forth to the world as Mrs. Slope, he might still be able to say: "There, I told you so. Remember what you said and what I said; and remember also for coming years, that I was right in this matter,—as in all others."

He carried, however, his concession so far as to bring himself to undertake to call at Eleanor's house, and he did call accordingly, while the father and daughter were yet in the middle of their conference. Mr. Harding had had so much to hear and to say that he had forgotten to advertise Eleanor of the honour that awaited her, and she heard her brother-in-law's voice in the hall, while she was quite unprepared to see him.

"There's the archdeacon," she said, springing up.

"Yes, my dear. He told me to tell you that he would come and see you; but, to tell the truth, I had forgotten all about it."

Eleanor fled away, regardless of all her father's entreaties. She could not now, in the first hours of her joy, bring herself to bear all the archdeacon's retractions, apologies, and congratulations. He would have so much to say, and would be so tedious in saying it; consequently, the archdeacon, when he was shown into the drawing-room, found no one there but Mr. Harding.

"You must excuse Eleanor," said Mr. Harding.

"Is anything the matter?" asked the doctor, who at once anticipated that the whole truth about Mr. Slope had at last come out.

"Well, something is the matter. I wonder now whether you will be much surprised?"

The archdeacon saw by his father-in-law's manner that after all he had nothing to tell him about Mr. Slope. "No," said he, "certainly not — nothing will ever surprise me again." Very many men now-a-days, besides the archdeacon, adopt or affect to adopt the *nil admirari* doctrine; but nevertheless, to judge from their appearance, they are just as subject to sudden emotions as their grandfathers and grandmothers were before them.

"What do you think Mr. Arabin has done?"

"Mr. Arabin! It's nothing about that daughter of Stanhope's I hope?"

"No, not that woman," said Mr. Harding, enjoying his joke in his sleeve.

"Not that woman! Is he going to do anything about any woman? Why can't you speak out if you have anything to say? There is nothing I hate so much as these sort of mysteries."

"There shall be no mystery with you, archdeacon; though, of course, it must go no further at present."

"Well."

"Except Susan. You must promise me you'll tell no one else."

"Nonsense!" exclaimed the archdeacon, who was becoming angry in his suspense. "You can't have any secret about Mr. Arabin."

"Only this—that he and Eleanor are engaged."

It was quite clear to see, by the archdeacon's face, that he did not believe a word of it. "Mr. Arabin! It's impossible!"

"Eleanor, at any rate, has just now told me so."

"It's impossible," repeated the archdeacon.

"Well, I can't say I think it impossible. It certainly took me by surprise; but that does not make it impossible."

"She must be mistaken."

Mr. Harding assured him that there was no mistake; that he would find, on returning home, that Mr. Arabin had been at Plumstead with the express object of making the same declaration, that even Miss Thorne knew all about it; and that, in fact, the thing was as clearly settled as any such arrangement between a lady and a gentleman could well be.

"Good heavens!" said the archdeacon, walking up and down Eleanor's drawing-room. "Good heavens! Good heavens!"

Now, these exclamations certainly betokened faith. Mr. Harding properly gathered from it that, at last, Dr. Grantly did believe the fact. The first utterance clearly evinced a certain amount of distaste at the information he had received; the second, simply indicated surprise; in the tone of the third, Mr. Harding fancied that he could catch a certain gleam of satisfaction.

The archdeacon had truly expressed the workings of his mind. He could not but be disgusted to find how utterly astray he had been in all his anticipations. Had he only been lucky enough to have suggested this marriage himself when he first brought Mr. Arabin into the country, his character for judgment and wisdom would have received an addition which would have classed him at any rate next to Solomon. And why had he not done so? Might he not have foreseen that Mr. Arabin would want a wife in his parsonage? He had foreseen that Eleanor would want a husband;

but should he not also have perceived that Mr. Arabin was a man much more likely to attract her than Mr. Slope? The archdeacon found that he had been at fault, and of course could not immediately get over his discomfiture.

Then his surprise was intense. How sly this pair of young turtle doves had been with him. How egregiously they had hoaxed him. He had preached to Eleanor against her fancied attachment to Mr. Slope, at the very time that she was in love with his own protégé, Mr. Arabin; and had absolutely taken that same Mr. Arabin into his confidence with reference to his dread of Mr. Slope's alliance. It was very natural that the archdeacon should feel surprise.

But there was also great ground for satisfaction. Looking at the match by itself, it was the very thing to help the doctor out of his difficulties. In the first place, the assurance that he should never have Mr. Slope for his brother-in-law, was in itself a great comfort. Then Mr. Arabin was, of all men, the one with whom it would best suit him to be so intimately connected. But the crowning comfort was the blow which this marriage would give to Mr. Slope. He had now certainly lost his wife; rumour was beginning to whisper that he might possibly lose his position in the palace; and if Mr. Harding would only be true, the great danger of all would be surmounted. In such case it might be expected that Mr. Slope would own himself vanquished, and take himself altogether away from Barchester. And so the archdeacon would again be able to breathe pure air.

"Well, well," said he. "Good heavens! good heavens!" and the tone of the fifth exclamation made Mr Harding fully aware that content was reigning in the archdeacon's bosom.

And then slowly, gradually, and craftily Mr. Harding propounded his own new scheme. Why should not Mr. Arabin be the new dean?

Slowly, gradually, and thoughtfully Dr. Grantly fell into his father-in-law's views. Much as he liked Mr. Arabin, sincere as was his admiration for that gentleman's ecclesiastical abilities, he would not have sanctioned a measure which would rob his father-in-law of his fairly-earned promotion, were it at all practicable to induce his father-in-law to accept the promotion which he had earned. But the archdeacon had, on a former occasion, received proof of the obstinacy with which Mr. Harding could adhere to his own views in opposition to the advice of all his friends. He knew tolerably well that nothing would induce the meek, mild man before him to take the high place offered to him, if he thought it wrong to do so. Knowing this, he also said to himself more than once: "Why should not Mr. Arabin be Dean of Barchester?"

It was at last arranged between them that they would together start to London by the earliest train on the following morning, making a little *détour* to Oxford on their journey. Dr. Gwynne's counsels, they imagined, might perhaps be of assistance to them.

These matters settled, the archdeacon hurried off, that he might return to Plumstead and prepare for his journey. The day was extremely fine, and he came into the city in an open gig. As he was driving up the High Street he encountered Mr. Slope at a crossing. Had he not pulled up rather sharply, he would have run over him. The two had never spoken to each other since they had met on a memorable occasion in the bishop's study. They did not speak now; but they looked each other full in the face, and Mr. Slope's countenance was as impudent, as triumphant, as defiant as ever. Had Dr. Grantly not known to the contrary, he would have imagined that his enemy had won the deanship, the wife, and all the rich honours, for which he had been striving. As it was, he had lost everything that he had in the world, and had just received his *congé* from the bishop.

In leaving the town the archdeacon drove by the well-remembered entrance of Hiram's hospital. There, at the gate, was a large, untidy, farmer's wagon, laden with untidy-looking furniture; and there, inspecting the arrival, was good Mrs. Quiverful — not dressed in her Sunday best — not very clean in her apparel — not graceful as to her bonnet and shawl; or, indeed, with many feminine charms as to her whole appearance. She was busy at domestic work in her new house, and had just ventured out, expecting to see no one on the arrival of the family chattels. The archdeacon was down upon her before she knew where she was.

Her acquaintance with Dr. Grantly or his family was very slight indeed. The archdeacon, as a matter of course, knew every clergyman in the archdeaconry, it may almost be said in the diocese, and had some acquaintance, more or less intimate, with their wives and families. With Mr. Quiverful he had been concerned on various matters of business; but of Mrs. Q. he had seen very little. Now, however, he was in too gracious a mood to pass her by unnoticed. The Quiverfuls, one and all, had looked for the bitterest hostility from Dr. Grantly; they knew his anxiety that Mr. Harding should return to his old home at the hospital, and they did not know that a new home had been offered to him at the deanery. Mrs. Quiverful was therefore not a little surprised and not a little rejoiced also, at the tone in which she was addressed.

"How do you do, Mrs. Quiverful?—how do you do?" said he, stretching his left hand out of the gig, as he spoke to her. "I am very glad to see you employed in so pleasant and useful a manner; very glad indeed."

Mrs. Quiverful thanked him, and shook hands with him, and looked into his face suspiciously. She was not sure whether the congratulations and kindness were or were not ironical.

"Pray tell Mr. Quiverful from me," he continued, "that I am rejoiced at his appointment. It's a comfortable place, Mrs. Quiverful, and a comfortable house, and I am very glad to see you in it. Good-bye — good-bye." And he drove on, leaving the lady well pleased and astonished at his good-nature. On the whole things were going well with the archdeacon, and he could afford to be charitable to Mrs. Quiverful. He looked forth from his gig smilingly on all the world, and forgave every one in Barchester their sins, excepting only Mrs. Proudie and Mr. Slope. Had he seen the bishop, he would have felt inclined to pat even him kindly on the head.

He determined to go home by St. Ewold's. This would take him some three miles out of his way; but he felt that he could not leave Plumstead comfortably without saying one word of good fellowship to Mr. Arabin. When he reached the parsonage the vicar was still out; but, from what he had heard, he did not doubt but that he would meet him on the road between their two houses. He was right in this, for about halfway home, at a narrow turn, he came upon Mr. Arabin, who was on horseback.

"Well, well, well, well;" said the archdeacon, loudly, joyously, and with supreme good humour; "well, well, well, well; so, after all, we have no further cause to fear Mr. Slope."

"I hear from Mrs. Grantly that they have offered the deanery to Mr. Harding," said the other.

"Mr. Slope has lost more than the deanery, I find," and then the archdeacon laughed jocosely. "Come, come, Arabin, you have kept your secret well enough. I know all about it now."

"I have had no secret, archdeacon," said the other with a quiet smile. "None at all — not for a day. It was only yesterday that I knew my own good fortune, and to-day I went over to Plumstead to ask your approval. From what Mrs. Grantly has said to me, I am led to hope that I shall have it."

"With all my heart, with all my heart," said the archdeacon cordially, holding his friend fast by the hand. "It's just as I would have it. She is an excellent young woman; she will not come to you empty-handed; and I think she will make you a good wife. If she does her duty by you as her sister does by me, you'll be a happy man; that's all I can say." And as he finished speaking, a tear might have been observed in each of the doctor's eyes.

Mr. Arabin warmly returned the archdeacon's grasp, but he said little. His heart was too full for speaking, and he could not express the gratitude which he felt. Dr. Grantly understood him as well as though he had spoken for an hour.

"And mind, Arabin," said he, "no one but myself shall tie the knot. We'll get Eleanor out to Plumstead, and it shall come off there. I'll make Susan stir herself, and we'll do it in style. I must be off to London to-morrow on special business. Harding goes with me. But I'll be back before your bride has got her wedding dress ready." And so they parted.

On his journey home the archdeacon occupied his mind with preparations for the marriage festivities. He made a great resolve that he would atone to Eleanor for all the injury he had done her by the munificence of his future treatment. He would show her what was the difference in his eyes between a Slope and an Arabin. On one other thing also he decided with a firm mind : if the affair of the dean should not be settled in Mr. Arabin's favour, nothing should prevent him putting a new front and bow-window to the dining-room at St. Ewold's parsonage.

"So we're sold after all, Sue," said he to his wife, accosting her with a kiss as soon as he entered his house. He did not call his wife Sue above twice or thrice in a year, and these occasions were great high days.

"Eleanor has had more sense than we gave her credit for," said Mrs. Grantly.

And there was great content in Plumstead rectory that evening; and Mrs. Grantly promised her husband that she would now open her heart, and take Mr. Arabin into it. Hitherto she had declined to do so.

CHAP. LL.

MR. SLOPE BIDS FAREWELL TO THE PALACE AND ITS INHABITANTS.

WE must now take leave of Mr. Slope, and of the bishop also, and of Mrs. Proudie. These leave-takings in novels are as disagreeable as they are in real life ; not so sad, indeed, for they want the reality of sadness ; but quite as perplexing, and generally less satisfactory. What novelist, what Fielding, what Scott, what George Sand, or Sue, or Dumas, can impart an interest to the last chapter of his fictitious history? Promises of two children and superhuman happiness are of no avail nor assurance of extreme respectability carried to an age far exceeding that usually allotted to mortals. The sorrows of our heroes and heroines, they are your delight, oh public! their sorrows, or their sins, or their absurdities; not their virtues, good sense, and consequent rewards. When we begin to tint our final pages with *couleur de rose,* as in accordance with fixed rule we must do, we altogether extinguish our own powers of pleasing. When we become dull we offend your intellect; and we must become dull or we should offend your taste. A late writer, wishing to sustain his interest to the last page, hung his hero at the end of the third volume. The consequence was, that no one would read his novel. And who can apportion out and dovetail his incidents, dialogues, characters, and descriptive morsels, so as to fit them all exactly into 439 pages, without either compressing them unnaturally, or extending them artificially at the end of his labour? Do I not myself know that I am at this moment in want of a dozen pages, and that I am sick with cudgelling my brains to find them? And then when everything is done, the kindest-hearted critic of them all invariably twits us with the incompetency and lameness of our conclusion. We have either become idle and neglected it, or tedious and over-laboured it. It is insipid or unnatural, overstrained or imbecile. It means nothing, or attempts too much. The last scene of all, as all last scenes we fear must be,

> " Is second childishness, and mere oblivion,
> Sans teeth, sans eyes, sans taste, sans everything."

I can only say that if some critic, who thoroughly knows his work, and has laboured on it till experience has made him perfect, will write the last fifty pages of a novel in the way they should be written, I, for one, will in future do my best to copy the example. Guided by my own lights only, I confess that I despair of success.

For the last week or ten days, Mr. Slope had seen nothing of Mrs. Proudie, and very little of the bishop. He still lived in the palace, and still went through his usual routine work; but the confidential doings of the diocese had passed into other hands. He had seen this clearly, and marked it well; but it had not much disturbed him. He had indulged in other hopes till the bishop's affairs had become dull to him, and he was moreover aware that, as regarded the diocese, Mrs. Proudie had checkmated him. It has been explained, in the beginning of these pages, how three or four were contending together as to who, in fact, should be bishop of Barchester. Each of these had now admitted to himself (or boasted to herself) that Mrs. Proudie was victorious in the struggle. They had gone through a competitive examination of considerable severity, and she had come forth the winner, *facile princeps*. Mr. Slope had, for a moment, run her hard, but it was only for a moment. It had become, as it were, acknowledged that Hiram's hospital should be the testing point between them, and now Mr. Quiverful was already in the hospital, the proof of Mrs. Proudie's skill and courage.

All this did not break down Mr. Slope's spirit, because he had other hopes. But, alas, at last there came to him a note from his friend Sir Nicholas, informing him that the deanship was disposed of. Let us give Mr. Slope his due. He did not lie prostrate under this blow, or give himself up to vain lamentations; he did not henceforward despair of life, and call upon gods above and gods below to carry him off. He sat himself down in his chair, counted out what monies he had in hand for present purposes, and what others were coming in to him, bethought himself as to the best sphere for his future exertions, and at once wrote off a letter to a rich sugar-refiner's wife in Baker Street, who, as he well knew, was much given to the entertainment and encouragement of serious young evangelical clergymen. He was again, he said, "upon the world, having found the air of a cathedral town, and the very nature of cathedral services, uncongenial to his spirit;" and then he sat awhile, making firm resolves as to his manner of parting from the bishop, and also as to his future conduct.

> "At last he rose, and twitched his mantle blue (black),
> To-morrow to fresh woods and pastures new."

Having received a formal command to wait upon the bishop, he rose and proceeded to obey it. He rang the bell and desired the servant to inform his master that if it suited his lordship, he, Mr. Slope, was ready to wait upon him. The servant, who well understood that Mr. Slope was no longer in the ascendant, brought back a message, saying that "his lordship desired that Mr. Slope would attend him immediately in his study." Mr. Slope waited about ten minutes more to prove his independence, and then he went into the bishop's room. There, as he had expected, he found Mrs. Proudie, together with her husband.

"Hum, ha,—Mr. Slope, pray take a chair," said the gentleman bishop.

"Pray be seated, Mr. Slope," said the lady bishop.

"Thank ye, thank ye," said Mr. Slope, and walking round to the fire, he threw himself into one of the arm-chairs that graced the hearth-rug.

"Mr. Slope," said the bishop, "it has become necessary that I should speak to you definitively on a matter that has for some time been pressing itself on my attention."

"May I ask whether the subject is in any way connected with myself?" said Mr. Slope.

"It is so, — certainly, — yes, it certainly is connected with yourself, Mr. Slope."

"Then, my lord, if I may be allowed to express a wish, I would prefer that no discussion on the subject should take place between us in the presence of a third person."

"Don't alarm yourself, Mr. Slope," said Mrs. Proudie, "no discussion is at all necessary. The bishop merely intends to express his own wishes."

"I merely intend, Mr. Slope, to express my own wishes,— no discussion will be at all necessary," said the bishop, reiterating his wife's words.

"That is more, my lord, than we any of us can be sure of," said Mr. Slope; "I cannot, however, force Mrs. Proudie to leave the room; nor can I refuse to remain here if it be your lordship's wish that I should do so."

"It is his lordship's wish, certainly," said Mrs. Proudie.

"Mr. Slope," began the bishop, in a solemn, serious voice, "it grieves me to have to find fault. It grieves me much to have to find fault with a clergyman; but especially so with a clergyman in your position."

"Why, what have I done amiss, my lord?" demanded Mr. Slope, boldly.

"What have you done amiss, Mr. Slope?" said Mrs. Proudie, standing erect before the culprit, and raising that terrible forefinger. "Do you dare to ask the bishop what you have done amiss? does not your conscience——"

"Mrs. Proudie, pray let it be understood, once for all, that I will have no words with you."

"Ah, sir, but you will have words," said she; "you must have words. Why have you had so many words with that Signora Neroni? Why have you disgraced yourself, you a clergyman too, by constantly consorting with such a woman as that,—with a married woman — with one altogether unfit for a clergyman's society?"

"At any rate, I was introduced to her in your drawing-room," retorted Mr. Slope.

"And shamefully you behaved there," said Mrs. Proudie, "most shamefully. I was wrong to allow you to remain in the house a day after what I then saw. I should have insisted on your instant dismissal."

"I have yet to learn, Mrs. Proudie, that you have the power to insist either on my going from hence or on my staying here."

"What!" said the lady; "I am not to have the privilege of saying who shall and who shall not frequent my own drawing-room! I am not to save my servants and dependents from having their morals corrupted by improper conduct! I am not to save my own daughters from impurity! I will let you see, Mr. Slope, whether I have the power or whether I have not. You will have the goodness to understand that you no longer fill any situation about the bishop; and as your room will be immediately wanted in the palace for another chaplain, I must ask you to provide yourself with apartments as soon as may be convenient to you."

"My lord," said Mr. Slope, appealing to the bishop, and so turning his back completely on the lady, "will you permit me to ask that I may have from your own lips any decision that you may have come to on this matter?"

"Certainly, Mr. Slope, certainly," said the bishop; "that is but reasonable. Well, my decision is that you had better look for some other preferment. For the situation which you have lately held I do not think that you are well suited."

"And what, my lord, has been my fault?"

"That Signora Neroni is one fault," said Mrs. Proudie; "and a very abominable fault she is; very abominable and very disgraceful. Fie, Mr. Slope, fie! You an evangelical clergyman indeed!"

"My lord, I desire to know for what fault I am turned out of your lordship's house."

"You hear what Mrs. Proudie says," said the bishop.

"When I publish the history of this transaction, my lord, as I decidedly shall do in my own vindication, I presume you will not wish me to state that you have discarded me at your wife's bidding — because she has objected to my being acquainted with another lady, the daughter of one of the prebendaries of the chapter?"

"You may publish what you please, sir," said Mrs. Proudie. "But you will not be insane enough to publish any of your doings in Barchester. Do you think I have not heard of your kneelings at that creature's feet — that is if she has any feet — and of your constant slobbering over her hand? I advise you to beware, Mr. Slope, of what you do and say. Clergymen have been unfrocked for less than what you have been guilty of."

" My lord, if this goes on I shall be obliged to indict this woman — Mrs. Proudie I mean — for defamation of character."

" I think, Mr. Slope, you had better now retire," said the bishop. ' I will enclose to you a cheque for any balance that may be due to you; and, under the present circumstances, it will of course be better for all parties that you should leave the palace at the earliest possible moment. I will allow you for your journey back to London, and for your maintenance in Barchester for a week from this date."

" If, however, you wish to remain in this neighbourhood," said Mrs. Proudie, "and will solemnly pledge yourself never again to see that woman, and will promise also to be more circumspect in your conduct, the bishop will mention your name to Mr. Quiverful, who now wants a curate at Puddingdale. The house is, I imagine, quite sufficient for your requirements: and there will moreover be a stipend of fifty pounds a year."

" May God forgive you, madam, for the manner in which you have treated me," said Mr. Slope, looking at her with a very heavenly look ; "and remember this, madam, that you yourself may still have a fall;" and he looked at her with a very worldly look. " As to the bishop, I pity him !" And so saying, Mr. Slope left the room. Thus ended the intimacy of the Bishop of Barchester with his first confidential chaplain

Mrs. Proudie was right in this; namely, that Mr. Slope was not insane enough to publish to the world any of his doings in Barchester. He did not trouble his friend Mr. Towers with any written statement of the iniquity of Mrs. Proudie, or the imbecility of her husband. He was aware that it would be wise in him to drop for the future all allusions to his doings in the cathedral city. Soon after the interview just recorded, he left Barchester, shaking the dust off his feet as he entered the railway carriage ; and he gave no longing lingering look after the cathedral towers, as the train hurried him quickly out of their sight.

It is well known that the family of the Slopes never starve : they always fall on their feet like cats, and let them fall where they will, they live on the fat of the land. Our Mr. Slope did so. On his return to town he found that the sugar-refiner had died, and that his widow was inconsolable : or, in other words, in want of consolation. Mr. Slope consoled her, and soon found himself settled with much comfort in the house in Baker Street. He possessed himself, also, before long, of a church in the vicinity of the New Road, and became known to fame as one of the most eloquent preachers and pious clergymen in that part of the metropolis. There let us leave him.

Of the bishop and his wife very little further need be said. From that time forth nothing material occurred to interrupt the even course of their domestic harmony. Very speedily, a further vacancy on the bench of bishops gave to Dr. Proudie the seat in the House of Lords, which he at first so anxiously longed for. But by this time he had become a wiser man. He did certainly take his seat, and occasionally registered a vote in favour of Government views on ecclesiastical matters. But he had thoroughly learnt that his proper sphere of action lay in close contiguity with Mrs. Proudie's wardrobe. He never again aspired to disobey, or seemed even to wish for autocratic diocesan authority. If ever he thought of freedom, he did so, as men think of the millennium, as of a good time which may be coming, but which nobody expects to come in their day. Mrs. Proudie might be said still to bloom, and was, at any rate, strong; and the bishop had no reason to apprehend that he would be speedily visited with the sorrows of a widower's life.

He is still Bishop of Barchester. He has so graced that throne, that the Government has been averse to translate him, even to higher dignities. There may he remain, under safe pupilage, till the new-fangled manners of the age have discovered him to be superannuated, and bestowed on him a pension. As for Mrs. Proudie, our prayers for her are that she may live for ever.

CHAP. LII.

THE NEW DEAN TAKES POSSESSION OF THE DEANERY, AND THE NEW WARDEN OF THE HOSPITAL.

MR. HARDING and the archdeacon together made their way to Oxford, and there, by dint of cunning argument, they induced the Master of Lazarus also to ask himself this momentous question: "Why should not Mr. Arabin be Dean of Barchester?" He of course, for a while tried his hand at persuading Mr. Harding that he was foolish, over-scrupulous, self-willed, and weak-minded; but he tried in vain. If Mr. Harding would not give way to Dr.

Grantly, it was not likely he would give way to Dr. Gwynne; more especially now that so admirable a scheme as that of inducting Mr. Arabin into the deanery had been set on foot. When the master found that his eloquence was vain, and heard also that Mr. Arabin was about to become Mr. Harding's son-in-law, he confessed that he also would, under such circumstances, be glad to see his old friend and protégé, the fellow of his college, placed in the comfortable position that was going a-begging.

"It might be the means, you know, Master, of keeping Mr. Slope out," said the archdeacon with grave caution.

"He has no more chance of it," said the master, "than our college chaplain. I know more about it than that."

Mrs. Grantly had been right in her surmise. It was the Master of Lazarus who had been instrumental in representing in high places the claims which Mr. Harding had upon the Government, and he now consented to use his best endeavours towards getting the offer transferred to Mr. Arabin. The three of them went on to London together, and there they remained a week, to the great disgust of Mrs. Grantly, and most probably also of Mrs. Gwynne. The minister was out of town in one direction, and his private secretary in another. The clerks who remained could do nothing in such a matter as this, and all was difficulty and confusion. The two doctors seemed to have plenty to do; they bustled here and they bustled there, and complained at their club in the evenings that they had been driven off their legs; but Mr. Harding had no occupation. Once or twice he suggested that he might perhaps return to Barchester. His request, however, was peremptorily refused, and he had nothing for it but to while away his time in Westminster Abbey.

At length an answer from the great man came. The Master of Lazarus had made his proposition through the Bishop of Belgravia. Now this bishop, though but newly gifted with his diocesan honours, was a man of much weight in the clerico-political world. He was, if not as pious, at any rate as wise as St. Paul, and had been with so much effect all things to all men, that though he was great among the dons of Oxford, he had been selected for the most favourite seat on the bench by a Whig Prime Minister. To him Dr. Gwynne had made known his wishes and his arguments, and the bishop had made them known to the Marquis of Kensington Gore. The marquis, who was Lord High Steward of the Pantry Board, and who by most men was supposed to hold the highest office out of the Cabinet, trafficked much in affairs of this kind. He not only suggested the arrangement to the minister over a cup of coffee, standing on a drawing-room rug in Windsor Castle, but he also favourably mentioned Mr. Arabin's name in the car of a distinguished person.

And so the matter was arranged. The answer of the great man came, and Mr. Arabin was made Dean of Barchester. The three clergymen who had come up to town on this important mission dined together with great glee on the day on which the news reached them. In a silent, decent, clerical manner, they toasted Mr. Arabin with full bumpers of claret. The satisfaction of all of them was supreme. The Master of Lazarus had been successful in his attempt, and success is dear to us all. The archdeacon had trampled upon Mr. Slope, and had lifted to high honours the young clergyman whom he had induced to quit the retirement and comfort of the university. So at least the archdeacon thought; though, to speak sooth, not he, but circumstances, had trampled on Mr. Slope. But the satisfaction of Mr. Harding was, of all perhaps, the most complete. He laid aside his usual melancholy manner, and brought forth little quiet jokes from the inmost mirth of his heart ; he poked his fun at the archdeacon about Mr. Slope's marriage, and quizzed him for his improper love for Mrs. Proudie. On the following day they all returned to Barchester.

It was arranged that Mr. Arabin should know nothing of what had been done till he received the minister's letter from the hands of his embryo father-in-law. In order that no time might be lost, a message had been sent to him by the preceding night's post, begging him to be at the deanery at the hour that the train from London arrived. There was nothing in this which surprised Mr. Arabin. It had somehow got about through all Barchester that Mr. Harding was the new dean, and all Barchester was prepared to welcome him with pealing bells and full hearts. Mr. Slope had certainly had a party ; there had certainly been those in Barchester who were prepared to congratulate him on his promotion with assumed sincerity, but even his own party was not broken-hearted by his failure. The inhabitants of the city, even the high-souled ecstatic young ladies of thirty-five, had begun to comprehend that their welfare, and the welfare of the place, was connected in some mysterious manner with daily chants and bi-weekly anthems. The expenditure of the palace had not added much to the popularity of the bishop's side of the question ; and, on the whole, there was a strong reaction. When it became known to all the world that Mr. Harding was to be the new dean, all the world rejoiced heartily.

Mr. Arabin, we have said, was not surprised at the summons

which called him to the deanery. He had not as yet seen Mr.
Harding since Eleanor had accepted him, nor had he seen him
since he had learnt his future father-in-law's preferment. There
was nothing more natural, more necessary, than that they should
meet each other at the earliest possible moment. Mr. Arabin
was waiting in the deanery parlour when Mr. Harding and Dr.
Grantly were driven up from the station.

There was some excitement in the bosoms of them all, as they
met and shook hands; by far too much to enable either of them to
begin his story and tell it in a proper equable style of narrative.
Mr. Harding was some minutes quite dumbfounded, and Mr.
Arabin could only talk in short, spasmodic sentences about his love
and good fortune. He slipped in, as best he could, some sort of
congratulation about the deanship, and then went on with his hopes
and fears,—hopes that he might be received as a son, and fears
that he hardly deserved such good fortune. Then he went back
to the dean; it was the most thoroughly satisfactory appointment,
he said, of which he had ever heard.

"But! but! but——" said Mr. Harding; and then failing to
get any further, he looked imploringly at the archdeacon.

"The truth is, Arabin," said the doctor, "that, after all, you are
not destined to be son-in-law to a dean. Nor am I either: more's
the pity."

Mr. Arabin looked at him for explanation. "Is not Mr. Harding
to be the new dean?"

"It appears not," said the archdeacon. Mr. Arabin's face fell a
little, and he looked from one to the other. It was plainly to be
seen from them both that there was no cause of unhappiness in the
matter, at least not of unhappiness to them; but there was as yet
no elucidation of the mystery.

"Think how old I am," said Mr. Harding, imploringly.

"Fiddlestick!" said the archdeacon.

"That's all very well, but it won't make a young man of me," said
Mr. Harding.

"And who is to be dean?" asked Mr. Arabin.

"Yes, that's the question," said the archdeacon. "Come, Mr.
Precentor, since you obstinately refuse to be anything else, let us
know who is to be the man. He has got the nomination in his
pocket."

With eyes brim full of tears, Mr. Harding pulled out the letter
and handed it to his future son-in-law. He tried to make a little
speech, but failed altogether. Having given up the document, he
turned round to the wall, feigning to blow his nose, and then sat

himself down on the old dean's dingy horse-hair sofa. And here we find it necessary to bring our account of the interview to an end.

Nor can we pretend to describe the rapture with which Mr. Harding was received by his daughter. She wept with grief and wept with joy; with grief that her father should, in his old age, still be without that rank and worldly position which, according to her ideas, he had so well earned; and with joy in that he, her darling father, should have bestowed on that other dear one the good things of which he himself would not open his hand to take possession. And here Mr. Harding again showed his weakness. In the *mêlée* of this exposal of their loves and reciprocal affection, he found himself unable to resist the entreaties of all parties that the lodgings in the High Street should be given up. Eleanor would not live in the deanery, she said, unless her father lived there also. Mr. Arabin would not be dean, unless Mr. Harding would be co-dean with him. The archdeacon declared that his father-in-law should not have his own way in everything, and Mrs. Grantly carried him off to Plumstead, that he might remain there till Mr. and Mrs. Arabin were in a state to receive him in their own mansion.

Pressed by such arguments as these, what could a weak old man do but yield?

But there was yet another task which it behoved Mr. Harding to do before he could allow himself to be at rest. Little has been said in these pages of the state of those remaining old men who had lived under his sway at the hospital. But not on this account must it be presumed that he had forgotten them, or that in their state of anarchy and in their want of due government he had omitted to visit them. He visited them constantly, and had latterly given them to understand that they would soon be required to subscribe their adherence to a new master. There were now but five of them, one of them having been but quite lately carried to his rest, — but five of the full number, which had hitherto been twelve, and which was now to be raised to twenty-four, including women. Of these old Bunce, who for many years had been the favourite of the late warden, was one; and Abel Handy, who had been the humble means of driving that warden from his home, was another.

Mr. Harding now resolved that he himself would introduce the new warden to the hospital. He felt that many circumstances might conspire to make the men receive Mr. Quiverful with aversion and disrespect; he felt also that Mr. Quiverful might himself feel some qualms of conscience if he entered the hospital with an idea that he did so in hostility to his predecessor. Mr. Harding therefore determined to walk in, arm in arm with Mr. Quiverful, and to ask from these men their respectful obedience to their new master.

On returning to Barchester, he found that Mr. Quiverful had not yet slept in the hospital house, or entered on his new duties. He accordingly made known to that gentleman his wishes, and his proposition was not rejected.

It was a bright clear morning, though in November, that Mr. Harding and Mr. Quiverful, arm in arm, walked through the hospital gate. It was one trait in our old friend's character that he did nothing with parade. He omitted, even in the more important doings of his life, that sort of parade by which most of us deem it necessary to grace our important doings. We have housewarmings, christenings, and gala days; we keep, if not our own birthdays, those of our children; we are apt to fuss ourselves if called upon to change our residences, and have, almost all of us our little state occasions. Mr. Harding had no state occasions. When he left his old house, he went forth from it with the same quiet composure as though he were merely taking his daily walk; and now that he re-entered it with another warden under his wing, he did so with the same quiet step and calm demeanour. He was a little less upright than he had been five years, nay, it was now nearly six years ago; he walked perhaps a little slower; his footfall was perhaps a thought less firm; otherwise one might have said that he was merely returning with a friend under his arm.

This friendliness was everything to Mr. Quiverful. To him, even in his poverty, the thought that he was supplanting a brother clergyman so kind and courteous as Mr. Harding, had been very bitter. Under his circumstances it had been impossible for him to refuse the proffered boon; he could not reject the bread that was offered to his children, or refuse to ease the heavy burden that had so long oppressed that poor wife of his; nevertheless, it had been very grievous to him to think that in going to the hospital he might encounter the ill will of his brethren in the diocese. All this Mr. Harding had fully comprehended. It was for such feelings as these, for the nice comprehension of such motives, that his heart and intellect were peculiarly fitted. In most matters of worldly import the archdeacon set down his father-in-law as little better than a fool. And perhaps he was right. But in some other matters, equally important if they be rightly judged, Mr. Harding, had he been so minded, might with as much propriety have set down his son-in-law for a fool. Few men, however, are constituted as was Mr. Harding. He had that nice appreciation of the feelings of others which belongs of right exclusively to women.

Arm in arm they walked into the inner quadrangle of the building, and there the five old men met them.   Mr. Harding shook hands with them all, and then Mr. Quiverful did the same.   With Bunce Mr. Harding shook hands twice, and Mr. Quiverful was about to repeat the same ceremony, but the old man gave him no encouragement.

"I am very glad to know that at last you have a new warden," said Mr. Harding in a very cheery voice.

"We be very old for any change," said one of them; "but we do suppose it be all for the best."

"Certainly—certainly it is for the best," said Mr. Harding. "You will again have a clergyman of your own church under the same roof with you, and a very excellent clergyman you will have. It is a great satisfaction to me to know that so good a man is coming to take care of you, and that it is no stranger, but a friend of my own, who will allow me from time to time to come in and see you."

"We be very thankful to your reverence," said another of them.

"I need not tell you, my good friends," said Mr. Quiverful, "how extremely grateful I am to Mr. Harding for his kindness to me,—I must say his uncalled for, unexpected kindness."

"He be always very kind," said a third.

"What I can do to fill the void which he left here, I will do. For your sake and my own I will do so, and especially for his sake. But to you who have known him, I can never be the same well-loved friend and father that he has been."

"No, sir, no," said old Bunce, who hitherto had held his peace, "no one can be that.   Not if the new bishop sent a hangel to us out of heaven.   We doesn't doubt you'll do your best, sir, but you'll not be like the old master; not to us old ones."

"Fie, Bunce, fie! how dare you talk in that way?" said Mr. Harding; but as he scolded the old man he still held him by his arm, and pressed it with warm affection.

There was no getting up any enthusiasm in the matter.   How could five old men tottering away to their final resting-place be enthusiastic on the reception of a stranger?   What could Mr. Quiverful be to them, or they to Mr. Quiverful?   Had Mr. Harding indeed come back to them, some last flicker of joyous light might have shone forth on their aged cheeks; but it was in vain to bid them rejoice because Mr. Quiverful was about to move his fourteen children from Puddingdale into the hospital house.   In reality they did no doubt receive advantage, spiritual as well as corporal; but this they could neither anticipate nor acknowledge.

It was a dull affair enough, this introduction of Mr. Quiverful; but still it had its effect. The good which Mr. Harding intended did not fall to the ground. All the Barchester world, including the five old bedesmen, treated Mr. Quiverful with the more respect, because Mr. Harding had thus walked in arm in arm with him, on his first entrance to his duties.

And here in their new abode we will leave Mr. and Mrs. Quiverful and their fourteen children. May they enjoy the good things which Providence has at length given to them!

CHAP. LIII.

CONCLUSION.

THE end of a novel, like the end of a children's dinner-party, must be made up of sweetmeats and sugar-plums. There is now nothing else to be told but the gala doings of Mr. Arabin's marriage, nothing more to be described than the wedding dresses, no further dialogue to be recorded than that which took place between the archdeacon who married them, and Mr. Arabin and Eleanor who were married. "Wilt thou have this woman to thy wedded wife," and "wilt thou have this man to thy wedded husband, to live together according to God's ordinance?" Mr. Arabin and Eleanor each answered, "I will." We have no doubt that they will keep their promises; the more especially as the Signora Neroni had left Barchester before the ceremony was performed.

Mrs. Bold had been somewhat more than two years a widow before she was married to her second husband, and little Johnnie was then able with due assistance to walk on his own legs into the drawing-room to receive the salutations of the assembled guests. Mr. Harding gave away the bride, the archdeacon performed the service, and the two Miss Grantlys, who were joined in their labours by other young ladies of the neighbourhood, performed the duties of bridesmaids with equal diligence and grace. Mrs. Grantly superintended the breakfast and bouquets, and Mary Bold distributed the cards and cake. The archdeacon's three sons had also come home for the occasion. The eldest was great with learning, being regarded by all who knew him as a certain future double first. The second, however, bore the palm on this occasion, being resplendent in a new uniform. The third was just entering the university, and was probably the proudest of the three.

But the most remarkable feature in the whole occasion was the excessive liberality of the archdeacon. He literally made presents to everybody. As Mr. Arabin had already moved out of the parsonage of St. Ewold's, that scheme of elongating the dining-room was of course abandoned; but he would have refurnished the whole deanery had he been allowed. He sent down a magnificent piano by Erard, gave Mr. Arabin a cob which any dean in the land might have been proud to bestride, and made a special present to Eleanor of a new pony chair that had gained a prize in the Exhibition. Nor did he even stay his hand here; he bought a set of cameos for his wife, and a sapphire bracelet for Miss Bold; showered pearls and workboxes on his daughters, and to each of his sons he presented a cheque for 20*l.* On Mr. Harding he bestowed a magnificent violoncello with all the new-fashioned arrangements and expensive additions, which, on account of these novelties, that gentleman could never use with satisfaction to his audience or pleasure to himself.

Those who knew the archdeacon well, perfectly understood the cause of his extravagance. 'Twas thus that he sang his song of triumph over Mr. Slope. This was his pæan, his hymn of thanksgiving, his loud oration. He had girded himself with his sword, and gone forth to the war; now he was returning from the field laden with the spoils of the foe. The cob and the cameos, the violoncello and the pianoforte, were all as it were trophies reft from the tent of his now conquered enemy.

The Arabins after their marriage went abroad for a couple of months, according to the custom in such matters now duly established, and then commenced their deanery life under good auspices. And nothing can be more pleasant than the present arrangement of ecclesiastical affairs in Barchester. The titular bishop never interfered, and Mrs. Proudie not often. Her sphere is more extended, more noble, and more suited to her ambition than that of a cathedral city. As long as she can do what she pleases with the diocese, she is willing to leave the dean and chapter to themselves. Mr. Slope tried his hand at subverting the old-established customs of the close, and from his failure she has learnt experience. The burly chancellor and the meagre little prebendary are not teased by any application respecting Sabbath-day schools, the dean is left to his own dominions, and the intercourse between Mrs. Proudie and Mrs. Arabin is confined to a yearly dinner given by each to the other. At these dinners Dr. Grantly will not take a part; but he

never fails to ask for and receive a full account of all that Mrs.
Proudie either does or says.

His ecclesiastical authority has been greatly shorn since the
palmy days in which he reigned supreme as mayor of the palace
to his father, but nevertheless such authority as is now left to him
he can enjoy without interference. He can walk down the High
Street of Barchester without feeling that those who see him are
comparing his claims with those of Mr. Slope. The intercourse
between Plumstead and the deanery is of the most constant and
familiar description. Since Eleanor has been married to a clergyman, and especially to a dignitary of the church, Mrs. Grantly has
found many more points of sympathy with her sister; and on a
coming occasion, which is much looked forward to by all parties,
she intends to spend a month or two at the deanery. She never
thought of spending a month in Barchester when little Johnny
Bold was born!

The two sisters do not quite agree on matters of church doctrine,
though their differences are of the most amicable description. Mr.
Arabin's church is two degrees higher than that of Mrs. Grantly.
This may seem strange to those who will remember that Eleanor
was once accused of partiality to Mr. Slope; but it is no less the
fact. She likes her husband's silken vest, she likes his adherence
to the rubric, she specially likes the eloquent philosophy of his
sermons, and she likes the red letters in her own prayer-book. It
must not be presumed that she has a taste for candles, or that she
is at all astray about the real presence; but she has an inkling that
way. She sent a handsome subscription towards certain very heavy
ecclesiastical legal expenses which have lately been incurred in
Bath, her name of course not appearing; she assumes a smile of
gentle ridicule when the Archbishop of Canterbury is named, and
she has put up a memorial window in the cathedral.

Mrs. Grantly, who belongs to the high and dry church, the high
church as it was some fifty years since, before tracts were written
and young clergymen took upon themselves the highly meritorious
duty of cleaning churches, rather laughs at her sister. She shrugs
her shoulders, and tells Miss Thorne that she supposes Eleanor
will have an oratory in the deanery before she has done. But she
is not on that account a whit displeased. A few high church
vagaries do not, she thinks, sit amiss on the shoulders of a young
dean's wife. It shows at any rate that her heart is in the subject;
and it shows moreover that she is removed, wide as the poles
asunder, from that cesspool of abomination in which it was once
suspected that she would wallow and grovel. Anathema maranatha!

Let anything else be held as blessed, so that that be well cursed. Welcome kneelings and bowings, welcome matins and complines, welcome bell, book, and candle, so that Mr. Slope's dirty surplices and ceremonial Sabbaths be held in due execration!

If it be essentially and absolutely necessary to choose between the two, we are inclined to agree with Mrs. Grantly that the bell, book, and candle are the lesser evil of the two. Let it however be understood that no such necessity is admitted in these pages.

Dr. Arabin (we suppose he must have become a doctor when he became a dean) is more moderate and less outspoken on doctrinal points than his wife, as indeed in his station it behoves him to be. He is a studious, thoughtful, hard-working man. He lives constantly at the deanery, and preaches nearly every Sunday. His time is spent in sifting and editing old ecclesiastical literature, and in producing the same articles new. At Oxford he is generally regarded as the most promising clerical ornament of the age. He and his wife live together in perfect mutual confidence. There is but one secret in her bosom which he has not shared. He has never yet learned how Mr. Slope had his ears boxed.

The Stanhopes soon found that Mr. Slope's power need no longer operate to keep them from the delight of their Italian villa. Before Eleanor's marriage they had all migrated back to the shores of Como. They had not been resettled long before the signora received from Mrs. Arabin a very pretty though very short epistle, in which she was informed of the fate of the writer. This letter was answered by another, bright, charming, and witty, as the signora's letters always were; and so ended the friendship between Eleanor and the Stanhopes.

One word of Mr. Harding, and we have done

He is still Precentor of Barchester, and still pastor of the little church of St. Cuthbert's. In spite of what he has so often said himself, he is not even yet an old man. He does such duties as fall to his lot well and conscientiously, and is thankful that he has never been tempted to assume others for which he might be less fitted.

The Author now leaves him in the hands of his readers; not as a hero, not as a man to be admired and talked of, not as a man who should be toasted at public dinners and spoken of with conventional absurdity as a perfect divine, but as a good man without guile, believing humbly in the religion which he has striven to teach, and guided by the precepts which he has striven to learn.

THE END.